CLASP

OF THE

KING

Books by R.R. Brikho

A Will Forsaken
Clasp of the King

The Soul Seeker
A Deserved Death

R. R. Brikho

CLASP

OF THE

KING

Book One of
A Will Forsaken

An Ambition Publishing Novel

This is a work of fiction. All of the characters, organizations, and events portrayed in this novel are either products of the author's imagination or used fictitiously

Cover Illustration by Arief Rachmad
Edited by Grace Fabbri

An Ambition Publishing Novel
Published by Ambition Publishing

ambition.pub

Hardcover ISBN 979-8-9989634-0-7
Paperback ISBN 979-8-9989634-1-4

Our books may be purchased in bulk for promotional, educational, or business use. Please contact your local bookseller or Ambition Publishing by email at support@ambition.pub

Printed in the United States of America

To those listening to their ambition, continuing towards their dream while it seems so distant. Keep going. I believe in you.

𝕬cknowledgements

Writing *Clasp of the King* was a long and arduous experience, and there are many people who were necessary to its creation. The project has been a dream of mine since I was a young child. I've penned numerous stories in loose notebooks I found around my childhood home, most of which are now long forgotten. What may come as a shock to some people, however, is that fantasy novels were probably the smallest influence on my writing. In this age of electronic media, most of my inspiration came from video games, films, and televisions shows. Media like Star Wars, *Game of Thrones* on HBO, *The Walking Dead*, and *Mount and Blade: Warband* are a few examples of the type of media that inspired me.

Any sandbox video game I could get my hands on became a vehicle in which I could worldbuild. The initial conception of Lonus began when I was about nine or ten years old and would spend hours playing *Minecraft: Pocket Edition LITE* on my iPod. A few years later, I started a community on a game site called Roblox. During that time, I wrote much of the groundwork lore for Lonus. There were many people in that community, and although I do not know most of their names, they know who they are, and I would like them to know how grateful I am to have been able to share my youth with them.

I would like to give a tremendous amount of gratitude to my editor, Grace Fabbri. Without her, I would not have been able to bring my world out as soon as I have. She possesses extraordinary skill with the English language, and I am happy to have her as my editor.

This project also would not have been possible without the people who supported it on Kickstarter: Bernie Meyers, Jennifer Meyers, Alex Wingblad, David Fabbri, Padre Yousif, Colin S, Dain, Ghilas Diaconescu, Kelly Lester, Brad Lester, Joe Yvorra, Mackenzie Pierson, Florentina Nitschke, Robert McCutchen, and Stephanie Stewart. I hope you all enjoy the story.

Contents

CLASP

OF THE

KING

A passage from a piece long forgotten

O o k o s

Ooks River

Mozny
Boshk
Suttonsda
Seprola
Dazhokda
Signy
Minisda

O s m j o r n i a

Kuremdod
Kurembrog
Polesgel
Belar
Kylndod

The
Akos
Sea

Remedaed

Loli

Tiuv

Bivdkop

Polans

P o m a

Conee

Luron

Waern

Lindaed

M j o r n

Nar

Nara

River of Nar

Feinnesa
Dorthu
Fisk
Wenay

Edrais

Edrovith's Plateau

Oureux

Bek d'Lifa

High Beak

Mur

Osgud

Bay of
Avon

Avonsgatte

Ulanai Wastes

Low Beak

Yhourn

Prologue

here were seven pyres, and three were lit. Religious men wearing simple gray robes and crudely made sashes stood behind these braziers. It was almost midday, and at that time the grand door of the Academy d'Ava stood open, allowing a wood scent to emanate out into the courtyard.

The braziers stood on a platform that preceded the doors. Sets of steps led to this platform, and at the bottom was an army of men that stood with beastly stature. A row of priests stood upon the platform, chanting hymns and staring down at the army below them.

In the forefront of these beastly men was an even larger figure. He was considered a hero among his people and worshipped as a god. He held himself with so much poise that it seemed as though one could throw a mountain at him and it would not disturb his posture. The air around him stung; yet if someone were to stand near him, they would feel as if they were being made stronger.

Taking sure steps, he alone climbed the stairs and made his way toward the door. One priest stood before him, and his gaze stabbed the beast-man with a captious glare. He stuck out his hand to halt him.

"Wait, Monster of Yhourn."

The priest's hand had touched the giant Yhournishman. He looked at his hand with a face of revulsion and wiped it on his robe-covered thigh. The Yhournishman, Enok, did not look to be insulted. He simply stared, waiting to hear what the priest had to say. The priest squinted at Enok as if he was analyzing every little spot on his face.

"Go on, barbarian. Enter the Academy."

The row of priests parted and allowed Enok to enter. Two other Yhournishmen took the place where Enok had been standing. One of them was the same height as all the other Yhournishmen, but unlike the rest, he was not wearing armor. His robes were not similar in style to the priests', but they were constructed with a similar simplicity. He wore them loose, with their lapels open, revealing his musculature underneath.

The robed Yhournishman possessed an obvious vitality, but the other Yhournishman standing beside him possessed an even more remarkable figure. Even relative to the others, he was *tall*. At his side hung an axe, and, unlike his robed brother, the only garment covering him was the hide of some large, scaly reptile that wrapped around his waist in the shape of a skirt. He wore mail chausses underneath and leather boots to cover his feet. His torso was exposed, his muscles bulbous and cable-like. They both had beards and full heads of hair; but the first Yhournishman kept his hair short and his beard trimmed, whereas the second left both untamed.

After Enok entered the building, the larger man stepped forward, but the smaller man extended his arm to stop him.

"Gannok, allow our father to meet with the bird in peace. They are good friends."

Gannok curled his lip and crossed his arms.

"None but the Yhournish are friends of the Yhournish, Restan."

All the priests had blue sashes, except for one in front, who had a silver sash. That silver-sashed priest's eyes were focused, squinting at the brothers in the same manner as he had squinted at their father. Restan had certainly seen eyes like these before. They held the look that he himself had possessed so frequently in his life: the look of a curious man. Gannok, however, undoubtedly took it another way. That priest did not chant with the others; it seemed that his purpose was to watch the Yhournish. Gannok was angered by his stare.

After an uncertain amount of time, the fourth pyre was lit. Still, Enok had not left the Academy. The Yhournishmen were now muttering amongst themselves, likely discussing what could be happening inside. Restan himself had not been told what it was that his father had come to discuss. He was good friends with the bird, too—yet the bird had only wanted to speak to Enok.

The fifth pyre was now lit. Gannok had grown restless. He pounded his feet and stared down the priest in front like a bear eyeing a deer. The priest held his head high.

"What is taking so long in there? What matter could they be discussing?" yelled Gannok.

The crowds stopped their muttering and looked at Gannok. They watched him with caution; however, the priest with the silver sash seemed entirely undisturbed. He continued to stare at them with the same glare. Gannok walked forward, and again, Restan stuck out his hand to stop him.

"You will not stop me again, brother."

"Allow Enok a bit more time," Restan said.

They spoke Yhournish when they talked to each other. Whenever they did, the priest winced as if it caused him pain.

Gannok shoved past Restan and walked forward, climbing the steps, his demeanor tense. Upon reaching the top of the steps, Gannok met the priest face to face. The priest did not move. He was frail, but despite that, he did not flinch. The large, monstrous stature of Gannok covered the priest in its shadow. He puffed his chest out—but still, the priest did not budge.

"I am going inside, Priest."

The priest stuck his hand out to halt Gannok. Despite how foolish the action was, Restan was impressed. Gannok could have clobbered that priest without effort, but the priest still had the courage to stop him.

"You will not enter. The Prophet Ava, long may he live, has ordered that only Enok enters—and so, only Enok shall." The priest raised his hand and made a waving motion. "You are in my light, barbarian. Move out of the way."

Gannok's face reddened, and he gripped his axe. The rows of priests halted their chants and stared at Gannok, shocked. The silver-sashed priest lifted his other hand high. He made another waving motion, but this one seemed more intentional, more formal. Lines of heavily armored men flooded into the courtyard. Feathers hung from their backs like wings, and in their hands were long pikes. They held their pikes at their sides and surrounded the

Yhournishmen. They stood at the ready, unmoving in their stances.

"Gannok! Come back here, now!" yelled Restan.

Gannok grimaced and released his hand from his axe. He stepped away from the priest and climbed down the steps to rejoin his people. The priest kept his chin high, donning a sardonic smile.

The sixth pyre was lit. It had grown colder, and clouds had formed up above them. The sun had almost fully set, and small pockets in the crowd of Yhournishmen had finally sat down to rest; however, the Yhournishmen near Restan and Gannok still stood straight, with an intimidating discipline.

Those that were sitting began to form circles, each of them surrounding a different Yhournishman who spoke to them as if he were telling them stories. Beside them was another Yhournishman who carried a banner. Each circle had its own unique banner. The Yhournishman who stood beside Restan and Gannok carried Enok's banner, which was adorned with a sigil that depicted a scorpion. Impaled on the sharp point of the scorpion's pincer was the head of a Terukian, pointy-eared and grinning smugly.

Gannok kept his eyes forward. He stared at the priest as if he were building up the courage to walk through him and enter the Academy.

"Priest!" Gannok shouted. "Tell us the nature of the meeting! Why must it take them hours to finish?"

Enok had told Restan and his brother that each clan was supposed to bring a small party from their respective armies. Restan did not know the exact reason why, but assumed that Enok had ordered it as an assurance to the Phoenicy that they would act if anything untoward were to happen during the meeting. They could have brought only Restan, but Gannok had wanted to come.

The priest stared down at them. For a moment he did not respond, but eventually he erupted into laughter. Once he noticed Gannok's angered eyes, however, he sighed and cleared his throat.

"None of the priests were told the nature of the meeting. It pains me deeply that our Prophet has deemed a lowly barbarian to be honored with his knowledge; but sadly, such is the case. Do not annoy me with any more emotional eruptions. Keep your words behind those untamed lips or my paladins will tame them for you."

Gannok growled. Restan stuck his arm out once more to hold him back, but Gannok had already expected it and whipped his hand away, pointing his axe toward the man.

"What is your name, Priest?"

"Ha! You wish to know my name? It is Aswold, Pyre Elder of Magnanimity. Did you hear that? *Magnanimity*. Do you even know what that word means? It is something you brutes will never have."

"Aswold! You ought to know that my brother Restan's greatest strength is speaking sense to me, but my sense may soon be running out. If you do not hold your tongue, I will rip your stupid head from your twiggy body."

Aswold grinned once more at Gannok; however, his face soon returned to the same judgmental glare as before. He kept quiet, and the priests resumed their chanting.

The final pyre was lit. The sky was pitch black, and the only light that could be seen was that which came from the pyres themselves. Their flickering fire gleamed over Aswold's face. The Yhournish began to set up camp in preparation for the night. Gannok paced around. He looked as if he were going mad. He once more climbed up the steps, and Aswold stuck his hand out to stop him—but this time, Gannok's sheer size meant he was able to knock the priest away easily, and he continued to walk toward the large Academy doors.

The priest whistled twice, and the men who surrounded the barbarians readied their tall pikes. The paladins were ready to stick the Yhournish where they camped, and Gannok halted once he caught wind of this. Aswold shook his head.

"Brutes will always be brutes. You simply cannot reason with them. They will never listen; especially not a sand-bathing scorpion sucker like you."

"I am tired of you, Priest. I will speak to my father myself—"

"Do not be naïve, brute! This is the holiest site in all of the world, and you think I will allow a *second* heathen within?"

"If you choose to attack me or my people when I walk through those doors, all of the priests that stand around you will die. You will die. Some of my men shall die, perhaps, but *all* of your men in their glittering steel plate will be killed. This site will be a graveyard, and this building the crypt where their bodies shall lie."

"And here I thought your brother was the poet! I never knew an idiot could speak such colorful words."

The priest raised two of his fingers, and the armored men took two steps forward. He grinned like a madman, glassy-eyed, clearly uncaring as to whether or not violence was to break out. Gannok returned a similar stare to Aswold.

A white streak of light lit up the sky. At first, it looked like lightning, but it did not zig-zag around in the frantic manner that lightning does. For a brief moment, the dark sky was replaced with a light more blinding than the sun. It hit the Academy d'Ava directly, drawing the stares of all the men, Yhournish and priests, while it dominated the sky above.

They felt a rush of emotion that filled every part of their bodies, as if they truly stored love in their hearts or passion in their fists—then this emotion was ripped from them almost immediately. Lightning struck for but a moment; however, this felt like an eternity. It felt like a terrible loss. It felt like a void of obscure and painful nothingness. Soon after the strike of light, a deafening boom erupted from the Academy. It sent a shockwave into the ground. Some of the standing Yhournishmen stumbled, and some of the pike-armed paladins fell, causing a break in their formation. The priests fell to their knees, stopping their hymns. Gannok stared at the priest, and the priest stared at the sky above. A bird flew around and circled the men in the courtyard below.

Gannok gripped his axe and sprinted toward the doors of the Academy.

Aswold's face tensed, and he whistled with his fingers once more. The soldiers ran toward the Yhournishmen and stuck their pikes forward, ready to impale them. The Yhournishmen stood up and swung their cleavers and war scythes at the soldiers, hacking at them. It was a mess of blood and steel being thrown about. Bodies began to pile up in the courtyard. Restan ran, following after his brother.

The priests that had presumably lined the walls in prayer within the building now lay on the floor, clobbered into broken messes. Some stood with candelabra impaling their chests, others were dismembered; but none were alive. Restan could hear wailing coming from deep inside the Academy. He had never heard his older brother cry.

He ran around the corner and was met with a vast number of books, all lined in rows and columns, stacked high to the ceiling.

A pair of large gates stood at the other side of the room. Restan went straight for them.

Gannok knelt on the ground, weeping, holding their father's possessions in his arms. Gannok looked up at his brother, and Restan's eyes went wide. It was as though he could not open them wide enough to comprehend the event. Aside from the items in Gannok's arms, there was no sign of their father.

Restan knelt, staring at the spot where his father had last stood. Gannok got to his feet and turned around, clasping his hand around his axe. Tears began to well up in Restan's eyes.

Enok, their father and god, was dead.

Althalos

lthalos's neck was locked under the arm of another. His opponent squeezed tightly and attempted to unbalance Althalos, but Althalos kept one hand on his opponent's elbow and his other hand on their hip. He tried to turn out, but his opponent resisted him. With a pull and a twist of his torso, Althalos threw his opponent onto the ground.

"Yes! Althalos, pin him!"

In the frenzy of the scramble, Althalos hurriedly got on top of his opponent. With one arm under theirs and his other arm cradling the wrestler's head, Althalos forced his opponent's shoulders down.

"One! Two! Three!" the crowd screamed in unison.

Althalos stood up, his opponent still lying on the ground. Althalos extended his arm.

"You have to teach me a thing or two. How did you get so good at wrestling?" said the other wrestler as he reached for Althalos's hand.

Althalos pulled him up. "Hrodolf, I honestly do not know. One day, I was being beat up by all the older boys; then I became the older boy."

Hrodolf nodded. "I suppose I should wrestle more, then."

Althalos grinned. "Exactly."

They stood in an area of their village where the dirt was softer. The sun was setting, yet the night bugs had not yet begun to harass the crowd. They kept far away from the village center as the adults would have no doubt attempted to shoo them off from their fun.

The handful of villagefolk that surrounded Althalos pushed out another lad to challenge him. He was short, about a head shorter than Althalos, and he held a frightened gaze. There was no meat on him, just skin and bones.

"Are you serious?" Althalos asked. "Who pushed him out here? Does he look like he wants to wrestle?"

No one responded. Althalos eyed the crowd.

"You just want to see him beat up, huh? You should be ashamed of yourselves."

Althalos stormed off. Hrodolf followed, reaching for the one who had bested him.

"What, Hrodolf?"

"They were trying to make him tougher. It was for his own good."

"That is not the way to make someone tough. Do you think that experience would have made him wish to fight again, or to run and hide from conflict?"

Hrodolf looked away. "You are right. If he wishes to wrestle, it'd be best if he came around to it on his own."

Althalos nodded.

"Where are you storming off to?" Hrodolf asked.

"To Jethr's."

"Oh, was he not with us? He usually comes to wrestle."

"He is building up the courage to ask Marsi to be with him. I think tonight will be the night."

"You jest! He has been saying he was going to ask her since he learned to speak. What makes you so certain?"

"I could see it in his eyes, I suppose. He seemed really sure of it this time."

Jethr's home was stone-built, just like the others in Dorthu. It had a thatched roof and a fenced enclosure that kept in their chickens. Jethr, a heftier lad, stood with his arms posted on the fence. He stared down at the ground. Althalos thought he looked like he was sweating. Jethr always stressed about putting anything into action.

"So, you are finally going to do it, Jethr?"

Jethr straightened up. "Well…"

"Oh, you're kidding," Althalos muttered.

"It's not the time, y'know? It is rather late, and I think she may already be in bed."

"Jethr…" Althalos placed his palms on his face and shook his head, "…you know better than any of us that Marsi refuses to sleep until it is much past dark. Go on and talk to her. She is probably playing with her mutt."

Jethr turned to stare at his chickens.

Althalos walked forward and grabbed Jethr by the shoulders. He turned his friend to face him.

"Hrodolf and I are sick of seeing the two of you gawk at each other. She is going to say yes, so just go on and get this over with already."

Jethr shook his head. "You really think so?"

"Is it not obvious?" shouted Hrodolf.

Althalos looked unamused. He pulled Jethr by his collar away from the fence.

"Alright, alright! I will do it."

Jethr fixed his tunic and headed toward Marsi's home. In Dorthu, everywhere was a short walk, so there were no secrets among anyone. There was a small table outside her house; her parents enjoyed eating outside, especially in the summer. Three stools surrounded the table. They stood at about knee-height and were made of the same local wood that every other piece of wooden furniture was made of in Dorthu. Marsi was outside, a stick in her hand. She looked down the road, and her furry dog rushed toward her.

"You better do it," whispered Hrodolf.

"I will tell her myself if you don't," said Althalos with a pat on Jethr's back.

Jethr stumbled forward. When Marsi saw him, she smiled. She had long dark brown hair, the same color as Jethr's and Hrodolf's. Althalos's hair was lighter, and he was the only one with any facial hair, even if it was only a faint stubble. The mutt continued to pester her for the stick in her hand, and she could hardly pay attention to Jethr with all the pushing the dog did.

"I suppose I should speak to you at a better time. Ser Scruff is a bit energetic, ain't he?"

"Toss us the stick, Marsi! We will play with Ser Scruff," yelled Althalos.

Marsi grinned and tossed them the mutt's stick. It fell on the ground in front of them, and the dog rushed for it. Hrodolf quickly snatched it and ran off, waving the stick in his hand. The dog followed. Althalos ran after him, and Hrodolf tossed the stick down the road. Ser Scruff launched himself after it.

"Jethr had better ask her this time. She's going to say yes!"

"He will. He has no excuse now."

"That was neat, you telling him you'd tell her yourself. He certainly knows it's going to happen now; you are not one to tell a fib to get your way."

Althalos grinned. The dog ran up to the two of them with the stick clenched between his teeth. He dropped it on the ground, and Althalos threw it once more.

"Althalos, I have been wondering," Hrodolf said, watching the dog scamper down the road. "Do you think there is anything for *us* out there?"

"What do you mean?" Althalos asked.

Hrodolf shrugged. "Priest Larmond often speaks of the Yhournish War and other such histories. Do you think we could ever rise to such prominence as the heroes of those stories?"

"Possibly," Althalos said. "The Prophet Avon himself was enslaved, and he rose higher than anyone else."

"Do you have any ambition for it?"

The dog ran back to them and dropped the stick. Althalos stared at the ground where the stick had landed. With an anticipatory look, Ser Scruff stared at Althalos; when he did not throw the stick, Hrodolf reached for it, throwing the stick even farther than before.

"I do not," said Althalos.

"Oh. What do you want out of your life, then?"

"I have not thought much of it. I just try to keep busy. I suppose I wish to live a good life with friends."

"I understand."

"What do you wish for your life?" Althalos asked.

Hrodolf grinned. "I wish to serve and become a hero. There is nothing here in Dorthu anymore, not since the mines were destroyed. It is unfortunate to have been born so late..."

Hrodolf paused; Althalos could tell he was struggling to say something.

"I am going to volunteer for Baron Rowe's guard."

"Are you kidding?" Althalos said. "When?"

"Whenever he comes next. I wish to see the world."

Althalos turned to Hrodolf and grabbed him by the forearm.

"When you do go, do not get yourself hurt. And do not forget us when you become a hero."

Jethr was back. The dog ran for him and dropped the stick. The lad had a wide grin on his face, and his arms were open wide. Hrodolf's jaw dropped, and so too did Althalos's.

"She said yes?" asked Hrodolf.

Jethr nodded, and the two erupted into cheers.

"I told her I would come back to grab Ser Scruff for her."

Jethr grabbed the stick that lay in front of Ser Scruff's pleading eyes and wagging tail. The three walked back to Marsi's. She was standing where she had been before, but now she had a slight smile on her face and looked to be recovering from blushing hard. She was naturally quite pale, so it was easy to turn her the color of a tomato. Jethr tossed her the stick, and she waved it in the air, catching the attention of Ser Scruff. She threw the stick, and Ser Scruff leapt for it.

"Finally, Jethr asked you! We sincerely never thought he would," said Hrodolf.

Althalos slapped the side of Hrodolf's arm with the back of his hand, shaking his head. Hrodolf looked surprised, but he shrugged it off. Jethr went a bit red himself, and so did Marsi. She stared at Jethr with admiring eyes.

"No, you are right, he did," said Marsi, raising an eyebrow at Jethr.

The four of them burst out laughing. Marsi patted Jethr on his shoulder.

"To be fair, though, he did profess his love to me already."

"What? When?" Jethr asked.

"When we were about a third the size we are now. Right over there, by the well."

Jethr snickered. "You know that does not count. We were children."

"And soon we will be elderly. You three know well how my old father will never stop mentioning how quickly life has passed. You know, you had more courage when you were younger!"

Jethr shook his head.

"What is your father doing, anyway? Usually, he watches us wrestle. He loves to tell us how he used to be the best wrestler in Dorthu," said Althalos.

"He lent his wagon to Adran," Marsi said. "Adran is heading to Wettay to sell crops, and then to Feninwich to visit family. His and Viula's toddler hasn't met his grandparents yet, so they are taking him to see them. My father is helping them pack."

"I have never seen Wettay or Feninwich," Althalos said.

"You haven't even seen Fisk," said Hrodolf.

"That's not true! I went there once to pick some herbs for my mother."

"I think you mentioned before that your mother does not have family elsewhere, Althalos, but doesn't she have any friends? Surely she would want to visit them at some point," said Marsi.

Althalos stared off. "I don't know."

"You and your mother came here when you were about five years old, right? That's what my parents tell me, at least," said Jethr.

"I think so. My mother does not really talk about it much." Althalos started to sweat. He looked up at the sky; the sun was setting. "I must beg my leave," he said. "I want to wake early to make it to Priest Larmond's sermon."

Marsi, Jethr, and Hrodolf waved Althalos off. His house was not even three buildings down the dirt path. It was a small home, like all the others. A large, fenced enclosure surrounded the left-hand side when one walked straight for the front door. He and his mother kept their chickens there. The chickens were kept for eggs and rarely butchered, for Althalos hated the feeling of killing the birds he had grown to love. When he had to do it, he would make sure their deaths were always quick and respectful, a concept that others in the village seemed not to care for.

His mother was nowhere to be found. Althalos reckoned she was out speaking with one of the neighbors, and that she would be back before night fell. He removed his dirtied clothes, rinsed himself with a small jug of water, and dressed himself before he went to bed.

Abba

ong green grass covered the rolling hills just before the beaches that flanked Kurembrog. The sound of crashing waves against jagged rock was a constant under the cliffs that held up the fortress's white walls. The fortress itself was separated from the rest of the town by a drawbridge that, when lifted, would render the keep almost impregnable. The drawbridge was connected to a permanent wooden bridge that led the rest of the way down to the bailey of Kurembrog. Burghers of all kinds dwelled within the bailey's white walls. There were smiths, merchants, laborers, priests, and ne'er-do-wells. One day, they would be Abba's subjects, if he could make his father proud.

Looking very much like a younger version of his father, Abba had fair skin, dark brown eyes, and hair that was a deep black with hints of brown. He was the firstborn son of Count Adar Kurem. Their realm, Kurem county, was named after their bloodline, and Adar was lord of it all.

The clashing of steel sounded in the sparring grounds.

"Son, do not fail to protect your offhand. And by Gol, stop showing your whole body to me, damn it! On guard!" shouted the Count.

"Forgive me, Father, it was a mistake," replied Abba.

"Cease your sorrow and strike me!"

Abba sent a quick strike to his father's thigh, but the Count side-stepped and struck his son in the face with his shield, sending him ass-first to the ground. The Count let out a sigh of disappointment and took off his helmet.

"You have a lot to do between now and the tourney so as to not embarrass yourself. Learn quickly, and do not disappoint me."

"Ah, Count Adar! I need a word with you."

It was Ser Mikhail. He was riddled with scars on his forehead and on the lower part of his neck. His left ear was missing, along with a few of his teeth. He had short, messy brown hair that was graying with age. Although he was fairly short, no one dared to mess with him because of his skill in swordplay.

"Very well, Ser Mikhail." Count Adar turned to look at Abba. "You know what you must do. Go on and continue your training."

Count Adar put away his sword and shield and went to follow Ser Mikhail to discuss their business. Countess Anita—Adar's wife and Abba's mother—stood above the rampart that overlooked the courtyard.

"Abba, honey! You need to pack for Belar," she called.

"Of course, Mother! I will be right there."

Abba removed his helmet and put away his arms. He went for the stairway and climbed up to the rampart, his tired legs pulling him up. He was not used to the ache his legs were experiencing. If it would not have made him look weak, he would have collapsed onto the stairs to rest.

Once he reached the top of the stairs, his mother approached him.

"Son, you have come of age. You need to be aware—"

"I understand, Mother. I need to look to the future. That is why Father is drilling me to perform well for the tourney."

"Yes, but I did not mean that. You will soon need to be ready for marriage. Your father and I have been looking for a suitable bride, and I hope I can trust that you will go through with it when the time comes."

Abba thought for a moment, and he replied reluctantly, "Mother, if it is what I must do, then I will do it."

"Good. That gladdens me. You make me proud, Abba—do not forget that."

Countess Anita hugged her son and turned away. Abba turned around and pulled open one of the doors. The halls of his father's castle were cold. It did not matter if it was summer or winter; the drab gray stone always gave the same feeling. He walked toward his room. The door was slightly open. Placing his hand on the handle, he slowly opened his door.

"BAH!"

Abba flinched. "What are you doing, Maric? Why are you in my room?"

Maric had similar qualities as his brother. He too had fair skin, brown eyes, and dark brown hair; however, his face much more closely resembled his mother, Anita. Their father often mentioned how it was widely known that their mother was the fairest lady in Nar. Like his mother, Maric was plenty popular with those of the opposite sex, and the fact he was good at anything he set his mind to did not hurt his popularity either.

"I came here to keep you on your toes. If you are fighting in a tourney, you should be more aware!"

"Har har. I am busy. What do you want?"

"I wanted to tell you I am going to compete in the tourney as well."

"You plan on fighting me?" Abba replied, his eyes widening.

"No, I am not planning on fighting you. I have wanted to fight in a tourney for a while now. But if it does come down to us fighting, well… I would hope you have gotten better."

Abba knew Maric did not mean to insult him, but he could not hide that he was displeased. His younger brother had always received preferential treatment, specifically from their father, so he could not blame Maric for his immature lack of tact. He decided to ignore his comment.

"Maric, I must do something. Please go."

Maric raised his eyebrows, but he nodded and left.

Abba's room was tidy. Imported silk curtains hung over his windows. His desk was in front of one of the windows, and on the desk there was a feather pen and blank parchment. His furnishings were made of an expensive pale oak. One of his walls was covered entirely in bookshelves, and not one gap was left on them. Books were piled on the floor and tables, scattered about; if only Abba had more shelves to fill! Nonetheless, the books—at least the ones on the shelf—were organized, kept in pristine condition in spite of how often they were read.

Abba walked over to the bookshelves and grabbed a book called *Ava's Lands*. There were notes stuck between the pages, more than any other book in his room. It was his favorite, and he had read it many times.

It told the story of the Prophet Ava. In truth, it was less about Ava and more of a general history book—it just so happened that Ava had played a pivotal role in every major event of the last few hundred years. Despite holding the title of Prophet, *zealot* was not a term that was used to describe him; he was a conciliator, the last member of a long-dead race of bird people. He knew the cost of war, and he wished for a time of peace. If only he had not left so many years ago.

Abba could not say how many times he had read it, but at the moment he was somewhere in the middle of the book. Ava's accomplishments were a marvel, and Abba spent just as much time reading the book as he did thinking about how much Ava had achieved during his lifetime. After pondering this for a while, Abba fell asleep.

"Get your arse dressed and get outside!" Ser Mikhail yelled, his voice firm and loud.

"Oh, alright—"

But before he could finish, Abba was grabbed and dragged out of bed.

"Apologies, m'lord, but you are moving rather slowly, and you have to hurry up. Get dressed. Go to the courtyard."

Before Abba could even ask why, Ser Mikhail had already left. Abba dressed himself and headed for the courtyard. A gambeson, dulled sparring swords, a nasal helmet, and a round shield sat on a wide table near the striking posts. The round shield bore the Kurem crest: two white serpents on an azure field, their heads turned toward each other. Ser Mikhail had his own shield that bore his personal heraldry, a simple per fess engrailed design with an azure-colored lower division and a golden upper division. He was already helmeted and doing drills on his own.

"Ready yourself," Mikhail ordered, raising his guard.

Abba fumbled to place his helmet on his head. He raised his dull blade. "Aye, I am ready."

The two gauged each other's distance. Mikhail swung a couple of light taps at Abba. In response, Abba blocked with his shield. Mikhail never showed much emotion when sparring. He was calm, with eyes that did not flinch.

Mikhail took a firmer strike at Abba's shield. Abba reacted in the same manner as before, and as punishment received a blow to the face from Ser Mikhail's shield. He stumbled backward. Ser Mikhail laced an arm under one of Abba's while he grabbed the other, then used the leverage to throw Abba to the ground.

"Abba, you will not sleep tonight if you continue to be so predictable. You must move more. If I hit you with one strike and you react one way, react differently next time."

Abba nodded and lifted himself up. He grabbed his shield and sword and brought himself into a proper stance. Ser Mikhail reached his sword forward and Abba met it with his own. Mikhail brought his sword high, keeping his shield forward and to the side. Swinging his sword forward, Abba engaged, but Mikhail's shield stopped him. Ser Mikhail returned with his own swing, which Abba blocked, retaliating with a stab of his sword. Ser Mikhail turned away from it, underhooked Abba's extended arm from behind, and threw his shield down to the ground so that he could circle his arm around Abba's neck. He yanked and threw Abba to the ground.

"You chose to thrust when I was too close. When you extended your arm, you exposed your back. If you did that in a battle, you would be dead."

Abba threw his sword away from him. Sweat rolled down his forehead as he tried to take in air. The throw had knocked the wind out of him, and he huffed desperately for relief. He refused to get up. The pain of fighting was so unbearable that he wished to just lie there, hoping Ser Mikhail would leave.

"Why are you not getting up?"

Abba rolled onto his side. "Ser Mikhail, why must I do this? I am no fighter, yet my father insists that I am to be one."

Ser Mikhail removed his helmet and placed it on the ground.

"For your whole life, you have known peace; but if you would take a moment to look at all the imperfections on my face, you would know that I have not. Your father does not like to speak about his time fighting the Ookosi—and rightly so, he has his own scars that were dealt to him from that time. Your father may grow annoyed with all that damned reading—"

Ser Mikhail paused.

"Your father knows how to be an effective lord, and you are his heir. You will inherit his same duty toward his vassals and subjects; you must be the protector of your people, and do not think you could protect them with such ineptitude in combat."

"But why must I be his heir? I am gifted when it comes to my studies, Elder Siemond says so himself. Would it not be wiser for me to do something more befitting my skill? My father was not my grandfather's firstborn, and yet he still inherited. Can Maric not be his heir?" Abba retorted with an ember of passion.

Ser Mikhail scoffed. "Elder Siemond… listen to me clearly. Elder Siemond neither knows nor cares for Osmjornish tradition—but that is all I will say of him. In your mind, how would you even go about relinquishing your inheritance? No matter your pleas, Adar will choose you as his heir. Once you inherit, would you abdicate? Osmjornish lords do not like those who step down from responsibility, and I doubt any of your family, peers, fellow nobility, or I would still hold any respect for you if you did."

Mikhail placed his hands on his hips and stared down at the mud, shaking his head. A look of disgust came to his face.

"You love to read stories of great heroes because you want to reflect their qualities. You mumble in your sleep, and it's all you mumble about. I met the Prophet Ava personally; his greatness was not handed to him, you know. He had to sweat and bleed to reach the heights he achieved. If you desire to be like him, learn how to fight. To stay weak willingly is dangerous, and it is perhaps the only danger a craven loves."

Mikhail picked up his helmet and left the courtyard.

Abba's face reddened with heat. He looked down in shame. One's first impression of Mikhail would likely lead someone to believe he was just a scar-riddled brute, but he was certainly learned. Abba wished for a moment that Ser Mikhail had not walked away from him so that he might once again stand up and train. But the knight was likely already off to fulfill some other duty—he was not one to waste time—and there was only one other person who might have been willing. Maric. He was likely attending a Phoenic prayer. Abba enjoyed learning about their religion, but Maric was more impassioned than most. Abba started off toward the bailey.

The Phoenic Temple in Kurembrog was whitewashed, just like the walls of the castle-town. Several spires surrounded its central monument. Unlike the rest of the buildings in Kurembrog, however, the temple was round. The large oak doors that stood between two of the spires were open, allowing for entry. Inside, the majority of the building was designated for seating, but about a quarter of it had been used as a pulpit for the priest and storage for the clergy. The local nobility sat in their own section, directly in front of the stage. Abba's father had mentioned that Elder Siemond had pushed for them to sit there so that he could make sure they would not miss a word. It was his belief that it was best for a lord to know his faith and know it well, for the benefit of his people.

Abba's mother and brother sat next to a man who was about a decade younger than Abba's father, with the dark hair typical of an Osmjornish man. There was a gap between him and Maric, a gap that Abba filled.

"Hello, Mother, Brother. Baron va Heddi."

"Welcome, Abba," replied the Baron.

Elder Siemond was giving the morning prayer. Despite his old age, he projected his voice throughout the large temple and waved his arms with passionate energy. He raised his hands to the heavens above, thanking the Phoenix and the prophets.

"What brings you here? You never come to sermons unless you have to. You're usually in bed 'til noon," whispered Maric.

"I came to ask if you would be willing to train with me for the tourney," Abba whispered in response.

Maric turned to face Abba, his head cocked, attempting to make sense of what he had just heard.

"You want to train? You? Of your own free will?"

Elder Siemond stared Maric and Abba with a heavy brow and returned to his prayer.

"Quit your talking and listen," ordered their mother.

"We thank the Phoenix for the light He has brought us. We thank Him for the enlightenment He has delivered us. The Phoenix has given you all good health. It has been so very long since we have seen a plague. Our people are strong! Our soldiers are well! With the good health of our people, our faith has been strengthened. More and more of Osmjornia is coming to accept the true faith. A number of temples have gone away with their false idols and accepted the Phoenix fully. Remember: it is *your* duty to lead us to victory! I am but a priest—*you* are the people who will bring about a Osmjornia that shall be saved. We are winning, yes, but do not allow our victories to give you an excuse not to do your part. Instead, be emboldened, and continue your devotion!"

When Siemond preached, he moved swiftly, his fists shaking with passion. The audience kept their heads up with pride. Abba looked around. The composition of the people in attendance was interesting. They were all young. There were a handful of people who were not, but the majority of those who attended were around Abba's age or younger.

"Maric, will you or will you not?" Abba whispered.

Maric grinned. "Of course I will help you, my brother, but do know it is only out of pity," he said, not in a whisper.

Their mother slapped Maric on the arm.

"I apologize, Mother." Maric looked down in shame.

It took a while for the priest to finish. Abba typically did not attend these prayers, as it was not the holy day. They were often the same as all the others in the week, unless anything so noteworthy occurred that Elder Siemond had to speak of it. The crowd began to break up. Maric and Anita rose to their feet to leave, but when Abba went to do the same, the Baron grabbed his forearm.

"Countess Anita, I wish to speak to your son about the importance of rulership. May I keep him here for a moment? I will escort him back to the keep myself once I am finished."

Countess Anita nodded and motioned for Maric to follow her. A short laugh burst from Maric the moment rulership was brought up.

"Abba. I have heard you are a smart boy with no love for ruling. That reminds me of myself when I was young," said the Baron, staring at Elder Siemond. "What is it that you want, Abba? Who is your ideal self?"

Abba flinched. He had not expected anyone to be interested in what he wanted, for it seemed to him that everyone wished to steer him toward whatever future they had envisioned for him. His father and Ser Mikhail wished to push him toward ruling. Though he was not against it, his mother wished to have him married. And even though he did find it preferable, Abba still noticed how Elder Siemond wished to lead him toward the priesthood. Abba attempted to speak, but all that came from him was nervous mumbling.

"You must be more confident and assertive if you ever want to achieve anything. I already know what you want," the Baron said.

Abba furrowed his brows. Baron va Heddi pointed to the Elder.

"You wish to live a life of learning. From what I have heard, it seems you've been drawn to the priestly practice. I would assume you took to it for the same reason I did when I was your age: like you, I was interested in the pursuit of knowledge above all other things. However, there is a fact that separates the two of us quite a bit. I was not born to be a lord. I was the second child of my father, Ser Hurdof va Heddi, and my brother was to be the next baron of Heddi. Sadly, my brother passed away early into his rule, and I inherited the title and responsibility of lordship. It was my knowledge of the world that helped me transition well into the role, but it seems your father neglects the value of the learned mind. We smart men can go down a few different paths, but for the most part they end up quite political. I want you to look at Elder Siemond and figure out what it is that he wants."

Abba stared at the Elder. He seemed drained and was slow to move. He let out a frustrated grunt and swiftly grabbed his hip.

"It seems he is motivated by his prayer," Abba said. "It gives him the energy and strength to overcome his age."

The Baron nodded. "Yes, that is surely plausible. But did you analyze his behavior in all lights? Did you take into account the crowd? Could it not possibly be that the Elder is motivated by the cheerful reaction to his speech?"

Abba's eyes widened with realization. It was surely the case, for as soon as the crowd had left, the Elder had shown his age. He must have truly cared about how the people saw him, and Abba understood why he would; he was the voice of the Phoenix in Kurembrog. He ought to have cared a great deal.

"There is your lesson from the wise Baron va Heddi," the Baron said, grinning.

The Baron stood up and motioned for Abba to follow him. He kept his back straight and shoulders wide; he took up space while he walked, and passersby made certain to not get in his way. It was apparent that he thought highly of himself.

They passed the market square. Some of the merchants waved to the Baron and thanked him for his efforts in improving the economy; others glared at him with contempt. He was not new to Kurembrog, but he had only been Count Adar's Master Treasurer for about a year.

Once the two reached the barbican that preceded the drawbridge to the keep, the Baron stopped walking, turning to face Abba and pointing toward the keep.

"Why is it that you and your family sleep there, and the rest of the people sleep in the bailey?"

"Well, it is because my family and I are of noble birth."

"Yes, that is true. But why is that so significant?"

Abba did not know what Baron va Heddi was leading the conversation toward. It seemed to be a conversation that would get him in trouble, even as a lord.

"Nobles live in keeps and burghers and peasants do not. That is just how it is, really."

"There is a cause for everything. Somewhere down your line of ancestors was an individual who amassed wealth, influence, and soldiers. That person did not receive those things on a silver platter, as nobles generally do; that person had to work for what they obtained. Take that into account, for you have been blessed with an easy life in comparison to those in the bailey. Work hard."

The Baron waved goodbye to Abba and walked toward the town center. Abba stared at the keep and took note of its qualities. It lay atop a rocky sea-stack, and on its far side was a wall on top of a cliff that Maric would often dive from. Abba had never done it; he was too scared. The shingles that covered the roofs of the buildings were a uniform dark blue. Abba turned around to look at the bailey. Lining the sprawling streets were small, crammed buildings. The only way to expand was upward. There was not a lot of space in Kurembrog; it was not a big town, and the space within the walls only allowed for so many buildings. Burghers dragged their belongings over their shoulders as they traveled to and from the market. Abba had never seen a commoner from the bailey carrying a book, and he would not have known if they were sold in the market. He lifted his head high and marched back to the keep.

Edit

ara's streets were filled with foreign merchants and Mjornish farmers looking to sell their wares. There were market stalls wherever market stalls could be placed, and these stalls were never left alone. The Narese coast was breathtaking. It was still warm and bright, being that it was midday in the middle of summer. The sun gleamed over the rocky coast of Nar and gave the bluffs a shiny golden hue, a stark contrast to the dark blue of the Akos Sea. The section of the city closest to its port was the oldest; some of its walls and round towers were crumbling with age. A few priests and peasants stood at a segment of the wall and prayed.

Edit and her father rode for the keep, where they were to meet Asbyorn Harferd, the King of Nar. They were being escorted by several knights, clad in engraved plate armor and armed with longswords that hung, sheathed, at their waists. On their right shoulders hung a long, orange half-cape.

Peasants would often call out to Edit's father to bless him with a pleasant day, and he would respond to these good wishes with a wave, a smile, and a toss of a coin to the beggar. Edit could not stand her father's habit of helping the strange peasants. It slowed down her meeting the King; so every time he gave a peasant a smile, Edit cringed, rolling her eyes. Her father had short ginger hair with fewer grays than one would have expected for his age, and a beard in need of a trim. His eyes still held some youth within them. Edit did not have ginger hair; hers was more auburn. Her face was sharper, too, with a much subtler nose than her round-headed father.

"Father, why do you show such kindness to these commoners? Other lords pay them no mind."

"I would prefer to live in a world where any person can smile and greet others kindly, rather than one where people feel the need to restrict their kindness toward others based on something so simple as who their father is."

Edit rolled her eyes. He always turned everything into a wise lesson or lecture.

"You know the King well, don't you, Father? What is he like?"

"The King inherited his kingdom at a young age, as you know, because of his father's untimely passing. His father was a good man, a good friend, and a good leader. Unfortunately, he was so preoccupied with administrative matters that he was not able to pass on those same traits to his son. King Asbyorn had a rough rule early on, and he has made many mistakes. But that is to be expected of a young lord. He has grown into a decent king."

Just before the gatehouse of the keep, there stood a man dressed in robes with golden strands sewn into their seams. Over his shoulder was a fine golden sash with various religious symbols woven into it. A gleaming platinum diadem with engravings similar to the symbols found on his sash wrapped around his head. His hair was a light gray that was hard to distinguish from the metal on his headpiece. His face was wrinkled like rolling hills, and his cheeks drooped like curtains.

The two parties met. Each of their respective guards shifted into a formation where they encircled Edit, her father, and the exquisitely clothed man. Edit frowned. Her father undoubtedly meant to have another one of his long conversations with this man.

"How are you, Orator?"

"Fine. I was hoping to speak with you," said the man.

"We will have to speak later; I must see His Majesty."

The Orator shook his head. "I am here to discuss your matters with the King in his stead. Sadly, he is ill and bedridden; he sends his apologies. I have a letter with his seal to confirm."

The Orator pulled out a letter that was tucked inside his robes and handed it to Edit's father. He examined the wax seal for a moment, but soon broke it and skimmed over the letter inside.

His eyebrows raised. Edit rolled her eyes; she had only a short amount of time before she and her father would go to the Midsummer festival in Belar, and now she might miss seeing the King.

"We both know that you coming here to discuss these matters is odd, Aswold. Why did he not send Barnut, or any of his other advisors?"

"Do not fret, Lord Venceslaus. They were all busy running other errands, and I had the time to attend this meeting for him."

Venceslaus peered at the Orator and signaled to one of his knights. The knight reached into a satchel and retrieved a note, which he handed to Venceslaus. Venceslaus nodded to his knight and passed the note to the Orator.

"The economic state of affairs in High Beak is looking fruitful. Our olive trees have finally matured and are back to producing enough fruit to keep up with demand after their destruction during the Yhournish War. Our wheat farming is going well, but it could be improved. We suffer shortages of clean water inland, but this is being handled with the construction of canals originating from the River of Nar. We will soon achieve the same prosperity we had before the war, thank Avon."

"Ah, yes. Nara is in need of grain. I find myself growing annoyed with the beggars pleading for bread. His Majesty can pledge men to help with your canal construction, so long as you set aside land for grain to be grown that will be sent to Nara exclusively. As for the olives, their destruction tarnished our economy years back; this is indeed a good sign for the healing of our kingdom."

The Orator's dull demeanor morphed into an intrigued one when he noticed Edit.

"So, is this your daughter? She looks just like your late wife. Her eyes are as blue as the Akos Sea, and her hair is like a fawn's."

"So it is, Orator. Now, may we take this discussion somewhere more private, so we might go into more detail? I am sure your joints ache as much as mine do."

"We can go to my study and speak there. Your daughter can wait in our library."

The Orator motioned for his bodyguards to follow them. They wore plate armor like Venceslaus's knights, but they had protrusions from their backplates adorned with feathers that resembled wings. Never before had Edit seen a knight wear those;

they must have been the Phoenicy's famed paladins. Edit, her father, and her father's knights followed. Edit curled her lip and looked down with disappointment when they turned to walk away from the keep. They headed instead for the Academy.

The Academy had its own set of walls that looked much like the old walls of Nara, but instead of crumbling under their own weight, they were sturdy and well-maintained, with segments replaced by new stone. They passed through a gatehouse into the ward of the Academy. Within the ward, there was a pair of large doors that were open, allowing entry into the building. A stone-brick platform stood outside the doors with steps leading toward it. Along the front wall of the Academy stood several pyres—four were lit—and a number of priests sung hymns with their heads down. Engaged pillars stuck out from the walls, and between these pillars, carvings of Viantse and other figures were present. They passed through the Academy doors. There was a massive rotunda with murals of war and holy rites above them. In its center, there was a grate open to the sky. Sunlight beamed through it, and as it did, it made a scene with the grate's shadow on the ground below: the shadow cut a scene that resembled a bird whose feathers burnt like flames.

"Ser Groent and Ser Jriton, you will accompany me to the study. The rest of you, stay here. Ser Elseharde, you will escort Edit to the library; go forward and take a left. It should be straight ahead," ordered Venceslaus.

"Yes, m'lord."

Ser Elseharde and Edit split from the main party. Ser Elseharde had a clean and maintained beard, his hair was kept short, and his dark brown eyes held no sorrow. To Edit, he looked no more than a few years older than herself.

"Why do you think the King was not present?" Edit asked Elseharde.

"Well, the Orator said he was ill."

"I forget the specifics of the Phoenicy's relation to the crown, but surely the Orator is no servant of the King."

"The relation between the two has been a bit confusing since Ava left, or so others say."

They passed through the double doors of the library, and Edit was met with the smell of old parchment. She had never seen so many books before. Countless bookshelves were lined up in rows on either side of her. Across from the entrance was another set of doors that looked to be made of some metal, probably bronze. There were markings above it that she could not decipher. A few paces forward from the library doors was a lectern made of wood; an older man in robes stood behind it, flipping through the pages of a large book with a bone pen in his hand. He made various markings as he went.

"Ah, hello there. I am Elder Bertram, book-keeper of the Academy. What are your names?"

Edit prepared to speak.

"The Duke Freihei ordered me to watch his daughter while he and the Orator went to discuss particulars. The Orator suggested we come here," said Elseharde.

"Ah, yes, of course. I could give you a tour of the library to pass the time, if you so wish. It is not often that the drudgery of stockkeeping is ever different."

Edit perked up. "Yes, we would enjoy that."

Bertram the Book-keeper smiled and beckoned for them to follow him. He went to the first row of bookshelves on the right-hand side of the room; they stood tall and proud.

"Since you are the daughter of Duke Venceslaus…"

The book-keeper scanned the shelves. He grabbed a library ladder and moved it to where some tattered books were kept. He leaned his decrepit body over it as if to catch his breath.

"Here is a complete chronicle of the history of all the noble houses, spanning around a thousand-and-a-half years in its scope. Our most notable prophet—Avon the Sword, blessed be his name—was a genius. He had this Academy built in the middle of Nara as a diplomatic tool. He foresaw the next prophet in a vision, and that the next prophet would be his own spawn. He did this to persuade our heathen ancestors to convert; to accept his rule, as well as to accept the Phoenix as their chief deity. He promised the nobles that their family histories would be recorded in their entirety so that Narese culture and history would not go into extinction. After Avon had taken over, there was no significant change in the daily lives of the commoners—well, other than that their religious education was now only to be conducted by Phoenic Temples. It was a situation similar to that of the Osmjornish."

Bertram climbed the library ladder with the passion of an ambitious young man. "There are so many families, it is hard to keep track of them all. Ah, yes, here we are—Freihei."

He smiled warmly as he reached for a book. It was far thicker than any of the other books, and he opened it with the care a mother cat would give her kitten.

"Avon favored the Freiheis well. Your family is among the oldest in the Kingdom of Nar, and rightly so. Your ancestors were one of the first to submit to Avon. I imagine it was a simpler time then."

"I heard there was more war. I certainly prefer the current peace," Ser Elseharde said.

"Peace is the time man prepares for war," Bertram said as he hobbled away from the ladder.

"Do you expect war soon?" asked Edit.

"Your father is a good man, Edit. I have survived many plots, but any attempts on the life of an old dog like me are a waste of time. You will not see a build-up to the feuds that are coming. Too many people nowadays like to play friend in case they need to be nearby to slit your throat as foe. Be wary of people here in Nara, especially the lords. Your father is one of the few good ones left."

Edit rolled her eyes. Her gaze landed on the set of bronze doors on the other side of the room. They had a trim around the doorframe that was etched in a language that felt familiar.

"What is behind those doors?" asked Edit.

Althalos

lthalos's eyes flickered open, beads of sweat already forming on his forehead. His hair was a tangled mess from the wrestling he had done the day before; it looked like the unkempt mane of a wild horse. He pushed himself up from his cot. His gaze fell upon a long stick propped up against the wall of his room. Beside the stick, a sharp rock lay nestled in the center of a pile of shavings. He reached for it, but halted.

"This can wait," he said to himself.

His mother was not home. Had she come home last night? He went to check her room, and her bed was left untidied. She typically fixed her bed every morning, and yesterday had been no exception. She must have been running late when going to see off Adran and his family. She always did make sure to show her face.

Althalos left the house. Their chickens pranced over to the fence, eager for Althalos's attention. One had a menacing stare, and Althalos knew it wanted grain. Althalos scooped some chicken feed from a sack that leaned against the inside wall of the house and brought it out to give to the chickens. He held his hand out over the fence so that he could pour the grain into their feed bowl.

The walk to the entrance of Dorthu was not a quick one. Althalos's home was on the other side of Dorthu, and even though it was a small village, it was large enough that Althalos could not see the entrance from his home. He walked past a few of his neighbor's houses, including Marsi's. She was not out yet. Althalos looked to the sky; the sun was low. She was an early riser and would usually be out feeding her hogs around this time. Althalos palmed his face. Her father had likely brought her to bid Adran's family off as well.

The idea of a family was strange to Althalos. He had his mother, but she was aloof and distant. He had never met his father, and his mother never spoke of him. Maybe his father was a dead soldier or a deadbeat rogue. If either were the case, it would not matter—Althalos did not know him.

A few of the neighbors began to open their doors. The older people of Dorthu had a joyless look to them: their arms drooped, and they held their heads down, their faces as blank as unwritten parchment. Althalos reckoned it was the destroyed silver mines that had put them into their gloom. They spoke about them often; the children never did.

The largest building in Dorthu was the Phoenic temple. Like most of the other buildings, it was built with stone—but its several spires that jutted into the sky reminded Althalos that it was surely a building the locals had not made. They did not have the means to cut the stone that composed the temple, and the engravings on its walls were a further reminder that it was likely built from the concerted effort of the Phoenicy. No one, not even Priest Larmond, was inside. It was not the hour for prayer, and the peasants had to tend to their animals and bathe. Althalos stared at himself in a mirror; his mother would surely give him an earful once she saw his uncouth appearance.

He passed the mill next. It was the only other large building in Dorthu. Althalos had to go to the mill often, but unfortunately, the miller was a prick.

Past the mill was the town square. No one ever set up a stall there; rarely was there ever a merchant who met Dorthu during their travels. In the center stood a small wooden podium. Their local lord, Baron Harry Rowe, would make announcements there whenever he would visit; yet he would only ever announce tax collection or punishment to wrongdoers. Ser Scruff lay on the podium with a stick between his paws. He chewed on his trophy like a wolf would a bone. Noticing Althalos, he stared at him, his tail wagging fiercely. Althalos smiled.

"Hey, boy! How are you? Nice stick, let me…"

Althalos grabbed the stick from Ser Scruff and chucked it to the other side of the town square. Ser Scruff bolted for it, and within seconds he was back in front of Althalos, wishing for more. Althalos knelt down and patted the mutt on his head.

"Sorry, boy. I wish I could play some more, but I have to go find my mother. Maybe I will play fetch with you later."

The village gate was just a turn past the town square. The wooden gate was open, and Althalos could see his mother lifting some boxes onto the bed of a wagon. She wore a faded yellow dress. Adran was helping his children into the back of the wagon. He had his toddler, Adro, and his daughter, Grita, who was a few years younger than Althalos, sit with their goods. Marsi and her father were there too.

The toddler was crying. Althalos's mother went over to him and patted his head.

"Don't you worry, little Adro. Grita has gone and seen your grandparents many times. You two are going to have plenty of fun in Feninwich," said Althalos's mother with a smile.

Little Adro stopped his crying, but he still had a pout and teary eyes, shaking his little fists with frustration.

"On the way... you can play with this!"

She pulled out a small, wooden toy knight and handed it to the young boy. Little Adro immediately perked up and reached for it. He pranced it around in the air, pretending he was a knight himself. His mother turned to lift another box.

"Althalos? Come help me lift this, it is quite heavy."

Althalos ran over to aid his mother. It was a large box filled with potatoes. Althalos squatted down and lifted the box onto the back of the wagon.

"Thank you, Althalos!" said Adran.

Althalos nodded. "Of course."

His mother stared at him with squinted eyes. Surely, she was going to scold him for looking as he did. Once they waved Adran's family off, she turned to him.

"Althalos, go and bathe in the river. And take your mound of dirty clothes and wash those, too. You always get so filthy whenever you wrestle."

He knew it.

"Of course, Mother."

He turned to head back home. He passed by the homes and the square, and soon he passed by the mill. Cristof, the miller, now sat outside.

"Oi! Althalos, c'mere."

Althalos sighed. "Yes?"

"You should tell Agnes to come by. She's a pleasant woman," said Cristof, grinning slyly.

"Cristof… My mother wants nothing do with you."

"Well, I don't want anything from that witch, either!"

"Witch? Have you placed your brain into the mill instead of grain? Do not insult my mother again."

"You're good for nothin'! Go away!" Cristof yelled.

Shaking his head, Althalos continued home. He grabbed his dirtied clothes as well as a set of clean ones to wear after he had bathed. Unlike the other villagefolk who preferred to wash at the stream closest to Dorthu, Althalos liked to hike a bit farther into the forest to another. Its seclusion within the brush gave Althalos a feeling of serenity. He poured a bit of the soft soap that they kept in a barrel into a bowl. With his clothes underneath his arm and the bowl in his hand, he walked over to the stream. He stripped himself and dipped his toes into the water. Although it was cold to the touch, it felt good in the summer heat. It was calming.

After just shy of an hour of bathing and laundering, the serenity that Althalos possessed fled from him. Smoke billowed into the sky from the direction of Dorthu. Althalos dropped his clothes at the stream and ran toward it. Faintly, he heard the yelling of men and the cries of his villagefolk. In the distance, over the hills and between the trees, he could see Dorthu.

Dorthu was burning. The straw roofs of the peasant homes had collapsed in on themselves. Livestock were bolting around, frantic and afraid. All the townspeople were either dead or dying. He heard faint galloping in the distance; whoever had done this must have been finished. Wails of townsfolk and the roar of the uncontrolled blaze filled Althalos's ears.

He dashed for his home, but it was unenterable. Its roof had already collapsed from the fire. He stood there for a moment, watching it burn. Had his mother returned home? She could be inside, and everything he had ever owned was inside, too. He tried to enter, but a flame roared up, discouraging him. Mutilated bodies lined the streets. Every building was in a similar state to

Althalos's own home, and he saw a man attempting to claw his way out from the burning rubble. Althalos ran over to aid him, but the man's hand went limp. Burns covered the man's entire body.

Althalos ran past the temple. There was another pile of slaughtered bodies, including Priest Larmond. The mill was burning down. He saw a mother shielding her baby in her arms, but both were impaled by a spear and lay lifeless on the ground. He saw a familiar stick on the ground, and next to it were the cut-up remains of Ser Scruff. When he made it to the village square, he saw the decapitated head of Hrodolf with a torn crimson cape near his body, gold stitching in its hems.

Althalos fell to his knees. His stomach churned and he wished to vomit. He reached his hand for Hrodolf. It didn't feel real. When he touched his friend's lifeless hand, he retched the contents of his stomach onto the ground. Who would have done such a thing? Why would they burn Dorthu?

Althalos's eyes landed on the torn crimson cape once more. The color of the cape confused him. He knew of no lords who had crimson banners. Were they foreigners? What band of foreigners would be so deep into the Kingdom of Nar that the people of Dorthu would not have heard of armed conflict first? Dorthu was nowhere near a border; they were in the middle of nowhere. Surely they would have known of any war before it met their village. The torn cape Althalos had found was incredibly well made—had they been attacked by a group of bandits that fashioned themselves as lords? Why would they burn a village and take nothing?

He stood up and walked over to the wooden gates where his mother had said her goodbyes to Adran and his family. Marsi lay dead with a gash across her chest, and her father was slumped beside her, a bloodied axe in his side. Althalos's mother was not there. His eyes darted around. The well near the entrance of the village had bloodied stone-brick near the rim of the well shaft. Althalos looked down the well, and the body of a woman dressed in yellow floated below. She was face down in the water. Was it his mother? He attempted to get a closer look, but while leaning over the wall of the well, his hand slipped on the blood that covered the stone-brick. He stopped himself. He did not wish to fall in.

He returned to the entrance of the village and faced Dorthu. He knelt down, staring at the remains of his home and his friends. His mother was dead. Marsi was dead. Hrodolf was dead. He did not see Jethr, but Althalos imagined he was dead, too. Even the damn dog had been killed. Everything Althalos ever had known and loved was gone.

Althalos grabbed the bloodied axe, slipped it into the space between his belt and his hip, and set off for Fisk, the sister village of Dorthu. Under different circumstances, he would have enjoyed the walk; but he could not get the thought of what had just happened out of his mind. It was a blisteringly hot day, but Althalos did not know if that was because of the weather, the heat from his village burning down, or his racing heart. Nature usually calmed Althalos's nerves, but the screams of his fellow townsfolk never left him, their voices lingering in the back of his head.

Beside the road, there was a wagon. Laid around the wagon were four bodies. Adran, Viula, Grita, and Little Adro had all been killed. A wooden club lay a few feet from Adran's body, and one of Viula's hands was cut, as if she had been trying to grab a sword. Grita and Little Adro were a few feet away. Grita's body was turned from the conflict as if she had been trying to flee. There was a deep wound on her upper back. Little Adro bore a similar wound.

There was a shovel in the back of Adran's wagon. Althalos began digging. He did not know how long he had dug, but he could not stop. He had to at least give some of the dead the respect of a proper burial. Maybe it would relieve some of the sorrow that had been placed upon him. He dragged Adran's family into the grave. Lifting the shovel once more, he tossed dirt onto their bodies. A feeling churned in his stomach, tickling his throat. He felt the urge to vomit, and his thirst harassed him, but he shoved his urge to the side so that he could finish his mission. He speared the shovel into the dirt once more; then, overcome with dizziness, he pitched forward and fell to the ground.

Althalos woke up dazed, with an aching head. He lifted himself up, squinting with confusion at his wet shirt.

"Glad yer awake, pisspot! Now tell me why yer sleepin' in the middle of the road."

"What?" His head was spinning. "The family, I—I knew them. Someone killed them, and killed my mother. Everyone in Dorthu…"

The man standing above him had short brown hair that was scruffy like the fur of a mangy dog, and his face bore a few scars. He extended a dirty, calloused hand to Althalos to help him up.

"I saw the smoke. I was headin' over there. What happened?"

"Someone burnt Dorthu to the ground," Althalos said. "I believe I am the only one who made it out alive."

The man looked down. His hand choked the neck of a canteen that hung from the side of his belt. He took a large gulp of the liquid inside.

"That is quite unfortunate. I knew some people there. My name is Gunter—what is yers?"

"Althalos. I need to bury them and get to Fisk—"

Althalos turned to look at the grave. The rest of the soil was already laid over it.

"Oh," he said. "Thank you."

"Do not thank me, boy. I can walk ye to Fisk if ye would like."

Gunter was a peculiar man. His hand never left his sword's handle, and he didn't ease up on his tense demeanor. The only time he ever smiled was when he told one of his occasional uncouth jokes.

Althalos stared down the road. Why him? Why must he be the one to be left alone? He knew things like this happened in the world; a few veterans of the war lived in Dorthu. But why would Dorthu of all places be burnt down? Only a sick cretin could have murdered innocent people so brutally. No reason could be good enough to justify it. This was evil. Justice had to be brought to whoever had killed his family. He felt the urge to cry, and he moved his fingers to wipe away his tears—but none had come.

"Boy, I'm speakin' to ye. When I speak to ye, ye answer."

Gunter had a strange accent. He certainly spoke Narese, but he must have not been from Fisk or any of the nearby villages.

"Wha—what? What did you say?"

"What did ye do in Dorthu?"

"Well, I... I cut timber. Tend to my chickens. I help my mother with housekeeping duties."

Gunter smirked. "So yer a good ceorl, ain't ya. Ha!"

"I may be a ceorl," Althalos said, "but you do not seem particularly significant, either."

Gunter's smirk left him.

"I am not. Let us head to Fisk, laddie."

"Before we do, why am I wet?"

"Now ye know why I called ye pisspot."

Fisk was a small village of a similar size to Dorthu. The same stream that ran near Dorthu cut through Fisk's center. Upon arrival from the direction of Dorthu, the village's Phoenic temple could be seen immediately to the right-hand side on a hill. Like the temple in Dorthu, it was extravagant, boastful, and tall. Across the road on the left-hand side was the tavern. It was made of wattle and daub, with a small stable and no shortage of carousers. Gunter fixed his gaze onto the tavern like it was the only thing to exist. The smell of human urine, shit, and moldy food hit the nose like a horse's kick.

"Ah! Helwig!" Gunter said. "Nice to see ye, friend."

Helwig let out a tired huff. "Gunter... I told you I cannot serve you any more ale."

"No, no! I am not here for myself. I found this boy passed out on the side of the road. He came from Dorthu—all that smoke in the air came from it burnin' down, he says! It would be a kindness for ye to bring him some salted meat."

Gunter reached into a pouch and beckoned Helwig to come accept payment.

"Dorthu is burnt down? Are you serious? Is it true, boy?"

Althalos nodded.

"Gol, this is a sad day. Do not worry about paying for the salted meat."

"If ye could bring an empty jack so that he may have some water, ye would have my thanks. Also, do take my coin and bring me some ale, Helwig," Gunter said, grinning.

"You cling to ale like a fly clings to horse dung. I will bring you some ale. Do not worry about fetching the water yourself; I will bring it."

"Thank ye, Helwig."

Helwig took the coin offered to him and strolled inside the tavern. He returned with two jacks in one hand and a small serving of meat in the other. When he gave Althalos his water, Althalos began to down it immediately.

"I didn't get ye the water to have you drink it in one gulp!" Gunter admonished Althalos.

"I'm thirsty," Althalos said, water dribbling down his chin.

"Ye will have a better chance of not makin' yerself sick if ye drink a bit slower. Eat the meat, too; ye need yer salts."

Gunter nodded his head in the direction of an empty table. They walked over to the table and sat, and Gunter once more beckoned Helwig to him.

"What do you want, Gunter?"

"Do ye remember the battle on the fields outside of Nara, when we sallied out to the Yhournish encampment and ransacked it?" Gunter said.

"How could I forget? I know you keep bringing it up because we drank all their ale that night. This night, that will be your only cup of ale. I am cutting you off."

Gunter pounded his fist on the table, and Helwig walked off. Althalos leaned on the table, staring at the meat and water with his leg bouncing up and down.

"Why are ye so restless, boy?"

"I cannot sit. I need to get help. I need to go to Wettay and tell Baron Rowe what happened."

"Baron Rowe... Ye can wait on Baron Rowe. Right now, we shall sit and rest. Let me tell ye somethin': yer foolish arse is lucky to be alive. If I had not been there to drag ye to shade and cool ye off with stream water after ye fainted, ye'd be dead. I'm surprised ye aren't pukin' yer guts out right now. Ye need to drink more water. Why the Gol were ye diggin', anyways? What did those dead bastards ever do for ye?"

"I knew them," Althalos said. "If I were slaughtered on the side of the road, I hope someone would bury me."

"Yer just a foolish child," mumbled Gunter.

Gunter waved Helwig down once more.

"Again, Gunter?"

"My friend, do ye have a room for me? I will need a nap once I'm done; I've had a long day savin' this brat."

"The boy can sleep in a room. *You* can sleep in the storeroom."

Before Gunter could raise his voice in protest, Helwig had already walked away.

Moments later, an outburst of laughter erupted a few tables down. Helwig was belly-laughing with all the other tavern-goers. He had his arm around a man dressed in robes, and the man was laughing, too. The robed man held a tankard of mead in one hand, and he was in the middle of chugging it down. Helwig raised his hand and implored everyone to come listen to what the robed man was about to say.

"Helwig, my dear friend, thank you for another night of laughter. I know you all see my face often in the tavern at night, but I have a serious announcement that warrants some degree of sobriety," the robed man said, grinning.

The giddy tavern-goers went quiet, looking at the man with expressions of curiosity.

"I am heading off for Nara. This will be the last time you see my face."

The crowd erupted into chatters. The robed man raised both of his palms, and the crowd fell silent again.

"It is about time for me to get up off my leisurely arse and do what I have wished to do for so very long. I have finished a dissertation regarding the deep corruption I have observed within the Phoenicy. Orator Aswold is pushing for himself to be known as a great reviver of the faith. You all know my thoughts on the Orator. He has ushered in many new practices, most of them bearing no foundation within the holy texts. But I will not bore you any further with the specifics—I will tell you a story, instead.

Our greatest Prophet, Avon the Sword, was not born into a family of wealth or power. In truth, he did not know who his parents were. The Viantse are much different to men in that regard—they are not birthed, they are hatched.

Viantse society was separated into two distinct tribes: the Upper Viantse and the Lower Viantse. The difference between them was quite simple. The Upper Viantse were winged, and the Lower were not. As history knows quite well, whenever there is a tribe that holds an advantage over another, rarely ever is there a people who do not abuse their gifts. The opportunity for power is too enticing; and with an advantage so great, the subjugation of the Lower Viantse was, to some degree, inevitable.

The Viantse customs were strange. One could own an egg, one could own the unhatched. Slavery was not forbidden there— it was quite normal. So when the old continent of Aerus was an archipelago of floating islands, the Upper Viantse would swoop down to the mainland and pluck up whoever they wished to own. It is quite hard to be free with no wings on an island in the sky.

Avon was found unhatched by an Upper Viantse. When he eventually did hatch, it was discovered that despite having been laid by a lower Viantse, he had wings.

The Orator Aswold believes that he himself is the one who rules from the heavens, free to do whatever he wishes to us. The institution he has inherited became his own island in the sky. Yes, he has reached the highest position within the Phoenicy, but where in the holy texts does it say the Orator is the speaker *for* the Phoenix, and not the speaker *to*? When the Narese temples were first formed, they appointed an Orator; but this Orator only relayed the word of the Prophets, they did not enact their own will. With Ava gone—whether you believe him dead or not—how could the Orator believe he has the right to make such overarching changes to the Phoenicy?"

The man paused to scan the crowd. The tavern-goers were leaning in, still listening attentively.

"After the war, the Orator urged for an increase in the tithes. It made sense at first; the Academy was raided and our temples burned. We had to fix the damages. But once they were fixed, why did the tithe stay? Where is this money going? I have spared you the glares other priests have given their laity at the expense of my own standing within Aswold's Phoenicy, and by doing so I have been shunned by those above me in the clergy. Aswold's system favors those with hubristic ambition.

Another change after the war were the requirements for induction into the Phoenic priesthood. Again, it was another reasonable change. The majority of our priests had been killed, so of course a loosening of standards was within reason: the will of the Phoenix must be preached.

Originally, priests had to know the Phoenix's will as well as fish did water. It surrounded their being, fully encompassing them. This standard made sure that any novitiates could do their duties. Furthermore, it made certain that those involved in choosing who became a priest had less opportunity to invoke their own opinions on the matter. There was a tradition of merit, and Aswold replaced it with a tradition of yes-men who see no issue in taking from your coffers to line their own. They concern themselves not with the benefit of the faith. Well, I say nay to that! I say we ought to bring the Phoenicy back to when it was just!"

The tavern-goers cheered, pounding their fists on the tables. Helwig patted his hand on the priest's back and smiled.

"Agathius! Agathius! Agathius!" they all said in unison.

Venceslaus

fter Ser Elseharde and Edit broke from the main party and went to the library, Venceslaus and the Orator headed for the Orator's study. Hymning priests dressed in dark woolen robes and blue sashes roamed the halls, gesturing religious signs. As the Orator passed each priest, the priest would halt their prayer and bow in respect. Venceslaus cringed at it. It was not the Phoenicy he had been brought up in.

They entered the Orator's study. Behind the Orator's desk, there was a stained-glass window that was twice as large as Venceslaus was tall. It was a round window with a circular arch of stone-bricks around it. It depicted Avon standing with the Phoenix behind him, posed in a manner that made his wings look rounded, resembling the corona of the sun. On the Orator's desk were several opened books, blank parchment, and a quill pen. The walls were lined with bookshelves, and there was a musky smell of old parchment in the air. The Orator sat behind his desk and motioned for Venceslaus to take the seat in front of him. The Orator's eyes shifted to and from Venceslaus's knights.

"It seems the further the war recedes into the past, the cleaner the armor of knights and garb of lords become," he said. "Venceslaus, there is something I must ask of you, and I would need you not to spread word of my request. Are these two men at your side trusted?"

Venceslaus squinted. "What is this request?"

The Orator rolled up a piece of parchment that rested on his desk and placed it into a drawer. From that same drawer, he pulled out a map that showed the whole of Mjorn; it marked the locations of various towns, hamlets, and castles. He pointed to Nara.

"Soon, Nara will be the epicenter of the political instability that has been growing in our region. A grain shortage has led to noncompliance by our subjects. As we have already discussed, I would be willing to pledge men to help build your canals in return for you setting aside grain to send to Nara so that we might remedy this. A few of the priests who serve in the city have heard confessions from the King's subjects—a number of them plan on storming the citadel."

Venceslaus stood up. His brows were tensed, and he wagged his finger at the old man.

"I thought priests were not to tell a soul of whatever tale any confessor had spoken!"

The Orator's guards placed their hands on the hilts of their swords; Venceslaus's knights reacted similarly.

"Please sit down and hear me out, Venceslaus," the Orator said.

After a moment, Venceslaus nodded to his knights. When they relaxed, so too did the Orator's guards. The Duke sat back down with a look of contempt on his face.

"It is my primary duty to defend our faith from any threat, and it is my secondary duty as an advisor of the King to defend our kingdom. I am only doing my duty. You are a lord of the people. There is not one person in this kingdom who is not aware of your reputation. The commoners' love for you is ever-present, which is why I am requesting that you—with your men present, of course—speak to the crowd when it eventually forms, so that you might dispel their anger. After we finish arranging our agreement regarding the construction of the canals, you can spread the word of how you brought grain to the people of Nara and saved them from starvation. You will be seen as a hero and a paragon amongst men. But there is one caveat to this: you would, of course, have to help Nara's guard if any violence were to break out."

Venceslaus looked down. His hand rubbed a golden pendant that hung from a chain around his neck.

"I am a faithful man, Orator. I cannot agree to that arrangement. Your plan is born out of a mockery of your faith. It is sworn by all priests to keep their mouths shut when it comes to speaking of one's confession. You are a man whose words bear no weight. I shall be off."

When Venceslaus stood to leave, the door swung open. A priest ran to the Orator's side and whispered something into his ear. The Orator's typically cold demeanor shifted to one of evident concern.

"What?" Venceslaus asked. "What have you heard?"

"It seems the village of Dorthu has been burnt to the ground," the Orator said. "There are no survivors. Even our priest who served the area has fallen. My messenger said we do not yet know who is responsible. This news will surely cause unrest soon enough, especially in Nara. I am begging you, Venceslaus—please help us keep order."

"Ha! You should know, magnificent Orator, you make for a poor beggar."

Venceslaus gestured for his knights to follow him. Together, they left the Orator's study.

"Ser Groent, go collect Ser Elseharde and my daughter from the library and take them to the citadel. I will be there to speak to the King himself."

Ser Groent nodded. Venceslaus left the Academy with his remaining knights following him. As soon as he had made it out of the courtyard, the passersby quickly caught wind of him. Naturally, they walked toward him, watching with awe and pleading for coin. Nara's people were frail, and the priests were easy to spot amongst the people. They could afford to be fat and to buy nice clothes.

"Hello! Good Duke of High Beak! Blessed be Avon that he brought you to me," a voice called.

It was a rotund man dressed in robes and a white sash. On top of his head was a vibrant blue cap with gold stitching at its hems. His robes were silk; they draped over his belly like curtains.

"Thank goodness! Our temple has had quite the trouble funding our food charities recently; the locals have been short with their tithes. Would you mind giving a donation? For the people, of course."

43

Venceslaus had not met this priest before. There were multiple temples in Nara, and Venceslaus knew their Elders; this one must have been new.

"Oh yes, the people do look to be hungry," Venceslaus said. "But you don't. Your stomach looks like it is nearly bursting."

Venceslaus walked over to the priest. He stuck his fist out and lightly knocked on the priest's belly.

"Why should I give money to the man who hides behind his faith to fill his own belly in the name of filling the bellies of others?"

The priest recoiled. Like an idiot, he sputtered around with no words coming from his mouth.

"I am a man of the cloth! I am the medium the impoverished use to fill their stomachs. I am the fork they bring to their maws!"

"A gold-plated fork, lacking prongs."

The Good Duke stormed off. It was a long march to the citadel, but this was not foreign to Venceslaus. He and his knights stormed through the gates of the citadel and went straight for the King's keep. Two guards stood at the doors of the inner ward. One of them held up a hand.

"Halt! What is your reason for entry?"

"To see the King, of course. Why is the keep closed off?"

"The King is not holding court today. He is ill; you can return with your matters another time."

"Have you not seen my face before? Rarely do I ever flaunt my status, but you are halting the King's most powerful vassal. I am not entertaining this. Move out of the way."

One of the guards placed a hand in front of Venceslaus. In response, Venceslaus's own knights puffed their chests up to the guard, their hands going to their sword handles. Venceslaus shook his head at his men. His men paused, then relaxed their hands from their swords. A man with raven-black hair and dark eyes was walking down the long hall that the keep's doors led to. He waved to Venceslaus, and Venceslaus pointed to him. The guards only noticed the man as he stormed past them to shake Venceslaus's hand.

"Duke! Halt—"

"Oh, shut it! He can come through," said the man.

The two guards did not say anything further. Venceslaus turned to his men and wagged a finger to one of them. The knight stood before him, awaiting his orders.

"Ser Jriton, take the rest of the men to the knights' chambers. When we are ready to depart, I will call for you."

Ser Jriton bowed his head and waved his hand to the rest of the knights. They entered the keep and left through one of the many doorways that attached to the main hall.

"We need to talk, Geder."

"Then let us talk, Venceslaus."

Adar

ount Adar awoke to his joints aching. He lifted himself out of his bed and onto his feet. His wife, Anita, slept with a calm beauty. Adar pulled up his trousers, put on his tunic, and laced his boots around his feet.

He stood taller than most other Osmjornish men, and his demeanor was as cold as a rulebook. When he said something ought to happen, it happened. Men both admired and feared him because of that fact. He was as cold as the winds that blew over the white walls of Kurembrog. Rarely, if ever, was he caught showing admiration for anyone but his wife. He was a ruler; that was who he was, and who he had to be.

He left his room and went to the rampart that overlooked the ward of the keep of Kurembrog. Abba was sparring with Ser Mikhail. Upon having watched for a brief moment, he turned away, grimacing. He strode back inside the keep and went down one of the winding halls of the castle. The court of Kurembrog was narrow, and parallel to its entrance was the dais that his throne stood on. It was old and made of a gray oak, the seat and backrest made of a tufted and blue-dyed leather. Waiting on one side of the throne was a bald, elderly man in dark woolen robes; on the other, a younger man who wore a pair of vibrant blue and purple trousers with a blue and purple tunic to match. Adar sat down on his throne.

"Elder Siemond, what is it you advise?"

The elderly man held a letter in his hand. On it, there was a red wax stamp with the seal of a fiery bird. The seal had already been broken. Elder Siemond extended the letter to Adar.

"Well, m'lord, as both your servant and a servant of our faith, I must inform you of the letter I have received from the Orator. His Greatness wishes to inform you that the King of Nar is ill, and that the Orator is temporarily taking up the responsibility of communication between you and the seat of Nar. His Greatness writes that your brother, Lord Geder, has been granted some time away from his duty as Master of the Treasury of Nar, and that he will make his way to attend the Tourney of Belar to watch his nephew compete."

"I have not seen my brother in years," Adar said. "It will be good to catch up with him. Baron va Heddi, what news do you bring?"

"I am pleased to inform you that there has been no trouble with the tax collection within your domain. Our people have continued to do well in the iron trade, and I have recently had the pleasure of talking to your other vassals and persuading them to pay more in taxes. I promised them that the coin would be sent toward the expansion of our docks, which would benefit the iron trade extensively. We have been dealing with an incredible surplus of iron, so instead of having it overflow our local markets, we can ship it off to make more coin."

Adar nodded his head in agreement. "That is wonderful. You did good work; that is a brilliant arrangement." Adar leaned on one of his armrests. "Unfortunately, I tasked Ser Mikhail with whipping Abba into fighting shape—so he is unable to attend this meeting. I did brief him on the matter I planned on bringing up, however, and he mentioned a separate matter for me to bring up as well. Since we are soon to depart for Belar, I intend to appoint an acting castellan. Mikhail suggested that I might vote in his stead on the matter; and being that you have impressed me, Jergi, I find it only fitting that you should take on the role."

Siemond cast his eyes down, his shoulders rolling ever so slightly forward. He shook his head but did not voice his apparent disapproval. Jergi, however, was ecstatic. He had a grin that spanned ear-to-ear and leaned forward to shake the Count's hand energetically.

"You will not be disappointed in your decision, m'lord!" Jergi said, shaking with childish excitement.

"Elder Siemond, I request that you accompany us to Belar, as we are to introduce Abba to his possible betrothed. If her father and I were to agree on terms, we would need you to be there to recognize it as a representative of the faith."

The Elder's posture straightened. He clapped his hands.

"Bless Avon! I will of course travel to Belar with you, m'lord!"

Adar grinned and stood up. "Alright. That concludes this meeting, then. Let us get back to our duties."

The Count left the two men and headed out through the court's large double doors. When he left the hall, he saw his wife, Anita, heading out for the rampart overlooking the castle's ward. She had dark brown hair that waved like the water that hit the rocks on the shores of Kurembrog, and her eyes brought him in like the warmth of a fire in the middle of winter. She smiled as Adar approached her. Adar reciprocated with a smile of his own.

"Good morn, m'lady," Adar said.

Anita grinned. "Good morn to you, my love."

The two walked out onto the rampart. Anita immediately went to look down below.

"The Good Duke has always been a good friend to you. It is so exciting that he has agreed to consider marrying his daughter to Abba!"

Adar smiled and crossed his arms. "It is always advantageous to be in the good graces of the Freiheis. Once married, we would have a great deal of influence on trade in the south; their fief of Bek d'Lifa holds amazing naval and trade opportunities."

Anita rolled her eyes and looked away from Adar. "You always find a way to bring up war or trade and never the excitement of the event. Our son is going to be wed, and of course you think about political power first."

"Yes, yes, you are right, my love. I should be focusing more on the excitement; however, the import of the politics of the decision cannot be understated. It is something we should have Abba realize. It is his duty to think like a lord, yet he thinks like a priest."

"You always speak of Abba with a disgruntled tone. When we first met, you were just like him, and I loved you for it. He is your son, you know. You ought to act like it."

Adar stared down the side of the rampart, mute. Anita sighed, storming off with a typical disappointment. He clenched his fists and stared at the sky with contempt. It was all very easy for her to say. She knew what Adar had done in the past, but she did not know how it ate at him. *Abba must be strong,* he thought. *Abba must do his duty. He must.*

Adar shook his fists loose and walked down the staircase that led down to the ward. He strode past Ser Mikhail and Abba sparring but avoided looking at them. A deep anger lingered inside him, and the only way it could be kept contained was by the omission of what agitated him most. He passed through the portcullis that protected Kurembrog. The pikemen who stood at the gates gave the Count a nod of recognition as he moved between them. His boots patted the old oak boards of the drawbridge. At the end of the drawbridge was an opened gate; it too was guarded by even more of the Count's pikemen.

Now in the bailey of Kurembrog, Adar made various turns until he had reached a street that tightened into a narrow alleyway. Down this alleyway and to the right was a doorway covered with a cut of tasseled, green fabric. He lifted the cloth and entered a room filled with a smelly, smoky haze. Various tapestries hung from every wall, and in the center of the room there was an elderly woman whose bones showed through her skin like a sheet covering a skeleton. She did not move to acknowledge the Count's arrival. She simply stayed seated and blew a cloud of smoke from her mouth.

"Neta. I once more ask of you a favor," Adar said.

The woman lifted an arm toward the Count, her palm facing up. Adar huffed his nerves from him and pulled his dagger from his belt. He slid the blade across his palm and squeezed blood into the decrepit old lady's outstretched hand. As soon as the blood made contact with her loose and wrinkled skin, it tightened around her arms. Her bones became less visible, while fat and muscle proceeded to grow around them. Her white, cobwebby hair grew fuller and took on an auburn hue. She straightened her posture and lifted her head, revealing a face that would make any man look twice. She tilted her head to the Count, her once-dead eyes now a youthful blue.

"What is it, boy?"

"It is about the future of my family. I need to know the state of their well-being when I pass. I need to know if they will be alright."

Neta grinned at Adar as if he were prey, chuckling and shaking her head. "Oh, Adar! You are a rotten fool for how often you visit me. You are already aware of the price. But so be it; I will start the ritual."

Neta stood up and walked toward a rotted wooden table that held an assortment of different stones, gems, and cups of powder laid in rows. She grabbed one of the cups of powder and sat down on the ground. Beside her was a smoking pipe; she poured the powder into its bowl and lit it ablaze. Moving the pipe to her lips, she proceeded to puff on it. A blue-gray smoke emitted from her nose when she blew out, and her eyes darted around in their sockets as if she were having a seizure. Her head leaned back, exposing her neck to the sky. She went limp. If Adar had not been through this before, he would have thought she was dead. She sat idle for a few moments, but then her lips began to move.

"The eldest brother shall fell his enemies with a tactic unseen by all but the youngest of the family."

Her head rolled around her neck like a writhing animal, eventually coming to rest.

"A united kingdom kept together by the prudent son."

Her head rolled once more and rested again.

"A war of flesh and flame that shall change the world forever."

She flailed once more. She squirmed around like a dying worm. Over time, she moved less and less, and for a moment she lay motionless. Eventually, she picked herself up and sat down in the chair.

"Have you received the answers you were looking for?"

"This prophecy seems to speak a great deal about Abba. But that last part about flesh and flame... it appears there will be a war in the future. I wager it will be the Ookosi again. Thank you, Neta," Adar said, staring blankly at the wall.

"Adar, by now you should already know that the prophecies can be remarkably different from what you expect. But, eh—you have never learned. They have never gone the way you wish, yet you still continue to visit me. You are like a dice-tosser; you are addicted to gambling, and the wager is your life," Neta replied, giggling.

"I must go. Have fun with what little youth I have given you."

"Farewell with what little you have left."

Meara

he streets of Belar were filled with beggars and peddlers, winding with no predictable order: one wrong turn could take you from a neighborhood where the inhabitants flaunted their vibrantly dyed clothes to one where they could not afford to cobble their shoes. Because of rampant poverty, it was not an uncommon sight to see a frustrated merchant chasing down a group of sticky-fingered orphans fleeing through the alleyways between the wattle-and-daub buildings. They would plead for help, but the guards rarely patrolled the streets here. They stayed where the money was.

A gang of children loitered outside a burnt-down cottage. They were filthy, their clothes tattered and soiled with a foul musk. They were standing around a boy who was about as wide as an ox, and who had a bit of stubble on his baby face. The rest of the children looked like imps in comparison. All of these imps had brought sacks of filched food and were presenting them to the boy. Meara, a scrawny girl, was the tallest of them all, and she presented the fullest sack.

The piggish boy, Luka, grinned at the sight, proceeding to take the sack from Meara's hands. He opened it and saw what Meara had brought: a plentiful amount of bread and fruits.

"Do you all see this? This is what you all should bring to me!" He snatched a sack from one of the other children and opened it. "There is barely any food in this one! You should be ashamed of yourself, you know. How are we going to stay fed if you bring me nothing?"

A tiny child at the outer edge of the crowd nibbled on a piece of bread. When Luka noticed, he dropped the two sacks in his hands and stomped his way over. He kicked the small child to the ground, leaving him bloodied and scraped. The child began to cry, and soon the crowd surrounded him.

"How dare you! How dare you eat before handing me food! How dare you steal food from the others!"

The crowd shouted and cursed at the small child. While the rest of the children continued their beatings and beratement, Meara reached into her sack and ripped a few tiny pieces of bread from her loaf. She began to eat, refraining from chewing. Luka turned around and returned to where he had been standing, collecting all of the sacks of food and putting them in a pile. He beckoned for the children to gather around him.

"And now we shall distribute the food!" said the tyrant with a grin.

He would pass out quarter-loaves to the smaller children and half-loaves to the older ones. Upon acquisition of the redistributed bread, without fail, the children said *thank you, Luka* and ran off into their own groups. When the battered child made it to the front of the line, he was pushed aside without receiving any bread. Meara's heart sank. When she made it to the front, she gave thanks—and, as a reward for her effort in providing the most food, was given a full loaf. When Luka was not looking, she made her way to the battered child and ripped the loaf in half, handing part of it to him.

"What is your name?" Meara asked the young boy.

He did not speak. His eyes darted around, his arms hugging his body. Meara sighed and went off to her own corner. The area had a few empty barrels and boxes lying around, and she used one of them as a pillow. She leaned one of the box lids on its end to provide some sort of protection from the elements. The sky grew dark, and she pulled a blanket fashioned from pilfered tunics and trousers over herself. She closed her eyes and drifted off into a slumber.

Her eyes shot open. Luka was shaking her.

"Come with me, Meara," said Luka plainly.

She furrowed her brow at Luka, but eventually she let out a sigh and nodded. Luka beckoned her to follow him into one of the several alleyways that shot off from the road. Once they reached the alleyway, Luka halted, turned around, and faced Meara.

"That brat last night was quite disrespectful, was he not? Taking food from all of us like that?" asked Luka, his chubby face jiggling when he talked.

Meara nodded in agreement.

"He took food without a second thought for the others! Filling his gluttonous self. Bah, he was even bold enough to ask for more! Good thing I sent him aside, because his selfish arse had already had his fill."

Meara nodded again. Luka grabbed his own head and squeezed, before eventually relaxing his hand back to his side.

"Now, if you agree, why in Gol did you give him bread? You were hungry, no? You gave him half the damn loaf. I try to help you, and this is the disrespect I receive?"

Meara froze. "I... I wasn't that hungry. He didn't seem to have enough food."

Luka clenched his fists. "You're lucky you brought so much food to the rest of us last night. If you had not, I would have had to punish you. From now on, you will bring back that same amount of food, and you will only get a half-loaf, since you seem not to need a full one. Do not ever betray me like that again."

Meara nodded her head with a nervous speed as Luka walked away. She quickly went back to where she had been resting.

In the morning, she awoke again. The sky was bright and the sun warm. She tore herself from the ground and stretched. While all the other children went off running, she took the time to fold her makeshift blanket and tidy up. She grabbed a sack she had stored under a rock and went off to loot some more food.

She made her way to the road where all the peddlers sold their goods. Between her and the peddlers was a narrow passage through one of the old walls that was frequented by both peddlers and marketgoers. She locked her eyes on a well-dressed elderly man with a purse dangling from his side. He looked to be alone, and he was departing from the market, heading toward the passage. She waited while the old man inched his way toward the corridor. Once he passed through it, she went for him. The passage was crowded, and there was little room for movement; this only slowed the man further. His dangling purse was tied poorly and looked to be an easy snag. In front of the old man, there was a young couple carrying goods they had just purchased. Meara bumped into this couple, causing them to drop their goods. This caught the old man's attention; his curious stares lingered, slowing him down. Meara snatched his purse and dropped it into her sack.

After the theft of the purse, she kept her head down and made her way to the peddler stalls at the market square. People flowed into the square like a stream of coin for the traders. One of the stalls was managed by a fruit salesman. He had a tan complexion, a pointed jawline, and brown eyes. He wore what looked to be a tunic that came all the way down to his ankles and had a white cloth wrapped around his head, draping to his shoulders. His stall was filled with various apples, figs, and all sorts of other fruits. Meara waved to the man and pointed at the fruit.

"You look a bit young to be in the market by yourself," the man said.

His accent was strangely non-foreign, yet he was so obviously a foreigner.

"I may be a bit young, but I have coin, and I want some fruit," Meara said. "And you look too foreign to sound so Osmjornish."

He chuckled. Meara noticed a small scar on his cheek peeking out from beneath his shawl.

"My parents were of a noble family in Low Beak. They fell from grace and decided to move to Belar. I was born and raised here. I still wear my people's clothes because it makes me stand out as a trader; customers expect that I will have something they have never seen before."

Meara squinted, nodding in understanding. The man was a clever businessman. She grabbed one of the figs and examined it.

"How much for one of these?"

"A half-groschen for a fig."

"I will take four."

Meara reached into her sack and opened the pilfered purse, grabbing two pieces of groschen to hand to the trader. The trader gave a subtle bow, and Meara put four figs into her sack. She wandered around the marketplace, making subsequent stops at the various stalls, acquiring loaves of bread, vegetables, and dried fruits as she went. With each stop, the sack grew. Meara soon felt its crushing weight pulling down on her shoulders.

She hauled her loot out of the market square with a proud gait and a smile that was visible to all. However, she soon noticed that the old man she had stolen from earlier was standing in the distance. She put her head down, trying to avoid making eye contact with him. A man stood in front of her; she only noticed him after she had already bumped into him. He stopped her from leaving.

"What are you up to, little one?" said the large man with a smile.

He was dressed in a green tunic with gold stitching at its hems. His boots did not have a speck of dirt on them; they were certainly not working shoes. He had short dark hair, and his face was clean-shaven.

"I... I was just at the market, picking up food for my mother."

"Well, would you open your sack? I would love to see what you got! I bet you are a shrewd haggler. Let's see if your mother will think you spent your coin well."

Meara winced. "I just got some dried fruit and bread; that's all, really."

The man waved the old man over, and as the old man came near, armored men with maces followed. He snatched the sack from Meara.

"Hey! That's mine!"

Meara reached for the sack, but the armored men held her back. The man she'd been speaking to opened the sack and sifted through the food. Once his arm was deep within it, he pulled out a nearly empty purse. The old man pointed at the purse and shook his finger.

"Ah, so it was not only food in the sack," the man said, tossing the purse back to the old man.

"That is my mother's purse! You cannot just take it!" Meara exclaimed.

"No, child. That is my father's purse. Furthermore, you were the one who took it. Do you have any idea who I am?"

Meara shook her head.

"I am Lord Hedmond Kyln, Regent of both the Duchy of Belar as well as the City of Belar. You just stole from my father, Duke Tedi Kyln of Belar."

Meara raised her eyebrows, and her shoulders slouched down. She tried to inch back, pointing her feet away from Hedmond. When the armored men caught wind of this, they stepped closer. Meara realized there was no way that she would escape them, so she straightened her posture. The old man, Duke Tedi Kyln, had a deep frown on his face, his heavy brows weighing down his elderly eyes.

"Cut the bloody thief's hands off. Damn you, wretch!" yelled the old man, raising a trembly, shaking fist.

"Ha! No, Father. In your old age, you forget that she is far too young for such a punishment."

Hedmond faced Meara. He reached into the sack and tossed her a loaf of bread.

"This is all you get to keep; the rest will be confiscated. If you dare to steal again, I may just cut your hands off."

Althalos

hen the inn-goers ended their applause, they huddled around Agathius and raised a toast to him. Agathius shook his fist with glee, accepting drinks from his fellow townsfolk. He would always refer to those who spoke to him by name, and they looked at him with a smile. Althalos felt the urge to speak to the man, so he stood up and walked over to Agathius.

"Where are ye goin', boy?" questioned Gunter.

"Priests are well-connected people, aren't they? They are also men of charity, so people would come to them for refuge. If anyone has heard anything, it would be him."

Gunter dragged his eyes away from Althalos and back to his cup.

"Go on, then. Speak to the priest."

Althalos nodded. The inn-goers were still huddled around Agathius. Some moments, they would be quiet; others, they would be laughing so hard that they lost control of their limbs. Althalos wormed his way through the crowd. When he had made it halfway, he attempted to wave at Agathius to gain his attention. Agathius did not notice.

"Yes, yes, I know that it is out of character and that you all wish for me to stay longer, but I must ready my belongings for the road. I have delayed this journey for far too long."

Agathius handed his drink off to another man, and the man downed the drink with inhuman haste. The crowd cheered as Agathius turned away; as he left the crowd, Althalos followed.

"Hey! Hey!" yelled Althalos.

Agathius turned around and noticed Althalos.

"Oh, you are the boy that sat next to Gunter. You don't look familiar; what is your name?"

"My name is Althalos. I come from Dorthu. Has anyone come to your temple for refuge? There has been a massacre."

"This is the first I am hearing of this," Agathius said. "Dorthu, you said? That is very sad news. I knew the priest there. Unfortunately, you are the only refugee from Dorthu that I have met. What did the attackers look like?"

"I did not see them up close—I was on the outskirts of Dorthu when I first heard the screams—but when I returned, they had already left. I found this torn red cloth there; I imagine it is from a bandit."

Agathius raised his brows. "It surely cannot be. Be careful, boy. Hide that away."

"Why? What do you mean?"

"That is the color of the Harferd family. Strange—they must have come from the opposite road. They did not pass through Fisk. Maybe they were avoiding us."

"Harferd? As in King Harferd's house guard? Are you sure it could not belong to some bandit?"

"Oh, I am certain it is from someone in the employ of the Harferds. I know the color quite well, and that pattern surely is too gaudy for a bandit to afford. I would be surprised if it was not from the Harferds."

Althalos's fists tightened and his face turned red. He felt hot, his body jittering as he gestured.

"I need to go to Lord Rowe. It cannot be that he accepted Dorthu being burnt to the ground. What lord would accept that?"

Agathius raised his hand. "Are you sure that you want to do that? You have never left Dorthu, I presume?"

"No, never."

"Right. You have only seen Baron Rowe now and then. I am under the employ of Lord Harry Rowe. Now, I do not answer to him, but I do have to speak to him often. I do not know why Harferd knights would attack Dorthu—the last I heard, the

Harferds and Rowes were quite close—but I would still be very careful when speaking to Baron Rowe."

"Why are you so sure the King did this?"

"Like all other priests, I was taught in the Academy. I have seen Harferd banners countless times. Whoever dyed that cloth used the same color dye that is used on those banners. Once you see enough heraldry, you can easily discern whose are whose," Agathius said. "I feel sympathy for you, Althalos. I would not recommend going alone to Wettay—I would offer my aid, but I have to get to Nara. In any case, you would need a great deal more help than I could give. Ask Gunter if he would help you. I wouldn't bet on him, but it may interest him. I will be at the temple packing for my departure tomorrow if you need me again. May the Phoenix watch over you, and the rest of those from Dorthu."

Agathius bowed and waved farewell to Althalos. Althalos waved back. Gunter still sat at the same table, staring at his drink as if his gaze was going straight through it. He would tap the edge of his cup every so often, then continue off into the same deep stare.

"So," he said, looking up when he heard Althalos approaching. "Ye have come back, boy?"

Althalos held out the red cloth so that Gunter could see. Gunter grabbed it from his hand.

"Why are ye handing me this?"

"Agathius told me the cloth comes from someone in service to the Harferds. You fought at Nara. Does this look the Harferd colors?"

Gunter tossed the cloth on the table.

"I fought with a lot of Harferd men, and they would wear this color. This one probably came from a knight; a cape like this would be costly."

"Gunter, the people who burnt down Dorthu could not have gotten far; there is time to go to Baron Rowe and catch them. Will you help me?"

"Huh? I saved ye once already, boy, and ye now ask me for another favor? Be off—ye can get killed on yer own."

"Fine, I will. You can wallow in your drink alone."

Gunter stared at his cup. His lip quivered, almost as if he had tasted something sour.

"Wait, pisspot," he said. "Come back here."

Gunter's grimace left him. He looked concerned, his eyes downcast, flicking back and forth across the tabletop. Althalos could tell that thoughts were going quickly through his head. After a moment, he looked up at Althalos, squinting at him.

"I'll go with ye. Ye've got some fight in ye, but yer stupid. Ye can barely handle the sun, let alone someone with a weapon."

"Thank you, Gunter."

"Do not thank me."

Althalos nodded. "Agathius said he would be leaving for Nara tomorrow."

"He's annoyin'," Gunter said. "How about ye go talk to him and tell him we will leave with him."

Althalos nodded. He walked over to the Phoenic temple across the road. He stepped through the spires and opened the doors to the building. The walls were mostly pale, bare, and composed of gray stone-bricks; but they were graced with several stained-glass windows that depicted various religious scenes and figures. In the center of the room, Agathius stood, shifting papers from his table to his satchel. At his side, there was a boy dressed in robes writing notes. Like Agathius, the boy held himself up straight; but he moved awkwardly, as if he did not know how to properly control his limbs.

"Ditwin, I gave you the sermons for the coming weeks, correct?"

"Yes, Brother Agathius."

Ditwin's voice perplexed Althalos. It was much deeper than he had expected. Althalos paused, but he had already caught Ditwin's eye—both he and Agathius turned to greet him. Ditwin smiled and waved, extending his hand for a handshake. As Althalos moved closer, he noticed how shaky the boy's hands were, as well as the height difference between Ditwin and himself.

"Hello there, and you are...?"

Althalos shook Ditwin's hand. "I am Althalos. Agathius, Gunter agreed to come with me to Wettay. I was thinking we could leave with you and split off at Wettay."

"Oh, that is wonderful news! But remember, Althalos, I am leaving at sunrise. I cannot wait for anyone. The matter I am handling is of the utmost importance. When I am done, the Phoenicy will be forced to fix the issues it produces. Be packed and ready."

"If you go, who will run the temple here?"

"Me, of course," chimed Ditwin.

"You look a bit young for a priest," Althalos said.

"Do not let appearances fool you," Agathius said. "Ditwin may look young, but he has gone through all the rites of the priesthood. He is a brother of the faith. He is my lesser and I am his greater, and if anyone knows the faith well, it is Ditwin. In fact—how old are you, boy?"

"I am nineteen," Althalos said.

"Ha! That would make Ditwin older than you. He just turned twenty a few days ago."

Althalos chuckled. "He is half my size!"

"I may be small, but that is of no consequence to my age," Ditwin said. "What I lack in body, I make up for in mind."

"You two are unlike any of the priests in Dorthu. Why is it that you and Agathius are so different?"

"Most minor priests nowadays grew up during the war. The older, more distinguished priests were the only ones who survived that war," replied Ditwin.

"Ditwin, like you, was born during the war with the Yhournish, but you both were too young to remember much and thus do not understand how the war affected the faith," Agathius said. "These men bear no sadness; they are cowards. The men of faith who survived the war were the craven Brothers who hid away and did not take up arms in defense of the faith.

There were a large number of good priests that fought, and a number of them possessed magic. The children of Enok went for them first—that is one of the reasons why there are not many mages in the Phoenicy. Those who did not have magic stayed locked away in a family member's castle or some other fortification; and that way, they survived. Many of my good Brothers died, and that allowed the cowards that did survive to take their place in the Phoenic leadership. Those same cravens trained the next generation of priests and gave them their rites, but they perverted the way in which we traditionally went about training priests. Most priests now would have been quickly ousted and mocked before the war, for they are nothing better than pompous street criers. This is one of the reasons I must go to Nara," Agathius said, staring into Althalos's eyes with a fiery zeal.

Ditwin shakily handed a pile of notes to Agathius, who immediately stowed them in his satchel. His hands continued to tremble while he attempted to write down the transfer of notes.

"Ditwin was born with a hand tremor. I offered him some fennica flower, but he refused. It does not seem he was meant for writing, yet he still decided to become a priest."

Agathius squinted, then threw up his hands.

"I almost forgot…"

Agathius walked toward one of his desks and pulled open a wide drawer. Inside, there was a random collection of knickknacks, quill pens, and strange rocks. He pulled out an object that was wrapped in a tattered, deep blue cloth. He removed the fabric and revealed an arming sword with a pommel in the shape of an eagle's head. Ditwin's eyes widened. Althalos's expression held no less surprise.

"Agathius, I did not know you kept a sword," Ditwin said, staring at the blade.

"Ditwin, my boy. When I said many of the good Brothers who fought in the war died, I did not mean *all* of them."

Edit

he Book-keeper stared at the closed bronze doors on the opposite end of the entrance to the library. He scoffed to himself and turned around. Edit stared at him, confused.

"Are you well, Elder?" she asked.

"Oh, I am alright," he said. "Every time I look at those doors... I am reminded of the past."

"What of the past?"

"The war started in that very room. Rarely, if ever, does anyone enter—very few are allowed. Only I, the Orator, and the Pyre Elders may, but I am the only one who ever does. Despite the value of the room, they never go in. It would have been better if they did—what we could learn in there is invaluable. Yet they refuse to."

"What is in there?" asked Edit. "If the room is full of books, could you yourself not read them and then teach their contents?"

"Heh. It is not so simple. What would be learned inside could not be read from a book."

"What would you learn from?" asked Ser Elseharde.

"It is no matter," said the Book-keeper. "Talking about that room brings me discomfort."

Ser Groent marched into the library. He carried his helmet between his arm and his side. He was around the same age as Edit's father, or slightly younger. He always had a tired, distant, look in his eyes, but he never sounded glum.

"Lady Edit! Ser Elseharde! Lord Venceslaus has ordered me to take you to the citadel!" he yelled from across the room.

"Ser! This is a library!" yelled Bertram the Book-keeper.

Ser Groent laughed, then walked over to meet with them. Ser Elseharde extended his hand to the knight, and Ser Groent took it.

"Thank you for retrieving me from babysitting duty, Ser," Elseharde said, giving a sly smile to Edit.

Edit pushed Elseharde on his chest. "Quiet, you. I will tell my father if you aren't kind to his only daughter."

"Hah! Edit, you should do it for the fun of it. Elseharde has never been flogged, and it is apparent," said Ser Groent.

Ser Groent was clean-shaven on both his scalp and face. On his face, there was a scar that went from the attachment of his ear to the center of his cheek. He led the two out to the Academy's courtyard and to the stables. Upon noticing the knight, the stablehand waved him over and pointed him toward two horses.

"Over there, Ser," said the stablehand.

Ser Groent made his way over to one of the mares and mounted it. Ser Elseharde mounted the other, and once on top, he held his hand out to aid Edit in mounting the back of his horse. The party galloped out of the courtyard and into the streets of Nara. They passed wandering burghers and beggars. For the most part, the crowds paid little to no attention to them, but occasionally a beggar would scream profanities at them with a waving hand; when Edit's father was not around, they were not fans of the wealthy.

The quality of the buildings improved as they neared the citadel. The homes near the Academy were dilapidated, and the buildings by the citadel were not new, but they were well built and better maintained. Just outside the citadel's gates was the bustling Narese market square. As expected, there were far more guards here than anywhere else. The gates were open, but Edit could not see the keep past the crowds of people and steps. Above the gate were several crenellated towers that jutted into the sky. They were painted a light gray that looked yellow in the shining sun. In front of the gates were two guardsmen dressed head-to-toe in chainmail with kettle helmets on their heads. They both wore a blood-red, short-sleeved surcoat with the sigil of a boar holding the broken shaft of a spear in its maw. In their hands were spears; they rested the butt-ends on the ground while they stood in place, unmoving.

"Hail! What is your reason for entry?" one of the guards asked.

Ser Groent waved to the two guards.

"This is the Lady Edit Freihei, daughter of Lord Venceslaus, and we knights are in service to Lord Venceslaus. He ordered us to join him in the citadel."

The guard nodded and stood off to the side, allowing the party to enter. Just past the gates was the ward of the citadel: in the middle was a square podium built of slabs of stone, and within it was an engraved map of Mjorn.

"Go around the map; the Narese nobility hate it when others step on it," said Ser Groent.

Ser Elseharde and Edit did as Ser Groent said and avoided trampling the map. They headed toward the double doors that allowed entrance into the inner ward of the citadel; the doors were wide open, and another pair of guards stood outside of them.

"Aye! Who are you three?" asked one of the guards.

"We are with Lord Venceslaus," said Ser Groent.

"Oh my Avon… We are not going to argue with you as we did with him. We cannot let you in—King's orders. He is not taking court."

"I do not see my father here. Where is he?" asked Edit.

The guard shook his head. "Your *father* is with the treasury master. He is fine; and thank Avon he took him of our hands, or else we would have to argue with him all day."

Behind the two guards, two ladies walked forward. One had black hair and wore a crimson dress, and the other had blonde hair and wore a velvety blue dress. Both of the women's garments were noticeably expensive; Edit had only ever seen a similar quality in material and tailorship in her own wardrobe.

"Why are you two buffoons preventing this lady from seeing her father?" asked the dark-haired woman.

The faces of the two guards straightened up, as did their posture.

"Queen-Consort Olena. We halted these three from entering the keep by the order of His Majesty. They are with Duke Venceslaus."

"When did the King order you to not let the Duke of High Beak's companions enter?"

"The Head of the Guard said that the King did not want anyone to come in for court. We were not to allow anyone to enter unless they lived or worked in the keep."

"You are daft. Let them in," ordered the Queen-Consort.

The two guards looked to each other, then backed away to the sides of the entrance.

"Malaina, take these three to Duke Venceslaus and Lord Geder; I am going to return to my quarters and tend to the King."

The blonde-haired woman curtsied and beckoned Edit and the knights to follow. They dismounted from their horses and continued forward.

"So, you are the Lady Edit?" Malaina asked.

"I am." Edit curtsied.

"Oh, there is no need to curtsy to me—you are the daughter of a Duke, and I am the sister of a Baron," Malaina said, giggling at Edit's gesture.

Edit's face colored. "What are you doing here in Nara, then?"

"I am the personal tailor of the King and Queen-Consort. There is a great deal more use for a tailor in here Nara than there was in my older brother's barony."

"Of what lands is your brother Baron?"

"Harry is the Baron of Wettay."

Ser Groent winced. "Lady Rowe, I am sorry to be the one to inform you of this, but Dorthu was burnt to the ground. None survived. That is why Venceslaus went off to the citadel without us."

Malaina's eyes widened. She stopped in her steps. Edit and Ser Elseharde stopped just behind her, stumbling a bit while his eyes went wide.

"And that means that Priest Larmond has passed away. Apologies," said Malaina, a tear running down her cheek.

"No need to apologize, m'lady. I knew people from Dorthu, as well. From the war."

The tears that flowed from Malaina's eyes wettened her hands while she wiped them away, attempting to compose herself.

"A moment, please." She sniffled.

Before them was a large, lackluster stone building. Edit had expected the keep to be grand—the King was one of the most powerful people in the world, after all. But there was a round building that connected to the keep that was more interesting than the keep itself, with engraved columns on the outside of its walls.

The doors of the keep were open, and when they entered, they were hit with the smell of cinnamon. Candles lined the walls; they must have been the origin of the scent, for the smell became stronger when they grew nearer. In between each candle was a banner with the Harferd Boar, as well as tapestries that displayed scenes of war: horses, knights, and rivers of blood. The sound of muffled yelling echoed from down the hallway.

Edit's father was standing with his arm resting on the wall and his fist balled up, shaking in the air. He was speaking to another man who wore a gold coat with black stitching that resembled vines. His hair was dark black with hints of gray, and his eyes were as black as a candleless dungeon.

"This will be news to the people sooner or later—and when they are informed of it, it will become a problem," said the man. He had a harsh accent, speaking his words clearly and quickly.

"I'm very well aware of that," said Venceslaus. "But as it stands, the Orator seems to have no intention of handling the issue other than pleading with me to use my standing with the people to remedy the King's own poor governance."

"Father," Edit interrupted. "If you could help, then why don't you?"

"I was wondering the same thing. Why is it that you won't, Duke Venceslaus?" said the man.

"I will explain more in private, Edit. The Orator has never liked me, and I do not trust his judgement or direction."

"Ha! If anyone other than you were to have said such a thing, they would be apprehended," said the man.

Upon closer inspection of his coat, Edit realized that the stitching did not depict vines; they were snakes.

"Unfortunately, speaking plainly has become unpopular in Nar nowadays. Geder, we ought to finish our earlier conversation; Edit, if you would wait outside—"

"Ah, yes, your daughter's betrothal," Geder said.

Edit's eyebrows raised in shock. "What? You are marrying me off without even speaking to me about it?"

"I was going to discuss it with you after we had gone over everything," Venceslaus said, sighing.

Geder raised his hand. "Apologies, Lord Venceslaus. It was not my intention nor my place to be the messenger of this information. I assumed you would have already informed your daughter of the betrothal."

Edit scowled. "He should have."

"It was never set in stone, so there was no reason to inform you of it," Venceslaus said.

"And to whom is it that I am supposedly going to be married?"

"Abba Kurem," Geder said. "My nephew and heir to my brother, Count Adar Kurem. They hold lands off the Osmjornish coast."

Edit frowned. She felt as if there were a knot in her chest. She shook her head, turning on her heel and storming off down the hall.

"Elseharde!" Venceslaus called. "Follow her."

"Yes, m'lord."

When Edit left the keep, she found a spot on the stone balustrade that lined the steps to the building and plopped herself down onto it. She huffed and sulked, staring at the ground. She people-watched in the courtyard, counted their steps, noticed their choice of clothing—anything to get her mind off of the news that she had just been met with.

If her father went through with it, her life would be uprooted. She would have to leave her home to live wherever that *Abba* lived. Osmjornia was cold, and Edit hated the cold.

Elseharde exited the keep. He looked around the courtyard for a moment; then, when he found her, quickly walked over found a spot on the balustrade beside her. He sat silently for a moment as he awkwardly gesticulated, attempting to form words. He let his arms fall to his side and sighed.

"Edit, you know this is the way of things."

Edit glared at Ser Elseharde.

"You know what I mean," he said. "You are a girl born into nobility; it is the duty of daughters such as yourself to be married off. It is as much a duty as it is for myself to risk my life for the life of your father."

"I was born into nobility; I did not choose to be a Duke's daughter. You chose to become a knight. Our duties are entirely different."

"Heh, you are right." He hesitated for a moment, then continued to speak. "It may not be appropriate for a person of my status to say this; but as someone who has lived through true hardship, I must. I have chosen to work hard, day and night, to get to where I am. That hard work has given me the freedom to choose my path. What have you done, Edit? You were blessed with being the daughter of the highest-honored Lord in all of Nar—more honored than even King Asbyorn—yet you have obtained no skills and have lived an easy life full of entertainment and socializing. I can tell you only care for status; it was evident by the disappointment on your face when you saw Orator Aswold this morning instead of the King."

Edit's blood boiled. She was furious, but she could think of nothing to say to Elseharde, so she stood up from the balustrade and stormed off.

"What in Avon did you say to her?" berated Malaina, going out of the keep after her.

Malaina rushed toward Edit and called her over. Edit ignored Malaina, but eventually, Malaina caught up to her and grabbed her by the hand.

"What do you want?" snapped Edit.

Malaina crossed her arms and stared Edit down. "I understand you are frustrated, but I am not the one who wronged you. So don't you dare treat me as if I did."

"I apologize," Edit replied, speaking in a calmer tone. "What do you want?"

"Walk with me."

Elseharde tried to follow, but Malaina shooed him away. "Tell the Duke that Edit is with me, and leave her alone."

She looped her elbow through Edit's, their steps falling into sync. "He was out of line, saying that to you."

Edit did not respond.

"I hope you don't mind me asking, but—if you don't want to take on the role of a Lord's daughter, what *do* you want?"

"Does it matter?" Edit said sourly. "I have no choice. I was born into this."

"Were you listening to what I said earlier? I am a Lord's daughter as well, but I have not been married off."

"So?"

Edit's attitude seemed as if it hit a nerve in Malaina, her eyes going cold for a brief moment. It looked like she swallowed down whatever angry reaction that was about to come from her.

"*So*, I know exactly what you are going through. I, too, was to be married off—but I did something with myself, and I earned a status that many would envy. Sure, I was ridiculed by my father at first, but he learned to accept it in time."

"But your father was only a baron. My father is a duke. Would that not make it much harder for me to attempt to do the same as you?"

"It would be *much* easier. My father was only a baron, and he was far hungrier than your father for status. Marrying off his children was probably his strongest tool to achieve that aim. Your father is known far and wide, even in other kingdoms; he already has his status and renown. Gol, he may even be supportive of you finding your place in the world."

"I suppose."

"If there was one thing that you truly enjoyed, Edit, one thing you would truly be happy to do, what would it be?"

Edit stared down at her shoes, pondering the question. What did she enjoy? As Elseharde said, it was true that she did not have any real skills she could claim. She only cared about status. The question of marriage had never occurred to her, not in any real sense; she was the only child of her father, the Duke of High Beak, and was naturally the heiress to his demesne. That was the only future that she had ever envisioned.

"I wish to be free, Malaina. That is all."

"Then I recommend you figure out what freedom means to you."

"Freedom is power over one's own life…" Edit paused. "My life has never been under my control. It has always been decided by my father. It has been this way for so long that I quite honestly do not know my own will."

"Ha! Do not fool yourself, Edit. You can only suppress the thoughts of what you want for so long. Sit and think about what you want from your life; it will come to you. Will you be in attendance when King Asbyorn holds court tomorrow morning?"

"I thought he was sick. How do you know he is holding court tomorrow?"

"Do not worry about that; he is feeling better. Pay attention, Edit. If you seek power over your own life, then observe the behavior of the people who have power over theirs."

Edit nodded. Malaina curtsied, so Edit returned a curtsy of her own. The two parted ways.

Edit looked back and saw Ser Elseharde still waiting at the balustrade. She dragged her feet back to him and stood beside him, refusing to look him in the eyes.

"Take me to my room," commanded Edit.

Elseharde narrowed his eyes at Edit, but bowed anyway. He motioned for her to follow him. They re-entered the keep and made their way toward a stairway. Elseharde placed his hand on the pommel of his sword. He made sure to direct his sheathed blade away from the walls. They climbed two stories up and walked down a long hallway. At the end of the hall stood a guardsman dressed in mail.

"Hail, knight. What is it that you require?" the guard asked.

"I am here to deliver the Lady Edit, daughter of Duke Venceslaus, to her chambers."

The guard nodded and began to walk down the hall, motioning for them to follow him. Near the end of the corridor, the guard opened a large door. Elseharde thanked the guard and held the door open for Edit. Together, the two walked inside. Edit turned around and stared Elseharde down.

"What is it that *you* need?"

"I wanted to apologize for speaking out of turn. It was not my intention to insult you," Elseharde said, bowing his head.

Edit looked away, gritting her teeth. "Elseharde, please go."

Elseharde bowed and exited the room.

Adar

dar exited the witch's abode. He walked with haste, keeping to himself while he walked back to his castle. He never waved to the children or spoke to their parents as he traveled through his town. Adar's philosophy was simple: he had a duty. One was required to do their duty, regardless of their own desires. As Lord of Kurembrog, Adar's only duty to his people was to provide them their protection, not to be friendly toward them. While they would cry out for his acknowledgment, Adar would often ignore them. Some of the townsfolk that had heard Adar speak knew his philosophy quite well and would refrain from asking for a helping hand. Instead, they would deliver him a face of contempt. Very rarely did Adar ever spend time in the Kurembrog bailey; consequently, many of his subjects did not know what he looked like. Oftentimes, the cries for his acknowledgment were from the poor burghers that took him to be some rich merchant who might toss them a coin as charity. The commoners had a smell to them, and Adar disliked it. He thought their odor to be a manifestation of their position in life.

Adar's posture was firm and straight. He would never take a step that deviated from the quickest path to his destination. If someone were to interrupt him with something stupid, like light-hearted banter, then he would berate them—especially if it were not befitting of their position in society.

Adar noticed Baron va Heddi walking toward the town square, so he hailed him over.

"Ah, greetings, m'lord!"

"Jergi, what brings you to the market?"

"I oft walk down to the merchants to make small talk so that they know I am a friendly face," Jergi said. "It is hard to prevent disputes during tax collection if those from whom you are collecting tax hate you."

"I suppose that is not a waste of effort," Adar said, squinting.

The Baron put his hand on the Count's shoulder and smiled. "You know I do not waste time, friend."

Adar recoiled away from the Baron's touch, brushing his hand off of his shoulder.

"How were Elder Siemond's prayers?" Adar asked.

"To be honest, m'lord, I honestly cannot tell you what that priest went over today. I was too busy explaining the world to Abba, with the hope that he would be more excited to become Count of Kurembrog."

"I did not ask you to speak to my son," Adar snarled.

"M'lord, your son is now more eager than ever. I believe it would serve your interests well if you left me more responsibility to counsel Abba."

"That responsibility is Ser Mikhail's alone. You will cease asking about this. My son needs to be a strong leader and fearsome general, not a pestering book-keeper!"

Adar stormed off. As he walked away, Adar heard the Baron call after him.

"Adar! When you go speak to him, you will be glad that I did!"

The Count held up his hand and waved the Baron's voice away while he strutted toward his castle. As he walked away, his expression was sullen. He cursed the Baron's name under his breath, keeping his eyes fixed on the gatehouse that led to his castle. He wanted to forget the Baron's deviance and the disgust it had brought him. If things just went the way they were supposed to, then the world would be free from tragedy.

Adar delved into deep thought, constantly questioning the meaning of the witch's words. He wished to know if he was correct in his interpretation. Every time he went to see Neta, he made certain to recollect the words verbatim; his obsession led him to repeat the words in his head until he had them written down. The cost of the prophecies was too great to forget them. He had to get it written down, and soon.

Adar redirected himself toward the temple. When he got there, the temple was almost empty, with just a few lone commoners praying the in the pews. Elder Siemond stood at his podium handling some loose pieces of parchment, stacking them on top of one another. When he saw the Count, he bowed, acknowledging him.

"Welcome to the temple, m'lord."

"Siemond, grab a blank sheet of parchment and write something down for me."

"Alright, m'lord."

The Elder grabbed a blank sheet and placed it in front of him. He nodded to the Count, signaling he that he was ready to begin.

"Write down 'the eldest brother shall fell his enemies with a tactic unseen by all but the youngest of the family'."

The Elder stared off for a moment but wrote it down soon after.

"Next line: 'a united kingdom, kept together by the prudent son'."

The Elder wrote down the line, but shifted his gaze to the Count.

"Did you see that witch again?"

"Just write this down, Siemond. Next line: 'a war of flesh and flame that shall change the world forever'."

The Elder wrote it down.

"You really should not be seeing her, Adar. You know her price. I wish the Phoenicy had never agreed to let her live. Her death would bring you peace."

"Siemond, I understand that you are my spiritual advisor, but I needed to see her. Do not question me on this matter again," Adar replied, possessing an unyielding stare.

"Very well, m'lord. What do you believe this prophecy to mean?"

"I do not know what to believe of the first line. Abba is not known for his ability to make war. And what of the *youngest of the family*? Does it mean Maric?"

"M'lord, my heart is with the boy, but my brain tells me that he is not a warring lad. I would not put much thought into these prophecies—they never served you well."

74

"These prophecies can be interpreted in many different ways. I understand your skepticism, but that is why I had you write them down. We will discuss this later; but for now, that note will stay with you to ponder over."

Siemond had to know of the prophecies. If he found out that Adar had kept them from him, Siemond would be displeased. The Elder squinted at the third prophecy written on the paper.

"This one is troubling. 'A war of flesh and flame' seems like every war, but it is probably more symbolic than that. Flame could refer to the Phoenicy, but I have no idea as to what 'flesh' may symbolize."

"Aye, that particular prophecy is unnerving. We ought to keep these a secret between us two for now."

"Aye, m'lord," the Elder said, bowing.

The Count exited the temple. He kept his head down; there were a number of commoners around, and he did not wish for his time to be wasted. He sped up his gait in order to reach the castle sooner, for being surrounded by the commoners gave him a sense of rising dread.

He passed by the gatehouses and entered the ward of his castle. Abba was standing at the sparring grounds, staring at a sword on the ground. Maric was there as well, and the two picked up their swords and began training. Abba was beaten again, and again, and again, and again, but he would always pick the sword back up and continue. For the first time in a long while, Adar smiled. Despite the Baron falling out of line, he seemed to have caused a tolerable outcome. Adar's heart was warmed while he watched his two sons train.

"Quite a shocking sight, innit, m'lord? You will be even more surprised that Abba was the one to ask Maric to spar with him. He wasn't forced to," Ser Mikhail said.

"It is shocking."

Adar's smile returned to his regular callous expression. His heart began to pound; he let out a huff, trying to calm himself down. The Baron had spited him. The Baron had embarrassed him. How could the Baron influence Adar's own children more than Adar could? He balled his hands into fists. Mikhail, still smiling, shot a glance at Adar; but when he noticed Adar's expression, he ceased smiling.

"You seemed proud for a moment, m'lord, but now you look dissatisfied. What troubles you?"

75

"Despite my desire for Abba to grow into his duty, this situation bothers me. Why did he suddenly decide to commit to training now? It seems out of order, out of his character," Adar said. "I have tried to get him to do so for as long as I can remember. I believed he would never take the initiative."

Mikhail grinned. "Do you remember that skirmish, the one that began our last conflict with the Ookosi?"

"The one where we were ambushed? What about it?"

"Before we engaged the Ookosi, we believed that it was going to be a victory with little effort on our part. It made sense; we were under the belief that the particular band with whom we were engaging was just a small group of Ookosi raiders who had no particular renown or allegiance to anything but coin."

"Until we soon realized that they were not a band of raiders, but rather a very disciplined band of warriors. Where are you going with this?"

"That belief we held was wrong," said Mikhail. "Adar, sometimes we are wrong."

Adar stood still, his face joyless. "That is the nature of the Low Ookosi. They are unpredictable roaches. I have known my son for his whole life, and he has only been predictable. He has always shunned the sword and found an unseemly comfort in books and reading. Mikhail, keep an eye on Abba and who he speaks with."

"Do you suspect someone of trying to influence him?"

"I do not suspect; I know. I have told them to cease their attempts. Just watch the boy."

"Of course, m'lord," replied Ser Mikhail, bowing deeply and departing.

Adar leaned against one of the pillars that held up the balcony overlooking the ward. His brows furrowed while he watched his sons sparring with their swords. Maric held himself together quite well. His stance was not perfect, but it was damn close to it. He wasn't too narrow in his footing, allowing him to circle Abba while Abba attempted his own attacks. Abba, on the contrary, moved poorly. He did *not* attempt to circle Maric, for he would get frightened by Maric's ripostes and shuffle backward, giving Maric an open target for striking. It was tradition for the eldest son to inherit, but what mattered more: the eldest or the most capable? The question reminded Adar of his own inheritance; of how his brother, Geder, had been passed up in favor of Adar.

Adar lamented the days when Geder had been named heir of Kuremdod. Life was much simpler and freer then.

Over and over, Abba was struck down by Maric's blade. Maric's will to be a tenacious swordfighter was mature compared to Abba's newfound drive. Adar scoffed at Abba, expecting his unexpected determination to pass—yet Abba continued to get up each time he was struck down. After a while, Maric called off the sparring. He helped the visibly displeased Abba up off the hard soil of the training ground. Adar shook his head and left for his keep.

Upon entering, he made his way to his study. He opened the door and immediately pulled out the chair at his desk and sat down. In the center of the room, there was a stone brick fireplace. Around its hearth lay numerous ornaments left by numerous past Lords of Kurem. These ornaments were all unremarkable, however, when compared to what was displayed on the mantel. The piece was a warmaul, and its design was anything but domestic. Its shaft was straight and made of a lightweight gray stone with an engraved ribbing running along it. At the butt of the shaft was a silver cap that took the shape of a bulb, and etched into it was a language that looked notably old.

The head of the maul was the most peculiar. It was quite large, or at least larger than any maul made in Osmjornia. It was not made of steel—it was made of a dark black stone that, despite the labors of several past Lords of Kurem, could never hold a shine. It would tarnish immediately after any attempt to polish it. It soaked up any luster; it was as though light was afraid of it.

Adar stood up and walked toward it. He gawked at it, face filled with awe. Often, he would place a candle near its head just to see the flame go from a bright yellow to a darker, more desaturated hue. The weapon itself was not heavy, but it felt as if it drained strength away from one's muscles the longer it was held. He placed a finger on the maul's head. He left it there until he felt his strength begin to fade.

"I wonder who had the endurance to wield you in battle," Adar muttered to himself while he backed away toward his desk.

He sat back down and scanned over his desk. He reached his left hand for a sheaf of papers. After flicking them straight, he began to read over them.

The Lineage of House Kurem
King Mecidar the Serpent-Slayer
The Founder of Kurembrog. Slayer of the Twin White Serpents. Succumbed to old age.

Petty King Kurem of Kurembrog
Son of Mecidar. A quiet and peaceful rule. Succumbed to old age.

Petty King Hagdar the Firebrand
Son of Kurem, elder to Kurdar and Mecidar II. A vociferous opponent of the Empire of Nar. Succumbed to Illness.

Count Kurdar the Kneeler
Son of Kurem, younger to Hagdar, elder to Mecidar II. Bent the knee to the Empire of Nar. Succumbed to Illness.

Count Mecidar II
Son of Kurem, younger to Hagdar and Kurdar. Of no renown. Succumbed to old age.

He continued down the list. Nothing was recorded regarding the maul. He set the papers down and brought his hands to his face, rubbing his eyes tiredly. The maul was important once before, and now its importance was lost to obscurity. His father had never told him its origin. Maybe he had intended to, but he had never had the chance; Adar had learned of his inheritance and his father's death at the same time, when he returned to Kurembrog after meeting with his then soon-to-be wife, Anita Demenstin.

Adar grabbed a couple of the other papers stacked on his desk and went through them. There were a number of letters addressed to him each coming from either an advisor or vassal. One of the papers was titled 'A Semimonthly Record of Customs Duties'. Adar flipped through some of its pages. He reached a page that concerned the iron custom duties that Adar's lands had received for the year thus far. In the first five semimonths, there had been a steady increase of the rate of exports—but over the course of the next two semimonths, there had been a stagnation in the export of iron. Adar pursed his lips and placed the paper down.

The manors whose exports had stagnated were also the highest performers, and all were under the tax supervision of Baron va Heddi.

Adar stacked the papers on top of each other and shifted them to the right-hand side of his desk. To his left-hand side was a map of Osmjornia. He pulled the map toward him and began to look at the manors that were under Jergi's supervision. Two were on the route to Belar. Heddi was a strange fellow; he was learned and usually kept to himself unless he wished to give advice. He never went to the taverns or inns of Kurembrog. He was the type to stay secluded in his chambers, presumably taking, examining, and apparently *falsifying* records.

A knock came from the hall.

"You may enter!" yelled Adar, turning his head to face the door.

It was Elder Siemond.

"Hello, m'lord," he said, ducking his head as he entered the study. "I believe I may have an idea as to what the 'flesh' in the prophecy refers to."

"Well, what is it?"

"It may be a reference to the growing hedonism in our lands. Venereal disease is running rampant—we both know it increased by a large margin after the war. I believe the prophecy to reference a great Phoenic judgment upon those of licentious behavior."

"Ah, that could very well be the case. The great vice of the flesh. We have lost a great deal of warriors to their savage desires. How goes your persecution of those who committed Phoenic delicts?"

"Our temple has imprisoned several whores who now await penance. The townspeople are dissatisfied, but this only serves as a reminder of how wicked Kurembrog has become."

"Interesting," said Adar, turning his eyes away from the Elder, his face settling into a blank expression. "Well. Good work, Elder Siemond."

"Thank you for your praise, m'lord. However, I do have a request."

"Speak plainly, Elder."

"Abba is a very gifted boy, but it is apparent that you do not believe his gifts are suited for lordship. If I may ask, if you do pass him over in favor of having Maric inherit, would you give him the freedom to come to the Academy? It would be a firm step—"

"So you've come to insult me, have you?"

"It would be a compliment, not an insult. I would never insult you. I am just affirming that which we both know—that Maric is better suited for rule, and Abba is better suited for the cloth."

Adar gritted his teeth. "I will consider this, Elder. Leave me be so that I may brood on it."

Venceslaus

et us return to our previous conversation," Geder said, looking off down the now-empty hall, then turning back around. He spoke quietly and with urgency. "Venceslaus, I still do not see why you are so against pledging troops to Nara. I understand that it is not necessarily your duty, but it would greatly help your standing with Asbyorn and the rest of the court. I worry that you are only deciding not to do so because of your disdain for the Orator."

"Do not mistake me for a fool that forgoes reason to spite his enemies," Venceslaus said.

"It is a ridiculous idea, and it only stands to benefit the Orator. The people love me; if I betray them, I betray everything that I have ever stood for. The Orator knows of my opinion of him. If my reputation were to be tarnished, he would be gladdened."

"The entire Narese court knows your opinion of the Orator," Geder said, smiling slightly. "To be quite honest, a great number of them are displeased with him as well."

"Are they, now?" said Venceslaus, glaring at Geder.

"They are. His decision to step in and speak in place of Asbyorn is, well... distressing. The members of the Crii d'Nar fear their influence over the affairs of the realm have been lessened by this precedent. The Orator has no obligation to listen to the Crii— and over the past week, it has become apparent that he has no personal interest in listening to anyone else, either."

"Asbyorn has been sick for a week? What is his illness?"

"He is feeling better," Geder said. "He will hold court tomorrow."

Venceslaus looked down the hall. It had been about a month since he had seen the King. Asbyorn had grown up to be a sort of *disinterested* fellow when it came to ruling. He enjoyed the benefits, leisure and luxury of his position, but did not seem to understand its true purpose: leading his people to prosperity.

"I believe you find yourself in a position of immense influence," Geder said. "The rioters *will* listen to you. They trust you. Also, it would avail you of the ability to help both yourself and the Crii."

"How so?"

"Well, you may not like the sound of it, but you would be in the perfect position to shift the blame for the burning of Dorthu, coupled with the commoners' poverty, on whoever you believe deserves it most."

Venceslaus stepped back. Ser Groent's eyes went wide, but he stood firm.

"You are mad, Geder. I understand what you are insisting, and I refuse to humor it any longer."

"I insist nothing; I only wish to inform you of an opportunity," Geder said, shrugging. "There are many strange things afoot. It is best to know how to protect one's interests in such times."

"A man who uses treachery to combat treachery is still treacherous. Now is not the time for such a conversation."

"Well, my apologies for bringing it up. I took you to be a man of action," Geder said.

"To risk my life and my family's lands for such a plot—"

"Venceslaus, I have a stake in this as well. You are the father of my nephew's soon-to-be betrothed—I wish only for the *stability* of your lands. Ruling is no easy task, I am sure, but I imagine it becomes even more difficult when certain groups in power are not keen on you continuing to rule."

"No more of this, Geder. I will not hear it."

"I understand. But if you need assistance from me, do feel free to ask."

Geder turned and began to walk away with a slow strut. He was the type of man to carry himself as if he owned whatever hall he was in. Courtiers knew to shy away; Geder would bump into them if they didn't.

Ser Groent stepped toward Venceslaus. "He does not care for honesty."

"No, that he does not," said Venceslaus. "The lords who cling to Asbyorn are the biggest snakes of them all. That poor boy does not even have a hold over his kingdom."

Ser Groent kept his eyes down.

"Merr, how are you faring?" Venceslaus asked.

Merr Groent's eyes wandered up to the ceiling. He paused for a moment.

"I wish I could say I am doing better. Last time I was here, my Glysi was with me. It is hard to go forward some days. How are you faring, Vences?"

"There is not a night I do not spend fighting tears. I think of Edesa often, especially as I am now arranging Edit's betrothal. I try to keep Edit safe—she is all I have after Edeslaus and Edesa passed—but... I cannot connect with her the way Edesa did."

"It is a shame how Edit saw her go. Such a thing would trouble even the most heartless Yhournish raiders."

"After Edeslaus died, Edesa was never the same," Venceslaus said. "And Edit has become so closed off—I do not know if she will ever come back out of her shell. She keeps her thoughts occupied with vain matters."

Venceslaus motioned for Ser Groent to follow him. Together, they strolled through the halls and made a turn toward a stairway. They climbed up a floor and made their way to two shut doors. Before the doors stood a guard covered in mail. He had a crimson cloak draped over his shoulders, and he rested his hand on the pommel of a sword that hung from his waist.

"Greetings, Duke Freihei. What is your business here?"

"I wish to discuss matters that have arisen during my visit to the capital with the Crii d'Nar."

The guard nodded and turned to open the doors. Past the doorframe was a table, occupied by several individuals. Ten seats in total surrounded the table: one seat at each end and four on each side. On the left side, two of the four seats were occupied, and on the right, all of the seats but one were occupied. The seat farthest from the door was the most remarkable. It was a humble version of the King's throne. But it was not the King who sat in it. A bald man dressed in a dark orange jacket with black horses sewn in raised his hand to halt the discussion and pointed to Venceslaus, acknowledging him.

"Everyone! Duke Venceslaus is here!" He beckoned Venceslaus to him. "Please, Vences, sit."

Venceslaus grinned and nodded to the man. He pulled out one of the seats and sat down.

"Thank you for allowing me a seat at the Crii, Great Chancellor Barnut."

"It is always a pleasure to have an old friend at the table. I know you would not have entered into a meeting without a just reason—what matter do you wish to discuss? We have just finished deliberating our last topic."

"The village of Dorthu has been razed. The Orator pleaded with me to pledge troops so that I might help deal with the social upheaval that he fears is coming soon."

"Yes, we have received word of the Dorthu massacre. Will you heed his plea?"

"I think it is foolish. It will only serve to create more distrust between the lords of our kingdom and the commonfolk."

"I agree with the Orator's suspicions of a potential uprising. I have it on good authority that groups of individuals have been sharing their discontent with the current state of the kingdom at various taverns within Nara. Your support would be a great help; however, I will not belittle your concerns. This is a very delicate matter in need of much deliberation."

"Thank you," Venceslaus said. "Is there any news regarding the perpetrators of the massacre at Dorthu?"

"Unfortunately, no. We do not suspect Yhournish raiders, as there have not been any sightings of them past Avon's Wall or the southern mountains. It is likely to be some large bandit group; but oddly, there has been no word of survivors."

"Odd indeed," said one of the men seated on the left side of the table, closest to the door.

"What do you have to say, Great Dignitary Loffreaux?"

"Well, Barnut. If it were a bandit group, why would they raze a village? Why would they murder everyone? Would it not be more in the nature of a bandit to plunder and rape, not burn and flee?"

Loffreaux spoke Narese, but he pronounced his words in a round manner. He seemed to put too much emphasis on O's and had a very throaty way of speaking.

"Bah! Loffreaux, please quit your outlandish deductions. Brigands are known for being unruly and carefree. Would it be terribly surprising if they decided to kill everyone? They are not exactly the most moral of people," piped up another man.

"Great Marshal Donas, please be more respectful when addressing another's point."

Donas laughed and shook his head. He refrained from speaking.

"Thank you," said Barnut.

Barnut placed both of his palms on the table and stood up to address them. He looked stressed, his shoulders rolling forward. He let out a sigh.

"Because there are no survivors, we are without any evidence. It is incumbent upon us as dignitaries of the Crii d'Nar to find the perpetrators. Because we can only speculate at this time, we should not denounce any of the points brought up by our *equals* in these meetings. We need all the ideas we can get."

Lord Loffreaux and Great Marshal Donas nodded in agreement. A younger man with a sharp jawline and ginger hair who sat next to Donas raised his hand.

"We ought to send scouts to the barony to see if there are any remaining witnesses. If it *was* a group of bandits, I find it unlikely for there to be none living," he said. He had a drawl to his speech. "And if that is what this seems to be, then it only follows that we ought to see things for ourselves before we take a record of what happened. No brigand is that thorough."

"Agreed, Great Dignitary Urbaed. Garnering information is our priority. Any more ideas?"

Everyone at the table looked leisurely around at one another. None of them raised any further matters to the table.

"As King Regent of the fatherland of Man, the Kingdom of Nar, I shall now conclude Crii d'Nar. We began with discussing various tax and treasury matters and have decided that we are to slightly ease the tax burden we have placed upon the tradesmen guilds and merchants, despite Great Treasurer Geder's protest and early departure from this meeting. Afterward, we discussed the grain shortage and how to deal with potential uprising within Nara. And to end, we discussed the massacre of Dorthu, and we have concluded with no contention that we have too little information to point to a potential culprit. We have decided to move forth with sending our own scouts to reap information. Is there any protest to the conclusion brought forth?"

No one spoke.

"And are there any other matters anyone believes we ought to discuss before closing Crii d'Nar?"

No one raised a matter.

"Very well. I hereby declare today's Crii d'Nar concluded. You are all free to depart."

Everyone stood from their seats. Donas, Urbaed, Loffreaux, and the rest made their way to the door. Venceslaus stood up and made his way to Barnut.

"It has been a long time, Barnut."

"Aye, it has, old friend."

Venceslaus waited until the rest of the Crii had fully left the room before turning to Barnut.

"I did not want to bring this matter up in front of the Crii, for I do not trust them all," whispered Venceslaus.

"What is it?"

"The Orator should be met with suspicion. You are supposed to act on the King's behalf—yet when I came here to meet with the King, the Orator met me in his stead."

"He did?" asked Barnut. "The Orator rarely even sits at his spot at the Crii—and he told me nothing of your arrival. This is troubling."

"Aye, I never knew the King to be so pious. Even when he was in the Academy, he was a... free spirit."

"He did not have the same vigor as his father, but it does make sense. King Matnus would be a poor choice to compare oneself to."

"He was a great man, and a good friend."

"Aye." Barnut nodded.

"I had the pleasure of seeing the Great Treasurer prior to this meeting," said Venceslaus.

"How displeased did he look? He was rather frustrated when he stormed out of here."

"I honestly saw no sign of it. We discussed the Orator's plea. As expected, he agreed with the Orator—but I do not fault him for it."

"Whatever happens in Nara affects everyone in the Crii. It is natural for him to want your help."

"I understand why, but he is an underhanded fellow. He brought up my daughter's betrothal in front of her. He claimed to have assumed she was already aware, but I do not entirely believe him."

"I take it you had not told her, then?"

"No, I had not. Unfortunately, she didn't take it very well. But it is what's best for her."

"You already know I had a similar issue when Derud was coming of age. He refused to marry anyone. It was a hard time getting him to go through with it."

"I think Edit will be different. She will sulk about it, but she will understand."

"Aye, she always has been much sounder in the head than Derud."

Barnut turned around and stepped toward a table that was placed near one of the walls. He grabbed a paper and handed it to Venceslaus. Venceslaus examined it, squinting. He shook his head and raised his brows.

"Our King has certainly neglected his people," he said dryly.

"So you see why I, too, have resorted to pleading for your help. I'd like to put out these embers before they grow into a potentially incredible blaze."

"These accounts are terrifying, Barnut. The imports of grain and vegetables have steadily fallen over the past year. What do you think has caused this?"

"This."

Barnut grabbed another parchment and handed it to Venceslaus.

"That Geder is mad! Why hasn't the King stopped this increase in the cost of tolls?"

"The issue isn't Geder's doing, though Geder was quite ecstatic to enact it. This is the doing of our dear King himself. He wants to build more infrastructure in Nara. The majority of the Crii d'Nar has already spoken against his choice of means, but he overruled us and enacted it anyway. I believe it would be wise for you to discuss this with him. Our King has always had fatherly respect for you."

"I am surprised he has not listened," Venceslaus said. "He has the same respect for you."

"It seems my position as Great Chancellor has soured our relationship. He now sees me as another advisor to be ignored." Barnut smiled.

Venceslaus shook his head. "I will deliberate over these records in my chamber. Farewell until tomorrow, Barnut."

"Farewell, Vences."

The two waved their goodbyes, and Venceslaus went off, Ser Groent following closely behind him. As they marched down the hall, servants bowed and curtsied to Venceslaus in passing. They soon made it to the hall that held their chambers; when the guard there noticed them, he stood down, motioning for the Duke and Ser Groent to follow him. He showed them to the Duke's room, and the two entered.

"Much obliged," said Venceslaus to the guard.

The guard bowed and went off.

The room was quite large. The bed was made of an unchipped, dark-stained oak. Its mattress was exceptionally comfortable. To the left-hand side of it was a desk. Venceslaus placed the parchments he was given on top of it and lit a candle. He sat on a hip-height stool and continued to examine them. Merr wandered around the room, examining the decor. Paintings of Asbyorn lined the walls. They all depicted a strong and triumphant King standing over his enemies with a sword in hand.

Merr laughed and pointed at the paintings. "That boy has never seen battle, yet he has paintings like this?"

Venceslaus smirked. "You do not understand, Ser Groent. It is a metaphor."

"Oh, is that what we've decided to call it?"

"I suppose. It sounds like an explanation that someone with no experience would give, doesn't it?"

Groent let out a belly laugh, then continued to look around. Venceslaus grabbed a blank sheet of parchment, a bone pen, and ink. He started to copy some of the information from the records. The pen tip went fast; Venceslaus was no slow scribe.

"What did you write, m'lord?"

"A solution. It may be too late—but it is a solution nonetheless."

Venceslaus waved Ser Groent over. Merr shook his head.

"It looks like a good plan. I hope the King listens with an open ear."

"Aye."

Althalos

gathius snatched up the sheath and secured it to his waist. With careful attention, he slid the blade into it. The craftsmanship of the sword far surpassed the simple scabbard with its carved pommel and spiraling black marble grip. The quillons, wavy and bent toward the blade, caught the light and gleamed. Despite a few small chips, the sword was clean and free of any debris. While it hung from his right side, Agathius kept a firm grip on the hilt, holding it as delicately as if it were a fragile newborn.

"Ditwin, I shall take my leave now."

Agathius removed his sash and placed it over Ditwin's shoulders.

"I, Agathius, Elder of Fisk, relinquish the position of Elder to my Lesser and now equal. Elder Ditwin, it is now your duty to serve the followers of the Phoenix in their faith. You are to be an example and mentor, guiding those who follow you in the footsteps of the Phoenix. Bow your head in recognition of this responsibility."

Ditwin's eyes widened. He bowed immediately.

"I accept graciously!" said Ditwin, shaking while he rose back up. "Elder, I thought I was to act only in your stead, not take your place."

"I do not plan on returning to Fisk, my boy," said Agathius with a peculiar finality in his tone. Then he turned away. "Take me to Gunter, Althalos."

Althalos exited the building, following the priest. The way Agathius moved made it seem like nothing could trouble him; he always kept his head high and a slight smile on his face.

The two made their way back to the inn. Gunter was sitting at the same table he had been when Althalos left, staring at the ground like a sad puppy. Agathius walked up to Gunter, grabbed his cup, and drank. Gunter's eyes shot up, half-filled with shock and half-filled with boiling anger. He slammed his fists on the table.

"Ye damned priest! How dare ye drink from my cup!"

Agathius grinned. "Gunter, over the years, you have drunk from many cups that were not your own; I am simply returning the favor. A drink for a drink."

Gunter grumbled under his breath. "What do ye want, priest?"

"I wanted to come and thank you for helping this lad. It was a truly noble act."

"I don't care for the lad. And I didn't do it because it was some *noble act*. Fuck yer noble act."

"I am glad you are helping him, Gunter. I know your heart will be glad of it, too."

"Fuck my heart, fuck ye, and fuck off."

"He doesn't seem to like you very much," Althalos said, turning his head to Agathius.

"Of course I don't like that fuckin' priest. That always-joyful priest. He needs to fuck off and leave me alone for once. Always been a fuckin' pest," interrupted Geder.

"Gunter wasn't always this insufferable, you know," Agathius said. "It was the war. It changed all of us."

Althalos tilted his head. Agathius had fought in the war? Althalos had met quite a few priests, but none of them had fought in the Yhournish War. Every time it was brought up, they would thank the Phoenix for granting them safety. But Agathius being a fighter was not shocking, Althalos supposed; his whole demeanor was proof of it. He didn't speak like the priests Althalos had known, either. He never used fancy language and would even curse. From a first impression, he and Gunter could be taken to be much alike; yet, in truth, they were entirely different. Agathius was happy, and Gunter was not.

While Gunter sat sulking, Agathius looked to the sky with indomitable hope. Being around Gunter in this state was unbearable, it felt like one was around wilted flowers and boring gray skies. But when around Agathius, it felt as if one was an unstoppable stallion charging toward the sun.

"Gunter has been through a lot," Agathius said.

"Ha! Aren't ye supposed to be educated, ye annoyin' priest? And the best words ye can come up with are *a lot?* I have been through shite and mud and blood and dirt. Fuck off!"

Agathius pulled Althalos aside. His eyes were firm, and the way he stared at Althalos made it seem he was about to say something serious.

"It may seem like I am pestering him for no good reason, but I want you to listen clearly to what I am about to say. Stay away from Gunter when he is drunk. He becomes very irritable and bad tempered. I wanted you to see for yourself." Agathius turned toward Gunter. "Hey, Gunter! After your heart is mended, then maybe we can get you to stop being such a drunk!"

Gunter slammed his cup against the table. "How many fuckin' times do I have to say it? Fuck off, priest!"

He stood up and stormed off toward a shack behind the inn, yelling profanities at the priest as he went.

"Althalos, do you know how to fight?"

"Of course."

"Ha! Are you being serious? Most boys your age say they can, but when they go out and fight in a battle, they're left cut up in some other person's field to be forgotten about. Have you ever fought anyone before?"

"I wrestled the other boys in Dorthu. I did fairly well, actually."

"But have you ever fought anyone with a weapon?"

"Well, no," Althalos said. "Not with any real weapons, at least. Sometimes, when I was younger, I would fight with sticks that fell from the trees in the Dorthu woods, but that's all."

"So you have no training whatsoever. If you want to avenge your village—"

"Avenge? You are a priest, and you speak of vengeance? Would meting out punishment not be the responsibility of the temple?"

"When your priest in Dorthu spoke, what did he proclaim to be your duty? Apart from listening to and obeying the teachings of the temple, that is?"

Althalos could not answer.

"Now, my boy, what did your priest say was the duty of the temple?"

"Well, many things. It would be quite difficult to list them all."

"Attempt to list them."

"Moral justice, education, the dissemination of current events… What are you trying to say, Agathius?"

"Did Avon ever go to a temple? Did a temple ever seek justice for Avon and all the others persecuted? Did the Phoenicy even *exist* in Avon's time? No. In fact, the temple as it stands now resembles much of what Avon sought to tear down: a corrupt group of rhetorical pundits who seek to advance their own benefit at the expense of the well-being and lives of men like us."

"Why are you telling me this?"

"I am only preparing you, Althalos. You do not seem like one to run from adversity, but I believe it is worthwhile to know how to defend yourself. I will spar with you on our way. When we depart, you are to continue training with Gunter."

Althalos nodded.

"Now, do you have somewhere to sleep?" Agathius asked.

"Yes, I do. Helwig is allowing me to sleep for free at his inn."

"Enjoy what will probably be your last night in a bed for quite a while. I will see you tomorrow."

Althalos waved goodbye to Agathius and returned to the inn. Being that it was late, it was getting quite busy at the inn. Helwig directed him to his room.

The door creaked as Althalos pushed it open. The room had a musty odor. A few storage boxes and pots were inside. The room was barely any better than a shed. Helwig probably did not expect many visitors to his inn. Althalos undressed and left his sweaty clothes to dry while they hung over the backrest of a chair. Afterward, he fluffed the pillow and lay down on the bed. He closed his eyes, and over time they began to sink under their own growing weight while he fell asleep.

Heat crept up on him until he felt like he was stuck in an oven. His eyes opened, and everything was on fire. Gunter was lying unconscious. Althalos tried to shake him awake, but after feeling for his pulse, he soon knew he was dead. To his left knelt a man, screaming as he stared at the flesh being seared off of his own hands. Althalos walked toward the man. Behind him, Helwig and Agathius had both been stabbed and were bleeding out in the Fisk commons. Althalos ran forward, but he stumbled and fell. When he picked himself up, he heard Ditwin's screams. Two crimson-cloaked men repeatedly stabbed Ditwin in his back, then dropped him to the ground. Althalos stumbled his way up to his feet and sprinted toward Ditwin, yelling at the crimson-cloaked men with rage. At that moment, one of the men hit Althalos in the head with his pommel. They held his mother, Agnes, above him. They slit his mother's throat. Althalos screamed while his dying mother fell onto him.

Althalos's hand rushed for his right cheek. It was raw and stung.

"Why in Gol are ye screamin' like a bitch, boy?"

Sweat rolled down Althalos's face. He was still in bed—he was drenched in sweat, and the covers had been twisted about. He'd been dreaming. Gunter had slapped him awake.

"Nothing," he said. "No reason."

"Ye scream like a bitch over nothin'? I am going to have to kill the bitch in ye, then." Gunter took Althalos's hand and lifted him unceremoniously out of bed. "That fool priest is about to leave. Hurry yer slow arse up, boy."

"Why are you such an arsehole?" asked Althalos, squinting at Gunter, still barely awake.

"Arseholes survive. Get going, boy."

Althalos exited the inn and began to search for Agathius. He spotted the priest on the other side of the village, fixing a satchel onto a horse while Ditwin handed him his bags. Althalos could overhear the two priests discussing the trip.

"Althalos! About time! I was about to head off without you," called Agathius, finishing tying up his satchel. He paused for a moment as if he were about to say something else, but he sealed his lips before he spoke.

"What were you about to say?" asked Althalos.

"Well, I was going to ask if you were all packed, as I see you have no belongings on you."

"It is alright, Elder. This is everything that I have left," replied Althalos, staring at the ground.

Gunter strutted up to the party and whistled at the priest. His clothes were disheveled, and his greasy hair was being blown about by the wind.

"Let us stop talkin' and get goin'. I don't want to waste any more time," he said.

Agathius smiled. "Oh, Gunter. I like you more when you're sulking."

Gunter ignored him.

Agathius patted his horse, then grabbed the reins to lead his sumpter while they walked out of the hamlet. After fully leaving Fisk, it began to smell less and less of ale and more and more of dry grass and tree bark. The party barely left any tracks in the packed-dirt road, for the heat kept the path dry and dirt fine, making it easily blown away. Agathius gazed at the sky, and Gunter glared at the ground. The bags on the sumpter shook as he clopped along. Agathius motioned with his palm to Althalos and beckoned him over.

"We ought to begin some training. Shall we, boy?" asked the priest.

"Yes, I would enjoy that."

Agathius halted and wrapped his horse's reins around a tree. He grabbed two sticks that were about the same length and tossed one to Althalos.

"Hit me," said Agathius.

Carefully inching closer, Althalos stepped toward Agathius. He slashed his stick down at the priest, but the priest easily evaded and sent a strike back that Althalos only narrowly dodged. Althalos sent another strike, but Agathius sent a riposte back at him. The fast-moving air from behind the stick blew Althalos's hair to the side. Althalos backed a safe distance away and extended his stick back out in front of him. He sent a flurry of attacks, but Agathius just danced away. When Althalos began to huff, he was slammed in the back of the knee by Agathius, forcing him to kneel. Agathius pointed his weapon at the downed boy.

"You need a lot of work, Althalos. It is unwise to act quickly when you do not know how. Understand that you will lose to me—but if you think out the movements now, while training, then you will remember them again when your life is threatened," said Agathius, grabbing Althalos's hand and lifting him up.

Althalos nodded and let Agathius pull him to his feet. The pair raised their sticks once more and began to spar again. Their sticks clacked against each other while they blocked each other's strikes. Agathius paused and changed his stance. He sent a cross-cut; but before he could connect, Althalos closed the distance, hooked his arm over Agathius's sword hand, and used his leg on the same side to hook behind Agathius's. Althalos's momentum sent the two to the ground, with Althalos ending up on top.

A few yards away, Gunter burst out laughing. Agathius laughed too, reaching his arm out to Althalos. Althalos grabbed his hand and pulled the priest up to his feet. Agathius untied his horse from the tree, and they continued to walk.

"Althalos, my boy, what was growing up in Dorthu like?"

"There was not much to do other than work the land. We were very poor. Honestly, I did not think I would ever leave my village."

"Ah, yes. Even before the events of the past few days, Dorthu had a very unfortunate fate. I remember a time when it was quite a remarkable village, but that was long before you were born. I visited there often."

"I have always heard stories from the few older villagers there," Althalos said. "Dorthu used to do quite well until the Yhournish destroyed our silver mine."

"Aye, it is a shame how the war destroyed such a beautiful village. But Dorthu has been rebuilt once; it can be rebuilt again."

"Ha! What are ye talkin' about, ye dumb priest? Ye've heard the boy's story. Dorthu is gone. No one survived—"

"We do not know that, Gunter. Althalos is here—who is to say that everyone else is dead?" retorted Agathius.

"Ye are too hopeful, Agathius. They might as well be dead. And Fisk is the nearest village to Dorthu. Surely, if anyone were alive, we would have seen them by now," Gunter said, frowning.

"Gunter, we have lived damn near the same life, yet you are so bitter. You must learn to have faith."

"And what has faith ever done for me, eh?"

The sounds of fluttering hummingbirds and rustling branches kindly entered the ears. They passed over a cobblestone bridge that overlooked a small stream. Agathius held out his hand and motioned for the party to stop.

"Let us take a quick rest here. It is past midday, and my horse needs to be watered."

Green shrubbery conquered the sides of the road, and off to the right of the bridge's end was a narrow path that led to the stream. The stream was clear, and Agathius led his sumpter to it. The horse pawed at the water and began to bob his head up and down, splashing water all over his face. Agathius smiled with a childlike grin and scratched the horse's neck.

"Good boy, Face-eater!" praised Agathius.

Althalos stared at the horse with bewilderment while Gunter paid them no mind at all. The horse was a very tame and happy steed that pranced alongside Agathius.

"That horse looks much too friendly to be named Face-eater," said Althalos.

"Are you sure?" asked Agathius, grinning with all of his teeth.

Gunter marched away, muttering profanities under his breath about stupid priests and ugly horses. Agathius ignored him.

"Come closer, boy," he said, motioning to Althalos.

As Althalos neared Agathius, the horse's loose bottom lip tightened up, and his relaxed, swaying tail went tense. The sumpter's eyes tracked Althalos, and when he grew even nearer, his ears flattened, and he bared his teeth. Agathius put out his hand to stop Althalos from coming any farther.

"He has actually eaten several faces, hence his name. But he has never tried to consume any of my flesh. He is rather protective of me, in fact."

Althalos backed away from the strange stallion, and eventually, the steed went back to its friendly and playful mood. The horse was dun colored, and the only noteworthy mark on him was the white star on his forehead. The priest's eyes glinted with a fatherly pride while he baby-talked his stallion. Althalos envied the connection Agathius had with his beast.

"Where did you find that strange sumpter?"

"Heh, he is not a sumpter; he is a rouncey. A very versatile creature. He can plow a field, then, very soon after doing so, help you kill a man. I found this beauty riderless, attacking Yhournish warriors during a battle near Avonsgatte."

Agathius grabbed Althalos's hand and placed it onto the horse's cheek. Face-eater gave Althalos a similar looked as he had before, but once he noticed Agathius's hand, he untensed.

"Why does he treat you the way he does?"

"It sounds peculiar, but I believe the reason to be that I helped him slay a few Yhournish warriors that were attacking him. They likely killed his previous rider; I found the mutilated remains of a Muric knight bearing the same colors as Face-eater's caparison."

96

Althalos sat on a flat stone near the stream, staring into the flow of the water. He reached for the red cloak and examined it. He did not know what he was looking for, but he wished to feel and look at it to remind himself of what happened. It troubled him. He knew he had to do something about it, but he did not know what. What would happen after he spoke to Baron Rowe? He crushed the cloth in his fist and dropped his head toward the ground, staring morosely at his feet.

"What troubles you?" Agathius asked. "Also, that bloodied axe at your side—you ought to cover it up with that rag. You do not want to bring attention to it in Wettay."

Althalos covered the axehead. "Dorthu troubles me. What do I do when we find out who did it? And how do I attain justice for what happened?"

Althalos picked up a rock and hurled it toward the stream.

"Ye kill them all, boy," Gunter said.

"But they wear the King's colors. We are speaking of treason," said Althalos.

Gunter began to laugh so hard he placed his hand on a stump to keep balance. "Treason? Fuck treason. They killed your fellows. Your *mother*."

"Gunter is a bastard, but he is right," Agathius said. "My last instruction to Ditwin was to inform Fisk of the massacre. The commonfolk will want justice for this. We will reach Wettay soon, and you must announce the news of the massacre there. I do not trust the Elders of most villages to be in possession of just hearts. It will be in your best interest to tell the people yourself."

"Is yer horse done playin' with the stream water yet, priest?"

"Aye. Let us get back to the road."

Meara

eara returned to the dilapidated houses where she and the other orphans had taken refuge. Her slow gait and slumping posture only made her sadness more apparent to the others. With her spirit defeated, she held the single remaining piece of bread in her right hand. She tried to shoo away the thought of the beating Luka would give her once he found out she had returned empty-handed.

She saw the orphans huddled around Luka, as they always were. Luka was pushing around some of the younger children, and shouting could be heard from the crowd. In the center, two young children were bludgeoning each other with their fists. One of them, a boy a few years younger than Meara, was pushed down to the ground while the other child began to beat him unconscious.

Luka's large belly jiggled while he laughed and pointed at the boy being battered. After a few seconds of apparent enjoyment, Luka grabbed the child on top of the other orphan and pulled him to the side, slapping a piece of bread into his hand and giving him a pat of approval. Before Luka could speak, the skin-and-bones boy ran off, devouring the bread like a starving dog would devour a small animal.

"If you want more food, fight!" Luka yelled.

He continued to laugh, but stopped abruptly when his eyes met Meara's. He looked her up and down, then gritted his teeth and balled his hands into fists.

"Meara! Where is all the food? Where is all the damn *food?!*"
His face had gone completely cold, any trace of his earlier
enjoyment gone. "Come here, Meara. Hand me the bread."

Meara inched closer to him, moving as slowly as she could.

"Hurry up, damn you!"

Meara sped up, striding quickly toward Luka. She flinched as
Luka ripped the bread from her hand and threw it into the pile
behind him. He stared at her, his eyes burning with anger. He
slammed his palm into Meara's face, and Meara's frail body fell to
the floor. Luka began to kick her.

"I!"

He kicked her.

"Told!"

He kicked her again.

"You!"

And he kicked her again.

"Not to *fuck up!*"

The crowd of children stared at Meara, slack-jawed, their eyes
wide with horror. A child tried to take a step toward Meara, but
Luka glared at him until he backed away. She lay motionless on
the ground, her head spinning from the pain. It was all that she
could think about. Luka took a seat and sighed.

"Meara, you will not be allowed to eat with the group any
longer."

Meara turned her head to look at Luka through the blur of
tears in her eyes.

"If you do try to come back, I will beat you even worse.
But..." He smiled. "...if you bring me twenty groschen, you may
be allowed to return."

Meara's face dropped to the dirt. Luka got up. He grabbed her
and dragged her battered body away from the crowd. When he
turned around and began to walk over to the pile of food, the gang
of children backed away from him. They all gawked at Meara while
she lay motionless on the ground. One of the children—the
mute—ran toward Meara and began to shake her in an attempt to
get her up.

"And you can go with her, too!"

Luka threw a rock at the duo, sneering at them. It landed
beside the mute boy. He was still trying repeatedly to pull Meara
to her feet. She planted her hands on the ground, her arms shaking

as she tried to lift herself up. She felt a dull and tender pain in her chest.

Eventually, she got back to her feet, tears running down her face. Her expression was blank. Together, she and the boy walked away, Luka yelling profanities behind them. The boy was tugging at Meara's hand, but she ignored him, continuing instead to aimlessly wander. In time, they reached the outer walls of Belar. Meara found a crate to sit down on.

Belar's walls were built of old and weathered stone. Guards leaned against the gatehouse while talking nonsense in order to pass the time. A rich merchant or noble was a rare sight here; they never stayed, they only ever passed through. The majority of the poor lived in this area, but not many people were seen wandering around. During the day, they went to the market to beg and pickpocket, just like the orphans.

The mute boy tugged on Meara's arm.

"What do you want?"

The boy frowned. He pointed in the direction they had come from, then pointed to his mouth, making a motion with his hands like he was trying to mime eating food.

"You want food? You're hungry?"

The boy nodded. He was jostled roughly by a passerby; Meara grabbed the boy's hand and pulled him closer to her, her chest aching where Luka had kicked her.

"I am, too," she said.

She squeezed his hand once, fiercely, keeping her eyes trained forward. She couldn't bring herself to look at his face while she spoke.

"We will just have to find a way to get food together," she said.

The guards at the gate had stopped a wagon that was filled with barrels. It looked like they had ordered the wagon-drivers to open the barrels as they climbed up to inspect the cargo. When the barrels were opened, the guards pulled out several pieces of cured meats. One of them smiled to the other and climbed down, throwing a few in a sack by his post and then waving the drivers off.

Clopping along the road, the horses pulled the wagon to a back alley and parked behind a building. Meara's eyes stalked the wagon like a mountain lion would a deer. The wagon-drivers descended from the wagon and strolled along the building's back wall before entering through a door.

As soon as they entered, Meara rushed up and briskly walked toward the cart, the boy following suit. She scraped past a table and swiftly snagged a sack that had been left on it. She made her way to the wagon, opened a barrel, and rummaged around inside it, tossing cured meats into the sack. She kept digging and digging until her hand hit something hard. It was a small wooden chest wrapped in a brown rag. She lifted it up to shake it so that she could attempt to hear what was inside, but her sense told her it would be conspicuous to do so; so instead she covered the barrel, placed the chest into her sack, and scurried off.

The men exited the building, their coats and sacks bulging awkwardly. They locked eyes with Meara. She turned the corner, her sack over her shoulder, and ran. The drivers began to lift one of the barrels—the very barrel that Meara had thieved from—and found it lighter than it had been only moments before. After a brief moment of confusion, the wagon-drivers turned in the direction that Meara had run off.

Meara could only focus on one thing: running as fast as she could. She heard yelling and arguing from behind her, and it grew only louder as they started to run after her. The weight of the chest and cured meats was slowing her down. The boy was keeping up, but she directed him to grab the sack and run down another alley while she attempted to lead the wagon-drivers away.

The wagon-drivers passed the alley the boy had hurried down, but they didn't turn; they still kept running toward Meara. She took a right, and then a right, then a left, then another right, eventually finding herself at a dead end before a hip-height stone wall overlooking a road below.

"Thieving brat! I will slit your throat!" yelled one of the wagon-drivers.

"Where is the sack?" asked the other.

They must not have noticed the boy running off, she realized. She revealed the piece of cured meat in her hands.

"I… I only took this," said Meara, presenting the cured meat to the wagon-drivers, bowing her head in faux remorse. "I am but a starving orphan. I beg you to be merciful."

One of the men—the bigger of the two—laughed. "Do you take me for a fool, child? You were rummaging around in my barrel. Where is the chest?"

He pulled a dagger from a dangling scabbard that hung from his waist and brandished it toward her.

"N—no... No, I wasn't," murmured Meara.

She stepped backward, stumbling when she made contact with the short wall behind her. The large man chuckled as he inched toward Meara. He pointed his dagger directly at her, then mimed slitting his own throat with it. Meara looked behind her, peeking down at the street below; then she looked back at the large man, and she jumped.

She barreled through the air for a moment before hitting the half-built wooden overhang below her, which she broke straight through. She landed on a table covered with tapestries. A plank fell on top of the tapestry merchant, knocking him down. He clutched his head, groaning with pain. Meara winced.

But her guilt didn't stay her for long. She looked up through the hole in the overhang at the large man staring down at her, then clambered down off the table and darted out of the shop. She could hear the man cursing as she evaded him, his voice growing quieter and quieter as she gained distance.

Eventually, she turned down an alley, then collapsed to the ground behind a crate, heaving in as much air as possible. Her muscles ached from the pain of the landing and her prior beating. She was used to running, but not in such a battered state.

In the distance, she could see the small boy carrying the sack over his shoulder. Meara's eyes widened, and she beckoned wildly to him. He tried to run to her, but the weight of the sack restricted his movement to a slow trudge. When he made it to her, he dropped the sack with a loud thud. A measure of her energy returned to her with the excitement of seeing him—Meara pounced on the boy and hugged him.

"You are safe! Thank Esu," she said.

She picked up the sack and opened its neck, peering inside. The pieces of cured meat were still there, as was the small chest. She looked around for a moment; then, deciding the area was safe enough for her to examine it, she removed the chest from the bag.

The chest was of a decent size. When she picked it up, she could hear the sound of metal clanging within it. She placed it down on the ground, then she gently undid the latch and lifted the chest lid. Within the chest were dozens and dozens of Belarish groschen. The boy looked back and forth between Meara and the groschen, stunned. He tugged on Meara's arm, trying to get her attention—but she closed the chest hastily and threw it back into the sack.

"We need to find a place to hide this," she said.

The boy tugged on Meara's arm again, more insistently.

"We are not going to bring that to Luka," Meara said firmly.

The boy's face grew confused. He tried to reach for the chest, but she swatted his hands away.

"Quit it! We both know very well that he will just hog it for himself. It will not help the other orphans, and it certainly will not help us."

She looked around the darkened alley, trying to find a place to stow the sack. Rats scurried away from piles of discarded debris: it was a rotten landscape of food scraps, torn fabric, planks of wood, and stones. She grimaced. It wouldn't have been a good place to store the cured meat—the damned rats would steal their food—but for once, food was not her priority.

She took the boy by the hand and pulled him toward one of the piles. She moved a few of the broken boards that were piled atop one another and stuck her sack under the little cover she had built. Afterward, she covered the structure with more boards, a loose tapestry, and some broken stone bricks to weigh it down.

Once the sack was sufficiently well hidden, she handed the boy one of the pieces of meat. Together, they sat down across from each other on the ground and began, with great speed, to eat. She reveled in its taste, for she had only been surviving off of bread and fruit for as long as she could remember. The boy consumed his piece like he had not eaten for a week.

"I cannot remember the last time I ate meat," Meara said, her knee jostling the boy's leg. "Maybe it was a good thing that Luka kicked us out after all, huh?"

Being out from under Luka's finger, away from him, she felt as though she was able to relax for the first time in a very long time, however minutely. It wouldn't last forever, she knew—the groschen would run out eventually, and they'd be back to begging—but it was a reprieve that she wanted to hold onto for as long as she possibly could.

"We need to find a way to get rid of him," she said, her mouth full of food.

The boy slowed his chewing, pulling his face into a twisted expression.

"Don't give me that look," she said. "Think of how many orphans have starved to death because of him, or have been beaten by him, or have been thrown to the guards after trying to take back their food from that pig. Luka has never left the comfort of sitting on his fat arse to find food. I do not even think he knows how."

An idea sprung into Meara's mind, and she reached out, grabbing the boy's wrist.

"We can use the groschen to get rid of him. We can pay someone to scare Luka off, or if need be… we can use the groschen to have him killed!"

The boy looked at Meara, his brow furrowing. He tried gently to pull his wrist from her grip.

"The only problem," she continued, "is that we don't know anyone who could do it. Or I don't, at least. And if we use the money to find a way to bring the other orphans with us, Luka will just find a way to bring them back."

The boy stopped moving. He seemed to be considering Meara carefully for a moment—then he flopped down onto his back and began to rub his belly, closing his eyes and breathing deeply as if to signal that he was too tired to continue the conversation. Digesting such an abnormally large amount of food was tiring her out, too, she realized; and it was starting to get late in the day. They'd hidden the sack, but they still needed to find a safe place to hide themselves.

Meara shifted her focus to finding anything that would give the two some cover from the elements. She wandered down the alley, eventually finding a building that was covered in foliage. It looked to be untouched and uninhabited, so she walked toward the large wooden door and placed her hand on it, attempting to push it open. At first, it felt like it was pushing back at Meara— but after a brief moment of struggle, the door squeaked open. It got caught on the floor, and Meara had to use what little strength she had left to lift the door up a bit and move it over the lip on which it had gotten stuck. She shimmied through the gap she'd made and into the room behind it.

The only light in the room was what shined in from the door. When Meara walked in, she was immediately caught in a cobweb. She wiped the tiny webs off herself and examined the room. There were several empty crates with their lids open or discarded completely. It was a mess; it looked as if a twister had swept through the room and scattered every item across the floor. But still, it was cleaner—and safer—than sleeping in the alleyway. She ran back to the boy, who was now sitting on an upended crate, throwing pebbles at the side of a building.

"Hey!"

He shifted his attention to Meara. Meara pointed to the pile of rubble and pretended to heft something across her back. The boy nodded, uncovering the sack and throwing it over his tiny shoulder. He wobbled toward Meara, struggling under the weight of the bag. Taking pity on him, Meara snatched the sack and threw it over her shoulder, making her way toward the building.

"It looks as if it has not been used in years!" she said, shimmying back through the gap in the door, then watching attentively while the boy followed suit. "We can stay here for a while."

She dropped the sack in the corner. The boy ran to the crates and put two side by side, then climbed on top of them. Meara shut the door and barred it with a plank. The floor was made of packed dirt; there were a spade and some other tools in the middle of the room. With the spade, Meara began to dig a small hole. The boy stood and watched.

It took her a painful hour to dig the tiny hole. Her bones and muscles ached with every movement she made, so she took a moment of rest after every few shovels. Once she was done, she was drenched with sweat and aching all over. She went to the sack and pulled out the chest, her arms trembling, and threw it into the hole. She motioned for the boy to come to her, and together, the two pushed the dirt back into the hole.

"I do not even know your name," she said, once they had finished. She was sitting back against one of the walls; she reached over for one of the broken handles from one of the tools on the floor and handed it to him. "Will you write it in the dirt?"

The boy grabbed the handle. He wrote something.

"*Gol?*" Meara said, incredulous. "You were named after Gol?"

The boy nodded.

"What a strange name to have! Your parents must—"

Gol's expression saddened suddenly, and he looked down at his feet.

"Oh," Meara said. "I'm sorry. I didn't mean to upset you."

He shrugged, his eyes still trained on the ground.

"My father was a carpenter," she offered, "and my mother helped with his trade. They were bringing some utensils to the market when a knight rode past them on the road. My father told him to use more caution when riding, because he had almost run into them."

Gol looked up slightly.

"The knight drew his bludgeon and struck my mother and father down. But they did not die from the blow itself—their wounds grew diseased, and they passed away a few days later. I still... I still remember the odor."

Gol stared at her for a moment, then came over and sat down beside her. He rested his small head on her shoulder. It was funny—she could go a long time without thinking about them, her parents, and almost convince herself that the grief had passed; but, retelling the story, she realized that it still hadn't. Gol slipped his hand into hers and squeezed it tightly. Together, they wept, tears slipping quickly and silently down their faces.

Abba

bba allowed himself to drop to the ground and lie down, gazing off into the sky. His eyes had no thoughts behind them, for at that moment he had no energy left to do anything other than simply exist. Maric came into view above him, extending his hand. Abba accepted it. Maric yanked Abba up to his feet and brushed some of the dirt off of Abba's back.

"I have a lot of work to do," Abba said.

"You have nothing to worry about," Maric said. "It is your first tourney; Father is only being hard on you because you represent him. I will make sure you are prepared."

"It is more than that. Every year, he is more and more disappointed. He always watches me, and I can feel his contemptuous eyes. He does not like me, Maric. Even when I am doing this willingly—something *he* forces me to do—he is disappointed."

"Don't say that," Maric said.

"No. I saw him watch me. He couldn't bear the sight of me."

Maric shook his head. "That isn't true."

"I have seen it myself," Abba insisted.

"Well," Maric said, smiling, "if you are such a disappointment, then I suppose that makes me the future Count of Kurembrog."

Spluttering, Abba shoved Maric's shoulder. "You shut your mouth!"

Maric chuckled, stepping away from Abba as he went to place his sword onto a rack. Abba followed suit, returning his own sword. Then he sighed, walking away.

"What?" Maric asked.

"Nothing."

Maric grabbed Abba by his elbow, halting him in his tracks.

"What is wrong?" he asked sternly.

Abba paused, wringing his hands together. "Do you really think there is a chance that he would not pass the rulership of Kurembrog to me?"

"It happened to Uncle Geder," Maric said.

"I cannot even say that I *want* to be the heir to Kurembrog; yet now I wish to win this tournament just so I can prove to Father that I am capable of it. I want him to be proud of me like he is of you—like he is of Mikhail, Siemond, and everyone else. But that is a foolish desire. I have no skill with the sword whatsoever."

"Abba, I told you we will train together. I meant what I said. On our journey to Belar, we will practice our dueling every day," Maric said. "But you *are* right. You have much to work on before you are ready to take part in the tourney."

"Why are you helping me?"

"Well, Father has always emphasized the importance of duty, and you are the presumptive heir. As your brother, I hold it to be my duty to help you…"

Maric paused.

"…and I do not truly wish to be heir, either."

Abba narrowed his eyes. "Somehow, I do not believe that, considering how closely you follow Father's way."

"Despite how he treats you, our father is still a wealthy and strong ruler. There are things to be learned from him. I only wish to be able to have the same prestige when I am older."

Abba kicked a rock. "We never talk about things like this. Why do you not want to be heir?"

"The idea of being stuck within the walls of Kurembrog forever does not sit well with me. I do not want to inherit power; I want to earn it," Maric said. "What about you? Why don't you want it?"

"I have read many stories of battles, knights, dragons, Viantse, foreign mountains, plains, and forests. I have this… unrelenting urge to see the world. I do not wish to be stuck behind these walls, either."

Together, the pair walked off toward the keep. When they entered, they parted ways. Maric went toward his room, and Abba went toward the hall. When he entered, he did not see his father; but he did see his mother, Anita. She sat on a gray oak bench with a blue linen draped over it and was occupied with reading a note. As her hands traced along its words, her eyes were anchored to the paper; but when she heard Abba approaching, she looked up and smiled.

Abba's mother was only slightly younger than his father—but, unlike his father, she still seemed to keep a fair bit of youth in her eyes. Many young girls and ladies in Kurembrog attempted to emulate her fashion in hair, makeup, and dress. Whenever she would walk into the bailey, all of the women would spend the next day trying to look like her. She was a standard of beauty amongst the ladies in Kurembrog. She wasn't Osmjornish in the slightest; she didn't have the dry face or the brooding attitude. She lived her life very simply, not caring much for the life of a rich Osmjornish noblewoman and instead longing for the days she'd spent hunting with her brothers in the Demenstin forests.

Abba had been taught that it was common for Osmjornish lords to marry into families that held lands within the Kingdom of Nar, and that it was often touted as an expression of solidarity and love for their kin in the south; but in reality, it was a political tool for the Osmjornish to receive aid in case of invasion from the crude Ookosi, and for the Narese lords to leverage aid, materials, and money from their soon-to-be extended family. Elder Siemond had taught Abba the first truth, and Ser Mikhail had taught him the second. In his father's case, House Demenstin was a relatively poor family in the south. Adar had married Anita out of love, for he had courted her prior to being named heir.

"Hello," Anita said, leaning up and pressing a kiss to Abba's forehead. "Have you packed?"

"No, I asked Maric to train with me. I shall pack before I go to sleep."

Anita tilted her head, an expression of confusion and amusement in her eyes. "You did? Voluntarily?"

"Yes, Mother, voluntarily," Abba said, shifting his weight back and forth between his feet. "Where is Father?"

"Well, that's nice," she said, smiling, a mischievous light twinkling in her eyes. "I imagine Mikhail nearly died of shock when he saw you."

"*Mother*," Abba said. "Father. Where is he?"

"Yes, yes, apologies," she said. "I believe he went to his study. But wait here for a bit—you know how your father can get when he is brooding away, reading his stories and looking at his trinkets and such."

Abba sat down on the bench beside her. "I have always found it odd how Father berates me for loving histories. Is he not the same as I am? He is always looking at that damned hammer, in any case."

Anita sighed. Normally, she might have slapped Abba on the thigh or pinched his ear for cursing; but this time, she didn't seem to notice. "I often think that Maric has inherited the traits that your father forces upon himself, but you have inherited the traits that are truer to your father's heart. He sees a great deal of himself in you, you know." She took his hand in hers and pressed it. "You are both good boys."

"I fear I will do poorly in the tournament," Abba said.

Anita scoffed. "This stupid tournament is nothing. Your father still has many years left in his rule; you will have much time to attain the skills to please him."

"You are right, Mother."

"But you must still try your damndest to win," she said, smiling.

"Why does Father care so much about fighting, anyway? Why must I be able to fight?"

"Do you know how many Ookosi raids have occurred this half-year alone?"

Abba shook his head.

"About eleven unfortunate pillagings—but the number almost doubles if you consider failed attempts. The only reason they have failed is because we have strong warriors like your father and Ser Mikhail protecting us."

"Well, they are only bandits, no? They are not organized armies with fierce drudna."

"Abba, there is a certain naïvety that comes from seeing the world through words on paper," Anita said. "When you see the world with your own eyes, you will notice it is not so clear. The Ookosi are not just bandits. They may be crude, but they are not simpletons. Their raids are a demonstration that they are ready to invade us at any moment. They long for warmth, and your father knows this. The Ookosi are waiting for us to be weak, and he fears with you being heir that you will not be equipped to handle this issue."

It was true that Abba had seen very little of the world with his own eyes. He had ventured around with his father to many of his vassals' manors and to the other lands that made up Osmjornia, but he had never left his birthland. All he knew were the cold, rocky coasts and forests that sprawled across the eastern half of Osmjornia. He had seldom ever been on a boat, and when he had, it was only to travel to the various sea-towns that lined the coast. He was a shy cat and secluded himself away from others to read his stories. Only the Phoenic Elders would pay him any attention: scholarliness was a priest's profession.

As if on cue, Elder Siemond came walking down the hall, waving to Abba, then stopping to bow to Anita.

"Countess," he said.

"Elder," she returned, a little coldly.

The Elder turned to Abba. "Well, hello there, Abba! How are you doing today?"

"I am well. And you, Elder?"

The Elder placed his hands on his hips. "I have certainly had a busy day, what with our Phoenic recitations and my meeting with your father. How are your personal studies faring?"

"I have not paid much thought to them recently. I am training for the tournament in Belar."

"Yes, yes, of course, the tournament. How could I have forgotten? How goes your training?"

Abba crossed his arms and looked away from the priest. "Well, I have improved a little bit. But it is quite difficult to get better quickly."

"The path of the sword is a very grueling one. Naturally, those who have followed the path of the pen are not accustomed to the fatigue of the body, for they have only ever trained their minds. It is often a waste of energy to do both, as it is quite rare to see an individual who is capable of mastering both the pen *and* the sword."

The Countess Anita glared at the Elder; then she stood and, without ceremony, stormed off.

The Elder watched her as she walked down the hall. "I do not think your mother appreciated the wisdom I shared with you."

Abba squinted at the Elder. "You have always been supportive of me in my studies, but you do not think I am suited for fighting. Why?"

The Elder shook his head, seemingly surprised. He fumbled with forming words, taking a moment to recollect his composure.

"I never said that, Abba. I only meant that I believe you are naturally more suited for scholarly endeavors."

"Well, thank you for your input; but I will be Count of Kurem, and I must take the path of the sword earnestly. I intend to speak to my father on this matter."

The Elder shook his head, gritting his teeth.

"Of course. Your father is in his study. I pray for the best of luck to you when speaking to him."

The Kurembrog halls were built with drab stone bricks. The only adornments that hung upon them were flickering sconces and banners of the twin serpents. It was not a bustling castle filled with courtiers rushing to please and obtain favor from some lord or lady, but rather a calm castle with the occasional servant roaming down its halls. It was cold and did not elicit much admiration. The servants did not pay Abba much attention, either—they kept aloof, gazing past the heir-apparent without acknowledgement.

Before long, Abba found himself at his father's study. He knocked on the door.

"Enter," said the Count.

Abba rarely ever visited his father's study. There were plenty of books that lined the shelves around the room, but cobwebs had formed over most of them. Abba's eyes wandered with a hungry curiosity. His father sat at his desk, reading a piece of parchment, his face emotionless.

"What is it that you want, boy?" Adar asked.

"Father, I wish for some thoughts on how to improve my chances of winning the tournament."

Adar stared at the maul that hung above the mantle.

"If you wanted to improve, you would be hacking your sword at a pell instead of speaking to me. Dueling is not a study like reading or writing; I cannot simply tell you something that will miraculously make you a great fighter. To learn, you need to fight."

"And what if I grow too tired to swing my sword?"

Adar broke out into a fit of laughter.

"Do you not realize how foolish that question is? What do you think your opponent will do when you are *too tired* to swing your sword? He will slice your thin little neck."

"Yes, Father," Abba replied, staring at the floor with shame.

Adar turned to look at Abba, but once he noticed Abba's shame, he placed his palm on his face and shook his head.

"Are you womanly, boy? Pick your head up and show a proud chest. Do you think the next Count ought to be such a sorrowful sod? No, you will not command respect looking toward the ground. How could you lead men into the battle when you lack dignity?"

Abba continued to look toward the ground.

"Gol! Are you deaf? Look me in the eyes, damn you! You will not survive the throne of Kurem if you cannot look a lord in his eyes. Begone!"

Abba frowned. "Father, I apologi—"

"Begone now! Begone!"

Adar shooed Abba out of the room and shut the door behind him. A single tear rolled down Abba's cheek, but he wiped it away before any courtier could notice. He stared at the floor of the empty halls of Kurembrog, defeated. He exited the keep and went to the ward.

Due to the hour, few people were training in the ward. In the distance, there stood a pell. It was chipped in several places and had noticeable wear. Abba walked toward the pell and began hacking wildly at it, going on for several minutes until he dropped. He huffed and puffed but could not muster the same fervor.

He picked himself back up, but instead of attacking the pell like a feral animal, he recollected himself and put his waster up into a high guard. He began slashing at the pell. He imagined the pell was a person: the wide end being the front of the duelist's body and the thin end being their sides. His hands moved as if the pell had a sword itself, contorting his body in a way that looked like he was reacting to the pell's imaginary attacks. Abba's waster parried an imaginary blow and immediately went into a cut from above. He drilled this single movement dozens of times.

He sat down for a moment. He did not know how to continue, so he began to hack at it again with the same movement. Then, he added an undercut that followed his overcut. By the time he grew tired of his drilling, his hands felt as if they could barely lift the waster into the air.

Leaning on one of the courtyard walls was Ser Mikhail with his scar-ridden face, grinning while he watched Abba swing at the pell. He walked toward Abba and sat down on a stool behind him. Abba noticed him out of the corner of his eye, but all of his effort and energy were directed toward maiming the pell. Ser Mikhail continued to watch Abba swing until Abba once more could barely lift the waster.

"Oi, Abba. It looks like you have the spirit of a warrior now."

Abba ignored Ser Mikhail and continued to slash at the pell.

"I do not mean to interrupt your training, but I do want to applaud this change of effort toward the sword. This type of training will do you well."

Abba continued to slash.

"Every night, you are to do this same exercise. Continue to add different movements to it, but keep the starting movement the same. That will be your best chance at winning the tournament."

Abba dropped the waster and huffed as he turned toward Ser Mikhail. Beads of sweat covered his forehead. He walked toward Ser Mikhail and sat down next to him.

"Thank you, Ser Mikhail."

"It pleases me that you have finally attained this level of passion," Mikhail said. "Granted, you will still have much trouble in the tourney. Simply working on a single movement will only slightly improve your chances. But for you, any improvement is beneficial."

Abba nodded, stood up, and marched to the pell. He continued to hack away at it while Ser Mikhail sat, grinning. Soon enough, Abba had dropped the sword again, collapsing to his knees.

"You may end your training for tonight. This was your first victory, but tomorrow I want to see this passion and determination again."

Ser Mikhail extended an arm toward Abba, dragging him up to his feet. He patted him on the back and waved him off.

Abba lugged himself back inside the keep, turning his tired body toward his room, stumbling as he made his way toward his door. When he entered the room, he saw a servant readying his wooden tub. A fire was lit under it to keep the water warm. The servant was a girl about the same age as himself, and Abba always found it hard to stay composed around her. He looked down while he thanked the servant and undressed. He stepped into the tub and began to scrub.

After cleaning himself thoroughly, the servant handed him a towel. He dried and clothed himself. The servant girl departed, and Abba picked up a satchel. He went through one of his drawers, grabbing a few tunics, a few pairs of trousers, and other necessities for the trip. He closed the satchel and placed it on his bed. His bookcase reeled in his attention, and he picked himself up, making his way to the bookcase. He grabbed *Ava's Lands* and wrapped it in linen. He opened up the satchel and stored the book inside.

Abba could not stop his thoughts from straying toward his books, but his tired mind halted him. His head ached and swirled, and his chest felt like it had caved in. He plopped himself on top of his feather bed and stretched out his arms. Abba was so exhausted that it felt like labor to pull his sheets and coverlet over himself. His heavy eyes drew him to sleep.

Edit

dit awoke to Phoenic calling bells in the morning. There was a knock on her door, so she dragged herself out of her bed to answer. "You may enter!" she yelled.

A servant girl entered, immediately giving a curtsy.

"I am here to prepare you for court, m'lady."

The servant held a folded dress in her arms. It was made of a golden fabric with orange trim. Edit walked over to touch the fabric: it was soft.

"This is a beautiful dress," she said.

The servant smiled. "I presented this dress to your father. We both thought it fitting for a lady."

Edit allowed the servant girl to strip her down to her undershirt and braies. She first fitted Edit into her hose and then fitted Edit into the dress. The servant helped her lace it from the back.

"What is your name?" Edit asked.

The servant girl paused momentarily, but soon returned to lacing Edit's dress.

"It is Loressa Lossefi, m'lady. Apologies for my surprise—not many lords or ladies have ever asked me my name. My father is the lord of a manor in Nar, but you likely will not recognize my house."

"It is of no matter, Loressa," Edit said. "Do you have any aspirations?"

"I—I would like to be married someday."

"Really? Why is that?" Edit asked, frowning.

"Well, I wish to have many children. Every lady I have known has been married and had children. I enjoy children, and I assume I would enjoy being a mother as well."

Loressa fitted the cord into the last ring of the dress and fastened it, pulling the cord tightly through the rings. Edit let out a huff as she felt her insides compress. She gazed at herself in the mirror, shifting her hips from side to side, examining how the dress looked on her. Loressa took Edit's hand and had her sit down. She brushed through her hair. At times it stung, her hair being yanked as the brush caught on knots that had formed in her sleep. Afterward, Loressa fitted a pair of matching shoes on Edit's feet. Edit stood up and Loressa curtsied as she pointed toward the door.

"Your father has already made his way to court, m'lady. I will walk you to Ser Elseharde so that he may escort you there."

Edit nodded, but her eyes were once more straying to the mirror. She could not stop herself from goggling at how the dress fit on her. She shook it out of her mind, stood up, and followed Loressa out of the door. Ser Elseharde was waiting just outside. Edit joined him, and they ambled on toward the court.

Plenty of knights, courtiers, servants, and templemen were also en route, the pair bumping into several different people while they worked their way toward the throne room doors. The throne doors were almost indistinguishable from large walls as they were unwieldy, large, and looked as if they would take over a dozen men to push open. They were likely made of oak, and were stained a deep red. Everyone walking in was forced to stand shoulder to shoulder as they made their way through. With all of the flamboyant colors the lords and ladies were wearing, it looked as if a river made of a rainbow flowed into the court, dispersing to the sides.

When Edit finally crossed, she gaped at the hall. Several stone pillars lined each side of the crimson rug that ran all the way to the throne. The first pillars—those nearest to the doors—had several notable landmarks engraved into them: the peninsula of High Beak, the River of Nar, Edrovith's Plateau, and Mount Kalarn. The second pair of pillars depicted men hunting wild elk and fighting off beasts like enormous bears, wyverns, and serpents. Many of the men that were carved into the second pair were made to look dead, with only a few standing triumphant over the beasts. The third pair of pillars showed people building towns, forts and castles with farms surrounding them. The fourth pair of pillars depicted scenes of war. It showed Mjornish men slaughtering other Mjornish men, with only one man standing, unharmed, on top; he had the head of a boar hanging from the tip of the spear in his hand. Massive Mjornish armies were carved into the fifth pillars, clad in crude armor armed with shields and spears. The sixth pillar showed carved Mjornish men and Yhournish warriors slaying Terukians, a race of humanoid beings with sharp jaws and even sharper ears. This pillar, too, had a Mjornish man standing triumphant, and he was surrounded by his cheering army, their weapons pointed to the sky.

The seventh and final pair of pillars showed the Mjornish people celebrating. As one's gaze drew up to the top of the pillar, one would see lords and ladies surrounding a Mjornish man, banners depicting the pierced head of a boar hanging behind him. He was surrounded by flames and was being crowned by a man who had a bird's head and wings protruding from his back. They stood on equal ground, but above them was the Phoenix. The flames below it were its wings.

Past the pillars was a black marble dais. The crimson rug led all the way to the throne itself. The throne paled in comparison to the pillars that surrounded the hall; it was a simple chair with red tufted cushions. The King was nowhere in sight, but about five individuals stood on top of the dais. Their dress was far more flamboyant than any of the others in the room, and they were protected by several knights who were lined up at the bottom of the dais. The knights stood attentively, with their arms resting at their sides.

Edit's father stood immediately in front of those knights. He was dressed in bright colors, similar to many of the other rich aristocrats in the hall, but the quality of his jacket and vibrancy of its dye far surpassed them all. He wore a bright orange jacket with gold stitching at its hems. His ginger beard almost disappeared when looking at him from a distance, but once Edit and Elseharde grew near, his inviting smiled peeked through. He opened his arms wide.

"Good morn, my little lamb! And good morn to you, as well, Ser Elseharde."

"Good morn, Father," replied Edit.

Ser Elseharde bowed and stepped forward to clasp Venceslaus's forearm. Then he turned to Ser Groent, who stood to the side of Duke Venceslaus, and shook his forearm, too. Together, the group all turned to face the throne just as a tall gentleman with blond hair stepped out from the flank of the dais. Upon his arrival, Edit noticed that everyone had grown silent and bowed their heads. Her father put his palm on the top of her head and gently applied force to let her know to follow suit. Never had she bowed in such a manner to another.

A crown made of some type of white metal weighed down his head, its luster almost blinding Edit. He wore a blood-red jacket with trim that was similar in color to the crown. He walked at an uncomfortably slow pace. It looked deliberate, like he was doing so to elongate the period of silence. The only thing that could be heard was his footsteps while everyone refrained from speaking.

He put his palm on the armrest of the throne and sat down. He certainly had the face of a king: clean, with a serious look in his eye. If he'd had any joy in his expression, he would have been a good-looking man; but the strange nothingness behind his stare made Edit uncomfortable.

A knight stepped forward, raising his right palm to the court.

"All raise your heads! King Asbyorn Harferd! The King of All Men and Lord of Nar!"

Everyone raised their heads. Quiet chatter began amongst the crowd. The knight that had called out stood in the center of the rug that led to the dais. He began to walk up to the top of the dais, turning to face the crowd. He held a tall spear in his hand that, from butt-end to tip, was made of a blinding white metal similar to that of the King's crown.

He slammed the butt-end of the spear on the floor, causing a reverberating echo to be heard in the throne room.

"All of you, quiet! Find your order in line to announce your grievances to the King! All of those who lack offense, place yourselves off to the side!"

The people on the throne room floor began moving around, looking like a colony of marching ants. The majority of the individuals in the room relocated themselves off to the side, leaving a small number of people lined up on the rug. The line was comprised of individuals of all social strata, with the notable exception of any clergy. There were peasants, craftsmen, aristocrats, merchants, and paupers that brought up their own personal troubles one by one. Eventually, a man dressed in an inky black tunic with hair that was a similar color stood at the front of the line. He looked like he was Narese, but his tunic was of a foreign design.

"Speak your grievance," stated the knight.

The man nodded and smiled. "Certainly, Ser Knight."

The man spoke a bit slower than a typical Narese person, putting emphasis on his R's and I's. The people near the dais tilted their heads in confusion, and the King chuckled. He raised his palm and stood up from his throne.

"Rarely does a gentleman from Aerus show his face in my court. What brings you here?"

"Your demesne is quite remarkable. I bring you a proposition."

"You announce a proposition before you announce your name? Our Aeric brethren have always had peculiar priorities. What is your name, *ser?*"

"Nay, not a ser. I am Prinz Afonices."

"Afonices? And what does that mean?"

"I am named after Afon, our first prophet."

"Avon," said the King. "Our prophet's name is Avon. Nevertheless, the Fatherland welcomes all Men to announce their concerns to our court, regardless of any misguided beliefs they might hold. Declare your proposition."

"As you wish, Sire. I am lord of a coastal fief that has been plagued by piracy. I propose a trade with you, for our protection."

The King shook his head and chuckled. "I do not wish to offend you, but your Aeric tongue sounds like gibberish to my Narese ears."

Prinz Afonices smiled tightly. "Pirates prey on my shores. I beg you for protection, and in return, I shall provide you with grain."

"Ah… Protection…" Asbyorn sat back onto his throne. "The price of our great kingdom's protection has always been the proclamation of one's subservience to the crown. Bend the knee."

Afonices stepped forward. "My demesne has, at each moment of its history, been free from Nar. Your people are in dire need of grain. Sire, I wish for you to simply consider it to be a transaction over a feudal contract."

"I have stated my terms. Accept or depart."

The peasants in attendance gasped. Around half of them stormed out of the throne room, and the other half erupted into chatter. Several of them began to murmur "ill-fit" or "simpleton King". The knight slammed the butt of his spear on the ground once more. The Great Chancellor Barnut walked, forward away from Asbyorn's side.

"Hold your tongues or be detained by Ser Bertram the White Spear!" he said.

The peasants quieted their chatter. The King held out his open palm and pointed at the Prinz. Edit's eyes were wide with amazement at the ability of the King and his men to control the crowd. He did not even need to speak, for his court knew how to speak for him.

"Afonices, what is your decision?" asked the King.

"It seems your response has insulted your subjects, and it has done the same to me. I shall petition other lords."

Asbyorn laughed. "Of course... It occurs to me that I have not asked which principality you hail from. What is the name of your domain and the name of your family?"

"I am a Lex, Sire. Prinz Afonices Lex. I hail from Saxvalsen in southern Aerus."

Asbyorn tapped his fingers on his chin while Afonices spoke. He never looked Afonices in the eye; he would always talk to the air around him. It looked as if Asbyorn held Afonices to be someone irrelevant and undeserving of his attention, rather than the independent and sovereign lord that he was. Afonices stood square to the King with an upright and proper posture, while Asbyorn slouched back into his throne. The Prinz waited for the King to respond, lapsing into an almost ticklish silence.

"Why are you still here?" asked the King, raising a brow at Afonices.

"What?"

"I reject your proposition. Begone."

The crowd erupted into chatter once more. Afonices adjusted his tunic and cleared his throat.

"At the hour in which you grow to your senses, the proposition will still be open."

Venceslaus brought his palm to his face and shook his head. "I knew that man's father," he said to Edit, his voice quiet. "He pledged men to help defend against the Yhournish in the war. This is quite a shame."

Edit ignored him and gawked at the King. The amount of influence he held would lead anyone to envy him. He sat calmly as the pinnacle of power in all of Mjorn. Holding court seemed boring to him. He could stare at the vaulted painted ceilings and answer *yea* or *nay* without care for his subordinates' grievances and go about his life. He was the ultimate arbiter of what happened in Nara. Edit wished to hold at least a portion of that power for herself one day.

But the King also seemed tired and absentminded. Perhaps his fatigue was due to the ailment from which he had recently recovered, but it still put a sour look on his face. The King never looked a commoner in the eye and often dismissed their pleas entirely. It was no matter to the King if the grievance brought to the court was urgent or important, for he met it with the same dry attitude he had afforded the Prinz. His indifference gave him the guise of being superior to all others, and no matter how true it might have been socially, it still left a sour taste in Edit's mouth.

After the last few petitioners had finished with their proposals and complaints, the throne room floor began to clear as people departed. Eventually, there was only a relatively small number of individuals left in the throne room. The group was composed of those with the highest prestige in Nara: the Freiheis and their present retainers, other high nobility and their own retainers, the King's personal guard, members of the Crii d'Nar, the Great Chancellor, and the King himself. Venceslaus made his way up the dais and nodded to Ser Bertram. Ser Bertram returned a nod of his own and allowed him up. The King looked at Venceslaus and smiled.

"It has been a long time, Uncle Vences."

Venceslaus grinned broadly. "It certainly has been, Sire. I do not recall ever introducing my daughter to you. Edit, introduce yourself to the King."

Edit walked shyly over and curtsied.

"Nice to meet you, Edit," he said. "How many years old are you?"

The King's eyes looked dead, as though there was no soul behind them. His smile looked forced, like it was a labor to keep a grin. He would have otherwise been an exceptionally handsome man if it had not been so unsettling to look him in the eye. There was also a strange red tinge in his hair, just below where his crown rested. Edit stared at him for a second, her heart racing with an instinctive fear.

"I—I am seventeen years of age," she mumbled.

"Which means I would have been about nine years old when you were born! And you would have been only a year old during the war…"

Asbyorn stared off at the throne room doors, his gaze empty.

"I miss your dear father," said Venceslaus. "It is a shame you had to grow into the throne without his guidance. King Matnus was an exceptional ruler."

Asbyorn looked at Venceslaus. When they made eye contact, Venceslaus recoiled. He stared at the King and squinted.

"Are you still unwell? You look… odd."

"The ailment was severe; I am still recovering," Asbyorn said. He smiled, but the expression did not reach his eyes. "It will take much more than a puny disease to put me down, I assure you."

"Of course, Sire. Long live the King of Man," said Venceslaus, grinning.

The two laughed for a moment. Edit inched away. The King's demeanor repelled her. His mannerisms also seemed manufactured: his reactions were slow, his laugh was hollow and unnaturally grand, and his posture was entirely unchanging while he sat in his chair, staring at the throne room doors.

"There is something I would like to discuss with you in private, Sire," said Venceslaus.

"Of course, Vences. Bring it up after the Crii later today. Now, however, I must go—there are some private matters I neglected while I was being nursed by the Queen."

Venceslaus bowed, and the King nodded him off. Edit, Ser Groent, and Ser Elseharde all followed the Duke as he walked down the dais. Edit sped up to her father and tugged at his arm.

"Something is strange about him," whispered Edit.

"He has the whole of Mjorn depending on his judgment, and he has not even been granted a proper rest after his ailment. Strangeness is to be expected. Do not speak of the King in such a manner again. Some may take it to be an insult toward His Majesty."

They made their way to the entrance of the keep. Lady Malaina stood by the door making conversation with a few of the servants, Loressa included. Malaina waved to Edit with a smile. Edit looked at her father, and her father gave her a nod. Edit smiled and turned to Lady Malaina, greeting her with a curtsy.

"That dress looks wonderful on you!" said Malaina.

"Thank you, m'lady! I am quite fond of it."

"I was hoping you would be—I had seen it made myself."

Edit's jaw dropped.

"A dress from the royal tailor? I am honored!" Edit replied, curtsying once more.

Every dress Malaina had worn was exceptionally grand: stitchings of various flora and fauna, bright and rare dyes, and fabrics softer than rose petals. Today, she wore a dress that looked as if it had been formed from gold. It had birds sewn into it with black thread. She had a shawl as blue as the sky resting on her shoulders, and this shawl had white birds sewn into it to complement the black birds on her dress. Malaina put her hand on Loressa's shoulder. Loressa blushed.

"I only received the commission. I instructed my apprentice Loressa to cut and sew it."

"I wish you would have told me you made this so I could have given my thanks sooner, Loressa!"

Loressa cheeks became even more rose-colored.

"Would you like to take a walk in the royal gardens with us?" she asked. "Lady Malaina seeks inspiration."

Edit turned her head to her father, and the Duke gave her another nod of approval. She turned back and smiled.

"I would love to."

Adar

dar dragged himself out of his bed, Anita still sound asleep at his side. He walked to the mirror that stood in the corner of his room. There was a bowl of water, clean pair of braies, and tunic on a small table next to the mirror that were prepared every morning by a servant, at Adar's request. Adar dipped his hands in the water and began to adjust how his hair rested on his head. He changed out of his nightwear and put on his clean clothes. He looked at a few pairs of trousers and jackets, choosing a pair of blue trousers and a black jacket. He topped off the jacket with a blue cloak that had the two white Kurem serpents sewn in. He strapped up his boots and exited his room.

It was early in the morning. Adar, despite being obsessed with his duty, thought of going back to bed: it was long since he had dreamt, and he longed for his dreams to return. But he never allowed himself to get more rest. Once Adar was up, he did not stop until he went to sleep at the end of the night.

He entered the throne room. Baron va Heddi and Ser Mikhail were present. He walked to his throne and took his seat. The three waited for a moment in silence, and soon enough the Elder Siemond entered.

"Now that Elder Siemond has arrived, we may proceed. Do any of you wish to share anything before we get started?"

"Your boy, Abba, has a newfound passion for the sword. I believe if you praise it, at least to a small degree, it will provide him with even more motivation to train," said Ser Mikhail.

"This is good, but I do not see the use in my speaking to him now. Your praise will suffice."

Elder Siemond raised his hand. "If I may, Sire, I am concerned about falling attendance at my recitations. I request more support with spreading the word of the Phoenix."

Adar sighed. "Siemond, you have lived in Osmjornia for over a decade now. A good number of the Osmjornish still cling to the old gods; it would cause great discomfort in my realm to push proselytization so fervently. It will be easier for everyone if you conduct your temple the same way as other Osmjornish Elders did."

"Lord Adar, we both know how the other Osmjornish Elders failed in ridding the people of their belief in the old gods. Need I remind you of the past? Need I remind you of your promise?"

Adar held his tongue. Ser Mikhail and Jergi kept their eyes down.

"I remember," Adar said. "I will think about that matter. Does anyone else have any matters to bring up?"

"M'lord, I have written up a plan for how the docks shall be constructed once I start my work as acting castellan," Jergi said.

Adar looked the Baron in the eyes. "This is one of the matters I wanted to discuss. I find it more appropriate to appoint a true castellan instead of shoving the work off to you. You have enough to deal with."

Baron va Heddi was visibly taken aback; he blushed deeply. "What compelled you to make this change?"

"It is better to have a man fully dedicated to a single position than it is to have a man partially dedicated to two positions. I am doing my duty as Count."

"But Sire, who will take up the position?" asked Siemond.

"I have a few candidates in mind. We will reconvene after I have collected them, and they will petition the court if they are interested. After we vote, Ser Mikhail and Jergi will travel to Belar with my two boys. I will stay back with Lady Anita and Elder Siemond while we wait for my brother to arrive."

The Baron pursed his lips. "Why must I travel to Belar? Should I not oversee the construction of the docks?"

"I want you to do your duty as Steward of Kurem and audit each village you pass through on your way to Belar. You can hand off your plans to the newly appointed castellan, if you wish."

The Baron looked down and shook his head. "Alright, m'lord."

"Any further matters to discuss?" asked the Count.

Everyone stood silent.

"Dismissed."

The Baron stormed out of the throne room, while the Elder Siemond gingerly walked down the dais, following the Baron out. Ser Mikhail stayed behind.

"Why have you suddenly chosen to remove the Baron from the position of acting castellan?"

"I was going over customs accounts yesterday, and I noticed potential evidence of embezzlement. I do not wish to formally charge him until I am completely certain of any wrongdoing. I will let you know which route to travel on, but I want you to pay very close attention to the Baron. As of now, I do not trust him."

"And what is your plan, m'lord?"

"I will travel along another route and investigate the accounts of the Baron's fiefs. If I find evidence further proving his hand in the embezzlement of iron, I will have you arrest him once we meet in Belar. I will use Geder's stewardship knowledge; it is a blessing that we will see him in Belar."

"Understood. The Baron has always seemed to have quite the greedy temperament."

"Aye."

The two stepped down from the dais and exited the throne room, parting ways. Mikhail went to the ward, and Adar went down to the gatehouse. He trudged his way down the drawbridge in a hurry, as he did not wish to be among his people for long. He arrived at the town square, where dozens and dozens of market stalls were propped up. Guardsmen were scattered about in order to keep an eye on potential misfits; thievery had recently been on a decline, but it never fully went away.

He turned toward the bailiff's office. At first glance, the bailiff's office looked no different to any other building that surrounded the town square. It had a stone foundation and stone-brick walls on the first floor, and the upper floor was made of wattle and daub. The only characteristic that separated it from the other buildings was a sign outside that had a painting of a scale with the word *BAILIFF* written beneath it. He entered the office to the sight of a lady sitting behind a table. She was focused, copying information from one paper to another; but when she saw the Count, her eyes opened wide.

"Welcome, m'lord!" said the lady.

"Is the bailiff in his office?"

"He is! Would you like me to call him down for you?"

"No need."

Adar walked past the woman and went up the stairs, opening the door of the bailiff's study without knocking. The bailiff, who was sat at his desk, jumped out of his seat at the sight of the Count.

"Oh, Gol! You scared the life out of me, m'lord," said the bailiff.

"How are you faring with your work?" asked Adar.

"It is the same shite every day—nothing I have not dealt with before. Has an issue arisen?"

"I have performed the duties of castellan of Kurembrog for a while now," Adar said. "But I have ambitious plans to better our infrastructure, and for that, I need a permanent castellan. I am going to nominate you for the position."

The bailiff bowed. "Thank you for your consideration, m'lord! I will serve you well."

"Rise, bailiff. It is not set in stone—I am deliberating over other nominations. You are to go to the keep in the evening. I will reconvene with my advisors, and we will discuss which of the nominees we ought to declare castellan of Kurembrog."

"Aye! I will be present."

"Good. I will see you then."

Adar turned around and exited the bailiff's office. He left the town square and walked down the road toward the docks. The dirt road sloped down toward the sea, speeding up Adar's strides. From inside the bailey, the docks were preceded by a gatehouse that was built to defend against any potential sea invasion, a common Ookosi and Aukstariczemic practice. The Count walked through the gatehouse and entered the port of Kurembrog.

Some of the wharfs and piers were crumbling from age and overuse. Planks were splintered and floating in the water. Despite their quality, there was never a dock that was not in use. There was always a ship sitting moored, unloading and loading cargo, or having repairs done. Adar stepped onto one of the piers and beckoned for a man to come forward. He had a long gray beard that covered his shoulders and chest, and he could be seen barking orders at people coming on and off of the docks, but once he saw Adar approach, he turned his head toward the Count and smiled.

"Hello, m'lord," said the man.

"Hello there, dockmaster. How are you?"

"My firstborn is wedding a beautiful young lady! It delights me that I shall be a grandfather soon," the man said with a grin that stretched from ear to ear.

"That is wonderful, dockmaster—but I was asking about the docks, not your personal life."

The dockmaster's grin dissipated into a blank expression. "Oh, yes, I should have known. The docks are busier than ever, and we are in need of more space for ships to berth."

"I am glad to hear that. I have always noticed that men listen to you when you speak; you garner their respect. The position of castellan is open, and I would like for you to be one of the nominees considered."

The dockmaster stuck out his hand to Adar. Adar grabbed him by the forearm and shook it.

"I will not disappoint, m'lord."

"Good. Be at the keep in the evening when my advisors and I reconvene. We will make our decision then."

The dockmaster nodded. Adar went back up the road, but before he passed the lower gates, he turned around and stared at the coast. There was plenty of unused space to the north, but the rocks underneath the keep made it impossible to build docks there. His eyes wandered to the sea. It was vast, so vast nothing but blue could be seen past the harbor.

"One day, I will make it right," muttered Adar.

He turned around and headed back up toward the keep. Ser Mikhail was waiting in the ward. The marshal was sitting down on a log inspecting armaments, organizing them into two piles: one was neat and carefully placed, while the other was haphazardly tossed into a chaotic mess.

"Hello there, m'lord. We need to repair or replace some of these arms. They are chipped and warped."

"What are you inspecting them for?"

"For the road! I want to make sure the two potential heirs to your lands are properly equipped."

"Thank you, Ser Mikhail." Adar smiled. "I nominated two men that will do fine in the position of castellan. They will be here by evening."

"Aye, very good. And who would they be?"

"The bailiff and the dockmaster."

"The dockmaster makes sense for the immediate future, but what does a dockmaster know other than ships? On title alone, the bailiff sounds more suitable."

"Whoever is elected, it does not matter. Neither are of the aristocracy, so removing them from their post would be no issue. I only care that it is not Jergi who becomes castellan of Kurembrog. He is a brilliant man, but an ambitious one, with loose morals."

"Aye, m'lord. I trust your wisdom, and I will support whoever aligns with your goal. I have always been wary of that Hedden, and I certainly believe it possible that he is scraping from your plate."

"He has been acting outside of his responsibilities of late. He wants more power, certainly. In the meantime, I am going to return to my study—it is around the time Siemond is to bring me the news."

"Alright, m'lord."

Adar passed Ser Mikhail and entered the area of the ward where Maric and Abba were sparring. To Adar's surprise, Abba had gotten marginally better. He was not as often caught by surprise now that he had become privy to Maric's tricks, but he continued to be bested by his younger brother. After a moment of observation, Adar frowned. He stormed over to Maric and snatched the waster from his hand.

"Stop going easy on your brother, Maric. He has you by two years and is still shite in comparison to you."

Adar turned to Abba.

"I will show you a real fight."

Abba held his waster up, hands trembling. He stepped forward to engage his father, but Adar sent the tip of his waster to Abba's hand. Abba dropped the wooden sword and squeezed his hand in pain. He stared at his father and then his waster. Abba grabbed the waster and attacked once more. Adar did the same move again, ending the bout in the same manner as the last. Adar threw his waster to the floor.

"Damned child! I did the same thing twice, and you still could not see it coming the second time? You have much to learn."

Adar turned around and stormed back toward the keep, refusing to face his son. He walked up a staircase to the rampart that overlooked the ward and stared off to the sea, his back turned to his sons. His hands squeezed the stone brick crenel in front of him while he lost his mind to a daydream. He thought of Abba getting beaten bloody in the tournament. He thought of his son injured, of his death. The thought of his weak son pained him, but he could not decipher whether it was a pain of the heart or a headache.

He tapped his palm on the crenel and turned away. He walked back into the keep, down the hall and to his room. He opened his door to see his wife fixing her dress. She smiled at the sight of Adar.

"Hello, my love," Adar said, walking over and kissing her temple.

"Hello, m'lord," Anita said, smiling. "What have you done this morn?"

"I revoked Jergi's appointment to acting castellan."

Anita's eyes widened.

"Does this trouble you?" Adar asked.

"You revoked Jergi's position as castellan so soon after appointing him? What compelled you to insult him this way?"

Adar shook his head. "As a lord, I must make sure my vassals' power is regulated. I cannot allow a man like Jergi to have such a vast amount of authority."

Anita stared at Adar with her hands on her hips and her chin tilted down. Adar could feel how tense she was. She turned around and sat down on their bed.

"I know when you are hiding something, Adar," she said. "There has to be a reason for this decision. You would never negligently appoint someone just to revoke their position, unless something came up immediately after appointing them. What happened?"

"Trust for now that it was the right decision."

"Adar, *tell me*."

Adar sighed. "I suspect him of embezzlement. I have Ser Mikhail keeping an eye on him to see if he is actually doing anything nefarious."

"Ser Mikhail? Is he not heading to Belar so that he might train Abba?"

"Yes, of course. Why would that have changed?"

Anita put her palm to her face. "So Jergi will be traveling with us to Belar?"

"No, we are staying behind to meet with Geder. But Jergi will be going to Belar with Ser Mikhail. Why are you asking so many questions, Anita?"

Anita took her palm off of her face and let out a deep sigh.

"Because, Adar, it sounds like an ambitious criminal is going to be traveling alone with the children of the lord who just insulted him. *Our* children. Does this not arouse concern in you?"

Adar put his hands on the table in front of him. He shook his head and grabbed the back of a chair, pulling it out in front of him and sitting down while he rubbed his eyes.

"My love, they will not be *alone* with the Baron. Ser Mikhail will be with them."

"I do not like this, Adar. You usually have more tact. Why would you take such a risk? Could you not have waited to revoke the position until after the tourney?"

"Embezzling customs is one thing; embezzling the Kurem coffers is another. I will not give that snake the chance. Anita, I will not be questioned again. Farewell, my love."

Anita stayed silent while Adar left, slamming the door behind him.

Elder Siemond was walking down the hall with scrolls in hand. Adar put his arm around the priest's shoulder and directed him to follow. They made it to Adar's study, and the two sat down together. Adar nodded to Siemond, and Siemond began to read.

"The Ookosi have been hunting and riding along our northern border. It has reached the point where there have been bouts of shouting between them and several of your vassals."

Adar shook his head and flicked his wrist, urging the Elder to continue.

"Aeric sea merchants have been purchasing quite a large amount of steel from our forges. We have also heard that there have been quite a number of arguments between the lords there. I suspect our trade is booming partly because the Aeric states are preparing for war."

"Hm... interesting. Is there anything else that I should be informed of?"

The Elder shook his head.

"Well then, thank you for the news, Elder. I will see you later this evening, during council."

Elder Siemond stood up, bowed, and exited the room, leaving the Count alone in his study. Adar's eyes wandered around. He stared at his reflection in the corner of the room; then his eyes slowly journeyed over to look at the maul that hung above the mantel. He walked over to it and brushed his fingertips along the maul's head, feeling the strength leave his hands the closer and longer he was near it.

"Why would someone make a weapon out of ordustone?" he muttered. "What would be its purpose?"

He walked back to his desk and went over the same account he had read earlier, as well as the history of his family. He could not tear himself away from the documents, looking over them again, and again, and again, and again. When he had first entered his study, light had been peeking through the window, but now the sun was low. Upon noticing the encroaching dusk, Adar jumped up out of his seat and hurried to the throne room.

Ser Mikhail, Pyre Elder Siemond, Baron va Heddi, the bailiff, and the dockmaster all stood waiting for the Count's arrival. The Countess Anita also waited in the throne room, but she stood off to the side, not intervening in the council meeting. She locked eyes with Adar and scowled at him. Adar ignored her.

"Where have you been, m'lord? We have been waiting," said Elder Siemond.

"Apologies, I got lost in my reading. I was stuck in my study looking over the reports about the Ookosi from our border with Minisda. Shall we begin? Were there any matters that have arisen in between our meeting this morn and now?"

Everyone stood silent.

"This shall be a quick meeting, then. I have brought forth two nominees for the position of castellan: the dockmaster and bailiff of Kurembrog."

Baron va Heddi stepped forward. "I still wish for you to reconsider revoking my appointment of acting castellan, and so I nominate myself for the position."

Adar put his hand on his forehead and wiped it down to his chin, shaking his head in disgust. He grimaced at the Baron. "Do not provoke me, Baron. I deny your nomination. Do not speak of any more foolishness, or you shall be dismissed from the meeting."

Baron va Heddi took a step back and kept his eyes down.

"Alright. Now that we have returned to reality: we have two nominees. The dockmaster is very experienced in managing the docks themselves, and I have no doubt that this experience will transfer smoothly to the general duties of castellan; although, naturally, this will take time. The bailiff, on the other hand, does have direct experience in managing issues within the bailey, but he does not have any experience managing docks, which shall be our main focus in the near future. We are planning to expand our docks to deal with the demand for our raw ore and refined metal trade. We have been receiving a large influx of raw ores from the eastern Osmjornish states, and we have seen an increase in demand from Aeric and Narese merchants for these raw materials, as well. I wish for the dockmaster and the bailiff to present their own arguments as to why they should be appointed, starting with the dockmaster; then the council will discuss who we plan to appoint to the position of castellan. Dockmaster, you may begin."

The dockmaster stepped forward and bowed.

"Thank you for the nomination, m'lord. I do not know if you all are aware of my history, but I have been much more than just a dockmaster. I have traveled all over the Mjornish and Aeric coasts. I have seen many lands, and I have had many ships at my command. I know the sea trade like the back of my hand, and, by extension, the influence it has upon the cities whose ports I have frequented. I have led ships into battle, and I know how to fortify a port in case of war. Indeed, I am not experienced in the other more general affairs of a castle, but I have decades of experience in organizing men. I know this would be an easy task with the bailiff under my leadership."

Adar leaned forward. "If the Ookosi were to attack tomorrow, would you be confident in your ability to lead the garrison in defense of Kurembrog?"

"Aye, it would be no matter for me. I have done so with other towns before," said the dockmaster, holding his head high.

"I like that response. And you, bailiff, what is your argument for appointment to the position of castellan?"

The bailiff stepped forward and cleared his throat.

"I have always been a simple man. I do my job, and I do it right. I am not as well traveled as the dockmaster, but I have been the bailiff of Kurembrog for years, and I know the city well. I know the names of every man in the garrison, and I am no stranger to battle, either. I have a good idea as to how the surrounding territories operate from reports I have seen over the years, and it would not be difficult to extend my responsibilities to those areas. Running a city is much more complicated than running docks, and I have experience in the management of *all* parts of Kurembrog."

"How would you begin the expansion of the docks?" asked Adar.

"As I would any other construction project. I would have engineers draw up the plans and then see how the cost would affect the rest of the castle, as well as try to project how much money the ports would bring. I would then choose the plan that was the most realistic."

"Ah, I see. I will now have both of you ask each other one question. Dockmaster, you may go first."

"Bailiff, you said you know the names of every man in the garrison. Do you know them because you speak to them daily, or because you handle their payroll?"

The bailiff pursed his lips, then grinned at the dockmaster.

"Either way, Madalbert, I still know their names. Have you ever looked at the payroll for the dock workers, or do you simply not care enough to pay attention to the coffers of Kurembrog?"

"Of course I have looked at the payroll. I know, for example, that you pay my workers far too little for the work they are breaking their backs doing. The docks are crumbling, and we do not have enough workers because of how low their payment is. The few workers that do stay only do so out of loyalty to me. Do you ever leave the bailiff's office, Tragileit?"

"I said only one question, dockmaster," Adar said.

"Apologies, m'lord."

"Now, I want you both to conclude with your reasons for being appointed castellan. Dockmaster, you first."

"Well, I know your lands and people quite well, and I know that your biggest concern is invasion by the Ookosi. Gol, it is the reason you were kept from this meeting. You need a man who can inspire troops, and a man that can make the Kurembrog port a marvel. I can tell you care much about the port's future—why else would you nominate me?"

Adar nodded. "And you, bailiff?"

"I feel it is quite clear that I am the one for the job. It is the position just above my own, and I already have the proper experience for it. Furthermore, the dockmaster is a commoner, whereas I am of noble birth. Naturally, it should go to me."

When the two had finished, Adar sat in his seat and looked back and forth between the two. The dockmaster was witty and cared for the people, which would go a long way when it came to keeping morale high in the castellany. Not only that, his experience in war pleased Adar. The bailiff knew the work of castle management well, and he was quite frugal, which also pleased Adar; however, Adar knew that Tragileit rarely ever left his office, and considering that he was rarely ever seen by the people of Kurembrog, it would likely make rallying troops to defend against a potential Ookosi invasion more difficult.

Then, Adar remembered: Tragileit's familial lands bordered Jergi's fiefs. Adar stood up.

"And now we vote. With careful consideration, my vote shall go to the dockmaster."

The dockmaster smiled. "Thank you, m'lord."

"I believe the bailiff's frugality and care are good traits for a castellan. We never know how a grand construction will turn out. My vote goes to the bailiff," said Elder Siemond.

Ser Mikhail shrugged. "I know Madalbert well; he speaks true to his history. My vote goes to him."

"And you, Jergi?" asked Adar.

"I would like to protest the appointment of either of them, for in my eyes they are both similarly qualified. I shall abstain from voicing my vote."

Adar glowered at Jergi for a moment, then turned his head to the dockmaster.

"Dockmaster Madalbert, by majority vote in the council of Kurem, I announce you castellan of Kurembrog; and, by the nature of the position, a fellow councilor."

Althalos

 tall stake-wall could be seen the far distance. Certainly, they were nearing Wettay, Althalos thought. Face-eater happily clopped up the dirt path with Agathius by his side, the two of them gaining distance from Althalos. Gunter, who had been lagging behind, grabbed Althalos by the arm and pulled him off to the side of the path.

"What?" Althalos asked.

"Ye were doing a lot of wrestlin' earlier. Have ye ever choked someone before?"

"As a joke, maybe."

Gunter grabbed Althalos by the shoulders and pulled him in front of himself. He wrapped his arm around Althalos's neck, using that same arm to grab his other bicep. Then he used that other arm to grab his shoulder. Althalos clawed at his neck, beginning to see stars.

Agathius turned around.

"Unhand the poor boy!" he yelled.

Gunter laughed and released him. "Now do it to me."

"Alright…"

Althalos went behind Gunter and loosely wrapped his arm around his neck. Gunter grabbed Althalos's wrist and elbow and shifted his arm so that the inside of Althalos's elbow met Gunter's trachea.

"Grab yer bicep, boy."

Althalos did.

"Now use yer other arm to grab yer own shoulder, behind my head."

Althalos did this as well.

"And squeeze."

Gunter's neck was already so compressed that his voice could only barely make it through the choke. Gunter tapped on Althalos's arm, and Althalos understood that he wished to be free. Althalos released him, shaking his head. They continued walking toward Wettay.

"Remember to hide yer top hand so whoever ye use it on can't grab it, boy. Ye could use yer village-boy wrestlin' with it, too."

"And what do I owe you for this?" Althalos asked.

Gunter smiled briefly, but shook away his grin soon after. "Some damn quiet."

Gunter sped up to match Agathius's pace. Althalos followed suit.

When the party reached the stake-wall, the guards did not halt them; instead, they gave a subtle bow as they passed, due to the habit and sash that Agathius wore. Wettay was an open but small town. It was rather flat compared to Fisk and Dorthu, so the temple there sat at the same level as all the other buildings. Likely to compensate for the local terrain, the temple's central spire could be seen from far outside the entrance of the village. There were plenty of trees and shrubbery along the road, and this road split the small town in half, running from the western side, bound toward Fisk and Dorthu, to the eastern side, bound toward Feninwich and Nara. Once they came upon the town square, Agathius halted and turned to face Althalos and Gunter.

"What is it, Elder?" asked Althalos.

"This is where we will part ways, Althalos. I must make haste to Nara."

"It was an honor meeting you, Elder. I cannot thank you enough for traveling with us."

"It was an even greater honor to help you with what little I could. Justice will be delivered to those who have killed your kin, and I will make sure that Nara knows that it was the King's men who did it. Do not waste time when seeking justice, Althalos."

Agathius mounted Face-eater and steered him away, heading westbound down the road.

"Finally, we are rid of that bastard priest! After ye talk to that Baron and figure out what ye plan to do, come find me. I will be gettin' a jack at the inn."

Gunter marched toward a building that ran parallel to the road. Althalos shook his head, disappointed.

Althalos started to examine each of the buildings in town. It was his first time out of Dorthu, and he wished to understand the other villages in his area. Most of the buildings and people were unremarkable, but two buildings stood out: the Phoenic temple, and a large manor house encircled by stake-walls that likely housed the Lord of Wettay. Althalos figured he would walk over to the manor house. The road split off through the town market toward the temple and the Baron's manor house. In the distance, by the gate to the manor house, five guards wearing yellow tabards could be seen. There were even more in the market. Althalos decided to meander around the market, looking at random stalls with no intention of purchasing anything so that he might eavesdrop; but he could barely hear anything, only picking out a few words like *Harry*, *traveling*, *Nara*, and *shortage*. His curiosity overpowered his reason and caution, and he found himself straying closer to the guards than he had intended.

"Halt!" yelled one of the guards.

Althalos turned around, doing as the man said.

"Why are you looking at things you do not have the means to buy?" asked the guard.

"What leads you to think that I do not have the means?" Althalos retorted.

"Look at your raggedy clothes—and you do not even have a purse. Go on your way, and stop grazing the stalls!"

Althalos nodded and backed away, turning toward the inn. The sun was now low in the sky, and the inn was bustling with activity. Men, and the occasional woman, could be seen drinking and socializing. It was much larger than Helwig's inn: it looked less like a repurposed home to serve drinks, and more like it had been built with the purpose of serving drinks in mind. A large and proper sign hung on its wall, marking it as an inn.

When Althalos stepped inside, he immediately saw a long bar with a barmaid tending to visitors. The building was packed with revelers, but once Althalos looked down the bar, he immediately noticed a sulking Gunter downing ale. Althalos walked up to him and sat down on a stool. Gunter did not acknowledge Althalos, continuing to stare at the bar counter in silence.

"Gunter?"

"What do ye want, boy?" Gunter motioned for the barmaid to bring him another jack of ale.

"I overheard that Baron Rowe is not here in Wettay."

Gunter gritted his teeth. "How does that help me?"

Althalos tensed. "What do you mean?"

The barmaid returned, dropped the ale off in front of Gunter, and scurried away. He looked like he was staring straight through the jack and countertop, entirely distracted.

"Ye are still a boy. Ye do not know the torture of this world."

Gunter's arms dragged forward as he attempted to lift the jack and down its contents into his mouth.

"Are you well, Gunter?"

Gunter grinned, crow's feet forming at the corners of his eyes.

"Am I well? Wellness is as foreign to me as the Yhournish wastes. I have seen it myself. I have been near it. Yet every time I try to grasp it with my own hands, I lose somethin'. Ye do not know, boy. Ye have not seen war. Ye have not seen your brethren slaughtered. Ye have not seen men whose blood is not your own, but ye have bled and sweat so much together ye can hardly tell whose blood and sweat is whose—ye have not seen those men die."

Gunter dropped his jack onto the counter, staring deeper into nothing. A tear fell from one of his eyes. He clenched his hands into fists.

"Ye have not commanded those men to die for ye. I was not some sellsword lookin' to shed blood in return for a mark or two—I led a band of brothers. I led those who I considered my kin to their deaths. I used to revel with my brothers in the inns, merrily skippin' and dancin' with the women who frequented the bar. Now, every time I am in one, I see them skippin' around me, but instead of smilin' and havin' fun, I see their mutilated and unrecognizable faces tauntin' me. They speak to me and blame me for their deaths. I grew up a poor boy at the wall. I was raised by my father; my mother died in childbirth. I had no love for him. He would drink and beat me. That band of brothers was my *real* family, and I killed them all."

Five men entered the inn, all dressed in shiny and ornamented plate armor, with their helmets removed. All of them wore crimson capes, and one of their capes hung tattered.

"Gunter..."

"Leave me alone, boy."

"Gunter, men with crimson capes," Althalos whispered firmly.

Gunter continued to stare dejectedly at the bar.

Althalos snatched a loose rag that rested on the counter and wrapped it around the head of the axe, covering the crimson cloth. One of the men walked up to the counter and motioned for the barmaid to come over. He looked a bit younger than Gunter, with only a few sporadically placed gray hairs in his black beard. He had no blemishes on his face, aside from his ugly smirk.

"I will take five tankards of your finest mead. You shall bring them to our table."

The man slapped a few coins on the counter and pointed to the table of soldiers. When the young barmaid put her hand over the coins to grab them, the soldier placed his hand atop hers and smiled.

"You are a beautiful young lady. There will be more coin in it for you if you accompany me to my room past midnight."

The barmaid grabbed the coin and gave the soldier a quick smile, but when she turned away, she looked down, her smile soon vanishing. She dropped the coins off to an older man behind the counter, and they began to discuss something. The older man started to talk faster, making more erratic movements with his arms. He looked annoyed with the barmaid. She kept looking over to the table, her blue eyes filled with distress. She looked to be around Althalos's age, and her youth clearly did not help limit the attention she received from the drunk men at the bar. The soldier turned his head to Althalos, and his frayed cape swung around his shoulder.

"Boy, why don't you have a jack in your hand? Are you poor?"

Althalos's eyes did not move from the cape. "I am only looking to have some water, ser."

"Ah, so you're a prissy cunt."

The soldier turned around and walked back to his table. Althalos's eyes tracked the man. Eventually, the barmaid brought the party's drinks to their table. The soldier with the tattered cape grabbed her by the hand and pulled her near. His arm wrapped around her hips, and his hand rested on top of her ass. He motioned for her to come closer, and he began to whisper something into her ear. She had a smile on her face, but her body shook with nerves. After the man was done, he smiled and handed her a pouch that looked to be filled with coins, and when she left the table, he smacked her behind. Her eyes went downcast and she handed the purse off to the same older man behind the counter. He overheard her say something about the third room, the older man replying that she ought to give him a "good time".

The soldiers drank and drank. They were the loudest revelers; their uncouth hollering could be heard all throughout the inn. Several inn-goers departed after a while. Some of them walked up to the older man to complain about the ruckus. The older man attempted to assuage their frustrations, but it came to no avail. He did nothing to remedy the situation. It was like the sight of the soldiers brought him joy. He grinned whenever any of the soldiers came to the bar to prattle.

Althalos stood up and walked toward the exit, choosing a route that would allow him to eavesdrop on the soldiers. Unfortunately, there was very little useful information that he could hear. They only nattered about bedding women, argued about who was more affluent, and joked about each other's cocks. For a moment, they mentioned Nara, but this soon passed in favor of more debaucherous topics.

Althalos left the building and sat down on a log outside. He watched the doors. To the side of the log, there was an empty burlap sack. He grabbed it. He briefly uncovered the axe to use its blade to cut into the sack, making eyeholes. He then kept the altered sack at his side.

Two of the soldiers left the inn, but neither of them had a tattered cape. Althalos figured that the knight with the tattered cape would soon appear, so he scoured around for an empty building to hide himself away in. Not too far from the inn was what looked to be an abandoned storehouse, standing by the western entrance to the village with very little foot traffic around it.

The moon had almost neared its highest point, and the last remaining soldiers finally left the inn. They wobbled as they walked, leaning on each other while laughing about trivial matters. The one with the tattered cape waved goodbye to the others, stumbling over to a secluded bush. He fiddled around with the straps around his buttocks, almost as if he was getting ready to relieve himself. Althalos stood up and tiptoed his way around the storehouse, toward the soldier in the bushes. Eventually, the soldier was able to lower his braies. He squatted and proceeded to defecate under the cover of the bush. Althalos put the sack over his own head, tiptoeing toward the soldier. The man grabbed an old cloth that was tucked underneath his armpit and began to wipe. When he was done, he tossed the rag away, pulling up his braies and beginning to fasten his leg armor.

Althalos's arm wrapped around his neck.

The man thrashed like a boar stuck in a net. Althalos made certain that the choke was secure, and that the man could not reach Althalos's top hand. As Althalos squeezed tighter and tighter, the man fought harder and harder, slowly going limp.

Althalos hastily pulled him back to the storehouse, awkwardly bumping into the door as he did. Althalos placed him so that his back was leaning up against a pole. The man started to squirm, but his expression was very slow and confused while he gazed around the room. A rope lay on the floor, so Althalos used it to constrict the soldier's torso and neck. The soldier was moving more. Althalos removed the rag and red cloth from the axehead and wound up the rag, tying it between the man's top and bottom teeth. After a moment had passed, the soldier fully regained his senses. He stared at Althalos's sack-covered face with a burning disgust. He tried to leap out of his bindings, but failed to do so, so he settled instead for muffled, angry grunts.

Althalos sat down and stared at the man, unsure of what to do with him. He knew he had to question him, but he did not know how. The soldier had a small satchel hanging on his waist, so Althalos opened it and searched around inside. Some coins and two keys were all that the soldier carried with him. Althalos grabbed the keys, tied the soldier up tighter, and exited the storehouse. He scanned around. Very few people were out this late, and the moon was still almost at its highest point. Althalos crept his way back to the tavern, tiptoeing up the steps toward the rooms. He put the key into the lock of the third room, fitting it snugly. He turned the key, and the door unlocked.

The room was what one would expect from an inn: the bare essentials. There was a bed with its headboard against the back wall, a chest next to it, and a small table to the left of the door with a candle on top. Althalos closed the door quietly behind him, hurrying to the chest and opening it with the other key. The chest was mostly filled with a few tunics and trousers, but there was a flat leather bag shoved in the corner. He grabbed and opened it. He sifted through its contents. There were many notes and letters, but none said anything of Dorthu. One was written using what looked to be monikers.

To the Black Wolf,
You and the Sword are to accompany the Gray Bear and his men. Lead them to the place we discussed. Do not allow anyone to survive. You are free to use whatever means necessary to secure their end.
The Ultimate

Althalos grabbed another note. This one was addressed to someone named Irold. He then grabbed another note, and this too was addressed to Irold. Althalos deduced that Irold and the Black Wolf were likely one and the same: the knight with the tattered cape. Right as he placed the note down, the room's door opened. It was the barmaid. Althalos still had the sack on his head. She looked at Althalos, pausing and glancing away with a dazed look on her face. Althalos immediately ran to her, slamming the door shut and putting his hand over her mouth. She looked scared, but at the same time a little relieved.

"Allow me to explain why I am here. Will you scream if I uncover your mouth?"

The girl shook her head.

"Alright," said Althalos, taking his hand off of her face.

"Wh—Where is he?"

"Do not worry about that. That man deserves what will happen to him."

Althalos looked up and noticed the girl was visibly distressed: she was shaking, and her eyes darted back and forth.

"Do not fear. I must make certain that I can question him. He…"

Althalos paused and swallowed his spit.

"…he and his companions killed everyone I know. They slaughtered the people of Dorthu like they were swine."

"The King's men massacred a village? That is absurd! Why would they do such a thing?"

Althalos took the sack off his head and revealed his face. The girl tilted her head with another dazed look.

"You were at the bar earlier, were you not? Next to the man who tried to solicit me?"

"I could tell you did not wish to talk to him."

"But why did you help me? Do you understand the position you have put me in? He was supposed to be in this room tonight, and now you have kidnapped him. Who do you think his companions will come for first? And what do you think my father will do to me when he discovers I did not go through with his demands? One night of torture is better than the punishment I shall receive now. I did not ask for your help."

"I never meant to assist you," Althalos said. "Just tell them you went up to the room, but you did not see the man. The last people who to see him were the soldiers, and they saw him go to a bush to relieve himself. This will bring both of us enough time."

"And what if you are wrong?"

"Then I will reveal my hostage and flee, your name will be cleared, and his companions will hunt me down."

"How can I trust your word? What is your name?"

"Ah. I—I am Althalos d'Dorthu, and my word is the last thing that I have. You can trust me."

"An interesting name," she said. "I am Lina d'Wettay. I will go along with your plan, Althalos, but you must keep your word."

Althalos nodded, scurrying out of the room.

Meara

eara and Gol woke to Phoenic bells ringing. She had never really cared for the bells. Her parents had always told her that the temple was just for show, for barely a soul practiced Phoeni in Belar. She did not like going around the temples, either. The priests gave charity—food and the like—but it was not worth the risk.

Meara grabbed the sack of food and stuck her hand inside, pulling out one of the cured meats. She undid the wrapping and ripped it in half. Gol ran over, his hand extended, and Meara handed him one of the halves. Together, the two orphans ate happily, but it was not long until Meara grew antsy, wanting to leave. She never felt safe staying in one place for long; if she always moved, she could never be found. The only reason she had stayed around Luka for so long was to avoid the loneliness she had inherited from the death of her parents.

"We need to figure out what to do with those groschen," Meara said. "Luka has hurt too many of us. The other children will never stand up to him."

Gol frowned, crossing his arms and looking down. He was bouncing his leg with a nervous energy. The two finished their cured meats, and Gol let out a burp.

"Ha! I think that is the first noise I have ever heard come out of your mouth!"

The boy smiled. It lingered on his face for a while, but soon it dissipated into a blank stare. Meara stood up and removed the plank from the door, unlocking it. When it opened, the sunlight that beamed through it was blinding. They both put their arms up over their eyes and squinted; it took a moment before their eyes adjusted to the light.

The two of them walked out of their newfound home. They made their way back to the area near the gatehouse, making certain to stay at the fringes of it. They feared being seen by the cutthroats they had stolen from the day prior. Meara kept her eyes on the same alley that the wagon had entered through. The wagon was now gone, and the alley now contained several loitering men. They all looked to be grizzled ne'er-do-wells, staring around and giving belligerent looks to any passersby bold enough to walk too close. Meara tapped on Gol's shoulder and pointed to the marketplace.

"Go and get Luka's attention. Then do this."

Meara put her finger into the dirt and wrote out the number twenty. She tapped her palm and pointed at Gol.

"Write the number twenty in the dirt, tap your palm, and point at Luka. He should understand."

Gol wrote *20* in the dirt, tapped his palm, and pointed at Meara.

"Yes! Good, you understand. Now go run off and find him!"

Gol hurried off toward the marketplace. After he left, Meara returned to watching the alley. She stood up and walked toward some crates that were closer to the gatehouse to get a better angle of sight. The buildings that lined the road running perpendicular to the alley were all shops of some sort. There was an armorer, a smithy, an unmarked warehouse, and a general store. In between the smithy and warehouse was a large fenced-in area. Unfortunately, the fences were too tall to allow someone to see over, so Meara inched closer. She tried to make it look like she was just strolling over to a well that stood on the other side of the road that ran by the shops.

Those shops were to her left, now. She looked at the fence out of the corner of her eye. There was a small hole from a plank that was warped, allowing a tiny window into the fenced-in area. Inch by inch, she crept toward the fence. There were not many people outside, as most people were busy praying. They did not pray to the Phoenix, however: the Phoenic recitations on their holy day happened at about the same time as their regular Esic prayer. Esic prayer took place every day, but on the Phoenic holy day, those who followed the faith used the bells as a way to tell the time. The streets would fill by the next bell.

Meara peeked through the tiny hole. Several men stood around, surrounded by crates. The crates were filled with pieces of metal and loose tools. In the far corner, a few barrels stood, likely originating from the wagon. The majority of the men looked to be workers, although a few did carry bludgeons. Those men were heavily blemished, scars covering their faces.

She recognized one of them. It was the large man with the dagger that dangled from his waist. She made sure to get a good look at him. He was hefty, much like Luka, and walked around as though he owned the place, also much like Luka. If he was walking somewhere, he did not need to ask anyone to move—they just got out of his way. He was bald, with a dark mustache and ugly, beady black eyes. Fat sagged from his chin, and he was dressed in a thick jerkin.

"You fuckin' cunts did it! I hoped I would've calmed down today, but unfortunately for you fuckers, I am still pissed!"

He pointed at two men, the wagon-drivers that had ridden the crates into the alley. They walked forward. He put his hands on both of their shoulders and pushed them down to the ground, making them kneel.

"You had one fuckin' job! You let that bitch take our groschen!"

He slapped one of the wagon-drivers in the face, sending him to the floor. He lifted the other by the collar, yelling at him for several minutes. He cursed the wagon-driver's mother, father, any extended family he had, any animals his family owned, and any future children that he would have. The man pushed the wagon-driver away, putting both of his hands on his head.

"I swear to Esu, I want to gut you two fuckheads. Find the bitch! Find my groschen!"

The wagon-driver that had been slapped rose up, pointing a shaky finger right at the fence.

"I think somebody is watching us," said the wagon-driver.

The large man squinted at the fence; then he grinned, exposing his decaying teeth. He undid the dagger from his waist and threw it at the hole in the fence. It missed, landing only a tiny distance away from Meara's eye, causing her to fall back. She struggled to get up, then ran toward the well. She looked behind and saw the men exit from the general store. Three of them ran toward her, including the large man who had thrown the dagger at her.

Meara passed the well, running past dozens of homes and stores. She turned her head to look, and she saw that only two of them still followed her. The fat man had disappeared. She smirked; he must have gotten tired. She traveled down a narrow road and passed through a corridor that led into the town square. As she turned, the Phoenic bells rang twice, and all the residents left their homes, and all the temple-goers left the temple.

The town square was filled with people. Merchants began to sell their wares. Meara disappeared into the crowd, losing the two men chasing her. She kept low, and she watched the two men.

Suddenly, the fat man was back. He held Gol by the back of his shirt with one hand. Gol tried to kick and make a commotion, but the man's grip held firm. Meara noticed several guards looking at the large man, but none of them went forward to apprehend him. The large man walked off with Gol in tow, out of Meara's sight. Meara's legs went out from under her. She fell to the ground, tears forming in her eyes.

Her only friend had been taken.

A shadow crossed over her. She looked up and saw the Low Beakish merchant that she'd bought wares from the day before leaning over her. She looked straight up at him and began to shrink away in fear. He extended his hand to her. She hesitated, waiting for him to attempt to strike her—but he had been kind to her, she remembered, the last time they had encountered each other. After a moment, she accepted his hand. He pulled her up to her feet.

"Do not fear, little girl."

His fingers were abnormally long. Meara stared at them for a moment. She did not comment on them, however, finding it more tactful to stay quiet. She brushed herself off. Her muscles were tense, and she turned her back to the merchant while she wiped away her tears.

"I never asked you for your name. What is it? And what troubles you?" asked the merchant.

"Why do you care?" Meara said. Furious tears returned to her eyes; she blinked, trying to will them away.

"Why would I *not* care?"

Meara stared at the ground. The man's eyes grew sterner and more focused.

"Does it have anything to do with the man who just caused a ruckus dragging away that boy?"

Meara winced, beginning to step back.

"Do not go," said the man. "I can help."

"How could you help? *Why* would you help?" asked Meara, once more wiping the tears from her face with the sides of her fists.

"I am simply doing my charity as a devout follower of the Phoenix," he said.

Meara turned her head, confused. She did not know if the Low Beakish people followed the Phoenic faith, and skepticism filled her. She was skeptical not of his religiosity—she couldn't have cared less about that—but she was skeptical of his willingness to help her. She was only alive because of her skepticism and carefully thought out action. It would not be wise for her to accept this man's generosity; but her heart was filled with desperation.

"How could you help? What do I have to do?"

"Slow down, lass. See that building over there?"

He pointed to a building that was on the fringes of the town square.

"Once the town square closes, go to the second floor of that building. I cannot help you until then, but do not worry—the lad is unlikely to be dead, if the two of you have done what I suspect."

Meara's head turned. "What do you suspect?"

"Never mind that, little pickpocket. Go to that building in the evening and you will get the help you need."

Meara nodded and walked away. The man went back to his stall as one of the passersby began to browse his goods. She scurried back to where the group of orphans had taken shelter. Luka still sat on his food sack throne and was surrounded by his child subjects. One of the children pointed at Meara as she walked back to the group. The boy shouted, "It's Meara!" and went to tug on another child's arm. The crowd of children parted, allowing Luka to view Meara's arrival.

"Well, look who returns!" Luka called. "Do you have my twenty groschen?"

Meara's heart sank. "So, Gol did not tell you about the groschen?"

"Gol? What do you mean, Gol?" asked Luka.

"The mute boy. Gol. I told him to tell you that I have your twenty groschen."

Luka stood up and shot his chubby arms into the air. He danced his way to Meara, putting his hands out in front of him.

"I always knew you would make me proud, Meara! Where are my groschen?"

Meara shook her head. "I will give you double the groschen, but I need your help."

Luka sighed and dragged his feet back to his throne.

"Wait! You will not need to do anything; I only need the help of the other children."

Luka stopped, turning around. "For what?"

"Gol... they took him. I can give you forty groschen easily, but I can also promise even more if we can snatch it from the people who took Gol."

Luka turned around with a greed-filled grin, rubbing his hands together. "And what do I... have to do?"

"Just distract them for me. I will do the rest."

"Alright, Meara," Luka said. "I will allow you to stay with us tonight, so we can carry out your plan tomorrow. But do know— if I do not get my forty groschen, I will have these children beat the life out of you."

The group of children looked at Meara. They were skin and bones, shivering like scared cats that would jump at a pin drop. Meara walked over to one of the buildings that surrounded the area in which the orphans loitered and squatted. She rested there, thinking, until the sun had grown low. A few of the children came over while she waited, asking questions about the plan, so Meara quickly explained it to them.

Before long, it was dark. Meara stood and left for the town square. At this hour, the square was empty, for the night trade was done in the brothels and bars. Meara walked past several empty market stalls toward the building the Low Beakish man had pointed to. She knocked on the door, and it promptly opened. The Low Beakish man smiled at her warmly.

"Come in, dear."

He stood out of the doorway so Meara could enter. She crept through the door, making sure to examine every corner in case there was a surprise waiting for her to arrive. She was met with nothing but a table and two stools, one of which had been pulled out by the Low Beakish trader. The trader grabbed a lockbox and placed it in front of her.

"Open it," said the man.

"I—I do not know how."

"You are a thief, yet you do not know how to lockpick? I suppose I really do have a great deal to teach you."

He walked to a table and grabbed what looked like a set of keys. He threw them down to the floor and pointed at them.

"Use one of those to unlock it."

"But that will take forever—there must be fifty keys on that ring!"

The trader grabbed the box and sat down on the floor next to Meara. He pointed to the wood and then to the metal. He turned the box upside down and pointed to a touchmark that was stamped onto the metal bits of the box.

"The wood grains; the metal. Do you see this? It is a marking from a Osmjornish forge. These keys are skeleton keys, and they are a great tool for lockpicking—but your true best friend in lockpicking is your own intelligence."

He grabbed several keys and held them up to Meara's face.

"Because the box is from a Osmjornish forge, it is most likely the case that one of these keys will open this lock. Try it."

Meara grabbed the key ring and, one by one, put each of the keys the trader had pointed out into the lock of the lockbox. Soon enough, one of the keys opened the box. Inside the box was a piece of paper, and the paper had drawings of common touchmarks with notes indicating their regions of origin. She scanned it for a while until the trader took it from her.

"So, you can read?" asked the trader.

"Only a little. My parents were teaching me some words, and I recognize the Mjornish alphabet. But the other ones I cannot make out."

He turned the paper so that Meara could see the markings.

"These other touchmarks are from all over Lonus. Marks from Aerus, Ookos, every region of Mjorn, Low Beak, Teruk, Uusuk, Eith—even Krenki and Yhournish touchmarks."

Meara grabbed the paper from the trader. "Why are you showing me this?"

"I am going to assume that you stole something from someone you should not have stolen from. I am also going to assume that you still have whatever it is you stole. I do not mean to alarm you, but they are more than likely torturing your friend right now. Since he is a child, he is likely to talk soon and let them know where you hid what they are looking for; and if he does, they will kill him immediately. However, if he is still alive, then he is also more than likely going to be behind a locked door. I will lend you these keys and lockbox so that you may quickly retrieve your friend."

Meara stared at the trader. "He will not talk."

"Nonsense, he is a child. He will talk soon. You need to hurry and retrieve him."

"No, he will not. He *cannot*. He is mute. The cutthroats are probably getting angry with him."

The trader stared back at Meara. "I suppose your friend's muteness has saved your life, then. But I can only imagine what he is experiencing."

Meara stood up and walked toward the door, stopping before she opened it. She turned to face the trader.

"Where did you learn how to do this?" she asked the man.

"My father. He was not the most honest man, and some of his dishonesty rubbed off on me."

Meara nodded and, taking the box with her, exited through the door.

She walked back to the other children and plopped herself down in her normal spot. Luka strolled over and pointed at the box.

"You know the rules, Meara: whatever you bring in is everyone's to have. Hand over the box."

"Luka, if you want your groschen, then you better let me keep the box."

"What is in the box, then? Is it my groschen you said you already have?"

"No. It is something that will help you get all the groschen you want—but only if it stays in my hands. If you take it, you won't ever get the coin you want."

Luka shook his head. He walked back to sit by the other children. When he spoke, every orphan was quiet. If they were not quiet, Luka would beat them. He was always loud. It was like he had to be louder than everyone else. He would try to make the other kids talk to him, but Meara knew they only responded so that they would be spared from his wrath. When a child did not respond, he would grow bored, pointing at random orphans and forcing them to fight each other. Most of the time, they would comply, because it was better to get beaten by a scrawny kid of the same age than someone much older and much larger like Luka.

Meara made sure to keep her distance from Luka that night. He did not pay her much mind after their conversation about the lockbox, but she was still on edge. In time, Meara fell asleep.

Venceslaus

fter parting ways with Edit, Venceslaus went straight for the Crii room with Groent and Elseharde. It was too early for a meeting, yet he knocked on the door anyway and awaited entry. No one answered. After waiting a bit longer, he knocked once more. Still, no one answered. He waited a bit longer for fear of being regarded as rude, but he eventually grew so tired of waiting that he knocked another three times.

"M'lord, I do not mean to question your actions, but could it be that you are knocking on the door to an empty room?" asked Ser Elseharde.

"No, it cannot be. Barnut nearly lives in the Crii room. For as long as he has been a member of the Crii d'Nar, he has sat in this room brooding over the kingdom's future," said Ser Groent, putting his hand on Venceslaus's shoulder.

Urbaed walked past them and knocked on the door; but still, no one answered. Venceslaus looked down at the ground. There was a small droplet of red on the floor. He pointed at it, and they all stared at the droplet. Ser Groent put his hand on the handle of his sword and attempted to shove open the doors. The doors seemed to have been blocked, so Ser Groent and Ser Elseharde tried to kick them open. The doors only budged a bit.

Through the crack in the door, several items of furniture could be seen, stacked and barricading the room from the inside. They pushed the furniture out of the way as quickly as they could and made their way through. A trail of blood led to the King's Crii seat, and when they made it to the seat, they saw the body of Great Chancellor Barnut bathed in his own blood. His wounds were fresh; his eyes were still somewhat alert, darting erratically around the room. He was trying to say something, but his tongue lay right next to his body, so he just awkwardly mouthed and gurgled. He could not move, for his joints were lacerated. He was still alive and writhing in pain. Venceslaus felt the urge to vomit, tears rising unbidden to his eyes.

Ser Groent choked his sword's handle as though it was the neck of the murderer himself. Urbaed looked down at the body of Barnut. He looked squeamish, as if it was the first time he had ever seen such wounds. Ser Elseharde pointed at the blood splatters. They trailed from Barnut out of the doors of the Crii d'Nar. Venceslaus's hands shook, and he fell to his knees.

"My brother is dying right before me, and I cannot even ask who wronged him…"

"The blood trails out into the hallway. It is fresh, so the perpetrator must be near," said Ser Elseharde, running to the doors.

Venceslaus put his hand up, and Ser Elseharde yielded. Ser Groent helped the Duke to his feet. Venceslaus began to examine the table. Documents were spread around; they concerned the fate of Dorthu, as well as the tolls on the roads. He looked at Barnut's hands. They were empty, but a bone pen did lay in the pool of blood beneath him. Barnut's eyes had stopped moving. His chest was no longer rising and falling, and he had stopped squirming. At some point between when Venceslaus had stood up and when he had turned back around, Barnut had drawn his last breath.

"Lord Urbaed, did you see anyone come down the hall?" asked Venceslaus.

"I did not, Lord Venceslaus. We need to run down that murderer—he is still loose!"

Ser Elseharde walked to Urbaed. "You came from that direction, did you not?"

Elseharde placed his hand on his sword's handle.

"Take your hand off your sword, Elseharde," said Venceslaus. "Ser Groent, stay by my side while I investigate the room. Ser Elseharde, inform any guard you see roaming the keep that there has been a murder. Go and follow the blood trail."

156

Ser Elseharde nodded and ran out into the hallway.

"Forgive Ser Elseharde for his accusations. He is jumpy, for he has never seen battle," said Ser Groent to Urbaed.

Lord Loffreaux, Great Marshal Donas, and the other councilors had entered the room. They all stared at Barnut's body in shock. Donas knelt down to look at Barnut's mutilated body. He felt his pulse.

"The Great Chancellor is dead."

"He only just died. When we entered, he was still moving. Well, as much as he could move with his body injured the way it is. Whoever did this wanted him to suffer for a long time," said Ser Groent.

"Who could have killed him?"

Venceslaus turned his head to the door. He remembered that they had found it barricaded from the inside. The killer could not have barricaded it and escaped through that door.

Lord Loffreaux walked around the room and examined the blood splatters. He stared at one for a while. He moved toward the window that was on the opposite wall to the doors and looked outside.

"Did you notice the blood splatters, Lord Venceslaus?"

"Yes, Lord Loffreaux. I sent Ser Elseharde to run down the halls to find the perpetrator and notify the guards."

Lord Loffreaux looked at the windowsill, then looked at the ground below the window. He turned around and pointed at the window. The bells of the keep rang three times, indicating an emergency.

"The murderer did not exit through the halls. The blood splatter showed movement toward Barnut, not away from him. He exited through the window."

Lord Loffreaux grabbed a cloth from his pocked and dabbed it on the windowsill. He displayed it to the rest of the Crii d'Nar, revealing a blood-red dot. The Great Marshal put a palm on his face and shook his head. He stood up and put his hand on Lord Loffreaux's shoulder.

"For once, I am thankful for Lord Loffreaux's analysis. I am going to gut the fucker that killed the Great Chancellor. He will suffer more terribly than Barnut."

Great Treasurer Geder Kurem entered the Crii room. He gaped at the scene. There was a manic shock in his eyes. Before he said anything to the Duke, he looked down at Barnut, then slumped into a chair.

"I may have butted heads with Barnut, but this is very unfortunate." Geder was silent for a moment; then he stood up, the manic expression returning to his face. "Why are you all just standing here gawking at a dead man? Should you not be searching for his murderer?"

"It is better that they stay here," said Venceslaus. He walked over to the documents on the table, picking them up and examining them. "It is my suspicion that the motive for the murder has to do with the investigation of Dorthu. Barnut was killed while examining these documents."

"Folly. We knew nothing of what happened in Dorthu. Why would someone kill the Great Chancellor when we knew nothing?" Donas asked.

"Because it is a warning to not look any further."

"Venceslaus, you have an astute mind, but I am not convinced. There could be countless explanations as to why he was assassinated. The position of Great Chancellor can be polarizing, and these are trying times," added Loffreaux.

Venceslaus put his palm to his forehead. "I am not a believer in coincidence. Yes, it could be anything, but he was so set on investigating Dorthu that he was doing so in his free time—what else do we have to go off of? The massacre of Dorthu was strange in its own right, and this is even stranger. The two have to be connected."

Ser Bertram Rowe, the White Spear, entered the room with several guards following behind him. He was not strikingly muscular, but he was well-built. His height made him seem wirier than he was. The armor he wore was made of finely polished steel that gleamed in the light and had crimson accents painted onto it. The spear for which he was known never left his hands; he used it as a walking stick wherever he went. He was accompanied by Ser Elseharde, who pointed to Barnut's body. Ser Bertram knelt down to examine the Great Chancellor, eventually standing up to address the room.

"Every one of you will be detained and questioned, but I will give you all the respect you deserve and allow you to be detained in your own chambers. Furthermore, I will need to be informed of any suspicions you may have as to the motive of the killer. I will allow you to stay a bit longer to mourn your acquaintance, but if you decide to leave now, we will immediately go into questioning."

"I am ready to present my suspicions." Venceslaus pointed to the papers on the table. "We ought to take these. I believe them to be important evidence."

Ser Bertram nodded and put his hand on Venceslaus's shoulder, leading him out of the Crii doors. He allowed Ser Groent and Ser Elseharde to follow. They walked back to Venceslaus's chambers, and the Duke sat down in a chair. Bertram did not sit down, preferring to wander around the room.

"Duke Venceslaus, where were you leading up to the murder?"

"This morning, I was in the throne room—you saw me there. After speaking to the King, I left through the main corridor. Then my daughter left to accompany your sister. I went to the Crii early to speak to my good friend Barnut. I knocked on the door many times, but no one answered. Eventually, we noticed a drop of blood on the floor, and by then we knew that something strange was happening."

"Why did you wish to speak to him?"

"To further discuss the matter which we spoke about yesterday. I also rarely see him, considering how busy we both are."

"Did you notice where the drop of blood came from?"

"It formed a trail, but I am unsure of which direction it had come from. Ser Elseharde ran out to investigate."

"Yes, he did; that was when he found me. The trail was lost in the crimson rugs of the throne room."

"Barnut was attacked in the throne room?"

"No. There was no such scene; in any case, I was there, and I did not see anything of the sort. We will leave off with this: what are your suspicions?"

"I believe that Barnut was targeted because of his intention to investigate Dorthu."

"And why is that?"

"During the Crii yesterday, we had discussed the matter of Dorthu, and the majority of us were not convinced that bandits were the cause. It was not a raid; it was a massacre. The aim was to wipe Dorthu away, for reasons which I do not know."

"How can you be so certain that it was not a group of bandits?"

Venceslaus fumbled about with the papers. "Bandits want things of worth, but nothing of worth was taken. The temple was untouched; all of its precious metals were still present."

"Interesting. Do you have anything else to add?"

"The nature of his murder was gruesome, Ser Bertram. They cut his joints so he could not get up, and they cut out his tongue so that he could not yell for aid. They left him there to suffer, and I imagine they did so as a warning. They kept him alive for us to see. I doubt it could be related to anything other."

Ser Bertram nodded. "Alright. I will take your suspicions into account. I will be off now, Good Duke, but I will return a bit later once I have spoken to the rest of the suspects. See you soon."

Duke Venceslaus nodded, and the White Spear soon departed. Ser Groent and Venceslaus sat down, looking over the documents together. There was no solid proof that Barnut's murder was tied to the Dorthu Massacre, but Venceslaus felt it deep in his bones that it was the case.

"Ser Elseharde," asked Venceslaus, "where did the trail of blood lead?"

"M'lord, I found droplets of blood all the way down the hall that leads from the Crii to the throne room."

"Interesting."

"Do you know of any enemies that the Great Chancellor could have had, m'lord?" asked Elseharde.

"Barnut was not a man with many enemies. People adored him. He was never too stern, and was known to be quite friendly."

They continued to talk about the murder for a bit longer, but the conversation shifted once they had exhausted all possible ideas. They were held in the chamber for around another hour. Eventually, the White Spear returned. Ser Bertram sat down beside the Duke.

"It is terrible what the Great Chancellor—your friend—has endured, Venceslaus. You were the first to make it to the door; did you see anyone in the halls nearby?"

"No, Ser, the halls were empty. Unusually empty, perhaps. There are typically more people about, if I remember correctly."

"Aye, usually there are. Are you sure? Identifying any potential witnesses is of the utmost importance, m'lord."

"I am sure, Ser," said Venceslaus.

"It was brought to my attention by some of the councilors that there were courtiers loitering in the halls. Are you saying that they are being... less than honest?"

Venceslaus turned his head with heavy brows. "Are you implying that *I* am being less than honest?"

"No, of course not. I was only asking if you trusted the accounts of the councilors."

"I suppose I do. A number of them been on the Crii for quite a while."

"Ah. Well, I am clearing you of suspicion, Duke Venceslaus."

"What? For my safety, Ser, what is the reason you are clearing me of suspicion?"

"Purely because of the blood trail. It starts at a point between the throne room to the Crii room; since you did not come from that direction, it could not have been you."

The Duke shook his head and stood up, his two knights standing at his side. Venceslaus extended his forearm to Ser Bertram; they grasped each other's arms and shook.

"Before I depart, Ser, have you found any suspects?" Venceslaus asked.

Ser Bertram shook his head. "Not as of yet. We do have a witness from the King's courtyard who claims to have seen a man dressed in black attire fall from the Crii window, but he seemed to disappear once he hit the ground."

"Has anyone else been cleared of suspicion?"

"The only other councilor who has been cleared is Geder Kurem."

"And why is that?"

"He came from the same direction as you did. It is known that he likes to take the long way to the Crii room; he never was an enjoyer of the Crii meetings."

"Ah. Thank you, Ser Bertram."

Venceslaus, Groent, and Elseharde all departed from the Duke's chambers. They walked down the halls, marching back down to the entrance of the keep. It was filled with guards, each of them standing with poise, their chins raised high, their hands resting on their sword handles. Typically, a number of them would bow upon the Duke's arrival; but at this moment, they refused to move.

"Elseharde, retrieve Edit and bring her back to her quarters. You will leave with her and Geder Kurem for Belar as scheduled.

I will go and speak to Geder to notify him that I will be staying in Nara to investigate Barnut's murder myself."

"Yes, m'lord." Ser Elseharde bowed, marching off to find Edit.

Venceslaus turned down the hall and walked off toward the royal chambers. They had to walk up three flights of winding stairs. Guards were everywhere. The last time Venceslaus had seen so many men in armor with crimson capes was fifteen years ago, during the Yhournish War. The keep was filled with an army.

When they reached the royal chambers, a guard stopped them from moving forward.

"Halt! The individuals in these chambers are under investigation."

"I am here to see Geder," said Venceslaus.

"Oh. Well, he was recently cleared. We will have to escort you to his room. I cannot let you freely go about."

"That is understandable. Take me there."

The guard escorted Venceslaus and Groent to Geder's door. He waited in silence while the Good Duke knocked.

"Enter!"

Venceslaus opened the door. Geder sat at his desk counting coins. He turned his head to see who had entered the room; but once he noticed it was Venceslaus, he resumed counting his coins.

Geder's room was drab and gray. He did not have many furnishings, and the furniture he did have was well-used, with papers piled on every surface. His bed was a mess, his sheets and coverlet falling off the sides of the mattress. His pillows looked as if he had thrown them into the air, and they had landed in random spots. One of the brick walls was painted entirely white, with Osmjornish letters painted on it in black. Venceslaus could read Osmjornish, but the writing was so messy that Venceslaus could not decipher what it said. His rugs were misaligned, and his only painting was unleveled. The only thing that looked to be in order was Geder's clothing, but even his hair appeared unbrushed.

"It seems you did not kill the Great Chancellor either, eh?" asked Geder.

"Of course not, Geder." Venceslaus walked to Geder's side, looking over his shoulder. "What are you doing?"

"I am going over a batch of recently minted currency. This is just a random sample of one hundred coins, and because they are consistent in weight and stamp quality, I will thankfully not have to have the whole batch remelted and restamped."

"Ah, I see," Venceslaus said. "Geder, I came here to tell you that I will not be able to accompany you when you depart for Belar with Edit tomorrow. Can I trust that my daughter will be well taken care of?"

"Are you not going to Belar?"

"Oh, no. I will meet you there on the day of the tourney. I simply must handle some business here before I leave."

"Ah, very well. I will see to it that your daughter is perfectly safe and comfortable on the journey."

"And tell Count Adar that I will be a bit late."

"I will," said Geder, grimacing.

"You have my thanks, Geder."

"Of course, Duke," Geder said, returning his attention to his coins.

Venceslaus exited the room with Ser Groent, walking in the direction of their chambers. He thought Geder's reaction to his brother's name was a bit strange; nonetheless, it was not out of the ordinary for Geder to be a bit peculiar.

"For some reason, it seemed he took offense when you mentioned his brother," said Ser Groent.

"That Geder is a strange fellow," Venceslaus said. "He does not seem to like when his brother or his home is brought up. I oft forget that tendency of his."

"Aye, quite strange indeed."

Althalos

he night was dark, and Althalos's head was growing ever heavier. He snuck his way back to the storehouse where he held the tattered knight hostage. When he walked in, he was met with the sight of the knight violently shaking in an attempt to free himself from the rope. The rope looked to be loosened, so Althalos grabbed a pitchfork that leaned on the wall and held the prongs to the knight's neck. His hands quivered.

"Hold still, you demon."

Althalos stared down the knight like a wolf did prey, though his heart panicked like a jumpy squirrel. If the knight were to make it out, Althalos would die. There would be no chance for him to beat this man in a fair fight. Like Gunter and Agathius had said, he had no real fighting experience.

The knight stopped his thrashing, and when he did, Althalos went behind him to tighten the rope back up. When Althalos came back around to face him, the knight smiled through his gag.

"Fuck you, *Black Wolf*," Althalos said.

The Black Wolf squinted at Althalos with confusion. He tried to speak, but the gag was tied too tightly for him to form intelligible words. He gestured with his chin several times, signaling for Althalos to remove his gag.

"If you scream, I will stab you in the throat with this pitchfork," Althalos said.

He ungagged the tattered knight. A large grin formed on the knight's face.

"Who is the Black Wolf?" the knight asked.

"Maybe you will know the name Irold more intimately," Althalos said.

Irold's grin left him. "It is quite rude to go through another man's belongings, you know. When I am out of here, I am going to have you worse than flogged, boy—know that. Who are you?"

Althalos stared down at Irold. He felt warm. He wanted justice, but he did not know what to do. Baron Rowe was not there, so he could not just drag him out and present Irold to him. If he did such a thing now, the village headman would probably side with the other knights, anyway.

"Boy, is there anything up there in that head of yours? Quit your staring."

"You killed everyone," Althalos said. "Dorthu is burnt to the ground, and it is all your doing. Everyone is dead. You killed mothers, fathers, babies, animals. You left nothing there. Why?"

Irold snickered.

Althalos crashed his fist into Irold's face. Irold's head whipped down with the punch. Althalos punched him twice more, and red began to drip down from Irold's nose. He shook his head and cursed under his breath. He stared at the ground, refusing to look at Althalos. His face was reddened and raw.

"You know, I thought you were a bit of a bitch—but your punches *do* have a sting."

Althalos wound up the rag and gagged Irold once more. He grabbed a few empty sacks and placed them by Irold, resting his head on them and placing his legs on top of Irold's.

"I am going to rest now," Althalos said. "But I am a light sleeper, and if I feel you squirming around again, I swear I will kill you."

Althalos grabbed the axe and clasped it near his chest. Irold did not respond, he just hung his head. Eventually, Althalos fell asleep; but as expected, he barely had any rest that night. His heart could not stop racing, leading him to wake several times just to keep an eye on Irold. The knight was always in a deep slumber.

The temple calling bells rang, waking Althalos. He examined Irold, making sure he was still tightly bound. The knight was wide awake with purple bruising all over his face, though one of his cheeks was still red and raw. He sat quietly. Althalos went over,

165

tightened the ropes just in case, and went for the storehouse door. He creaked it open carefully.

There was no one in the streets; the entire town must have been in attendance at the Phoenic temple for recitations. Althalos hurried off toward the inn and peeked through a window into the common room. Through it, he saw Gunter passed out face-first on top of a table with no one else in sight. Althalos crept through the door and tiptoed over to Gunter, shaking him awake. Gunter startled awake, sucking in a strangled breath and whipping his head around to look at Althalos.

"Oh, fuckin' shite, don't ye sneak up on me like that, ye cunt," said Gunter, rubbing his reddened eyes.

"Gunter, I found one of the men who slaughtered Dorthu," whispered Althalos.

Gunter shook his head and walked behind the counter toward a basin of water, dumping his hands into it so he could scrub the drool and vomit off of himself. He grabbed a rag and dried off.

"Where did ye spot him, boy?"

"Follow me, and I will show you."

The two exited the tavern. Althalos led Gunter to the storehouse, holding the door open for him. When Gunter stepped inside, he immediately stared at the tattered knight, his eyes going wide with surprise.

Althalos walked in and shut the door behind them. He passed Gunter and knelt down next to Irold. The knight stared at Gunter. Gunter moved closer, and when he got a better look at the tattered knight's face, he looked uneasy.

"Boy, how in Gol did ye subdue this man?" asked Gunter, while Irold smiled through his gag.

"I crept up on him while he was undoing his trousers, and I did that strangle you taught me."

Gunter sat on top of a crate. He did not take his gaze off of the tattered knight, clenching his fists while he stared down at the man.

"Ungag him," said Gunter.

Althalos ungagged him.

Irold turned his head to Althalos. "So, you know this sad sap?"

"Gunter..." Althalos said. "You know this *monster*?"

Gunter stared fiercely at the bound man. "Irold used to employ me. Before I started my own band of brothers, I was in his company."

Irold's grin grew even wider. "Gunter! How nice to see you again. It is unfortunate that it is under such conditions as these, but it is nonetheless wonderful to know you have not killed yourself yet."

Gunter gritted his teeth. "Ye connivin' shite. I left ye because ye were a rapin' and murderin' lunatic. Ye will always find an excuse to kill."

"Gunter, it may be true that I had done terrible acts when you knew me last, but I am a different man now. I have found the light! I have been rebirthed in the Phoenix's flame. I am a reborn man, leading a holy life!"

Irold spoke in a peculiar way when he began to discuss his holiness. It was like he found the idea of being a good man humorous. It was a mockery. He cared nothing of who he killed; it seemed to be *funny* to him. Althalos squeezed the axe shaft like a vise, inching toward the tattered knight. Gunter put his forearm in front of Althalos, halting him, and they stared at each other for a brief moment until Althalos eased up. Gunter stepped closer toward the knight, and the knight turned his head and smiled.

"You were drinking yourself to delirium last night, were you not? I thought it was you next to that boy over there. You did not realize I was right next to you, did you, Gunter?"

Gunter stared blankly at the Black Wolf. "If there was anyone heartless enough to slaughter his fellow countrymen, it would certainly be this man."

Irold shook his head. "Gunter, I have *changed*. Quit it with the *slaughtering fellow countrymen* shite."

There was a strange emptiness to Irold's black eyes. He looked annoyed.

"You killed everyone I ever knew and burnt Dorthu to the ground. You are mad," said Althalos.

"For the last time, boy, I did not kill your fucking mud-wallowing people. You fucking roach—I will have you hung for this offense."

Althalos removed the ripped cloth from the head of the axe and held it up before the knight. The Black Wolf's eyes darted back and forth between the cloth and the axe until he could not contain himself any longer. He smiled; then he erupted into a hysterical-sounding laugh. Gunter put his palms on Irold's mouth and nose and firmly pressed down, smothering the knight. When

Irold noticed his lack of air, he began to thrash violently. Gunter removed his hand, and Irold heaved for air.

Gunter snatched the torn cape from Althalos's hand, wound up the cloth, and gagged the knight again. He drew a dagger from his waist.

"What are you going to do, Gunter?" Althalos asked.

"First, I am goin' to undress him of his *very* expensive armor. Then, I am goin' to find out why he slaughtered Dorthu."

"Why would you need a knife to question him?"

"I am not questionin' him, ye fucking dolt, I am *torturin'* him. If he just so happens to tell me about Dorthu, then I guess it's a merry fuckin' benefit to you, isn't it?"

"Don't torture a man for me," Althalos said. "It is unjust."

"It ain't for ye. Irold does not know what the word *just* means, anyway. Shut yer mouth and take his boots off, will ye?"

Althalos walked over and removed the knight's boots. The two of them began to unlace and unbuckle all of the plate armor that covered the knight's body, loosening some of the rope to free an arm or a leg. Without struggle, the pair unarmored the knight's limbs; but once they got to his torso, Irold jumped at his chance to escape. He kicked Althalos over, and the boy stumbled and fell by the side of a crate. The crate was against one of the walls, and when it was knocked to the side by Althalos's weight, it uncovered a hole in the wall behind it. A few rats nibbled on some kernels from a ripped sack of grains there. Althalos stood up to the sight of Gunter punching the knight in his jaw. Irold went down immediately. Althalos unclipped, unlaced, and unlatched the remaining armor pieces and tossed them all into a pile. Gunter grabbed a sack and poured its contents out onto the floor, handing it over to Althalos. Althalos put the armor into the bag.

"Sneak past the guards and find a spot to hide this outside of the walls. Guardsmen piss about during temple recitations, so ye should have no issue gettin' past them."

Althalos neared the door, but he turned back before he opened it. "Ask him who the Grey Bear, Sword, and Ultimate are. He had a note."

Gunter nodded, putting a sack over the knight's head to help muffle the sounds. He put his dagger to the knight's arm and began to cut. Irold thrashed, and Gunter did not speak a word. Althalos closed the door behind him.

He looked toward the western gate. A single guard stood there. Althalos placed the sack behind a stack of crates and looked around for a way to divert the guard. His effort was unnecessary, however; as Gunter had predicted, the guard walked away from his post. He looked around to make sure no one was looking, then pranced off behind a building. Althalos picked up the sack and made a break for the western gate.

Now outside the walls of Wettay, Althalos trudged toward the forest. There was a large oak that towered above the tree line. The sounds of crunching leaves and branches followed him while he labored toward that tree. The winding roots of the great oak created ridges in the dirt. There was a small ditch off to the side of the tree, and those same roots were exposed there, creating a small crevice. He tossed the sack inside the crevice and ripped several branches off of a few small trees to throw on top of the hole. Once he had deemed it sufficiently concealed, he turned back toward Wettay. He took his time on the way back, making sure to enjoy the calmness of nature before he returned to whatever Gunter had done to the knight.

Once he made it back to the western gate, two guards had returned to their posts.

"Halt!" said one of the guards. "State your business in Wettay."

"I just left to go for a walk," Althalos said.

"What? I did not see you," said the guard.

"Fucking Gol, I have seen this boy around. How did you not see him? Boy, did you go through this gate?" asked the other guard.

"Yes, I did."

"You fucking dolt. You left your post again, did you not? I will make sure Lord Rowe beats your arse for this. You may pass, boy!"

Althalos walked through. Behind him, he could hear the other guard trying to excuse his absence by saying that he had needed to relieve himself, but the other guard dismissed him, saying he ought to have grabbed another guard to cover for him.

The streets were filled with townspeople. Knights with crimson capes were going up to seemingly each and every passerby, talking to them as they went. Althalos kept his head down while he made his way toward the town center.

"Oi, lad! Have you seen a Narese man in plate armor with black hair around here?" asked one of the knights.

The knight was bald, with a gray, grizzled beard. His hair was disheveled, but his skin and teeth were clean. He had a stare that seemed to oft overstay its welcome. He did not take his eyes off of Althalos.

"Were you fellows not hogging all the ale at the inn last night? I would be surprised if *he* even knew where he was," said Althalos, giving them a side-eye.

The trio laughed, and the gray-bearded man patted Althalos on the back with a smile.

"What is your name, boy?" asked the gray-bearded man.

"My name is Althalos."

"Althalos of…?"

"Althalos d'D—" Althalos paused and pretended to clear his throat. "Apologies, Ser, it seems a ghost stole my words. I am Althalos d'Fisk."

"Ah, d'Fisk… What brings you to Wettay, Althalos?" asked one of the other knights. He had brown hair and blue eyes. He snickered after he finished speaking.

"Well, I am only staying for a moment. My destination is Nara."

"Oh, really? Why?"

"I—I wish to take up the Elder's habit."

The man snickered again. "Why the Gol would you want to live such a boring life? Reading books all day."

The gray-bearded man put his hand up, and the man stopped his laughter. "The boy is working toward a dream—and it is a noble dream, at that. Boy, do not listen to that pompous arse over there." The man gave Althalos a coin. "Use this to pay for your travel."

"Thank you, Ser. If I may ask, what is your name? I only wish to thank you for your generosity," said Althalos, looking down so that they would not see his disgust.

"I am Ser Ernest, and there no need to thank me. I am simply tending to the flame," said the gray-bearded man with a smile.

"Ser Irold is probably drunk out of his mind with a whore somewhere. He'll turn up in time," said the last knight.

Althalos waved goodbye to the trio of knights and left to wander around the town center. He did not want to make it obvious that he was going to and from the storehouse, as he did not know who owned it. It did not look used, but it was surely someone's. He walked around until the knights went off on their way, and when the coast was clear, he returned to the storehouse.

Gunter jumped to his feet with the swiftness of a rabbit once the door opened, pointing his dagger—blood dripping from its tip—at Althalos. Once he realized it was only Althalos, he turned around, returning to Irold. The knight's right forearm was riddled with cuts and burns. Gunter had a lit candle beside him and was holding his dagger's blade above it. The knight also had chunks of skin removed from his legs. What Gunter had taken was placed in a pile by the knight's bare feet. Irold's eyes were bloodshot, and his brows furrowed. Althalos could hear his muffled groans from under his gag.

"What did he say?" asked Althalos.

"A whole lot of nothin'." Gunter pulled Irold's head up by his hair. "Confess yer murders, ye fuckin' roach."

"Ungag him."

Gunter ripped the gag from Irold's mouth, and Althalos crouched next to him. Tears ran from Irold's eyes.

"That knight with the gray beard is the Gray Bear, isn't he? It would have to be one of them, and he is the one in charge."

Irold grinned. "Their names don't matter. Do you really think this is going to end well for you? I know who you are. Gunter will be easy to find. He cannot stop himself from getting drunk—"

Gunter squeezed on Irold's raw, burnt leg.

"Fuck! Fuck, fuck, *fuck!* Fuck, that hurts! Fu—"

Gunter placed his palm on Irold's mouth, waiting until the knight quieted down. Once Gunter removed his hand, Irold let out a sigh.

"Mmm—I do not know your name yet. Gunter just calls you *boy*. But that does not matter. You undoubtedly traveled through Fisk first, complaining about your dead family and friends all the while. I can travel back and find your name there," he said. "I really think you will be quicker to kill. If it were my choice, I would kill you myself, but it seems I am going to take a while to heal up thanks to that drunk."

Gunter slapped him. "Confess to killin' Jurrod."

"Oh, Gunter," said Irold. "You still have not moved past that, have you? Does it rile you that you do not know what happened to that lousy churl?"

Althalos looked at Gunter. "He is not going to say anything. Let us leave this arsehole alone for a while. Maybe a moment of peace will bring him the courage to speak."

Gunter gagged Irold and took Althalos with him outside.

Abba

bba woke up to the sound of the Phoenic temple bells. He rubbed his eyes and stared at the ceiling, his stomach churning. He did not know if it was due to excitement or fear, for the outcome of his travel to Belar was still left to be written.

He dressed himself and grabbed his packed belongings. Once he left his room, he headed out for the ward. He was met by his father, Count Adar; his mother, Countess Anita; Ser Mikhail; Baron va Heddi; and his brother, Maric.

"Abba, Maric," said Anita, taking them both by the hand, "you shall travel with Ser Mikhail and the Baron to Belar by yourselves, for your father and I must wait here to meet your Uncle Geder. But do not fret—I will meet you in Belar before the tourney begins."

Ser Mikhail nudged Abba toward his steed, and Abba stepped forward. He secured his bag onto the saddle of his horse, then climbed up onto the horse's back. The rest of the party followed suit.

Adar grabbed the reins of Ser Mikhail's steed. "I shall walk you to the outermost gatehouse that leads to the road that heads toward Belar. Abba, make sure you train day and night. You must not bring shame to the Kurem name."

Abba nodded, and Adar led the horses down to the gates. Once they reached the outermost gate, Count Adar released his hand from the horse's reins and waved them off.

The Kurembrog countryside was filled with rolling hills and vast rye fields. The skies were thick with clouds that floated north. Every so often, they passed by the occasional farmhouse; Abba and Maric made sure to wave to any peasant that was outside. The roads were quiet, smelling of dirt and dung. The breeze that passed filled Abba's nose with the smell of straw. Sparsely grown trees lined the road, and in the distance was a heavily wooded green forest.

The four were soon surrounded by trees. Tree limbs crossed above them in a lattice of branches and leaves. The road twisted and turned much like how a snake would, avoiding the large rocks and hills in its way. Small streams and felled logs were a common sight. Wild Osmjornish Elk watched the party while they moved through the forest. Abba enjoyed watching them graze. He gawked at the rabbits and birds, and in his head, he would test himself by stating the names of their species. Rarely did Abba ever get a chance to see the fauna he had read about so often.

"Oi, Abba! Never seen a bull before?" taunted Maric.

Abba ignored him and continued to name the animals in his head. Once he ran out of animals to name, he began to stare at the leaves and wild plants. He then did the same thing again, trying to name the common flora. He did this for about an hour until he ran out of flora to name. He smiled, for he had not stumbled on any of the names; and, as far as he remembered, he had named them all correctly. They passed over a several creeks that flowed down into the Kyln River, and Abba named these, too. He began to name them out loud. Maric looked up and groaned.

"Abba, you are making me even *more* bored."

The Baron and Ser Mikhail smirked.

"Stop caviling and go back to daydreaming if it bothers you so much," Abba said.

Maric ignored Abba and turned to Ser Mikhail. "Do you know how much farther it is? We have been riding for hours!"

"Maric, stop whining. We will be crossing a toll bridge soon, and then we will meet the first village on our route," said Ser Mikhail.

Maric groaned again.

They made it to a narrow river. A bridge crossed over it, with a small wooden tower guarding the bridge. Two guards stood side by side, crossing their pikes to bar any passage across the river. They wore the Kurem crest on their tabards.

The party's horses trotted toward the bridge. Once the guards saw Ser Mikhail's face, they immediately uncrossed their pikes and stood to the side of the bridge, allowing them to pass. Ser Mikhail smiled and nodded to the guards as they rode by.

The trees were much denser on this side of the bridge, and the shrubbery along the road was almost impossible to see through. Smoke could be seen over the tree line in the distance. Baron va Heddi spurred his horse forward, trotting a bit faster toward the smoke. Soon, they reached the entrance of the village. Baron va Heddi dismounted from his horse.

"Lord Hedden!" greeted one of the peasants.

The Baron waved to the peasant with a smile, then he walked off toward a building that was a bit larger than the rest.

There were purple banners hanging everywhere. There was a yellow hyacinth flower at the center of all of these banners, standing strong and proud. Abba then remembered that the Baron often wore purple, and his eyes widened with realization.

"Ser Mikhail, is this a fief of the Baron's?"

"One of three. I thought you of all people would have been aware of that," Ser Mikhail said.

"I do not know much of his family; his house is not in my history books."

Ser Mikhail chuckled. "News always moves faster than the pen writing it down. His father was a wonderful knight and a good friend of mine. He was knighted after defending our realm from several Ookosi raids. He was awarded his fiefs after an incident with their previous lord. Your grandfather granted him the fiefs as a way to make up for the incident, and because he was the only reasonable choice. He died shortly thereafter. He was a good man."

Ser Mikhail dismounted his horse; Abba and Maric did as well. They grabbed the reins of their horses and led them over to a fenced sparring enclosure, tying their horses to a hitching post before they entered. Ser Mikhail leaned against a pell and scratched his beard. He pointed at the two brothers, then pointed at the wasters that hung from the saddles of their horses.

"There is not much for any of us to do while the Baron is performing his duties, so you two may as well use this time to train."

Abba nodded and walked to his horse to grab his waster. Maric did the same. Abba raised his wooden sword, staring at Maric. He waited for his brother to act, but Maric did not move. Abba's chest felt as though it had been weighed down by bricks, his nerves harassing him. He knew that he ought to move around and circle his opponent, but his feet felt as if they were part of the ground, or as if they were stuck in deep mud.

Maric's waster zipped past Abba's face and whacked him right in the rib. Abba stumbled and lost his footing. He caught himself and planted his feet firmly on the ground. He brought his waster into a high guard, and Maric did the same. Abba swung his wooden sword down, but Maric parried it, returning a strike of his own. To Maric's surprise—and certainly to Abba's surprise as well—Abba parried the strike; however, it was of no consequence. Maric returned Abba's parry with a thrust of his waster, jabbing the tip of his wooden sword into Abba's stomach. Abba fell to the ground, heaving for air.

Maric stuck his hand out to Abba, and Abba accepted it.

"You had me for a moment, but you think too much."

Abba squinted with confusion. How could someone *think too much*? All he did was think. It seemed mad that someone could win anything without thinking. He wanted to call his brother stupid, but he had just been beaten by him. Maric always bested him in fighting.

"What do you mean, I think too much?"

"Do not do what you just did. Just act. Just *do* something."

Abba looked off to Ser Mikhail, and Ser Mikhail shrugged. The knight walked forward and grabbed the waster from Abba's hand, then pointed it at Maric. Ser Mikhail swung his sword at Maric, but Maric parried it. After that, it was hard to keep track of what was happening. So much movement in such a short span of time; it all happened so quickly. Sometimes they would get into brief exchanges that consisted of attacks that followed attacks that followed attacks. Eventually, Ser Mikhail planted Abba's waster into the ground and turned to him.

"What did you see, Abba?"

"I do not know, it was all so much. So much movement."

176

"All we did was react. We reacted in the manner in which we had been trained. The reason I told you to repeat that one movement was to foster a natural reaction in you. Think when you drill, but stop thinking when your life is on the line. Just react."

Abba nodded and grabbed his waster from the ground, going back into a guard. Ser Mikhail gave a thumbs up to the brothers, and they began sending strikes at one another. The knight turned around. He was walking away.

"Oi! Ser Mikhail! Where are you going?" yelled Maric.

"I am going to find the Baron," Ser Mikhail yelled back. "Continue on with your training."

Ser Mikhail left them. Abba and Maric sparred for a brief moment, but after a few bouts, Maric planted his waster into the ground. He began to walk along the same path as Mikhail, leaving Abba behind.

Abba ran up to Maric and put his hand on his shoulder. "Where are you going?"

"Do you not want to explore, Abba? We have been cooped up in that castle for almost our entire lives. You might be content with reading about the world, but I wish to see it."

"Brother, we need to spar…"

"No, *you* need to spar."

"But you said you would help me!"

"And I did!"

Maric walked away.

Abba did not want to be left alone, so he went after his brother. Maric was heading for the building that the Baron had walked off toward. The Baron stood outside speaking to his bailiff, and Abba noticed that Maric was eavesdropping on them. He was leaning against one of the walls of the building, trying to act as if he was just resting, but he was looking in the Baron's direction.

Abba leaned beside him, and Maric shook his head to him in silence. Abba understood that Maric wanted him to be quiet. They overheard the Baron talking about iron, customs, and other matters, but it was hard to hear clearly from such a distance. After a while, Abba grabbed Maric's arm and tried to pull him away; but Maric yanked it back, continuing to listen. Abba overheard the Baron saying something about a burning village and coins, but he could not discern whether they were speaking about the same topic or not. They leaned in closer, trying to get a better listen; but soon two palms covered both of their mouths. They struggled and squirmed, but once they looked up, they saw the scarred face of Ser Mikhail. He dragged them back to the sparring enclosure.

"Are you two fucking idiots? Why in Gol would you spy on the Baron? Whose idea was it?"

Abba looked at Maric, and Maric looked at Abba. They both refused to say a word. Ser Mikhail put his hands on his head and sighed.

"What did you hear?"

Abba opened his mouth, but he hesitated to speak. He cleared his throat. "I heard him mention something about iron and customs, and something about a burning village and coins, but I could not make out what else."

Ser Mikhail put his finger in Abba's face. "You never heard *anything*. Do not even think of repeating what you heard. You interrupted the privacy of a lord in his own fief. I am disappointed. Both of you should be sparring—you have a damned tourney in a week!"

Abba put his head down in shame.

Maric handed Abba his waster. They made eye contact, giving each other a nod. This time, Ser Mikhail stayed to watch them spar. He made them train until one of them collapsed—typically Abba—giving them a brief moment's rest afterward. He would jump in and train with Maric until Abba stopped huffing and puffing.

Eventually, the sky grew dark, so they grabbed their satchels and departed. Ser Mikhail brought them to a house, finally allowing them to rest. The village buildings were quite nice to look at. They were made with cruck frames, with exposed framework inside. The two brothers threw their wasters to the floor and collapsed onto their cots. Maric stared up at the ceiling and moaned. Abba shuffled around inside his bag, grabbed *Ava's Lands*, and began to read.

"Abba, you are so *boring*." Maric turned his head to Ser Mikhail. "Could you tell us a real story about war, Ser Mikhail?"

Ser Mikhail grinned. "You want to hear of battle, Maric?"

Abba rolled his eyes and turned toward the wall, continuing to read.

"I can tell you of the Kurem Struggle twenty years ago."

Abba paused, marking his spot in his book and closing it. He turned to face Ser Mikhail.

"Twenty years ago," Ser Mikhail began, "we were invaded by an Ookosi warlord. It came as a surprise to us; there had never been an Ookosi attack so large before. Yes, there would be the occasional raid party that attacked one of our border or coastal settlements, but this was different. They did not take and leave; they took and stayed. Once we realized they were building fortifications around our northern settlements, it was almost too late."

Ser Mikhail paused.

"Please continue, Ser Mikhail! We never hear stories like this," said Maric.

Abba smiled to himself. He had read of the Kurem Struggle. For once, Ser Mikhail was teaching them something that Abba already knew, and Maric did not.

"I paused for a reason. I was thinking. You do not often hear such stories, and for good reason; but I believe you should know at least a little of the past. There are many things—many *issues*—that the two of you will inherit, and you ought to be ready for them. Your father may seem distant, but there is reason for that. The Ookosi do not believe in our faith. Not only that, they find it deserving to be culled. They are quite firm in their roots, and they dislike that we are different. As a consequence, they sought to conquer us."

"You said it was sudden," said Abba. "Why would they attempt to do so out of nowhere?"

"I... I could not tell you why. The past is the past. There was a great deal of confusion, and much bloodshed as a result of that confusion. It was a hard war. It was winter, and there were many casualties. The Ookosi fight very chaotically. It was hard to predict their movements, and on top of that, they attacked the roads, making sure we could not feed our people. Many died. I earned the moniker 'the Sword Seer' during the war; it was given to me by Ava himself."

"You knew the Prophet?" Abba said, sitting up.

"I fought beside him. The battle that ended the war was the Battle of Volk Hill. The Ookosi were fortified on top of the hill, and only Ava could reach them. He could keep warm with his magic, but at such high elevations, the air gets very cold. He fought well, impaling the Ookosi warriors and drudna with his javelins and burning them with his flames, but it took a heavy toll on him. He allowed a group of men to break through to the top of the hill, but the men reinforcing the rear fled. I do not know why; maybe they mistakenly retreated, or were afraid of what would happen once they reached the top. Nonetheless, they were weak and gave in to the cold. They did not make it. I do not blame them, really. But unlike them, the men who charged forward did not die. They were wounded, of course, but they survived. At one point, I was the only man on the hill able to walk. None of the Ookosi warriors could strike me, and I made sure that none of them could strike my brothers. They all made it home. Ava flew down to me himself and gave me his gratitude."

Maric grinned. "I have struck you before, Ser Mikhail. I suppose that means I am better than any Ookosi warrior!"

Ser Mikhail laughed. "I suppose you are; but that was when my life was not in danger. Though, one's life is always in danger when one holds a sword."

"I always found it strange that my book never said why the Ookosi invaded. What faith do they follow?" asked Abba.

Ser Mikhail looked down. "I... am not familiar with it."

"Oh," replied Abba. He could tell that Ser Mikhail was avoiding the question—but he didn't know how to press further.

Ser Mikhail went to his room to put his belongings away. When he did, Abba turned over in his cot, attempting to fall asleep; but Maric had begun throwing a rock at the wall. Abba placed his blanket over his head in an attempt to muffle the noise, but it could not quiet the sound of the constant thudding.

"Maric, quit that," Abba said.

"I cannot."

"Why?"

"I cannot sleep."

"You cannot sleep because you keep throwing that damn rock at the wall—and neither can I," Abba said. "You are keeping yourself awake. Just put your head down on your pillow and close your eyes."

Maric dropped the rock to the floor and stared at the ceiling. "Alright, Brother."

Abba shut his eyes. Before falling asleep, he would often try to picture the stories he had heard or read during the day. That night, he imagined Ser Mikhail's story. He filled in the gaps of what Ser Mikhail had told them. He was fighting the Ookosi, the

180

formidable warriors that they were. He struck them down and pulled his comrades to safety. He felt victorious; yet when all was still, he heard a cry from afar. A man, disfigured, *howled* in pain. He screamed; oh, he screamed. It was deafening, growing so loud it forced Abba to open his eyes.

Maric was screaming. Ser Mikhail came running out of his room, while Abba tumbled out of his cot, rushing over to shake his brother awake. Maric's eyes shot wide open, his gaze darting wildly around the room.

"Gol, Maric! What is wrong?" asked Abba.

Sweat dripped down Maric's forehead. He heaved for air and pulled himself into a seated position. He used his sleeve to wipe the sweat off of his forehead.

"Abba, your brother has been having nightmares recently," said Ser Mikhail. "He does not remember what he sees."

"Is that why you were trying to avoid sleeping, Maric?"

Maric looked at Abba and gave him a tiny grin, beads of sweat dripping down his face to the floor.

"Do not worry about me, Brother."

Then, without another word, Maric turned over and went back to sleep.

Edit

dit followed Malaina and Loressa to a large, open gate. Through it was a network of paths, lined with flowers and grasses. A wall with arched openings separated the gardens from the keep's outer courtyard. The flowers smelled sweet and fruity, and the grass sprawled all over. There was a gardener trimming the grasses, carefully only cutting enough to keep the plants from encroaching over the sidewalks.

Statues were placed at regular intervals within the sea of green and specks of petals. They were sculpted from black marble and had golden crowns on their heads. Most of them depicted men; although, a statue in the middle of the path was of a large, birdlike figure that stood tall, its wings relaxed, two swords in its hands. Its crown was not gold like the rest. It was made of a shiny white metal that was blinding when the sunlight reflected off of it. It looked just like King Asbyorn's.

Malaina walked over to the statue and leaned over its base, staring up at it.

"I always love looking at this statue of Avon. It is my favorite depiction of him," said Malaina.

Edit walked to her side. "It is a rather grand statue, but what is that crown made of up there? It looks like the same material as your brother's spear."

"You do not know of chausilver?" asked Malaina.

"Oh, so it is chausilver?" Edit said. "I know of it; I just have never seen it before."

"Your father never bought you any chausilver jewelry? What is the use of his money, then?" Malaina said, laughing. "It is a wonderful metal. And yes, it is what my brother's spear is made of. Our father had it made from a small vein of ore that was found in Wettay; it was a trophy of his. It took the entire vein to produce that spear. The metal is a terrible pain to work with. It reacts to almost everything. Whether it be the heat of the furnace, the anvil on which it was formed, or even the hammer that formed it, it can react and destroy any progress that the smith might have made. They could have made five more spears, if it was not such a rebellious material. But chausilver's beauty and properties are second to no other metal."

Loressa walked past the statue of Avon and gazed at the flowers. She knelt and smelled a few. Several birds flew down and perched in one of the several bird baths in the garden. Loressa's eyes were tied to the flora and fauna; she rarely looked at the statues.

"Loressa likes to take her inspiration from the plants and animals. I believe she does so because she grew up in Nara, and so has rarely seen the beauty of nature."

"Whereas you prefer the look of these materials?"

"Naturally. I grew up in Wettay. I never saw materials such as this until I had made a name for myself. This metal is a wonder, and I wish to find a way to use it in my own articles of clothing."

They walked past the statue of Avon toward a fountain in the center of the garden. The three of them sat down on its side and admired the waters. Edit's eyes wandered, eventually falling onto the keep itself. A man stood just inside one of the windows. He leaned out, looked around, and then jumped.

Edit screamed. She leapt to her feet and ran over to one of the arched openings to get a better look. The man tumbled through the air, but before he hit the ground, he faded away into a cloud of black smoke.

"Edit! What is the matter?" yelled Malaina.

"Someone just jumped out of one of the windows," Edit said, pointing at the window that the man had leapt from.

"What?" Malaina ran over and stared where Edit was pointing. "Oh, Avon! That is the window of the Crii!"

"I do not see the person who jumped," said Loressa, peering over at the ground below the window.

"He disappeared... into a puff of black smoke."

Malaina looked at Edit as if she were mad. "Black smoke?"

"I—I believe so. Should we go over and see if whoever fell is there?"

"Oh, Gol, of course not! We must stay here and be witnesses. I would rather a man find the body, in any case," Malaina grumbled. "So many lazy and entitled men roam these halls; they would probably accuse us of orchestrating the suicide, even though we were on the ground."

Edit thought Malaina's reasoning was strange and an inappropriate response to the situation. A man had just attempted to jump to his *death*. Edit's conscience tugged her to go see what had happened, but Malaina's domineering and disinterested character dissuaded her from leaving.

Frowning, Loressa stared off toward where the man had fallen, but she soon turned away to look at the garden plants once more. Malaina also wandered off. She resumed staring at the statues as she had been before, pointing at one of the hands of the depicted kings. She beckoned for Edit to come closer. She pointed at painted white lines on one of the gloves.

"I suspect chausilver used to be a common fashion trend in Narese history. Look at the gloves; if they were fitting for a King of Nar in the past, then they must still be fitting for a King of Nar in the present. I want them!" said Malaina, turning around with an ecstatic look on her face.

Edit gave a false grin. She could not produce a real one after seeing a man die only a moment before. She found it strange how Malaina could change her focus with such little regard for what had just happened. Edit felt uneasy around her now, and she tried to hide her discomfort with a smile.

"They would be a wonderful accessory," Edit said.

"Accessory? They would be a statement! I would present my palms with pride if I had them. To be so affluent as to form chausilver into a thread and sew it into one's garments... it would be very symbolic. Very powerful."

Within moments of finishing her sentence, the keep's bell rang three times. Guards began to run in the direction of the Crii room. Malaina ignored them and continued to look at the statues, walking past the central fountain and making her way to another

184

large statue that stood in the middle of the path. It was carved into another birdlike figure, its plaque engraved with the name *Ava*. The statue wore what looked to be a steel crown that was finely polished to a shine. Edit assumed the statue-maker had wished to make it look like chausilver, but it was a cheap imitation. He was posed with his right foot stepping over a large rock. He held his left hand with its palm facing up, and in it was a white marble carved flame that, from their angle, looked to be hovering.

"His crown does not look like Avon's," said Loressa.

"He was only given a crown on his head to please the clergy," said Malaina. "He forsook Narese tradition and kept it after he disappeared. It is a shame. We could have melted down the deserter's crown and reused it."

"Is speaking of the Prophet in such a manner not blasphemous?" said Edit.

Loressa turned her head to Edit, wide-eyed.

Malaina laughed. "It would only be blasphemous if a priest were present. Do I see one? Of course not! They are too busy picking the pockets of commoners."

Malaina was disgusting, but Edit refused to voice her disgust. At first, Edit had taken her to be kind; but she was too brash with her words. There was an awkward silence while Malaina stared at the statue of Ava. She walked past it, looking toward the last statue.

"This one is boring. No real grandeur," said Malaina.

"This is of Matnus, no? He and my father were great friends, I have heard," said Edit.

Without responding, Malaina turned around and began to walk back to the keep.

Edit and Loressa followed. Loressa seemed shier when around Malaina, like she did not want to receive her attention. Malaina's carefree gait was peculiar compared to the rushing of the guards in the halls. Whatever chaos was happening did not seem to matter to her. The guards paid the group of women no mind.

The King's bodyguard, Ser Bertram, came walking by.

"Sister, halt!" ordered the knight.

Malaina turned her head with an exhausted expression. "What do *you* want, Brother?"

"Where were you three just now?"

"Out in the gardens. Why?"

"Did you see anything strange?"

Edit stepped forward. "I saw a man dressed in black jump from a window. It was strange; he seemed to disappear into a puff of black smoke."

Malaina raised her brow at Edit.

"Did you see anything else? Could you identify who jumped?" Ser Bertram asked.

"No. It was too far away."

"Malaina, where are you three headed to?"

"To my room. Quit being so nosy."

Ser Bertram shook his head, looking down at his feet. "Alright. Thank you for your statement. I am heading to the royal chambers, so I will walk with you until we part. Stay in your room until this is all over."

The group continued to walk together. When they were about halfway down the hall, Ser Bertram split off from the group. The three women continued by themselves, stopping before a door. Malaina opened it, holding it open for the girls so that they could enter.

Edit walked over to one of Malaina's windows, placing her hands on its windowsill. Through the window was the coast of Nar. The waters were clear, and the sand of the beach was white and powdery. A slight breeze brushed through the yellow curtains. Turning around, Edit noticed that Malaina's room was impressively decorated. No wall was bare, and trinkets made of rare metals were neatly displayed on all of the furniture. The bedcurtains had impressive stitching that showed a woman from a town in the woods traveling to a city. Malaina had clearly tried quite hard to make the space look grand, and she had succeeded; although, it seemed to be a bit much for a bedroom.

Loressa looked a bit tired, but she did not sit down, despite there being more than adequate seating in the room. Edit pulled a stool out and took a seat herself. Her legs ached. Loressa stared at Edit with horror. Malaina turned around, narrowing her eyes once she saw what Edit had done.

"You are an aggravating child! Did I say you could move my furniture?"

"What? I only sat down. I did not mean to insult you, Lady Malaina."

Edit stood up. Malaina pointed at the stool and then pointed to where it had stood before.

"Move it back!"

Edit looked to Loressa, but Loressa just kept her head down and her eyes glued to the floor. It seemed that this was her typical response to Malaina's behavior. Edit pushed the stool back to where it was. Malaina shook her head, stomping over to shift the stool only *slightly* away from where Edit had placed it. Malaina stormed away, a sort of riled energy rolling off of her. She stared out of the window and let out a huff. Edit wandered around the room while Malaina's focus was occupied, looking at her decorations. She made sure not to touch anything, so as to avoid another crazed reaction.

"Loressa! Bring me the fabric I picked out yesterday."

Loressa scurried over to a trunk. After she opened it, bright and flamboyant silks as well as other textiles were revealed. She meticulously picked through the trunk so that she would not make a mess. When she found what she was looking for, she pulled out a crimson-colored fabric.

"Give it here! Hurry!" said Malaina.

Loressa hurried over to present the cloth to Malaina.

"This shall make a wonderful dress. Loressa! Hand me my equipment!"

Loressa once more scurried away, returning with an assortment of tools while she kept her head down. Malaina walked over to a table and placed the fabric flat on top of it. She dipped the tip of a bone pen into a vial of ink, marking pieces of the fabric. She would go back and forth between periods of staring at it and periods of manic work. It was as if no one existed around her while she worked; but to be fair, it was possible that no one else *ever* truly existed to her. She made numerous cuts with shears in hand, and eventually, the fabric was ready to be sewn.

Once Malaina had begun the sewing process, her progress slowed down significantly. A loud knock was heard on the door, and Malaina closed her eyes and let out a breath. She stabbed Loressa with a look, so Loressa ran over to the door and opened it. On the other side was Ser Elseharde. He bowed as the door opened.

"Hello, Lady Malaina. I am here to retrieve Lady Edit."

Malaina sighed and pointed at Edit. "Go…"

Edit raised a brow briefly to Malaina before turning away to meet Ser Elseharde. He held the door for Edit, and together, they departed from Malaina's chambers. The walk was quiet, as neither went to start a conversation with the other. The activity in the halls had lessened by quite a bit, and the pair made it back to Edit's chambers without running into anyone else. Elseharde shut the door behind them.

"You and I are departing for Kurembrog tomorrow. Make sure you are completely packed for the trip."

Edit raised a brow to Elseharde. "Why so soon?"

"Your father wishes it to be so. Just be ready to travel by tomorrow morn."

Edit looked down. "Do you know what happened to the man that fell out of the Crii room window?"

Elseharde froze. "You saw the murderer jump out of the window?"

"Murderer? I thought the man ended his life. Who was murdered?"

"The Great Chancellor," Elseharde said. "Someone mutilated him and left him to die in his own blood."

"What? That is horrible! How did that happen?"

"We do not know. What else did you see?"

"All I saw was that he jumped, and that there was a cloud of smoke that appeared before he hit the ground. Does that mean anything?"

Ser Elseharde sat down. "That is very strange. I do not know what to say about that; although, it is also strange that he jumped from the window in the first place."

Edit stood up and began to pack her belongings. She sifted through her things and organized them along the wall of her room. Most of the items in her bag were not even unpacked yet, so she had very little work to do. Ser Elseharde fiddled around with the pommel of his sword, screwing it and unscrewing it. Edit turned to Elseharde.

"So, when should I be ready to board the ship?"

"Third pyre. I will wake you up if needed and escort you to the docks."

Edit nodded. "I shall be up."

"Alright."

Ser Elseharde bowed to Edit and exited her chambers. She finished folding her remaining clothes into one of her satchels. Afterward, she undressed and grabbed a change of looser garments. There was a small shelf on the other side of the room with a limited but varied assortment of books. She reached for one that was titled *The Heroic Deeds of Nar*. Quickly flipping through the pages, she eventually found a story about a knight and a noblewoman being attacked by a beast that she thought she would enjoy. Before long, however, she grew bored. The knight was the one fighting the beast, while the noblewoman was reduced to almost nothing—her only trait of any importance was her beauty. Edit put the book down, rolling her eyes and flopping back onto the bed. She stared at the ceiling. She did not typically have trouble sleeping, but she reckoned it was the murder keeping her awake. Over time, she convinced her body to fall asleep.

She dreamt of a noblewoman traveling the countryside. Eventually, the noblewoman wandered into a forest. She was quickly covered by the brush's shade. All she could see were the tiny plants that sprouted around her. She journeyed further into the dimly lit woods until she stumbled upon what seemed to be the den of an animal. There was a rocky overhang above her, and dripping from it was a peculiar liquid.

She crept inside, her eyes scanning around. The head of an animal zipped past. The noblewoman stumbled back, regained her footing, and drew her sword. Once more, the animal lunged forward; but this time, the noblewoman stepped to the side and slashed off the beast's head. The head was that of some strange snake with a humanlike nose. She scanned around the den to see if there was another nearby. A vine brushed her shoulder, so she turned her head to examine it. In the dim light, the vines looked brownish; but upon closer inspection, they appeared to be a dark pink. There was a slimy residue left on her shoulder. She stepped back, looking at the body and severed head of the beast once more. It was an amalgam of flesh, she realized. She could not tell what made it up, but it did not look to be born of any natural process. Another beast appeared and pounced at her. She fell while the beast locked its jaws around her neck, shaking as she died.

Edit's heart was racing, and her eyes shot open. Feeling sweaty and warm, she threw her blankets off of her. She sat up to the sight of Elseharde in her room.

"Get up, sleepy," he said. "Did you have a nightmare?"

Edit angrily rubbed her eyes with her fists and shook her head. "Do not worry about me, Elseharde. I will be ready soon."

Ser Elseharde nodded and left her chambers. Edit grabbed some clothes and dressed into something more appropriate. After she left her room, she let Ser Elseharde lead her down to the courtyard. They hopped on a horse together and rode through part of the city, soon arriving at the docks.

Geder Kurem stood there, waiting, his arm resting on one of the dock posts. The two of them made eye contact. Edit shifted her gaze away. Geder held a stare that lasted a bit *too* long.

Once they reached him, Edit and Elseharde climbed down from their steed.

"It is a pleasure for you both to join me in my travel to see my family—and it is a special pleasure to have my nephew's possible betrothed under my protection." Geder smiled.

Edit had not realized how cold Geder's eyes were until that moment. She looked down shyly and walked toward the plank that led to the ship, turning around to take one more look at Nara before she left. She noticed her father hurrying to them with Ser Groent.

Venceslaus walked up to his daughter and hugged her tightly. He put both of his hands on Edit's shoulders and smiled. Her father had a glint in his eyes.

"Do not worry, my dearest. You will be safe with Ser Elseharde. I will meet with you before the start of the tournament in Belar. Safe travels to you."

"Be safe, father," Edit said. Then she leaned in and whispered into her father's ear. "The man who fell from the window disappeared into a puff of black smoke. I saw it myself."

They made eye contact, and her father nodded.

Venceslaus

enceslaus watched the ship disappear beyond the horizon, then he turned back with Ser Groent and walked back to the keep. He passed the gates and headed for his chambers. Once the pair had made it to the Duke's room, they looked around the halls and shut the door behind them. They shut the window, too, and stood in the area of the room that was farthest from any opening to the outside.

"What do you intend on doing next, m'lord?" Ser Groent asked.

"What we know thus far is that someone came from the hall that led directly from the throne to the Crii room and killed Barnut. Then he jumped from the window and disappeared into a puff of black smoke."

"A puff of black smoke? Strange. Do you suspect divination?"

"It is one possible explanation. It could also be the result of one of those smoke bombs from the Sealands. We would have to see the site where the murderer fell for ourselves to know for certain."

"Aye. Shall we go look now?"

"No, you shall go on your own and scout the scene. I am unsure of how anyone could have survived such a fall unscathed, but make sure to look for any imprints on the grass or shrubbery below to see if the man landed or ran anywhere," Venceslaus said. "I have a feeling that whoever committed this crime acted in collusion with others, and I believe the safest route for us to take is to have me poke and prod for information from the man leading the *official* investigation."

Ser Groent bowed. "Alright, m'lord. I will scout out the scene and report back to you with what I find."

Venceslaus nodded to his knight, and the two exited the Duke's chambers. They parted ways: Ser Groent headed toward the courtyard, and Venceslaus headed toward the throne room. King Asbyorn sat on his throne, and Ser Bertram stood to his side. Venceslaus marched his way over to the two and knelt before the King.

"I am sorry for your loss, and for our kingdom's loss, Sire."

"Arise, Good Duke Venceslaus," said the King, fatigue in his voice. "It is a tragedy. I have already sent word to his family; his funeral will be held in two days."

"Bless Avon that we have a knight such as Ser Bertram in your service to lead the investigation into the Great Chancellor's death."

Asbyorn frowned, making eye contact with Venceslaus. "I received no rest last night; I could not bring myself to sleep knowing that a man whom I had considered an uncle was killed in such a sudden and horrific manner. The murderer will suffer a fate worse than execution."

The King clenched his fists and squeezed, having to take a deep breath to calm down. Venceslaus stepped forward to the dais, but the White Spear stepped in front of the king, blocking Venceslaus's way. Venceslaus took a step back, wide-eyed.

"I apologize, but I cannot allow you to come any closer," said Asbyorn.

"Of course, m'lord. I understand. It is only natural for you to be more guarded after such a horrific event. If I may ask, why do you think he was killed?"

The King scoffed. "I do not know. That is why I am being so cautious. The most probable reason is that the Great Chancellor had an enemy who caught up with him. We are investigating such a scenario."

"Interesting. M'lord, I do not mean to question your suspicion, but have you ever known Barnut to be a man with many enemies?"

"Ha! You have lived longer than I, Duke; do you not expect a man in such a high seat of power to have a few enemies? I am surprised that you of all people would be so naïve."

"Of course, Sire. How foolish of me," Venceslaus said. "I will see you once more, when the Crii begins. I wish to contribute the cost of Barnut's funeral."

Venceslaus bowed and turned away, leaving the throne room. As he exited, he saw Lord Loffreaux. Loffreaux noticed the Duke and waved to him. Venceslaus waved back. Loffreaux always seemed to carry a look of superiority on his face, and Venceslaus did not like it much. Loffreaux had grown up affluent and powerful, the same as Venceslaus, but he had allowed it to go to his head. He always spoke with a tone that implied he knew more than whoever he was talking to. It did not matter how learned someone was, Loffreaux would never concede to being wrong. He was not an idiot, but he was too stubborn to be useful.

"Hello, Duke Venceslaus."

"Hello, Lord Loffreaux. How are you faring?"

"It is an awful tragedy. Barnut did not deserve to die such a brutal death. I always told him to watch his back. You never know what mad bastard could have it out for you."

"Aye. But he never did have many enemies; he was a well-liked man. Who could have committed such a grotesque act?"

Loffreaux nodded. "Barnut was a good man, and he was good for the kingdom. He stopped that Geder from getting into the King's ear too much. He was also good at stopping Donas from interrupting. That mad idiot. He always wants to quiet me down and speak his nonsense."

"I have noticed an unpleasant dynamic between the two of you. It is obvious you do not agree with him much."

"That I do not."

Venceslaus nodded, looking away down the hall. "I have to get matters handled before I leave. I will see you another time."

"Aye. Goodbye, Venceslaus."

Venceslaus walked down the hall, passing by a balcony that overlooked the courtyard. Lord Urbaed stood there. He looked as if he was lamenting while he looked down at the courtyard grounds. Once Venceslaus grew closer, he noticed that Urbaed was looking directly at the ground where the murderer must have landed. Venceslaus walked to the balcony balustrade, leaning over it next to Urbaed.

"Y'know, I had mixed feelings about Barnut; but Gol, he never deserved to die such a death," said Urbaed.

"Aye. Barnut was a childhood friend of mine. I cannot fathom who would have a personal grievance with him."

"They say the assassin disappeared into a puff of smoke when he fell. What do you think of that? Do you think he could have been one of those Terukian soul seekers?"

"It could be many things. The murderer's escape was similar to that of a soul seeker, but everything else seems too messy for it to be one of them. Like the trail of blood, for example. You came from that direction. Did you by chance see a man dressed in all black walking with Barnut?"

"I... I do not recall, really. I did see Barnut walking past me in quite a hurry, though. He could have met with someone farther up the hall, but I was busy discussing matters with one of my subordinates."

The Duke raised a brow at Urbaed, turning his head back to the courtyard. He pointed to the area under the window. The path that was near the wall had delicately cut shrubbery lining its side, but behind the shrubbery was a small grass path where the assassin could have landed. The Duke's old eyes could not see the area in detail; his vision blurred.

"Which way do you reckon he went?" asked the Duke.

"I was wondering the same thing," said Urbaed. "As much as it pains me to do so, I tried to put myself in the shoes of the assassin. What route would be best for an escape? I do not think he would go through the front gate. He would probably cross past the royal garden and climb down one of the walls that lead to our beach."

Venceslaus shot his eyes to one of the short walls. "Did you receive word of any ships sailing from the beach?"

"I would not know, but I doubt it. Word would have come by now. The king's ships would have questioned why they weren't docked in the harbor."

"Hm. I will ask Ser Bertram if any ships left the harbor when we see him for the next Crii."

"I can see how much you care for justice," Urbaed said.

"Barnut was my friend. I feel as if it is my duty to figure this out."

"You are a good man, Vences. Ser Bertram had questioned me to see if I believed you had committed the act, and I let him

194

know that I never even thought of suspecting you. He told me that he believes the blood splatters completely absolve you of any suspicion, and I agreed in entirety."

Venceslaus smiled, placing his hand on Lord Urbaed's shoulder. "Thank you, my friend. I never once suspected you, either."

Lord Urbaed smiled, and Venceslaus departed from him. Venceslaus shook his head at himself. He had lied; his lack of suspicion had not been true. But it was now. Urbaed's concern was palpable.

Walking inside, Venceslaus noticed that the halls were empty. Tears started to form in his eyes. He shook his head. Though it would be expected of someone to cry for the loss of a childhood friend, the courtiers could not have cared less for that. If he was seen weeping, then gossip about him would surely chatter in the halls, and Venceslaus would not suffer that. He wondered to himself how cruel the murderer must've been to kill a good man in such a manner. The question ran through his head several times. To Venceslaus, the murderer had to be a member of the council, or have access to information from it, for who else would have killed Barnut? Where else would conflict arise between him and anyone else? Barnut's job was to manage the kingdom, and he had made it his life's purpose. He spent years away from his family to serve the King, and rarely, if ever, was there a time when he dedicated his ambition to something *other* than the betterment of the Kingdom of Nar. He was the Great Chancellor before he was Barnut.

Venceslaus walked out to the courtyard where the Great Map of Lonus was carved into the concrete. He walked toward it. A gold token on the coast of Mjorn signified the location of Nara. He walked along the coast, his eyes fixed on the southern tip of Mjorn: High Beak. He longed to go home; his old bones ached, and he was tired of dealing with the burden of politics.

He went to look north, toward Kurembrog. He clenched his fists. He was annoyed with himself that he had let his daughter go off with the protection of just a single young knight, and it bothered him even more that he could not think of a better plan before sending her away. It was not that he did not trust Geder, but he would have preferred to be with her himself.

Ser Groent stepped beside Venceslaus and stared down at Kurembrog with him.

"What did you find?" asked Venceslaus.

"Nothing. No imprints of a body or feet landing in the grass. No residue from any smoke. Absolutely fucking nothing."

"Strange... Nothing pressed into the ground when a man fell three stories? Surely there would have been some evidence of an impact."

"No impact, and no soot."

Ser Groent kicked a rock away from him.

"Are you alright, Ser Groent?"

Ser Groent sighed. "Barnut was a good man, and his death... it just reminds me of my wife, and how violent her death was. Would you think it foolish to say more lives have been lost to the cancerous politics of Nar than were lost in the Yhournish war?"

"Ser Groent... You know better than to ask me that. Every life that was lost in the Yhournish war was a consequence of the politics of Nar."

"I suppose. Bastards."

Venceslaus faced his knight. "Search for more clues in the two directions the murderer could have fled. We will reconvene after the Crii and discuss what we have found."

Ser Groent bowed. "Have fun with those arseholes."

The Duke shooed his knight away, laughing at Ser Groent's profanity. He enjoyed how honest Ser Groent was. He acted as a genuine man, unlike many of those in service to the nobility.

Venceslaus meandered about, stuck in his thoughts. He asked several of the guards if they were present in the courtyard during the murder. The majority had said they saw nothing, but one had, and he attributed the others' lack of attention to them being *lousy cunts*. They discussed the matter, and everything he said seemed to corroborate Edit's statement.

In time, however, Venceslaus had to pause his investigation, as the Crii was about to begin. He marched through the halls all the way to the room where his dear friend was murdered. He knocked on the door, and Ser Bertram opened it. All the Crii members sat around the table. There was an air of discomfort in the room. Venceslaus could tell that many of them did not wish to be there, as their eyes would often jump to the spot where Barnut's body had lain. It irked Venceslaus that they had not met somewhere else, but there would be no avoiding it: this Crii room had been the same room used for the King's meetings ever since the days of the Empire. Asbyorn sat in the same seat that Barnut had sat in just the day before. It was not an odd thing in itself, but it was odd to see the empty seat next to him. Venceslaus's heart grew heavy. Asbyorn beckoned Venceslaus to the table and pointed to the seat across from him at the other end.

"There, Good Duke. Sit."

Venceslaus sat down at the end of the table.

"Now, we may begin. Do not be worried. In my heart, it feels wrong to host the Crii in the room where Barnut has so recently been murdered; however, I believe that Barnut would have wanted us here as a statement to the perpetrator that the Crii d'Nar cannot be intimidated. With that being said, the Crii may now commence. The first matter to be discussed will be the murder itself."

The King's voice was relaxed and dry, and the longer Venceslaus observed him, the more he was inclined to agree with Edit's observation the day prior. He seemed *strange*.

"Fortunately, we have, using both evidence and witness statements, found all members of the Crii to be free of any suspicion; furthermore, we have also found evidence of a possible perpetrator. Barnut had long been the diplomat who would speak for my father when it came to foreign matters, and as we all know, it became quite common that he would travel in my stead to foreign lands to discuss trivialities with foreign diplomats. We have reason to believe a foreign actor has murdered Barnut, and we base this suspicion on the barbaric method of murder, as well as the technology used to flee from the scene. An individual gave testimony regarding his witness of a man dressed in black fleeing on the beaches of Nara, and at some point, he must have headed toward the harbor and hidden as a stowaway on one of our departing ships. Does anyone have anything to bring to the table that they believe will help the investigation?"

The Great Marshal Donas huffed. "You think that funny-speaking prince *Aw-vonnie-chess* had anything to do with it? He is a foreigner, and he wore the color black."

The King squinted at Donas. "He fits the description, but it seems strange that he would flee as a stowaway."

"Did the witness notice what type of character boarded that ship? Perhaps they were Aeric men—they could have certainly been in on the affair!" Loffreaux said, raising a finger.

Donas raised his chin. "Loffreaux, that is the first smart thing I have heard come out of your mouth in a long while."

Donas gave a little clap, and Loffreaux snarled at him.

"No more stabs at Loffreaux, Marshal Donas," said the King. "I imagine it *could* be the Prinz Afonices. I did not take him to be a cruel man, yet he does fit the description; I would have to discuss with my witness to see the nature of the crew aboard the ship he fled on. However, there is one fact that does not make sense: who would have bled him and why?"

Lord Urbaed looked at Venceslaus and shook his head with disbelief.

"May we answer this question first, Sire? Who is the witness? Would it not be natural for us to have the witness give testimony before the Crii?" asked Urbaed.

"Well, yes, it would be; but I have been on this Crii for many years, and anonymous witness statements are not unheard of. Perhaps the witness fears for his life. I remember, a time long ago, before King Matnus—"

The King raised his palm, and Loffreaux stopped talking.

"We understand your point, Lord Loffreaux; there is no need to ramble. Lord Urbaed, we must ascertain that the witness shall not be harmed. I will not reveal who he is until we have the perpetrator in custody. This assassin killed a man whom I considered as close to me as an uncle; I shall not risk any chance of losing someone who can help me apprehend him."

Adar

t was a warm day, but not too warm. It was as if the sun was only barely grazing the land. A gentle breeze brushed over the dry grass. The Countess followed behind the Count as they turned around to head back to the keep. She grabbed his hand. Adar held her hand with a loose grip, staring off into the distance in deep contemplation.

"Adar, are you sure it was right to leave the boys with Jergi?"

"No, it is not; but it *is* right to leave the boys with Ser Mikhail. If any treachery occurs, I see no future where Mikhail does not lop off the Baron's head. The Baron should know that well."

Antia clasped Adar's hand. "I suppose you're right."

They continued on back to the keep. After passing the gates, they were met by Madalbert. Adar beckoned him to join him and his wife on their walk. They climbed up to the top of the keep's walls to gaze at the docks. Adar leaned over one of the crenels and pointed up and down the coast.

"We need more docks, new docks. The old ones have greatly slowed down our ability to export raw materials. If you have any recommendations for improvements, now is the time to share them. But, first and foremost, the docks must be built so that we may begin accruing more revenue."

"Aye, we ought to build at least two more docks; but after that, we must rebuild our current ones. They are almost unusable and have caused plenty of trouble for the workers. Just last week a man died because some rotted wood collapsed from under him. He hit his head on the way down."

"It would greatly boost the morale of the workers," Anita said. "Adar, you are a wonderful ruler, but you and your people have a strained relationship. I think this is a good idea."

"I will throw in new workhouses for them as well, so long as the amount Jergi projected us to make rings true. Maybe even hold a feast upon its completion," Adar said.

"Aye, good idea," said Madalbert. He rested his arm on a crenel.

"Figure out the costs for this, Madalbert. I will agree to whatever amount of coin is required as long as there is some purpose to it; but do not go mad with the budget. I still need a war chest in case of an Ookosi invasion."

"Of course, m'lord. I will use the coin wisely," said Madalbert, bowing.

Adar nodded and took Anita's elbow, pulling her away from the crenelations. They left Madalbert and walked back to the keep. After walking for a while, his chest began to tighten up as if his lungs were being crushed by a boulder. He collapsed to his knees, almost pulling Anita down with him. He desperately gasped for air while his heart pounded like a war horse's hooves pounding the ground. Anita frantically tried to help him up, but Adar did not have the strength to stand.

"Breathe in through your nose and out through your mouth slowly, Adar," Anita said. "Breathe!"

Adar did as his wife said. He felt only a bit of relief, but it was enough for him to get up. It was still hard to breathe. Gasping for air, he went to hug his wife, but Anita pushed him away from her.

"Did you?" asked Anita, her eyes stabbing Adar.

"Did I what?"

"Did you see that damned witch again, Adar?"

Adar's heart sank. "I—My love, I—"

"Oh, *my love*. I asked for you to not see that crone! What was so urgent that you had to speak to her?" said Anita, tears forming in her eyes.

"I asked her about my legacy."

"You asked her about your *legacy*? Are you serious? You know what she is doing to you—she is taking your life. You have given her so many years of your life in return for words you could never interpret. You could have seen your legacy with your own eyes, if you had stopped seeing that witch. Why do you gamble with your life? Why do you hurt me so? And what about Abba and Maric? Every night I share your bed, and every night your lungs sound more and more rotted. You frighten me, Adar."

"I—I am sorry, my love."

"No, you are not. You know how much it pains me, and yet you still continue to do it. I know your love for me rings true, but you cannot move beyond the past."

"Anita, you know what I have done. How could I ever move past it? You do not understand."

"Like Gol I don't! You could move past it by not making your misdeeds in vain," Anita said, before she stormed off.

Adar went to chase her, but even moving his arm forward left him out of breath. He leaned against the wall and instead shambled his way back to his study. He stumbled through the door, almost falling over. An old walking stick—one his father had used when he was much older than Adar—leaned against the wall. Adar grabbed the walking stick and used it to prop himself up. He made it to his study seat and sat down. Once more, he lamented at the hammer.

"Fucking Gol!" yelled Adar.

His body felt like he had aged a decade. In reality, he was only in his late thirties. People his age still moved well, yet he could barely move his arm from his side. Any action drained his energy from him. He squinted at a mirror standing in a corner of the room, his face a blur. He wanted to look at the hammer, but he shunned the thought. He worried that if he touched it, his heart might stop, or his lungs would fully close him off from any air; he did not truly understand how the stone it was made of worked. Fatigue set in on him, and he passed out in his study. He awoke to Madalbert leaning on his desk, shaking him awake.

"Are you alright, m'lord?"

"I'm—" Adar hacked. "I am fine, Madalbert."

Madalbert raised a brow at Adar. "You look like you have suddenly contracted some sort of infection. Are you sure you are alright?"

"I am *fine*. What is this paper?"

"This is the cost of the build."

"How did you come up with it so quickly? I only just told you of the project."

"Adar… Look outside your window."

The sky was black.

"I—I thought I had only shut my eyes," Adar said.

"You must have fallen asleep, m'lord. Please read over this paper."

Adar quickly skimmed over the paper. Everything seemed in order with what the two had discussed earlier, so he began to prepare his wax stamp. After stamping the paper, he returned the paper to the castellan. Madalbert bowed and prepared to leave, but before he could turn around, Adar grabbed his arm.

"What do you think of that hammer, Madalbert?"

"The hammer? I dunno. It looks quite strange with that rock as its head. Why do you ask?"

"It *is* strange. I have been searching all these documents for its origin, but to no avail. My brother knows nothing of it, either, and my father never spoke to me about it. I was hoping you knew. You are around the same age as my father."

"To be honest, this is my first time seeing it, m'lord. I never saw your father wield it."

"Ah, well. Thank you, anyway."

The castellan bowed and exited Adar's study. Adar sat for a while as he continued to lament at the hammer. Propping himself upright with the walking stick, he left his study; but before he exited, he grabbed a cloak and covered his head with a hood. He shambled down his corridors, taking momentary rests so that he could catch his breath.

He made it out of his keep and past the gates. It was gloomy: a fog smothered the air, and the faint light of lanterns were the only noticeable items in his view. Occasionally he tripped, and the act of pulling himself up with his walking stick forced him to take the time to catch his breath. He made it to the town square, turning off toward an alley. Neta's door stood before him, and he entered.

Adar gagged at the smell of burnt minerals and animal flesh. Neta sat in a trance-like state. It took a moment for her to notice Adar, and she grinned at his arrival. Adar's face was lit with anger. She blew out a flame that filled the room with a disgusting aroma, smiling at Adar.

"Did you come here to give me more of your life, boy?"

"You damned witch! I feel as if my body is decaying. What did you do to me?"

"What did I do to you? Did I bring you into my home? Did I pull out *your* knife and cut *your* palm? Do not be a fool, boy. You did this to yourself. These are the consequences finally coming to you."

Adar lifted his walking stick and pointed it at the witch, but his hands shook, and the weight of the stick led him to stumble over. He dropped his walking stick and tumbled forward onto the dirty floor below. He reached for the stick and tried to pull himself up. The witch let out a guttural laugh.

"You are the same foolish boy as you were years ago. I warned you of what would happen to you if you did this. You have given away that which gives you life. It is a miracle you have lived for so long. Your blood is... very potent."

"Damn you, witch. How can I reverse this?"

"Why would I help you reverse it? You ought to be grateful you are alive, with the state you are in."

"Tell me how to save myself, or I *will* kill you."

Neta turned her head away from Adar and fiddled with some of her herbs and minerals.

"You can barely move. You will not kill me."

"You know I am the only reason you are still alive."

"You are also the only reason I feared for my death in the first place."

"I will tell them," Adar said. "I will tell Siemond I care for your services no longer."

Neta gritted her teeth.

"Pyre Elder of Harmony. What an unfitting title for such a disgusting man," she said. "Find some chausilver and file it down into a powder. Mix the powder with something viscous, like honey or molasses, and ingest it. It will make your blood stronger, but it will also use up your life even more quickly. If you feel as if your insides are going to explode, consume ground ordustone mixed in water. Do know, Adar, you will be dead in at most a month no matter what you do. So use your time accordingly."

Adar spat on the ground and left the witch, stumbling back to his keep.

He made it to his room and picked up a lockbox that rested on top of his dresser. He opened it and fumbled around with the jewelry that was inside. He found a pair of earrings made of chausilver and dragged himself back out of the room. He shambled toward the kitchen, grabbing a small pot of honey, a wooden mixing bowl, and a spoon. His shaky body bumped into courtiers on the way out, clumsily tripping over himself as he went back to his study.

He placed the items on his desk, pushing papers out of the way to make room for them. Desperately, he searched his drawers and found a steel file. He reached for the chausilver earring and held it up, growing less shaky once he held it in between his fingers. He started to file the earring, holding it over the wooden bowl so that the shavings would fall down into it. It was going fine at first, but then the chausilver sparked, burning a bit of his finger. He winced, but he kept going. The reaction seemed to destroy about half of the earring.

Thankfully, he shaved down the rest of the earring without any further reactions, saving a decent amount of powder. He poured the honey into the bowl and mixed the contents with the wooden spoon until the metal was spread evenly about. He consumed a small portion of its contents. Immediately, he felt a rush of warmth. The weight lifted off of his chest, and he could finally breathe properly again. Adar stood up and walked about. His tremors had disappeared, but he could feel his muscles tensing and his body heating up. His head pulsed with pain. His eyes darted toward the hammer, and in a frenzy, he rushed for it. He placed his palm on the maul's head, and slowly his symptoms began to abate.

He took a deep breath.

"A smaller dose. A smaller dose..."

The door opened, and Anita walked inside. She stared at Adar, his palm gripping the hammer's head. She looked down at the desk and walked over to examine the silvery mixture in the bowl.

"I went to my room and saw my jewelry box open," she said. "What did you do to my mother's earrings?"

"I am saving my life, Anita."

Anita's face reddened, her expression turning angry. "You damned yourself to Gol the first time you spoke to that witch."

"Anita, I beg your forgiveness for what I have done to your earrings, but I must live and see that my boys are well off—"

"I do not give a damn about the earrings! I lost my mother already, and now I am seeing you slowly deteriorate in front of my own eyes! Every morning, I wake up, and I hear you struggling more and more to breathe. You probably overlooked it yourself with your obsession of being a *strong* ruler. Why do you need to consult a witch about your future? Why can you not have faith in yourself?"

Adar shook his head silently.

"Well, I hope you can already tell that if you see her again, it will likely mark the end of your life," Anita said. "Did she say whether or not you will fully recover? Did you even ask?"

"She said—she said I will be fine. I just have to drink this mixture daily. Do not worry, my love."

Anita exhaled quickly, tears springing to her eyes. She stepped toward him, but then she stepped away. "I am so tired of this, Adar. Sleep by yourself tonight."

She slammed the door of the study behind her as she left. Adar shook his head. He knew very well why he had such little faith in himself. He could not escape it. Every morning, he would tell himself the same thing. He was not Adar; he was the Count of Kurembrog, Lord of the White Coast, descendant of Mecidar the Serpent-Slayer. Yet he never felt he deserved to sit on the throne. His older brother, Geder, was *meant* for the throne. *Geder* was the eldest, raised from his birth to be the Lord of Kurembrog. But Adar had been picked over him.

He had spent much time thinking about his father and the position he had put Adar in. He never said why he did not choose Geder, despite all the years it was said that Geder was sure to inherit. It irked him. Geder never spoke of it, either, but Adar assumed he just did not want to talk about his greatest loss. It went against Osmjornish tradition, but there was no law in Kurembrog that said the first son had to inherit. There was nary a day that Adar did not feel as if he were an imposter, and he felt it was his duty to disassociate from who he was—from what he had *done*—and remake himself into how he ought to be.

He let go of the hammer, and the symptoms soon returned. He once more placed his hand on the hammer and felt them disappear. He took the hammer off the mantle. There was a leather strap rolled in the same drawer that Adar had fetched the file from. He cut the strap so that he could tie it around the maul, using the ridges on its shaft as a means to secure it. Once he was sure it would not fall off, he slung the hammer over his shoulder so that it could hang on his back. He scoured the room for a bottle. He found a few glass bottles but shook his head in frustration: they were too small. Eventually, he found a clay bottle and poured the honey and chausilver mixture into it. He sealed it with a cork and held it at his side.

Afterward, he went to go walk back to his chambers. When he opened the door, he noticed his wife was not present, and this set a sinking feeling in his heart. It almost felt worse than his inability to breathe hours prior. He set down the maul on the mattress beside him, but he could not sleep that night. He figured it was the energy from the honey and radiating effects of the chausilver that made it hard for his mind to rest.

Soon, the dawn of morning brought light to his eyes, while the crowing of roosters filled his ears. He stood up and ventured for his throne room. He was met by the Castellan Madalbert and the Elder Siemond. They gave him a confused glance while he dragged himself onto his throne with the ordustone hammer still slung across his back.

"You really are... *fascinated* by that hammer, aren't you, m'lord?" asked the Castellan.

"He always has been, but I have never seen him lug it around outside of his study. Are you alright, Adar?" asked the Elder.

"Do not worry about my habits. I am fine. The hammer is a wonderful piece, and I imagine if I carry it around, someone may come forth with information that elucidates its origin."

"Aye, makes sense," said Madalbert.

"We may begin with today's meeting," said Adar. "There will be no formal vote, as there are not enough members of the council present, so we will instead discuss matters relating to my departure for the tourney, as well as the improvement of our docks. Do you two have any pressing matters that are related to your positions on the council?"

Madalbert shook his head.

"Well, Adar, there is one matter I believe we ought to discuss. A small sect of Dievic pagans has been found in the villages around Kurembrog. I ask for your help in bringing them before the justice of the pyres," said the Elder.

Adar sighed. "Siemond, we have discussed this many times. If you think I am going to suffer a revolt when the Ookosi may invade at any moment just to satisfy your austere adhesion to the Phoenix, then you are wrong. Within the bailey is fine, but if we are going to proselytize the villagefolk, then I do not think either of us will last long. The faith simply does not have the same strength there as it does in the cities of Osmjornia."

Siemond did not look pleased.

"Now, I have personally approved of the budget Madalbert brought to me yesterday; but before you bring up any protest to the cost, Elder, there is a high projection in tithe revenue from the sea trade. You can look at the sheet, if you would like."

"That is tolerable, so long as the merchants are being held to the tithe."

"Do not worry, Elder, I will make sure of it," said Madalbert.

"Now, we must discuss my departure. When the Elder and I leave for the tourney, Madalbert, you will be the only councilor present in the city. This will be a good test of your effectiveness as castellan. I will have the bailiff work closely by your side as an acting treasurer, as well as the head of the garrison as acting marshal. This is just to make sure you are capable of upholding the responsibilities of the position."

"I will not disappoint, m'lord."

"If anyone has anything further to bring up, we may continue. I have nothing left to say, so we may leave if there are no further matters to discuss."

Neither Madalbert nor Siemond brought up a matter.

"Perfect. You are dismissed."

Abba

 rooster was crowing, disturbing what little real rest Abba had gotten that night. He rubbed his tired eyes and sat up. Maric was sitting up in his bed, already wide awake. Ser Mikhail was out of bed and dressed in his armor. He hurried the boys to their feet, rushed them to dress, and pushed them out the door.

The peasants were collecting hay, and the Baron stood outside, waiting for the three to exit. They grabbed their horses' reins and walked them to the outskirts of the village, mounted their steeds, and departed. They passed the Baron's fief, going deeper and deeper into the brush. To Abba, much of the woods looked like the same woods they had already passed on the way to the Baron's village, and it was hard to occupy his mind on the journey. Maric fell asleep on his horse—as expected—and the horse just continued on as if he was not there.

They passed by an uncountable number of trees, streams, birds, ferns, and foxes. Abba would look at just about anything to keep his mind even somewhat stimulated. The Baron and Ser Mikhail continued forward, as though nothing existed but the trail. Ser Mikhail looked like an attentive hound, keeping an eye on the road. Jergi looked back at Abba and Maric, and this momentarily broke Ser Mikhail's attention. Jergi looked forward and grinned.

The trail was winding, with sprawling wildflowers and scattered broken branches at its flanks. Ultimately, the repeated instances of the same flora and fauna on the trail led Abba to fall asleep on his horse as well. He eventually awoke to his steed stomping on the ground, and before them was a large split tree trunk that crossed over the trail. Ser Mikhail looked around, dismounting from his horse and motioning for the others to follow. Abba climbed down and walked toward the tree trunk, placing his hand on it.

"It's rotted," said Abba.

"Then it will be easy to clear. We only need remove a portion, and we will soon be able to continue on."

Maric climbed down from his horse, wiping groggily at his eyes, and grabbed a hatchet that was strapped to the side of his saddlebag. He began hacking at the log. Jergi and Abba joined in soon after. Ser Mikhail stood at the ready, his hand resting on his sword's handle, watching the forest in case of an ambush, but there was none. Soon, they cleared the log and remounted their steeds, galloping past the rotted remains of the log. They passed by another of the Baron's villages. The Baron collected information from one of his own subjects in a conversation that lasted a little over an hour, but soon the party had departed again into the thick Kurem forests. Over time, the brush began to open up. Abba could see the blue sky above him once more.

"This opening marks the border of Kuremdod and Pelesgeb. Do not start trouble here, children. It will mark a diplomatic crisis that neither Jergi nor I wish to deal with," Ser Mikhail said, turning his head toward Maric.

Maric threw his hands up in disbelief while Abba laughed, pointing his finger at his brother.

"Pelesgeb is a nice, calm land, but we should ride straight through it. No point in stopping anywhere," Jergi said.

Ser Mikhail nodded.

They continued to ride through the opening, soon reaching another stretch of brush. The next few days of travel were unremarkable, consisting of training while the horses were watered, munching on their packed bread and salted meat, and packing and unpacking their tents. Eventually, they neared a fork in the trail. An old farmer and a younger man were hauling harvested crops from the south in a small wheelbarrow. They were walking toward the northern offshoot of the road. Ser Mikhail smiled and waved to the farmers, and the two Pelesgebic men reciprocated, greeting them loudly.

"Why are you grinning like that, Ser?" asked Maric.

"The Pelesgebic are a kind people, but damn do they know how to wage war," said Ser Mikhail. "It is an irony of their people, and also the reason I told you not to cause any problems during our time here. They are as hard as their land. They will gut you."

"There isn't much to do here. What else are their children going to do besides wrestle and hit each other with sticks? The land is locked from the sea, and they only have one stream large enough to sail down the Kyln," said Jergi.

"I read that they make amazing pies," said Abba.

Maric turned his head quickly to Ser Mikhail, his eyes going wide.

The knight shrugged. "They do."

They continued down the southeastern bend of the road and pushed through the woodlands. After about an hour, they passed through the village that the farmers must have originated from, but they refrained from stopping. They waved to villagers while they passed through. Ser Mikhail was right; they seemed to all be very kind to outsiders. They met the brush once more, spending about another half-hour riding before Maric stopped his horse. Jergi rolled his eyes with annoyance, and Ser Mikhail put his hands up.

"Why are you stopping?" asked Ser Mikhail.

"I have to relieve myself," Maric said.

"Well, by looking at the sky now, we might as well set up camp. Clearing the path earlier must have taken more time than we thought," said Jergi, sighing as he dismounted.

Ser Mikhail dismounted as well. The party led their horses off the road to the side of a large boulder, unpacking their tents. They pitched them in a circle while Abba dragged a log and some tinder to the center to make a fire. Maric went off into the woods, disappearing from the party.

"Why is he going so far away?" asked Abba.

"Perhaps he wanted some privacy while he pulled down his trousers," said Jergi, smirking at Ser Mikhail.

The party continued to set up camp for about another quarter-hour. Maric had still not returned. Abba wandered around the perimeter of the camp, looking in each direction in an attempt to find his brother. He waved his hand to Ser Mikhail, and Ser Mikhail followed.

"What is it, Abba?"

"Maric has not returned yet. It has been quite a while."

Ser Mikhail gazed around. "I thought the same. Grab your sword, boy."

Abba shook his head and ran for his saddlebag. Mikhail pointed at Jergi.

"Watch the camp. The shitter went missing."

Jergi nodded.

Ser Mikhail and Abba headed in the direction of where Maric had split from the camp. It was brush, brush, and more brush. The brush grew thicker. Abba's hand brushed past a tree trunk, and he recoiled away the second it touched it. It did not feel sappy; rather, it was wet. The bark did not feel rough; it felt smooth. He scowled at his hand. Whatever it was that had come from the tree was a strange, gooey substance that Abba did not recognize. He wiped his hand onto some scattered leaves on the ground in an attempt to dry it. There was a strange haze in the distance, and Ser Mikhail stared off into it.

"Let us venture in. That bored boy is probably exploring this oddity."

Abba nodded, and the two headed into the haze.

Abba had read about plant grafting in one of his many books, but he never had the opportunity to have a garden. He was to be Count of Kurembrog someday, not a gardener. Or rather, that was what his father had told him. Elder Siemond, on the other hand, had told him that a priest he knew had grafted a tree that bore several different fruits. It was an interesting thought to Abba; it was like creating life, in a way.

As they plunged farther into the woods, he was reminded of what he'd read. In the haze, the plants were warped and growing into one another, as though someone had taken all the plants in the forest and directed them to grow together in a jumbled web. It got worse the deeper they ventured in. As they went, more and more of the ground was covered by a strange pink fungus. The roots of the trees looked like discolored intestines, and transparent white goo drained from them like streaming sap. It smelled putrid, like the rotted remains of a rat or fish that had been left in the sun. The plants squirmed like worms or snakes.

"Do not touch anything," said Ser Mikhail.

"Alright," replied Abba.

They continued into the odd woods until they saw what looked to be a gray willow tree on a hill. The grass there was curled, and leaves of the tree looked to be flexing up and down. Maric lay in the curly grass in an unconscious state. Abba sprinted toward the base of the tree and tried to shake him awake, but his brother did not open his eyes. Abba saw that his chest was still rising and falling, still breathing, and he prepared to drag him away. Ser Mikhail ran over and slung the boy over his shoulder. Abba stared at the ground where Maric had been. A small, half-eaten, pustulous fig rested on the ground. Abba reached to pick it up.

"Do not touch that rotted filth!" Ser Mikhail shouted. "We need to get your brother back to the village!"

Ser Mikhail grabbed Abba by the arm and led him forcibly out of the odd wood. When they returned to their camp, they were met with the sight of Jergi sitting on a log by the fire, relaxing and examining documents. Ser Mikhail tossed Maric on the back of his horse and mounted.

"Get on your horse, Jergi! We need to head to the village!"

Jergi stumbled as he stood up, his eyes widening when he noticed that Maric was unconscious.

"Abba and I will go ahead. Jergi, lead Maric's horse behind yours."

Jergi nodded, running over to Maric's horse to grab its lead. He pulled the horse over to his own and mounted. Ser Mikhail and Abba galloped toward the village with haste, soon reaching the outskirts. A pair of guards stood there with lanterns in hand.

"Quickly! Present your priest, we have a sick child!"

The Pelesgebic guards beckoned the party to get off of their horses and led them to their temple. It did not look like a real Phoenic temple. It looked like a simple house. If Abba hadn't been directed to it, he never would have noticed that it was there. The only thing of note were the very large double doors, as well as several wooden idols spread about. At first, Abba thought that the chimney was a Phoenic spire, but then he noticed the barely visible gray smoke in the night sky above.

The inside was also completely different to any temple he had ever been in. There were more unrecognizable carved idols spread around. Abba could not determine the significance of them, for he had never read of anything of the sort in his books. He knew that the people of other lands worshiped their own gods, like the Ookosi with the Diev and the Terukians with their Koroark, but

212

he had thought that all Osmjornians followed Phoeni. This temple, however, seemed to suggest something different.

Ser Mikhail scanned the room. When he saw the priest, he brought Maric over to him.

"Priest! Help this boy, I beg of you."

The priest turned around and looked at Maric. He squinted and waved for Ser Mikhail to come closer. He pointed to the ground in front of him, and Ser Mikhail placed Maric down. The Pelesgebic priest put his hand on Maric's forehead and then placed his hand on Maric's chest.

"He has a fever," said the priest. "What happened to him?"

"We found my brother in a strange area of the woods. It was… disgusting. He was passed out next to a piece of half-eaten fruit."

"Strange area of the woods? Where did he go?" asked the priest.

"We were heading east until we set up camp off the road. This lad wandered off to relieve himself. There was a vast, grotesque section of woods hidden deep within the brush. We had to drag him out," said Mikhail.

The priest's eyes widened while he stared at Maric. "How large was that section of the woods?"

"I have no idea. I could not see the end of it."

The priest gritted his teeth. "Rechmann! Bring this boy some ugosa root! That should take his fever down."

"What is wrong, priest?" asked Abba, staring at Maric.

"Your brother has done something very dangerous," said the priest. "Though, do not fret; it is a good sign that he is still alive. It means that he must have only ingested a small amount of whatever it was that he ate. A few months ago, a number of our youth were running about in the woods and stumbled upon a similarly infected bush. A number of them ate from it, as that particular plant species was safe to forage from; but unfortunately, they could not discern whether or not its berries were diseased, as the plant had not shown any signs of blight. Despite that, all but one of them survived."

Abba's heart grew heavy. "How many berries did he eat, that boy who died?"

"About a handful."

"Fuck!" Mikhail placed his hands on his face, pacing back and forth.

"That rot is spreading. It used to be only a single infected tree, then a small cluster of trees; but we thought it was showing signs of shrinking, not spreading. To hear you speak of its vastness is immensely concerning."

A priest—Rechmann, Abba assumed—rushed a piece of ugosa root to the Elder. The Elder grabbed the root and pried Maric's mouth open. He squeezed the juices of the root into Maric's mouth. For a long moment, they waited; Maric lay on the ground, unmoving, as if dead.

Then he began to open his eyes.

Ser Mikhail exhaled.

"I am honestly quite surprised the child is already awake. I would keep an eye on him, for the children that ventured into the woods took much longer to recover. He must be blessed by Esu!" The priest smiled, laying his hand on Maric's forehead.

Abba squinted. He did not recognize the name the priest had used. He looked at Ser Mikhail with confusion, but Ser Mikhail just glared at him, as if to warn him off of asking any questions. In the center of the room, there were seven pyres, as well as several wooden carvings of birds. Many of the people present in the temple would walk around and routinely raise the wooden figurines above their heads and toward the sky. The priests, too, were dressed nothing like the priests of Kurembrog. They wore robes of varying shades of brown with no sashes shawled over their shoulders. They had a golden pendant of a flaming feather around their necks amidst a sea of several other pendants that were silver in color. Abba shook his head in confusion.

"Priest, what do these wooden figurines signify?" he asked.

The priest chuckled. Ser Mikhail scowled.

"Where are you from, boy?"

"I—I am from Kurembrog."

The priest chuckled once more. "Well, that makes much more sense. I thought I recognized Mikhail the Sword Seer. I take it you are the two sons of Count Adar, then? Has your father not taught you your Osmjornish history?" said the priest. He grinned at Ser Mikhail. "Has the boy never left Kurembrog? Even in your countryside, some of the locals still follow the Diev. Strange."

Abba looked down with embarrassment. He had not read much about the Diev. There were no books on it in Kurembrog, only mentions of the Ookosi following the pantheon.

"We can discuss matters of faith later," said Ser Mikhail. "We thank you for your help, priest."

"You Kurem-folk are interesting people," the priest said. He turned his attention back to Abba. "Your brother is breathing, so you may prepare him for departure. Take this ugosa root. If any more symptoms arise, squeeze some of the root juice into the boy's mouth. I hope your voyage is safe and swift."

"Thank you, Elder," said Abba.

"And I believe a small debt from the Count of Kurem to our humble village is in order, seeing as we just saved the son of Lord Adar himself."

Ser Mikhail sighed. He nodded his head.

"Thank you."

He lifted Maric up and over his shoulder. They left the temple, and Abba waved the Elder goodbye. As they departed, Ser Mikhail muttered under his breath. Jergi was doing the same, but his tone was different. Mikhail sounded tired, and Jergi sounded irritated. The party hurried to their horses. Mikhail lifted Maric's limp body over the back of his horse. Mikhail grabbed Maric's horse's lead and walked over to his own horse, mounting it.

When they returned to their camp, Mikhail carried Maric into his tent, setting him down carefully on the ground. Maric was still weak, groaning as he tried to move his body.

"You stay still and rest," Mikhail said.

Jergi went back to looking over the documents he had been examining before he was interrupted. Abba sat next to him, staring off in the direction of the anomalous woods.

Ser Mikhail returned and sat next to Abba, staring off into the woods with him.

"You have read many books, Abba. What do you think is over there?"

Abba shrugged. "I have never read of such a thing."

He twiddled his thumbs. He wanted to ask more questions about the priest and the temple, but he was unsure how to approach the topic.

"I never knew the country-folk worshipped the Diev," he said, sneaking a glance at Ser Mikhail's face. "Why was their temple so odd?"

Ser Mikhail sighed. "You are far too curious for your own good, you know."

"What do you mean?"

"What I am yet to say may put me to a pyre—but you deserve to know what it is that you will one day inherit from your father," Ser Mikhail said. "In your father's lands, his subjects are kindred to the Phoenicy; but that was not always the case. Because of intermarriage between those from Nar and the Osmjornish, the Osmjornish adopted the Phoenix into their pantheon. However, not all followers of the Phoenix have the same deep connection with the Phoenicy—the temple and the priests, I mean. The Phoenix is not their only god; it is one of many."

"Why did no one teach me this?" Abba asked.

Ser Mikhail paused for a moment.

"Elder Siemond insisted. Your father was to not tell his sons anything of Kurembrog's religious history, and all the religious texts in the library were to be sealed away. And, as I said, all of your father's subjects are kindred to the Phoenicy, so he did not see the utility in you learning about our ancestral faith."

Abba thought of what the priest had said to Maric, and the unfamiliar name he had used. "Who is Esu?"

"Esu is the highest of all in the Diev. She is a goddess, and she is said to be the mistress of dreams, visions, time, and space," Ser Mikhail said. "But that is all that I will share with you. Your father will have my arse if I continue, and I do not wish to hear the Elder Siemond's complaints."

Abba nodded and stood up. He walked to his tent and lay down. He turned over and stared at Maric's tent through the small gap in his tent flap. That made him nervous, however, so he rolled to his other side, trying to cease worrying for his brother. He covered himself with his blanket and stared at the sky through the slit of his tent, naming the constellations in his head. Soon enough, he grew so bored and tired of counting that he went to sleep.

Althalos

lthalos and Gunter stepped out of the storehouse and meandered about the town. Gunter's hands and clothes had much less blood on them then Althalos would have expected. The mercenary's eyes were resolute; he did not look like a man that was afraid to inflict pain on another. What type of man was Gunter? How could he so readily hurt someone? Althalos felt a bit uncomfortable walking with him, but he felt *more* uncomfortable anywhere else.

Gunter walked over to a small water barrel and dunked a rag inside. With the wet rag, he scrubbed his hands clean of what little blood was on them. He held onto the rag while they walked, only to toss it into a bush once they were a few legs away. They reached a well, and Gunter reeled in the bucket to pour some water into a small cup.

"Did ye get the names of any of the other knights? I want to be certain I do not know them."

"Just one," Althalos said. "Ser Ernest."

"I do not know a Ser Ernest."

Althalos stared off toward the town square. The knights stood there, chatting to each other. It seemed they had taken a break from searching. Althalos's throat felt like he had swallowed a rag. He gulped and turned to Gunter.

"That was not the first time you have ever done something like that, was it, Gunter?"

Gunter grimaced, taking another drink of water only to slam the cup on top of the well's wall, the hollow wooden cup making a thud on impact. Gunter walked away. He was heading toward the inn. Althalos would have followed him if Gunter had not seemed so angry at him. He also feared seeing the girl once more. The thought of her outing him for what he had done made his heart race. Althalos had choked a man to the point of unconsciousness, dragged him to a storehouse, tied him up, and was complicit in his torture—and she knew about it. There was no world in which that was not a serious crime.

What would people think if they knew what he had done? Sure, Irold was a murderer, but Althalos's actions were grotesque as well. What would Althalos's mother think? He could not imagine that she would be permissive of him doing such a thing. She had always told him to be kind, and he agreed with her. He did not like it when people hurt people. But what did he think was going to happen with Irold? Was he just going to keep him in the storehouse and ask him nicely to confess what he had done? Althalos wished it could have been so easy.

"Lad!" a voice called after Althalos.

Althalos turned. Coming toward him was an older man dressed in a priest's habit. His robes were a dark gray and his eyes were inquisitive. His expression made it clear that he was either angry or annoyed with Althalos and was planning on giving him a stern talking to.

"I do not remember your face," said the priest. "Where were you this morning during recitations?"

"Oh, apologies. I missed the recitations this morning, unfortunately," Althalos said.

"The Phoenix shall deem you honest. Most would have said that *I* was the one who missed them in the crowd; but I do not miss anyone, lad. What is your name?"

"Althalos d'Fisk."

The priest tilted his head once he heard Althalos's first name. "Ah… Althalos d'Fisk. Althalos is a very unique name, boy. It is an interesting one."

"To be honest, Elder, I have never put much thought into my name. I am just a peasant."

"I come from a noble house, where a strong name is an important thing. Althalos is a strong name. It comes from the language of Avon. Your parents must be quite devout."

218

"Oh, yes," said Althalos.

"Are you not so devout? Why were you not present?"

Althalos stared at the ground. "I... I had an *issue*, and I felt the need for some privacy."

"And what was this issue?"

Althalos paused for a moment longer, thinking for something to say.

"I—I was ill. I did not wish to condemn the chamber pot in the inn to such a poor fate, so I went into the woods to... handle my business."

The priest's expression was a mix of amusement and disgust. It was as if he could not decide whether to laugh at Althalos's imagined predicament or to feel sorry for him. He nodded his head and turned away so that he would not make eye contact.

"Well, lad, that is understandable. Thoughtfulness is not a named virtue, but it is a virtue nonetheless. I hope the Phoenix grants you relief."

Althalos could feel the priest's discomfort, so he bowed, giving the priest an opportunity to depart. As Althalos also walked away, he noticed Ser Ernest coming toward him. Althalos's heart began to race.

"Just the man I was looking for!" Ser Ernest said, smiling widely. "I realized I never asked you if you had the necessary pass to travel to Nara to become a priest."

Althalos gulped. "Well, no. I was meaning to meet with our village priest, but he left for Nara before I could speak to him."

Ser Ernest squinted his eyes, his fingers pattering on his sword's handle. He shook his head.

"Oh, yes, of course. Agathius is the priest of Fisk, is he not? We had already planned on heading over to Nara—I can take you with us so that you might meet him on his way."

Althalos looked away. He did not want to travel with them, but Ser Ernest would be expecting a gracious acceptance of such a generous offer.

"Oh, thank you! That will surely make the trip quicker."

"Yes, it will. It would be a long walk to Nara, otherwise," he said. "I overheard the priest questioning you about your absence at recitations, and I heard your answer. To be entirely honest, I was coming to question you myself, because I found your absence to be quite suspicious. You are new to Wettay, and you say you wish to be a priest; yet you miss a recitation? And what with Ser

Irold's disappearance... but you have explained all. I do apologize for thinking you could have done such a thing, even just for a moment."

Althalos shook his head. "I do not fault you for trying to find your friend. Have you discovered any information as to his whereabouts? I imagine it would be hard to remember his plans for the evening, given that you all were having such a grand time."

Ser Ernest's eyes lit up, as though a thought had pierced his brain.

"Ah! I do believe I just remembered something. He said he was going to shag that pretty barmaid last night. Ha! I commend you, boy. This is a good lead."

"Of course, Ser Knight."

He turned away with great speed, as if going to leave; but then he paused and turned back.

"You know what, lad, I think you should come with me. Makes no sense for me to let you wander. When we find Irold, we will leave immediately. We have been in this village for too long."

Ser Ernest put his hand on Althalos's back and pushed him along. As they strolled to the inn, Althalos could not take his mind off of what Ser Ernest was planning. Maybe the knight wanted to keep an eye on him.

When they entered the inn, Althalos saw Gunter drinking at the bar, his head down. He looked to be in a similarly dejected mood as he had been the night before. Ser Ernest rested his hands on the bar counter. A man's voice could be heard yelling from the other side of one of the doors behind the counter. Ser Ernest pounded his palm on the countertop. The innkeeper stuck his head out from the room, his face red with fury; but when he noticed the knight, he wiped the anger from his face, instead smiling brightly.

"How can I help ya, Ser Ernest?" asked the innkeeper.

"I wish to speak to your barmaid. I cannot find my companion, Ser Irold, and your barmaid was... discussing matters with him last night. I reckon she was the last to see him."

"Aye! Yes, yes. I was just speaking to her about that." He turned toward the door. "Lina! Get out here! A gentle knight wishes to speak with you!"

The barmaid opened the door, wiping tears from her eyes. As she inched her way to the knight, she kept her eyes downcast. The innkeeper glared at her, jabbing her arm with his finger. She picked up her head and smiled tightly.

Her eyes shot at Althalos, then shot back to the knight. Silently but emphatically, Althalos shook his head.

"The knight wants to hear about what happened with Ser Irold," said the innkeeper.

"Oh, Ser Irold. He was supposed to meet with me last night, but he never returned to his chambers." She looked at Althalos once more. "I am concerned for him. Do you know where he is?"

"Ah, interesting. You sound a bit unnerved. But I imagine that is due to your *concern* for Ser Irold's well-being."

He placed his hand on the barmaid's shoulder.

"Do not worry, darling. I will find your knight for you," said Ser Ernest with a smile.

Althalos tried to keep his head down. He did not want Ser Ernest to see the disgust on his face. He did get a glance at Gunter, though. He was not trying to hide his revulsion in the slightest, slamming his cup down on the table and turning his head to the knight.

"Ye disgust me," muttered Gunter.

Gunter turned his head back to his cup. The innkeeper, barmaid, and knight all stared at him, dumbfounded expressions on their faces. Ser Ernest walked up to Gunter and put his palm on the bar counter, next to the mercenary's cup.

"And who are you?" Ser Ernest asked.

"What does it matter to ye?"

"I am one of the King's knights!" said Ser Ernest with a stern and dutiful look.

Gunter gave the knight a similar look. "Well, I am a drunk! I just wish to drown myself in my cup and not talk to ye!"

"You are lucky I am a devout of the faith. Any other knight would have gutted you for this insolence. May the Phoenix bless you with a more *agreeable* temperament," said Ernest, grimacing.

Gunter slumped down on the countertop and pretended as if he were snoring. Ser Ernest sighed and went back to the barmaid. He said something to her that Althalos could not quite make out and turned around. He pulled Althalos by the elbow, and they left through the front doors.

"I must go speak with my other knights—wait here for my return," Ser Ernest said.

He left. Althalos looked to the inn and thought about going in to grab Gunter, but he did not know if he was actually drunk or not; if he was, he would be deadweight. He watched Ser Ernest walk to the town square. Only one of his knights was there, and the two of them discussed something for a moment before turning and walking to the manor house. Once Althalos was sure Ser Ernest could not see him, he walked back to the storehouse. He entered to the sight of Ser Irold still bound to the pole. He pulled the gag from Ser Irold's mouth.

"Tell me what you did, in the order you did it, when you arrived in Dorthu."

Irold looked confused. "Why in Gol does that matter?"

"It ought to matter to you. The more you talk, the longer you will live."

Irold grinned.

"I already know that it was you and your companions who killed everyone in Dorthu," Althalos said. "I want to know how you went about it, and what you thought about while you did it."

"My thoughts? You want to know my *thoughts*, boy? I just killed them! I did not think anything. I just stuck 'em with my sword, and they fell."

Althalos balled his hand into a fist.

"Oh? Did I strike a nerve again with you, lad? Are you going to hit m—"

Althalos stomped his boot onto Irold's maimed leg, mushing and mashing it with his foot. Irold screamed in pain. Althalos stuffed the ripped cape into his mouth to quiet him. Tears streamed from Irold's eyes; but then he laughed. He *laughed* under his gag.

"You are a monster," Althalos said. "Do you feel no remorse?"

Irold tilted his head with confusion. Althalos ungagged him again.

"I was doing my duty," Irold said.

"How was your cape torn?"

"Some young cunt with a very sharp axe swung at me and cut it off. He almost had my leg; but he could barely swing an axe, so it was no fun at all to kill him. He was not a challenge."

"His name was Hrodolf," Althalos said, seething.

"What?"

"The boy you killed. His name was Hrodolf. He wanted to become a soldier. He was a friend of mine."

Irold rolled his eyes. "What a friend he was. That axe you carry around—it was his, I imagine? I barely remember the thing."

"Do you not stop to think for a moment why you are killing people? Is the most pressing concern of yours how enjoyable a kill is?"

"Most do not understand. Do you not have any activity that you find enjoyable?"

"Yes, but—"

"So you know the feeling it gives you in the end, then. That feeling of triumph."

"Do you mean to say you get that joy from killing?"

"You say that as if it is wrong," said Irold. "I am doing my duty! I have no choice. Is it so terrible that I enjoy it, too?"

Althalos grimaced at the tattered knight before gagging him once more. He could not bear to hear his voice any longer. He grabbed a couple of marks from the knight's satchel and made sure his bindings were still tight. Then Althalos left the storehouse, heading for the town square. At that time of day, it was very busy; it seemed like every peasant in the village was out in the square looking for things to buy.

Althalos felt like he had hit a dead end with Irold. The man simply did not think about his killings. How could he be useful if he did not care to remember anything? He looked off to the manor house. Ser Ernest was there, addressing his knights, but Althalos could not really tell nor hear what for. They would grow restless sooner or later, he knew; and as time went on, Althalos's concern grew. They already knew his face. When Althalos made his run, he would have to cover it.

He went to a tailor's stall. Several items of clothing were laid out on the stall table: braies, trousers, tunics, hoods, and scarves. Althalos browsed through a few, then he picked up a navy-blue cloak. He held it up and presented it to the tailor.

"How much would this cost me?"

"A quarter mark or so, lad."

Althalos nodded and handed the merchant a mark. The merchant nodded with wide eyes, giving Althalos three quarter-marks in return. Althalos threw his new blue cloak over his shoulder, waving goodbye to the tailor. He meandered through town. He wanted to wait a bit before returning to the storehouse, for his anxiety was growing. He leaned against a street pole and people-watched for almost a half-hour. He kept a keen eye on the manor, making sure that Ser Ernest and his posse were not watching him.

In time, he went back to the storehouse. Irold was squirming in his bindings, but once Althalos entered, he stopped moving. The light that shined through the cracks of the storehouse was dimmer than before; it was growing late. Althalos put the cloak on, then fixed the axe so that it would stay on his back. He walked up to Irold, looking down at him. He made sure the knight's bindings were tightened once more and exited the storehouse.

He walked to the inn, taking his hood off and heading inside. He walked up to the counter. Lina was there, and she saw him out of the corner of her eye. She stumbled on her words as she spoke to a bar-goer before regaining her composure and continuing to talk with the customer. Althalos walked to the bar. Lina poured the customer a jack of ale and turned to Althalos.

"H—Hello there, A—" She paused before speaking further. "What can I get for you this evening?"

"Hello. I would just like an ale and whatever soup you have today."

Lina nodded. She turned around and bent over to grab the ale jug. Her shirt rode up a bit, and Althalos noticed purple bruises all over. His heart sank with guilt, and his stomach churned. She turned around and poured him a jack. Althalos tried to catch her eye, wanting to whisper an apology, but Lina ignored him. She ladled some soup into a bowl and placed it in front of him. He could not tell what the soup was made of, but he was famished, so he scooped it quickly into his mouth.

It was around this time when the knights had entered the bar the day before. He gazed around the room to confirm that none of the knights were present. It seemed they were not so merry this night. Another gentleman stood between Althalos and Gunter, so Althalos moved his meal next to Gunter and stood beside him. Gunter's cup was empty, and he laid his head down on the counter. Althalos shook Gunter's shoulder, and Gunter gave him a stare out of the corner of his eye.

"Be discreet, boy," he said.

"I thought you were in a drunken coma," whispered Althalos while he gazed at his soup.

"I can't drink at a time like this…"

"Then why is your cup empty?"

"I poured it out, ye churl."

Althalos chuckled, finishing his soup. "Sure you did, Gunter."

"I'll beat the piss out of ye when we are done, boy. What do ye want?"

"He knows nothing," whispered Althalos. "He does not care."

"I should have let ye know that mad dog does not care for anythin' but killin'. Whoever is his superior would not need to direct him much, other than to lead him to his destination."

"Aye, he has a wicked sense of right and wrong," Althalos said.

Gunter yawned and reached for Althalos's jack.

"What in Gol, Gunter?"

"Were ye goin' to drink that, boy?"

Althalos stood quiet.

"Of course ye weren't. Ye only ordered it to blend in."

"Did you hear of anything?" Althalos asked.

"No, lad. We should depart. That man is worthless trouble."

Althalos stared at Lina, then back down at the counter. "We cannot."

"What in Gol do ye mean, we fuckin' can't, boy?"

Althalos shook his head. Out of the corner of his eye, he noticed one of the knights entering the inn. He stepped away from the bar. Gunter went to yell at Althalos, but he noticed the knight and returned to brooding on the bar counter. Althalos gazed out of the window so that he could watch the knight with the side of his eye. The knight walked up to the counter. It wasn't Ser Ernest, but rather one of his underlings. He talked to Lina for a moment, and she handed the gentleman a key. He thanked her and exited the inn. Gunter stood up and began to stumble toward the inn's doors. He glared at Althalos, nodding for him to follow. Althalos waited a moment before he made his exit.

Gunter shambled around like a man with mush in his skull, but it seemed his eyes were fixated on the balcony that preceded the rooms on the second story of the inn. The knight was up there, and he was headed for the room that Irold had bought. Althalos loitered by a street pole a few yards away from Gunter. He leaned back onto the pole and waited until the knight had entered. At this point, Althalos put his hood over his head and strayed further away so that he could get a better angle on the door.

After a moment, the knight stormed out, rushing down the stairs. He sped past Gunter and Althalos. He was not running, but his stride was fast and his pace hasty. His destination was the manor house. Gunter darted a look to Althalos. He stumbled around town with seemingly no direction, but Althalos noticed that he was gravitating toward the manor house. Gunter lifted a palm to Althalos, and Althalos took the palm as a sign to stay back. The mercenary pretended to crumple to the ground beside a building along the road to the manor house, keeping his head low to the ground. He looked like a drunkard dozing off.

A dozen or so minutes passed by, and the trio of knights exited the manor house and headed toward the nearest building. They knocked on the door, and a peasant woman answered. They barged in, and Althalos could hear her begin to scream. Soon enough, the three exited. They went door-to-door. If no one answered, then they knocked the door down and ransacked the building. They slowly encroached toward the inn, which stood on the other side of the town.

Gunter stood up and drunkenly stumbled back to Althalos. He pointed at Althalos, stabbing the air with his finger in direction of the storehouse. Althalos turned around and hurried toward it. He crept through the door. Irold was attempting to flee once more, but again, he could not break free from his bindings. Gunter barged through the door after him and pulled Althalos to his side.

"We need to kill that whoreson now, boy! We need to fuckin' go!"

"We have learned nothing. This murdering bastard has told us *nothing*," said Althalos, clenching his fists.

"Are ye daft, boy? Ye should have fuckin' killed him a long time ago. Once ye were sure he had nothin' of use to say, ye should have put him down right then and there! Where is that axe? Get yer vengeance on that sack of shit now—we have to leave!"

Althalos pulled the axe out from under his cloak and walked toward Irold. He choked the handle, staring at the Black Wolf's beady and soulless eyes. The tattered knight grinned through his gag, tilting his head to show his neck. Althalos lifted the axe. Tears began to run down his face, and his arms dropped to his sides.

Torchlight shone through the cracks in the planks that made up the thin storehouse walls. Althalos could hear clamoring steel plates. Gunter ran toward the door and put down the wooden drawbar. Althalos rushed over, pushing crates in front of the door and forming a barricade. The knights knocked on the door. Althalos and Gunter kept quiet while they leaned against the barricade. Gunter kept his hand on his sword's handle. The crates rattled and shook. Gunter pulled out his sword and kept it free at his side.

"Oi! Ye arseholes need to stop tryin' to knock down my door!"

The shaking stopped.

"Allow us entry and we shall refrain from doing any more damage!"

The voice sounded like Ser Ernest.

Gunter glanced at Althalos and pointed to Irold. Althalos ran back to the axe. He had to kill him. What if Irold freed himself? They were already outnumbered. Althalos tried to lift the axe up once more, but his heart dissuaded him. Irold was bound. To kill a man while he could not defend himself was dishonorable. And even if Althalos did free him, Irold was in no shape to fight with the state that his legs and arms were in. The door started to shake once more, and one of the old planks splintered off, creating a view to the outside.

"Ye fuckin' crimson cunts! I'll fuckin' kill ye!" Gunter shouted.

"Unbarricade the door now, you lousy drunk!" yelled one of the other knights.

Althalos stumbled to one of the walls and pulled one of the crates back. The hole he saw before him was big enough for both him and Gunter to get through. A hand extended through the door and attempted to lift the drawbar, but Gunter stabbed through the hole. A loud wail of pain was heard from the other side.

"Damn you to Gol! We will burn you on a spike!" roared Ser Ernest.

Gunter ran toward Irold and lifted his sword, but before he could kill him, the door behind them was knocked down. Two knights were pushing down the stacked crates with their swords drawn. Althalos dove through the hole, and Gunter followed. They sprinted away, but Althalos turned his head to look back. A knight, presumably the one Gunter had stabbed, was on the ground bleeding out in front of the storehouse door. Gunter yanked on Althalos's arm; the knights were running toward them.

There was a single guardsman at the western entrance of Wettay, and Gunter bum-rushed him to the ground. He started whaling on the guard's face and pulled his dagger out, but once he noticed that the guard was unconscious, he urged Althalos to continue following him.

He was about to kill that guard, Althalos thought. *The guard did nothing other than be there.*

They headed into the woods, making several random turns in an attempt to get the knights off their tails. They ran under fallen tree trunks, jumped over small streams, cut through sprawling bushes, and hid behind one of the numerous boulders that were scattered about the forest. Althalos saw the orange light of torches into the distance. Gunter put a single finger over his lips and mouthed *be quiet.* They crouched down, and Gunter watched. Althalos noticed once more that Gunter's hand never left his sword.

Dozens of shining orange flames peered through the tree branches. Gunter put his hand on Althalos's back, pushing him down.

"If we need to flee, don't let yer head pop up. They'll notice ye. Move from side to side," whispered Gunter.

Althalos nodded and continued to watch the torchlight in the distance. Two of the king's knights roamed around, looking behind anything large enough for someone to hide behind. Althalos tried to count how many men in yellow tabards there were, but there were too many to count. Gunter pulled Althalos's arm and made a motion with his hand. He mouthed *stay low,* motioning for Althalos to follow. They duckwalked away from the boulder, making sure to avoid any loose branches that could break and alert the guards with their sounds.

After a while, they lost sight of any torches moving about in the forest. They crouched behind a fallen log. Gunter was tense, looking around like an alert owl. They were still surrounded by brush, but the woods were much thinner and more open than before. The moon was up above them. Althalos relaxed a bit.

A bush rustled. Gunter jumped and presented his sword to it. A man stepped through, his armor clanging. He wore crimson on his back, and his eyes were filled with angry malice.

"You killed my brother, you wretch. You killed my brother! I am going to damn you to Gol!"

He drew his sword and charged at Gunter. Gunter parried a swing. The knight had no beard. He had long brown hair and blue eyes. He was much larger than Ser Ernest.

"Do not intervene, boy! This man will kill ye!" shouted Gunter as the knight pressured him away.

Every time Gunter changed his stance, the knight addressed it and changed his as well. It seemed at times that Gunter was outclassed by the knight, although it was by only a small margin. Their swords swung at each other faster than Althalos could understand. The knight had tears in his eyes, slashing at Gunter with gritted teeth.

"You stabbed Uther in the neck! I am going to let your guts roll from your fucking body, you cunt!"

The knight parried each swing of Gunter's sword, leading Gunter to stumble in his footing as he stepped backwards. Althalos chucked a stone at the knight's head, but he aimed too low and hit him dead in the chest. It glanced off of his armor, catching his attention. His eyes shifted to Althalos. Gunter took the moment to slash at the back of the knight's calf. He roared in pain. The torchlight grew nearer, as well as the stomping sounds of countless soldiers.

"Ser Ulrich!" yelled Ser Ernest.

He wielded a sword with a wavy blade; each curve was highlighted by the torchlight. He dashed at Gunter while the guards retrieved Ser Ulrich, pulling him away. Gunter ran off, and so too did Althalos. They jumped over streams, rocks, fallen logs, and whatever else was in their way. Althalos drew his hatchet and swung it at the trunk of a tree that was split in its center. The trunk splintered and separated, the top part of the tree falling behind Gunter and Althalos. Some of the pursuers tripped over it, but it only halted them momentarily. The rest of them ran around the tree. Althalos's foot hit what was probably a rock, and he fell face first to the ground.

His heart raced. Surely, this was his end. Oh, what it was to survive a massacre—and then die a couple days later.

He started sweating. After lifting himself up from the dirt, he rolled himself to his side. The brush was lit ablaze in a golden fire. A few guards lay dead, their torches on the ground. Gunter stared at the fire, pulling Althalos up but seemingly unable to pry his eyes from the sight. Althalos looked at where he had fallen; there was a ring of dead grass and mushrooms at his feet.

"Stop gawkin' and fuckin' run!" Gunter yelled, yanking him forward.

Althalos ran with Gunter. They ran as fast as they could. The fire behind them drowned out the guard's torches, and they lost the sound of yelling men pursuing them. They made it back to the road and crossed to the other side. Gunter was looking for something. They made it to a tree, and they stopped. The both of them were panting for breath.

"We need to get back to runnin'. Why the hell are ye tired, boy? Yer young, this should be nothin' for ye."

Althalos looked behind them. "They will hunt us, Gunter."

"Aye, boy, they will. But ye were already marked for death when ye decided to nab Irold. Gol, ye were marked for death even before that, but ye got lucky and threw yer second chance at life away. I do not blame ye, though. Those men deserve to die."

Althalos did not reply. Gunter stared down the road.

"Where do ye think ye can get justice for yer village?"

"I can only think of Nara. Agathius is going there."

"Alright, then," Gunter said. "Let us go to Nara."

Althalos kept his head down. The pair walked down the side of the road, heading off in the direction of Nara together.

Meara

eara woke up to a bright and clear sky. She pulled herself upright and walked to the lockbox, grabbing it. She marched over to Luka and the other children. This had to go right; she had to get Gol back. She placed the lockbox on the ground and sat on it. She stared at Luka, and Luka raised a brow at her. She crossed her arms.

"Are you going to say something, Meara? Or are you just going to sit on that chest?" asked Luka.

"I am ready to go," replied Meara.

Luka's fat cheeks raised into a grin. "Well, alright! You heard her, children! Follow her and do as she says!"

The crowd of orphans erupted into mutterings. They turned to each other in confusion. Meara understood; Luka would never relinquish control of them to someone else. It was actually quite funny to see their dumbfounded looks. They were uncertain. Luka stepped forward.

"A group of sick villains has kidnapped our *friend*—that little boy who never spoke. I need you to do as Meara says, or you will be beaten for not coming to help your friend in need."

Luka wiped his eyes as if he were crying, but when Meara squinted to get a better look, she noticed his eyes were dry.

"We are going to save him! And we are going to take their gold as revenge for their cruel act!"

Meara sat back and stared at Luka, frowning. When he spoke, he gesticulated broadly, his fat arms jiggling as he moved. Meara stood up and walked away from the group. The pack followed her. She told them to split into three different groups so that the guards would not stop them. The guards never liked when they all huddled together; a few children could be seen as a group of friends, but a large mob was likely a bunch of tiny, starving ghouls ready to pounce on any oblivious passerby. The guards knew the children could be dangerous. Their hands were not clean. Not all of them were bad, but rarely ever had Meara met a child that had not done something bad in order to get a meal. Some were worse than others, though: like Luka.

The groups all met at the gatehouse. Meara instructed them to gather up rocks. Then she stood on a wagon and addressed the crowd of starving orphans.

"Hello!"

The orphans stood quietly.

"You all know me; I am Meara. I need you all to listen very well. If we fail, then G—the mute boy will die."

Meara adjusted her feet and cleared her voice.

"With the groups of three you are in right now, you will stand and throw rocks at the building I am going to sneak into. Only one group at a time will throw—and once they reach the attention of the guards, they will run away. Once those guards are out of sight, the next group will throw rocks. When that group gets pursued, they will run off, and when their pursuers are out of sight, the next group will replace them. If your group is being chased, run away. When you have gotten away, come back here and meet up with your group. Do you all understand?"

The kids laughed, beginning to grab rocks. They pretended to aim them at houses and giggled with each other. One boy almost chucked a rock.

"Do *not* throw until I say! If you mess this up, Luka won't get his coin! You do not want to anger Luka, do you?"

The crowd went quiet. All of their attention went to Meara. She pointed at the buildings that the wagon had parked behind. She stepped down and came closer to the children.

"I need you all to listen. We cannot lose any more of us to those cutthroats. Do as I say, and continue to do it until I am out of there. I will be going in alone to save our friend. After enough of those evil men have been drawn away, some of you will need to stay around to take the boxes of coin back to Luka."

The crowd of orphans still stared at Meara attentively. Whenever she mentioned Luka, they winced. Meara walked down the road toward the general store and warehouse. She pointed at the buildings and waved a group of children over. They readied their arms. As they held the rocks, their face were transformed by an intense, juvenile excitement. She walked back to where the children were grouped up and told them to hide behind the wagon.

Meara stared at the alleyway, gripping the lockbox tightly in her arms. Some of the passersby noticed the gang of children, but before they could call the guards to stop them, Meara yelled for them to start throwing. Windows cracked. The pitter-pattering of glass shards hitting the ground filled the ears. A number of miscreants exited the warehouse and rushed the children, but the group fled. As Meara expected, the criminals ran after them. She rushed another group to replace the one that had fled, and soon the volley of rocks was heard again.

"You all are the third group. I am going to run over to the warehouse. When the group out there is chased off, replace them."

The children nodded, and Meara smiled. She ran over to the alleyway and peeked inside the fenced-in area where the wagon-drivers had been. No one was there. She ran inside. A door opened, and she heard footsteps leaving through it. Meara crouched behind a crate. A number of criminals left the building, yelling as they went. She could not hear the thuds of rocks anymore. She stood up and walked to the door. A foot stepped out, and a man pushed the door open, its hinges squeaking, unoiled metal on metal. He had already seen her. He was not a large man, but he was a *grown* man: certainly larger than Meara. He bore a club in his hands.

"Stupid bitch…" said the man, raising his club.

He marched toward Meara. She stumbled backward, falling. Meara dropped the lockbox and crawled back, bumping into a wall. The man prepared to swing. Next to Meara's hand was a hammer. She grabbed the hammer and slung its head into the outer side of the man's knee. She heard a pop, and he crumpled to the ground, dropping his club. She stood up and stared at the man. As she was about to walk away, the man reached for a dagger; but before he could unsheathe it, Meara slammed the hammer into his skull in a panic. He stopped moving. Meara did not know if he was dead or just unconscious.

She retrieved her lockbox and ran into the building. It smelled like burning coal, and Meara's skin felt like it was cooking over a fire. There was a stairway leading up to the second floor. They certainly would not have kept Gol here; there were too many normal people about. Smiths were pouring molten metal into molds. They stared at Meara, confused.

Meara ran upstairs. There were a few doors, but only one with a lock. She checked the others, but it was the only locked door she could find. Meara tried to open it, but it did not budge. She examined the lock and found a maker's mark on the front of it, so she opened the lockbox and looked for the same maker's mark on the document. She whittled down the number of potential keys to just a few, soon finding the proper one.

Gol was inside, bloodied and bruised. He had been kept in the dark, the only light in the room coming from the now-open door. His eyes lit up. He looked as if he had suddenly come out of a deep dejection. Meara ran over to him and put a finger to her lips, signaling for Gol not to say a word. He had two black eyes and a busted lip. His arms were severely purple. There was a knife on a table next to him, so she used it to cut the boy free from his bindings. She hugged him, but Gol whimpered in pain as she squeezed. Meara released him quickly. She grabbed his hand, retrieved the lockbox and keys, and ran out of the door, heading down the stairs. She looked through the open door; the fenced-in area was filled with members of the gang, looking down at their unmoving acquaintance. The sound of pelting stones was gone. *Had the children stopped?*

One of the men noticed her and pointed. She dashed toward the front door, avoiding the furnaces and many workers. She could hear them running after her and Gol. None of the other orphans were outside. Her heart almost jumped out of her chest. They had *abandoned* her. She ran, pulling Gol along with her. He could barely keep up at first, but when he looked back at the men chasing them, he gained the strength to run. They ran through the alleys, losing the gang of men.

Eventually, they made it back to Luka and the others. He was sitting on a sack of food, grimacing at the ground. As usual, he was having the children fight each other for his entertainment. Luka noticed Meara. He stood up, looking like a growling mutt.

"Do you have my groschen, you lying bitch?" Luka snapped.

Meara's eyes widened. She had overlooked the groschen, for the only thought in her mind had been to save Gol. She closed her eyes, putting her palms to her face. She scowled at Luka.

"You left me there. You left me there without any time to get your damn coin! Why did you leave me there, Luka? Why didn't the other children stay?"

Meara looked around at all the orphans, glaring.

"It looks like everyone is here! Why did you leave Gol and I?"

Luka puffed out his chest proudly. "Well, unlike you... I actually *care* for my friends."

"Heh. Of course, Luka. Is that why you starve the others and eat all the food?"

The orphans kept their heads down. Luka gritted his teeth and stared at Meara.

"I am the only one making sure that everyone gets fed. And *everyone* is alive and fed, no?"

No, they were not—but Luka did not know that. He did not care to know. The children would never tell him, and they would never rise up against him. He was too big and strong, and he had always been their leader; none of them knew any different. Luka did not know how many children had run away, trying to find food on their own. Many of those children had died, for they did not have the strength to pilfer. Luka did not know how many of them had crawled away to die in some hole, bleeding out from within from the beatings they had suffered for his *entertainment*.

Luka walked over to Meara, leaning in close.

"I will forgive this, and I will also forgive you for not bringing me back *my* coins; but I will only do so if you give me the groschen you already have. It is the least I can do after leaving you back there to fend for yourself."

Meara turned her head and stared at Luka with confusion. "Mercy is not common from you, Luka. Why the sudden change of heart?"

"What do you mean, *not common?* I have always been kind!" snarled Luka.

"I will... I will give you the groschen," Meara said.

Gol tugged at her arm. He stared at her, his brows knitted with concern.

"Thank you, Meara," Luka said. "I will be waiting for it."

Meara turned away. She took her time while she strolled away, walking through the market square and perusing the stalls. She kept watch for any ne'er-do-wells, as the gang of men earlier could very well still have been searching for her. The Low Beakish trader's stall was not where it had been before; he must have left. She stared at where the stall had been. The trader was a kind man, and rarely ever did Meara run into kind men. She frowned. She would have liked to have given him a proper thank you and goodbye. She wondered why he had not told her that he was leaving.

She went down one of the many alleys, taking several turns that almost seemed random. Gol stuck to her side like a stray dog. They eventually made it back to the shack. She opened the door and went to the spot of dirt where she had buried the groschen. She did not want to dig it up, but she felt as though she had no choice. Even though Luka was a terrible person, she felt safer with him than she did on her own. Strength in numbers, she thought. The gang would be out for blood; they had to be searching for her. She would've rather been surrounded with the orphans, facing the gang together, than trying to survive on her own.

Gol frowned, sitting in a corner and watching as Meara uncovered the chest. She turned around and scowled at Gol; but her outward appearance was a facade, for she was grinning in her mind at the sight of him. She was gladdened to have him back with her.

Meara lifted the chest and set it down in front of her. She opened it, and all the coins were still there. She thought of all that she could have bought with the coins—meat, fruit, clothes, and a ride away from Belar—but she immediately threw those thoughts out of her mind. She had to survive.

She picked up the box and held it at her side. Gol tugged at her arm.

"What do you want?" barked Meara.

Gol glared at her and pointed at the chest.

"What? What about it? Do you not want me to give it to Luka?"

Gol shook his head and tugged at the chest. Meara yanked it from him.

"What has gotten into you, Gol?"

Gol shook his head side to side and pointed at his bruises. He opened his mouth as if to speak, but he closed it soon after. Meara ignored him and left. The shack was at a dead end in the alley, and Meara headed for the exit. Luka was there. He had followed her? How could she not have seen him? She placed the chest down, squinting at Luka, her hands resting on her hips.

"Hello, Meara!" said Luka, giddily waving his fingers to her.

"Why—Why did you follow me?"

Gol inched away, back to the shack. He was shaking, goosebumps forming all over his skin. A large man was walking down the alley toward the shack. He stopped to stand next to Luka. He grinned, his smile ugly. His teeth were rotten and dirty; Meara was amazed she could notice how ill-maintained they were from such a distance. He had a large dagger that hung from his hip.

It was the same man that had pursued her before.

She trembled. She tried to speak, but she could not think of what to say.

"What is it, Meara? Are you going to give this gentleman his coin back, or not?" yelled Luka, smirking.

Meara looked at Gol. He collapsed to his knees and grabbed his head again, huffing for air. She pulled him close; she could feel his heart jumping in his chest. His frail body still shook, and he felt cold to the touch. Luka and the brute walked forward. Gol retreated in response, and Meara went with him.

"Stop your moving!" yelled the brute.

Gol and Meara froze.

"Take the groschen—but please, leave us alone!" Meara cried.

The large man snickered. "You poor dumb cunt. I am taking the groschen, and I am taking you, as well."

Luka put his hands on his hips. "Meara, you do not seem to enjoy my company, so I imagined that you would enjoy the company of this *gentleman* far more…"

He grinned, his eyes glinting with madness.

Meara's eyes shifted to the brute. She stepped backward again until her back bumped into the stone brick wall of the shack. Gol clung tight to her, crying at her side. Luka and the brute were only a few feet away.

"I'll put you to work," said the man. "You're going to work off what you stole from me."

Meara's eyes widened. The man went to grab her, and she turned to flee; but she reacted too slowly, and he had her in his hands. She tried to scream for help, but he put his hand over her mouth, squeezing his palm over her jaw until the pain forced her to stop. Gol ran away like a scared dog. He stood at the end of the alleyway, stopping to take a look back at Meara. Tears shone in his eyes. Then he ran away.

Meara screamed against the man's palm, her voice breaking. For a moment, she kept fighting; kicking her legs uselessly in the air and thrashing back and forth, trying to bite at his hand.

Then her arms went limp at her sides. Her body sagged in the brute's arms. She did not know what she felt; she was already trying to forget it. All she could think about was Gol at the mouth of the alley, running away, and the fear encroaching on her like black fog. It was like her mind was trying to protect her from her own feelings; from the grief and pain she knew she was about to endure.

Edit

hile the winds pushed Geder's ship out to sea, Edit stared at the coast. Ser Elseharde joined her at her side, placing his hands on ship rails. The ship was made of a dark brown oak, the boards creaking whenever someone walked on them. Oars extended from its sides, but at this moment, the winds were favorable, so the rowers could relax. The winds made it quite chilly on the ship, and the air around them smelled both sweet and musty. Ser Elseharde sighed, looking down at the hull ripping through the waters below.

"I hate the sea," he said.

Edit smiled. "The sea is fine. There is a sort of unbound beauty to it. It sprawls on and on, and you can go wherever you wish."

"You must not sail often. On a ship, you must go wherever the winds permit you; and if you try to row off too far, your sailors will probably starve before they can get back to land, leaving your ship to float away unbound."

Edit's smile disappeared. "Thank you for ruining the sea for me, Ser Elseharde."

"The pleasure is mine, m'lady."

Edit stepped away from the rail, but Elseharde stepped close, stopping her.

"Just a moment, Lady Edit. You must stay within my view. After what happened to Barnut, I do not trust you to be alone.

Whoever Barnut's enemy is, they are also the enemy of your father."

"But why would anyone go after me?"

"If someone were to take you, then they would have plenty of leverage over your father. You are the only thing he cares about."

"Ha! Of course, he *cares* about me. That is why I am on this ship without him, and that is why he did not even ask me if I wanted to marry this *Abba*."

She looked at the front of the galley. The bowsprit figurehead was carved into a depiction of the Phoenix; Geder stood before it, looking with longing to the north. He was dressed in blue, and his hair was neatly combed. Edit looked up to the sails. They were blue, with two white serpents facing away from each other.

"I thought the white serpents were supposed to face each other," said Edit.

"Geder modified his heraldry after he was passed up for Adar in the succession for Kurembrog. He had the serpents face away from one another in a passive rebellion against his father. To this day, I hear Geder will still complain of it."

"Why was he passed up?"

"I do not know, but Geder does have a reputation of not being able to keep friends for long. Maybe his father had had enough of him."

"Ah," Edit replied, nodding.

"I am going to go speak to Geder's sailors," Elseharde said. "Stay here. I will not be long."

Elseharde stepped away from the rails to wander around the top deck of the ship, making small talk with the sailors as he went. He seemed to acquire a knack for speaking to people that he did not have when speaking to Edit. The sailors erupted into laughter when Elseharde spoke to them, and others started to gravitate toward him. *People found Elseharde funny?* Edit had never noticed; he was always so serious around her. She could hear them teasing each other as if they were brothers, even though they had only just met.

In contrast, Geder stood by himself. She did not see any of his subordinates coming to him for a laugh. Her father's knights would often hang around him to talk about trivial matters or to joke about current happenings, but Geder's subordinates did not. Edit did not remember him not having such a cold demeanor before; he seemed different from when she had first met him. He had a resolute expression, staring north toward his home. He beckoned a few of his sailors to him, and they stood at attention. When he talked, he pounded his fists in the air—whatever he spoke of was surely something that he was passionate about. But Edit's staring and judgment had lasted a bit too long; Geder had noticed it and beckoned her forth. She dragged her feet over to Geder. Something in her head told her to take her time and be wary of the man.

She begrudgingly presented herself to Geder with a curtsy. He returned her gesture with a lackluster bow. His smile was manufactured, as stiff as metal. He pointed at the waters, motioning for Edit to join him and watch the sea.

"How do you like the waters, Lady Freihei?"

"They are fine, I suppose."

Geder rested his arm on the side rail, turning to face Edit. "Nothing about the waters draws your interest? I do not believe you."

It seemed as though his accent grew harsher at sea. Edit rolled her eyes.

"I never said that. I said they were fine."

"Whenever someone down here says that something is *fine*, either whatever it is does not truly matter to them, or they are omitting the rest of what they want to say. I do not think you are indifferent to the sea, for you were staring at it quite a bit back there when you stood with Ser Elseharde."

Edit gritted her teeth behind her lips.

"I also do not believe that you, as a lady from the beautiful shores of Bek d'Lifa, could ever be indifferent to the sea."

"What makes you think that, Lord Geder?" replied Edit, turning to face the sea.

"I come from a similar background as you. I too come from a coastal town, and I have long looked at my shore with fervent pride. I could not fathom that you would not do the same, for the shores of Bek d'Lifa are far more beautiful than the shores of Kurembrog."

Edit nodded. "I suppose the sea is beautiful."

For a moment, she thought that if she agreed with Geder, then he would leave her alone.

"Aye! It truly is. Have you ever been to Kurembrog? I think you would enjoy it greatly."

"I have not."

"The rocky shores are magnificent. It is the second most beautiful coast; the first being the coast of Bek d'Lifa, of course."

Edit shrugged.

"Well," he said, after a moment of uncomfortable silence. "It has been a pleasure talking to you, Edit."

"Likewise."

Once Geder left, Edit let out a sigh of relief. Geder walked with his chest puffed up; he seemed to need to have it known that he was in charge. Some sailors gave him a look of disgust after he passed them, but Edit never noticed any of them be bold enough to do it to his face. Elseharde was still chatting with the sailors. Edit grew ever more bored; there was nothing for a lady to do on the ship to keep herself occupied. She did not think there was even another woman aboard, so she kept to herself by the rails. Edit stared off at the sea.

Geder was right—she had omitted some of the truth.

The sea was vast. Edit had seen people from all over the world in Bek d'Lifa. She had seen Ookosi, Aeric, Low Beakish, and Krenki people. There were even times where she had seen Elven merchants unloading their cargo to be sold. The beauty of the sea was not in the sea itself, but the unique people it might bring.

The sky grew dark, so Edit turned to head toward her bedchambers. Ser Elseharde caught up to her, clearly planning to escort her there. But as soon as she entered the room, a sailor said something that drew his attention. He laughed, leaving Edit to herself so that he could jest with the sailor. The door shut behind him.

Edit went for the wardrobe. She dressed herself in something comfortable, stretched her arms, and jumped onto the featherbed. She pulled the coverlet over herself, letting her eyelids grow heavy until the darkness drifted her off to sleep.

She awoke to a loud knocking on her door. Edit sat up on her featherbed and rubbed her eyes.

"Enter," Edit muttered, still half asleep.

The door opened, and Geder filled its frame. He walked inside, extending his hand to Edit.

"I wish to show you why I find the sea to be so beautiful. I beg that you join me in watching it under the night sky."

Edit, not wanting to make Geder angry with her, accepted his invitation. She walked with him back onto the deck and perched her hands on the side rail. He pointed at the stars that filled the sky and named their constellations.

"Do you see it? That one makes the shape of a rose."

Edit did not believe him; but when she looked up at the sky, her eyes went wide. It *did* resemble a rose.

"Oh! It does..." She hesitated to speak further, but she was growing bored of speaking with a plain tone. "I always wondered how the stars came together to form constellations."

"Do you wish for me to name them for you?"

"No, thank—"

Edit sighed.

"You might as well, Lord Geder."

"Wonderful," said Geder, smiling.

They stood next to each other while he pointed to several constellations, outlining with his finger how the stars made their shapes. He pointed out a sword, a shield, a warrior, the phoenix, and several others that Edit could not keep track of. He continued to name them, and Edit got lost listening to how many he could name. It impressed her, to some degree; she continued to listen and let him name them, for it made her night at sea a little less boring. Geder extended his hand to Edit and waved for her to accompany him. She followed his lead. He led her back under the deck to the rear of the ship. They entered a room, and he walked to a window.

"When I am traveling back home, I prefer this view. It is much easier to see the Kraken. That it is why I made it my bedchambers."

Edit squinted.

"Where is the Kraken?" she asked, holding her finger up as she attempted to trace the stars.

Geder grabbed her hand and put his pointer finger atop Edit's. She stared at the lord with wide eyes while he traced the legs of the Kraken. He smiled at Edit; and for some reason, his smile felt even colder than before. He looked down at her as if he were hungry.

"Do you see it?"

"I—I do," muttered Edit.

"Is it not beautiful, Lady Freihei? The way the night sky shines on the sea?"

"It... It is..."

"Beautiful like you, Lady Freihei."

Geder grabbed Edit's hand, and she froze. He pulled her close, grabbing her at the small of her back. Because she was so surprised, she was not quick enough to pull away when Geder kissed her. Her eyes stayed open, frozen wide and staring through him. He moved his hands lower, making a lewder advance. Her heart raced, and she pushed him off of her.

"What is wrong with you?"

"What do you mean?" asked Geder.

"I am to be betrothed to your nephew. Why would you make an advance on me?"

"I saw how you reacted to the news of your betrothal. You neither know nor care for my nephew."

"That does not matter!" Edit said, stepping farther away from him. "This... This is inappropriate."

"It is certainly not traditional, but what does that matter? I never was treated properly within the traditions of my land, and as I understand it, the traditions of your land have not been particularly kind to you, either. As a consequence, we ought to do whatever we want."

Edit felt the urge to vomit in her mouth. *Geder was insane.*

"I must go back to my chambers," Edit said, her heart pounding through her chest. "I cannot accept that this happened."

"Refuse to accept it, if you like; but tell none of it. They will question your decency if you do," Geder replied, smiling sardonically.

Edit's face grew hot, and she stormed out of the room. She entered her chambers and slammed the door shut behind her, making sure that it was locked. After lying on her bed for an indeterminate period, she sat up; she was unable to sleep. She stared at the wall with deep consternation, shuddering while the thought of Geder making an advance on her was still in her head.

She did not wake in the morning, for she did not sleep. There was a knock on the door, but Edit did not answer. Whoever it was knocked again, harder; yet Edit still did not open her door.

"Edit! Are you well?"

The voice sounded like Ser Elseharde. Edit stood up and walked to the door. She opened it, and she saw Elseharde. He tilted his head with concern at the sight of her.

"You look like you have not had any sleep," he said.

"I am fine. I had trouble sleeping."

"Ha! Well, I did, too. I was partying with one of the sailor lads here. It is a pleasant crew, indeed."

Edit ignored Elseharde.

"What is it, Edit? What happened?" Elseharde asked. "Are you still angry at me for speaking the truth to you in Nara?"

"Elseharde, leave me alone."

"You need to tell me what happened!"

Edit hurled a pillow at Ser Elseharde, hitting him in the face. He stared at it, shook his head and left, closing the door behind him. Edit felt a bit of guilt for throwing the pillow, but she wanted to be left alone, and she did not know how to show how much she needed him to go.

Edit had stayed in her room for several hours. Hunger filled her, but the thought of running into Geder once more scared her away from a meal. She thought of telling Elseharde, but fear of her chastity being questioned brought her an even greater deal of anxiety. What had she done to deserve this misfortune? How ever could there be a man so vile as to make an advance on a girl who was to marry his nephew? Did her father know the type of man Geder was?

There was another knock on her door. Again, she refrained from responding to the knock. Elseharde opened the door with bread and soup. He placed it on her bedside table and pointed at it.

"Eat."

Edit ignored him.

"I will force you to eat it," he said.

Edit glared at Elseharde and continued to ignore him.

"Your father told me to protect you, and I swore to serve him. Believe me when I say I will force you to feed yourself."

Edit mocked Elseharde, using her hand as a puppet and caricaturing his voice with her own. She grabbed the bread and ate a bite of it. Elseharde dragged a stool over and sat down.

"Tell me what happened," he said.

Once more, Edit ignored Elseharde, chewing louder to drown out his interrogation.

"Edit. If something has happened, I need to know."

Edit slurped on the runny soup so loudly that it drowned out his words entirely.

"Dammit, Edit! What is the matter with you?"

Edit stared down at her sheets.

"Geder is a vile man."

"What are you saying?"

Edit kept quiet. Ser Elseharde drew his sword and pointed it at the door.

"I will kill him right now if you do not tell me what you mean."

Edit glared at Ser Elseharde, but his action put her at ease.

"He made a pass at me," she said. "Nothing happened, but I fear what the repercussions might be if word gets out that I entered his room alone."

"Fuck! Are you serious?" Ser Elseharde sheathed his sword and began to pace around the room. "What was the extent of his advances?"

"He kissed me," Edit said, looking down at her hands. "He... well. He attempted to bed me."

"Fucking arsehole," Elseharde spat. "You are not to leave this room without me at your side, Edit. Do not act strangely around him, either. He is a snake. You must treat it as if it never happened."

"Treat it as if it never happened? He attempted to bed me! I am to be betrothed to his nephew! If he were anyone else, he would be apprehended," snarled Edit.

"But unfortunately, he is not *anyone else*. I will inform your father when I see him again, but you must keep quiet about it until then. The people are unlikely to believe your word over the Master Treasurer's, even if you are the Good Duke's daughter. Gol, the people would have an unsavory amount of fun spreading gossip of the Good Duke's only daughter being a tart."

"You are not comforting me at all, Elseharde."

"I am your protector, not your comforter."

Edit waved Elseharde away, hurling head backward onto her pillow. While Edit lay down, Elseharde continued to sit on the stool.

"You will be fine, Edit. Although, there is something far more frightening in store for you..."

Edit lifted her head to look at Ser Elseharde. "Like what—"

A loose cushion was catapulted at Edit. She threw her arms in front of her, and it bounced off of them onto the floor. She furrowed her brows, shaking her head.

"What in Gol was that for?"

"You threw one at my face this morning!"

Edit reached for a pillow to throw at the knight and hurled it at him with great speed. "Do not make me laugh, Elseharde! This is serious!"

Elseharde stared at the pillow she had thrown at him with a dumbfounded expression on his face. "Did you just assault a knight?"

He lifted the pillow and whaled it on Edit. She began to laugh as he did, growing less tense. She grabbed another feather pillow to return blows at her knight.

Venceslaus

he King placed his palms on the Crii table and let out a huff. He was paler than Venceslaus remembered him being in the past; his skin looked as if his blood had been sucked from him. He had a tired, shaky demeanor. Venceslaus told himself that this could have been from the stress of his position and previous sickness—but for his relatively young age, the King looked pitiful. He moved well, but his movements were forced and jerky. It was like he had lost the natural intuition of how to walk.

The Crii covered the topic of the informant for some time with much back and forth. It was inconsequential. No one conceded their position, so they hovered around the discussion until the King exercised his absolute power to move on to the next discussion. The king tapped his fingers on top of the table, making eye contact with Venceslaus.

"The next matter we are to discuss is the Good Duke's involvement with our potential revolts. How do you wish to aid us, Venceslaus?"

Venceslaus furrowed his brow. "I never committed to such an agreement."

"Well, I imagined you would have had a change of heart, no? After Barnut's passing, who else would be qualified to help deal with it?"

Great Marshal Donas looked at Asbyorn with a zealous stare. "It would not take me long to put down a crowd of rowdy peasants."

The King rolled his eyes and turned his head to Donas. "Part of what makes someone qualified to be helpful under such circumstances is their ability to end a revolt before it even starts. You need to be well-liked by the people. That is a quality that you do not possess."

Great Marshal Donas's brows furrowed hard with anger. He stared at the tabletop.

"I fear I cannot help you the coming revolts, m'lord," Venceslaus said. "I have duties elsewhere."

Asbyorn leaned forward, his fingertips splayed and propped on the table.

"*Duties elsewhere?* What of your duty to your King? What foolishness is this?"

Venceslaus laughed. "Are you being serious, m'lord?"

Asbyorn stared Venceslaus down, and Venceslaus rubbed his eyes.

"Have you forgotten the millennia-old oath of fealty my forefathers have sworn to every Narese king since Avon? Have you forgotten the words I said to you on the day of your coronation? When did I ever swear to an oath that said I was to be your reeve? This is absurd. If you truly need men to come to your aid, I will send men your way; but I will not be the face of the problem *you* have caused."

The others in the room stared at Venceslaus, their eyes wide with concern. They must have been astonished at Venceslaus's pluck, for none of them would have spoken out against the King in such a manner. When compared to Venceslaus's name, their fancy titles were, in truth, merely de jure compensations to say that they were at a similar degree of power to the Good Duke. Venceslaus did not need permission to speak at the Crii, for he just spoke. No one had the means to stop him, either. His name was his shield.

"I suppose you simply do not care for the integrity of your kingdom anymore," Asbyorn said. "Why do you even attend these meetings, Venceslaus?"

Venceslaus recoiled. "Why? I have always been present on the council; you, and your father before you, appointed me. Are you insinuating that you wish for me to depart?"

"Aye, I am. I did appoint you, for you were beneficial to past discussions of the Crii; but I believe you have exhausted your usefulness, Duke."

Venceslaus stood up with indignation. "Never would I have thought that I would see the day where the King of Nar would expel a Great Dignitary from the Crii. There is no such custom that would support this. How dare you, Asbyorn?"

Venceslaus shoved his seat back under the Crii table.

"No such custom? Look long and hard at the fashion atop my head," scoffed Asbyorn.

Venceslaus stormed out of the Crii room with Ser Groent at his side, exiting the keep entirely to take a breath of fresh air. Within him arose an anger that rarely surfaced. He rubbed his eyes, trying to ease his stress.

"I am no less shocked than you, m'lord. The King is acting entirely out of custom. He has proven he finds the traditions and precedent of the Crii worthless," said Ser Groent.

"Aye, it puts me in a sour mood. Let us find a place to discuss this in private." Venceslaus rubbed his eyes once more and sighed. "Actually, we ought to find our King's informant."

"Is that not risky, m'lord? The King is very riled up."

"We are already absolved of wrongdoing, so any risk incurred would only be from the murderer himself."

"The King is willing to forego tradition. He might take it as you undermining him, especially since you have been ousted from the Crii."

"That is of no matter to me. I will deal with the backlash once I find out who killed Barnut. I have lost faith in the King's investigation, and I cannot sit by and wait for an answer that I do not truly believe will come."

"I understand. I will follow whatever it is that you will, m'lord."

Venceslaus extended his forearm to Ser Groent. They grabbed each other by the forearms and shook, looking at each other with resolute eyes.

They left the courtyard, passing by the courtyard gates. As they walked past the commoners, their reactions to the Good Duke were no different than they had been before. They shouted his name and praised him. Venceslaus waved to them with a smile. Crowds were strange; they had a mind of their own. At times, they would surround a lord, not allowing them air to breathe; but for Venceslaus, they afforded him ample space.

When they made it to the docks, there was a sea of workers before them. Venceslaus walked toward one of the workers, waving for him to come over. When the worker noticed him, he did not waste time to come and greet the Good Duke.

"Good Duke! I am honored that you have given me time out of your blessed day!" exclaimed the worker.

Venceslaus clasped the man's forearm. "The pleasure is mine. I came here to discuss the unfortunate event that happened yesterday. Do you have a moment?"

The worker looked away. Venceslaus squinted. He was looking at a man that was barking orders at his peers. He turned back to Venceslaus and nodded.

"I suppose I have the time. My boss won't notice that I am gone; but if he does, I hope you can make it right for me."

Venceslaus nodded. "Of course."

He waved for the worker to follow him to one of the docks. Venceslaus pointed at it.

"Have there been any reports of strange activity on the docks? Stories of hasty stowaways, or of ships leaving earlier than planned?"

"Those things happen quite often, Good Duke, almost weekly. You should ask my boss. He would know more than I."

Venceslaus stared off toward the horizon, shaking his head in disagreement. "Do you know who was working the docks yesterday, at around midday? If something odd did happen, it would be more beneficial to have an eyewitness, not your boss, to corroborate our own suspicions."

"Well, I was not present yesterday, but I know someone who was."

"Well, take me to him," said Venceslaus, smiling.

"Did the King's Champion not come here himself yesterday to find a witness?"

"We have some additional questions of the utmost importance."

The worker nodded. "Alright, then. I will bring you to him."

The worker guided Venceslaus and Ser Groent to a man that was busy tossing offloaded cargo onto the back of a cart. He smelled of rotted grass and sweat. He turned his head, noticing

Venceslaus. He smiled. Venceslaus extended his arm forward to shake the man's hand.

"This man here is Emmer," said the worker. "Emmer, this is—"

"You do not need to introduce me to the Duke of High Beak! Everyone knows the only *decent* aristocrat."

"Thank you, lad," Venceslaus said. He knew he ought not to speak further, but he was still rankled by the King's behavior, so he continued. "Most Narese aristocrats are pompous cunts. I should not like to be associated with them."

Emmer burst into laughter, extending his arm out to the wall to catch himself. It took him a moment to regain his composure, but he was eventually able to brush the laughter away and keep his focus on the Duke.

"Apologies. I am not used to nobility saying such things."

"I'm afraid I am not here to revel," Venceslaus said. "Our Great Chancellor was murdered yesterday, and I heard you were working the docks at the time of the murder's escape."

Emmer grimaced. "Yeah, and...?"

His sudden change of attitude was startling.

"And I wish to find the perpetrator. Did you notice any odd events that day, like a stowaway, for example, or a ship leaving far earlier than planned?"

"Eh, yeah? But I was asked these same questions yesterday, you know."

"I just would like to hear it from the source itself."

"Ah. Well, the only ship that left hastily was that funny-talking Aeric Prince's ship. I heard something about that simpleton King insulting him, so maybe he got prissy and killed the Great Chancellor—but I am only a dock worker, what in Gol would I know," said Emmer, slinging another sack into the back of the cart.

Venceslaus shook his head.

"Thank you for your time, Emmer," he said, tossing the worker a coin.

Emmer caught it, shoving it into a purse that hung at his side. Venceslaus walked off and beckoned for the dock worker that had led him to Emmer to follow.

"That lad seems quite critical of the King and his Crii, no?"

The worker's eyes widened. "I—I would not know about such things, Good Duke."

Venceslaus grinned. "Do not worry about me, lad. The King is an arsehole; I do not care what you say of him."

The worker chuckled. "I never heard Emmer say a good thing about a noble. He always complains about them."

"He does, does he? When does this usually happen?"

The worker tensed up. "Uh... I do not know. Every so often?"

"I see. He ought to be careful, for if a noble other than myself had heard him, he could have been in a great deal of trouble."

The worker nodded solemnly. "Right, yes. Thank you for being so considerate, Good Duke. But I'm afraid I must get back to work now."

"Oh, of course, get on with your duties. Mjorn is nothing without the commonfolk," said Venceslaus, smiling.

The worker smiled back and waved goodbye; Venceslaus reciprocated with a wave, then walked away with Ser Groent to the town square. He turned a corner into an alleyway. They loitered there for a moment. Venceslaus placed a hand on Ser Groent's shoulder.

"Ser Groent, keep an eye on that Emmer. See if he interacts with any groups. I do not trust his testimony that it was the Aeric Prinz."

"Who do you believe it was, Vences?"

"I am unsure, but I do have a hunch. If insurrection is truly brewing, then maybe it was the insurrection that killed Barnut."

Ser Groent nodded. "After I escort you back to the keep, I will observe Emmer."

"Thank you, Merr. I will be in my chambers. Report to me with what you find."

The shook each other's forearms and headed back to the keep. Once they passed the gates, Ser Groent bowed to his Duke and turned around. Venceslaus climbed the stairs, journeying down the halls to his bedchambers.

He entered his room and locked the door. He grabbed a piece of parchment and walked over to his desk. Venceslaus began to write down the facts of the murder, starting with the time of the murder, moving on to Barnut's execution, the trail of blood, the escape through the window, the disappearance of the killer into smoke, the lack of impact from the supposed landing, and the alleged witness. He lifted his bone pen up from the parchment and squinted at it, trying to think of possible explanations for each occurrence.

The two that seemed the most significant to him were the trail of blood and the man's disappearance into a puff of smoke. The trail implied that the murderer had come from the throne room, which could support the Prinz as a valid suspect—but that was a stupid assertion. The Prinz did not have a strong enough motive to kill the Great Chancellor. As for the smoke, the lack of impact ruled out any notion of a Terukian smoke device, so, in Venceslaus's eyes, it must have been related to some form of divination. Who could have done such a feat? It would certainly have had to be someone magically adept. From what Venceslaus had seen, teleportation was not a common skill amongst mages. If it was teleportation, then that would further absolve the Prinz; if the murderer could teleport, why would he bother running back to the docks and risk being seen? The perpetrator could have teleported anywhere.

Venceslaus clenched his fists, releasing them to rub his eyes. He had nothing to go off of. He could only wait for Ser Groent to finish his investigation and hope that he discovered another lead.

It took hours for Ser Groent to arrive at the Duke's chambers. The moon was high in the sky, and Venceslaus had refused to sleep. Ser Groent entered the room and tossed a black cloak on a chair.

"The people are certainly unhappy with their King," he said.

Venceslaus squinted. "What came of observing Emmer?"

"It seems that stinky whoreson is the voice of a small group of rebellious chatterers. They were drunk off their arses, celebrating Barnut's death. They called for the King's death next."

"Did any worthwhile information come of it?" muttered Venceslaus.

Ser Groent nodded. "Surprisingly, yes. One of the other gentlemen in the group drunkenly confessed to being the King's informant. They were paid off by an outside source to tell the tale that the Prinz hurriedly left the docks. That fact was true, but the Prinz apparently left because of frustration with the King, not because he was fleeing the scene of any wrongdoing. He saw no reason to stay a moment more in Nara. He had paid for his ship to be held for a few days, for he assumed that the King would not reject his proposal in the manner he did."

"Who was this outside source?"

"I do not have a name, but Emmer did boast loudly that he would see the man once more in a tavern to retrieve his payment tomorrow night."

"We shall go there together, then. We shall dress as commoners and revel with the commonfolk."

"Aye, we shall, though I am concerned about the peasants. Aswold and the King were correct in one thing, at least: there *are* talks of rioting. So be aware that I will not hesitate to drag you out and set us on a horse to Belar upon the slightest hint of revolt."

"Of course, Ser Groent. I am doing my duty as a friend of Barnut, but I understand the times we are in. To think the King wanted me to strike down the coming riots. What a damn fool."

"This city is full of them."

"The *Crii* is full of them. Get your rest, Ser Groent. We must be ready for what is coming on the morrow."

Ser Groent exited, heading down the hall toward his own chambers. Venceslaus changed into a nightgown and tucked himself under his blankets. He rolled to his side, drifting off to sleep. He dreamt of his daughter and only of his daughter. His mind dwelled on unfortunate thoughts. He knew she was safer on her way to Count Adar than she was here: the nobility there wasn't being murdered. But what if something had happened?

The sun shined in his eyes. Venceslaus propped himself up. At his age, it hurt for Venceslaus to get up in the morning. His bones ached, and it felt as if his joints ground against one another. He would often wake up to some new part of his body in pain. He reckoned it was from his tossing and turning at night; he had not been a sound sleeper for a long time. He brushed his old mane with his fingers and stood up. A servant lady was waiting, and he requested for her to start a bath. His nightgown clung to his skin; his worry for his daughter must have caused him to sweat through it. The servant lady had just finished bucketing the water into Venceslaus's tub, so he walked over, dipping his finger in the water. It was warm. She turned around to grab a rag and soap, but Venceslaus put his hand up.

"It is alright. I will bathe myself."

She nodded, placing the bar and rag back down on side table that stood just beside the tub. He dipped his old body into the water, allowing himself to melt in comfort. The warmth of the water relieved him of some of his pain, so he made certain to enjoy the moment. It was the joyful peace of a warm bath.

He lifted himself out of the tub and grabbed a linen to dry himself off with. There were some clean undergarments on the side table. Venceslaus grabbed them and dressed himself. He opened his door, informing the servant lady that he was finished and that she could have the bathtub drained. Rays of sunlight seeped through the window, and Venceslaus walked over to it so that he could bask under it. He tried to think of what to do in the meantime, before he met with Ser Groent in the tavern. Typically, at this time, Venceslaus would be heading straight to the Crii.

He decided to leave his room. He marched down the stairs and crossed through a large, open gate. He used to go to the gardens often with Matnus and Barnut when they were children. They used to play there. They were not bad children, but they did frequently infuriate the gardeners with all their running and hiding. Venceslaus walked past Ava's statue and went straight for Matnus, placing his hand on the base of his old friend's statue. He held his head down in lament.

Adar

dar watched over the dock workers while they started their construction of the new port of Kurembrog. He grinned, his hand brushing the head of the ordustone maul while he reached for the crenel in front of him. His bottle of chausilver honey clung to his hip, bobbing when he moved. Madalbert was at his side, and the old sailor also grinned at the construction.

"I was a bit skeptical at first, but the people's response to the port improvements have been overwhelmingly positive," said Adar.

"Aye. They are also very happy with the payment."

"Usually, the people are impossible to please when it comes to payment," said Adar, grinning.

"That they are. The only unfortunate aspect of the construction is that we are making less money while the docks are being improved—it's slowing down the loading and unloading—but most of the captains at the docks understand the benefit. We only had one captain raise his voice to the new dockmaster."

"Good. I am glad everyone is happy with the construction. I cannot wait for my brother to arrive in the middle of this. He will be impressed indeed."

"Aye, he will, but I imagine he'll also be quite skeptical. He has always been cheap."

Adar smirked. "As is the nature of a man who likes money in his chest."

"I should return to overseeing the construction," said Madalbert, bowing with respect to his liege.

Adar returned the castellan with a pat on his shoulder. "Aye, you may depart."

Madalbert stepped away from Adar, journeying down the steps that led to the keep's gatehouse. Adar looked down at his palms. They were trembling. He opened his bottle of chausilver honey and let it drip down into his mouth. He quickly gulped, feeling a surge of energy erupt within him. He clutched his hammer and stepped away from the walls.

It was early in the morning, and Adar begrudgingly dragged himself to the temple; but before he left the keep, he realized he still had the hammer with him. Huffing with frustration, Adar turned around and went for his room. He grabbed a cloak to wear, draping it around his shoulders in order to keep the hammer hidden underneath.

When he entered the temple, Elder Siemond looked shocked at his attendance. He stared at him until he sat down. The priest regained his composure and continued his recitations. Adar felt the urge to fall asleep, but he refused to do so. In Adar's eyes, if he fell asleep, he would look like a vicious sinner in front of Elder Siemond; so Adar dealt with Siemond's old voice until the recitations were over. After Siemond finished putting his notes and holy texts away, he went to greet the Count, taking a seat next to Adar.

"Hello there, Adar! What... What, er... What brings you back here?"

"No need to hesitate with asking me where I have been, Siemond. You are my court priest; I expect you to push me to attend recitations."

The Elder smiled and placed his hand on the Count's shoulder. "Why have you not been at recitations, then, Adar?"

"You already know why, Siemond. They are boring, and you are going to repeat them to me whenever you bother me in my study anyway," said Adar, smirking.

The Elder grinned. "I suppose. But what brings you here today, then, if you do not feel the need to be present at my recitations?"

"The Lady Anita is angry with me, and I wish to stay out of her way. I do not know what to do in the meantime, so I am electing to have my face seen by my people."

"You do not seem to enjoy being seen," Siemond said.

Adar clenched his jaw. "It is my duty. I must do it every now and then."

Siemond stared up toward the rotunda of the temple. "How do you think Abba will do in the tournament?"

"What does that matter?" Adar asked. "If he trains well, he could avoid embarrassing himself."

"Maric *is* more gifted when it comes to fighting."

Adar glared at Siemond. "Do not dare to ask for Abba to become a priest again. He needs to become strong, not to shrivel away into books. What use is his intelligence if he cannot fend off those fiends from the north? Is he going to kill a drudna with a book in hand? With a pen?"

"Maric is strong, and Abba would be safe in the Acadamy d'Ava."

Adar choked the armrest of his seat. "My boys were born in Kurembrog and raised in Kurembrog. I will not have them live their lives the way my brother and I have. They will both live and support one another in Kurembrog."

"I see. How *traditional*," Siemond said. "Your brother has done well for himself down in Nara."

"Aye, he has, but that is of no matter. It could have been different for him, had he stayed. Different for Kurembrog."

The Elder looked at the Count's back, seeing the hammer-shaped bulge that lumped through his cloak.

"You have the hammer with you," said the Elder, scoffing.

Adar did not say anything. The Elder shook his head.

"You are the sole reason Kurembrog has not fully been embraced by the Phoenix. Every time I try to give you guidance, you shun me. I am beginning to question your faith."

"You question my faith because I will not allow you to take my son?"

"I do not question your faith because of that. It is apparent you are obsessed with the past, carrying that hammer around the way you do."

"I do not carry it with me because of the past," Adar said.

"Then why do you?"

Adar gave Siemond a blank stare. "My... penchant for knowledge has caught up with me. I will die if I do not carry this hammer."

Siemond shook his head, giving Adar a wide-eyed stare. "What are you talking about, Adar? Does this have something to do with that damned witch?"

"Aye."

"I knew this would happen in time. You just could not give her up, could you? I felt my hand grow weaker when I touched that hammer. What is in that bottle on your hip?"

"Chausilver. Mixed with honey."

The Elder huffed out a breath, shaking his head. "You are brewing potions, are you? Do you not understand how dangerous that could be? You endanger your soul and your people for your own selfishness; you must repent immediately. I thought you felt a duty to your people."

"How does penance benefit me, Siemond? I am dying, and my land needs a proper heir. How in Gol's name does *penance* afford me a proper heir?"

"*Gol's name?* Invoking the name of a pagan god, are ye? Yer soul needs to be saved."

Adar chuckled at the priest's slip in accent. "Focus on saving the souls of the whores you persecute. I have more important matters to deal with."

"More important than your faith?" asked Siemond, recovering his neutral voice.

"My children will always be more important than any faith," barked Adar.

The Count shot out of his seat, storming out of the temple with his hands balled into fists. Upon planting his foot on the ground outside the doors of the temple, his knee buckled. Adar fell and clutched his knee in agony. Once he garnered enough strength, he tried to stand up. There was a stick next to him, so he grabbed it and used it to prop himself up. His hands gripped the end of the stick, looking rougher and looser than they ever had before. Repulsed by the look of them, he stumbled again, and once more he clutched his aching knee. He propped himself up and stumbled for the outer walls of Kurembrog.

Once he made it to the outer stables, he beckoned for the stablemaster to bring him a horse. He climbed on top of it and journeyed out of Kurembrog. He rode to the countryside, taking a turn north on the road. His head wobbled tiredly. It was hard for him to keep focused on ride while his energy was leaving him so rapidly. Blue banners with white snakes stood off into the distance. He rode through his village and dismounted at what looked to be a simple home with a tall spire erected in the middle of it. Adar dragged himself through its doors.

The Elder inside was surprised at the Count's entrance, rushing to him in an attempt to provide aid. Adar accepted his help, but once the Elder made the attempt to guide him to the Phoenix, he reared away. Adar's eyes stared at a wooden figure.

"I do not care for the Phoenix. Take me to Esu."

The Elder looked at Adar with shock, but he nodded and guided the Count to the idol of Esu. Adar knelt down, clasping the idol of Esu in his hands and raising it above his head. He brought the figurine back down to his knees and sat with his eyes closed.

"I dreamt that you would come back," said a voice from behind him. "But I assumed it was just a dream."

"I am here; your dream was true," Adar said.

"I have not seen you in this temple in over two decades, Adar. Why are you here?"

"I am making my peace, Elder Tadhg."

"Why now?"

Adar did not respond. Instead, he kept his eyes closed in desperate focus. Tadhg sighed, walking around the room, preparing candles to burn. Eventually, he pulled a rug beside the Count and knelt beside him. He grabbed a figurine of his own and worshiped next to Adar.

"It brings me joy to see you again, old friend, despite everything that has happened."

Adar opened his eyes. Tadhg looked the same as ever: black hair and a long, braided beard that reached almost to his belly button.

"Those happenings torment me to this day," Adar said.

"The Conversion of Kurembrog dealt much anguish to all of us."

"The Conversion was necessary for peace."

"It was necessary for your woman," Tadhg said.

Adar snarled and closed his eyes again, continuing his worship.

"No need to be angered by the truth, Adar. What is done, is done. You know it yourself."

"And what of it? It was the only way to keep my lands safe."

"Your fornication with the Lady Anita Demenstin was the cause of your ills. To keep her—and to keep your unborn son—you had to announce the Phoenix as the sole deity of Kurembrog. If you did not, her father would have come for your head."

Adar choked the figurine. "Refrain from dredging up my past, Elder."

"Accept it, and perhaps you will be saved from Gol."

"If I had not converted Kurembrog, you would have been dead. Whether it was by the hand of my bitter father-in-law or by the damned Ookosi, we *all* would have been dead if I had not done what I did."

"At least you understand your hand in our woes. You always had an honest heart."

Adar lifted up the idol of Esu, and Tadhg left him to worship on his own. About an hour passed, and the sun hung in the middle of the sky. Tadhg returned with candles, placing them around the temple. He went to the base of the central spire. Several stone statues of the Phoenix surrounded it, and in its center, a fire was lit. Tadhg smothered its flames. Adar's eyes opened for a moment, noticing this, but he kept his mouth shut. Tadhg came back around to Adar, leaning on a table that stood behind him.

"Do you remember when we were all lads, you and Geder and I?"

Adar smirked. "How could I not? Every day, I wish I could go back to that time."

"In those days, I thought you would be the one to become a priest. Life does not care for our expectations, does it?"

"No, it does not. Geder was to be Count; I, a priest; and you... I thought you would be found dead in a brothel. Ha!"

Tadhg smiled. "And now you are the Count, I am the priest, and Geder is the womanizer. I laugh about it, sometimes. The changes we three have gone through."

Adar shook his head. "I could never laugh about it. When Geder was refused his inheritance, it changed everything. It changed Osmjornia."

"Geder stopped caring for much of anything after being refused the title of Count."

262

"Our father wanted what was best for our homeland, but he never did show much care for his own children. I pity Geder. Our father pulled the rug out from underneath my brother's boots for reasons I still do not know. At least Geder made a name for himself in the Kingdom of Nar. His position rivals that of even the most powerful Osmjornish noble."

"Aye, it does. But, like you, he renounced his faith to do so."

"I beg you to cease talking of it," Adar said. "I am here now. Geder has chosen his path. I imagine he still worships in secret, as do I."

Tadhg shook his head. "I doubt that. Even before being stripped of his inheritance, he was never the most faithful follower."

"Oh, folly. You never were, either," said Adar, grinning.

Adar began to hum the names of his family and close advisors, refraining from mentioning Siemond and the Baron va Heddi. He held himself in silence until Tadhg touched the hammer that was hidden by Adar's cloak.

Tadhg yanked his arm back. "Why do you carry the Molotokdar?"

"The what?"

"That ordustone maul on your back. The Molotokdar. Why are you carrying it?"

"It helps me deal with the complications I have suffered after my visits to Neta."

"Adar, is that why you look so frail? There is a reason why she was ousted from the temple. She perverted our faith. She uses our methods of healing for her own heedless and nefarious goals. Why have you been seeing that witch?"

"She was our priestess," Adar said. "I longed for our childhood. It felt natural to go back to her."

"But why her? Why would you not come to see me instead?"

Adar kept quiet.

"Adar, why have you chosen to suffer at the hands of that witch?"

"I wished to know if my family would be alright," said Adar, sighing.

Tadhg shook his head. "You never did care much for your legacy; although I suppose I do not know you as well as I once did."

Adar continued to pray to his Goddess. His arms trembled as he lifted the idol again. He shed the Molotokdar from his back, allowing himself the strength to pray. Tears ran down his cheeks. Every so often he would cough and grunt. Tadhg stared at Adar with pity. Tadhg was only a few years older than Adar, but at this moment, Adar sounded like a dying man. He hacked and hacked. His hands trembled once more, so he placed the idol down and reached for his bottle; but before he could grab it, everything went dark. Time slowed.

Then Adar sprung up with electrifying energy. His skin burned, red hot in color. Tadhg snatched his seared hand back, and Adar fell, landing by the Molotokdar. He grasped the hammer, and his skin returned to a normal color once more. Tadhg held the bottle in his hands, and Adar's lips tasted of honey.

"Tell me… of the Molotokdar, Tadhg," muttered Adar.

"You do not know the story of the Molotokdar? Did your father not tell you of it?"

"Nay. There are no records of it, either. What is it?"

"There never were records; its story has been passed down orally for centuries by your forefathers, and it is your duty to tell its history to your seed in turn."

"Then why was I never told of it?"

Tadhg shrugged. "I have no insight into this matter, but I imagine your father refused to tell you after your conversion. I wonder if he told Geder."

"Why would Geder not tell me?"

"I do not know. I can tell you, though, if you would like."

Adar stared at the Phoenic figurines near the base of the center spire. "There will be no need for that. You may tell Abba once he becomes Count of Kurembrog."

"Very well, Adar."

"It is nice to see you again, old friend, but please refrain from speaking to me any further. I wish to make my peace."

𝔄bba

he first thing Abba did when he woke up was check on his brother. Maric was still asleep. His breathing sounded labored, but he seemed much better than he had been the day before. Abba kept his brother company until Ser Mikhail whipped the tent flap open. He tossed Abba his waster and motioned for him to follow him to a ring of rocks that had not been there yesterday. Abba stood at one side of the ring and Ser Mikhail stood at the other. Ser Mikhail nodded to Abba, and the both of them drew their wasters.

Ser Mikhail did not allow Abba to circle him. He kept him in front, and whenever Abba attempted to flank, Ser Mikhail retaliated with his wooden blade to cut off Abba's advance. Abba attempted to circle him again, but Ser Mikhail engaged him, sending strikes with his waster to pressure Abba away. Abba tried once more to attack Mikhail, but the knight's waster struck Abba's hand. Abba released his sword, letting it fall to the ground.

"I won't be fighting the damned *Sword Seer* in the tourney! Why are you making this so difficult?"

Ser Mikhail pointed at Abba's waster, then pointed at where Abba had stood at the beginning of the duel.

"Go back, now. If you think that was any kind of display of skill on my part, then you must read less and fight more," said Ser Mikhail as he returned to where he had started.

He threw his waster out of the ring of rocks. "Get in a guard," he ordered.

"But you have no sword—"

"I said get in a damn guard, boy!"

Abba presented his waster in a high guard. Ser Mikhail walked toward him.

"Grab your waster! This is an unfair fight; I have the reach advantage."

"*Unfair?* Gol, you must learn humility," said Ser Mikhail, strutting toward Abba with the confidence of a badger.

Abba slashed downward, but Ser Mikhail evaded it with footwork alone. Abba once more sent a cut down, but again, Ser Mikhail evaded it. The boy thrust his sword forward, but Ser Mikhail stepped near, grabbed the hand Abba was using to hold the handle of his sword, and shoved the side of Abba's head, throwing him.

"Reach advantage? You have to be able to touch me to have a damn reach advantage."

Abba stumbled to his feet. He slashed his waster again at Ser Mikhail. The knight rolled under the cut and rushed toward Abba. He wrapped his arm under Abba's sword arm, grabbing Abba's shoulder. After he grabbed Abba's wrist with his other arm, with a turn of his hips, a duck with his shoulder, and a reap with his leg, he threw Abba flat onto the ground.

"Do not complain about my methods of teaching, boy. You are always going to be terrible at whatever you do the first time you do it. Such is the nature of knowledge. Now, this isn't your first time fighting, but it *is* your first time taking fighting seriously. I would not expect you to know how to sail a ship if you had never sailed one before, let alone expect you to sail it better than a captain who has had his sea legs since he was a lad. You have a lot of work to do. Accept that."

Abba pushed himself off of the ground. He grabbed the waster that was outside the ring and handed it to the knight before retrieving his own. Ser Mikhail grinned and raised his waster. They sparred that morning until Maric arose from his tent. He coughed heavily, and Abba dropped his waster, running to his aid. His skin was warm. Maric shook his head and lay back down, shucking his blankets away from him. Abba sat beside his brother while he groaned in pain. Maric mouthed *fuck off*, then grinned tiredly, rolling slowly over onto his side and looking away from Abba. Abba stood up and scoffed.

Jergi came up behind him and stared down at Maric. "If he can curse his brother, he can travel. Throw him on the back of his horse and tie the reins to Ser Mikhail's steed."

"He can crawl on his own damn horse," said Abba.

Jergi chuckled, giving Abba a push on his shoulder. "Come on, help your brother."

Abba sighed and lifted Maric over his shoulder. His knees struggled under his weight. Abba's neglected muscles and unconditioned bones ached as he trudged toward the horse. He threw his brother onto the horse's back and went back to his tent to pack. Jergi and Abba did the majority of the packing, for Ser Mikhail sat to the side, jotting something down on a piece of paper. Jergi huffed and marched toward Mikhail.

"What in Gol is taking you so long? Come on and pack."

"Jergi, I am doing my job and writing a report about the anomaly. I will help in a minute."

Jergi shook his head and stomped away. Abba finished packing his tent and then went to work on his brother's. Once he had finished, he attached the packs to their respective steeds and mounted his horse. Ser Mikhail finished his writing, quickly put away his tent, and mounted his horse. As soon as everyone was ready and mounted, they continued to travel east down the road and away from Pelesgeb.

By the next day, they had finally crossed into the eastern half of Osmjornia. Vast fields of green stretched up to the horizon while sparse trees peppered the landscape. Abba lost himself, staring at the landscape. He was used to the dense forest near the coast; he had never seen so much open land. They did pass by a few villages, though Ser Mikhail preferred to camp out in the open fields, saying that he would rather train with Abba where it would not disturb the locals.

A few nights passed. In the distance, there was a stretch of brush; and to the south, where the Kyln river flowed from the mountains in the east to the Mjornish coast in the west, there was an even thicker forest. Along the road there was shrubbery.

Once, they came upon a young, thin woman. She had her palms up, begging for help. She pointed off to the side of the road where man lay on his back, clutching his side.

"Please help my husband! I beg thee for help!"

Abba went to dismount, but Ser Mikhail put a hand up to him.

"Stay on your horses, lads," said Ser Mikhail, turning to the woman.

The knight dismounted his horse, keeping himself within three sword lengths away from the woman. While she begged, she inched forward, holding her hands out as she tried to pull the knight's hand toward her.

"Come! Why are you not coming! Are you devoid of empathy? Come here!"

"Keep away, miss! What happened to your husband?"

She stabbed a dagger at Ser Mikhail's face, but he blocked her arm, shoved her in the face, and grabbed her wrist. Ser Mikhail hugged his other arm underneath her shoulder from behind, making sure to pressure his head in the space between her shoulder and head. The 'husband' stood up and ran for Ser Mikhail. The woman tried to pull her arm back, so Ser Mikhail let her, pushing her hand back to her stomach, following with a yank and twist to send her to the ground. He kicked her away from him, and the man swung at Ser Mikhail with a club. He stepped away, narrowly avoiding the swing, and whipped out his dagger.

Three other men emerged from the bushes around them. Ser Mikhail wrapped his arm around the man's club arm and stabbed him in the torso with his dagger, throwing him onto the woman. He pulled out his longsword and readied it into a guard. He held his blade high while the men rushed him. They attempted to circle him, but Mikhail made sure to keep the dead man in between them. One of them stepped over the body, and Ser Mikhail rushed him, quickly cutting down the man while he stumbled over his comrade. Another went for Ser Mikhail. He had an axe and round shield, and he pursued the knight with his shield covering him well. He swung at Ser Mikhail, and soon after, the other man was behind Ser Mikhail, readying his sword to strike. Jergi just stared while Abba dismounted his horse. He pulled his steel sword out of his sheath and ran to help Ser Mikhail; but by the time he had reached the knight, Ser Mikhail was already pulling his sword out from one of the two men he had just killed.

"I told you to not dismount, Abba!" yelled Ser Mikhail.

"I thought you were going to get hurt!"

Ser Mikhail shook his head. The knight seemed to stare off behind Abba for a moment, but he brought his eyes back to the dead. The woman crawled out from under the dead bodies and ran away, wailing.

"You reckon we should go and grab her? She did try to kill us."

Ser Mikhail shook his head. "No, let her run. If there are others, she can let them know not to terrorize anyone else on this road."

He turned his head back to the four dead men.

"Three of them are Ookosi, but the supposed *husband* is not. I would say these are just highwaymen, or maybe a very poor band of Ookosi raiders. Get back on your horse, Abba. We must keep going."

Abba nodded, returning his sword to its sheath. Ser Mikhail and Abba mounted their horses, clopping on the road forward. The horses reared away from the dead, whinnying once they grew near.

"Woah there!" said Ser Mikhail, patting the mane of his horse. "Don't worry, girly. They can't hurt ya."

Abba stared at the dead men on the road.

"Ser Mikhail, how did you know it was an ambush?"

"I didn't."

"Then why were you so cautious?"

"Greed and desperation manifest in any way imaginable. You don't know how often people die attempting to perform a good deed."

Abba grabbed his reins and leaned back. The wind gently strung along the grass beside the road, and the rays of the sun forced Abba to squint. He had begun to sweat, but he was unsure of whether it was due to the heat or the anxiety from the sudden ambush.

They made it to the woodlands. Their horses trotted gingerly along the road, passing through a few more villages on the way. The locals would often greet them with quick hellos and goodbyes while they rode through.

Maric started to twitch. He raised his head and groaned, gazing around him. He bobbled on the back of his horse like a limp sack of potatoes. He looked down at the horse's legs trotting below him.

"Ugh, my back hurts," grunted Maric. "You could have... you could have sat me behind one of you."

Ser Mikhail halted his horse, dismounting. He patted Maric's face and sat him upright. Maric flopped back down and groaned once more.

"You can sit up by yourself, Maric," said Ser Mikhail.

"He shouldn't have eaten that damned fruit," complained Jergi.

Ser Mikhail gazed off into the sky and pointed to a plume of smoke. After a brief moment of obvious thought, he beckoned the others to follow.

"The smoke is in the direction of Woldhom. But that plume is quite large, no?" said Jergi.

"Aye. I wonder what they are burning," replied Ser Mikhail.

Jergi turned his head to Abba. "What are your thoughts on it, Abba? What do you infer?"

Ser Mikhail raised a brow at Jergi, but then he looked back at Abba as he also awaited a response.

"Er... I dunno. We will have to see once we get there."

"I like that response. Never assume you know a situation before seeing it," replied Mikhail.

"Eh, it lacks experience," said Jergi.

Ser Mikhail shook his head. "No, I think you are mistaken. Enough experience will lead you to understand there are many explanations for every event."

"Where there is smoke, there is fire. Why would there be fire?"

"No one could know for certain until they got there."

"But one could infer. It could be a campfire, a burning building, or even a wildfire."

"Maybe you can make inferences like that in the field of finance; but as a warrior, it is a quick way to die."

Ser Mikhail drew his sword and pointed it forward. He reached for his helmet and put it on.

The town stood still. No one roamed the streets. A single building was ablaze. A body, mutilated and dismembered below its ribcage, rested on the road at the entry of the hamlet. Ser Mikhail stared at it, frowning deeply at the sight. He dismounted and used his sword to shift the head of the victim to the side, shaking his head at the sight of the corpse's face. Abba rode past body, wincing in anticipation of seeing the wound; but there was nothing there. There was no blood. Instead, skin stretched from underneath the ribcage where there should have been spilled guts and broken bone.

Abba heard rustling, and he turned to look behind him. Maric was awake. He stared around the village, lifting his head up to do so.

"Where're all the commonfolk?"

Abba and Jergi dismounted. Maric attempted to dismount as well, but his weak arms collapsed under him, so he clung tightly to his horse instead. Ser Mikhail knocked on a door. No one answered, so he attempted to open it. It did not budge. He pushed on it, waited a moment, and then stepped away only to slam his foot into the door. It opened. Abba peered inside behind Ser Mikhail. It was empty, so Ser Mikhail went to the next building, and then the next building, and then the next building.

Abba walked through the first door Ser Mikhail had opened. How could the door be so stuck if no one was inside? He looked around, making sure not to touch anything that he was not supposed to, for he felt strange enough searching through someone else's home. He looked out of one of the windows. The wood frame around it was chipped and scratched. There was a thick slime on it that seemed to imply something had been dragged *through* the window.

Abba left the house. Ser Mikhail was walking toward the burning building, so Abba joined him. It was a round stone-brick building with what had probably been a thatched roof before it had caved in on itself. Some of the bricks were collapsed inwards, too, and a moaning could be heard inside. Abba went forward to get a closer look through the bricks, but Ser Mikhail grabbed him by the forearm and dragged him back to his horse.

"Get on your horse."

"Why'd you pull me away?"

"I don't trust it."

"Do you think those Ookosi marauders had something to do with this?"

"I do not know."

"There was moaning coming from inside that burning building," Abba said, turning around to try to look back at the village.

"Abba, listen: *never stick your nose in a stinking pile of shit.* Something very odd happened here. We are leaving."

They mounted their horses and rode through the hamlet. Abba had not noticed it before, but there was a trail of blood and flesh that led away from the burning building and toward the dismembered body, but it disappeared about a quarter of the way there. Had it crawled out? Had the wound healed somehow? The thought made Abba's skin feel strange, as if bugs were crawling all over him. Maric groaned again, stretching out his arms with such a great intensity that he almost fell off of his horse. Abba scowled at him, slowly shifting his gaze back to the road.

They rode for another several hours. The sky grew dark, so they set up camp for the night. Ser Mikhail announced that they would reach Belar the following day. Abba felt himself growing nervous at the thought.

The next morning, Maric looked much better. He was up and packing his own tent. They mounted their steeds and set off. Maric seemed to be habitually looking behind him. Was he fascinated by what had happened in Woldhom, too? But he had barely even been awake then; how could he be so interested now? Abba tried to keep an eye on him, but for some reason, staring at his brother began to make him feel uncomfortable, so he shied away. Ser Mikhail and Jergi rode in front, keeping their eyes on the road in front of them. In little time, they saw big gray stone walls on the horizon.

Ser Mikhail raised both of his hands to the sky. "Welcome to Belar, lads! Behave well here; this town is large, much larger than Kurembrog."

They rode to the gates. The guard halted them, extending his palm.

"Do you have your pass?"

"Aye," Ser Mikhail said, reaching into his satchel to hand the pass over.

The guard looked over at it, nodding. He handed it back. "Two groschen a head."

"*Two* groschen? That is double what the commonfolk pay," said Jergi.

"You lot don't look like commonfolk to me," replied the guard, snickering.

Ser Mikhail tossed the guard a bag of coin and rode past him.

"Petty whoresons," he complained. "They will make any thug a guard in Belar."

"Belar is too large and too poor to have guards of any quality. The damned Kylns keep all their money tied to the mines and ship it downriver," said Jergi.

Once they were inside, Abba gazed around. There was a well and a few wagons spread about. The only guards he could see were standing at the gates; once they passed through, they could go about without the prying eyes of a guard on them. Abba looked around. He did not see any spires. Usually, the temple was much more visible in a town—but maybe this one had grown too big.

A man of a similar age to Jergi stood in the distance. As they neared the merchant square, the gentleman held his arms out wide. He wore dark blue trousers and a tunic, both with green stitching. His hair was short and black while his face was clean-shaven. He smiled wide, white teeth behind his lips. An older man stood by his side. His lips moved, mumbling something to himself. He was bobbing a purse up and down with an almost infantile fascination on his face. Ser Mikhail gave the gentleman a quick forearm shake and nod, whereas Jergi embraced him, making small talk during their greeting.

"The Kylns welcome you to Belar!" said the man, his gaze shifting to Abba and Maric. "You two are Adar's boys, yes?"

"Aye, we are. Who are you?" asked Maric.

Abba scowled at his brother.

"I am Hedmond Kyln, Regent of Belar. When I saw you in the last Osmjornish Diet, you were not this cheeky, Maric…"

"Was that not around eight years ago? I would have been half as old as I am now," Maric said.

Hedmond ignored his comment. "Hello there, Abba! How have you been?"

Abba paused, looking at Maric. "I have been well. How have you been?"

"Wonderful. You lot have rooms in the keep. I will meet up with you later to talk about the tournament, yes?"

Ser Mikhail nodded. "Aye."

Althalos

lthalos's stomach grumbled. The soup he had eaten earlier that day was doing little to fill him now. He grabbed his gut, applying pressure to distract himself from the pain. He felt oddly cold, even though the sun was sending wrathful heat to his skin. On the surface, he was unquestionably feeling the heat; but there was also a strange internal chilliness that he had never felt before. He felt more sluggish than usual as well. He assumed it was because he had eaten almost nothing at all that day.

Gunter pulled out the dagger that hung from his waist and ventured deeper into the woods. Althalos followed his lead. After walking for a while, Gunter stopped, pointing at a long, narrow streak of stamped-down leaves with his dagger.

"Ye see that, boy?"

Althalos crouched down. "They're leaves."

"They're *tracks*. Have ye never hunted, boy?"

"Hunting is the business of huntsmen and lords. I am a peasant."

"Those lords bleed the same color as ye and I," Gunter said.

"Are you saying I should just go out and poach? I would be imprisoned, or worse."

"I've not been caught yet," Gunter said. "I'm goin' to go find a chokepoint in the tracks. Follow me and learn a thing or two, boy."

Gunter followed the tracks, stepping by putting his heel down first, then rolling his foot forward until his toes touched the ground. After walking for several yards, they found that the tracks led between a pair of boulders. Gunter grinned while he looked around him. There was a patch of milkweed; he scurried off to the patch and plucked some. He wrapped a few of them together, forming a makeshift string. Scattered around the woods, there were a few small saplings. Gunter gathered a few twigs. With his newly collected materials, he began to assemble some form of trap in between the boulders. He placed the remaining twigs and milkweed into Althalos's hand.

"Make a snare, boy."

"I do not know how," Althalos said.

"I just did it right in front of ye. Are ye blind or somethin'?"

Gunter yanked the twigs and milkweed from Althalos and placed them down. He carved small lips into two of the smaller sticks, then he went to a sapling that had sprouted along the tracks. His fingers looped a string around the top end of the sapling branch and tied the other end onto one of the smaller sticks. With some of the remaining milkweed string, he tied a noose and attached it to the small stick that was tied to the sapling. Afterward, he stabbed the other small stick into the ground and pulled the stick with the noose to anchor it onto the stick in the ground. The sapling branch bent as he did, bringing the string into tension. He propped the noose open with some sticks and pointed at the trap.

"See here, boy. Very simple. It looks just like the other one. We will make several of these and place them all 'round these tracks so we can eat. Go on and make a few more."

"Sure, Gunter."

Althalos walked off and pulled out his hatchet. Once he had collected enough sticks from the saplings, he went for the milkweed. He tied the milkweed into thin strings, much like how Gunter had done. He placed everything he had collected in front of him, staring at them while he attempted to remember how to assemble the snare.

First, he found a sapling along the tracks; then he used his axe to cut lips into the smaller sticks. He anchored the one of the sticks into the ground and tied the other to the sapling. He brought the string into tension by hooking the lipped sticks together, taking a step back to look at his creation.

He cursed at himself, for he had forgotten to tie the noose. Althalos tied some more milkweed string into a noose and attached it to the snare. He turned around. Behind him, Gunter was lying at the base of a tree. He was sound asleep and snoring. Neither of them had slept that night, but Althalos only realized he was tired when he saw Gunter sleeping. He sought a tree trunk of his own to rest his head on.

Suddenly, the sun was shining in his eyes. Gunter was jumping around hysterically, a dead rabbit in each of his hands. Althalos rubbed his eyes. When the mercenary realized Althalos was awake, he strutted over and held the carcasses in front of Althalos's sleepy eyes.

"These aren't the only ones, boy! We got a few more. We are eatin' tonight!"

Althalos smiled. He stood up and wandered around, collecting firewood. He placed some stones in a circle and attempted to light a campfire with a stick and fire plow he had made from some wood he'd chopped. With manic haste, Gunter rushed over and yanked the fire plow and stick from Althalos's hands.

"Yer goin' to get us killed, boy," said Gunter, digging his hands into the ground.

"What are you doing?"

"I learnt a thing or two in the war. There was a man who taught me how to start a concealed fire. Those Harferd whoresons will be searchin' for smoke in the sky, so we have to make sure they don't see ours."

He continued to dig the hole into the ground. Once he finished, he dug another hole that fed into the main hole. Afterward, he moved the rocks that Althalos had placed around the top of the main hole and tossed some firewood in it. He handed Althalos the stick and fire plow and walked back to the trunk he had rested his back on before. Althalos set the fire quickly. Gunter raised a brow.

"So ye *can* do somethin' yerself," he snickered.

"Are you going to gut the game, master hunter?"

Gunter dragged himself up, snarling. One by one, his dagger cut into the skin of the small game. He removed the fur and disemboweled them, walking over to a small stream to wash their carcasses. Althalos blew air into the fire to keep it going, and Gunter came back with a few clean strips of meat in his hands. He stabbed each with a wooden stick and stuck them over the fire.

A few strips of meat were left to the side, for there was not enough room over the fire to cook them all at once. Althalos stared at the fire; memories of his friends, mother, and village flickered like flames in his mind.

"The meat'll be done cookin' soon, boy. No need to stare down the rabbits."

"What is war like?" asked Althalos.

"War is war. Whatever you think of when you think of the word, it is worse."

"What was the Yhournish war like?"

"Do not ask me about that," Gunter said.

Althalos stared into the fire. "Why are you helping me?"

Gunter shrugged. "Well, ye can't even kill a man who killed everyone ye ever knew. Ye were goin' to die if ye went by yerself."

"But why does that matter to you?" asked Althalos, turning to face the mercenary.

Gunter, too, stared into the fire. "Pay no mind to that, boy."

Soon, the rabbits and squirrels were fully cooked. Gunter passed a piece to Althalos, and they began to chew. Once they had filled their stomachs, Gunter went back to setting snares around their camp. Althalos walked over to a tree trunk that had split and fallen over. He took out his axe and cut off a chunk of wood. While he sat beside the fire, he went about chopping away some of the wood from the chunk he harvested. He chopped it down to a small rectangular prism. Normally, he would have used a whittling knife for something so small, but the axe would have to do. He chopped away the top of the wooden prism into something that vaguely resembled the head and beak of a bird. Below it, he chopped into it a torso. It was hard to get the fine details in with the axe, but the general shape was there.

"Why're ye whittlin' one of those birdmen?"

"Viantse? I dunno, I am just fond of Ava."

"*Fond of Ava?* He left us. All the shite we have to deal with today is because of him. What happened to *Dorthu* is because of him."

Althalos stopped his carving. "My mother always had positive things to say about him."

"Well, yer mother—" Gunter stopped himself. "I was there when that... barbarian king, or whatever he was called, was killed. I saw that bird fly right off after. They said Ava himself killed him, but they never found a body. They said Ava was the strongest ma—*thing* that ever lived, but he left his own kingdom to suffer rape and murder. They…"

A tear ran down Gunter's cheek. He stared into the fire, wiping it away almost as soon as it had formed. Althalos cut some more material off of the wood block, and soon the legs of the small carving of Ava had taken shape. The mercenary walked into the woods. Althalos made sure not to stare.

After some time, he finished the general shape of the carving. Gunter had still not returned, so he stood up and walked in the direction Gunter had gone, his body scraping through branches and shrubs. Before him was a small creek, and Gunter's sword rested on the rock bed beside it. It was clean of any blood. Gunter was slinging rocks across the water.

"Ye should wash that axe, boy. Even if ye did not draw blood yerself, it will still paint ye as a less-than-decent lad."

"The blood will stay. It is proof."

"Ye look like a crazy axe murderer with it."

Althalos grabbed a stone and slung it across the water alongside Gunter. He skipped it twice over. Gunter scoffed at his achievement. The mercenary's next rock skipped thrice over.

"Competitive, are you?" Althalos asked.

"I survived many battles by bein' a better fighter than others."

"Makes sense," said Althalos, skipping his next rock four times over.

"Heh."

Gunter sent a rock out across the creek. It skipped ten times over.

Althalos shook his head and dropped his rock to the ground. He sat down by the water. Gunter joined him. He still felt cold, but after eating, his body had thankfully begun to slowly recover its heat. The sun still baked them. Cattails surrounded the creek. Small rabbits hopped around on the other side and came to the creek's flowing waters to drink. A large stick slammed onto Althalos's lap. He spun around, looking for where it had come from. Gunter stood above him with a stick readied at his face.

"We are fightin'."

Gunter whacked his stick on Althalos's thigh.

"What in the Gol—Gunter!"

Althalos stood and thrusted his stick forward, but Gunter slapped it down and whacked him hard.

"Ha! This is why I am helpin' ye, boy. Ye are a shit fighter."

Althalos sent a cut with the stick at Gunter's stomach, but Gunter bashed it aside and pushed Althalos back.

"Good," said Gunter.

Althalos sent a flurry of strikes at Gunter, but he blocked them all.

"Stop," Gunter said. "Ye are shite at the sword. Ye need to learn yer basic guards."

Gunter held his hands near his head with the stick's fictitious blade pointing behind him.

"Day. Repeat it," said Gunter.

"Day," repeated Althalos.

The mercenary fully extended his arms above his head. Althalos did the same.

"High day."

"High day," repeated Althalos.

Gunter brought the stick down to his side, the tip of it pointed forward toward the ground.

"Night."

"Night."

Gunter nodded his head. "Good. When ye thrust yer blade forward, have yer front foot step forward with it. Also, do not cut straight up and down like ye are; it is easy to block. Cut at an angle."

Althalos nodded and readied his stick up into Day. They fought each other. Bout after bout, Gunter bested Althalos. In their next duel, Althalos grabbed Gunter's arm with frustration.

Suddenly, his cheek felt raw. Althalos shook his head and looked around to see what he was hit with, and he saw another palm being sent to his face. He winced back, letting go of the mercenary's arm.

"Why are you slapping me?"

"Why are ye *grabbin'* me? We are swordfightin', not wrestlin'. I won't be tossed by ye, boy."

Althalos shook his head. "I was only making it fair. You were winning."

"Ye mistake why we are swordfightin'. Ye aren't supposed to try to win here; ye are supposed to swordfight. Ye can already wrestle fairly well, but why in Gol would that matter if a man can stab ye?"

"But if it helps me, should I not then wrestle?"

"Oh, my—quit thinkin' about wrestlin', boy. Ye won't get better at swordfightin' if all ye do is wrestle. Ye must fight with a sword to be good at the sword."

Althalos readied his stick up into a guard. "Fine."

They sparred for about another half an hour or so until the sun fell low. The two threw the sticks to the ground and returned to the campfire. After putting out the campfire, they picked up what little belongings they had. Althalos pushed dirt back into holes they had dug for the fire pit.

"Good thinkin', lad. We shall travel at night from here on out, so we have the benefit of the dark."

The pair continued to walk off into the forest, avoiding any roads. Gunter would always make sure he was a distance away where he could see it, but not too close to where he would not be able to hide. Whenever a caravan, a group of soldiers, or even a noise came from the road, Gunter would stop and yank Althalos by the shoulder to the ground with him. They would drop to their stomachs and hide behind some form of cover. Gunter's eyes always had a manic anxiety to them; he seemed to know fear intimately. Now, like before, Gunter's hand never left the handle of his sword. Althalos thought of Gunter's mannerisms a bit differently now; for if this bombastic mercenary was so brazen as to do the things he had done the day prior to help Althalos, then he would have surely made enemies in the past.

After long hours of walking, Althalos saw a tall hill in the distance. The top of the hill shone bright with the light of dozens of torches, all spiraling their way up to a walled fortification. Gunter stared at it for a moment; then he spat on the ground and walked toward it.

"Why did you spit on the ground?" asked Althalos.

"I fuckin' hate Feninwich. Have ye ever been, boy?"

"I never left Dorthu, except one time to Fisk—but that was barely even a visit."

"Why didn't ye kill that cunt back there? He killed everyone ye ever knew."

Althalos looked down. "I have never killed a man before. I froze."

"I'll have to drill the bitch outta ye, boy."

"What is it like to kill a man?" Althalos asked.

Gunter's neck tensed. He turned his chin away, tapping his fingers on the pommel of his sword.

"Well... I never enjoyed it. But it does feel a lot better than havin' your people killed."

"I would imagine you are right about that."

As they grew closer to Feninwich, travelers became increasingly common. Gunter's manic expression returned. It seemed that they were doing more hiding than walking; it felt like every time they took two steps, Gunter would force them to wait for some indeterminate amount of time. They walked. They hid. Althalos cursed under his breath, growing annoyed with Gunter's caution. The mercenary's eyes darted around like a squirrel watching for predators.

"If they were headin' for Nara, those bastards would have gotten to Feninwich before us. They had horses, and we took too damn long to get here. We'd best stay away from that hill. They're probably waitin' at the gate, ready to shoot an arrow in our chests."

It took them a great while to journey around Feninwich. Constantly going up and down the hills put great strain on their legs. Because he refused to take a rest, Gunter kept going on the path, and Althalos showed no sign of wanting to stop either. Guards with torches patrolled the roads. They stared deep into the woods every so often, as if something very important lurked deep within. Althalos and Gunter did not want to take the chance that it was them they were looking for.

The pair made it past Feninwich without being stopped by an ambitious guard; however, Gunter still did not ease up. He would frequently look behind him at Feninwich, triply making sure that no one was following them.

Raindrops tapped Althalos's face. Off of the road to his left, there was a cave. Althalos pulled on Gunter's arm.

"We should get out of this damn rain."

Gunter went to pull his arm back, but he stopped once he realized that it was in fact raining. He conceded and followed Althalos to the cave. They peered inside, searching for anything hiding within. Thankfully, there was nothing there.

"I will take watch," said Gunter.

"Alright. But when you feel the need to sleep, wake me up so that I can take the next watch," Althalos said.

Gunter smirked. "Shut the fuck up. You would only get us killed."

Meara

he man tossed Meara into a room and locked the door. She pulled herself up to a sitting position, staring at the dust from the ground that clung to her legs. The room was mostly empty, except for a single sack resting in the corner. The ground was hard and did not help to take the ache from Meara's bones. Muffled shouting and musical instruments could be heard from behind the door. Meara wanted to rest, but because of the loud noises and conditions of the room, she just lay down and stared at the cobweb-covered ceiling above her.

The door slammed open, and the brute that had dragged her into the room stood in its frame. She instinctively pulled herself back into the corner in an attempt to get away. He crouched down and grinned at the girl, grabbing her arm. Meara yanked her arm away from him. She shivered with fear; the man's grip was like a vise. He yanked her over to him.

"You killed one of my men, you bitch. You caved the bastard's head in. You *owe* me."

She could feel herself shaking. She tried to pull herself back to the wall.

"Ha! You're not gettin' away from it."

He yanked her to her feet, led her out of the door, and dragged her through the halls. The music and sounds grew louder. He passed through a door. Before them was a scene of excess lechery.

There was a group of men sitting on benches and chairs, all of them obviously drunk, and several women stood at different points throughout the room, chained by their wrists. Most of the women's eyes were devoid of any emotion; they moaned, but the noises they made sounded manufactured.

Meara stumbled back, trying to pull her arm from the man's grip, but he grabbed her by the back of her head and forced her to stare at the room. Tears formed in the corners of her eyes. She winced, blinking the tears away, and turned instead to glare at the large man with proper contempt. A few of the women looked in Meara's direction. Some gave her looks of pity, but others clearly could not even summon that emotion.

"You will pay back with what you took," said the man, "and you won't complain."

Meara tried to look away again, but the man's hand forced her to view the room.

"Don't look away, lass. That's you! That is how you will pay me back," said the man, grinning. His breath was hot on the back of her neck. "What's your name, lass?"

Meara could not speak. For once, she felt she understood what it was like to be Gol.

The brute snickered. "Won't matter soon, anyway. You're to get a new name. We will make you a proper woman here, lass; but first, you will act as my servant."

He shoved Meara through another door. Inside the room was a woman sitting on a stool. The brute pulled another stool next to her, putting his hand on Meara's shoulder to forcibly push her down to sit.

"This will be your mentor, lass. Her name is Leisa. Listen to whatever she says. She is one of my favorites."

The man walked away from them. The woman painfully maintained a smile until he left the room. Once he did, her eyes darted to Meara, her smile instantly disappearing. Her expression was transformed by sorrow. It seemed she too pitied Meara; but Meara found it difficult to look at her, and so she decided to stare at a wall instead. Meara shivered, but she did not know whether it was from cold or fear.

"What is your name?" Leisa asked.

Meara refused to answer.

"You do not need to speak to me," said the woman. She reached out a hand, moving as if to touch Meara's hair. Meara reared away from her.

Leisa leaned in. "But please, just do as they say. If you don't, it will only make things worse," she whispered.

Meara scowled at the woman and moved away, still trembling. The woman did not stop her.

"I have seen many girls come here. Some came willingly, but most did not. I have always felt sorrow for them. Those who disobey Hrodert, no matter whether they come here by choice or by fate, are all punished the same. Please, if you wish to survive, I beg you to just do as he says," Leisa said. "You are filled with an angry fire; I can tell by your eyes. It is not an easy life here for any of us, but if you fight—I am going to beg you once more, please just do as they say. You will not last long otherwise."

It was not worth Meara's time to talk to this woman. Each time Leisa pleaded with her, it brought the taste of vomit to her mouth. Hrodert was no different than Luka. This woman, and all the other women, were just like the orphans; they clearly thought it safer not to seek their freedom, and instead had spent their lives slaving for someone who cared nothing for them.

"Hrodert can be very nice," Leisa said. "Just do as he says, and you will see."

Leisa had empty, lifeless eyes. They looked like as if someone had stolen them from a corpse and placed them in her living eye sockets. They were like gray pebbles, entirely devoid of life or shine.

Leisa handed Meara a pair of shoes. Meara refused to take them. Leisa insisted, trying to shove them onto Meara's feet.

"You can't walk around here without shoes," insisted Leisa, smiling.

Meara frowned at her.

"Hrodert will wonder where you got the shoes, but you can just tell him they were from me! He will understand."

Meara gritted her teeth and kicked the shoes off her feet. She understood what the woman was trying to do, and she wanted no part of it. This woman was *nothing* like her. She was not Meara's friend or confidant. Meara despised this woman and her weak attempts to make her like her—to make her *weak* like her. Leisa stood up and grabbed the shoes, handing them to Meara.

"Please, take them. I know what it is like to be in that room that you were in, and to walk these halls with nothing on your feet. It is belittling. It makes you feel as if you are nothing. Please, just take the shoes."

Meara turned her head to the woman with a curled lip. "Belittling? They use you, and you think a lack of *shoes* is belittling? I never had shoes when I roamed the streets; but at least out there, I was not tormented by those foul men. You make me sick."

Meara turned away, keeping her distance from the woman.

"It is going to happen anyway," Leisa said, her voice pleading. "There is no getting around it. Accept it, and you will at least be allowed to keep some of your dignity. It is much better to do it willingly so that you can keep something so simple as a pair of shoes. If you do not behave, then you will be treated like less than shite. Lass, use your head!"

She was no different than the children who would take any opportunity to appease Luka: the ones who were given a little more bread than the others; the ones who told him what he wanted to hear; the ones who repeated the same words Luka had barked at the other children. If she was to be plucked from one tyrant's flock and placed into another, she would be the same person. Meara would not tolerate a life like Leisa's.

She looked around the room for anything that she could use to escape. Leisa placed her hand on Meara's own.

"Please do not try to leave. I suffered greatly from a past attempt of my own. There is no leaving this place. It is much better than out there, in any case! You never have to worry about starving." She clasped her hands around Meara's thin arms. "It is terrible to go through life not knowing when your next meal will be. Here, you will always be fed! You will always have water and shelter from the elements. It is not as bad as it seems."

"Stop talking to me," Meara snarled.

The woman frowned, shaking her head. "Your disagreeableness will be the end of you, lass. I warned you what would happen if you didn't listen. You may leave the room and find your way back to Hrodert."

Meara stormed out of the room. She hoped she would have a chance to just hurry out of the building, but once she passed through that door, several men armed with clubs and messers turned to look at her. She was being watched. If she were to try to escape by running past them, she knew she would end up dead, or worse. She walked with small strides, looking around to take in the room before returning to Hrodert.

It was large, with many curtains. There were various recessions in the walls, likely where the working women would bring the foul men that visited this place. She noticed only one door. A guard stood in front of it. Whenever someone would knock, he slid open a peephole and decided whether or not to allow them entry. This usually involved the handling of some coin, the guard sometimes pocketing some for himself. Other guards kept an eye on the customers, making sure they were not damaging the working women; or at least making sure that they would still be healthy enough to continue working.

Meara recognized some of the visitors. Several of them were loiterers that hung around the town square or the Phoenic temple that gave refuge to orphans. They stared at Meara like perverted and hungry dogs. If a visitor got too rowdy, perhaps from drinking, or just from their despicable nature, a guard would toss them out. None of them drew their weapons. Maybe it was because all the customers were unarmed, or maybe it was because drawing blood would bring a mess bigger than the blood itself.

One of the guards stared at Meara with a furrowed brow, pointing his chin at a hallway. Meara took it as a sign to keep moving. She went back down the hall, past the small room from which she had come. Past that door, Hrodert was sitting down at a table. There was a slice of meat on his plate—a steak. Meara only ever eaten meat a few times in her life, but she had often smelled it when traveling through town. At times, she had thought about stealing some, but it did not make sense to do so; she had nowhere to cook it. Placed next to his own was another plate of steak. He noticed Meara and smiled at her, pulling out the seat next to him. He waved her over, and she slowly walked to the table and sat down. She stared at the floor.

"Come on, lass. I am not a terrible man. See, I have made you some food. Please enjoy it with me."

Meara refused to pick up the fork and knife that sat next to the plate. Hrodert looked down at her feet. He grimaced, then shook the expression away.

"So, you did not accept Leisa's gift? When I spoke to her about bein' your mentor, she seemed very excited to help you *acclimate* to your new home. It would have been better if you had just taken the slippers, lass."

Hrodert would put emphasis on the words he used that were longer or more obscure than average. It seemed he enjoyed *sounding* higher class, but he was surely nothing of the sort. Meara refused to answer; she also refused to eat. Hrodert grabbed the fork and shoved it into Meara's hand, closing her fingers around it.

"Eat, lass. I did not make this meal to have it go to waste," said Hrodert.

Meara reluctantly started to eat, partly out of fear, and partly because she was truly hungry. The steak tasted better than anything she ever had before. She found it hard to *truly* enjoy it with everything that was going on around her, but she attempted to do so. Hrodert smiled and continued to eat his steak. Some time after the two of them finished, Leisa walked in and took their plates. Hrodert smiled at her.

"Thank you, Leisa." He turned to Meara. "How did you like it, lass?"

Meara did not answer.

"You will soon begin to answer me, lass. If you want to continue to enjoy *delicacies* like this, then you will need to do as I say. Leisa! Put the slippers on her feet."

Meara recoiled. Leisa walked over and shoved the slippers onto her feet. Meara tried to kick her hands away, but the brute's hand wrapped around her neck.

"Put them on. Be thankful for my kindness."

Leisa tied the laces of the slippers on Meara's feet.

"Say thank you, lass."

Meara refused. Hrodert tightened his grip around her neck. She felt her airway begin to constrict, so she desperately opened her mouth. A gargled *thank you* escaped Meara's lips as she tried to form words. The man immediately released Meara and smiled at her.

"Of course, lass. I am always glad to help. Unfortunately, you will now have to go back to your room. I believe you need some time alone to think of how fortunate you are to have come under my protection. Leisa, escort her."

Leisa grabbed Meara's arm and dragged her back to the room. Once Meara was inside, Leisa closed the door. Meara immediately unlaced the shoes, kicking them off. She would never accept a gift from that pervert. She thought of the stories she had been told about girls her age being taken and put in places like this, but she had never thought that she herself would have been taken.

There was no sunlight in the room. It was windowless, more like a small closet than a room of any real size. She felt herself growing ever more tired. Over time, she began to lose all sense of it. It felt as if she had been left in that room forever.

Her restless mind tried to think of things to do. She began to throw the shoes at the wall, but soon enough this grew boring. Every so often, one of the women would peek through the small peephole in the door, but never did they try to open it or speak to her. Meara imagined they were only checking to see if she was still alive. Sometimes she would try to listen through the door, but it always sounded like the same disgusting cacophony one would hear in a brothel. There was never any quiet in this place. Whenever they fed her, they gave her scraps; but that was no matter. Meara was a street urchin. Hunger was something she was used to.

Eventually, the door did swing open. It was Leisa. She looked at Meara's feet and gasped, rushing to put the shoes back on her. Meara scurried away but Leisa grabbed her by the leg and yanked her near.

"Please do not refuse this gift another time. Hrodert will be very angry with you if you do. And his anger is something you do not want to bear, I promise you that."

Meara, annoyed with going through the same routine once again, allowed Leisa to put the shoes back on her feet. She pulled Meara up and led her through the doorway, walking her out to the common room to show her around.

"This is where you will spend most of your time," she said, pointing around the room. "But, if you are really lucky, the visitors will like you and want to spend more time with you."

She pointed to the recessions in the walls that were blocked by curtains.

"If that happens, you will take them to one of those room while one of the guards accompanies you. Hrodert makes sure we are all safe here," Leisa said, smiling.

The more this woman spoke, the more Meara could not stand her. She stared around at the women in the room. They were busy with the very actions Leisa had alluded to. Meara turned her eyes away and instead gazed around the room in search of an exit. She was stuck. It suddenly dawned on her; perhaps Leisa's *mentorship* had all been designed by Hrodert to break her spirit. Meara gripped her hands into tight fists.

"What are you looking at, girl?" Leisa asked.

"I'm—I am only looking around. I have never been in a place like this before."

Leisa nodded. "Yes, of course. It is certainly something to get used to."

She grabbed Meara by the hand.

"Follow me."

Leisa took her to the front door.

"Do not think you will be stuck in this room forever! If you behave well, you will be able to leave and go about the town as you like," she said, the same unnatural smile on her face. "But do know—it is the law here to carry a card such as this with you."

She pulled out a small piece of paper. It was a prostitute's card; it had Leisa's name on it, denoting her as a prostitute, as well as the names of a few others that were referenced as witnesses of her profession.

"But do not go near that Phoenic temple. The followers there will recognize you and berate you. They are very intolerant of our profession."

She pulled Meara away from the door. Meara stared at it. She longed for escape. She longed for *freedom*.

Leisa brought her once more to the back of the building, taking her through the women's dorms and showing her around.

"It is unfortunate that you are so young," Leisa said, "but that means Hrodert will care more about keeping you safe!"

Meara shuddered. The more she thought about it, the more certain she became—Hrodert had told Leisa to speak to her this way; to desensitize her to the brothel, and to bribe and frighten her into listening to him. She refused to pay any more attention to this broken-minded woman.

Leisa brought her back to Hrodert. When he looked down and saw that Meara was wearing the slippers, his grin stretched from ear to ear.

Edit

hey landed on the shores of Kurembrog. Edit stared at the white walls of the castle with awe. It was far windier up in Kurembrog than it was in the south, where the winds gently pushed the waters up onto the sandy coasts. While the ship was coming to port, Edit noticed the docks were under reconstruction. A crowd of workers were huddled around what looked to be the location where a new dock would be built, lugging stones and wood posts. Geder looked astonished at the number of men assembled to work on this grand project.

A man with a cloak was waiting at the wharf when they docked. He a bit older than Geder, with thinning skin and graying hair. His back looked as if it were beginning to hunch forward.

"Adar?" Geder said, his accent becoming sharper.

Geder climbed down the gangplank and hugged his brother. Edit frowned. If this was Adar, the father of the man she was to marry, then she surely could not imagine being happy with his son. He looked old and decrepit, his facial expression very severe.

"Is he ill?" Edit whispered to Elseharde.

"I have no idea," Elseharde whispered back. "From what your father told me, he is a good bit younger than Lord Geder; but he looks much older, doesn't he?"

Edit stepped down the gangplank with Ser Elseharde. Adar splayed his arms wide and embraced Edit.

"Ah! You must be the Good Duke's daughter! I hope you had a comfortable journey," he said. He had a much thicker accent than his brother.

"Thank you, m'lord, I did," Edit said. "You have a wonderful land here. I can tell that you administer your duty as Count with great care."

She was lying. Edit already knew she could not stand the winds of Kurembrog. She did enjoy the walls, but the lands around her seemed dull, even though it was summer. She could tell the Count was satisfied with her response, however. He perked up when she said the word *duty*.

"I thank you for your kind words. I try my best," said Adar.

Edit smiled. "My father seems to like you well."

"For that to come from your father is indeed a high compliment. He is a man of great renown and admiration."

"When it is my time to take my seat at Bek d'Lifa, I will rule just as my father did."

Adar's face shifted—he made a noise that almost passed for a cough, but that could have been a half-disguised laugh. He turned to Geder.

"It has been far too long, Brother. There is much that we ought to discuss. Madalbert, guide the lady and her knight to their quarters."

Adar said this in Osmjornish. It took Edit a moment to figure out what he had said, for she was not used to speaking their tongue; but she had studied it relatively extensively in Bek d'Lifa. Her father had thought it important for her to know the languages of the world, being that most of their wealth had come from foreign sea-trade.

The man she assumed was named Madalbert nodded, and Geder walked off with his brother. Madalbert brought them forward and off of the docks. Together, they walked through the city. Edit had to lift up her skirt repeatedly so that she would not step in any of the cow shit that littered the streets. The people here looked no poorer than the people of Nara, but no richer either.

Madalbert led them up to a gate. Past it was a drawbridge and another gate up top. The climb was steep. Once she made it to the top, she stopped to lean on a wall, for her ankles ached. Madalbert urged them along with haste. Edit was sick of all this stomping around and traveling. Almost a week ago, she had been hurried into a room in the citadel of Nara; now she was being hurried into a room in the keep of Kurembrog.

When they reached her room, she went straight for the window. Resting her forearms on the windowsill, she stared out into the waters. She thought of the sun, bright and beaming down onto the crystal-clear waters of Bek d'Lifa. She remembered the sight of townsfolk walking around on the white sand beaches. Her longing for home grew more and more severe. She blinked. She saw the dark blue waters rushing for the rocky shores of Osmjornia. She sighed, and Elseharde walked over to look out of the window with her.

"What are you sighing about?" he asked.

"I long for home, Elseharde. I hate that I have been dragged here to do something I do not want to do."

"I long for Bek d'Lifa as well."

Edit turned to him. "Why did Lord Adar laugh when I said I would rule Bek d'Lifa just like my father?"

"Heh. You need to learn more about the world, Edit," Elseharde said. "The Osmjornish would not be very happy if a woman held a seat of such power."

Edit grimaced. "Does he think that his son will take High Beak from me? He must be a fool. My father would never agree to that."

Ser Elseharde frowned and stared at the waters below. He was sulking, Edit realized, his expression surprisingly adorable—he really must have wanted to go home, too. But her gaze lingered for a little too long; when he turned, he looked like he had felt her eyes touch him.

"Are you alright?" Elseharde asked.

"Of course," Edit said. "Why would I not be?"

"You were staring."

"Am I not allowed to stare?"

"I suppose it's alright. A bit creepy, but you have always been a strange one," said Elseharde, smirking.

She pushed his shoulder. "Shut up."

"Yes, m'lady," said Ser Elseharde, going cross-eyed.

"Oh, quit it! You have become a fool this past week. Go talk to one of the other knights. I want to brood in peace."

"Unfortunately, I can't," he said. "We have to depart for Belar soon. We will only stay here for a night; by dawn, we will be riding out to a small inland port on the Kyln river to row toward Belar."

"So, I have to wake before dawn? I was hoping to finally get some real rest now that the world isn't bobbing up and down."

Ser Elseharde chuckled. For a time, he left her by herself in her room; but once she was ready to leave, he was ready to do his duty as her protector. The day was unremarkable. They had already eaten lunch on the ship, for they had arrived past midday. One of Adar's plentiful courtiers guided Edit and Elseharde around the town, giving them a tour. The town arose within her a natural loathing; it was almost like a darkened and dirtied rendition of Bek d'Lifa.

When the night grew dark, Edit and her knight returned to the keep for supper. In attendance were Edit, Ser Elseharde, Count Adar, Countess Consort Anita, Pyre Elder Siemond, Castellan Madalbert, and many other courtiers that seemed to hold some sort of significance. The table appeared to be made out of the same wood that the lumber stacked in the dockyard had been made of. Several golden candelabra gave them the light they needed to see their utensils before them. A man dressed in a white apron came around with wooden plates in hand, sliding them onto the table and spacing them about evenly in its center. Count Adar stood up.

"Good evening, everyone! I am pleased to share another meal with you all today. It is an even further honor to be sharing this meal with the Lady Freihei, her sworn protector, and, of course, my dear brother Geder, who just arrived in Kurembrog today. I wish for you all to treat our guests from the south as your kin. Now, we shall pray for our blessed supper."

Adar sat down in his seat and closed his eyes, keeping his brow downcast at the tabletop. Everyone else had held their heads down in a similar way as Adar. The Elder Siemond stood up and led them in a religious recitation. He told stories that any Mjornfolk would have known, for they were said before every meal. He told stories of when the Prophet Avon, long ago, had gone through starvation during his time as a slave under the ruling High Viantse. Edit had heard this recitation so often that she had learned to tune it out until the food had been served. When Siemond finished his recitation, everyone said their thanks, and the white-aproned man removed the lids from the platters he had placed around the table.

"Do enjoy the Osmjornish boar! It tastes much better than the boar of the south."

Edit and Elseharde chuckled. She looked over to Geder, who sat to the left of Ser Elseharde. Geder was staring at the ground, visibly trying to contain his laughter. Eventually, he erupted, and his brother patted him on the back until the laughing subsided.

Edit felt something touch her shoulder. Wincing back, she noticed it was just Elder Siemond. He gave her a welcoming smile.

"So, you are the young lady to whom Abba is to be betrothed? A good Narese girl! A proper follower of Phoeni too, I presume?" He spoke Narese.

Edit shrugged. "Well, I have always tried to be a proper follower. I attend my recitations."

The Elder nodded. "Good. At least you have heard the words of our prophets. Kurembrog is the only half-proper town in all of Osmjornia; all the rest are tainted by heathen influence. Personally, I am from Avonsgatte."

Ser Elseharde grinned. "You don't speak like you're from Avonsgatte. You speak too *proper.*"

"Ha! Of course I speak properly! I was taught in the Academy d'Ava itself. I used to be quite the ruffian when I was younger; but as I grew and learned, I realized that the world was ill, and that that illness needed to be addressed with the utmost seriousness and caution."

The Elder continued to ramble with zeal, and Edit just nodded in agreement to avoid any admonishment. She stared over at Elseharde, trying to make it clear on her face that she was begging for a reason to leave. Ser Elseharde grinned, almost as if he enjoyed the sight of her being annoyed. Glaring at the knight, she looked back at her meal. Loud music was being strummed and pounded in the hall. The commotion made Edit's muscles tense. The music of the south was much subtler.

She leaned over to Ser Elseharde, whispering to him. Together, the two of them stood up and left the hall.

"Do you actually have to relieve yourself, or are you just sick of them?" Elseharde asked.

"They are too loud," Edit said. "I wonder what a Osmjornish wedding would sound like."

"I can guarantee, at least from what I have heard, that Osmjornish gatherings do not get much quieter than this."

"Gol! I dread it."

"Maybe you can convince your future husband to allow you to stay in Bek d'Lifa."

"*Allow me?* I will do as I please."

They walked through a doorway that led to a rampart that overlooked the coast. Edit stared at it for a moment, but the dark sky and waters arose within her unpleasant thoughts, so she elected to turn around and gaze upon the bailey. The temple in the town looked to be a nearly identical reconstruction of a temple she had passed in Nara while she was on her way to the citadel.

"Have you been to Kurembrog before? Or any of the other Osmjornish states?" she asked.

"No, this is my first time this far north. I was knighted only recently. Until this trip, I had not traveled far from Bek d'Lifa."

"Where do you come from, Ser Elseharde? I do not think I have ever asked you."

"I am from a small hamlet a little ways north of Avonsgatte," said Elseharde, grinning. "We don't speak like those nutters, though. Fortunately."

Edit giggled. "They are quite brash with their language. A very crude people, no?"

Elseharde looked down. "Crude like the Yhournish who raped them. It is difficult to truly blame them for how brash they are; I imagine only the toughest of them survived after Avonsgatte fell to those savages."

"That Elder Siemond seemed far too mild-mannered to be from Avonsgatte, then," Edit said.

Ser Elseharde shook his head. "Do not share that I spoke of him in such a way, but that bastard is probably of a noble family and used the Academy as a *justified* means of fleeing from Avonsgatte's defense. They left us and our families to be slaughtered."

His expression sharpened, and his lip curled. Edit looked over at Elseharde, placing her palm on his forearm.

"Are you well, Elseharde?"

Elseharde turned around to look back at the bailey. "When I was but just three years of age, I saw my father murdered in front of me. And my mother... Those damn Yhournish brutes did worse to her. I did not become a knight to go north, Edit. I became a knight so that I might one day go south and kill as many Yhournish savages as I can."

Edit grabbed Elseharde's hand. Elseharde shot a glance at her, his filled with concern, and pulled his hand quickly away.

"I thank you for your comfort, but if anyone were to see us holding hands, they would assume lechery."

Edit took Ser Elseharde's hand again. "To Gol with them. Let them assume. You saw your family slaughtered; you deserve some comfort."

Ser Elseharde stared down into the crevice that stood between the motte and bailey.

"Thank you, Edit. I never knew such a rich brat like you could be so kind," said Elseharde, slyly grinning.

Edit slapped his shoulder. "I will comfort you, but I will also hit you for the stupid things you say."

Elseharde smiled. The two of them held hands and watched the happenings in the bailey, gravitating closer until their hips were touching. Ser Elseharde looked at Edit with concern, but Edit just smiled and leaned in for a kiss.

Elseharde jumped away, eyes wide. Edit could almost feel his anxious heartbeat pounding the air between them. She stepped closer again, but he stepped away, looking down into the crevice below them and sighing with frustration.

"Edit, your father would hang me. I would be stripped of my title and forced to leave Bek d'Lifa. I *beg* you. Be mature and respect my wishes. You are a wonderful lady, but it would be inordinate for me to accept your advances."

Edit frowned, flicking a pebble that rested at the top of a crenel into the water below.

"Not only does my status restrain me from doing what I want, it also restrains those around me from doing what they want," she said. "Everyone believes status is power, but really, it is just a chain, a hindrance on my freedom. I wish I could do without it and be free. I will never be able to do what I want. It is as though my will means nothing."

"There is no way of getting around it, Edit. You are a lady. You have a duty to your family that you must uphold. It is dangerous for a lowborn like me to meddle with the affairs of lords and ladies."

"I am tired of you telling me about duty," Edit snapped.

She stared down at the water in the crevice. Its ripples were illuminated by the torchlight above, like a wavy, dark rug with dim yellow-orange swirls on its surface. She flicked another pebble into the waters below. When it landed, it made even more ripples.

Ser Elseharde took her arm and pulled her away, leading her back to the keep.

She could feel herself blushing, but her heart had stopped racing so quickly. She hunched over with disappointment and embarrassment. He brought her back to her seat at the table. The Elder was up talking to the courtiers about faith, and when Edit walked back in, he gave her a wave. She dragged her hand up, waving back.

The Countess beckoned her over. Edit looked to Elseharde, and he nodded. Following Edit, Ser Elseharde stood at her side while she took a seat next to the Countess.

"Hello, Edit," she said in Narese, a friendly smile on her face. "Welcome to Kurembrog."

"Lady Anita, thank you," Edit said. "I was not aware you spoke Narese."

"Speak it? I am *from* the Kingdom of Nar. My family has land on the border that the Kingdom of Nar shares with my husband."

"So, you're long used to the climate here, then," Edit said.

"Certainly. How are you enjoying it thus far?"

"Oh, it's wonderful here."

Anita chuckled, looking down at the pork on her plate. She picked through it. The meat was untouched. She placed her fork back onto the plate.

"No need to tell a small untruth, Edit. Bek d'Lifa is far more exciting and beautiful than anywhere in Osmjornia. Also, don't tell Adar, but the Narese boar tastes far better."

The grin on Anita's face seemed to invite honesty.

"I would much rather be in Bek d'Lifa than here, if I am to be honest," Edit said, smiling tentatively. "It sounds like you have been to Bek d'Lifa before. When were you there?"

"Oh, I never have. I've been to Nara once, and the beaches there were beautiful; they said Bek d'Lifa was even more appealing. Osmjornia has its points of beauty, but it is often overcast, and the weather here never gets as warm as it does down there. The grandest thing about Kurembrog is that its walls are painted white…"

It was hard to find a wrinkle on Anita's skin, and her eyes were not glassy and cloudy like Adar's. There were no spots of gray in her dark brown hair. Almost everyone around Edit, other than Elseharde and Anita, had raven black locks.

"Do they not whitewash their walls in your family's lands? It is very common in High Beak to do so."

"Oh, no. My father's castle is quite small, not grand like those in the south."

Edit fiddled with the fork in her hand. "You're a noblewoman, as am I. What is it like to have your life arranged for you?"

"What do you mean?" asked Anita.

"Well, arranged by your father with marriage and all."

"Ah," Anita said, a knowing smile appearing on her face. "My father was not the sole decider of my fate. In fact, it was mostly my own doing that led me to be married to Adar; my father only finished the deal. But do not fret, young lady. Abba is a nice young man with a pure heart and a thirst for knowledge. I imagine you will find him quite interesting to talk to."

Edit nodded. She closed her eyes and rolled them beneath her eyelids. Then she looked at the Countess and smiled.

"I cannot wait to meet him," she said.

Anita placed her hand on Edit's shoulder and returned a smile of her own.

Adar came over and whispered something into his wife's ear. She stood from her seat and followed him out into the hallway. Edit stayed back and observed the room. Even with Ser Elseharde by her side, she felt alone. If this had been her family's hall in Bek d'Lifa, she would have felt no discomfort in reveling with her lady friends and other courtiers while drinking wine and eating seafood from the Bay of Avon. She could not motivate her legs to dance with the people here, and she could not convince her hands to shake the hands of others. The nearest reminder of home was Ser Elseharde, and after what had passed between them, he had kept himself closed off and cold.

Indeed, she was alone.

Adar

dar pulled his wife away, going into a side room. Geder awaited the two of them. The room was small with a few chairs scattered about, three of the chairs surrounding a small table. Adar sat down on one of the chairs.

"Please, sit," said Adar, his voice raspy.

His wife and brother both sat next to him.

"Adar, you look horrid. What happened to you?" Geder asked.

Adar nodded. "That is the matter I wish to address. We must talk about the inheritance of Kurembrog and the rest of my holdings." He coughed as he finished his sentence.

"Adar... what are you insinuating?" asked Anita.

"I feel as though my muscles are now thread on bone, and that my bones are nothing but brittle twigs. My body is decaying. I am dying."

Geder shook his head. "Stop this madness, Adar. You are scaring your poor wife. What illness do you have that is so terrible you could not recuperate from it?"

"I would not dare bring up the idea of succession to you if I did not believe it necessary. You more than anyone are aware of my integrity, Geder."

Anita stared dully at Adar. "Integrity? Yet, such integrity could not keep you from seeing that beldam."

"You have been visiting Neta?" Geder asked.

"She is the last thing that remains from my great sin," said Adar.

Anita hunched forward, covering her face with her hands. Adar attempted to lift himself up, reaching for his cane. Geder tried to help him, but Adar shooed his hand away, using the walking stick to carry his weight. Anita looked up at him and glared. With regret, Adar stared at his feet. He tapped his cane onto the ground.

"It will be set down in writing that Abba shall inherit Kurembrog. There will be no question of it. My heir is chosen."

Geder shook his head. "How long do you think you are for this world?"

Adar removed his bottle from his belt and held it up, feeling the weight of it in his hand. "Not long."

Anita erupted from her seat and fled from the room. Geder placed his hand on his brother's shoulder, patting his back; then he walked away from Adar.

"Stay, Brother," Adar said. "We can discuss this matter further without my wife."

"What else needs to be discussed?"

"Once I die, the proselytization of Kurembrog bears no significance. I wish for you to tell your nephews of their religious heritage. I would hope you'd bring Tadhg to aid with this."

"Heh... You want that promiscuous priest to inform your children of our forefathers' faith?"

"You *will* have Tadhg inform them of their heritage," Adar said. "They must know the treachery I have done so that it will never happen again."

"The Pyre Elder out there won't be too pleased with that."

"Then do not tell him. He shall be ousted and replaced by a Dievic priest once Abba is crowned. As for—" Adar huffed. "As for the other advisors. Inform Abba that Madalbert and Ser Mikhail may stay."

"What of Jergi?"

"If Jergi has not been arrested by the time of my death, then I wish for you to inform Abba to look for a more *prudent* treasurer."

"Arrested?" Geder asked. "What do you mean, arrested?"

"It is but a hunch, for now; but I suspect malpractice."

"I am the one who taught him the art of bookkeeping, and I have always known him to take his trade quite seriously. I have no doubt that he would be willing to cross someone in some other manner—but with bookkeeping? I do not believe it."

"We both know our preconceptions may lead us astray from the truth, Geder. I have not yet arrested him, because there is no hard proof of it—but the records do not make sense," Adar said. "In any case, I must get to my study. Enjoy the rest of the dinner. Give my apologies for my absence to Lady Edit."

"Alright, Brother," Geder said, furrowing his brow.

Adar stood and left the room. He walked up a staircase that led to the hall his study was attached to, passing a door that exited onto the keep's outer walls. After looking around to see if anyone was nearby, he walked down the stairs and toward the bailey. Once he entered the bailey, he mounted a horse and rode once more out to the countryside. His horse galloped in the direction of a large rock that overlooked the Kurem coast. A man in robes stood on top of the ridgeline; he was smiling at the sight of Adar's arrival.

"Adar! I am pleased to see that you have truly decided to go through with this."

"Do not congratulate me, Tadgh. I gave you my word, so I must fulfill the duty I have given myself."

Tadhg looked out at the sea. The sky was peppered with stars. Adar's legs shook while he tried to walk down the ridge. Tadhg grabbed his arm, guiding him down to the shore. Adar's boots stomped on the dirt below him while he stumbled around in an attempt to maintain his footing. Tadhg's feet were bare. The tide almost reached Tadhg's toes, so the pair halted to watch the waves. Adar grasped onto Tadhg's shoulder while he kicked off his boots, shedding his cloak next. It took him a moment to build up the courage to remove the bottle from his waist and the hammer from his back.

"Even in summer, Osmjornia is still terribly cold at night," Adar said.

"Ha! You'd think that being born and raised here would've made you used to it by now. Wait 'til you get into that cold Kurem water!"

"Gol... fuck that. But I must, I suppose," said Adar, stripping himself to just his tunic and trousers.

"Keep your braies on. I do not want to see a noble cock."

"As if you didn't see more cocks in one day in those brothels than I did in my entire life," snickered Adar.

Tadhg put a finger up. "I came for the women! It is much different. If I could avoid seeing a cock, I would."

Adar patted Tadhg's stomach while he shivered from the cold Kurem night. "You even made your gut so large to avoid seeing your own!"

"Oh, carry on, Lord Cunt."

Adar shot a glare at Tadhg.

"I said carry on, Lord Count!"

Adar erupted into a fit of laughter. "I missed having you around, Tadhg!"

Tadhg grinned, leading Adar into the sea. They journeyed from where the tides tapped their toes to where their knees were submerged deep into the waters. Adar shivered, but Tadhg did not waver to the cold. The priest scooped some water into his hand and poured it over Adar's forehead.

"I wet thy forehead in preparation of washing your vices from you. May your vicious thoughts be cleansed from your mind and may you return wholly to your faith. I beg that Esu may accept that forgiveness is suitable, for the sake of your soul when you enter her dream."

He scooped to more handfuls of water and poured each of them over Adar's arms.

"I wet thy limbs to cleanse the wrongdoings they have dealt to others, and I wet them to cleanse the wrongdoings you have dealt to yourself. May the fornication, thievery, and idolatry of a lesser god over Esu, and your war against your own soul, be forgiven. I pray your soul will be saved from Gol."

Elder Tadhg stepped to Adar's side and held him at his back.

"Adar! Accept Esu as your true Goddess once more! Commit yourself to doing right by your faith and soul! Proclaim your faith and reject your vices! Do you accept?"

"I accept!"

Tadhg dunked the Count into the water below, holding him under. Right as he began to squirm, Tadhg ripped him from the sea. Adar huffed air into his lungs, unable to fill them fully. Tadhg must have noticed Adar struggling to breathe, for he dragged him back to shore and grabbed the bottle Adar had placed on the dirt. He popped the cork from it and poured a drop of the chausilver honey into Adar's mouth. Adar's desperate breathing slowed down.

"Breathe, Adar. Stress will only kill you sooner."

"I am soon to die, and I must make sure my children are prepared. I cannot afford *not* to stress, in my situation."

"Your blood deal with Neta is what's draining you of life," Tadgh said. "Stress will make your heart race and quicken your end."

The water steamed off of Adar while his skin grew hotter. He dove for the maul and held it in his hands.

"You—you gave me too much. Barely a drop can be consumed, or else I will suffer even worse symptoms."

"It is a shame that the time you have left is so short," said Tadgh. "I have missed you, friend. Keep the bottle and maul nearby. Hopefully, you can come to terms with the mistakes you have made in your life."

Adar sat and stared into the water. Tadgh joined him, and together, they gazed into the Akos Sea. Thoughts knocked on the door of Adar's mind, thoughts that Adar had long shut the door to. Memories of when he was first lustrated. He remembered the joy of that day. He remembered studying his faith, and he remembered discussing the differences between his and Anita's religions with her when she first came to Kurembrog with her father. He struggled to stave off his tears. His last happy memory was when he had met with Anita that one night after returning from the war; little did he know that it would ruin what he would have expected to be his happiest memories going forward. His wedding with Anita, the birth of Abba, and the birth of Maric were all tainted reminders of his past.

He looked at his hands. He could not blame anyone but himself, for the forced proselytization of his people was of his doing. The imprisonment and expulsion of priests who refused conversion were by his cause. It still astonished him how an innocent act of love when he was young could have produced such an unfortunate outcome. He was hated, and he deserved it.

Elder Tadgh placed his hand on Adar's shoulder. "What are you thinking about?"

Adar looked up. "I am mourning my long-dead soul."

"You did what you could, no matter how vicious or terrible it was. You are seen as a traitor to the faith by many—but even if that is true, it does not matter now. I remember when you first met Anita. She was a good lass then, and she is a good woman now. You can not blame a young man for pursuing someone so perfect for him."

"That love has condemned men to death."

"Either way, those men were condemned to die: either by war or by holding onto their faith. Anita's father would have attacked our lands. Though I am not a proponent of thinking like this, fewer people died because of your conversion. You have condemned yourself to be hated. I know your heart well, Adar. You have suffered enough."

"My actions were vicious. I am past forgiveness for what I have done to you and the people of Kurembrog."

"Forgiveness is not for you to be concerned with," Tadgh said. "It is Esu's responsibility. Quit your sulking and focus on what you must do with what little time you have left. You were the catalyst for the perversion of the Dievic faith, but now you can be the catalyst for its purification. You are the gate to Osmjornia, and you have the power to influence all the lands connected to the Kyln river. You can revert the faith back to what it was, to what it ought to be."

"I suppose. But I cannot do it myself." Adar faced Tadgh. "I want you to guide my children in healing Osmjornia. I will write in my will that you hold the authority over their religious teachings. If I pass before I return, Ser Mikhail will hold my will. When I reach him in Belar, I will hand it over to him."

Tadgh's eyes were wide. He bowed his head to Adar. "Thank you for this honor, m'lord."

"Tadgh, you may call me friend. No need to refer to me as your lord."

"Thank you, friend. I will escort you back to Kurembrog. You ought not to travel alone."

Adar attempted to move his limbs forward, but they were still weak. Tadgh grabbed his arm and led him up the ridge. When the reached the top, they noticed a strange event unfolding before them. Yards away from their feet were several dead rats surrounding a living snake. One rat was left standing. It leapt at the snake with ferocity. The snake lunged for the rat, but its fangs missed it by a hair and only bumped the rat away. The rodent turned for the snake and jumped for its slender body, chomping into the flesh of the snake. It writhed and squirmed until the rodent lost hold, lunging once more. It missed, and the rat lunged for its head, sinking its teeth in. Unfortunately for the snake, it could do nothing to get the rat off at this point. The rat viciously kept its jaws tight on the snake.

"Astonishing," Tadgh said. "I have never seen a rat fight a snake and win."

Adar stepped forward. He knelt behind the dead rats and stared at the rodent while it kept its maw around the snake's head. The snake was azure in color, a species native to Kuremdod. The rats were all albino and stood out in the dark grass. Upon further examination, the rat that had killed the snake was the smallest of them all. Not a hair on it was harmed.

"Nature is odd, isn't it, Tadgh?"

"Nature is nature. It is mankind who has made it to be odd. If you look at the world, the strangest things are what men do, building cities and the like. Nature has presented a beautiful story before us."

"Beautiful? I reckon it is quite sad. The rat's family is dead, and the lone rat must continue to live knowing this unfortunate event. I reckon if that rat were a man, it would not last long."

"It is beautiful because that rat, against all odds, was strong enough to take down the snake. The fact it is the only one to survive means it is special. Rats that will spawn from this one will be quite hardy."

Tadhg helped the Count up once more and guided him down the road back to the white walls of Kurembrog. The wind of the night chilled Adar, and he regulated his temperature by relaxing or tightening his grip on the Molotokdar. Specks of yellow-orange flame flickered in the distance. Once they made it to the steel portcullis of the easternmost gatehouse of Kurembrog, Tadhg stopped in his tracks.

"You do not wish to come into the city?" Adar asked.

"I cannot step within these walls so long as you still live. That Elder Siemond will find a way to lop my head off."

"I understand. Safe travels to you, friend."

Tadhg bowed to the Count and turned around, walking toward his hamlet. In Kurembrog, there were not many peasants walking the streets at this hour, but there were a few wanderers. Adar did not shy his eyes away from them; he waved to them. For most, their response was an instinctive disgusted look that morphed into a false smile. Some of them even waved back at their Count. Despite Adar's frail condition, he was in a joyous mood. He did not hasten his strides; he took a longer route, for he wished to look at his bailey one final time before he left for Belar. He even waved to his guards, which were the same guards he had always rushed past when he was once unwilling to talk. The chains he had placed upon his own wrists had disappeared after his immersion into the Akos, dissolving in its waters. He looked at his life with an old, revitalized light. It had been far too long since he had talked to Tadhg, and he was gladdened by it.

He walked up the drawbridge to his keep, walking through its many doors and halls until he returned to his room. Anita was there, waiting on the edge of her bed. She glared at Adar, but her expression quickly morphed into one of confusion.

"Why are you all wet?"

"I was in the Akos, my dear wife."

"You went for a night swim? In this state? You could have drowned."

"No. I was lustrated."

Anita put her hands over her face. "I cannot blame you for it, I suppose. But tell me you were not seen by anyone other than someone you trust."

"It was performed by Tadhg. He was the only one there."

Anita brought her hands down. "Oh. Did he... hold a grudge?"

"None. He accepted me as if I were the same friend he had eighteen years ago." Adar reached for Anita's hand. "My love, I am so dearly sorry for the torment I have brought you for our entire marriage. I wish I—"

"Stop." Anita took Adar's hand and clasped it. "You've changed—of course you've changed. I never expected you to stay the same after what my father forced upon you. Only a man with feeble principles could have done what was necessary without pain. You're not the only one who bears guilt for that day, in any case."

"No, love, it is my fault. I did not have to see you that day."

"Adar, I prayed that you would be alive to visit me after the war. The burden is not solely on you."

Adar smiled. He kissed Anita's hand.

"Our relationship has been tarnished by my guilt. I have been perhaps the worst thing to ever happen to the Diev; how ironic, for the offense to it was my marriage of love. Anita, would you like to take a walk on the beach with me early tomorrow before we leave for Belar?"

Anita smiled. "I would love to."

306

Althalos

lthalos woke up to the sight of Gunter snoring, his head resting on a sack perched against the wall of the cave. He laughed under his breath and stood guard for the rest of the night. When the morning sunshine woke the mercenary, Althalos still held his axe in his hands. Gunter rubbed his eyes.

"Rise and shine, watchman!" said Althalos, poking Gunter's leg with his foot.

Gunter jumped up, looking around manically. Once he realized he had fallen asleep, but that they were still safe, he sighed and leaned against the cave wall. He pulled his pack over and started to stuff some of his things back into it. Althalos returned his axe to his back and walked over to the edge of the cave mouth. He stared at the sky, and the sun made him look like a dark shade in the midst of its rays.

"Why are ye standin' up there, boy? Yer goin' to draw attention to us."

"I have never been this far from home. I wish to look at my country for a moment."

Gunter continued to pack away his things. "Southern Mjorn is nothin' special compared to what's out there. All that's here is rollin' hills, rock, and forest. *Yhourn* was a sight: empty, but beautiful, too, in a strange way."

Althalos turned around and leaned against the cave wall, crossing his arms. "What did it look like?"

"First off, there are vast wastelands of fine white sands, but then ye'd get to the parts where the large beasts roam in the gorges and plains of cracked ground. Those barbarians were not stupid. They knew how those beasts hunted, how they *thought*. They would use them to kill whole parties of Mjornish men without losin' a single one of their own. I only survived because I was the one commandin' them to go."

Gunter spoke to the ground, dead-eyed. Althalos did not want the man to dwell on the past any more than he already had, so he refrained from asking any more questions. Instead, he walked over to Gunter and stuck out his hand.

"Let's go."

Gunter shook his head, but he took Althalos's hand. Althalos pulled the mercenary to his feet and the two left the cave. Gunter trudged behind him. Althalos felt a hand on his shoulder.

"Yer goin' the wrong way. Let us follow the river 'til we make it to a shallow part, so we can cross over. If we follow at the side of the road, we'll eventually meet a toll stop."

"I bet you reckon the knights would be at the toll stop, yes?"

"Of course, why else would I steer away from the shortest path? Dumb boy."

"You are a very bitter old man."

"Old man? I'm only thirty-somethin'! What in Gol do ye mean, old?"

"Thirty? Your hair has grayed! I hope I don't look like you when I'm thirty," said Althalos with a sly grin.

"Don't ye make me slap ye, boy. Ye run yer mouth too much."

Althalos smiled, looking into the forest while they traveled away from the road. They made it to a river. Gunter pointed north. Althalos leaned forward and gazed over; at the foot of the bridge was the toll stop that Gunter had predicted.

"See that over there? They've been built near most of the bridges in Nar. That cunt King Asbyorn raised the tolls on every bridge that leads to Nara these past few years. Ye can't travel anywhere without him tryin' to take yer money."

Althalos walked toward the water and placed his hand in it. The water was traveling downstream, and the velocity of it seemed manageable for the two to walk through. He went behind a tree and removed his boots and under-stockings. Afterward, he put his trousers back on, rolled the hems up to his ankles, and put his boots back on his feet. Gunter did the same, and the two waded through the water. Gunter led the way, carefully using his feet to read the riverbed below and gauge its depth. Althalos followed his path, and soon the pair were across the river. They drained their boots of water and redressed themselves.

"Too many damn rivers in Mjorn," Gunter said. "Hopefully ye'll kill that King Asbyorn so that whoever else takes charge can remove these fuckin' tolls, and I won't have to walk through streams to save some damn coin anymore."

"I never even knew there were bridge tolls," said Althalos. "Why did he institute them?"

"I don't fuckin' know! Maybe he needed to bribe all the women he's been tumblin' with behind his wife's back to hold their tongues. To Gol with him!"

Althalos looked toward the sky. "Would the Phoenicy not have him atone for adultery?"

"The lords follow different rules than us commonfolk, boy. They will preach for ye to follow the faith, yet they don't follow it themselves. A bunch of liars, they are. I've walked in on too many lords havin' affairs in their war tents. Out of them all, there's only one lord in the Kingdom of Nar that I respect."

"Who's that?"

"The Good Duke," Gunter said. "That man doesn't waver to any lord. I regret that I didn't choose to fight under him during the war. Instead, I had to be a plucky young lad who wanted to fight in the fuckin' vanguard."

They reached another road. Gunter returned to his squirrelly behavior.

"It's two to three days' worth of travel between here and Nara, but it all depends on the activity on the roads. The lands around Nara get rockier and rockier the closer ye get to it."

"Rocky Mjornish coasts..." Althalos said. "I heard the capital was beautiful. Our priest always boasted about the grandness of the Academy d'Ava: the painted ceiling and the elaborate sculptures. I have always dreamt of seeing it with my own eyes. He also said the library was massive."

"Ha! Can ye even read the Viantse language, boy? That's what all of the books are written in."

"They must have some books in the common tongue; but I mainly look forward to just looking at the library itself."

"Don't think ye will see it. They don't let just anyone walk in there."

Clopping along the road was a pair of horses traveling east, towing a wagon behind them. There were crates overflowing with tools and manufactured equipment on the back of it. Althalos ducked before Gunter could push him down. Gunter laughed under his breath. There was a man steering the horses and another man with a sword at his side.

"They're carrying tools in their cart," Althalos said. "Do you think they're traveling from Nara?"

"Maybe."

"They've probably crossed paths with Agathius…"

Althalos jumped up onto the road. Gunter tried to grab him by the leg, but the boy slipped by. Alarmed, the man drew his sword, and the horses stopped in place.

"Hello there!" said Althalos, waving at him.

The wagoner stood up. "Why in Gol did ye jump in front of us, boy?"

"My companion and I were traveling west, and we encountered some ne'er-do-wells. We were split up from our priest. I was just wondering if you two had crossed paths with him."

"Yer companion? Tell him to show himself."

Gunter walked out, glaring at Althalos. He turned his head over to the wagoner. "So, yer from Avonsgatte?"

"Sure am! Could tell ye are, too, with how ye look."

"And not how I talk?"

"Did you see the priest?" Althalos asked.

"Why would we tell ye?" asked the man. "Ye could be highwaymen lookin' to rob a poor priest, for all we know of ye."

"Look, if you *have* seen him, he probably told you of what happened to Dorthu—"

Gunter grabbed Althalos by the head and put his palm over his mouth. His angry eyes told Althalos to *shut up*. The armed man almost jumped down to intervene, but the wagoner leaned into his ear and whispered something. He turned his head to look at Althalos.

"We were originally headin' over to Dorthu to sell some minin' equipment to one of the older locals. Agathius told us what happened, and he told me that a boy that looked just like you had survived."

Gunter took his palm away from Althalos's mouth, looking relieved.

"We're aimin' for Fisk, now—goin' to discount the tools plenty to help fix up Dorthu. I am incredibly sorry for yer loss, boy."

Althalos nodded to the merchant.

"Agathius also told us that it was the King who had massacred Dorthu. Steer clear of the roads; we passed a few knights travelin' toward Nara not too long ago."

"Thank ye," Gunter said.

"Of course," said the man. "Good luck!"

The wagoner used his reins to order his horses forward. Gunter watched the wagon as it left and pulled Althalos to the side of the road once it was out of sight. Dragging him behind him, he led Althalos deep into the woods.

"Why are we going so far from the road?"

"Because ye like talkin' to random travelers," Gunter said. "What if Agathius had not spoken to those men? What if those men had been devoted subjects of the King? Ye have lots to learn. Observe yer surroundings. Why do ye think I duck down whenever anyone passes by? I have seen everyday-lookin' men and women lie and kill on these roads. Ye got lucky that those gentlemen sympathized with yer cause, boy."

"They were people, like any other," Althalos said. "Do you not trust your fellow man?"

"I have *been* the fellow man that hid in the bushes to stab kind fucks like ye and those wagoners to death for their coin. Learn to listen to yer elders, boy. Yer own fuckin' king killed yer people, and he is supposed to be your strongest protector."

Althalos had a feeling of fear and repulsion whenever he was near Gunter, but also an odd sense of safety. He *felt* Gunter's drive for survival; and for some reason, Gunter had extended this drive to protect Althalos's own life, too. But he could not fathom why Gunter would bother joining him on this journey, and his evasiveness bothered Althalos. Gunter was a selfish and despicable man. Why would he help Althalos with anything? How could Althalos truly feel safe with Gunter without knowing the strange man's motivations?

"Gunter, I will ask you once more," Althalos said. "Why are you helping me?"

Gunter gritted his teeth and slung a rock at a tree. "Leave it alone, boy! Stop askin' me that same damned question. I am gettin' sick of it."

Althalos stopped in his tracks. "What aren't you telling me?"

Gunter choked the handle of his sword, and Althalos stepped back with fear. Gunter turned to look at Althalos, who stumbled back in fear. Gunter loosened his grip on the sword.

"Do ye think I chose to be a murderer, boy? Do ye think my sins do not haunt me? Ye remind me of myself when I was a young boy. Ye remind me of a young man who wished to do the world right: to rid the world of all its wrong-doers. When I was yer age, I served in the vanguard so that I could kill the Yhournish cunts who killed my friends. I served as a mercenary after the war to kill even *more* of those damned barbarians. I could not stop myself from takin' my anger out on them."

Gunter kicked some rocks.

"I have never done a right thing in my life, but everything I did taught me how to stay alive in this damned world. If I can watch ye and stop ye from makin' the same mistakes as I did, maybe my soul will be saved. But I am tired of talkin' about my past, boy. Do not ask me that question again."

After a few miles of silent hiking, they set up camp in another cave. Gunter allowed Althalos to take the first watch. When they woke in the morning, they immediately packed up and continued to travel. In time, it grew dark, and they had to set camp again. The repetitive routine—wake up, walk, camp, and sleep—was the norm for the next several days, and so too were the nightmares. Burning visions coupled with night sweats and gasps for air burdened Althalos's sleep. It was Dorthu, damned Dorthu. His dreams had always felt real, but even so, when he tried to stop the massacre in his own dream, he failed every time. If he had been present, could he have done something, or would he have been killed too? He asked himself that question every time he woke. They cleaned up their camp and continued on.

Large ridges became a more and more frequent sight in the landscape. Althalos's legs ached as he climbed, but Gunter showed no sign of fatigue. He had the endurance of a soldier who had marched through countless battlefields. Seeing this, Althalos refused to whine about the trek. The trees became sparser as the soil grew rockier. The next few days were only filled with the humdrum that came with travel.

312

Finally, they reached a vast opening in the trees. There were still ridges, but trenches had been dug between some of them. Some of the trench walls were collapsed, looking like mere ditches. Burnt tree trunks were scattered around. This wasteland stretched far to the north and south, but to the west, another stretch of rocky-soiled forest was in sight.

"There were many battles here durin' the war," Gunter said. "The Phoenic Elders used their knowledge of the magical elements to burn the forest that was once here. It was done to stop the Yhournish from reachin' the capital, but now it is an eyesore of the past."

They walked down from a ridge and through the barren trenches. Old and broken weapons were scattered around. Althalos stepped on what looked to be a large rock, but when it crushed under his foot, he realized it was the skull of a large man.

"What the—" said Althalos, recoiling in shock.

"Ye step on somethin', boy?"

"It looks to be someone's remains... a rather *large* person's remains."

Gunter kicked the cracked skull to the side. "Ah. That is the head of a barbarian."

He stomped it under his foot.

Grass sprouted between patches of the burnt landscape. There was the occasional cluster of young trees in view, but the rocky soil limited where they grew. They neared the edge of the old battlefield. The sky grew dark, and once more they sought shelter for the night. They entered an old trench underneath a large rock overhang, providing cover from above. Once more, they slept, and once more, they awoke. Gunter was sitting at the trench wall, fiddling with his knife. Althalos rubbed his eyes and stared at the ground, the sun shining down.

"We will make it to the city today. Make sure ye don't bring any attention to yerself. Ye are but a boy from... Wettay, we'll say. There is no gettin' around the fact that my accent is of Avonsgatte, so that shall remain the same. People will wonder why ye came so far to the capital. The Narese aren't fond of people like me, so keep yer voice to yerself and make certain not to make a scene. Do ye understand?"

Althalos nodded.

"Alright, I will speak to anyone before ye do. Let us get on our way."

They climbed out of the trench. It had rained during the night, so the mud squished beneath their feet while they journeyed through it. It clung to their boots like slime, and Althalos tried to stomp it off whenever they stepped over a dry patch of ground. They entered the forest. Before them were banners standing at the sides of the road: large and blood-colored, with a boar in their centers. The King's banners. The posts were vandalized with juvenile carvings and words of protest.

After another hour of traveling, the large walls of Nara could be seen in the distance. Two large statues stood at the sides of the gatehouse. They were both of two different men with swords in their hands, armored in stone-carved chainmail. Their helmets were conical, the style of Narese helmets of the past. The tall walls were adorned the King Asbyorn Harferd's banners.

Behind the walls, an incredibly huge white spire capped with a statue of a golden bird pierced the skyline above. Only the citadel was second to it in height. Numerous brattices were built along the walls. The walls had steep taluses, making climbing the walls almost impossible.

"We cannot go through the main gates," Gunter said. "I have no doubt the knights we angered in Wettay told them to watch out for us. And even if they did not, we don't have the papers to get in."

"Then how do we get in?" Althalos asked.

"I know of some tunnels that lead into the city. This city is so large that most guards don't care to patrol all of its many entrances and exits."

Venceslaus

enceslaus's wrinkled hand brushed over the smooth, black marble statue. He stared at the failed attempt to capture his dead friend's face. Matnus's carved face was stoic, and Venceslaus knew that if the old king were alive, he would have the statue torn down and carved again to show a joyful smile. As he moved his hand along its base, dirt clumped up onto it. Venceslaus slapped the dirt off his hand. The lack of maintenance for Matnus's statue was a show of blatant disrespect.

Lord Urbaed walked over to the Good Duke's side. Venceslaus stepped back, caught by surprise.

"Urbaed! Aren't you supposed to be in the Crii today?"

"If the King does not care for your opinion, he surely does not care for mine," Lord Urbaed said, smiling wryly. "Now that Barnut is dead, I am powerless in the Crii. I don't think the King will even notice my absence."

Lord Urbaed stared up at Matnus's monument. He grinned and looked back at Venceslaus.

"I was the ward of King Matnus, briefly. I am not sure if you remember."

"Oh, really? Little Cannen? You're new to the Crii, aren't you?"

"Yes, I have only been a member for a year. I feel as though that may be why I am often ignored; my tenure has been so much shorter than the rest of yours. They often act as though I am not even there."

"It is a shame. The northeast has always been overlooked, but you are all still subjects of the King. Were you not Asbyorn's friend when you were a lad?"

"No, I never had the chance. Matnus died not long after I became his ward. He wanted me to become friends with Asbyorn, but there was not much time to do so with Asbyorn studying at the Academy and such." Lord Urbaed fell silent for a moment, staring up at the statue before them. "Matnus should be smiling. He was a happy soul, always finding something nice to say about his fellow man."

"Aye, that he was."

"It cannot be said that his son has the same temperament. Once, I was concerned about being his friend—but now I am glad I am not. After he ousted you, he spoke many ills, ills that I do not deem appropriate for anyone to say of you."

"I am disappointed, Urbaed. Crii members are not to speak on the contents of their meetings, no matter the topic."

"Your honor is apparent, but those who do not care for tradition should not expect it to benefit them."

"He is but one king in a line of many. The tradition should be upheld for the sake of his line, not for Asbyorn himself."

"But what of our lines? Our input on the Crii means nothing to him. Do you not find it strange that Geder, a foreigner, has more influence than any of the King's landed vassals? We are due for another statue..."

"Urbaed, hold your tongue. If I understand correctly what you are insinuating, you ought not to say anything further."

"My intentions are not treacherous; I only speak what I believe to be the truth. Our Great Chancellor was just assassinated, and our *inept* king believes it to be some prince from Aerus. Why the Gol would that Aeric prince want to kill Barnut? The murderer was without a doubt a soul seeker; I cannot fathom who else would have the ability to disappear into a puff of smoke and leave no residue behind."

Venceslaus closed his eyes and sighed. "Do not be silly, Urbaed. It has been centuries since there was any conflict between Terukians and Mankind."

"They are expanding, and their emperor is a dreadful figure. What they are doing in the Sealands is frightful to me. With the talks of riots here, and with my own suspicions, I must follow my gut. If the Terukians invade, I will make sure my lands are ready."

"If you believe you must, then go," Venceslaus said. "I do not wish to be the one to tell you that you are wrong; it is better to be cautious than filled with sorrow."

Lord Urbaed nodded. They clasped forearms. Urbaed returned to the keep, and once he was out of sight, Venceslaus hurried out to the ward of the citadel. He beckoned the stablemaster to fetch him a horse, tossing him a coin. He trotted the steed through the streets of Nara, hurrying toward the grand gate of the Academy. A man dressed in plate armor with feathered wings attached to his back stood alone at its entrance. He held a spear in his hand and pounded it on the ground at the sight of the Good Duke.

"Halt! State your reason for entry," ordered the man.

"Hello, good paladin! I am Duke Venceslaus Freihei of High Beak. I only wish to make use of the Academy's library."

The man nodded, bringing his spear back and stepping off to the side. He planted the spear on the ground and signaled for Venceslaus to enter. The Duke nodded to the paladin and went through the gatehouse. He stared a bit at the paladin as he passed, for it was strange to have a paladin guarding the Academy's entrance; but after recent events, he assumed the heightened security was a cautious response.

He dismounted from his horse and climbed the countless brick steps to the entrance of the Academy d'Ava. He rushed past the countless priests roaming the halls and entered the library. Bertram the Book-keeper stood before him.

"Oh, Venceslaus! The Good Duke visits our blessed library!" said Bertram, holding his arms wide.

They embraced one another, holding the hug a bit longer than usual. The aged Elder patted Venceslaus on his back.

"It has been a long time," he said.

"Aye, it has. You have gotten older," said Venceslaus, grinning.

"You have, too. Ha! What brings you here? You never visit the Academy."

"I am looking for a book on Terukian soul seekers. Do you have any histories or descriptive texts on their methods?"

"Ah… What draws your interest to Teruk?"

"I am doing my own investigation into Barnut's murder. I beg you not to tell anyone of this."

"Good Duke, I trust you. You may have confidence in my silence; you have my word. Follow me."

They walked from the entrance of the library to the alcove where histories were shelved, Bertram's old body hobbling all the way there. He made Venceslaus look like a young man. The old priest's back was hunched over, and he moved as if his muscles refused to work. He stretched his arms up, struggling toward a shelf that was a bit out of his reach. Venceslaus came over to aid him.

"I don't need your help, boy." Bertram pulled over a small stool and stepped on it. He reached for the book, brought it down, and handed it to Venceslaus. "Sometimes it takes a little bit more work, but I am still capable in my old age, Venceslaus. Don't you forget that."

Venceslaus opened the leather-bound book.

"This text will have all that you need to know about the Terukian soul seekers," Bertram said.

The markings in it were in the Viantse language. Venceslaus looked up at the Book-keeper.

"I apologize for asking another favor of you, but you are far more capable at reading Viantse than I. Would you aid me in reading it?"

"Ha! Of course, Vences."

The priest took the book from Venceslaus's arms. They walked to a table with a bookrack on top. Bertram placed the book on the bookrack, opening it to the page where soul seekers were mentioned. His gnarled fingers traced the words on the page.

"Ah, yes, just as I remembered. I believe you said the puff of black smoke that had been reported might indicate that the murderer was a soul seeker, yes?"

"Aye," said Venceslaus.

"While that trick *is* a common one with soul seekers, it is not exclusive to them. Almost every magic-practicing society has some form or method of disappearing into thin air."

"So, strictly speaking, it would not have to be a soul seeker?"

"Aye. We even teach certain Elders here a similar sorcery. Of course, there are Terukian spies all about Mjorn, but I do not see a reason for them to attack here. They have stayed quiet while dealing with their own reconquests."

"So it could be anyone."

"Well, not anyone. Use of that particular sorcery requires a very specific elemental balance that most do not have. Of course, there is the possibility someone could use an assortment of potions to figure that out; but for one to even learn what their own balance is is a dangerous task, and one rarely achieved."

"Are there any records on those who have found their balance and would have been able to perform such sorcery?"

"Those records are sealed away for the sake of their protection. We do not wish to bring harm to those specific individuals. Although, the capacity to do magic is hereditary; I can show you the book that has records of which noble families tend to produce those who are gifted."

"Aye, that is perfect. Show it to me, please," Venceslaus said.

Bertram narrowed his eyes. "Before I do, tell me: Do you suspect malice from within the kingdom?"

"I do not know what to suspect. However, I know that the King's suspicions do not make any sense, and I wish to weigh all the possibilities before providing any argument to go against the King's word."

"Smart lad. As much as I loved that boy, he has grown into a simpleton when it comes to managing the affairs of his kingdom. If only Matnus had lived a bit longer to mentor him."

The Book-keeper led Venceslaus to another bookcase, fetching another book for him. Venceslaus opened the book and noticed it was in Narese. He nodded to Bertram.

"Thank you, Elder Bertram. May I borrow this record to copy down any necessary information? I only wish to have evidence if I need to present it to the King."

The Book-keeper hesitated before he spoke, but he soon sighed and caved in. "You are a man of due diligence, Vences. You may borrow the book. But if it is heard that you have lost it under my permission, Aswold would have me drawn and quartered. Return it as soon as you are done with it."

Venceslaus bowed. "You have my word."

The Book-keeper returned the bow. "Now get going," he said. "I have work to do."

Venceslaus carried the record in his hand, opening the flap of a small satchel on his side to place it within. He waved goodbye to Bertram, and the Elder returned him a heavily wrinkled grin only an old man could produce. Venceslaus marched out of the academy, rushing past any priest with the intent to avoid any discussion. He would have to meet with Ser Groent later, so he did not have the time that day to discuss frivolities with anyone.

The ride back to the citadel felt even quicker than the ride to the Academy. His horse trotted through the citadel's outer gates. Venceslaus returned his steed to the stablemaster and entered the keep. He continued to ignore any courtier he passed by, for his eyes were set on copying over the information from the record. Venceslaus entered his room, setting the book on top of a desk that was placed against a wall. The book was titled *A Record of All Families Who Hold Potential*. He laughed at the title and opened the book.

The pages were divided in order of the degree of potential. There was a small description explaining that families other than the ones stated in the book were to be avoided when the Phoenicy sought new Elders, unless they had demonstrated individual ability. It was a short treatise, and plenty of families had at least a low degree of potential, but Venceslaus had no interest in any of them. He flipped to the end in search of the families with the most potential. The first page referenced a family he knew quite well, a highly isolated house by the name of Blyker. Despite their potential, they were not suspicious at all. The Blykers had never cared to partake in the affairs of the Crii; the last time a Blyker had been in Nara was most likely during the Yhournish war fifteen years ago.

He flipped through more and more pages. The record must have been quite old, for the House of Kurem was still there. He flipped through more and more pages, seeing the name Lyrion, another old house now fallen from grace. The last page was dedicated to the Harferd family.

Were any members of the Lex family capable of doing such a thing? They were not in the record, but that did not clear them of the ability. Could it have been a Harferd? There were countless Harferds—by blood, not name—in Nara. Members of the Harferd family were so well known for spawning bastards that the Phoenicy regularly sought them out to recruit them into their clergy; or at least they had before the war. From what Venceslaus knew, most of them were dead. He pounded the desk with frustration. Matnus was a good man, he had no bastards, and Asbyorn's bastards were far too young to suspect.

Venceslaus fetched a piece of parchment and a bone pen while his eyes traced the pages, recording each family that possessed high potential. As he copied them down, his fingers ached; but he did not care. The nature of having old hands would not disturb him in his mission.

Once night had come, Venceslaus was long done with the record; he was simmering in his thoughts and waiting for Ser Groent. He left the original record and his copy on the desk and stared outside. The air was still. The door opened, and Venceslaus jumped. To his relief, it was only Ser Groent. His knight nodded to him, and Venceslaus followed him down the halls, heading for the exit. Venceslaus had brought with him a cloak, and Ser Groent had done the same. They made it to town and strode toward the tavern where they knew Emmer to be present.

The streets were quiet, but the tavern bustled with noise. It was overflowing with activity, a sprawling sea of revelers. Venceslaus and Ser Groent struggled to swim through the drunkards and carousers. The two could not find a table, so they settled for loitering by one of the walls. Venceslaus looked around for Emmer, noticing the squirrelly commoner sitting at a table in the corner of the room. A man in a black cloak sat down with him, his hood pulled up. He held out a pale, leathery hand, and in his hand was a pouch. That person must have been either the assassin or working with the assassin, Venceslaus realized, using Emmer to feed the King fiction. The pale man's cuff peeked out from under the black cloak that covered him.

It was *crimson*.

"Merr, we should stand at the far end of the bar nearest to Emmer. Maybe we can hear what they're discussing," whispered Venceslaus, leaning toward Ser Groent.

Ser Groent looked over to the end of the bar and walked toward it. Once the two of them had sat down at the bar counter, Ser Groent hailed a barmaid so that she could fetch them something to drink. Venceslaus feigned complaint with his knight, turning his head so that his ear pointed toward Emmer and the strange man. He could not hear a thing they said because of the merrymakers around them. In his peripheral vision, Venceslaus noticed Emmer accept the pouch, feeling the weight of it in his hands. After opening the pouch and looking inside, Emmer shook his head. He yelled something at the odd cloaked gentleman.

People started to watch Emmer. The cloaked man refused to raise his voice, remaining unbothered.

"He must die!" Emmer yelled with an untamed anger.

The cloaked man shook his head and stood up, walking away from the table and toward the exit. Emmer trembled with anger, squeezing his fists. He must have been quite easy to insult, Venceslaus thought.

Emmer climbed up onto the table and yelled something out to the tavern. Venceslaus's eyes dashed to Ser Groent, and he jerked his head in the direction of the door. Ser Groent nodded. They rushed toward the door while Emmer shouted for the man's head. There were a few rough-looking folks in the tavern, and they listened intently to Emmer's words. The revelers began to get riled up. Ser Groent and Venceslaus made it to the exit. A fight broke out behind them as they left.

The strange man was walking toward the citadel, but he did not take a straight path. Instead, he took many irrational turns, stopping in his tracks at some points. Ser Groent made sure that the two of them stood back far enough that they would not be noticed.

The strange man took one more turn down into an alley, smoke wisping away from it even though there was no fire. The two hurried over, and Ser Groent drew his sword. The tracks of the man stopped exactly where the smoke was now dissipating. Venceslaus spun around, hoping to find any more clues the man might have left behind.

"He saw us," said Venceslaus, pulling out a small dagger from his belt.

Ser Groent was slammed into a wall behind him while black smoke appeared once more. The cloaked man lunged for Ser Groent's sword and attempted to take his weapon from him. Venceslaus kicked the side of the man's knee, causing him to tumble to the ground. Ser Groent swung his sword at the man, but before it connected, the man disappeared into a puff of black smoke once more.

"Behind you!" yelled Ser Groent.

Without thinking, Venceslaus spun around and stabbed with his dagger, sticking it into the man's thigh. The man fell to his knees, clutching his leg. He tried to disappear once more. A chausilver pendant hung from his neck, and Venceslaus snatched it seconds before the man disappeared.

Ser Groent looked around in case the man reappeared, but he did not. Venceslaus stared at the pendant in his hands. *How could it be?* Ser Groent walked over and looked at it, recoiling once he had noticed what it was. The pendant was engraved in great detail, covered with features that would have required the finest and most expensive instruments to produce. Venceslaus rubbed it with his thumb and felt the grooves that formed the hairs of the animal it depicted. He touched its tusks with his index finger and gazed upon the divot that resembled a spearhead. He held a boar in his hand and disappointment in his heart.

"Do you believe what this implies to be true, m'lord?" Ser Groent asked.

Venceslaus sighed. "Unfortunately, I do."

Meara

he room that Leisa had brought Meara to must have been Hrodert's own, for it only contained a single large bed. Hrodert was sitting down on the bed, counting coins. The room was sparsely decorated. Few trinkets or keepsakes could be seen, and the only furniture that graced the room was the aforementioned bed, a side table, and a dresser. Hrodert placed his coins on his side table, stood up, and placed his hands on Meara's shoulders.

He had an unnerving grin on his face. Meara shivered, recoiling as his face moved closer to hers. His face smelled sour, and his breath smelled of rancid oil; he was so close to her that she could feel his hot breath engulf her face.

"You are a very special girl, did you know that?"

Meara did not respond.

"What other young girl would have had the courage to go and save her friend? I admire that about you..."

Meara squirmed away from Hrodert. Leisa barged into the room and beckoned for Hrodert to come over to her. The brute peeked through the door, sighing at whatever he saw. He hurried out. Meara stood up and walked quietly across the room, staring through the small crack in the door.

Hrodert marched over to a man dressed in purple. His large torso made it impossible to see the man's face. Hrodert looked flustered, moving his hands anxiously about. The man in purple shook his head, seemingly disappointed, and was handed a lumpy purse by Hrodert. Hrodert eventually stepped to the side, and the face of the man was revealed to Meara. He had clear skin and dark black hair; surely a lord, with how he was groomed and dressed. They ended their conversation, and Hrodert turned around, heading toward the room he had left Meara in.

Meara's eyes darted around the room. She saw a small bone pen on the side table and grabbed it. She sat down on the bed, hiding the pen under her thigh. Hrodert stepped through the door and grinned at Meara.

"Making yourself comfortable, are you?" he asked.

Meara shrugged.

"I want you to feel at home here."

The revolting man inched closer and closer to Meara. She sat still on the bed, tracking Hrodert with her eyes. As he grew near, her heart raced faster.

"You are going to enjoy it here; you have my word."

He placed his hand on Meara's chin and lifted it. Her heart jumped ever more.

"You will do well here, lass."

Hrodert pushed on her shoulder, putting her to her back. When he tried to climb on top of her, she gripped the bone pen and stabbed it into Hrodert's left eye. He screamed in agony and clutched at his eye socket while Meara rolled off the bed, snatched the seax from his waist, and slashed at his thigh. Hrodert fell about as gracefully as a bull that had just broken a leg. She ran out of the room and shut the door. Leisa stood out in the hall, open-mouthed, seemingly unable to speak. Meara pushed her back, passing by her. The moaning in the main room almost drowned out Hrodert's screams, but some of the guards came to meet her halfway. She ducked behind one of the women and darted for the front door. At this time, the guard up front was peeking through the slot in the door. She sent the seax through his back and pushed him to the side, barreling through the door. She ran past the man on the other side. In the distance, she saw the man in purple walking away, going toward a group of people. She made sure to run the other way.

She took every odd turn she could with no destination in mind. The only goal she had was to get as far away from the brothel as possible. The more she ran, the easier it became; but soon a painful shortness of breath caught up with her and forced her to stop. The part of town she was in was not one she frequented. It was near the Phoenic temple. Rarely ever did she or any of the other orphans go here. The temple did offer charity to the orphans, but there were stories of children disappearing whenever they accepted aid. A few goons loitered about. Maybe they had some relation to the brothel and Hrodert, she thought, preying on the small; but she wasn't frightened. Her fear had subsided and been replaced by a consuming anger.

She wanted Luka dead.

Meara stared at the ground with glassy eyes. The thought of stabbing Luka in his fat neck repeated in her head. She held a rock in her hand, and she found herself pounding the street with a relentless tenacity as if it were an enormous walnut that she had to split. Even the idea of hurting him brought her joy. Tears formed in her eyes. For a moment, she finally let herself cry, taking some time to catch up with all the pain the world had forced her to endure.

She would have to find a way to catch Luka alone, for he would undoubtedly command the little gremlins that surrounded him to rip Meara apart at the first sight of her. She tried to think more about how she would go about killing him, but the tears streaming down her cheeks interrupted her thoughts. Gol entered her mind, and she shoved the thought of him away. She had saved him, yet he had run away while she was being taken by Hrodert.

The only thing that interrupted her crying was the sound of her stomach grumbling. She had forgotten that she was hungry. She couldn't remember how long it had been since she had eaten the steak—days, surely, and nothing but scraps since then. She looked at the Phoenic temple, and the idea of accepting the temple's mercy drew her over. She watched her surroundings, making sure she wasn't being followed or watched.

A priest stood outside the temple, praying to something. Meara had heard the names the priest was chanting before, but she did not care to remember who the names referred to. None of the orphans really cared for religion, unless worshipping the pig counted.

Meara feigned a limp and stuck out her palms to the priest. "I beg of alms."

The priest looked down at Meara. "Of course, dear."

He rummaged through a sack that hung from his waist, pulling out a small piece of bread. He tossed it to Meara, and she smiled, bowing with gratitude before she devoured it. She turned to walk away, but the priest grabbed her by the shoulder. She flinched and pushed the priest off of her.

"You seem to be starving," the priest said. "If you are in need, just attend the recitations. I will give you more food."

Meara smiled. "Of course," she said, bowing again before running off as quickly as she could.

She felt like she was being watched by the people around her, so she hurried away from the Phoenic temple. She jumped over small dividing walls, climbed atop overhangs, and crawled through fences while she made her way back to the hideout she and Gol had discovered. She watched its perimeter from one of the alleyways surrounding it. A number of thugs wandered around, seemingly having commandeered the building for their own use. Gol was surely not there.

Walking away from the area, a hand stopped her in her tracks. She made a strange noise, almost a scream, but she stopped herself because she did not want to attract the attention of any of Hrodert's thugs. A man covered her mouth, spun her around to face him, and put his other finger to his lips, gesturing for Meara to be quiet. He wore the armor of a knight, and his face was terribly scarred.

"I only want ask you a question, lass. Do not be afraid; I mean you no harm."

He let go of her. She stepped away from him.

"You fled from a building," he said. "Not too long ago, a companion of mine left that same building. When you ran away, you looked terrified. I do not know what business my companion has in a building that would lead a young girl to flee with such urgency. What was the purpose of that establishment?"

He looked down at Meara's hands, and she did the same. Splatters of Hrodert's blood still painted her hands. She looked back up at the man.

"A brothel," she said.

"*Gol.*" The knight squeezed his fists, staring at the ground. "Did you hear anything that the man in purple said?"

"No, but I did see him receive something."

The knight perked up. "What did he receive?"

"Money, I think," Meara said.

"Money? For what?"

"I do not know. I barely even saw him—Hrodert was blocking his face almost entirely."

"Who is Hrodert?"

Meara grimaced. "A foul brute."

The knight shook his head, looking at Meara with a pitying expression. He reached into his purse and gave her a few coins.

"Thank you for the information, lass. Go buy yourself something to eat; you look like you're starving."

"What is your name, Ser?" Meara asked.

The knight gave Meara an exaggerated bow. "Ser Mikhail the Sword Seer, Marshal of Kurembrog."

Startled, Meara laughed at his bow. The knight waved goodbye to the girl, and she stared at the coins in her palm.

An idea sprouted in her mind. The pig was predictable; he always wallowed in the same spot. She hurried to the town square, threading her small body through the large crowds of adults that frequented the trade stalls. Passing right by the food stalls, she headed straight toward where the whittlers and wood carvers sold their wares. She stared at the knives that lay on top of the table.

"Get! You have nothin' for me, girly!"

Meara showed the merchant the coins in her hand. "I just took up whittling; I wish to buy some tools to help me with it. I only have a bread knife, and father says that won't work too well."

The merchant's expression changed. "Oh, er—well, of course. Take a gander at what I have to offer."

Meara picked up each knife individually, examining each one of them.

"I can provide you with a discount, if you buy them all. It is always best to have a set of multiple knives, as one each serves a different purpose," said the merchant, talking directly to the coins in Meara's palm.

"Deal," Meara said.

They completed the transaction, and the man stared happily at the gold at his hand. Meara knew she had overpaid for the set of whittling knives, but it didn't matter to her. After she killed Luka, she could retrieve the groschen he had stolen from her; it would be enough money to help her disappear.

She went over to an alleyway not far from where the orphans lingered. There was plenty of scrap wood on the ground; it had come from an old, burnt cottage at the corner of a crossroads that had been partly torn down. She grabbed a bundle of long, thin posts and shaped them into wooden spears with her new tools. Memories of her father guiding her hands along old pieces of wood with his old set of whittling knives came to her. Her eyes watered, but she shook her tears away so that she could focus on the work in front of her. The sharpening took an hour to complete. She had to hide now and then from the eyes of a wandering passerby or guard. Her arms throbbed and stung from the work, so she used her palms to massage the pain and soreness away.

There was a sewer drain beside the outer wall of one of the other buildings in the alley. She lifted the cover off of the drain hole and noticed that the plumbing curved under the road. The hole was big enough for someone to fall through. She threw scraps and dirt into the hole, filling it. Then she tucked the spears she had made inside. She placed the grate back onto the sewer hole and laid some planks over it to cover it from sight. *A wild hog needs bait,* Meara thought. She returned to the town square to find something to attract him.

A town crier was there, yelling the news to the square-goers.

"Hear me! Gentlemen and gentleladies of Belar, the Midsummer festival will begin in just a few days, and the tourney in but a week—so prepare your guts for ale and your eyes for bloody combat! Also, to anyone traveling out into the hinterland, be careful! There have been several reports of disappearances, as well as of growths of strange and noxious flora. Be on alert, and do not stray from the roads. And to say this one last time before the festival: Stop pissing in the damn water! The ale and wine guilds need *clean* water, not your piss!"

Everyone broke into conversation after the crier had finished. A few people muttered nervously about the disappearances. Others exclaimed their excitement for the upcoming festival. One man jokingly threatened to piss in one of the streams that cut through Belar again. Meara smiled with sudden joy, for the festival was perfect for her plans: she would lead Luka to her trap once the festivities began. The sheer number of people in the streets would give her plenty of concealment, allowing her to easily escape if any guards were to try to apprehend her for the killing.

But evening was coming, and Meara figured she would have to find shelter soon, unless she wanted to suffer a cold and restless night. If the merchant who had taught her how to pick locks was not out peddling his goods now, then he surely was no longer in

Belar. She laughed at the thought of breaking into his house to sleep in his warm bed—but then she slowly warmed to the idea. However, she would need the lockbox, and she had left it with the orphans. Cursing to herself, she stood up and walked toward their hideout.

The orphans sat around Luka, waiting for a boon. The lockbox was right beside him. She would have to sneak by and snatch it when he wasn't aware. When evening came around, the orphans splintered off into their own smaller groups while Luka sat in a corner, alone, to eat *their* spoils. Every night, this happened; Luka was a consistent pig. He could not bear to hear the whimpers and whines of starving children while he ate, but this did not stop them from coming up to ask for an extra portion of food. They would beg and beg, but he always grew annoyed with them, sticking out his chest and walking over to slap them. There was a time—once—when Luka was merciful to one of the orphans, giving him an extra loaf. It seemed that single act of charity had stuck with the orphans, convincing them it was worth the risk of a beating to have an extra meal.

Meara meandered about until she had reached the other side of the building. Luka's throne was too central for him to eat on, so he was a decent ways away from it, leaving the lockbox unattended. Most of the children, although not begging, did hover around Luka; everywhere he went, they were bound to follow. Clinging to the wall, she snuck around the building and peeked past the corner of its exterior wall. She could not even see Luka past the huddled children. She sprung toward the lockbox, snatching it. Angry shouting came from behind her, so she shot a glance backwards while she ran away. It was Luka; although, to her benefit—yet surely not the other child's—his yelling was directed at one of the orphans surrounding him.

Once she was a good distance away, she sat down to open the lockbox. To her delight, the skeleton keys and paper were still inside. She threaded through the crowd in the town square and went toward the merchant's home. She went through the keys, isolating the Mjornish ones. She tried them all, but none of them worked. She looked at the paper to help find the keys from Low Beak. There were only two, and both of them did not open the door. She grabbed her hair and cursed with frustration. After examining the lock for a few minutes, she noticed some strange foreign markings on it. She pulled out the paper and scoured for similar markings referenced in the guide. His lock was not from Mjorn or Low Beak, but rather from some foreign place called *Teruk*. The merchant must have been well traveled, Meara thought. She found the correct key and unlocked the door.

She entered the merchant's abode. Inside, it was astonishingly empty compared to how it had been before. Almost all of the furniture had been removed from the room, aside from the merchant's bed; it must have been too big to get out the door. After she locked the door behind her, Meara dove ungracefully onto the bed. She basked in how soft it was. It had been years since she had lain in a proper bed, and even back then, her bed was never as comfortable as this one. She dozed off almost immediately. She had never fallen asleep so quickly before. When she woke up, she was confused, despite how well she had slept. It must have been the comfort of the bed and the security of the lock that calmed her nerves enough so to allow her to sleep so soon. She decided she would stay at the house until the start of the festival, and for the two following mornings, the first thing she would do was to look out of the window that overlooked the town center to watch the booths being set up.

After three nights of rest, the booths were set up, and the festival-goers appeared, dressed up in bright colors. The Midsummer festival had begun.

Abba

he day was hot and dry, and the air in Belar stood still. Eastern Osmjornia felt different than Kuremdod; the sun shone more persistently here. The winds that etched across the Akos did not harass the people that lived so far inland.

Ser Mikhail walked toward the brothers while they sparred in the tourney arena. Jergi was laughing at Maric as Abba got the better of him for the first time. Abba struck his waster at the side of Maric's helmet. Maric fell, and Ser Mikhail shook his head.

"Your brother is still recovering from his affliction. Stop using his misfortune to overpower him and start using skill."

Maric picked himself up. "Do not worry about me, Ser Mikhail. I don't even feel this prissy boy's blows," he said, smirking as he attempted a strike at Abba.

Abba countered and disengaged.

"Maric, take it easy," Ser Mikhail said. "Your footing is off."

Jergi continued to laugh. "Maric has been telling Abba *not* to go easy on him the whole time. Do not chastise the poor lad for listening to his brother."

Ser Mikhail sighed. Across the arena, Hedmond Kyln returned, sitting next to Jergi. They discussed something in whispers, and Abba noticed that Ser Mikhail was staring at them with a hunter's eye.

Suddenly, Abba yelped, tumbling to the ground. Maric stood over him with his finger pointed at him, taunting his brother.

"Keep your eye on your opponent!" Maric said, laughing.

Ser Mikhail did not flinch; Abba thought he might not have even noticed that Maric had struck him down. Maybe he didn't notice because Abba losing a practice duel was nothing new; but his fixation on Jergi *was* new. Next to Hedmond was the same mumbling old man that had been with him when they arrived at Belar. Hedmond would often look over at the old man like he was checking to see if he was still there, only to return to his conversation with Jergi immediately after. Hedmond pulled out a paper and they discussed it. Abba shrugged it off, returning to his practice duel.

At one point, they ended up closer to Ser Mikhail. He only barely acknowledged them, taking the time to step away to get another angle to watch the duel; but even this acknowledgment was only momentary, since it seemed he was more interested in what the Baron was doing than he was in Abba and Maric. Ser Mikhail noticed Abba staring, and he shook his head.

"Come on, boys! If Maric can handle it, then you may as well pick up the intensity!"

Maric gave Abba a mischievous smirk. They went at each other for about another half hour.

"Ser Mikhail, Abba, Maric! We ought to head back to the keep! It is growing dark, and Hedmond just informed me that dinner will be done soon."

Ser Mikhail turned to the boys. "You lads ought to go and raid the Kylns' pantry. You will need to eat well for the tourney."

Hedmond beckoned for them to follow him, strutting toward the keep. Abba wondered if the rest of the Kyln family was just as smiley, for Hedmond always seemed to be grinning about something.

"So, little lordlings, are you two excited for the Midsummer festival?"

"Festival? What?" Maric spun around to Ser Mikhail and the Baron. "Father said nothing about a festival."

"Your father did not think it part of your duty to attend, *little lordlings*, so Ser Mikhail and I did not see the use of telling you about it," Jergi said.

Ser Mikhail did not say a word.

"I reckon Father did not want us to think of this as a party, but rather as something of great importance," remarked Abba.

"A party *is* important," said Maric, shaking his head.

"As for another thing of great importance," said Ser Mikhail, turning to Hedmond, "Woldhom is deserted. When we passed through, everyone was gone, and a building had been lit aflame; furthermore, there was a dead body—dismembered—at the entrance of the town, its wound covered by fresh skin. There was also a sort of plant exanthema afflicting the lands due east of our own."

"I will send scouts out immediately to Woldhom to gather more information," said Hedmond. "Where exactly did you see this... exanthema?"

"Pelesgeb."

"That sounds more your problem than ours—your neck of the woods."

"It spreads," said Ser Mikhail. "I would keep an ear out for any stories of its appearance."

Hedmond waved his hand dismissively. "You can tell me more after the feast. Today, I wish to be in a merry mood!"

They passed through a gatehouse built of dark gray stone bricks, and a portcullis made of wrought iron loomed above them. The keep itself was half-strange. For one, it was built out of wood; and although it was quite similar to the style of the villages, it did not seem as appropriate as stone for a lord's estate. Carved arches depicting mountains and beasts covered regular recessions in the walls. These recessions housed large wood sculptures that reminded Abba of some of Kurembrog's own; but instead of wood sculptures, they had stone statues of the Phoenix. A couple of the wanderers in the ward knelt in front of the wooden statues. But what perplexed Abba most was that he could not find a depiction of the Phoenix in any of the recessions. There was a not a single one.

After they passed through the large doors, they each briefly stopped by their chambers to drop off their belongings. Then they walked down to the keep's great hall. Courtiers rushed through the halls, carrying boxes, posts, fabric, and tools in their arms as the rushed to and fro. They moved with such haste that Abba and Maric had to jump out of the way several times to avoid getting trampled.

Instead of the cold stone brick that caged courtiers inside of the Kurembrog halls, the walls of the Belar keep were made of a warm and cozy dark wood. Despite it not being his home, Abba felt relaxed in this keep, his head beckoning him to take a long nap. The old man that clung to Hedmond's side shambled his way to the throne and climbed up.

Abba leaned toward Ser Mikhail. "Should Hedmond not stop him?"

Ser Mikhail snickered. "Stop him? It is his right. That old man is Hedmond's father, Duke Tedi. The throne is his."

The fireplace behind the throne roared with a heat that stuck in the room. It was a comfortable temperature inside, even though it was summer; although Abba was concerned that it would get uncomfortably warm once the rest of the feast-goers arrived. Abba and Maric leaned against the table and examined the room. Light from the wrought-iron chandeliers covered them. While the guests started to find their way in, Hedmond stood in front of Duke Tedi with his arms held wide.

"I welcome you to the Great Hall of Belar! We have food and drink from all corners of Osmjornia—please, do not hesitate to enjoy the feast."

The old man swung his legs back and forth like an entertained toddler while he stared at the ceiling. Hedmond took his seat at the end of the table. Abba, Maric, and the rest took their own seats. Maric poked Abba's side and leaned closer.

"That old man sure is strange, isn't he?" asked Maric.

"Aye, it is like he is... not present," Abba said.

The boys talked to and teased one another while they waited for the food. It took maybe a quarter of an hour for the maids to bring the first round of meals to the table. Abba and Maric held their heads down. To the shock of the boys, Ser Mikhail started a prayer. Abba opened his eyes and stared at the knight, only to see that everyone else's plates were already filled with wild boar, baked potatoes, salty fish, various kinds of cheese, southern olives, and a plethora of foreign fruits and vegetables. Many people wearing a large variety of colors sat at the long table. They all looked fairly similar, with dark brown to black hair and fair skin. A few individuals had bone-pale skin. Adar often said that all Ookosi people had skin as pale as snow.

Abba leaned toward Ser Mikhail, who was still in the middle of his prayer. "Are they Ookosi?"

Ser Mikhail glanced over to where Abba was pointing. "Probably. But do not make a scene of it here, Abba. Some families in Osmjornia marry into Ookosi families—we are very far east."

"Why would it matter how far east we are?" asked Maric.

"Things are different here," replied Ser Mikhail, staring at the tabletop.

As the night grew dark and the feasting continued, the more and more drunk the people became. Ser Mikhail refused to drink a drop of wine, still watching Jergi as closely as he had been earlier. The Baron was having a grand time, graciously accepting drinks, though he did water them down a bit. Feasts like these were probably Jergi's only time to let loose. Ser Mikhail stood up, grabbing his drink to bring with him. He had a smile on his face; though if one only looked at his eyes, it would not have been apparent. He walked over to Jergi. The two clacked their cups together, and Ser Mikhail wrapped his arm around Jergi's shoulders. The two of them were laughing about something, but Abba could not tell what. Ser Mikhail led the Baron out of the hall, and Abba stared at the pair as they left.

"Why are you staring at Ser Mikhail?" Maric asked.

"He has been watching the Baron all day, for some reason. Even back at the tournament grounds. I wonder what he is thinking about."

"I am sick of these revelers," Maric said. "Do you want to go and find out?"

"We really shouldn't follow them."

"Well, if you won't, I will."

As Maric always did, he went off to stick his nose in something he shouldn't. Abba sighed and followed his younger brother, carving through the crowd of feast attendees. Ser Mikhail and Jergi took a right. Not long afterward, a large thud was heard. Maric rushed over, peeking around the corner, and Abba did the same. Ser Mikhail was holding the Baron va Heddi by the collar of his shirt and pressing him into the wooden wall. Abba stood up to hurry toward the two of them, but Maric stuck his arm out, preventing his brother from moving.

"Wait," whispered Maric. "Let's see what this is about."

Abba nodded. Ser Mikhail grabbed Jergi by the face with his gauntleted hand.

336

"Have you gone mad? Unhand me!" yelled Jergi, clenching his fists.

"Under our laws, I could gut you right now," Ser Mikhail snarled.

"What? You are deranged!"

"That building you entered earlier—what was your purpose there?"

"I told you; I was handling business with a merchant who frequents Kurembrog!"

"Does he supply the brothels of Kurembrog with their women?" Ser Mikhail's grip tightened. "The ones here seem quite *young*, don't they, Jergi?"

"What are you going on about?"

Ser Mikhail slapped Jergi, the metal on his gauntlet clanking upon impact. A mark in the shape of his hand reddened Jergi's cheek. Ser Mikhail patted him down, then grunted with disappointment.

"You had a pouch filled with something. Where is it?"

Jergi's face went pale, his eyes wide. He tried to shake away his change in demeanor. "What are you talking about? What pouch?"

Ser Mikhail grabbed Jergi by the arm and spun him around, pushing his face into the wall. From his waist, he grabbed a leather strap and tightly bound the Baron's hands together. He grabbed him by his upper arm and led him back down the hall he had come from.

"You are under arrest under the suspicion of visiting a brothel that employs girls far too young for such work. Abba! Fetch me a guard."

Abba jumped at the sound of his name; they clearly hadn't been as stealthy as they thought. He revealed himself. "Al— Alright, Ser!"

Abba ran around the corner, noticing a guard dressed in blue patrolling down the hall. He waved him over and brought him to Ser Mikhail. Ser Mikhail told the guard to lead the Baron to the dungeon, and that he would return to the hall to speak with Hedmond about the matter. The guard nodded, leaving Mikhail with Abba and Maric.

"Why in Gol did you arrest the baron?" asked Maric.

"He is a criminal who allows crimes committed against little girls to go unreported."

"Oh," said Maric.

They returned to the Great Hall, and Ser Mikhail finally took a sip of his drink as he went for Hedmond. He pulled the regent to the side of the room.

"Pay attention, both of you," said Ser Mikhail to the boys.

"What is so important that you had to interrupt my pleasant feast?" Hedmond asked.

"By the law of Kuremdod and in recognition of our traditions, I have arrested the Baron va Heddi for entering a brothel under the suspicion that he is aiding in its operation. I humbly request that you hold him in your dungeon until we depart, so that he may face his due punishment for the crimes he has committed under Lord Adar's court."

Hedmond's eyes sharpened. "Do you have any evidence of this?"

"I have testimony. My investigation is not finished quite yet; I will be searching his room soon."

Hedmond shook his head. "I cannot accept this. Tradition has it that only a *lord* may arrest his own subjects if they have committed a crime against *their* laws. Never has it been that a man may be arrested by his peer."

Ser Mikhail looked at the entrance of the Great Hall. "Once Adar arrives, he will tell you himself; he gave me the command to arrest va Heddi once ample proof had presented itself."

"Ample proof? Of what?"

"We suspected him of embezzlement."

"Operating a brothel is entirely separate to embezzlement."

"Both are crimes under Kuremdod law," Ser Mikhail said. "Please hold him until Count Adar arrives."

Hedmond put his hand up. "Alright, but I cannot allow you to search his room until Lord Adar arrives. He will be here in a few days, I presume? We will sort out this debacle then."

Maric pulled Abba away while Ser Mikhail talked to the regent, leading him through the entrance of the Great Hall. He leaned against the wall.

"There are too many people in there," he said. "It is driving me insane."

"Are you alright, Maric? You seem to have regained your strength, but what of your head? Are you still woozy?"

"I have a splitting headache, but it should be gone in time for the tournament. Otherwise, I feel great. Better than before, even."

The two walked down the halls and left the keep. Abba was content on getting fresh air in the ward, but Maric did not stop. He went straight for the gatehouse. Abba sighed. He was getting sick of having to follow his brother everywhere. They both passed the gatehouse. Maric continued to walk down to the city below, but Abba stopped, caught by the view. Belar was much larger than Kurembrog, sprawling with an uncountable number of buildings and an amount of people that would make even a gregarious man queasy. He was shocked that he had not yet found the Phoenic temple while he walked through the city. The only building that could have been the temple was a decently sized building with a single spire in its center.

He shook his head. He was standing and thinking while his brother went off to only the Phoenix knew where. He walked down the the main road and wandered in the direction he believed Maric had gone. Abba reached the town square, and after a moment of looking around, he saw Maric staring down a road. Around them were crowds of people. A few passersby gave them strange, judgmental glares. He grabbed his brother's shoulder. Maric jumped at the touch.

"Do you remember where that building the Baron went into was? I thought I would, but my head is spinning."

"Yes," Abba said, "but what of it?"

"We should check and see what Jergi was doing there!"

"You're a snoop! That place is none of our business. You heard what Ser Mikhail was saying, didn't you?"

"You are such a do-gooder. This is the first time in years that we've been this far from home, and we are old enough to see things for ourselves now. Have some fun for once."

"We can look around, but let us just leave that—"

Maric went off, ignoring whatever Abba was going to say. Again, Abba had to run after him. Maric turned a corner and went into an alley. From the street, Abba could hear soft footsteps, then a loud bump. His impatient brother had probably tripped and fallen. Abba shook his head.

"Watch where you're goin'!"

Abba turned the corner to the sight of an unsightly man who was puffing out his chest at Abba's brother. Maric had fallen to his ass, and he was trying to climb to his feet. Another man muttered something to the one in front, but Abba could only make out the word *bitch*.

"Nah, these two can't be with her. Look at their clothes; they're *rich*, and it doesn't look like they're with anyone else, does it?"

The man pulled out his dagger. Abba reached for his side, but he did not have his waster; he had left it in his room. Maric hurriedly crawled back. As he did, he somehow planted both of his feet behind the man's ankles and pushed at his hips with his hands to send the man falling backward. This did not give Maric enough time to escape, however, and while Abba stood heavy and frozen, the other man dove at his brother with his own dagger in hand. Maric grabbed the man's wrist, halting his attempt at gutting him. There was a wooden rake to Abba's right that leaned against the side of the building. He grabbed it and rushed at the man on top of his brother. He swung it and swung it hard, hitting the man in the head. His limp body fell to Maric's side.

Finally able to stand, Maric got to his feet. With speed, he pulled his arm up. The other man swiped forward with his blade and cut Maric on his forearm. Maric tried to control this man's wrist as well, but the man pulled it back from Maric's grasp. Abba slammed the rake onto the top of the man's head, dazing him. He swung down once more to put his assault to an end.

Abba rushed to his brother's side. Maric was clutching his forearm, staring at the gash in its underside.

"Oh fuck, oh Gol! I need to wrap this."

Abba pulled out a loose cloth he kept in his pocket and wrapped it around Maric's forearm.

"I think I'm going to vomit," muttered Maric, clutching his head.

Abba pulled Maric out of the alley and yelled for a guard. Thinking no one had heard him, he yelled out once more; but once again, he was met with the stares of annoyed burghers. Abba found the whole thing strange. If they had been in Kurembrog, the guards would have stopped the fight before it even occurred.

Instead of waiting for help, Abba decided to take Maric back to the keep himself. When they reached the ward of the keep, Ser Mikhail was there, discussing matters with a few other knights. Once he caught a glimpse of the boys, he stormed over to them.

"Where the Gol did you two run off to?" yelled Ser Mikhail.

Noticing the bloody cloth around Maric's forearm, he grabbed it, shaking his head with distress.

"What happened?" he asked.

"We were walking around the town and Maric bumped into someone. They pulled their daggers and tried to mug us, so we defended ourselves."

Ser Mikhail put his palms to his face, then reached for Maric's forearm again. He unwrapped the makeshift bandage slightly to inspect the cut. It was wet with blood. He shook his head, confused, and unraveled the bandage entirely. He threw the rag to the ground and grabbed Maric's forearm, turning it around to inspect the whole of it.

"Are you two trying to trick me? Did you stick his arm into a butchered pig? There's no cut."

"What? No, the cut is right here—"

Maric looked down at the wound, or lack thereof, and moved his forearm around to inspect it the same way Ser Mikhail had. Abba stared at it, too, dumbfounded. Maric rubbed the blood at the site where the supposed wound had been, and there was no scratch or scabbing present. Smooth skin and wet blood were all that was there. Maric furrowed his brow at the sight of it.

"This is still surely blood, but where did you get it?" Ser Mikhail asked. "It can't be from a wound; you've not a mark on your skin."

"The thug cut him! I saw it happen!" Abba said.

Ser Mikhail grabbed Maric's forearm again and shoved it in Abba's face, yanking Maric with him.

"It would be impossible for him to have been just cut. This must be fake. The blood drips down; if it were another man's blood, it would look like a splatter. Stop trying to play a trick on me."

"We aren't playing a trick!" yelled the boys in unison.

"How in Gol would a large gash heal so quickly?"

"How should we know? All I can say is that Maric was cut in front of my eyes, and now he has no wound."

Ser Mikhail shoved Maric over in the direction of a well. "Lift yourself a bucket and wash that shite off your arm."

Maric walked over to it, rubbing the blood off of his forearm as he went. He rolled up a winch to lift the bucket of water out of the well. Part of the loose rag was dry, so he doused it in the water and used it to scrub off the blood that covered his forearm. He scrubbed it with a confused and merciless frustration.

Ser Mikhail turned toward Abba and leaned closer to him. "How did it go?"

"What? What do you mean?"

"You said you two had to defend yourselves. How did it go?"

"Well, Maric had fallen to his ass after he bumped into the first thug, but once he pulled out his dagger Maric somehow pushed him down. The other one jumped on him, and I hit him in the head with a rake. Then Maric was cut, and I whacked the other one, too."

"Enough with the getting cut," Ser Mikhail said. "What happened to the thugs?"

"I don't know," Abba said.

"Where did it happen?"

Abba told Ser Mikhail where they were assaulted, and Ser Mikhail told some guards. A couple of guards walked off in no hurry and left the ward. Maric returned to them with a slightly less bloodied arm. His confusion, however, had not left him, and he returned with the same dumbfounded stare he'd had before.

"How could I not have a cut?" he asked.

"Maybe it was your nerves," Ser Mikhail said. "Maybe one of those thugs cut themselves and bled on your forearm. Either way, consider yourself lucky; if you actually *had* been cut, you could have gotten an infection that might have killed you by the tourney day."

Edit

dit and the rest of the party waited for the Count and Countess. Once they had arrived, they rode away together into the Kurem forests. Edit rode on the back of a horse steered by Ser Elseharde. They were in the front of the party with the Kurems, while a single soldier walked in the front and a retinue of soldiers followed behind. Count Adar mentioned that they were heading for a small inland dock that would not be too long of a ride. However, before they had made it there, the Count directed the party to briefly stop at two villages along the way. Both of these villages hung purple banners with a yellow hyacinth flower for their charge. Their visits were quite short; the Count only aimed to collect reports while he passed through.

The forests of the Kuremlands were familiar for a reason that Edit could not discern. The inland port was ahead of them, and they dismounted to board a small boat docked there. A few servants waited at the port, and when the party had fully boarded, the servants walked back in the direction of Kurembrog. The boat was not large, but it surely was not little. It fit the party well, giving them enough room to store their belongings under their seats. A significant number of paddles lined the side of the boat, and Adar's retinue of men sat at these paddles, ready to row them upstream.

During the journey, Adar was quiet. It seemed talking pained him; but to Edit's misfortune, talking came easily to Geder. He would not stop yapping about nothing. Edit was surprised, for she had not initially taken him to be someone so desperately in need of attention.

"The deeper we go, the more Dievic it is," said Geder, speaking in Narese.

Adar huffed.

"Geder, I do not wish to hear about these backward pagans," snapped Siemond.

"Oh, I am just educating the southerners here. I know you are a very learned southerner, but the two we have from High Beak certainly have never heard of Esu."

"What in Gol is Esu?" asked Ser Elseharde.

"It makes me laugh whenever one of you southerners says Gol. *Gol* was in Esu. It is the whole Diev, if you will. Esu is a goddess in Osmjornia, and Gol is a god."

"Adar! Tell your brother to be silent!"

"My brother is not my subject, Siemond," Adar said tiredly. "I hold no power over him."

Geder muttered something under his breath.

"No, Gol is damnation," responded Elseharde.

"Gol is the god of torture, burning, suffering, *and* damnation. May I ask you, Ser Elseharde, where in the Phoenic texts *Gol* is written? It is a Osmjornish word in origin, and only Viantse and Narese words are present in the texts."

The loose skin of Elder Siemond's neck moved as he shook his head with disapproval. "Quit spoutin' nonsense, Geder."

Geder laughed. "Whenever Siemond grows angry, he speaks like he is back in Avonsgatte!"

Not wanting to listen to Geder's words, Edit stared off into the water and daydreamed. The name Esu was familiar, but she could not remember where she had heard it before. Geder continued to talk, and every time someone else would shift the conversation to another topic, he would always find a way to bring the focus back onto himself. It seemed to be like an art of a sort— a very annoying and repetitive art.

Eventually, night fell, and the soldiers' backs grew tired of pulling the boat upriver. They moored the boat to a tree and set up their tents for the night. Edit made sure to prop her tent as far away from Geder's as she reasonably could, telling Elseharde to stay nearby. She struggled to sleep, for the absence of a permanent wall and door put her on edge.

At some point during the night, she peeked out of her tent to see Geder staring off into the water, tossing a coin in his hands. He turned around, noticing Edit's stare. He gave her a smile, and she retreated into what little solitude her cloth tent brought. She slept very lightly that night, clutching a rock that she had found near her tent. When the bright Osmjornish summer sun peered through the gaps in the cloth tent, she awoke. She helped Ser Elseharde pack her tent and once more boarded the boat.

The retinue of men rowed even further up the river. Geder continued to be the unsolicited guide they neither wanted nor needed. Even the soldiers shot glares at the Count's brother while he spoke, but their peers would slap them on the back; their lapses in focus made the pull of the waters grow heavier.

A putrid odor entered Edit's nose, smelling of rotten fruit and spoilt fish. Edit shivered, goosebumps forming over her back and arms. She pinched her nose and winced. Count Adar, Geder, Anita, and a number of the soldiers did not even flinch. Instead, they stared around, looking for its origin. However, the same could not be said for Ser Elseharde and the rest; they gagged at the stench.

"What *is* that?" asked Ser Elseharde.

"It smells of death. You are a knight, no? Are you not used to the smell of death?" inquired Adar, turning his head over to the knight.

Ser Elseharde furrowed his brow. "You're right, but it smells far worse than that."

The Count grunted and swallowed his spit. He looked and sounded worse than yesterday. He had rashes forming on his face and arms, as well as other blemishes that had not been there a day prior. His condition was deteriorating at a rate that was almost noticeable in real time. He was a dead man walking.

"Now we are passing by Pelesgeb! I suppose it's something there that is causing this smell; I do not recall Pelesgeb or its people ever being known for smelling pleasant," said Geder, grinning.

Osmjornia did not smell nice at all, even in Kurembrog. Edit found it amusing that Geder could think Pelesgeb was any different. Even the buildings and forests of Pelesgeb looked no different from the ones in the Kuremlands; and at this rate, she did not expect Belar to look any different, either. She had at one point been excited to see the Midsummer festival in Belar, but her experiences thus far had soured that excitement into a rotten, foreboding feeling. She was losing faith that the trip would be any fun at all.

Geder would not keep his eyes off of her. Elseharde caught on to his excessively lecherous gaze and leaned himself between Geder and Edit to block his view. Another day of inane ramblings from an older man that stared for too long. Edit dreaded it.

Anita took a seat next to Edit.

"Do you have any dreams, Edit?" she asked.

Edit was surprised by the question. "No," she said. "I—I mean, nothing in particular."

"Surely you must have dreams. Everyone has dreams."

She knew it was a bad idea to answer truthfully, but at that moment, she couldn't stop herself. She was tired, and frustrated, and starting to feel too warm in the sun. "Any dreams I might have certainly do not consist of giving up my lands to some boy I have never met," she said.

Anita's face turned red. Geder looked over. Edit expected Adar to look over as well, but it seemed he had not heard her.

"Well, you would of course still have authority in Bek d'Lifa; and you will have some authority here in Kurembrog, too! It would not be as bad as you think," Anita said.

"Pardon my tone, m'lady, but what does Abba know of Bek d'Lifa? What does he know of the Bay of Avon, the olive trade, or even the Yhournish?"

Anita smiled. "Well, I would assume he knows quite a bit! He has never seen High Beak, but he has a vast number of books on those topics. He is fascinated by the history of Mjorn."

"To read something is not the same thing as experiencing it yourself," Edit said, gritting her teeth. "I do not understand why my father wishes to have me marry someone from so far away."

Anita sighed. "It is quite simple, really. Kurembrog is the gateway to all trade in Osmjornia, as well as a good amount of southern Ookos. High Beak is the gate to the west, and I mean that quite literally. Your father controls the gateway to all seafaring. He only wishes to construct a prosperous future for you, Edit."

Edit shook her head. "He is forcing me to give up my home to someone else. Bek d'Lifa is mine."

Geder sat down next to them.

"And Kurembrog was mine, but everyone on this boat knows what happened with that," he said, glancing at his brother.

Adar sighed. His sigh turned into a cough, the coughing to hacking, then the hacking turned into the Count gasping for air. He reached for a bottle at his side and consumed a drop of its contents. Geder stared attentively at the action, but he stayed silent.

Siemond looked quite disturbed during the journey. He stared off into the woods with disgust, making loud remarks about the Dievic followers. The other travelers on the boat spoke of repetitive nonsense that Edit had no interest in. The night came once more, and they camped at the side of the river, but the smell of death permeated their tents. They elected to travel in the night, for none of them could fall asleep with the smell that cursed the forest.

When the moon was directly in the center of the sky, they finally escaped the smell of the dead and found a place to set up camp. Elseharde made certain to pitch his tent next to Edit's. Again, Edit slept lightly. She awoke to the cooing of ringdoves. She dragged herself up to prepare for yet another day on the river. Elseharde once again packed their tents, tossing them on the boat.

"Soon…" Adar said, huffing to catch his breath. "Soon we will reach Woldhom. It is a distance from the river, but we shall visit there just a moment. I miss the taste of their honey."

Anita and Geder looked down, their expressions inscrutable. Siemond shook his head with disapproval. Edit watched carefully, trying—and failing—to understand their reactions.

It took a few hours to reach Woldhom, and when they landed, the smell of death returned to Edit's nose. They docked at a small port that stood at the side of a road leading into the hamlet. They stepped off the boat and walked toward the small village. Adar hurriedly shambled his way forward. When he reached the entrance of the village, he stopped in his tracks. Woldhom was entirely empty. No one roamed the streets. All the buildings looked untampered with, except for one. A house at the edge of town was charred and blackened. It looked as if a boulder had been launched from a trebuchet, collapsing its roof and tearing down one of its walls. Charred planks surrounded it.

A two-limbed creature crawled toward the party, scurrying and chattering its teeth. Ser Elseharde quickly drew his sword and sliced the creature's head clean off. It had the face of a man, but it was deformed; its teeth poked through its cheeks, and its jaw was offset. The head chattered once more, and it violently clawed at itself. Geder grabbed a large stone and slammed it down onto the creature's head; then he pulled out his own sword and thrust it into the body, keeping it in place.

"Hand me a torch! Hurry!" yelled Geder.

One of Adar's men ran to him, handing him a lit torch. He set the torch to the creature, then beckoned for them to retrieve some flammable items so that he could cover the thing in flames.

"What in Avon's name *was* that thing?" asked the Elder.

"You ought to know, with all that schooling you had at the Academy; shouldn't you, Siemond?" Adar asked.

"Go easy on the old man. Not every priest is a complete scholar in all things," said Geder.

"How did *you* know to burn it?" asked Adar.

"If you burn something for long enough, it'll eventually stop moving," Geder said.

Adar hobbled deeper into the center of Woldhom while the rest of the party examined the buildings, searching for any more strange creatures. Edit followed Adar, for she felt a similar curiosity toward the scene. Adar gravitated toward the burnt building, peeking inside the hole in its wall. The roof had collapsed into the building, and within its walls were strange growths. The walls were uniformly bowed out, as if something had grown within it and pushed them out. Near the charred walls, the growths on the edge looked to be dead, or more dead than the rest of the flesh. They must have tried to avoid the fire, for they curved back in toward the center, looking like the mouth of a sea cucumber. The growths in the center writhed. It reminded Edit of something, but she could not remember what it was.

Adar shook his head. "What misfortune has befallen this once fine village?"

In the distance, someone screamed. Adar's head perked up like an alert hound. Members of his retinue ran off into the woods. The moans and growls of several individuals were heard from the direction of the scream. Edit ran to the side of the road, but Ser Elseharde held her back, preventing her from running into the woods to investigate. The same retinue of soldiers that had run into the woods to investigate ran back to the road, yelling for the rest of them to head for the boat. Adar rushed everyone back on.

They ran down the steep road back to the port, loading the women on first. The men climbed on soon after they untied the dock lines.

"What are we running from?" asked the Elder.

No one answered. The retinue of soldiers went to their seats and immediately began to row away from the riverside. They made it about a dozen yards from the port. Adar looked around his boat; four men were gone.

"What happened? We left—" Adar broke off into a painful-sounding coughing fit. When he recovered, he said, "We left men back there!"

The moaning grew nearer, and something screeched; it sounded similar to the scream that they had heard. A hulking beast made of mended bodies crawled between two trees that stood on some raised ground on the riverbank, slamming its shoulder onto one of them over and over as if it were scratching an itch. It held a man in its maw and stared at the boat. Edit clung to Ser Elseharde's arm. Its head was an amalgamation of two bodies, and its mouth was a strange creation that used what looked like arm bones to form its jagged teeth. It was hard to tell what its legs were made of, for they all looked different. Metal plates and dark blue cloth stuck sporadically out through its skin. Nothing was uniform about the creature. Upon seeing it, everyone—even the women, Geder, the Elder, and the ill Adar—took a spot to row away from the beast. The beast did not follow, looking content as it chewed on the corpse in its mouth.

"Oh my," muttered Geder.

"We must inform Hedmond of this. No one can travel on this road. That beast must be hunted to prevent any more of this insanity," said Adar.

"We should put a hunt bounty on it," said the Elder.

"That beast will require more than just a hunter to take it down," Adar said darkly.

They rowed for hours. Night arrived once again, but no one wished to dock out of fear that the beast had been following them. Eventually, a number of the party's heads began to fall with a drowsy weight. Adar ordered that half of them should sleep while the other half rowed. As soon as the other half grew tired, they woke the others so that they could continue to row upstream.

Edit's eyelids were heavy, her head slowly lowering to rest on Ser Elseharde's shoulder. She dreamt of the beast that night. She dreamt of its monstrous teeth and misshapen arms and legs. She imagined that it darted for her, swiping at her with its grafted paws. She flinched awake in the morning, and this woke Elseharde next to her.

"Trouble sleeping again?" asked the knight, blinking blearily in the morning light.

"Bad dreams," Edit said.

Edit noticed Lady Anita staring at her out of the corner of her eye. Edit picked her head up off of the knight's shoulder and stared at the river.

"We will reach Belar soon," Adar announced. "I imagine the festival must have already begun. Be on your best behavior, everyone—we are the representatives of Kurembrog! Do not embarrass the twin serpents."

Geder grinned up at the gray stone walls of Belar, which were slowly growing nearer. Belar was not the prettiest city, but it was impossible to gauge its size by looking at the walls alone. Edit turned her head from one end of the walls to the other, but was unable to see the ends. She frowned. She hated the north of Mjorn. Every town looked the same. All of them had bland architecture. Everything was flat, and there were no rocky hills or cliffs where grand castle towns perched.

They docked in the port, and Geder helped tie the dock line to the side of the old stone Belar dock. The dock workers dragged a gangplank over to the boat, and one by one, everyone removed themselves from the ship.

Edit peeked past the crowd of people at the docks. Festival music rang through the crowd. Edit had never heard this type of music before. Several strange horns hummed deeply and resonantly. Music in High Beak was much more elegant, involving the usage of stringed instruments. The music in Osmjornia sounded as if it originated from a deep abyss.

Venceslaus

enceslaus paced around his room. His door had been barricaded by several pieces of furniture. Ser Groent was sleeping in a chair that faced the only window in the room. Venceslaus shook him awake.

"It is midday, Merr. I hope you are rested."

Ser Groent rubbed his eyes. "As rested as a man could be, with things as they are. I am surprised we are not dead already."

"Maybe stabbing our King in the leg borrowed us a bit of time."

"Maybe."

Venceslaus fetched the original record that he had taken from the library, placing it in his side satchel. He beckoned for Merr to follow him. They began to remove the furniture in front of the door. Once all of the barricades had been removed, Merr lifted up the drawbar and placed it on the ground. Venceslaus retrieved his keys and unlocked the door. Both of them stepped out of the room and locked it once more.

They climbed down the steps and left the keep, watching the guards. Despite the King certainly recognizing them the night before, no one attempted to stop them. It was strange. Maybe the King wanted to keep his deeds a secret.

They mounted their steeds and rode their horses down to the Academy. A paladin stood guard at the entrance, blocking their entry.

"Are you the same paladin that was here yesterday? I am here to return a book that I borrowed," Venceslaus said.

The paladin stepped to the side, allowing them to pass through.

"You would think the paladins would know you as anyone else knows you," said Merr.

"I suspect the Orator has something to do with their strange treatment of me."

They trotted their horses to a hitching post and secured their leads onto its rings. The two marched their way up to the top of the Academy steps. A priest at the entrance halted them.

"Remove your weapons and leave them at the door, knight," commanded the priest.

Merr grunted while he untied his sheath from his belt. The priest pointed to a small table, so Merr placed his sword upon it. He almost stepped inside; but again, he was stopped. He grinned. He removed his dagger from his belt and left it on the table. The priest permitted them through.

While walking toward the library, Merr looked around in awe at the Academy.

"I know I was here but a few days ago, but Go—" He stopped himself. "I mean, it is a marvel to look at."

"Ha! Merr, I never thought you would be one to stop yourself from speaking profanities," Venceslaus said.

"I am a fearing man, Vences. This building is a testament to the faith's power."

They entered the library. Bertram the Book-keeper stood in the same place as he had been standing the day before, his old hands scraping across some books. He looked like he was in deep contemplation. Venceslaus walked over to the priest's lectern. The priest did not notice the Duke, but Venceslaus waited to interrupt him out of respect for the old man's time and knowledge.

After a moment, Bertram looked up and grinned widely. Venceslaus returned him a grin and pulled out the record, placing it on a table that stood next to the Book-keeper.

Bertram's grin faded slightly. He pointed at Venceslaus's satchel.

"What do you have in there? I can feel it…"

Venceslaus looked around the room. "We should discuss it away from prying ears."

Bertram looked at Venceslaus with confusion, but he nodded and led the two to a side room. The room was small, but it overflowed with stacks of books, both open and unopened, with countless notes filling their pages. The Elder closed the door behind them, then stumbled his way toward a chair. Venceslaus helped him sit down.

"What is the reason for such secrecy?" Bertram asked.

"Ser Groent and I were tailing a man who was a leader amongst a group of peasants who are not too fond of the King. This man had a meeting with a black-cloaked individual. Once this meeting had ended, we tailed that dark-cloaked man to an alley where he disappeared... into a puff of black smoke. We fought him off, and I snatched a pendant from his neck before he fled."

The Book-keeper waved his hand at Venceslaus so that he would come near. Venceslaus reached into his satchel, waiting a moment before he pulled the pendant out.

"When you see it, you will understand my urge for privacy."

Venceslaus pulled out the boar's head pendant from his satchel. The priest stared at it, shaking his head in disbelief. Venceslaus went to hand it to him, but the priest pushed the Duke's hand away.

"I mustn't touch it. As I have been led on toward the fate that is old age, I have lost the ability to properly control divinations as I once did. Why would Asbyorn kill Barnut?"

"I have no words to explain it, but it surely cannot be anyone else. He has been acting strange, very strange."

"Flip it over, let me see the maker's mark. It was undoubtedly made here, but I wish to be certain."

Venceslaus turned it over. Bertram leaned in to examine it.

"Aye, it was made here. Did you see the face of the person who wore this?"

"I did not—his face was hidden by his hood—but he was the same height as the king and wore a crimson cloak."

"That damned boy."

"The fact he is colluding with those who want his head is even more baffling. Why would he work with them? It is as though he is plotting against his own kingdom. Only Avon could understand his motivations," said Venceslaus.

He placed the pendant back into his satchel, shaking his head with disbelief. The Book-keeper wagged his finger at Venceslaus and pointed at the satchel once more.

"Be careful not to show that pendant to anyone. You already know that people will kill for chausilver; but the King's pendant? More than just beggars and thieves will be after you."

Venceslaus nodded, marching out of the side room. He and Ser Groent exited into the courtyard of the Academy d'Ava. Before them, there was a crowd of priests and servants hurrying past the Academy gates. Venceslaus, knowing that it would take a long time to travel through the crowd, and seeing that even more people were coming, motioned for Merr to hurry with him over to the gate. It took them about a minute to get past the throng of people that filled the gateway. Once they were out, they saw what all the commotion was about.

A priest about a decade younger than Ser Groent was mounted on a dun-colored horse. A sword with an eagle-head pommel was strapped onto the horse's saddle. The priest held one arm up for all to see, parchment hanging from his hand like a banner. He looked insulted, pointing at the Academy with a zealous fervor.

"Be it on full display to the priests who have abandoned their faith!" yelled the priest.

There was a crowd of peasants and burghers filling the road, standing quietly and listening to the words the mounted priest was yelling. Venceslaus pushed through to the front of the crowd, lingering near the people standing opposite the Phoenic priests. The mounted priest was sashless, but he was undoubtedly a priest. He wore a priest's habit, but his righteous poise was what truly made it apparent.

"By the witness of the ever-living, I, Agathius d'Fisk, once Elder of Fisk, proclaim the Academy *damned*. Since the war just fifteen years ago, the surviving powers in the Phoenicy have perverted our faith to their own benefit and personal gain. Well, I say nay to them! I have copied my argument onto dozens of pieces of parchment just like these and spread them about in the crowds. Copy more! Spread word of the Phoenicy's wrongdoing!"

"This is heresy! Be silent!" said another priest, stepping forward.

A group of peasants took a step toward that priest, intimidating him into silence.

"These priests have been brought into a cloister where their prayers are intercepted by a ceiling before they can reach the heavens. They know not the religion they preach!" called

354

Agathius. "I ask you all one question; and this is a question that all good followers of the Phoenix shall know the answer to. What is the monetary obligation of all free-people?"

A few people in the crowd yelled "the one-seventh tithe."

"Aye! Many priests will claim that obligation is written in the Phoenic texts, but has anyone here verified that? There is no need to answer such a question, for I have the answer here. All of these priests, learned in the Viantse language though they are, know that the Phoenic texts never explicitly call for a one-seventh tithe! It was an obligation born of an argument about the seven pyres of Phoeni. One of these pyres, as I am sure all of you know quite well, is the pyre of almsgiving. Since it is one of seven pyres, the early Phoenicy and the Kings of Nar thought it fitting to institute a one-seventh tithe into law over a thousand years ago.

Now, I think this logic is flawed; but I am in the minority of priests who question the morality of how they are paid. With that being said, without arguing whether the people should or should not pay a tithe at all, the one-seventh tithe is the *only* monetary obligation free-people have toward the Phoenicy. In current times, and especially after the war, it has become commonplace for a priest to ask you for your spare coin in the name of giving it to the needy. However, the same hungry souls are always begging for food outside of these priests' temples. It seems like every week there is a new beggar on the street, but the priest to whom you gave your coin fills his stomach with expensive wines and meats. They wear their habits in the name of poverty, but within the confines of their garments is proof of their avarice!"

Venceslaus grinned. He liked the courage that the priest presented to the crowd. It reminded him of priests before the war, of how they would step in the face of anyone who dared to disrespect the faith. He had been a more devoted man then, and this Agathius gave him some hope. Agathius noticed Venceslaus's grin and returned him one back. Then he turned back to the crowd.

"The priests here think that I am speaking heresy! They think because I shed my sash, that my faith is elsewhere; but that is the furthest thing from the truth. My faith in the ever-living Phoenix above remains stalwart! Though they do not understand, it would be a disservice to my faith if I did *not* rebuke the Phoenicy for straying from the Phoenix!"

Mounted paladins rode their horses out of the Academy, and in the center of these steel-clad religious soldiers stood the Orator himself. By now, the crowd had grown larger than ever, so the Orator's bodyguards formed a square around him, quick to show the collected peasants not to get too close. Aswold stepped in front of Agathius's horse.

"What have we here, Agathius? Step down from that steed and cease this folly," ordered the Orator.

"When I relinquished my sash, I made a choice for myself: I am through with the Phoenicy. I cannot stand idly by and allow myself to be fed by a temple that recruits those who so brazenly disrespect the faith. The greed—"

"What a display of foolishness! Recant your words now! Recant in front of the crowd!"

Agathius refused to acknowledge the Orator's interruption. He turned his face to the crowd.

"Rebuke the Orator! He is at the helm of our faith's perversion. He steers our faith toward an unfortunate destination, guided by the ultimate sin of hubris. He speaks as if he is capable of no wrongdoing, yet he—"

A few of the Orator's bodyguards stepped toward Agathius. His horse bared its teeth at the soldiers.

"Wait. I will come down willingly," said Agathius.

The bodyguards stood back, holding their swords by their handles. Agathius dismounted, patting his steed on the neck and whispering something to it, which seemed to calm the horse.

Agathius locked eyes with Venceslaus. "Orator, I will go willingly; only allow that gentleman over there, the Good Duke, to lead my horse back to the stables."

"Ah, I do not think I will. I think my paladins will escort you and your belongings to the citadel themselves. You are preaching heresy, Agathius, in front of hundreds of witnesses. You will earn yourself an unfortunate demise unless you recant."

Agathius refused to speak any more to the Orator. The paladins bound the priest's arms and dragged him off toward the citadel. The crowd followed them, so Venceslaus and Ser Groent followed as well. The sun cooked them like a stove cooked meat, and the heat of the commonfolk grew more severe as the crowd increased in size. The Good Duke began to sweat; and whenever he bumped into Ser Groent, his steel armor burned at the touch.

A leader amongst the guards posted at the citadel gates called out for more members of the garrison to help push back against the coming mob. Venceslaus and Merr beat the Orator in his march to the citadel, and the guardsmen allowed the duo through. Venceslaus marched straight for the great hall; and soon, the Orator arrived, his paladins dragging Agathius inside. They threw the priest onto the floor in front of the King's dais. Asbyorn stepped unsteadily from his throne and looked down at the priest.

"What have we here?"

Aswold stepped between the King and Agathius. "Brazen heresy," he said.

"That is quite a hefty charge. What did he do?"

"He distributed parchment that defamed the temple and slandered his fellow priests while mounted on his horse in front of the Academy d'Ava. A grave offense!"

"Were there any witnesses?"

"It would not be hyperbole to say that there were hundreds. There was an overwhelmingly large crowd, and it only grew larger in following us over here. He created a spectacle! He is exacerbating our current issues with the commonfolk; I demand him to recant his words and to publicly proclaim that he was speaking falsehoods!"

"Ah," said the King, turning his head to Agathius. "Recant."

Agathius said not a word.

"Recant!"

The King gestured for one of his bodyguards to walk over to the priest. The guard stood Agathius up and grabbed him by his hair.

"If you wish a for chance at keeping your life, then recant this instant!" yelled the King.

Agathius's face was blank. He had no fear, nor sadness, nor even anger on his face. He was calm in the face of persecution. The King gritted his teeth and nodded to the guards.

"Put the priest in the dungeon. He shall have a formal hearing tomorrow; his fate shall be determined then."

A few guards retrieved the priest and took him away. Agathius did not fight against them. It was as though he had already accepted his fate; or perhaps he simply did not fear his death at all.

Venceslaus leaned toward Merr. "I want you to find out which cell he is being held in. I want you to speak to that man."

"Are you sure? The King surely is aware that we know he killed Barnut; I am not certain his dungeons are quite safe for you."

"He said he was from Fisk. I am curious what he knows of Dorthu."

The King walked with a limp as he exited the great hall. His complexion was even paler than usual. Ser Bertram followed the King out of the room, and Aswold marched over to the Good Duke, stopping when he stood almost face to face with him. His paladins kept themselves at his side, standing at the ready.

"Venceslaus, why would that priest ask for his steed and belongings to be moved by you?"

"I suppose I must have a trustworthy face," Venceslaus said.

The Orator wagged his finger at the Duke. "If I hear *anything* to suggest that you conspired with this priest to spread his heresy, then I will have you locked up next to him."

"You are grasping at nothing, Orator; this is the first time I have ever met that man."

"You poke your head in places you ought to avoid. Have a blessed day."

Venceslaus squinted at the Orator as he left the room. *What had he meant by that?* Venceslaus and Ser Groent hurried off to the Good Duke's chambers and unlocked the door. Entering with haste, they shut the door behind them.

"Do you truly believe that priest would know anything about the massacre at Dorthu?" asked Ser Groent.

"If anyone is likely to be able tell us what happened in Dorthu, it is him," Venceslaus said. "Once it grows dark, I will go off and find his cell myself. I want you to search his steed for any of his belongings. Prepare the horses to leave; I do not think it is safe for us in Nara anymore."

"I shall," said Ser Groent, bowing to his liege.

"I wonder if the King is even aware we stabbed him. He saw our faces, yet no one has come after us. It isn't as though he only acts at night; he killed Barnut in broad daylight. His limp cannot be a coincidence, either, but to face such an odd lack of consequences makes me feel as though stabbing the King was some strange dream."

"It is strange indeed. I will tell the stablemaster that we are heading for Belar; we had intended to leave for the tournament several days ago, and they know this," said Ser Groent. "I wonder how that Elseharde is doing. He is sometimes too brash for his own good, but he has a good spirit."

"Aye, you taught him well. He is a good lad; I trust him. It is apparent that knighthood is something he cares much about." Venceslaus sighed. "I miss my daughter. It is at times like this that I feel guilty. You have your own children at home. I am going to give you leave from your service to be with them after this trip. I have kept you from them over the years."

Ser Groent smiled. The knight and duke clasped forearms, then hugged one another.

"Thank you, Good Duke."

"Of course."

The two sat down to laugh over old stories and talk about history. They discussed other subjects of interest to them— economics, philosophy, and religion—and while they did, time seemed to wisp by like an arrow. Once night arrived, Venceslaus grabbed his cloak. They nodded at one another and exited the room, parting ways. Merr headed for the exit, and Venceslaus went deeper into the keep. The guards that were posted must have been tired and bored; their heads were down, and they were nattering to one another. Venceslaus laughed under his breath at the quality of men the King kept.

He crept his way through the halls, walking down numerous flights of stairs. Strangely, the dungeon had been left unguarded, so Venceslaus marched his way downstairs unhindered. He passed by empty cells and prisoners begging the Good Duke for his mercy, for freedom. Venceslaus paid them no mind, traveling deeper down into the dungeon until he found the man that he was looking for. Agathius was sitting down, staring up at the vaulted ceiling above him. He repeated prayers and continued to do so even when Venceslaus arrived, so the Good Duke waited until the priest was finished. When his prayer had concluded, Agathius smiled.

"I expected that you would come, Duke Venceslaus," said Agathius.

Venceslaus knelt next the cell bars. "Why did you name me as the person responsible for your belongings?"

"Because you would make good use of them. You are known as the Good Duke for a reason."

"That title means nothing, truly. I only try to treat each person I meet with compassion."

"You try; that is good. What noble in Nar could claim the same? A very small number, especially after Barnut's passing."

Venceslaus flinched. "How long have you been in the city?"

"I arrived only this morning. Word spreads quickly in the streets of Nara," said Agathius. "Why have you come, Venceslaus?"

"You expected me, yet you question why I am here?"

"I have an idea as to why you are here, but I have learned that asking questions often leads to a more fruitful understanding than any assumption."

Venceslaus looked down at his satchel, then he looked back up at the priest. He opened the satchel and pulled out the boar's head pendant.

"I snatched this pendant from the person whom I think killed the Great Chancellor," he said. "I came to you in the hope that you may know something about the Dorthu massacre."

Agathius stared at the pendant. He held concern in his brow, shaking his head at the sight.

"I do know of Dorthu. The King's men slaughtered everyone there—everyone but for one boy," said Agathius.

Venceslaus clasped the pendant in his hand. He gripped it so firmly that the boar spear pricked his hand, causing a rivulet of blood to flow down his wrist.

"Rise, Duke Venceslaus," commanded a voice of a man behind the duke.

Agathius stared behind Venceslaus. The Good Duke turned around and saw who it was: a man in shining armor who wielded a blinding white spear.

"It is a pleasure to see you again, Ser Bertram Rowe," said Agathius, getting to his feet.

"Venceslaus, you must come with me."

Venceslaus's heart pounded.

"For what reason?" he asked.

Ser Bertram placed his hands on the Good Duke's shoulders and faced him. He had a hard, resolute expression on his face.

"Because everything you suspect is true," Ser Bertram said. "But the truth is not so clear. The King's hands did slay Barnut; yet we still do not know who killed the Great Chancellor."

"What?" said Venceslaus, recoiling in distress.

"Follow me, and you will understand what I mean."

360

Venceslaus looked to Agathius, and Agathius nodded. The White Spear led the Good Duke down the royal halls and into the King's chambers. Inside, the King was alone. He looked to be asleep. Black collars were wrapped around his neck and wrists. A glass bottle with a mixture that Venceslaus could not identify sat on his side table. Ser Bertram locked the door behind them and took a seat on a stool next to the King's bed.

"What is going on here?" Venceslaus asked.

"Whoever has been controlling the King must have assumed I would not be able to do anything about the changes in his demeanor and actions," said Ser Bertram. "But while I swore an oath to obey him, I also swore an oath to guarantee his health. It took me a while to figure it out, but I became certain of what was afflicting him several months ago. He has been growing bolder."

Venceslaus inched his way around the room to the side of the bed opposite to the White Spear. He leaned in closer to stare at the King. The King's skin was pale, and it looked as though he had almost been drained of life. Venceslaus held his hand near the stone collars and felt himself growing weaker the longer he did.

"This is ordustone," he said.

"Every so often, right after our King falls asleep, he rises and leaves this room with a black cloak draped over his shoulders. Sometimes, he won't even bring it; instead, he acts *differently* around the citadel. Before the ordustone collars, he would rise every now and then, often writing notes. I caught a glimpse, once, of what he was writing. It was a command of treachery against himself."

Ser Bertram leaned toward a side table and opened a drawer. He held several of the letters in his hands, and he gave them to Venceslaus.

"All of these letters espouse treachery against the King of Nar," said Ser Bertram. "If you look at the signatures, you can see that they are all signed by the same man: 'the Ultimate'."

"A pseudonym," said Venceslaus. "Peculiar indeed."

"I have been placing these collars on him every other night to see if a response would come. But I am certain that whoever is controlling him is now aware of my actions against them; for after the first few instances of my collaring him, Asbyorn awoke and sought to make my sister his mistress."

Venceslaus's jaw dropped. "Who do you believe wishes to torment the king so?"

Ser Bertram stood up from the stool and placed the letters down on the side table. He looked at his spear, twirling it around in his hands. He grabbed it by the sharp end and pointed the butt of it at the King's flesh. Swirls of wispy helminths desperately writhed their way toward the spear. The King's eyes flickered, so Bertram swept the spear away from him. The King quickly fell back into his slumber.

"I studied at the Academy before I became a knight, and there are no records of the existence of these worms; but while I may not know exactly what they are, I know that his control depends on them. I am trying to rid his body of them, but I fear that their removal could kill him. It is getting even harder to put the cuffs on him, now. I put a sleeping powder into his medicine so that I could make certain he would not harm himself anymore."

"What can I do, Ser Bertram?"

"I want you to seek justice for Asbyorn," said Ser Bertram. "I cannot do so as openly as I would like. I hope that even if I may have to fight against you publicly, you will fight to rout out whoever is doing this to him."

Venceslaus walked over to the stack of letters on the side table. Bertram moved out of his way. One of the pseudonyms struck him; it was from a person using the moniker "the Serpentine".

"Who is the Serpentine?" Venceslaus asked.

"The letter makes it quite clear; you can deduce from there."

Venceslaus read the letter over quickly, his eyes flicking across the page. When he finished reading, he put the paper down on the table with great force. "Why did you not bring this to my attention sooner?"

"My loyalty is to the King. I knew that if you saw that letter, you would leave," said Bertram, his eyes downcast.

"I need to go to my daughter at once," Venceslaus said.

"Do not seek your own means of transportation. The King has ordered a watch to be kept on you, and he will apprehend you if you flee. I will prepare a ship for you."

Venceslaus hastily stuffed the letters into his satchel. "I am taking these. Ser Groent is inspecting the priest's horse; I must go."

"Be careful, Good Duke."

Venceslaus stormed out of Asbyorn's chambers, leaving the White Spear and the King behind. He ran down the halls and stairs to the exit of the keep. He could hear yelling coming from the direction of the stables, so he raised his hood and kept to the shadows. He crept toward a side window and peered inside.

Ser Groent had his sword drawn. He was fighting a duo of guards and a knight wearing a crimson cape. Venceslaus hurried around to the stable gates. They were wide open, and the dun-colored horse was nowhere in sight. Ser Groent slashed at the knight's unhelmeted face, gashing across his forehead. Blood spurted in the knight's eyes, and he attempted to wipe his face with no success. One of the guards successfully cut Merr; but in return, he cut the guard in the neck and kicked the other guard in the chest, sending him stumbling back. He grabbed the blade of his own sword and used it to help him thrust the tip of his blade through the guard's visor.

Suddenly, Ser Groent's eyes widened. Venceslaus looked down. There was blood pouring from a wound in Ser Groent's neck. He grabbed at the wound and gasped for air. Venceslaus ran to him, pulling the guard's dagger from his waist and stabbing him in the throat. Venceslaus went to Merr, falling to his knees and trying to pull his dying friend closer. Dark blood ran quickly over his hands.

"Merr... I—Merr... oh, Gol, I'm sorry," Venceslaus said, pushing a hand across Merr's forehead.

A gurgling sound came from Merr's mouth. He was trying to form words, but the blood had already filled his throat.

"It's alright," Venceslaus said. "Do not try to speak."

Venceslaus unclipped the straps keeping Ser Groent's breastplate affixed to his chest. He grabbed the knight's dagger and pulled his gambeson aside, revealing his left clavicle. He would not allow Ser Groent to suffer needlessly. With tears in his eyes, the Good Duke placed the tip of the dagger to Ser Groent's skin and thrust downwards. Tears blurred his vision.

"You are with Glysi now," Venceslaus murmured.

Torchlight illuminated the stable wall. Filled with adrenaline, Venceslaus got to his feet and ran. He crept along in the shadows and jumped over a small wall, then fled into the main streets of Nara. He looked up toward the sky. The moon was directly above him. Venceslaus ran to a manhole and climbed down into it.

Meara

*uka will die. Luka will die. Luka will die.* Meara told herself this while she stared at her reflection in the blade of whittling knife. She paced around the merchant's house in an attempt to build up enough courage to venture out and enact her revenge. The streets outside were flooded with people. She knew Luka would have the orphans running rampant in search of food to fill his stomach.

She exited the house to the sight of a sea of colors, ribbons, and banners. It was a cacophony of music and movement. The trade square overflowed with stalls and merchants trying to compete for the festivalgoers' attention. There were plenty of stalls with parade equipment around, and Meara headed directly for one that sold festival masks. The stall merchant waved to her, so she returned him a smile and walked over.

"Hello there, lassie! Looking to buy some masks for the festivities?" asked the mask merchant.

He wore a mask made to resemble an angry elf. It had pointed ears, and in its maw were jagged teeth. Its eyes were exaggeratedly large and bulbous. She looked around to make sure no one was watching her.

"Alright," Meara said.

After browsing the large assortment of masks, she noticed one that called to her: a wooden mask that had been carved to look as if it were a man's face, crumbling apart. Green flames were carved and painted at the edges of the mask. Satisfied with her choice, she showed it to the merchant and brought out coin to pay for it. The trader accepted her coin with a joyous grin and bowed.

"Frightening choice! The face of Gol himself," said the trader.

Meara smiled and turned away from the stall. She put the mask on her face and wandered through the crowd of people. Exactly as she'd predicted, orphans scurried around the square, standing out like sore thumbs. As she watched, a few of them were apprehended by the stall keepers and guards. She followed one of the more skilled pilferers, tailing him while he brought back a sack of food to Luka. Because of the number of people that filled the streets, Meara knew that Luka would move to a different hiding spot so that he could keep away from the eyes of passersby. But the child traveled quite a distance, and Meara was confused; this was the farthest away that Luka had ever camped from the town square.

The crowd thinned out the farther away they went. The child took a turn down an alley. She refused to follow him, so she instead decided to keep a careful watch on alley from the street. The orphan took another turn and disappeared behind a building. Meara went around the corner to cut the boy off. To her left was another alleyway. When she looked down it, she saw the pig.

She could overhear Luka's complaints: he was not pleased by the bounty that had been brought before him. He cursed at the children to bring him more food. Her fists tightened, so she took a step back and sat down in order to calm her mind. She watched the entrances to the alleys for about an hour or so, but she grew bored of waiting for the pig to reveal himself. Shaking her head, she followed one of the orphan children back to the town square.

She fetched a loose burlap sack that had been left at the side of a random storehouse. She wisped through the crowd of festivalgoers, pilfering as she went. She took one loaf of bread, some fruit, and some berries. She would walk past a stall, and with no apparent movement, whatever it was that she had found appealing in the stall would be inside her sack. Stealing was easy. The other children tried to force their way to food, but Meara did so with seemingly no effort. Her sack was full of it. She noticed a group of children standing and staring. She dropped the sack to the ground and propped it open so that the food inside was displayed to them. One of the children caught a glimpse of the food, so he crept past the festivalgoers, picked up the sack, and threw it over his shoulder. He ran back in the direction of Luka; but this time, Meara followed the boy into the alleyway, and just as he turned the corner, Meara snatched the boy, pushed him in front of the group, and took the sack from him.

Luka always went on and on about how he would be there to protect the children and that he was their savior. He would tell each child that if someone from the outside were to harm any of them, he would be the first to rise and defend them. In practice, this rarely happened. Whenever a child would come back with wounds or any signs of having been beaten, Luka gave excuses. He would say that it was not the right time, or that it would take too much energy to find the perpetrator. But what *really* mattered to Luka was food. The only time Meara had ever seen Luka get to his feet and do something was when his source of food had been threatened.

When Luka saw Meara take the sack of food from the orphan, he let out a beastly roar. He pointed his finger and sent all the children to chase after Meara. She grinned, running away. She knew she was faster than any of the other children, and it was no question that she was far quicker than the pig. She ran toward the town square and slipped into the festival crowd. The orphans chasing her dissolved into the mass of people.

Meara left the town square once she was sure that they were all scattered around; but before she left the crowd, she dropped the sack once more. When she saw the group of orphans go for it again, she yelled *thief!* at the top of her lungs and watched all the local guards run after the group of orphans in an attempt to corral them. This scattered them far and wide.

As she had expected, she saw Luka standing at the edge of the crowd. He anxiously tapped his foot as he scanned around, trying to see what was happening. Meara watched for a while, but none of the children returned to Luka. He was red with anger. It was at that moment that Meara revealed herself. She waltzed out in front of him, removed her mask, and gave him a wide smile. He stared at her as if he had seen a ghost.

He took his time walking toward her, gritting his teeth forcefully.

"Meara! I thought I was done with you, but here you are, right before my eyes!"

He broke into a sprint toward her. She began to run, too, choosing a long, circuitous route that took her around several different buildings. Again, she faced the pig, but this time he huffed and cursed, his feet dragging behind him. He walked after Meara, for he could not keep up with her. Meara walked backward into an alley. She passed the burnt-down cottage, then stopped.

"I could never *stand* you, you cunt!" Luka shouted, spittle flying from his mouth. "You have harassed me for as long as I can remember. The absolute disrespect I have received from you— how dare you, Meara! How *dare* you!"

He stomped toward Meara. Inch by inch, she stepped away.

"You have always been full of yourself, Luka," she said. "So full of yourself, in fact, that you forget to notice anything around you. You haven't even noticed the gift I brought you."

He faltered. "Gift?"

Meara pulled out a loose post and slammed it into Luka's side. He howled in pain. She hit him once more, causing him to stumble toward a pile of stacked wood that leaned against the alley wall. He did not stumble far enough toward it, however, and he was able to lift himself back up. She charged forward with the post in hopes of pushing him over again, but he barely stumbled. He was heavier than she had expected, which amused her for a moment; but the thought of her being unable to move him frightened her even more. She swung the post at Luka's head, only narrowly missing him. He clenched his fists with a primal anger. Meara swung again, but Luka grabbed the post and stomped on her foot. Meara yelped, stumbling backward.

Luka threw the post to the ground and slapped her, sending her face-first to the alley floor. Her ears rang.

He stared at the stack of planks and laughed. "Are you serious?"

He ripped away the stack plank by plank and revealed the trap that Meara had created. Still laughing to himself, he turned to Meara and grabbed her by the head, forcing her to look at it.

"Did you think you were going to stick me in that hole? Every plan you have ever had has failed! You are a dumb cunt. The only thing you are good for is filling my fucking stomach."

Meara couldn't help herself; she laughed. "You are right. I should have found a bigger hole to put you in."

Luka huffed and threw her to the ground. Meara's back and head slammed into the dirt, knocking the wind from her. Her vision blurred. She saw Luka reaching his hand toward her neck. He dragged her toward the spike pit she had created. She scrabbled against the ground, trying to prevent him from dragging her farther, but he pulled her along with frightening ease.

Luka screamed at her while he dragged her to the hole. He was yelling at her, calling her names, and telling her how useless she was. Furious tears formed in her eyes. She had fought, and fought, and fought, but there was nothing she could do. It had been a good plan; he was just too strong, too *big*, and he had overpowered her. She had come all this way for nothing. She could hear her heartbeat pounding in her ears; she looked up at the pale sky above her as he dragged her across the alley to her doom.

"You will not just sit back and painlessly die. You will *experience* your punishment," Luka hissed, his face barely an inch away from hers.

Meara stared off at the crowds, hoping someone would notice what was happening, but the festival was too busy and too loud. Nobody seemed to notice her at all. Luka's eyes were bloodshot, and his reddened face shook with bloodlust.

"Do you think any of them care about you? Do you think any one of them would stop their fun to help you, you cunt? *You are nothing.* You were never anything. The only thing you ever did that mattered was feeding me. And now," he said, "you are going to die, and that won't matter to anybody, either."

Luka squeezed Meara's skull even tighter and pushed her face toward the spikes; but before he could force her to make contact with them, he shot upright. He made a garbled, strangled-sounding noise. His arms pulled in close to his torso and shook awkwardly. Meara caught herself, grabbing the sides of the hole. She scrambled away from the spikes as quickly as she could—and to her complete surprise, she saw Gol standing behind Luka, jabbing one of her whittling knives into the pig's back. She must have dropped one in the alleyway, she realized, but she hadn't noticed that she'd done so.

Luka turned around, the knife still stuck in his back, and slapped the boy away. He began to beat the boy. Meara ran up to him, pulled the knife out of his back, and stabbed him again. He turned around in shock, then lunged for her. She tripped and dropped the whittling knife. He stomped over to her, his face contorted with rage. With all the might that remained in her, she slammed her foot into his knee. He squealed in pain, stumbling backward and tripping unceremoniously into the spike pit. Meara clapped her hands over her mouth.

He screamed and screamed, blood streaming in rivulets from his mouth. After a moment, the commotion began to draw the eyes of passersby. A cleaver that had been left outside near a cottage caught her attention. She picked it up, returned to the pig, and swung the cleaver down at his neck. The sound of his screaming dissipated into choked gurgling. Meara, consumed with a rage so intense that her vision began to tunnel, gripped the pig by his hair and continued to chop at his neck.

After his head was completely severed, she held it up and stared at it. Luka's eyes were glassy and lifeless, and his skin was pallid. Adrenaline was flooding through her, and she did not know whether she wanted to scream or laugh or cry. For some reason, she felt compelled to wrap his head up and carry it with her in a burlap sack. So, she did exactly that. She and Gol stared at each other. She looked down at herself, her hands and torso all bloodied, and when she looked up, she saw a guard walking down the road. He noticed her. Their brief moment of reunification and triumph was over. Meara placed the mask of Gol on her face, and they ran away into the crowded festival streets with the Luka's head in a sack hanging over Meara's shoulder.

After their escape, they found themselves at a stone brick balustrade that overlooked a part of the city below. The area was between two buildings and was incredibly secluded. None of the festivalgoers loitered there. They had lost the guard, so they sat and stared at the ground below. People filled the streets, flowing like a river. How could there be so many people, Meara wondered to herself, leading so many different lives, all with their own problems and futures? Gol's expression was difficult to read; she wondered what it was that he was thinking.

"Is it not strange, Gol?"

Gol turned, tilting his head like a confused dog.

"Is it not strange that what we went through today is not even thought about or known to anyone else in the world? None of these people know of it. Gol, I—" She caught herself, then turned to Gol, laughing sheepishly. "I did not mean to use that word that way. I will only use it as your name from now on."

Gol smiled.

"But these people do not know what we did," she continued, "and honestly, I do not think they would even *care* to know.

Children starve on the streets around them, and they turn a blind eye. That Phoenic temple is surrounded by perverted men who seek to prey on children. The lords of Belar do not think for even a *second* about bringing aid to the countless orphans on the streets; Lord Hedmond is far more worried about presenting a grand festival to everyone. And everyone else? They go toward the town square... They want to buy *knick-knacks*."

She removed the mask from her face, staring at it in her hands.

"This cost me the same as two loaves of bread. That coin could have gone toward feeding the needy; yet they choose to buy useless toys like this instead."

She handed the mask over to Gol.

"We will go back to the children. They have no one now, so we will replace Luka. We will treat them well. We will give them proper food, and we will allow them to grow strong. We will be champions for the children who have been forced to deal with the same hardships as we have. We will create a better future for them."

Meara tightened her grip on the burlap sack that held Luka's head. She looked down at the people below them once more, scanning around. She pointed to the alley where she had found Luka hiding.

"The children will be over there; we should go find them. We will show them that Luka cannot harm them anymore."

Gol nodded his head and smiled at Meara. Together, they stood up and ventured toward the alleyway. The darkness of night was beginning to fall over the streets of Belar. Meara and Gol entered the alley to the sight of the children sitting and waiting for their king to return. One of them noticed Meara and stood up. He had knife in his hand. The rest of them soon noticed her, and they too rose with a conditioned hostility.

Before the boy could run toward her, she pulled out Luka's decapitated head by the hair and pointed it at the children. His lifeless jaw drooped open, and blood dripped slowly from the wound in his neck.

All of the children dropped their weapons. They looked lost. They knew not what to do, so they allowed Meara to walk by them. She climbed up onto the same throne that Luka had once sat on, Gol at her side. The children stared at the girl, waiting silently for her orders.

Venceslaus

enceslaus's feet touched the sewer floor. He released his grip from the ladder and looked around in the vast darkness. With no means of lighting his way, he took a deep breath and attempted to remember his way out.

It had been many years since Venceslaus had last used these tunnels. The first time had been when he was a boy; he, Barnut, and Matnus had all played in these long-unused tunnels before they had come of age, pretending to be knights venturing deep into a great dragon's lair in search of treasure and renown. Nostalgia gripped him for a moment, but the feeling soon went away.

The last time he had been here was a far less joyous occasion. It was the day Ava had left, and the day the Yhournish chief Enok Vanok had been killed. The memories of the Yhournish rampaging in the streets of Nara recurred in his mind, and they smeared the smile from his face. He had used these tunnels to escape Nara that day, and he would do the same today.

It was pitch black, the lack of light taunting him whenever he would stumble over the occasional brick; but he shrugged off these moments and persisted in the dark. For the most part, he remembered the tunnels well enough, and he did not need to see to move about. Something that sounded like muttering was heard behind him, but no torchlight followed. The Duke's heart raced, and he hurried forward. The darkness gave him brief solace from the thought of his dead friend, but his pursuit brought the thoughts back. He wiped his eyes, struggling to fight away the tears.

Moonlight shined into the tunnel through an old grate. Venceslaus attempted to open it, but the hinges were rusted and refused to move. The shaking of the grate echoed within the tunnel, and the sounds of guards grew louder. Venceslaus spun around in search of a way to force the door open. A loose brick rested on the sewer floor. Venceslaus grabbed the brick and slammed it into the hinges of the grate. The collision of the brick with the metal grate rang out within the tunnels, and in between each swing, Venceslaus could hear the steps of guards getting even louder. Torchlight emanated, flickering from deep down in the tunnel. Venceslaus slammed the brick onto the hinges with all of his remaining strength.

The grate popped off at the top hinge. Venceslaus slammed the brick on the bottom hinge, and the hinge broke immediately. *The rust must have weakened it,* Venceslaus thought. He pushed the grate over and ran out of the tunnel and into the woods, making sure to take a rockier path to avoid any mud. He saw the guards exiting the tunnel behind him. One of them pointed to a set of tracks that Venceslaus had left behind. Venceslaus cursed to himself and began to tiptoe carefully across the rocky ground so as not to bring any more attention to himself.

One of the guards went to follow the tracks, but another guard grabbed him by the arm and pulled him back into the tunnel. Venceslaus let out a sigh of relief. He turned his back to the city of Nara and ventured deeper into the forest that surrounded it. After a walking for a while, he reached the Lende, a tributary of the River of Nar. There was a small house on its bank, and he dragged himself over to it. Desperate for rest, he decided to take a chance on the home. His old bones could not handle the prolonged exertion; he almost collapsed at the door of the home.

He knocked on the door, using his other arm to keep himself propped up against the door frame. The door creaked open. An older gentleman was behind it. He must have recognized Venceslaus, because he swung the door open and hurried him inside.

He pulled out a stool, aiding Venceslaus as he sat down. "The Good Duke, at my doorstep? How can I help you, m'lord?"

"I recognize you," Venceslaus said. "You are from the city, a shipbuilder—your name is Ehren, yes?"

Ehren laughed. "By Avon! You remember my name? How many years has it been?"

"Many. I see you have moved out of the city."

"It is quieter out here."

Ehren suddenly stood still, as if he had remembered something. He bowed deeply to Venceslaus, keeping his head low.

"Oh, Ehren! I am not your commander anymore. There is no need for such gestures," Venceslaus said. "You have welcomed me into your home, in any case; I am in your debt."

Ehren slowly looked up. "And under such strange circumstances, m'lord. You are wandering around in the middle of the night without any knights of yours to protect you—are you alright?"

"Arise, Ehren," Venceslaus said, frowning.

Ehren stood straight up and took a seat next to the Duke.

"You look sad," he said. "Quite sad. In shock."

Venceslaus did not respond. He only gave the man a sullen look.

"Lord Venceslaus, there is no need to share, but you must allow me to aid you once more. I will not allow you to suffer alone."

Venceslaus smiled through his frown. "That is very kind of you, but I only require lodging."

"I have a spare room. My son never visits anymore, so you can use his bedding."

"Thank you, Ehren."

Ehren went into another room. He spent some time in there, and after a few minutes of the sounds of tossed items and rustled bedding, he held the door open and beckoned for Venceslaus to come inside. Venceslaus entered and sat down on the bed. It was not the most comfortable, but he was so dearly grateful for Ehren's hospitality that the quality did not matter.

Ehren rested his forearm on the doorframe. "What is it that led you here, Good Duke?"

Venceslaus looked up. "Have you heard the news?"

"The news of the Great Chancellor? Yes, of course. Why?"

"His death had a far more malevolent origin than I could have imagined, and I was caught in the web of it. I was looking to find the man who had killed my friend, but it had only led me to more loss."

"I see," said Ehren. "What do you plan on doing now?"

Venceslaus bit his tongue, hesitating to answer. He had been harmed by so many unforeseen events that he was fearful of sharing too much, but he swallowed his fear. At that moment, Ehren was the only person capable of helping him; and if he *were* to help, then he deserved to be made aware of the danger that it would bring him.

"I need something I can sail up the river. Nothing grand, just small and nimble enough so that I can row upstream if need be."

"Are you sure, Good Duke? If the winds are unfavorable, rowing will take great strength."

"Call me Venceslaus—or Vences, even. I will be fine. I love river rowing. My legs are what ail me, but my back is strong," Venceslaus said with a wide grin.

"I imagine you need one soon; otherwise, you would have just paid for a ship to take you wherever it is you wanted to go."

"Aye. And I would be leaving now, too, if I wasn't unsure of my ability to stay awake."

"Take my personal skiff. I will have it prepared for you in the morning."

"Thank you for your kindness, Ehren," Venceslaus said.

Ehren smiled. "Thank you for yours."

Ehren left Venceslaus alone in the room to rest. He fell asleep quite quickly, although his dreams tormented him. He woke up the next morning in a cold sweat. He could not quite remember what he had dreamt about, but he figured it must have been related to Merr, Barnut, or even Asbyorn. He rose from the bed and walked toward the door, but when he overheard Ehren speaking to a man outside, he froze. He crept over to a small hole that was in the wall and peered through to see who was there. It was a gray-bearded man dressed in steel armor with a cape bearing the King's charge. His eyes wandered around, examining Ehren's home.

"I appreciate that you are taking time out of your day to speak with me, kind gentleman! I am Ser Ernest, and I was tipped off by one of the night-watch captains in Nara that a wanted aristocrat fled into these woods. You would not happen to know of anything of that, would you?"

"An aristocrat? Which one is wanted? There are many aristocrats in Nara."

"An older fellow with graying ginger hair. Venceslaus Freihei is his name."

"Oh! I know that name, but no lord as rich as he has come around here in a long time. I apologize for being of such little help to you."

"Well, how unfortunate. But if he truly is not here, then I presume you would not mind if we checked inside, would you?" Ser Ernest asked. "He has been known to bribe peasants, you see, and we want to be as thorough as possible in our search."

"Why would I let you enter my home? I do not know if you would ransack the place."

"I assure you, we will leave everything as we found it; we only wish to absolve you of any further suspicion. I should think it quite a nice proposal. Were you to deny us entry, I would not offer such a thing again."

Ehren turned around and looked at the house. Venceslaus's eyes widened. He ducked away from the hole in the wall and went quietly from room to room, looking for Ehren's back door. When he found it, he pushed it open slowly, careful not to make a sound. He saw the skiff Ehren had prepared sitting by the bank of the river, but he doubled back, looking around for a place to hide. If he attempted to flee on the boat now, then Ehren would surely be killed for housing a wanted criminal. There was a small hole that led into the crawlspace under the post-supported house. Venceslaus crawled into it and tucked himself behind a few barrels that had been stored there, craning his neck to listen through the floor.

"I cannot let you in, Ser. It is against the principles of the good people of Nar to allow others to step uninvited over their thresholds."

Ser Ernest sighed. "We are going to search your home whether you wish us to or not."

Ser Ernest walked forward, but Ehren stood in his way. The knight shoved him to the ground, and his men held him down while he cursed. Venceslaus felt the stomping of footsteps above him. The door swung open, scraping across the floorboards over Venceslaus's head. He could hear thudding and rustling coming from above him. The sounds soon stopped, and Venceslaus sat in the crawlspace, his heart pounding. He heard the knight's footsteps; loud at first, then slowly growing quieter as he vacated Ehren's home.

"Why are both of the beds in your home unmade? They both look slept in, and one is wet with a musk."

"My son rarely comes by anymore, so he is not here to make his bed," Ehren said, hesitating only momentarily. "I leave it as it is to remind me of the last time he visited me."

Venceslaus heard a disappointed huff.

"I will leave you to what you were doing, then... eh, what was it?"

"Ehren."

"Yes, Ehren. What is it that you do again?"

"I make boats, large and small. My father taught me the trade, and I taught my son. He now works as a shipbuilder in the capital. I am very proud of him."

"Ah. Well, if you do find the gentleman named Venceslaus, be sure to notify a member of the local watch. We will pay you handsomely enough that neither you nor your son will ever have to worry about making another ship to feed yourselves again. Do you understand?"

"Yes," Ehren said. "I will let you know if I see him."

Venceslaus smiled. Ehren's loyalty was impressive; he was surely the same soldier he had known years ago. The knights marched away, but Venceslaus stayed in the crawlspace for a while longer until he was certain that the men had wholly gone from the area. In time, Ehren's steps tapped above Venceslaus's head, and at this moment Venceslaus revealed himself. Ehren gave a sigh of relief and pulled Venceslaus out from the crawl space. The Good Duke brushed the dirt from his tunic and shook the shipwright's hand.

"Thank you, Ehren. You are a good man. When all is well again, I will guarantee you a grand prize in Bek d'Lifa."

"It is the least I can do for you, Venceslaus," Ehren said.

Venceslaus smiled and slapped a few coins in the shipwright's palm. "It is an order, lad. You shall be rewarded for your loyalty."

Ehren grinned. He led Venceslaus over to the skiff. He had packed a bag inside with all the necessary tools to set up a tent and light a fire. There was even a fishing pole, some bait, a loaf of bread, and a pot to boil water in. Venceslaus smiled and patted Ehren's back. After tossing his own pouch into the bag, he grabbed the oars that Ehren had retrieved for him and climbed into the vessel. After Ehren untied the skiff from a post, Venceslaus used an oar to push himself deeper into the river.

"Are you sure you will be able to row upstream?" yelled Ehren.

"Are you joking, lad? I have been rowing upstream in this river since I was a boy! I have conquered these waters time and time again; my age won't keep me from doing so now!"

Ehren saluted the Duke, waving him off as the boat drifted farther and farther from the riverbank. The only stress that would come from the first part of the journey would be the risk of being stopped. Venceslaus did not need to worry about the winds; at the moment, he simply had to float downstream. He rowed only to pick up speed, knowing that the current would aid in maintaining it. He passed by several villages on the bank of the river, but he kept his hood up and his head down. The most attention he received was a few passing curious glances.

It took him half the day to reach the River of Nar. He could see the rivermouth opening to his right and the River of Nar proper to his left. Venceslaus looked to the trees. As he had expected, Avon's Wind was in his favor. He hoisted his sails and sat back while the wind pushed him along. The winds gave some assurance that Venceslaus would make it to Belar in reasonable time, about a week and a few days.

Nearing nightfall, Venceslaus found himself at a point where another river fed into the River of Nar. Feeling the pressure of time, Venceslaus continued to sail forward. He wanted to pass Feninwich before setting up camp, for if there were anyone searching for Venceslaus this far from the city, they would likely be coming from—or heading toward—Feninwich. It was the largest town in that direction for a long while. The dark of night was something Venceslaus rarely found comfort in, but it was truly a blessing now; although he would need to set camp up soon, before it became too dark to see.

Venceslaus took down his sail and rowed to the riverbank. Before he climbed out, he tied a rope to the bow. Then he pulled the boat to shore and tied the bow to a tree. Using the supplies Ehren had given him, he pitched a tent and rested for the night.

He awoke the next morning drenched. He glared at the sky, but it was as bright as it had been the day before. The ground was dry, too; warm, even. Venceslaus smelled himself and recoiled. He must have sweated severely in the night. There was a change of garments in the bag, so Venceslaus stripped himself and walked over to the river to rinse his clothes in its water. Afterward, he hung the clothes on a branch and dressed himself in the spare clothes Ehren had packed. Still wet, he took his washed clothes and laid them out flat on one of the skiff's plank seats. He untied the boat and hopped in while it drifted off into the river. He hoisted the sails and sat back, enjoying the feeling of the hot sun warming his joints.

There was a toll bridge in the distance, so Venceslaus reached for his purse so that he could pay and pass quickly through. But as he looked forward, he noticed that the guards wore crimson. Venceslaus grabbed his now-dry clothes and quickly stuffed them into the bag, making sure they were out of sight. He tucked the bag underneath his seat.

A trio of guards stood at the toll bridge. They waved him over. Venceslaus took down his sail and rowed toward a small dock on the riverbank. One of them held out his hand, his palm facing Venceslaus.

"Stay seated. What is your name?"

Venceslaus looked up at the men. "Me name is Loidis! I'm just an old man travelin' in me last days."

The guards squinted at the the Duke.

"Is that an Avonsgatte accent?" asked the guard in front.

"Sure is, lad. Have ye been there?"

The guard in front grinned. The other two laughed to themselves.

"Gol, no! Who would ever wish to go to that pigsty? I can smell you from here," said the guard, holding out his palm.

"How much is the toll again?" Venceslaus asked. "That darn King keeps on raisin' it. It'll be somethin' one day, then double the next!"

"I wonder if Avonsgatte trash like you could even afford it."

Venceslaus gritted his teeth. He reached into his purse and pulled out a solid gold coin, placing it into the guard's palm.

"Where in Gol did you get this? Did you steal it?" said the guard, grabbing his sword handle.

"No, laddie. I saved up all me coin in me life, and I finally had enough to sail down the River Nar. Will this be able to cover the toll?"

The guards whispered to one another.

"Yes! This will be *just* enough."

"Wonderful!"

The guard in front made a shooing motion with his hand. Venceslaus raised anchor and hoisted his sails once more, setting off on the waters and waving goodbye to the men at the bridge. He shook his head, for an honorable man would have let Venceslaus know he had overpaid at the toll and given him his change.

His stomach grumbled, but he did not wish to stop while he was still making good distance on the water. Venceslaus waited until the sky had darkened to set up camp on the bank of the river. He readied a fire, grabbing Ehren's fishing rod so that he could catch something to eat. He caught a few fishes; nothing too filling, but he still smiled at the prospect of something meatier to eat. He had eaten too much of the bread, about a quarter of the loaf, and had grown sick of it. He grimaced. How quickly he had grown tired of it—and there were others who did not even have that small luxury. Sometimes, he felt guilt for his affluence, and this was one such time. But the feeling was fleeting. He committed himself to looking at the journey in a positive light; it was a way to separate Venceslaus the person from Venceslaus the Duke.

Althalos

unter walked over to a large grate that marked the entrance to a tunnel under Nara. There were tracks coming from the mouth of the tunnel, heading away from Nara and into the forest. The tracks must have been several hours old, but they were fresh enough that Gunter knelt down and stared at them for a minute or two before waving Althalos over. The grate that had once blocked off the tunnel was lying on the ground, its hinges broken, a suspicious-looking brick resting next to it.

Althalos stared off at the horizon, gazing toward the water. He tried his hardest to squint past the water to see the other side, knowing that Aerus was somewhere off in that direction. He could not fathom how such a vast amount of space could contain only water. The only bodies of water that he knew were streams around Dorthu.

Gunter dragged Althalos into the tunnel. They walked with no light to guide them, and the light that peered into the tunnel from the grate soon disappeared. They were effectively blind. Althalos could still feel Gunter's hand wrapped around his wrist. He heard a dragging sound, but he soon realized it was Gunter's other hand brushing against the wall of the tunnel. Rats scurried past their feet, and Althalos stumbled over what he thought was a loose brick.

"Is this the only way into Nara?" he asked.

"No, but this is the only tunnel that will take us someplace where we will have a bit of privacy," Gunter said.

"Why are there tunnels under Nara? Is this a sewer?"

"Used to be. Now, sometimes people use these tunnels for smugglin', or for less-than-honorable transactions."

"It's so dark down here," Althalos said. "Are there not better ways of smuggling things into the city?"

"Not really. The King has destroyed almost every pathway into Nara. He does not want to miss a single mark from anyone who enters the city."

They delved deeper into the tunnels. Gunter stopped, and Althalos could feel him rummaging around at the wall. He heard Gunter step on something, and then he heard the noise again. Gunter pulled Althalos's hand to the wall, and he felt metal. After further inspection with his hand, he realized it was the rung of a ladder. He could hear Gunter begin to climb up. The mercenary opened up a manhole, and light flooded into the tunnel.

As they exited the tunnel, Althalos stared around at the city. The paved Narese roads were finally beneath his feet. He could not stop himself from staring at the city in awe. There was so much stone everywhere: rarely ever was there a house made entirely of wood. In the distance, the tallest spire he had ever seen pierced the sky. It was surrounded by several smaller spires.

Althalos pointed to them. "Is that the Academy d'Ava?"

"Yes, boy. But do not worry about the Academy. Ye can walk past it once we find that fool priest."

Althalos nodded and followed the mercenary, feeling a strange rush of anxiety inside of him that he could not shake off. He was in Nara—the capital. Where would he go to get help? If the King was the one who had ordered the burning of Dorthu, then Althalos would have to avoid him. Agathius might be of help; he would know people in the city.

Gunter walked over to one of the buildings in the square, examined it for a moment, then grunted unhappily. The building had dozens of tables outside and a sign with a jack painted onto it.

"Are you saddened because the damn inn is closed?" asked Althalos.

"Shut it, boy!"

The sudden sound of yelling came from the direction of the citadel. Althalos turned toward the noise. The citadel gates were surrounded by a crowd of angry peasants. A line of guardsmen held them back, beating anyone who attempted to break past their wall of men. Althalos took off toward it; Gunter called angrily after him, but Althalos ignored him.

When he reached the crowd, Althalos waved at one of the disgruntled men.

"Hey! *Hey!*"

"What?" asked the peasant, turning to face Althalos.

"What is happening?"

"Where have you been, boy? Hiding in some hole? How can you not have heard what is happening? That Orator arrested a priest!"

Althalos stared at the citadel. "What was the priest's name?"

"Eh... Agg-uhh-teez? Yes, Aggateez! It was Aggateez."

"Agathius?"

"Yes, you stupid boy! Is that not what I said? Agathius!"

Althalos cursed to himself and walked back over to Gunter.

"Why do ye look like a sorry bitch?" Gunter asked.

"They arrested Agathius," he said.

Gunter laughed. "Of course they did. What did he think was goin' to happen, comin' up here to cause a ruckus?"

"Do you not care for what happens to him? He came here for justice, the same as I have."

Gunter gritted his teeth and looked at the crowd.

"That's different," he said. "Very different."

Gunter walked into the sea of shouting peasants. Althalos went after him. The mercenary waded through the people, pushing through to the front of the crowd. He tried to peek inside the citadel, but there were far too many people between them and the keep to see anything worthwhile. Gunter pulled Althalos back out of the crowd, standing at its perimeter.

"These rioters are useless. We shall wait until later, once the bards start singin' of the priest's fate."

Althalos clenched his fists. "The bards? The ones in the tavern you wish to go to? You will look for any excuse to drink, won't you, Gunter?"

Gunter grabbed Althalos by the face and squeezed.

"How many fuckin' times do I have to tell ye to watch yer tongue, boy? Ye can learn damn near everythin' about a town in one night in a tavern. Take it from a man who knows 'em.

Everyone of all statuses goes to them; and when they drink their hearts away, their secrets spew from their mouths."

Gunter released his grip from Althalos's face, and Althalos shook his head. They walked away from the crowd. A piece of parchment was nailed to a lamppost at the side of the road. Gunter leaned in to look at it, but after a moment, he turned to Althalos.

"Read it, boy."

"You cannot read your own tongue?"

"Education was not a priority in Avonsgatte."

Althalos ripped the parchment from the lamp post. It was an argument telling of all the misdeeds the Phoenicy had committed under the leadership of, in Agathius's phrasing, *Aswold the Arrogant*. It was a blatant protest against the temple. Althalos read it aloud, and Gunter shook his head.

"That priest is damned. They'll drag him straight to the stake."

Althalos dropped the parchment to the ground. "He must have come here knowing that he would die. Why else would he appoint Ditwin as his replacement?"

"That is true, boy. We should keep low and out of sight until nighttime. I have no doubt that those knights must be lurking around in search of us."

"Agreed."

The two waited until the sky was dark. In time, the roaring peasants grew tired of their protest, portions of the crowd breaking off little by little. It seemed that the majority of the peasants then went straight to the tavern. It was bustling. Of all the taverns Althalos had seen on his journey, this was bigger— and then some. Gunter and Althalos walked inside. There were no guardsmen or knights. Commoners boozed around, bumping their drinks to one another and making friends. The bards sang tales, singing ill of the King. They sang about the lack of food, and how much it hurt their bellies to see the knights, priests, and nobles filling their mouths with expensive meats. They sang of the tolls, and how much they hurt their pockets. One of the bards sang of Agathius. The crowd didn't care; they were too drunk to care.

Althalos leaned toward Gunter. "We ought to tell them of Dorthu."

Gunter gave the boy a crazed look. "Are ye mad? Ye wish to alert the King that the only survivor of the village he burnt to a fuckin' crisp is in the capital where he can be found and killed?"

"I feel as though I would have their protection," Althalos said.

"Their *protection?* They don't give a fuck about ye! They did not even know Dorthu existed until the town criers told of its burnin'. Once the king releases a bounty for yer head, oh… they will all be after ye like flies to shit."

"Then what in Gol do I do, Gunter? How can I attain retribution?"

"Ye wait."

"Wait until what?"

"Ye wait until enough of these bastards rise up on their own. They're already riled up. Ye could certainly rile them up more, get the thing done quicker; but they'll do it themselves eventually."

"We have no time to wait. They will kill Agathius any moment now."

"Agathius is going to die anyway," Gunter said. "I know that man. He would rather die a martyr than be saved; and he knows it, too."

There was discussion going on a few tables down about the Great Chancellor's assassination. A few of the tavern-goers gossiped about how it was a foreign noble from Aerus who had done it. Many laughed joyfully when they heard of the man's death, but Althalos did not understand why.

One of the particularly drunk peasants shouted, "Fuck the tolls, and *fuck* the Great Chancellor!"

When Gunter heard it, he looked down. After a moment, he wiped his eyes.

"You are saddened by his death?" Althalos asked.

"He was my commander in the war," Gunter said. "I served under him before I served under Irold. He came from a powerful family, but ye wouldn't have known it if ye spoke to him. He led the vanguard into Yhourn. He really did care about his people."

"I am shocked that you did not react with anger to their words," Althalos said.

"They are idiots. Idiots do not anger me. They know no better."

Althalos frowned. "Agathius angers you."

"Idealistic folks like him are different. I cannot fuckin' stand people who have seen the world and refuse to accept how it works."

"And how does the world work?" asked Althalos.

"The world is unforgivin'. It will take everythin' from ye, and it will give ye nothin' in return. It is ruthless."

"Yet here you are, miles and miles away from Dorthu. You brought me here to help me."

"Enough," Gunter said. "Stop suckin' my cock, boy."

Althalos stood. He walked around the tavern, listening for more news about Nara. He turned his head and saw a younger man sitting at the bar counter. Althalos walked toward him, but he stopped once he caught a whiff of his odor; the man smelled like he had just finished rolling around in wet grass. Althalos leaned on the counter and asked the bartender for water.

"The strange one just fucking upped and left. He gave me coin, but he told me to stop the riots. Why the Gol did I even listen to that cunt, anyway? He only gave me a wee bit of money," said the man.

"I told you he was strange, fella. I don't understand why you decided to work with him," said the man beside him.

The musty gentleman stood up and stepped forward, getting close to the other man. He stared down at him, his face illuminated with sudden anger.

"You do not understand? Of course you do not understand. Who the Gol would? I am the *only* one working my arse off to fix the shite they are *subjugating* us to!"

The other man shrunk back. "I did not mean it in that way, Emmer! I meant no offense!"

The tavern-goers around them began to back away. Emmer balled and unballed his fists, a vein poking out of his forehead.

"You said something, but you did not mean what you said? What caused you to make that comment, then? Absolutely nothing? Who in Gol is helping us? Who in Gol is helping *me!*"

"Emmer, please calm down. Let us talk this through."

Emmer stared blankly at the man. His fists unballed. "Outside. Now."

Emmer stood up and walked outside. The other man followed him out. Althalos followed them, too. Outside, Emmer stood in the middle of the road, a group of men around him. He beckoned the man closer. The man walked over, then stood and stared mutely at Emmer.

Emmer punched the man in the face. Then he punched him again. He punched him again, again, and again. He continued punching him until the man's head caved in. Cuts formed on Emmer's fists. Althalos inched closer, hoping to remain indistinguishable from the crowd that surrounded the tavern. A few people looked over in the direction of the fight, commenting on how brutal of an affair it was; but what struck Althalos was how no one cared to intervene or to speak out against Emmer's violence.

Althalos went up to a man who was watching the beating closely.

"Who is that man?" asked Althalos.

"What? Who are *you?* That is Emmer right there; how the Gol have you not heard of him?"

"I, er... I am not too fond of carousing."

"He is the people's voice. He makes sure everyone is doing their part in standing against the King's tyranny. He is quite the fella."

"I noticed," Althalos said. "Why do you follow him?"

"Are you daft?" said the man, pointing at the gentleman whose head had just been caved in. "He's brutal, but he gets the job done."

Althalos stared at the bloodied mess of a man that lay in the road. No one ran to stop or catch the man who had just murdered someone in the middle of the city for all to see. Althalos was stunned. He walked back to the tavern. He found Gunter sitting at the bar, staring at a jack of mead. He traced his finger around the rim of the drink and hummed a song. Althalos sat next to the mercenary and stared at him.

"What?" asked Gunter, after a moment of heavy silence.

"Nothing," said Althalos, turning to stare at the bar counter.

Gunter took a sip of his drink.

"You know," Althalos said, "there was no inn in Dorthu—"

Gunter slapped his hand over Althalos's mouth and held it there. Althalos nodded and pulled Gunter's hand off his mouth.

"You're right. I should keep my mouth shut; but I only meant to say that I had never been in a tavern before that day in Fisk, and now it seems I always find myself in one. Gunter, if you need to talk about anything, you can tell me. It is the least I can do in return for all that you have done for me."

Gunter nodded. He waved the bartender over and handed him a few coins. The bartender walked away and returned with a key. After the mercenary had finished his mead, he took the key off the counter and led Althalos to a room. Inside the room were two beds. Gunter lit a candle while Althalos went to lie down. He stared up at the ceiling.

"I cannot get the thought of my village burning out of my head," Althalos said. "The houses crumbling to the ground, my chickens killed, the dogs killed, children, my friends, everyone dead. Every time I sleep, I dream of it; and whenever my mind is idle, I find myself thinking of it."

Gunter lay on the other bed, staring up at the ceiling as well. "I have seen many Dorthus, boy. In war, it is somethin' ye get used to. I don't reckon ye are likely to understand it yet; although, if the world is goin' the way I think it is, ye had better prepare yerself to see many more such events," said Gunter with a lifeless, monotonous voice.

"I feel strange being here, in such a large town. Everyone here feels as though they do not truly exist. There are too many people here for them all to be real," Althalos said.

Gunter laughed. "There's an arrogance that comes from livin' in the city. Most of the people have no idea what is happenin' in the world, yet they think they are smarter than people like us. They might have read or heard a lot of things, but most of them haven't *seen* anythin'."

Althalos turned to look at Gunter. "I saw a man have his head caved in for saying something that was nowhere near offensive enough to warrant that punishment."

Gunter nodded. "That's the city for ye. People die for nothin' here."

"Aye," Althalos said.

Adar

dar's bones creaked like old floorboards while he dragged himself across the stone-brick pavement of the Kyln riverport. Anita hurried to his side, taking his elbow and steadying him. He ripped his arm away from her at first, but as soon as he locked eyes with her, he frowned and returned his arm to her.

The rest of the party strolled behind them. They stared at all the festivities around them: traditional games, dancing, brightly colored garments, and music. The blue banner of Count Adar was being carried by one of his retainers behind him. Geder, despite Adar's protests, carried his own banner that had the twin white serpents facing away from each other. They stepped through the gatehouse that preceded the keep. Regent Hedmond Kyln was before them, standing on top of a podium and shouting to other lords and their retainers. Adar caught the regent's eyes when he entered.

Adar turned his head and noticed Ser Mikhail, Abba, and Maric standing alone. He walked around the other parties to reunite with his two sons and advisor. When he noticed Adar, Ser Mikhail's eyes went wide with shock.

"Adar... What happened to you?" whispered Ser Mikhail. "Are you ill? Have you been injured?"

Adar coughed. "Do not worry about me, Mikhail. This condition is of my own doing. Where is the Baron va Heddi?"

Ser Mikhail stared at Hedmond, stone faced. "In the dungeon, awaiting judgment for his crimes."

"Ah, so you have found something? When I investigated his fiefs, I found no such evidence."

"We stopped at a few of his manors, but I assume he knew enough to prepare for prying eyes. I found nothing when it came to embezzlement or anything of the like. I even searched his chambers after arresting him, but I found nothing related to your finances."

"Then what did you arrest him for?"

"I spotted him leaving a brothel."

"Oh," Adar said. "I wish you would have waited, then. Going to a brothel is unlawful in the county, but it is only a minor offense."

"I have a witness that saw him leaving with *coin*. Now, I've never seen a man leave a brothel with more coin than he had before… unless he had a hand in its operation."

"Did you find the coin?"

Ser Mikhail shook his head. "He must have slipped it somewhere when I was not watching. But I have a witness I can use as proof; I just have to find her."

Adar sighed. "That will have to do for now, I suppose."

"Hedmond asked for you to corroborate my claim that my arrest of Jergi was under your command."

"I will inform him that it was."

Hedmond continued his speech, talking about the festivities and how he wished for everyone to enjoy their time in Belar, the *jewel* of Osmjornia.

"Midsummer is a wonderful time!" he bellowed. "We are gathered here to celebrate our Osmjornish heritage, and I have not seen such a mighty and varied lot of Osmjornish men and women since the last Osmjornish Diet!"

He pointed his hand to Count Adar, raising his voice even louder.

"I am greatly honored that Count Adar of Kurembrog himself is present!"

Only a few people clapped for the Count, and those few who did clap were quickly glared down. Hedmond grinned like a mischievous child during the whole ordeal. Adar grunted under his breath, and Ser Mikhail shook his head at the regent.

"Cunt. He knows I am not the most popular lord in Osmjornia—" Adar began, speaking under his breath; but he broke into a brief coughing fit.

Abba and Maric stared at him with curious concern. Their eyes communicated that they did not like what they saw, but they refused to look away. Adar turned away from them, his face burning.

Hedmond finished his speech, and the crowds all funneled into the keep. Members of each family loitered in the Great Hall, gossiping about the affairs in Mjorn. Hedmond sought out Adar himself, placing his hand on the Count's shoulder. Adar winced in pain, and Hedmond furrowed his brow at him. His eyes went to Geder, then back to Adar.

"What is the matter with you, Adar?" Hedmond asked.

"Please refrain from questioning me about my current state. I have explained it countless times, and I do not wish to dwell on it any longer." Hedmond was always blatantly disrespectful; every word that came out of the regent's mouth annoyed Adar. "I was told by my marshal that you wanted to hear that it was, in fact, I who ordered the Baron va Heddi's arrest. Any word Ser Mikhail speaks may as well be my own. What he has told you is true; I ordered him to investigate the Baron, and upon sufficient evidence of a crime, to arrest him."

Hedmond looked disappointed. "I see. Then I shall continue to hold him until your departure, as per our Osmjornish customs."

Hedmond walked away. Anita came up to Adar.

"He has always been an arsehole," said Anita.

"Aye. He has treated me like a scoundrel ever since I converted," muttered Adar.

Adar turned to Abba, beckoning for Edit to come closer.

"Abba, this is the Lady Edit Freihei. I wish for you to greet her as a lord would."

Abba nodded. He gave Edit well-choreographed bow. Edit looked unimpressed by the whole event.

Adar beckoned Ser Elseharde over. "Knight of Freihei, I would like for you to take my son and Lady Edit to the courtyard so they might get to know each other in privacy," he said in thickly accented Narese. "Chaperone them carefully."

Ser Elseharde nodded. He led Abba and Edit outside. Maric stayed at his father's side, staring at his father. Adar could feel the judgment in his gaze.

He sighed and turned to look at the boy. "What is it, Maric?"

"What happened to you?" Maric asked.

Adar knew he should've expected as much; his youngest son had always been blunt. "I took a risk that did not pay off in the end," he said. "I made a mistake."

Ser Mikhail placed his palm on Adar's back and leaned toward his ear. "I have more to report, m'lord, but it will have to be in private."

Adar nodded to his knight. The two walked away from the crowd, leaving Maric with Anita.

"What is it?" Adar asked, once they were ensconced in the silence of the hallway.

"On our trip, we camped in the woods near a village in Pelesgeb. Maric had to relieve himself, so I allowed him to go and find some privacy out in the trees. But he did not come back for a while. When Abba and I went to find him, he had fallen unconscious in the middle of a grotesque cluster of trees. We were able to discern that he had eaten one of their fruits. It had an effect on him, so we brought him back to the village to be treated. Within a few days, he was better."

"What? Describe where you found him."

"The foliage looked to be made of flesh, intestines. They were turgid abominations."

"This must have been Woldhom, yes?" asked Adar, coughing. "What else did you see?"

"Just before we entered Woldhom, we were ambushed by some Ookosi; and when we arrived to Woldhom, everyone was gone. There was a half-dismembered body that crawled away from a burning home. I informed Hedmond of it, and he sent out scouts."

"We passed through Woldhom as well. There was a beast there who killed a few of our men—and that thing you described, the half-bodied thing, it hid in the woods and lunged at us the moment we entered the village. Then we heard screams, and a few of our men went to investigate. The thing was *huge;* it was bigger than a bear. It had metal plates that looked as if they were made from armor, and pieces of blue cloth protruding from it that were the same color as Hedmond's banners. Those scouts Hedmond sent are surely dead. If only he had not run off as quickly as he did, we could have informed him by now."

"Aye," said Ser Mikhail.

"Has Maric made a full recovery?"

"I worry for him."

Adar's hand trembled. "What do you mean, you worry for him?"

"He and his brother were involved in an… altercation a few days ago. They ran off right after I arrested Jergi. Apparently, Maric wanted to snoop around and see the brothel for himself. Some thugs attempted to rob him, and he said he was cut on the forearm in the process. The two of them said the cut was deep."

Adar frowned. "I noticed no such injury."

"Aye. I took him to be jesting at first, but Abba corroborated it. I have never known Abba to be a jester. But I inspected Maric's forearm, and there was no wound."

"Abba would not lie," Adar said. "How strange."

Suddenly, Adar was wracked by another coughing fit. This one would not abate; he coughed until his ribs ached. He almost collapsed, but Ser Mikhail held him up.

"M'lord, you must tell me what ails you. You were not like this a few days ago."

Adar shook Ser Mikhail away and found a wall to lean on. He stared at the ground.

"My condition is the result of seeing Neta."

"I thought as much," replied Ser Mikhail, shaking his head. "What wisdom did you receive that was worth this?"

"She gave me three prophecies. Siemond possesses them in writing in his satchel."

"Oh, he abhors Neta. I am sure he was fuming once he heard that you had gone to her again."

"That is of no matter; he can do nothing about it now," Adar said. "One of the prophecies mentioned a 'war of flesh and flame'. Elder Siemond has his own beliefs about what it could mean, but after your report of the strange woods and what I saw in Woldhom, I am certain that this is the war of flesh and flame to which the prophecy refers. We must prepare for it, but I am not long for this world. So *you* must prepare Maric and Abba to deal with it. There is no one better than you to do so."

Ser Mikhail bowed. When he righted himself, his eyes shone with sudden tears. "I will do what I must."

"When I pass, find Elder Tadhg. We will need to revert Kurembrog back to the Diev. No lord in Osmjornia will answer a call to a diet if a Phoenic land of Kurem calls it," said Adar. "I wonder how quickly this ailment spreads."

"The priest in another village we passed through in Pelesgeb said that it had shrunk a bit before; but when we described it to him, he looked concerned. He said it was far larger than it had been. If that is any clue to its spread, then it is growing fast."

Adar clasped Ser Mikhail's shoulders. "I thank you for your service, Mikhail, both during my life and after my death. You have been my greatest and most trusted friend."

Adar's breathing began to quicken. He reached for the bottle on his waist and dripped a bit of its contents into his mouth.

"It is strange seeing you in this condition, m'lord," Ser Mikhail said.

"Ha! I have not been truly healthy for a long time. I have been mad in the head for almost two decades now. To be honest, having death so near in sight is truly liberating. It has allowed me to understand what is truly important," said Adar, staring at his almost-empty bottle.

Ser Mikhail looked off toward Maric, and Adar's gaze followed. Maric was waltzing around and speaking to others of his age in the Great Hall. He had always had a knack for making new friends quickly, despite being Adar's child. Adar could not stop himself from looking down in shame. He had always tried to push away the thought of how his conversion would affect his children. It had forced other lords to censor themselves in front of them. They would not bring their children around, for they were afraid the children would spout something to Maric or Abba that would force Adar to arrest them. How strange it was to be the sovereign of a land enforcing such detested laws.

The girls blushed around Maric, and the boys put their arms around his shoulders. Adar overheard them wishing each other luck in the tourney. Hedmond sat on his father's throne and watched the whole ordeal. Socializing was not Hedmond's strong suit; it was obvious he did not enjoy it. He rarely smiled unless someone was speaking directly to him, and once he had turned away, his smile would disappear as quickly as sugar in water.

"Maric is popular," Ser Mikhail said.

"I wish Abba was, too," Adar said. "He is too much like his father. It would have aided my reign if I could have been a bit more like Maric, I suppose."

They both chuckled. Adar held tightly to a wall to keep himself upright.

"You are likable enough for a lord," said Ser Mikhail. "Many still respect you from how you carried yourself in the war; and your men can see that you truly care for them, even though you do not often speak to them."

Adar shook his head. "That is not true. I wish I had spoken to them more, but I convinced myself that I ought not to. I beg you not to allow my children to continue my obsessive mode of thinking; it is what led me to the grave."

"You have changed, Adar. Not only physically, but in attitude as well."

"It is strange how nearing death can grant one a clearer perspective on life. Bring Maric over, would you? I wish to spar with him before the tourney tomorrow."

Ser Mikhail furrowed his brow, but he sauntered over to Maric without argument and led him back to Adar. Adar gestured to the doors with his head, and they left the keep and headed for the tourney grounds. Adar felt his body growing cold, so he shed the Molotokdar from his back. Ser Mikhail handed both Maric and Count Adar a waster. Maric held his waster up, readying himself.

"Father, are you sure you are in any shape to spar?"

Adar laughed and crept forward. He moved like an elderly man. Maric walked forward and lifted his waster to strike; yet he hesitated, avoiding a clear swing at his father. The Count slapped him with the flat of his blade.

"Do not hesitate. Even a wounded opponent can hurt you."

Maric recovered, sending a flurry of attacks Adar's way. Adar parried several of them; however, his sluggish arms were slow to keep up. He was hit in the arm and yelped in pain. Maric froze, but Adar only laughed and unclipped the bottle from his waist. He took another drop and winked at Ser Mikhail, tossing the bottle over to him.

"I should be alright now."

Adar moved as if he were a young man again. He was fast, swinging and stabbing at Maric. Huffing and puffing, Maric attempted to put up a defense against all the strikes that were being volleyed at him; he swung his waster at the back of his father's knee, sending him into a stumble. But Adar recovered, swinging again at his son. Maric parried, riposting with a swing and a thrust. Adar blocked it, putting both of their swords into a bind. In quick succession, Adar was disarmed and Maric half-sworded his waster, pointing the tip at his father's neck.

Adar smiled, putting his hands up. "I yield."

Suddenly, he felt himself grow dizzy. He felt hot, so he looked at his arms. His skin was reddened. Struggling to breathe, Adar scrambled to grab the Molotokdar off the ground. He walked over to the fence that enclosed the dueling area and leaned on it.

"I am happy with your performance, Maric," Adar said, slowly catching his breath. "You will do wonderfully tomorrow."

Maric smiled. "Thank you, Father."

"You may return to the great hall," said Adar, flicking his hand at Maric.

Maric nodded and placed his waster back on the weapons rack. He walked back to the keep. Ser Mikhail leaned on the fence beside Adar.

"Do you think that Freihei girl is taking a liking to Abba?" asked Ser Mikhail.

"I do not know. Anita will pry that out of him; I know he does not want to talk to me. I do hope it goes well, though. It would be the best thing to come to him. Venceslaus is an honorable lord, and he is also a caring father. I know he would want to make sure his daughter would be happy with her future spouse."

"Aye. From what I have heard, he has quite a good reputation."

Adar sighed. "Take me to Jergi. I wish to speak to him."

The two walked to the keep. They walked down the stone steps that led to the Kyln dungeon. The guards noticed the Kurem crest on Adar's tunic almost immediately and stepped out of his path, allowing him entry. Many brutes lunged their arms through the cell bars that flanked each side of the hall. The guard that escorted Adar and Mikhail bludgeoned away any hand that reached too far. The prisoners wailed in pain. Some of them received the message well and retracted their arms, but many of them did not, and met the same fate.

Jergi sat in his cell, throwing pebbles at the wall.

"Fuck you, Adar. Fuck you," said Jergi.

Adar coughed. "It is not the place of an administrator to run a brothel."

"You've no proof of anything. And if by chance I *was* running a brothel, it is legal in Belar, and we both know you do not give a damn about illegal brothels in Kurembrog. You could have shut them down for years, yet you leave them open. So who is truly the criminal, you or I?"

"The ones in Kurembrog don't employ children," stated Ser Mikhail.

Adar turned to Ser Mikhail, giving him a questioning look.

"My witness is a young girl," said Ser Mikhail. "She fled with blood on her hands. You did not see her, did you, Jergi?"

"My business is money. I am a book-keeper; I have no interest in the operations of brothels."

"Right, of course. So you are just doing books for the brothel, then? You are doing the books for an establishment that defiles children?" asked Adar.

"Ha! Shut your trap, Adar. You know nothing of what you speak."

"I will deal with your treachery after the tourney," Adar hissed. "I will have the rats tear through your chest and rip a confession out of you."

Jergi grinned at the wall like a madman. "I will be waiting in this cell. I cannot wait to tell you everything."

Adar did not like feeling as though information was being withheld from him, and this struck a nerve within him. Adar spat at the Baron and stomped away, leaving the dungeon with his fists clenched.

Althalos

lthalos and Gunter woke to the sounds of a mob. The rioters were running rampant in the streets, cursing at the guards who blocked them from causing trouble. The guards were stoic, for they did not respond to the crowd's shouts. Althalos stood up and stared out a window.

"The King doesn't want to piss the people off more than he already has, boy! If this were anywhere else, the guards would have beaten and arrested those men; but this crowd is too fuckin' big," Gunter said.

"Aye, it is," said Althalos. "This is exactly what we need."

"They are too damn loud. Makin' me lose sleep."

"You're like an old man," Althalos said, chuckling.

Gunter didn't respond; he was fixing his boots onto his feet. Althalos grabbed his axe and affixed it to his back while he prepared to leave. The mercenary stopped him, taking the axe away from him. Althalos was confused, and he grew even more confused when he noticed that Gunter was not carrying his sword at his side.

"We are not carryin' weapons today," Gunter said.

"You are strange, Gunter. In all the days I have traveled with you, your hand never left your sword; yet we are not carrying weapons today? Are you not afraid of being defenseless?"

"No," replied Gunter.

Gunter left the room. Althalos followed him. As they left the tavern, Gunter led Althalos straight into the crowd.

"We will follow them and see what happens," Gunter said. "Hopefully, we will hear somethin' new about Agathius."

Althalos nodded. They walked with the crowd for a couple of hours, playing along with their shouting. They turned a corner to the town square, and before them was a town crier standing on a wooden crate and shouting to the people around him. He held a horn in his hand and was using it to amplify his voice.

"Hear! Hear all! The Good Priest Agathius's trial has concluded! The Orator and the King demanded once more that he recant, yet he refused upon each chance the King afforded him. According to Phoenic-Narese customary law, the Orator—with the blessing of the King of Man—has sentenced this man to death. He shall be burnt at the stake in two days. However, the King has allowed him one final chance to recant in the time leading up to his execution; and if the Good Priest does recant, he will only suffer one hundred lashings and the removal of his sash. Peace be with ye, people of Nara!"

Althalos frowned. Gunter looked unaffected, and Althalos shook his head at his callousness. The crowd heard the news well, and they shifted their march directly for the citadel. It was a struggle to keep up with them, being bumped carelessly around by the mass of people. Althalos cursed at them in his head. But this anger was misplaced; he was truly angry at the King who would kill a man simply for wanting to restore integrity to the temple.

Althalos stopped and let the crowd drift off toward the citadel on its own. Gunter stopped with him, and the two watched the crowd while it mindlessly wandered throughout the streets.

"We have to talk to that Emmer fellow," Althalos said. "If they are going to kill Agathius, then we have to do something about it."

"That is not a smart plan, boy. He does not sound as though he is a good person."

"You said yourself that you're not a good person, yet you are still helping me."

"That is different."

"And what is different about it?"

"Ye ask too many questions, boy. Ye'll need to learn not to do that when ye go and talk to Emmer. I know I can't stop ye from doing what ye wish, but be warned: If ye make him angry, he will kill ye in the middle of the street, just like he did to that other gentleman."

Althalos walked back toward the tavern. He hurried along nervously while Gunter lollygagged behind. Shouting erupted behind them, and both of them looked over their shoulders to see a large number of guards pouncing on the crowd, beating them senselessly in the streets. They chained a number of them and led them back toward to the citadel they had been marching for. They shouted and shouted.

Gunter laughed while they walked back to the tavern. "I knew they would be apprehended. They are marchin' themselves right to where their enemy wants them. There's no one directin' the crowd; they all think they're doin' something, but all they're doin' is makin' themselves easy targets."

"I suppose that is true," Althalos said.

They returned to the tavern, and Althalos plopped himself down onto one of the benches that were scattered around the dining area. Gunter leaned against a post that stood next to the bench and stared at the crowd.

"Gunter, what are we supposed to do now?"

"That is a good question," Gunter said. "A very good question."

Althalos picked up a pebble and chucked it across the road. "We have traveled all the way to Nara to find Agathius—yet we are too late. He will die soon, and I will be left without guidance."

"Ye did not travel here for Agathius. Ye traveled here because that cunt in the keep over there killed everyone ye have ever known. Agathius is just another gentleman who agrees with yer sentiments. His death can aid yer cause."

"That is twisted to say."

"Why? 'Tis the truth. Men will die more readily for a martyr— especially for one as grand and vocal as Agathius."

"I suppose," Althalos said. "But it still is not right."

"Well, there is nothin' ye can do to prevent it, so ye ought to come to terms with it." Gunter looked off toward the tavern doors. "I have some business to take care of. Wait here."

Althalos waited until the mercenary was fully occupied by filling his belly with alcohol to begin looking around for something, or someone, that could help him. He spotted a man that was surrounded by a group of people who looked to be manual laborers, for their hands and faces were dirtied with soot and grime. The man locked eyes with Althalos. His expression grew more and more intense the closer Althalos came to him. Althalos's heart raced.

"What do you want?" asked one of the workers.

Althalos stood up straight, with his chin proud. "I saw you with Emmer last night. I would like to talk with him."

"Why the fuck would we let you talk to Emmer?" spat the worker.

The man who had been making eye contact with Althalos sighed. "Look, if you want to help the cause, we can give you a task. If you complete it, we will let you join."

Althalos gritted his teeth. "I did not come to you to be given a task. I came here because I am the only survivor of Dorthu."

The group of thugs fell silent, staring openmouthed at Althalos.

The man who had first spoken to Althalos shook his head. "What are you talking about, boy? There are no survivors of Dorthu. The King killed them all."

"All except me," Althalos said. "Agathius, that priest being executed, he knows me. Imagine what he would do to you if I spread the word that the people proclaiming support for his cause had turned me away."

"Emmer is here every night," said the second man, his expression tense. "It is hard to miss him. Now fuck off."

"I do not have that long. Where does Emmer work?"

"You ask too many questions. For your own good, leave it alone. Have a merry fucking day."

Althalos shook his head and left the group of men. He knew Gunter was likely to be deep into his cup, so Althalos had no reason to return to the inn. He decided to wander around to get a good look at the city. He walked through the streets, taking note of how different the city buildings were from those with which he was familiar. The buildings in Nara were rounder and more circular, with far more spiraling adornments than the boxy homes of the Mjornish countryside. After passing into a part of town that was a bit farther from the citadel, Althalos noticed that the style of buildings had transitioned into what looked to a be a mix of simple Mjornish architecture and the elegance of Narese stonemasonry. An old wall partitioned this area off from the rest, and it looked to be crumbling of old age with several patched holes in it.

Althalos gazed upon the wall. There were numerous engravings, indentations, marks from weathering, and countless other blemishes that Althalos could not quite identify. This wall was much thinner and not as tall as the outermost walls of Nara. Statues of birdmen were mounted on top, positioned to look as though they were guarding against external forces.

Althalos felt a tap on his shoulder, so he spun around. He stepped back, initially frightened; but once he noticed the man who tapped his shoulder was dressed in robes and a sash, he sighed a breath of relief.

The priest smiled. "I do not think I have seen you around here before. Are you from this part of town, lad?"

"Er, no. I am just traveling through from another part of Nara…"

"Well, if you have the time, I would love to invite you to come and listen to our daily recitations."

Althalos hesitated to answer. It would've been nice to take some time to go to a recitation, he thought. But before he could respond, he spotted a man standing a few paces behind the priest. He was dressed in plate armor who had a gray beard. The knight and Althalos locked eyes, and Althalos felt a spark of recognition. *Ser Ernest.* By some strange stroke of luck—or, rather, misfortune—the two of them happened to be in the same place at the same time. Ser Ernest reached for his sword, and Althalos ran off. He could hear Ser Ernest shouting for the guards, so he ran straight for one of the alleys, knocking down whatever he could reach. The guards tripped and stumbled behind him, but they still maintained a frighteningly quick pace. Althalos swore under his breath. That priest had seen his face, and so had Ser Ernest. Now people would be on the lookout for him.

Althalos turned down another alley and made it back to the main street. The tavern was in sight, and a large crowd stood in front of it. They were loitering around and talking to one another. Althalos wanted to listen to what they were saying; but for his life, he could not stop his feet. A few of the people noticed the running boy and huddled together when he ran past, forming a human wall behind Althalos. Ducking down, Althalos watched through the gaps between the people in the crowd. Ser Ernest stopped, too.

Althalos could see his head past a few of the shoulders in front of him.

"You are harboring an outlaw!" Ser Ernest yelled. "I understand that the tension in the air is high, but you must allow justice to be maintained! If you hand over the boy, I will reward you handsomely!"

A few of the people standing around Althalos looked at one another. Another boy of about the same height as Althalos was nearby; one of the older men leaned toward him and whispered something. The boy nodded and ran off. Althalos could see Ser Ernest peeking past the crowd.

"He is running away! Apprehend him!" ordered Ser Ernest to the guards that accompanied him.

The same man that had told the boy to run leaned over to Althalos and murmured in his ear.

"He wants to speak to you in the tavern. Go now."

Althalos glanced over at the tavern. Once he was sure the knight and guards had gone, he walked over. Upon entering, he could see Gunter at the counter, staring at his jack of whatever it was he was drunk off of. Emmer was sitting at a table. When he saw Althalos, he waved him over and pointed to the seat in front of him.

"Hello, Dorthu boy," said Emmer.

His smell grew worse the closer Althalos got to him; but he made an effort to hide his disgust, as he did not wish to upset the man.

"Hello, Emmer."

"You wanted to speak to me, eh? What can I do to help the only remaining d'Dorthu?"

"I—I do not know, really. All I know is that I want retribution for what happened in Dorthu, and it seems that I should talk to you about it," Althalos said. "I have been pursued by the King's men. They do not want me to share what I know."

"And what exactly do you know?" asked Emmer.

"I know that it was the King who ordered the killings in Dorthu, for it is his knights, the ones pursuing me, who massacred my home."

"What proof do you have?"

At that moment, Althalos stopped talking. He looked at Emmer, examining him with inquisitive and careful eyes, for

Gunter's words of caution had suddenly rung in his head like temple bells.

He leaned back. "How can I be sure you won't turn me over to the authorities?"

Emmer laughed. "Are you serious? I am an outlaw, just like you."

"Then why are you out in the open? Why are you free?"

"Because my followers shield me from the tyranny of the King. It is astonishing how loyal men can be when you feed their families better than any of the rich merchants they work for," Emmer said. "A man is loyal to he who feeds him."

A group of people entered, grabbing seats around the tavern. Althalos recognized many of their faces, for several of them were members of the same crowd that had helped him escape.

"They're loyal. They support you greatly."

"Those men are mine. This tavern and the street outside are my property. Gol, this whole section of the city outside of the citadel might as well be my domain. They hold me to be the lord here. *Me!* The fucking guards that patrol the streets know this. That is why they only grew the balls to arrest some of my men when they were near the King's gates."

Emmer twiddled his thumbs while he stared around the room. He sat in his chair like it was the throne of his great hall; but there was clearly a great juxtaposition between his status in society and the way he thought of himself.

"It seems you have created quite the kingdom here," Althalos said. "I wish to help you in your fight against the King, and I will tell you everything I know when it is safe for me to do so. But I just met you, and I do not know this town. Even mentioning aloud that I am from Dorthu could get me killed. So I hope that you understand my caution."

Emmer smiled. "I understand."

Abba

bba left the Great Hall with the Lady Freihei at his side. The Freihei knight, Elseharde, accompanied them, following at a slight distance. Edit looked forward with an unamused stare. For a while, Abba did not say anything to either of them; he felt a bit shy. Things to say dotted in and out of his mind, but none of them seemed like they had enough substance. He hadn't spoken to many ladies, for whenever there were social events he would simply give his greetings, then run off to some corner to study. But now, he was being forced to speak; the silence was too unbearable.

An idea popped into his head.

"Would you two follow me?" asked Abba in Osmjornish.

Edit shrugged. Abba led them to another side of the courtyard. There was a large gate, and Abba stepped through first. The knight and Lady followed. They stood on top of a retaining wall that overlooked the sprawling city. Abba rested his arm on one of the crenels.

"It is not the greatest of views, but Gol, Belar sure is vast," said Abba.

"Do not take this the wrong way, but the views here are very lackluster. Nara is far vaster than this town," replied Edit, shaking her head.

Ser Elseharde stared at both of them with a look of confusion on his face. He had curious eyes, and it was obvious he couldn't quite understand what was being said.

"Oh, I apologize. I can speak Narese," said Abba.

Edit's eyes widened. "Wow, your accent is good! It doesn't sound at all like your uncle's or father's."

"You said the views here are lackluster. You have seen the white walls of Kurembrog, have you not? As well as the rocks that line the shore?"

Edit grinned, beginning to chuckle. "Kurembrog's shores are nothing. I am from Bek d'Lifa! Our shores are covered—"

"—Covered with countless olive trees," finished Abba.

"You knew what I was going to say?"

"Well, I read a lot. The Kingdom of Nar is very interesting to me."

Ser Elseharde grinned.

Edit squinted at Abba. "Have you been to High Beak?"

"Well, no."

"But you have read a lot about it. What else can you tell me?"

Abba looked down, putting his hand on his chin to think. "It is common for people to think Avonsgatte is the southernmost city in all of Mjorn, because it is right on the southern border; but really it is Osgud at the tip of High Beak."

Edit laughed. "Anyone who looked at a map would know that. Tell me something that not many would know."

Abba spent another moment thinking of what to say.

"Well," he said, "your family was the first to bend the knee to Avon when he landed in Mjorn, which is why the Freiheis have long been one of the most powerful families in all of Nar, rivaling even the Harferds."

"Hmm, you're right. But that is simple, too. You said you like to study, so tell me more."

So Abba did. He built from where he had started. He listed off each successor from the first Freihei lord that submitted to Avon all the way to her father, Venceslaus. Abba talked and talked, and the more he spoke, the more Edit's eyes widened. She listened well, not interrupting Abba. Even Ser Elseharde was attentive. They stared with amazement at the depth of Abba's knowledge.

When he finished speaking, Ser Elseharde glanced at Edit. "Is he right?"

Edit looked to Abba. "I am surprised. I do not even know if you are right, but from what I do know, you did not contradict anything." She looked off at the city, staring at it with a deep concentration. "You passed through Woldhom, correct?"

"Yes, I did," Abba said.

"Tell me what you know about those strange growths there."

Abba tilted his head at Edit. "Strange growths? I did not see anything in Woldhom besides a dead body and a burning building."

"No strange tentacle-like growths? Nothing that looked like a mess of bodies?"

"No, none of that. The dead body was strange, though. It lacked legs, but underneath its ribcage where there should have been a wound, there was only skin." He paused for a moment. "Did you see any plant life there that looked peculiar?"

Edit shook her head. "I did not. Why do you ask?"

"In the middle of the forest, there was a patch of woodlands that had a terrible, foul odor—"

"Was it like Woldhom?"

"Hmm... faintly. But it smelled less like burning flesh and more like... decayed flesh."

Edit stared at Abba with intense curiosity. Abba did not understand why she was looking at him like that, but he enjoyed that she was being attentive to what he had to say. He told her of the scene. He told her of the intestine-like vines that had hung down from the trees. Abba continued on and on about how the oddity had looked. Edit did not break her gaze. He spoke for a good few minutes.

"The Academy probably has information about those things, with all those damn books in there," said Ser Elseharde.

"You two have been to the Academy? What was it like?" Abba asked.

"We were inside the library for a moment when my father was speaking to the Orator," Edit said. "We only spoke to the book-keeper there—"

"Bertram? Bertram the Book-keeper? What did he tell you?"

"Whoa, Abba, what's got you so riled up?" asked Elseharde.

Abba stopped speaking. He paced around and gesticulated to try and calm himself down.

"It is just... I always wanted to visit the Academy. There are so many books there, and they are all original copies. It has long been a dream of mine to simply sit and sift through the countless number of old books on the bookshelves."

"I don't even think that book-keeper has read all of them, and he is quite the aged man," said Elseharde, laughing.

Edit laughed, too. "No, he surely has. He knew exactly where each book was; that was a telling sign."

They returned to the courtyard. Abba looked to the festival. There were too many colors being waved around to keep track of. In Kurembrog, there were festivals like this; but they felt much more local, not as large and grand as this one. It was much more of a spectacle in Belar. But the soil was strangely fertile here, yielding enough grain to feed most of Osmjornia; it made sense that such a large city would sprout up here.

"Ser Elseharde, will you be fighting in the tourney?" Abba asked.

Ser Elseharde stared longingly at the tourney grounds. "I would love to, but I will be busy protecting Lady Freihei. I must forgo it."

"Ah, that is unfortunate. It would have been interesting to see how the Narese way of sword fighting held up against our own."

Edit walked toward the steps that led into the city. "Let's go see the festival."

Ser Elseharde hesitated, but he nodded and followed her. They marched down from the keep and went to the town square. Ribbons followed dancers, twirling in the air. Drummers beat their instruments and sang songs with deep voices. On the side of the street was a line of food vendors. Lady Freihei ran over to the stalls. Several peddlers noticed the well-dressed girl and began to push their wares into her face. Ser Elseharde put his palm up and told them to back away; when they saw the sword at his waist, they suddenly became very placid, smiling and bidding Edit off. Elseharde grabbed Edit by the wrist, but she yanked her arm away, giving Elseharde a look of discontent.

Abba stepped forward. "What's wrong?"

"Never mind it," said Edit, rolling her eyes.

She turned to look at a stall that was covered with masks. A gentleman wearing a mask stood behind it, presenting his wares in his hands. One of the masks was made of painted wood and depicted a beautiful young lady with long, flowing hair. Abba noticed Edit's desire to examine it, so he went over, took her hand, and led her to the stall. Ser Elseharde followed close behind.

Abba smiled at the man, and the man turned around, staring at Abba. There was a moment of strange, tense silence.

"Ah—hello? Are you alright, trader?" asked Abba.

"Oh, yes! Apologies. I was only daydreaming."

"Worry not," Abba said. "We saw your stall from across the square. These masks are beautifully made."

"Well, thank you, but I don't make them. I simply bring them here and hope the right one reaches the right person."

Edit gravitated toward the mask of the young woman. The trader watched her.

"You like the mask of Esu, do you?"

Edit paused as if she were frozen. Her eyes were wide. "I—I do."

Abba stepped forward, pulling out his purse. "I will pay for it—"

The trader handed her the mask, giving her a bow that seemed a bit strange. Then he glanced at Abba, tilting his head. "Anything wrong, lad?"

"No, no, of course not." Abba turned to Edit. "Are you happy with that mask?"

"Yes, I am," she replied.

She held the mask in her hands and stared at it for a minute or two. She did not put it on, however, which Abba thought strange. She only held it and continued to stare at it until the three of them had returned to the courtyard. Abba walked over in an attempt to look at it with her, but she inched away immediately, pulling the mask closer to herself as if she was trying to protect it. Abba glanced at Ser Elseharde. The knight shrugged.

The three of them spent another hour or so discussing an array of different topics. Abba lost track of time, for he was listening with full attention. But in time, it was obvious that Lady Edit and Ser Elseharde had grown tired of the talking, huffing and looking disinterested. The sky drew darker, and the two southerners bid Abba farewell and departed.

Abba walked over to a wall and leaned on it. He only had a few days until the tournament, so he knew he should be using his spare time to do something productive. Maric was nowhere to be found, but that was no matter; he did not need his brother to train. He patted himself, making sure that he still had his dagger in case a thug were to assail him on the street again.

It was a longer walk to the the tournament with all the people in the streets, but he made it eventually. A few people were there, training with their wasters. Abba figured they were either members of the city garrison or other combatants in the coming tournament. He waited around awkwardly, trying to find a chance to speak with one of them. To his luck, they were kind and offered to go a few bouts with him. Abba held up much better than he had expected; it must have been all the training he had been doing with Ser Mikhail, he reasoned. In time, dusk had arrived, and the others went their separate ways. Abba stuck around, waster in hand, facing a pell.

He practiced several combinations and performed numerous drills, switching to another once his mind had grown tired of one. It was a bit bizarre to stand in such an open space, alone, knowing that the empty seats would be soon filled with people eagerly watching his performance. Some would cheer him on, and some would roar for him to lose. But even when the seats were filled, there would still be only him and his opponent on the field.

He had his side-bag with him, and inside was his book, *Ava's Lands*. At that moment, he felt the sudden urge to reach into it and read it—but then he looked at the waster in his hand. Anyone with the ability to read could read that book, but to be someone who sought to become a spectacle that enticed attention was rare. Surely it was more noble to be a member of the few who labored alone in the field than it was to be one of the many onlookers watching them toil.

Abba spent the remainder of his evening training.

Althalos

mmer stood up from the table and called for someone to come over. It was a man, and he held a note in his hands. Emmer clasped the man's forearm, pulling him in for a hug. Then he thanked the man and shooed him away. After Emmer sat back down, he opened the letter, gently removing the wax stamp that sealed the note. He flicked the paper in his hands so that it would be flat and easier to read. His eyes went line by line, and Althalos sat patiently waiting for him to finish.

Emmer folded the note and placed it onto the table. "Can you read?"

Althalos nodded. Emmer pointed at the paper. Althalos picked it up and read it. It was a report of how much grain was being grown and traded in the Kingdom of Nar.

"Why are you having me read this?" Althalos asked.

"If you had seen the last report, then you would know that there was a slightly lower amount of grain coming into one of the hamlets over—" He grabbed the paper from Althalos, pointing at the imports of a random town. "—there."

"Where is that hamlet?"

"It is east of Nara. Dorthu's destruction led some of the grain merchants to turn around and head elsewhere. It seems if you kill people, then there is more grain to go around," Emmer said.

Althalos was revolted at Emmer's insinuation. He leaned back from the table and crossed his arms.

"Oh, stop it," Emmer said. "It would be a good story, a good line for a crowd to yell. *The King killed Dorthu so that he might feed you.* I like this. It would piss him off dearly, and the fact it came from my mouth would paint me as a hero. I would stand up and say there was no world in which I would kill one man to feed another. An amazing plan, is it not?"

Inwardly, Althalos laughed at the idea. He refused to show his true thoughts out of fear; but not only was it misguided, it was undeniably stupid.

"An amazing plan. But what if the truth is even more important? Why don't we push for the truth as to why Dorthu was massacred?"

Emmer stared at Althalos. "Are you an idiot? Althalos, what do you think the people care about more: the truth, or being fed? You cannot control how people look at things unless you *make* truth. If we saunter over to the King and ask, 'Why did you burn down Dorthu?' that gives him the advantage. He would be able to say anything. That is why we must insinuate something else."

Althalos watched Emmer's eyes. He was a strange man. When he spoke, he emoted quite intensely, whipping his head back and forth like a crazed person. Althalos recalled when Emmer's demeanor had changed earlier. If he was left to ramble, he would gesticulate normally; but if any argument came his way, he would stare the deviant down like a wild cat stalking prey. Althalos could not comprehend why anyone would want to flock to him, of all people. Maybe it was out of fear, or maybe they hoped that the scary bastard would win, and it would make things somewhat better for them to have been on his side. Or maybe Emmer was right, and they only wished to have food. Althalos had grown sick of speaking to the man, so he stood up.

"It is getting dark. I must get some rest for the night."

"Oh, naturally." Emmer flicked his finger to a man, and the man nodded to him. "This gentleman will watch your door for you."

Althalos clasped his hands together. "I appreciate your kind gesture, but—"

"You cannot refuse me. This man will protect you whether you wish it or not. Good night, Althalos."

Althalos looked at the man Emmer had appointed to be his bodyguard. He smelled terrible—the same as Emmer—and had a bushy black mustache and tired eyes. He was impressively large; Emmer must have been feeding this particular man quite well. Althalos turned around and walked toward his room. Gunter appeared to have already fallen asleep at the bar counter. Althalos shook his head. Gunter's habit was aggravating.

He walked up to his room, and the man shut the door behind him. He did not mope about his situation, for what harm could it be if Emmer appointed someone to protect him? After stripping himself of his outerwear, he climbed into his bed and wrapped himself in his blankets, allowing himself to drift off to sleep.

The world faded away, eventually shifting to a haze. Before his eyes was a whirl of color. He was sitting in a grassy field. The sky was bright and blue, and it pained him to look at it for any longer than a moment. There was a pungent scent of fruity summer flowers in the air. He looked around. In the distance was a large city; it was well over a few miles away, but its tall spires were still visible. It looked pretty from such a distance, but he far preferred the wilderness around him.

There was a dove in the distance, and its feathers were of a white that was similar to dull chausilver or quartz. Althalos felt drawn to the bird, so he walked toward it. It glanced at Althalos, and he halted. He did not wish to scare it. The bird did not move, and with some hesitation Althalos displayed his palm to it. He wanted the bird to hop onto his hand. When it finally did, it hardened into a white-painted woodcarving. Althalos stared at it, shifting it around in his palms.

When he finally took his eyes off of the woodcarving and looked up, he saw that he was surrounded by white flames. The grassy field he had been standing in was now charred, war-torn. The once-soft dirt was now packed firmly beneath Althalos's feet. He turned to face the city again, but he could not see it through the haze of smoke.

In the far distance, near the tree line, stood a figure wearing black robes. Althalos squinted his eyes to get a better look, but after only a brief moment, the figure disappeared. Despite this, Althalos still felt compelled to trudge toward the spot where the person had been. Initially, when he reached the white flames, they disappeared, allowing him to pass. But eventually, they refused. Althalos stuck out his hand, reaching for the fire, and flinched back. His skin felt like it was melting off. Wanting to avoid the flames, Althalos walked instead through an opening between two rows of fire, which led him down a steep hill. He stumbled his way down, and when he looked up, the flames were gone.

A strange creature appeared below him, fleshy and sour-smelling. It writhed like a disgusting amalgam of worms grafted together into a single entity. He felt compelled to touch it, but he did not understand why. He reached for it. It reached up to him. It had the head of a man, Althalos realized, and it opened its eyes to look at him. One eye was missing, and the other was almost fully liquified into a rotten soup. Althalos still reached for its hand, and his pointer finger came to touch the creature's.

Upon contact, the creature was engulfed in white flames. Althalos fell to the ground and stared at the creature while it screamed and squirmed in pain. Its flesh melted off of its body. It tried to crawl away from Althalos. Guilt surged in his chest; he had caused the thing pain. But before long, the flames returned, and the dark figure appeared once more. It was closer this time, but Althalos still could not make out any distinguishing characteristics other than its size. It had no face, and its whole body was a featureless black void. Around Althalos, an army of creatures arose, clawing themselves up from the charred soil. Some of the creatures were whole, with functioning limbs and a head on their shoulders; but others were much less whole, comprised only of a limb, a hand, or a single finger. The figure pointed at Althalos, and the army of creatures rushed him.

Althalos tried to run away, but he could not move. He was stuck in place. The mob of *things* ran at him, enraged. He shrunk back, preparing for them to tear him to shreds; but when they reached him, upon contact, they burned. This truth did not matter to them, however, for they continued to keep coming and coming until they pushed through the flames, clawing desperately at Althalos. He felt the heat of the flames and sharp bones of the creatures pierce his flesh.

He shot up out of bed and screamed. He was trembling and drenched in sweat.

Emmer's soldier burst into the room. "What in Gol wrong with you, boy?"

Gol was right; Althalos felt as if, in the dream, he had witnessed Gol itself. He did not answer the man, instead sitting on his bed and staring at the wall in front of him. Sunlight barely peeked through the window. Althalos had had nightmares only rarely before the massacre, and it bothered him that they seemed to be growing worse and more frequent.

A mirror stood in the corner of the room; Althalos walked over toward it to look at himself. He recalled that he used to carry a smile on his face more often, but when he looked at himself, he noticed that he wore the expression of a tormented man. He looked like *Gunter*. He laughed at himself when he noticed the resemblance.

He heard footsteps enter through the doorway, so he turned around to face his visitor. It was Emmer. He walked over to sit on Althalos's bed.

"I heard a scream," he said. "Are you alright?"

"Ah, yes. Only a nightmare."

"Of what?"

Althalos hesitated to answer. "I... do not quite remember. I just know that when I woke up, I felt an intense fear."

He had knowingly lied to Emmer. He did not trust this man even with the knowledge of his dreams.

"I never have nightmares," said Emmer.

Althalos squinted. "Do you have any fears?"

"Ha! Of course not; a good leader has no fear. And what am I to fear? I have been warned off of almost everything I have attempted, yet here I am, still standing, despite everyone's warnings."

Emmer still sat on Althalos's bed. Althalos could not tell what he was waiting for. The two stood in silence.

"So, Althalos," Emmer said. "Have you decided to show me the evidence yet?"

Althalos smirked. "I thought you did not care for the truth."

"I do not. But it will be much easier to mold a *new* truth if I have full knowledge of the situation."

Althalos would have been shocked if the people downstairs did not know how much of a liar Emmer was. They probably didn't care, Althalos thought, for they knew he would do absolutely anything to win. Althalos heart pounded with more distress the longer Emmer stuck around.

Gunter's bed was empty. Althalos went to leave.

"Where in the Gol are you going?" Emmer asked.

"I am searching for my companion. It looks like he did not return to his bed to sleep, so I must go out and find him."

414

"You do not need to search for him. Sit."

Althalos spun around. "What do you mean?"

"He came up here entirely drunk and annoyed the good lad that I put at your door. We moved him outside because he became increasingly belligerent."

Althalos clenched his fists. "You did what? He paid for this room!"

"You do not need him. You are under my protection now. This inn is mine; this room is mine; *you* are mine."

Althalos grabbed the blooded axe and went for the door. He attempted to walk past Emmer's soldier, but the man grabbed him by the neck and squeezed. As Althalos struggled in the man's grip, his vision started to darken, his heartbeat pounding in his head. In a frightened frenzy, Althalos grabbed the man's wrists and tried to pull them away from his neck. The moment he made contact, the man screamed and quickly released his neck. Where Althalos's hands had met Emmer's soldier's wrist, there was a fresh burn mark. It was as if his hands were hot irons that had branded the man.

Emmer stood up and stared at Althalos with confusion, walking over to the man to get a better look.

"You... Did you *burn* him? How in Gol did you do that?"

Althalos gazed at his own hands with confusion. After a brief glance at Emmer, Althalos turned and left the room. He hoped they had not hurt Gunter. Emmer's hotheadedness made Althalos worried for the mercenary. He went downstairs and searched all over for him. Gunter was nowhere inside the tavern, so Althalos went outside. The mercenary was leaning on a pole that stood at the side of the road. His face was bruised, but so were his knuckles. He had a bottle of ale in his hands. When he noticed Althalos, he chuckled.

"I warned ye about that Emmer fella."

"Gunter, I am so sorry," Althalos said. "If I had known that they were going to treat you this way, I would never have spoken to him."

Gunter raise his hand, his palm facing Althalos. "Quit it. I know ye would not. Ye have no brute in ye."

"Get up, Gunter."

"Why? What are we supposed to do?" asked Gunter, taking another swig of his bottle.

"We don't need Emmer. We can announce what happened to Dorthu in the streets. We can spread the word."

"Ha! The people here are under the spell of Emmer's tongue. If he tells 'em not to listen to ye, then they won't. Gol, ye never had a good idea in yer life."

Gunter lifted the bottle to his mouth once more, but Althalos grabbed it from his hands and threw it into the street. The bottle broke into dozens of little ceramic pieces. Gunter stared at it like his life had ended. But he did not have an angry expression on his face. Instead, he looked sorrowful.

"Did you come all this way with me to be a sorry sack of shit?" Althalos raised his voice. "Why the Gol would you come with me if you did not think justice was possible? Why are you even *here*, Gunter?"

Gunter's eyes were wet.

"I have seen many Dorthus," he said. "I have *razed* many Dorthus. I have been the knight in a tattered cape. I have killed innocents. I am a *murderer*, boy. Even when I try to do good, even when I try to do right, I fail miserably. I am not meant to be a good man. I am *meant* to be a sad sack of shit. And that's all."

Althalos frowned. "Get your arse up. Stop being a coward."

Gunter grimaced at Althalos. "What did ye say, *boy?*"

"You came all this way because you wanted to drink. There are people trying to kill us, and you are afraid. Well, I am afraid too, Gunter! But you only want to sit in the streets and cry like a craven."

"I dare ye to keep talkin'," said Gunter, his face reddening with anger.

"Oh, *now* you want to do something. Look at yourself! You're sitting in a puddle of ale in the street!"

Althalos kept pointing at the puddle for Gunter to look, so Gunter did. The mercenary looked at his reflection; in it, there was only a grizzled man overcome with grief. He grimaced once more and turned his head away. Then he huffed and picked himself up.

"I suppose ye are right," said Gunter.

Althalos was stunned. Gunter took the axe from Althalos and jumped onto a crate. He began to call out to passersby, garnering quite an amount of attention. Soon, a crowd began to form around the mercenary.

"Good mornin', people of Nara!"

The members of the crowd muttered to one another, their attention drawn only briefly before they turned back to their own conversations. Gunter stared at the axe in his hand. It still had the red cloth covering it. He shifted his gaze back to the crowd and raised the axe into the air.

"The King killed Dorthu!" Gunter shouted.

Everyone in the crowd turned toward Gunter. He had their ears now.

"Did he, now?" yelled a person in the crowd.

"Aye! He ordered the deaths of yer countrymen—women and babes, too. He had his knights *clip clop* over to Dorthu and slaughter those innocent folks."

"He's fibbing! He's from Avonsgatte!" yelled another in the crowd.

Gunter nodded his head, raising his hands into the air. "Aye, that I am. Avonsgatte born and raised. But that boy there—" Gunter pointed the axe at Althalos. "—That boy there is from Dorthu. I met him on the side of the road. He was passed out with a shovel lyin' beside him. It was a hot day, and that boy dug until he collapsed from the heat to make sure that a father, mother, *daughter*, and *baby boy* were buried proper. How many of ye have walked down a road and seen a murder, only to leave the victim to rot in the street? I know I have. I am from Avonsgatte, and that's just the way it is there, really. But that boy there was so sick of seein' his folk killed that he was willin' to die just to give them the proper respect. He *would* have died if I hadn't found him. No sweat was on his brow; he had worked so hard in makin' sure they were buried that he did not realize he was goin' through heat stroke! He could not bear to see his fellow folk of the Kingdom of Nar suffer such an insult to their dignity."

Everyone in the crowd stared at Althalos. He was so taken off guard that he did not know what to do with all the newfound attention. Gunter beckoned him to his side. Althalos walked up to the crate. Gunter stepped down and handed the axe over to Althalos.

"They want to hear ye talk now, boy," Gunter murmured. "Tell them what ye saw. Let them know yer pain; I know they share it with ye."

Althalos nodded. He climbed up onto the crate and cleared his throat. The crowd was silent, waiting to listen to what Althalos had to say.

"I am Althalos. Althalos d'Dorthu."

They still listened intently.

"I was born and raised in the village of Dorthu. Like most people there, I never really left. It was all I knew."

Althalos struggled to find more words to say. He remembered everything vividly, but he struggled to articulate it. Some members of the crowd began to mutter. Althalos examined the axe in his hands.

"I found this axe next to the body of my friend Hrodolf. They... cut his head off. But before he was killed, my friend managed to tear a piece from one of the knights' capes. That same fabric is what covers the head of this axe," Althalos said. "And if you were in the crowd yesterday, and you helped me evade *that* knight, then you will recognize that this cloth is the same color, with the same stitching, as the cape of the knight who pursued me!"

Louder muttering broke out among the crowd, but unlike before, the muttering was urgent, not dismissive. Several people were looking at Althalos with shock in their wide eyes.

"The King ordered the massacre and razing of Dorthu! I do not know why, but he did! There is nothing left to go back to. The buildings are gone, the temple has crumbled, my chickens are dead, my friends are dead, my *mother is dead!* Everyone there is dead, and I have been cursed with being the only survivor. They wished not to leave a single soul alive, and for what? They told you it was bandits, but the only criminals who rode into Dorthu were the *King's* men. They wanted to cover it up."

Althalos looked around. The guards were staring at him, but they kept their distance. Emmer was right; it was apparent that they were going to do nothing to enforce the law here. Althalos looked at the citadel.

"In the King's dungeon, they are torturing a great man. I heard that you all met this man a few days ago, the one who spoke ill of the Orator. I spoke to him before he left to travel to this city. I was not old enough to remember what it was like before the war, but I have been told that it was once better here. That this kingdom was a more just place."

Gunter climbed up onto the crate and took the axe from Althalos's hand.

"Who here fought for King Matnus?"

Many members of the crowd yelled *aye.*

"Who here had a loved one die for King Matnus?"

"Aye!" yelled almost everyone in the crowd.

"Would ye die for the Simpleton King?"

"Nay!" the crowd roared.

"But ye *are* dyin'. Yer starvin' so the King can eat lavishly. When have ye ever seen the King walk the streets of Nara? Never! When was the last time ye had a proper meal? I reckon quite a few of ye would even not be able to remember! Well, I say *fuck* the King!"

The crowd roared. Gunter stepped off the crate. Althalos walked over to Gunter and extended his hand. They shook forearms. Althalos stared at the mercenary with bewilderment.

The shouting crowd had begun to rush toward the keep. As they left, Emmer walked over. Gunter pulled out his knife, but Emmer simply laughed, walking forward with his hands up.

"Now, now. Don't you stick me with that knife of yours," said Emmer.

"Ye fuckin' snake. Don't ye come near us."

"We were poorly introduced. What is your name?"

Gunter pointed his knife at Emmer.

"Do not be so eager with that knife," Emmer said. "Those men in that crowd still fear me. They may look up to you momentarily, but they remember it is I who feeds them."

Althalos put his hand on Gunter's arm, pushing his hand down. Gunter struggled momentarily, but he eventually relaxed somewhat and put his knife away. Emmer pulled a stool over, sitting down. Althalos and Gunter sat on the crates behind them.

"It seems you are a smart man, so we are going to play this your way, now. But if you dare insult me again, I *will* have you killed. The lone survivor of Dorthu matters not to me."

"You are a strange man, Emmer. Why fight for something if you care nothing for it?"

"Oh, Althalos," Emmer said, smiling a strange, toothy smile, "you are even more peculiar than I."

Adar

dar climbed up the dungeon steps with Ser Mikhail following closely behind him. His fists were still clenched, even as he walked away. His hands began to tremble. Adar jerked his head in the direction of his chambers. They hurried to Adar's rooms and shut the door behind them.

The Count fumbled around his waist and grabbed his bottle, dripping a tiny drop of the concoction into his mouth. He shuddered. It always burnt his tongue whenever he ingested it. It felt as if he was swallowing shards of glass with the heat of metal straight out of a forge. He gagged and crumpled to his knees; it was becoming harder and harder to deal with the pain as his condition soured. Ser Mikhail went to help Adar up, but Adar shooed his hands away.

"Thank you, Mikhail, but I am afraid to say your aid is of little use. This episode of pain will end soon."

Adar held up the bottle and whirled it around.

"What have you been ingesting?" asked Ser Mikhail.

"It is a mixture of the expensive kind—chausilver ground into honey. It is near its end; and with its end, mine will come as well. The likelihood of us finding anyone willing to give up their chausilver is slim to none. Besides, there is not enough chausilver in the world to keep me alive for even a year. It is allowing me to live just a tad bit longer; but in truth, the chausilver is killing me, as well."

Ser Mikhail let out a huff. "Well, then. I had better guard that bottle with my life."

"This bottle is not worth your life," Adar said. "You are to continue to guide my sons. I will write out my will, and you will be the protector of it. And when my death *does* come, in due time, you will be the one to announce my will to all the lords of the next Osmjornish Diet."

Ser Mikhail bowed. "Of course, m'lord."

Adar sat on his bed and sighed. He stared at the Molotokdar in his hands, turning it over and examining the markings that were engraved on the maul head.

"It will be written in my will for Abba to be informed of the history of this hammer," Adar said."

"So, you have finally figured it out?"

"No. I visited Elder Tadhg, and he knows it; but I refused the knowledge, for I do not deserve it."

"You have spoken to Tadhg—"

"Elder Tadhg," Adar interrupted.

"Elder Tadhg, my apologies," said Ser Mikhail. "But… you have spoken to him? Why?"

Adar stood up and walked over to a table that had a pen and parchment resting atop it. He dipped the pen in ink, and he began to write on the paper. He focused intently.

"I have spoken to him, yes. I have been lustrated in the waters of the Akos, as well."

Ser Mikhail stared at Adar with worry in his eyes. "Why, m'lord?"

"Because whether I believe a bird or a goddess of dreams created the world is of no matter to anyone anymore. Anita's father is old, I am dying, and soon enough the old order for the conversion of Kurembrog will lose its significance. After my death, the people will fall back to the Diev. They will hearken to the writings of the druid Markyer once more, and my sons will learn of their faith."

"M'lord," said Ser Mikhail, looking down at his feet. "I'm afraid… I have already somewhat informed Abba of his heritage."

Adar looked up from the paper. "What? Why would you do such a thing, Mikhail?"

"It happened when we took Maric to the Dievic priests in Pelesgeb to be treated."

Adar stood up and began to pace back and forth. He had never shown such stress before, and his inability to contain it troubled him. He stared at the bottle; he surmised it must have been the effects of the mixture on his mood that had led him to be as easily disturbed as he was.

Adar shook his head. "How did he respond?"

"Abba was growing increasingly curious about the temple. He noticed the priests praying to Esu. I did not see the use of lying to him outright—I felt he would not trust me if he found out I had misled him so brazenly—but I did not tell him everything, I promise you that."

Adar's heart steadied. He returned to his table and continued scribbling. Adar noticed Ser Mikhail creeping up beside him, peering over Adar's shoulder to read what he was writing.

Adar was further elucidating how exactly he wished for Ser Mikhail to go about handling his children's inheritances. Even if Abba was to inherit, Maric still ought to receive a fief of his own, and Adar wanted to ensure it would be one on the coast, with some tall cliffs nearby. Maric had always been daring, and he had loved cliff jumping since he was a young boy. Adar also gave firm instructions for Ser Mikhail to continue training Abba and Maric, as well. There was another clause that Adar had earlier considered adding. He stared at the parchment for a moment; then he shook away his hesitation and wrote the clause down.

He signed the will, folded the parchment in half, then handed it over to Ser Mikhail. The knight stuck the document into a side bag that he carried on his waist. Adar stood up and headed toward the door. Ser Mikhail followed, but the Count turned around, placing his hand on his knight's chest.

Ser Mikhail stopped. "What is it, m'lord?"

Adar shook his head and lifted his bottle. "Nothing, really. I only wish to see the festivities alone. I feel as though I only have but a week or two left with this bottle, so… I want to have a bit of fun in my last days."

"M'lord, I cannot let you go out there by yourself. It is too dangerous for a man of your status to do so; you would be the target of every street dog."

"I know very well," Adar said. "But remember: you have my will. It does not matter if I go two weeks from now, or tomorrow, or even today. My reign is over. I can feel my body decaying, and I want to clear my head while I still can. You will not follow me."

Adar left the room. Just before he left, he saw Ser Mikhail instinctively step forward to follow; but he halted, keeping himself from doing so. Adar smiled at Ser Mikhail's loyalty. Then he left the Great Hall, hobbling his way down to the nighttime festivities.

Many men were boozing in the streets, calling out to women, making nasty, vulgar remarks about their cleavage and other assets. It annoyed Adar to see people reducing themselves to such base activities. The men disgusted him; their self-relegation to mindless hedonism was a life Adar could never have accepted for himself. The women there were not undeserving of derision either, for a few of them drunkenly accepted the simpletons' advances. Festivities, for some reason unbeknownst to Adar, always seemed to serve as a way for the masses to numb their minds entirely.

Adar stopped walking. It would have been nice to numb his mind, he thought; but he had always been rather straightlaced, and had never had any particular proclivity toward drinking. He had also known other lords who were drunks, and he had watched their children learn to hate them as they grew older.

Adar hoped his sons loved him.

He walked over to a group of minstrels. They were singing of Osmjornia. Their lyrics reminded Adar of how Kurembrog had been before he had converted it. They sang of the Diev and of many other things that Adar had ousted and censored. He smiled at the performance, and when they had finished, he was the most enthusiastic with his applause. He tried to yell for an encore, but he erupted into a fit of coughing. People began to back away from him, staring guardedly at Adar as if he were a diseased wretch from whom they might need to protect themselves.

"No, no, do not worry. I am alright, everyone," said Adar, beckoning for the people to come back.

But no one paid any attention to the Count. They walked past Adar, leaving him to pick himself up on his own. He felt his limbs grow heavier, so he took a seat and allowed himself to catch his breath. He wore the colors of Kurembrog, and he reckoned that that was the reason they were so uncaring toward him. Adar had a reputation for being a renegade, an apostate. But as he looked around, he noticed that the people were truly only focused on themselves. They drank for themselves, and their drunken actions were vain and blindly pleasure-seeking in nature. The drunken men gravitated toward any lady they thought would accept their attention, taking a polite "pardon me" as an invitation to initiate lewd conversation. They did not care if he was the Count of Kurembrog; in fact, they barely seemed to *notice*. The festival-goers were only concerned with themselves. They were drunks. Their pastime lacked class, Adar thought, propelling individuals time and time again into an environment that deadened them to their potential and made them into people far less impressive than they might've otherwise been.

But his thoughts about the drunks did not prevent him from enjoying himself a little bit. He watched actors dressed as ice trolls fighting on stage. Adar had never seen one before, and he wondered how accurate the well-made costumes were to the real beasts. He tossed a few coins to the performers to show his appreciation. A stray reveler bumped into him, and before Adar could stop himself, he turned on his heel and shouted at the man to watch where he was going. To his surprise, his voice was much raspier than before.

"Shut up, old man," said the reveler before he stumbled off.

Adar looked down at his hands, feeling hollow. He was not old, but he had aged. Whenever he moved, he was reminded of that fact. And he hated it very much. However, he did not feel justified in hating it. He deserved what had come to him. Every action he had ever taken had led him here; and he'd known the entire time where he had been leading himself to.

Adar looked around in search of more interesting events. A crowd was huddled around a dancer that spun flames in his hands. The dancer pranced around, hopping to stand on one leg. He tossed some torches into the air and caught one with his teeth while he juggled the others. Then he threw all of his torches in the air, catching and balancing one on his right palm, one on his left palm, and one right in the middle of his forehead. The crowd was amazed, erupting into cheers and roars at the finale. Adar, giddy from the sight, joined in on the celebration, too; but before long, his joints started to ache from the clapping. He clutched his hand for a moment, waiting for the most intense peak of the pain to subside before he pulled out his bottle and opened it. His hands trembled as he brought it to his lips.

However, as he raised it, the drunken revelers around him mistook his gesture for a toast. He was able to ingest a small drop, but people came running up to him, ale sloshing from their cups, to tap their drinks with his.

"Please, please. It is not a drink—" pleaded Adar.

But the townsfolk insisted. A group of drunken gentlemen missed their mark and slammed their drinks right into Adar's hand. His weakened body could not pull back from the collision in time, and his bottle dropped to the ground.

Adar stared at the bottle as it fell. It was as if time had slowed; or maybe it was the contents' effect on Adar's perception. Whatever it was, it completely captivated Adar. It was a strange thing, seeing one's life crash to the ground before one's own eyes. It started so high in the air, and it fell such a great length. He did not even attempt to catch it, for he knew he was too slow to do so. He flinched when it made contact with the ground; but to Adar's surprise, the bottle did not break. It stood intact, with only a small amount of the elixir spilling out onto the ground. Adar turned his head and saw a reveler reaching down to grab the bottle. Adar hurried toward him, but he tripped and stumbled onto the man. Together, they fell onto the bottle, and it broke. A dozen pieces rested in the spilled mixture.

Adar picked himself up and stared blankly at the bottle. The ground began to foam, and a strange haze emitted from the mixture. Adar instinctively took a few steps back. The rest of the festivalgoers around the broken bottle began to cough, but the haze quickly dispersed. He knew the reactivity of chausilver quite intimately; he could feel the burning sensation worsening within him.

He left the festival, finding a short stone balustrade to sit on. He laughed to himself, quietly at first; then he began laughing louder and louder as if he were surrounded by joking friends. His memories whirled around around his mind. Moments of the past returned to him as if they were happening at that very moment. He remembered when he had first met Anita. She had been such a beautiful woman—she still *was* a beautiful woman. He thought back to when they had danced at their wedding eighteen years ago and smiled at the thought. Leaning back, he felt his spine creak and ache as he adjusted himself into a somewhat bearable position. Each movement brought him a sting of pain that reminded him of his current situation. But despite that, he still smiled.

He felt relieved, to some degree. For he what could he do in the time he had left? He was unable to secure anything further for his children. He did not have the physicality or even the mental fortitude to deal with any issue at the moment. He could barely handle breathing, let alone manage a domain. Adar wanted to get up and walk back to the castle, but the desire to sit down and rest just a little bit longer overpowered that urge. He rocked his feet back and forth, tapping his heels on the side of the balustrade below him.

The moonlight shined above in the dark blue sky. The moon was an impressive size, symbolizing that tonight would be a night of good rest—at least, to those who followed the Dievic faith. While Adar was looking at the moon, he began to hum a hymn. The hums turned into words, and his mind was carried away by the song.

Oh, oh Esu, ease me to slumber.
Surround me with flowers,
ones that will calm.
Please do allow! I am ill, expired.
Nightmares are not desired,
Gol is the fiend.
Oh Esu, please let me dream.

Adar's muscles relaxed. His eyes were still open, and he stared at the city. He finally found comfort, not wishing to move from his spot. The roads were all lit, graced by the light of torches. Countless colors whirled around in the air, from spinning cloth ribbon sold by the festival merchants. He heard laughter; happy laughter, not debaucherous, mischievous laughter—the sound of people having fun with family and friends. He allowed these hopeful thoughts to act as a dream.

Adar looked down. From the balustrade, he had a view of the tournament grounds. He saw someone training. After squinting for a moment, trying to get a better look, he noticed the shade of blue the figure wore. It was Abba. Adar smiled, finally drifting off into a real dream. The dream was something pleasant, but it was interrupted by the feeling of someone scooping him up into their arms. He turned his tired head to look up at the person, and he saw the face of his knight staring off toward the castle.

"I told… I told you… to leave me be," Adar rasped.

"Adar, I swore many moons ago to protect you with my life," said Ser Mikhail. "If you thought I would not follow you into the city, in your state—well. Then you must not know me very well."

"Hah. Alright, Mikhail. You win. Take me back to my bed."

Ser Mikhail marched back to the keep, heading straight to the Count's chambers. He laid Adar down on the bed and removed any garments that would make sleeping uncomfortable, starting with his side bag and boots. But he stopped once he saw Adar's belt; or, rather, he stopped once he noticed what was missing from the belt.

"The bottle is gone," he said. "Adar, where did it go?"

Adar was already half-asleep, quickly disappearing into another dream. "You—you did not see me drop it?" he mumbled.

"No, I did not. Where did it happen?"

But before he could formulate a response, Adar had fallen asleep entirely.

Edit

s she walked away from Abba, Edit held the mask up in front of her. She did not look where she was going, so fully captivated by the mask was she. She blindly followed Ser Elseharde while she flipped the mask around, looking at its every detail. It had wavy, dreamlike hair that was painted black with hints of blue. The paint on the skin was not a normal shade of tan, brown, or even peach; it was a swirling combination of desaturated greens, reds, blues, and tans. It reminded her of the muted way in which her vision would sometimes get blurred in the process of closing her eyes.

"Elseharde, where do you suppose I could learn more about the character in this mask?"

"The trader said it was a depiction of Esu," Elseharde said.

"Esu is a goddess; Geder said that. I imagine those who follow the Diev have temples, no? I need to find one."

Without giving Elseharde the chance to interject, she headed toward the town. Begrudgingly, Elseharde followed close behind. She had her knight ask a few of the locals where the Dievic temple was, and after having their time wasted by a few drunks, one of them finally pointed them in the right direction. They left the festive town square and traveled down one of the many streets in Belar. The further they went away from the main festivities, the fewer people crowded the streets. Bek d'Lifa felt perfectly safe when walking at night, but the same could not be said about Belar.

Even where the streets were mostly empty, Edit still felt watched. Ser Elseharde made her feel safer, for he stood tall with an unconcerned expression despite their surroundings; but the city as a whole made her feel uneasy.

They stopped once they reached the building they'd been directed to. It appeared to be a house, no different from any of the other houses on the street.

"Doesn't look like a temple," said Elseharde.

"That's it?" Edit asked.

"Has to be—unless he was drunk, too, and he pointed me in the wrong direction."

It *was* bigger than the rest of the houses, and it had a wide set of double doors, so maybe it could have been a temple, Edit reasoned. After walking closer to get a better look, she noticed that the doors were painted with faint blue patterns that could barely be seen in the night. They entered.

Edit looked around, squinting her eyes. *This was a place of worship?* There were no seats for people to sit and listen to recitations. A few individuals sat by themselves, lifting and lowering wooden carvings. Murals of men, women, and strange creatures she had never seen before decorated the walls.

She walked over to one of the murals and gazed upon it. There were large sea serpents, tiny men surrounded by white sparks, monstrous brown bears, and depictions of circular mushroom formations in the ground. She tried to find something painted that resembled her dream, or what she had seen in Woldhom, but she was met with no success. Eventually, however, she saw the portrait of a lady: one with dark black hair that shined blue in the light, and a face that glowed with a myriad of colors. She reached out to touch it, but a priest grabbed her hand before she could.

"Do not touch," ordered the priest.

"Apologies," Edit said. "I am… drawn to this character."

"*Character?* Many are drawn to Esu at this time, girl. She is the Goddess of Dreams."

That felt like something Edit had already known. She stepped back to get a better look of the mural, then glanced down at her mask.

"Your way of speaking is foreign," said the priest. "You are from the south?"

"I am," Edit said.

"Not many southerners care to visit our temples. What is your name?"

"My name is Edit. Edit Freihei," replied Edit, giving a curtsy.

"I will remember your name. Now, Edit, how might I help you?"

"I had a dream—or, rather, a nightmare—a week ago. I saw this woman in my dream. She was standing in a patch of strange forest. If you have heard the stories of Woldhom, then it was exactly like that."

The priest stared at Edit with a new and profound intrigue. "You saw her in your dream? Have you ever dreamed of her before?"

"No, I have not. I have never dreamt of *anything* like this before," said Edit.

"This is concerning," said the priest.

"What arouses your concern?" asked Ser Elseharde.

"I would never expect two southerners such as yourselves to know the gods and goddesses of Osmjornia. There is no education of the Dievic faith in the south. It is forbidden by the Phoenicy and the King of Nar. She has never learned about the Lady Esu before; therefore, the simple fact that she has seen the Lady Esu in her dreams may be a frightening omen."

"Why?" asked Edit.

"Depending on your dreams, it could mean many things. Please recollect your nightmares, for I will need to know what they are to be of any help."

Edit nodded. The priest fetched a piece of parchment and pen and began to take down notes on what she was telling him.

In the middle of Edit's recollection, the doors opened behind them. It was Geder Kurem. He strutted straight over to one of the altars and picked up an idol, staring at it, seemingly not noticing Edit or Elseharde at all. Edit momentarily stopped her story and stared at him, but then she turned her face back to the priest and continued, speaking much more quietly than she had before.

When Edit finished, the priest let out a breath.

"It seems you do indeed have a connection to Lady Esu," he said. "Do either of your parents claim heritage from Osmjornia?"

"My father certainly doesn't. As for my mother, I know only very little of her. My father does not talk about her often. She passed when I was quite young. She—" Edit took a deep breath.

It always startled her, how close to the surface this sadness was; tears sprung to her eyes almost immediately. She tried quickly to blink them away. "—She ended her own life. It was very sudden."

Ser Elseharde pulled out a handkerchief from his side bag and handed it to Edit. She wiped her eyes and regained her composure.

"I am sorry for your loss," said the priest. "If you are able, I would ask your father whether you might indeed have any Osmjornish heritage. It would help explain why you are having these prophetic dreams."

Edit shuddered. "Prophetic?"

"Yes, prophetic. The Lady Esu shows visions to all. Some may be prophetic, and others may simply be lessons or gifts of knowledge to those whom she favors. However, because of recent events in Woldhom, I believe you are having the former."

Geder walked over to Edit and the priest. Ser Elseharde stepped forward, positioning himself between Edit and Geder. Geder grinned at him, patting him on a pauldron. Edit's stomach churned. Geder stared at her with a mocking smile.

"Why have you not told anyone of these dreams?" asked Geder.

"I thought they were simply nightmares," Edit said. "I did not think there was any significance to them."

"In the future, I would like for you to record them," replied Geder, stepping around Ser Elseharde.

"Why?" asked Elseharde, stepping in front of Geder once more.

Geder looked Elseharde up and down. "Ease yourself, knight. It would be for the sake of everyone's lives. I have read many books, and those growths in Woldhom are not a known force. They ought to be treated with the utmost concern and caution."

He paused.

"My brother, Adar... he often would visit a witch named Neta. She has the gift of prophetic dreams, and her dreams often came true. You have likely noticed his illness; his condition was caused by his transactions with the witch. Adar is notorious for interpreting these prophecies incorrectly, but in the right hands, they can be of immense utility. I think you should go see if any of your dreams align with the prophecies he received."

Edit did not know how to respond. She was just a lady from Bek d'Lifa; why should she of all people have been given this gift? Her eyes wandered back to the murals.

Elseharde huffed and stepped forward, getting in Geder's face once more. "I request that you leave the Lady Edit alone."

Geder laughed. Edit put her hand on Ser Elseharde's shoulder.

"Do not worry, Ser Elseharde. I believe Lord Geder came to speak with us with pure intentions. And I imagine it would be a good idea to speak to his brother to find out more."

Ser Elseharde gritted his teeth.

"Aye, I beg you to speak to Lord Adar as well. If we can put these prophecies together, then perhaps we can reach a more complete understanding of any danger to come," said the priest.

Edit shook her head. She readied herself to leave, taking Ser Elseharde's hand to lead him out. She glanced back at Geder, squinting her eyes at him. He noticed her stares and returned her the same unsettling grin he always did.

They took the same route they had taken to get to the temple on their way back to the keep. She tried to sort through her thoughts while they journeyed back. Ser Elseharde still looked displeased, like someone had insulted him right to his face.

"It is all a load of shite, Edit. Do not worry about any of it. You just had a nightmare; there is nothing outrageous or grand about it," grumbled the knight.

"Can you not see how strange this is? I have never seen nor heard of this Esu before, but now I see her in my dreams. This is too odd to be coincidence!"

"How could it *not* be coincidence? You have seen many faces in your life. Do you think you are incapable of imagining a lady who *happens* to look somewhat like that goddess?"

"It is not only that," Edit said. "In Woldhom... the growths that came out of that burnt house were the same growths that I saw in my dream. These things are abnormal. That thing that came out of the forest—that was abnormal. It was not like a bear or some other forest beast. It looked like it was made of a bunch of... of *dead people lumped together!* Elseharde, nothing happening right now is normal!"

Elseharde sighed. "Then I suppose you ought to go and speak to that Adar, then. Your mind has been made up, but I am not going to entertain this insanity. That thing in the forest was an odd beast, yes—but it *must* be a coincidence."

Edit did not understand why Ser Elseharde refused to believe her. He looked annoyed. They trudged forward, and he did not say another word. Maybe it was his dislike for Geder that was blinding him. Edit understood—Geder was an abhorrent man— but he was from Osmjornia. Surely he knew more than Edit.

Once they reached the keep, Ser Elseharde escorted Edit to her room. Edit took some loose parchment and began to write down everything she remembered of her dreams. Ser Elseharde rolled his eyes and leaned onto the wall by the door. She finished her record quickly, and she folded the parchment into a small square and placed it on the table. Turning around, she lit a candle that stood on her bedside table. Edit shooed Ser Elseharde out of the room and closed the door. Sitting in her bed, she prayed that she would receive another dream that night to reaffirm her suspicions. She lay down and pulled her sheets over her, letting herself drift off to sleep.

Edit did not dream that night. When she woke, she decided that she would go and seek out Count Adar anyways. However, to her misfortune, his knight informed her that he was feeling unwell and not taking visitors. She felt it would be a bit too bold to plead, so she left it alone. She and Ser Elseharde spent the day with Abba and Maric. They were nice boys; but still, Edit could not see herself with Abba. The next two nights and days were no different. Edit grew progressively more annoyed. She had to speak to Adar, but his knight stood firm at his door. She knew it would be wrong to disturb him while he was ill, but she was unsure of how else to convey the urgency of her need to speak to him.

There was an archery competition taking place in the city. Abba and Maric both wished to participate, putting their admission money into the organizer's bowl. Edit had shot a bow once or twice before, so she figured she would enter as well. Ser Elseharde stood by Edit's side, disinterested in the whole ordeal.

Maric looked over. "Oh! You're entering too?"

"I might as well," said Edit. "I don't want to just stand around and watch the two of you."

"Well, good luck!" said Maric.

Across from them was a straw target with painted markings. Excluding the three of them, there were four other competitors. They were all scraggly fellows who appeared to have a need for the prize money. The rules were simple: if your arrow hit the outermost ring, then you would get zero points; if your arrow hit the ring in between the outermost and the center circle, then you would get one point; if your arrow hit the center circle, then you would get three points; and if you missed the target entirely, then you would be disqualified. Each participator was only given three arrows. Because of the unequal number of participants, the organizer gave Edit a bye for the first round. He mentioned something about it being the *gentlemanly* thing to do. Edit gritted her teeth at the notion.

Maric was up first. He went against one of the other poor fellows. It was no competition. Maric hit all three of his arrows in the center circle, while the other hit one in the middle ring and two in the outermost ring. Abba was next. He did not beat his opponent as easily as Maric had, but the other lad did not seem like he had ever held a bow before. The next two competitors were both peasants, and both gave a lackluster performance. The one that did win only beat the other by one point, after hitting a lucky bullseye. During the round, Maric's eyes lit up.

"It will take no effort to win this! Did you see that?" he said.

"Don't get too excited. I still have not gone," Edit replied, smirking while she reached for the bow.

She was going against Abba. As another *gentlemanly* gesture, she was to go first. She lifted up the bow, pulled the bowstring back, and loosed the arrow. It hit the outermost ring. Disappointed in herself, Edit shook her head. Abba's arrow hit the middle ring, bringing him a point. Edit loosed another arrow and once more struck the outermost ring. She cursed at herself. Abba glanced over. His next arrow hit the outermost ring. She locked her eyes at the target; she could still win if Abba hit his next arrow in the outermost ring. She exhaled, loosed her arrow, and hit the middle ring. She sighed and shook her head; it had not been an incredible performance on her part, but at least it was now tied. Edit caught Abba glancing over once again. He lifted up his bow, and when he released his next arrow, the arrow landed with a thunk in with the wooden stand holding up the target.

"Disqualified!" yelled the organizer.

Edit's jaw dropped. She stomped over to Abba and glared at him.

"Are you serious? You let me win!"

"Maybe, but I did have a match right before you. I thought it would be wrong to win when I already had some practice, and you did not."

Edit shook her head and sighed. "It doesn't matter. Your brother is going to win regardless."

Maric went eagerly over to the bow. He was to go first, and with his first shot he hit a bullseye. With a lucky shot, the peasant that went up against him also hit a bullseye. Maric smirked, and with his next arrow, he hit another bullseye. The other peasant did too. Maric side-eyed him. He released his next arrow and hit another bullseye.

"I'd like to see you get lucky a third time," said Maric, turning his head to the peasant.

The peasant shrugged, and with his third shot hit another bullseye. The organizer laughed with amusement and exclaimed that the two of them ought to keep going until they broke the tie. And so they did. Edit could not remember how many shots Maric and the peasant had taken; but eventually, Maric's stamina waned, and he hit the middle ring. The peasant's, however, did not, and he hit the bullseye once more.

"Oi!" Maric shouted. "What's your name?"

"Ynov," replied the peasant.

Maric shook his head and walked over to the peasant. He stared at him for a moment, but then he extended his hand to him. They shook hands.

"Good work, Ynov," Maric said.

Ynov went on and beat Edit as well, receiving the prize money in the end; but Edit had not expected anything different after the show he had put on. She, Elseharde, and the brothers wandered around the festival for the rest of the day, eventually returning to the keep for dinner and to sleep. Edit dressed herself in her nightgown and went to bed.

In the cold and dark of a stone-brick room, blood puddled on the ground. A man knelt within its bounds, his knees reddened and wet. A knife lay in the puddle in front of him. His hands were bloodied, too, and he held his head down, staring at his stomach. His torso was a mottled red, blood streaming from his many wounds.

Edit woke up dazed, in a dreadful sweat. She wondered if it had been a prophetic dream or simply a nightmare. There had been no growths of any sort present, but she felt as if she recognized the setting in some way. But its familiarity could mean nothing, she supposed; Elseharde had suggested as much regarding the face of Esu. Maybe the dream meant nothing, and she was simply recalling a room she had seen before.

She got out of bed, and a servant readied a bath for her. Not too long after she had finished bathing and dressing, a knock was heard at the door.

"Enter!" Edit yelled.

Ser Elseharde entered, and at his side was Count Adar. The Count looked like a dead man who had just crawled from his grave. He shambled to the nearest seat and slowly sat down. He erupted into a fit of hacking, his arm wettened by the spit from his cough. Edit waited for him to finish coughing; then she smiled to Elseharde and inclined her head politely to the Count.

"Thank you, Ser Elseharde," she said.

Ser Elseharde furrowed his brow, as did Adar.

"Why are you thanking the knight?" Adar asked. "I told him to take me to you."

"Did Elseharde not tell you that I intended to speak to you?"

Adar shook his head. "No, he did not."

"Why have you come to my room, then?"

"I came to give you a—" he coughed again. "A… a gift. It is a necklace."

He pulled the gift from his side bag. The first thing Edit noticed was that it was silver. She looked off to the side, trying to hide her disappointed expression. She wore *gold*, not silver. Its pendants were of a design that Edit would've never worn; they were too round, and too bland. The engraving on it wasn't poor, but it was something anyone could have commissioned. It was *lowly*.

"I see. Thank you, m'lord," Edit said.

"Wonderful. It pleases me that you like it. It is a fine piece for a young lady," said the Count, wheezing.

"M'lord," Edit said, "I hope this is not impertinent of me to ask, but I have heard your condition was caused by your search for prophecy—"

"What in Esu's name? Who told you that? *Who?*" Adar launched up from his seat, but he soon sat back down, trembling terribly. He rubbed his forehead and sighed. "I apologize for my eruption."

"It was your brother," Edit said. "He advised me to speak with you."

"My brother... He knows better than to spout my secrets. Why did he advise you to speak with me?"

"I suspect that I have been having prophetic dreams—much like your witch, Neta."

"He told you her name, too?" asked Adar, raising his brow. "What makes you suspect this?"

"I have seen the Lady Esu in my dreams. I have seen the growths and beasts of Woldhom. I am certain they mean something, but I am not from Osmjornia, and I know nothing of Esu or what they could mean. Could you help me?"

Adar massaged his temples with his thumbs. "I... I am sorry. I do not know of how much help I will be able to be."

"Could you tell me about the prophecies Neta gave you? Maybe one of them could help me."

"I know them vaguely, but my head... I am barely capable of standing. And if I know one thing, it is that you need to know the prophecies exactly as they were given, or else you are going to interpret them incorrectly."

He started to hack once more.

"I do not want to bore you with the history of Kuremdod; but as a consequence of my actions many years ago, I had to perform certain duties to keep control of my lands. These duties involved eradicating Dievic worship from Kurembrog. I made a special request to the Orator to leave one Esic priestess alive, and he agreed. That priestess was Neta. Whenever I went to her for prophecy, I had to go to the Pyre Elder Siemond afterward and relay to him what she had foretold. He recorded those prophecies. Seek him out; he should be able to help you."

The Count stood up once more, and he stumbled again. Ser Elseharde hurried to catch him. Lord Adar landed into his arms. Ser Elseharde almost fell, but he caught himself and wrapped the Count's arm over his shoulder.

"Do you have a walking stick?"

Adar laughed. "A walking stick? That hardly matters at this point. My condition has been progressing at a rate that is difficult to believe. It has only been three weeks, yet I feel as though Gol is right in front of me—dropping stones in my path, waiting for me to trip and fall into dirt that will soon bury me."

Althalos

lthalos grabbed his own wrist and squeezed, yet he did not feel a burn. His palms were still warm, but he wondered if that was simply because it was hot outside. His hands looked exactly the same as they always had.

Gunter grabbed Althalos's wrist and began to examine it.

"What is wrong with ye, boy? Why're ye starin' at yer wrist?"

Althalos yanked his arm from Gunter's grasp.

Emmer laughed. "You should ask my mate over there what's wrong with his forearm. This boy here has some very hot hands. What a strange gift! And it seems the boy did not even know he had it."

"Hot... hands?"

"He melted the flesh off a man. A grievous injury, it was; I believe we are going to have to amputate his arm. You will repay me for this, Althalos."

Althalos held his hands out in front of him.

"Oh, enough," Emmer said. "You do not know how to control this newfound ability, and I would *definitely* not go around showing it off. The Academy will have you in their hands as soon as one paladin catches wind of your existence. You will become a wanted man."

"Seems he's a pretty wanted man already. We're off," said Gunter, grabbing Althalos by the elbow and pulling him away.

Gunter led Althalos to an alley. After peeking around for a bit, he looked at Althalos with intense, concerned eyes.

"Did ye know ye could conjure?" asked Gunter.

"Conjure? Is that what you think this could be?"

Gunter stood very close to Althalos. "Boy, ye are not to tell a single soul of this. If ye are ever to use this… *ability*, even on accident, ye are to cover yer face and run as far away as ye can."

"I cannot conjure! This is absurd," said Althalos, turning away.

Gunter rubbed his head with frustration and huffed. "Back when we fled Wettay, I saw ye light that patch of forest on fire."

"No, no, the knights dropped their torches. That is what caused the fire."

"Do ye think a torch could cause that blaze, boy? Use yer fuckin' head."

"There was brush all around," Althalos said. "It could have easily caught fire and spread quickly."

"Did ye see what ye tripped over? Did ye look at the ground?"

Althalos thought back to that day. He remembered how bright and blinding the fire had been at the moment it was lit. He thought about the terrain beneath his feet; what he'd seen on the ground when he'd fallen. His eyes widened.

"It was… a ring of dead grass and mushrooms. Gunter, are you implying what I think you are implying?"

"Aye. An Aeric ring."

Althalos's eyes darted about. He stared at his hands once more, then to the road, and then to the sky. He smiled.

"Thank you, Avon."

Gunter squinted. "Why are ye thankin' Avon?"

"Because now I have something I can use to get justice for Dorthu," Althalos said.

Gunter looked down at Althalos, grabbed him by the face, and pulled him closer.

"I want ye to pay *very* close attention, boy. There are very few people with this gift, and those people are part of the Phoenicy. If they arrested Agathius, then they are yer *enemy*. I hope ye do not think they will help ye. There is no other priest like Agathius. Ye do not know how to use yer gift, so do not think that ye'll last a second against any capable Phoenic mage. Ye have the talent, but without knowledge, ye will be smitten immediately."

"Have some hope, Gunter. Why would I have this gift if I was not meant use it? How is it not a blessing? How is it not a sign?"

"A lonesome hatchet does not need swingin'. Ye would not believe how many men think they're somethin' special, marchin' off to face someone who wishes to kill them. Ye do not know what *special* is, boy. This is yer naïvety speakin' once again. Ye must refrain from usin' magic."

Althalos shook his head.

Gunter clenched his hands into fists. "Ye have not listened to me this whole fuckin' time, boy! When will ye learn to stop questionin' the man who lost everything? I am tellin' ye not to make my mistakes—but here ye are, runnin' off to make them! Althalos, yer goin' to *die*, just like the rest of yer town!"

"It is hard to listen to you when all you do is run to the tavern when I need you most," Althalos said. "What else am I to do when you are busy drowning yourself in ale? I cannot stand your habit. Every time I need your help, you are preoccupied with your own sorrow."

"Shut yer trap, boy. Ye know nothin' of my sorrows."

"I know nothing of your sorrows?" Althalos laughed tonelessly. "I have already shed my tears for Dorthu. Now I wish to march and achieve justice against the people who murdered my villagefolk. How are you going to seek justice for what Irold has done? How are you ever going to redeem yourself if you run away at every chance to do so?"

Gunter unclenched his fists. Althalos stumbled back, expecting Gunter to slap him, but he did not. Instead, Gunter walked over to the street and beckoned for Althalos to follow him. Althalos did. Together, they walked down the road for a while, observing the passersby on the street.

"I am goin' to tell ye a story," said Gunter.

Althalos listened intently.

"During the war, there was a priest who traveled with the vanguard. It was not uncommon for priests to be present on the battlefield, but they mainly acted as doctors, or they launched projectiles at the enemy. The priest with us could not perform any spectacular sorceries, so he instead lit a torch as a sort of... *trick*. He was a good priest."

"What happened to him? Did he survive the battle?"

"Aye, he did."

"Do you think he would be able to teach me? Where is he?"

"A grave somewhere. The Orator ordered his death after the war. Aswold has grown quite comfortable with the amount of power he has achieved. Agathius and I spoke very few times after the war, but when we did see each other, he spoke often of Aswold's seizure of power and the dark secrets behind it," Gunter said. "It was a strange time then. There was an internal effort to be rid of anyone who was a threat to the Phoenicy, and Agathius was one of the few who slipped by. He's a lucky idiot, blessed with the inability to do magic. Any priest worth somethin' spoke out against the Orator; but Agathius was smart. He waited, speakin' only to those whom he trusted. Yet now he has the bright idea to go to his death."

"I'm sorry for your loss," Althalos said.

"A loss is a loss. I don't think about it," Gunter said.

Althalos looked at his feet as they walked down the road. "Do you know of anyone who would be able to teach me? Someone like Agathius who survived?"

"No."

Althalos swore under his breath. He briefly wondered if he could teach himself, but he shooed that thought away. His gift was destructive. If he had truly lit that whole patch of forest on fire, then he was at significant risk of burning himself. Althalos doubted his ability to control it. With no one to help him, it might as well have been useless. He shook his head.

"Gunter, I'm going to go and get something to drink. May I have some coin to pay for it?"

Gunter pulled out a coin from his purse and shoved it into Althalos's hand.

"Order a drink for—" Gunter paused and flicked his wrist at Althalos. "Never mind."

Althalos walked back to the inn and sat down at the bar. The bartender came over, wiping grime from the plate in his hands.

"Hey there, lad. How can I help you?"

"I would just like some water, please," replied Althalos, pulling out the coin Gunter had given him.

The bartender shook his head. "No need. You're the only survivor of Dorthu, yes? The least I could do for you is to bring you some water. Do you want any stew?"

Althalos smiled. "Yes, I'd like some stew. Thank you."

After pouring water into a cup and scooping some stew into a bowl, the bartender returned to Althalos and delivered his meal.

Althalos bowed his head and used the spoon the bartender had given him to scoop the stew into his mouth. He hadn't realized it, but as soon as he saw the stew, intense hunger churned in his stomach. It was similar to the hunger he'd felt after fleeing Wettay. He put the spoon down and stared at the stew. Shaking his head, he grabbed his water and sipped it while he turned to people-watch. There were plenty of people around, but this bar always had plenty of people. Many of the faces were ones that Althalos had already seen before. What did they do to get by?

He turned to the bartender. "Excuse me, bartender? Do you have a moment?"

The bartender glanced at Althalos, pausing while he cleaned some cups. After he placed them down, he walked over to the boy.

"How can I help you?"

"I have always wondered: with all the different people that visit a place like this, what strange stories have you heard?"

The bartender laughed, wiping his hands on a rag. "Strange stories? I have heard many. This place is the capital of gossip in Nara. There have been so many fights here that have left men either bloody or dead I'm surprised people still want to come here for a drink. I don't even want to think of some of the more severe stories."

"C'mon, tell me one of them!"

"Oh, alright…"

The bartender leaned over the counter and told Althalos about the bar fights that had happened in the inn. While he told them, he'd get interrupted now and then by some other bar-goer, and he would head off to tend to them. Once there was another lull in business, he would return to Althalos and tell him some more stories. After a while, however, he began to constantly glance at the same corner of the room. Althalos turned to take a glance of his own. A man sat in that corner. The bartender was watching him like a worried deer.

"Why are you staring at him?" asked Althalos.

"No reason."

The bartender turned around and hurried over to a stove and water barrel. Dirty dishes and utensils were piled up near it, and he dunked a rag into the water barrel, picked up a dish, and poured some bran onto it. He scrubbed, moving as if he were being rushed. He kept his full attention on the dishes, and after he was done scrubbing them, he went off to rinse them. Once he was done, the bartender disappeared, rushing away to the back of the inn where the kitchen was; however, the lull had become a rush, and he was forced to return to the bar counter to attend to the customers.

When he was done with them, he glanced around the room. He stared once more at the man, but Althalos refused to interrupt him this time. Once the man in the corner finished his drinks, he stood up with a gang of a few men and left the inn.

Althalos leaned toward the bartender. "Why were you staring at that man?"

"You need to mind your business," the bartender said, his demeanor still fidgety and nervous. "This place is no good for people who don't mind their business."

"I only wish to know for my own safety. I don't know anyone here; I do not wish to come across the wrong person. You were looking at that man like he was despicable."

"He is a fucking devil," said the bartender.

"How so?"

The bartender sighed. "He works for Emmer. Emmer has done plenty of good for us, but he is also a bit mad when it comes to choosing who will serve under him. He is content with working with murderers. He likes how it makes him *look*."

"How does hiring murderers make him look good?"

"Because they kill who he tells them to. And if they're killing people that the people here want dead, then nobody cares. That's all I'll say. Talking about it will make *me* the next one stomped out in the street."

The bartender walked away. Althalos stood up and walked out of the inn. Emmer was outside; Althalos saw the man walk over to him, and Emmer embraced the killer as if he were a brother. Althalos could not understand Emmer's actions. How could he say he wanted justice when he surrounded himself with people who were entirely unconcerned with it? Althalos marched over to the peasant lord. Emmer looked over his shoulder and noticed Althalos. He smiled at the boy. Althalos glared at him with judgment.

Adar

dar exited Edit's room and shambled straight for the courtyard. He grinned, delighting in Edit's interest in Esu. Ser Mikhail wrapped the Count's arm over his shoulder, helping him down the steps to the first floor of the keep. They exited through the large doors of the keep and met a crowd of tournament participants, family members, and spectators standing in the courtyard. It did not take long for the courtyard to fill with people. Hedmond Kyln sat in his seat, grinning, while the crowd circled around him.

The sun was excessively bright that day, but Adar's body generally felt more sensitive as his conditioned worsened. He felt heavier than usual, but he knew that he had lost quite a bit of weight the past week or so. He was skin and bones. He felt as if his muscle would soon be gone, fully degraded. He struggled to keep himself upright, his back crumpling forward under the weight of his upper body. Ser Mikhail led him over to the spot where the rest of the Kurems stood.

Abba and Maric stood at the front. Abba had a stone-cold, stoic demeanor to him, while Maric stood with the same spunk he carried every other day. They both wore their tournament armor, and Adar felt a surge of pride in them. Geder stood near the back of the group, displaying little interest in the tournament as a whole. His eyes strayed around like a bored child's. Anita was smiling, and Adar could tell she had the same delight within her as he did, gazing at their boys; however, when her gaze crossed over to him, her expression changed immediately to one of fright and sadness. Adar's heart sank. He truly wished he had never made his transactions with Neta. If he could only have let his fears go... He had hurt his wife, and it hurt him even more to remember that he could have stopped himself from doing so. But there was no point to his regret; he would be gone soon, and there was nothing to be done about it. He shook his head in an attempt to clear away his worries and enjoy the day as fully as he could.

"Good morning!" Hedmond called. "I thank you all for attending the first day of our Midsummer tournament. Today, we will begin with the dueling, and we shall end with a grand melee!"

The crowd roared. The competitors hit their arms together and howled. Hedmond let them go on. Adar assumed the regent wanted to bask in the applause.

Hedmond raised a hand. "I thank you for your enthusiasm! Now, today shall be a grand day. These duels will cement which family produces the most skilled swordfighters in all of Osmjornia. I hope each contender is ready for their duels, for they are soon to commence! As for the prize..."

One of Hedmond's servants walked over to him, holding a box in his hands. He gave the regent a bow and presented the box to him. Hedmond opened the box and grabbed a charm from it, holding it in his palms. After admiring it, he held it up for the crowd to see.

"In our mines far to the east, we have retrieved a collection of charms like this. They are beautiful, and they are made of minerals that are few and far between. This particular charm is made of ordustone; you can feel its power when you hold it in your hands. The victor will win this charm!"

The crowd applauded while Hedmond placed the charm back into the box. Adar stared at the ground and thought of the ordustone maul. He realized with a jolt that he did not have it on his back. Staring around with confusion, he turned his head and noticed that the lady Edit and Ser Elseharde had joined their group. He smiled at them, and Edit gave Adar a friendly wave.

"We shall start off the day by heading toward the tournament grounds. Each family will occupy their tents, and one of my servants will go around and notify each family's competitors of who their first opponent is."

Hedmond went on about what would happen during the day. It took him quite some time to finish, for he was interrupted several times by loud cheers from the crowd. Again, each time, he allowed it. When Hedmond finished, he pointed the crowd over to the tournament grounds, and everyone hurried toward it. Ser Mikhail tightened his grip around Adar, and they began their descent to the city.

The Kurem family was the last to arrive, for Adar had greatly slowed their travel. Abba and Maric hurried into the tent. There were a countless number of tents scattered around, each as colorful as the crowd members themselves. The competing members of each family were clad in their families' colors; however, compared to the Kurems and Kylns, their plate armor was far more abused, and their visages far less groomed. Some looked savage, but this did not strike fear into Adar, for their looks were just that: looks. Adar's boys had been trained by the best swordsman in all of Mjorn. The Count looked at Ser Mikhail, feeling sentimental toward the man.

"Mikhail, thank you for always being by my side."

Ser Mikhail looked down, taking a moment to respond. Adar could see his lips moving, struggling to form words.

"Of course, my liege," he finally said. "It is my duty."

Abba left the tent, and Maric exited the tent soon after, heading over to stand by his brother's side. They discussed something quietly for a moment.

One of Hedmond's servants came over with a note in his hands. "Count Adar Kurem! Your son, Abba, shall participate in the third match. Maric shall be in the eighth. It is a single-elimination tournament, so if either of them is eliminated, he will not have any further matches. Does this make sense?"

Adar nodded.

"Perfect!"

The servant left the Kurem tent to go around and inform the other family heads about the format of the tournament. At that moment, Adar noticed his sons, Lady Edit, and Ser Elseharde walking over to the tournament grounds. His sons leaned on the side of the fence that surrounded the dueling area, gazing at their soon-to-be battlefield.

"Ser Mikhail, do you think Abba will do well?" Adar asked.

Ser Mikhail shrugged. "He might, if he does not lose this newfound attitude. He knows the fundamentals. He just needs to apply them."

The tournament was to take place in a large, oval-shaped coliseum with seating all around. The nobility sat on one of the longer sides, and there was a large blue overhang that sheltered the aristocrats from any potential shift in weather. Adar looked to the sky. It was calm, sunny, with no sign of coming rain. Geder stood a short distance away. He was immobile, staring at Adar with an expression of shock on his face. He clearly had not been anticipating such a sharp, visible decline in Adar's health. But after a moment, Geder shook his stare away, coming to aid Ser Mikhail in delivering Adar over to the stands. Anita followed. When they arrived, they met the Regent Hedmond, Duke Tedi, and several others who were already seated, waiting for the event to begin. The regent waved at Adar, but Adar only nodded, for his arms were bound to Geder and Ser Mikhail while they led him to his seat. They all sat down, joining the rest in their wait.

A man walked to the center of the coliseum with a horn. He blew into it, and its loud hum beckoned the attention of everyone in the stands. Adar could barely see him from such a distance, but he could hear his voice. The man called for the fighters of the first match to come forward.

The first name called was a young knight from Pelesgeb. He wore green and waltzed over to the announcer with the swagger of a farm boy. Comparatively, the other fighter looked almost frail. His colors were brown, he was very thin, and he entered the arena with his helmet on. Adar could not make out any sigils that would have indicated who his family was, but that could have been due to his poor eyesight. The announcer led them both over to the middle of the arena and had them shake each other's hands. They were then led to opposing sides of the dueling area, and the announcer pointed to the Regent Hedmond. Hedmond stood up, walked over to the railing of the stands, and cleared his voice.

"Commence!" he commanded.

The two fighters walked over to one another with their weapons drawn. The man with no visible sigils held his sword down, and the Pelesgebic knight noticed. Once the Pelesgebic knight had closed a bit of the distance, he aggressively rushed forward and went for the thin man's head. The thin man stepped to the side and riposted the attack, striking the knight's shoulder.

He tried to turn around to get the thin man in front of him again, but the thin man kicked him in the hip, then brought their swords into a bind. The thin man threw the knight to the ground. The knight's sword flung out of his hands, and the thin man kicked the sword away. He put his knee on the downed fighter's chest, lifted his sword hand high, and repeatedly struck the pommel of his sword on the knight's helmet. The announcer rushed to push him off of the knight.

"Cease!" yelled Hedmond.

The thin man stood up and stood to at the announcer's side. The Pelesgebic knight stumbled in his attempt to stand. The announcer walked over and pulled him to his feet. He led both of the fighters to the center, grabbed the nearest wrist from each of the fighters, then raised the thin man's hand into the air. Usually, people would cheer after winning a duel, but the man stood with a stoic posture.

Adar leaned over to Ser Mikhail. "How strange. Even with all your duels, you'd still lift a fist in victory."

Ser Mikhail grinned. "Maybe he does not count it as a victory. It looked like a very easy fight for the lad."

"What is the name of his family?"

Ser Mikhail shrugged, turning to look at Hedmond. Hedmond also shrugged.

The announcer brought out the next two fighters. One was another younger man who wore dark orange and black. He walked with an obvious bravado, and he stared down his opponent. The other fighter wore light green, walking into the arena with a similar sense of superiority. They stared each other down, leering menacingly at each other. Hedmond sighed and rubbed his forehead.

The announcer pointed to their starting positions, and the two went over to where they were supposed to be. They put their helmets on their heads, and once they were both ready, Hedmond stood and commenced the fight. They quickly rushed toward each other. From the look of their energy at the start, Adar expected it to be an exciting match, but that could not have been further from the truth. The two fighters looked to be gasping for air only a few strikes into the match. The crowd soon fell silent, and Adar felt his eyes growing heavy.

The fight lasted for an excruciatingly long time. Fortunately, the fighter in light green tripped and lacked the stamina to lift himself up. The fighter in orange and black fell on top of him in an effort to keep him down. The announcer called off the fight, and the two young men stood up.

"They misled the crowd with how they carried themselves before the fight," said Adar.

"They misled themselves," said Ser Mikhail. "Those two must have been scared out of their minds."

"They certainly were! Ha!" laughed Hedmond as he stood up and leaned over the rail.

The announcer raised the hand of the man who wore orange and black. After the fight concluded, Hedmond walked to the seat behind Adar. After he sat down, he patted Adar's shoulder. Adar winced in pain.

Hedmond frowned. "Adar, what ails you? You look no better after your days of rest."

Adar looked down. "It is just… a condition I've developed."

"How unfortunate," said Hedmond.

The Regent looked forward and pointed. The target of his finger was Adar's son, Abba. His son wore his tournament armor proudly and held his sword firm. Adar eagerly leaned forward in his seat.

The announcer extended his arm toward the other fighter. That fighter wore a black tabard with a single red line going from his left shoulder to right hip, walking out with a ferocity similar to the two boys prior. Abba stared at his opponent with stoic resolve. He seemed different; he seemed at ease, *confident*. Adar grinned.

Hedmond stood up, lifting his hands up high. "Commence!"

The knight quickly sprang forward. Abba stood still, waiting for his opponent to draw nearer. The knight prepared to send a strike at Abba, but he pulled his hand away before he could. Abba was unflinching. The knight began to circle Abba, and Abba responded by keeping the knight in front of him. To Adar's shock, Abba thrust his sword forward, and the knight stepped back. Almost as quickly as he stepped away, however, he slashed his sword at Abba. Abba parried and stepped off to the side, sending a cut of his own to the side of the knight's helmet. The knight stumbled to the side, and Abba tried to close the distance. Unfortunately, he did not make it in time; the knight turned and swung his sword at Abba's chest. The impact only slightly knocked Abba off his footing, but that allowed the knight to send a flurry of strikes at him. Abba was pelted with swings. Adar brought his hands to his face with worry.

Boots stomped up onto the platform, and a man wearing the Kylns' blue stood with two other guards at his rear. The man had a mangy face and scraggly hair. He walked right up to Hedmond and whispered something in his ear. Hedmond looked concerned, and he looked at Adar.

"Apprehend him," said Hedmond.

The two guards walked straight for Adar. Ser Mikhail stood and unsheathed his sword halfway. Adar put his palm on Ser Mikhail's hip and shook his head.

Adar turned to Hedmond. "What is the charge?"

"My guards have interrogated Jergi Hedden," Hedmond said. "Adar, you are charged with counterfeiting groschen."

"That is preposterous! Adar would never do such a thing," said Anita, erupting from her seat.

"The apostate who forcefully converted his fellow countrymen is too morally upstanding to counterfeit coin? Don't be foolish," Hedmond said.

Ser Mikhail still stood, hand on blade, his brow furrowed. Adar grabbed his knight's sword handle and pushed it back into its sheath.

"Let them take me. There is no point in making a fuss," he said.

Anita stepped in front of Adar. "I will not let you take him. You cannot trust Jergi! Adar *imprisoned* him; of course he would try to pin some sort of crime on him!"

"The evidence is enough to jail him for the time being. But I am not freeing Jergi, either; we will hold a proper trial and see if his charges have merit," said Hedmond.

Geder patted Anita's shoulder. "Do not worry. I will go with them to the dungeon and make sure Adar is treated with respect."

Anita, still visibly upset, said nothing.

"It is alright, dear. Just let them take me," said Adar.

The guards lifted Adar up and led him to the steps. Ser Mikhail followed behind, but Hedmond put his hand on the knight's chest.

"We can't have everybody go with Adar."

Ser Mikhail looked to Adar.

"Aye, stay—" Adar went into a fit of coughing. "Stay and watch the boys. They need your guidance."

Ser Mikhail shook his head, wiping his face with his hand. He sat back in his seat.

Geder looked over to Hedmond. "Let me carry my brother. Your guards don't know how to prop him up without causing him pain."

Hedmond nodded and allowed Geder to walk over to Adar, slinging his brother's arm over his shoulders. The guards led Adar and Geder down to the keep. The mangy-faced one followed close behind, but he split from the group after they reached the bottom of the steps. The commonfolk in the tournament stands stared at Adar while he was hauled away. Most of them kept quiet, but a number of them yelled curses at Adar. A smattering of hate-filled laughter patterned around the crowd, and it was loud enough to reach Adar's ears. He stared forward, feeling a strange bliss. He knew he would not make it a night in a cell. What would be the use of protesting? It did not matter if he died a month from now, a week, tomorrow, or even today. The future was certainly already written, and nothing Adar could do—especially now—could change it. Abba would become the new Count of Kurembrog. Ser Mikhail was capable enough to make sure his realm was safe.

They passed the gates that protected the courtyard of the keep. The halls were empty; everyone was likely in the arena, watching the tournament. Adar looked at Geder's face and saw that he was smiling broadly.

"Why do you smile, Brother?"

Geder did not answer. He helped Adar down the stairs.

The prison was filled with thugs. They walked over to where Jergi was being kept, and Jergi looked as if he had just bathed. He had a servant in his cell grooming his beard. Adar had never seen him look so well taken care of before, and he stared at the steward with a dumbfounded expression.

Jergi looked at Adar, grinning just like Geder. Adar's heart began to race. He looked back at Geder. One of the guards that had led them down to the dungeon opened one of the cells. They placed Adar inside, and the guards left him alone with Geder. Jergi rested his hands on the bars of his cell.

"How shocking. The Count of Kurem in a cell."

Adar's eyes darted back and forth between Jergi and Geder. He settled his eyes on Geder, turning his head with confusion.

"What is this?"

Geder walked over to the wall that was between Jergi's cell and one next to it. The Molotokdar leaned against it.

"I am doing what must be done. You have stained Osmjornia with your selfish desires. It fills me with sorrow that I must do this to my own brother, but I can not let the consequences of your rule worsen the state of the world—especially not with what is coming."

"What are you talking about, Geder? Did you have a hand in my arrest?"

Geder choked the Molotokdar's handle. He looked down, his face filled with sadness. He reached for his pocket, taking out a small note and holding it up for Adar to see.

"Neither of us truly agrees with Elder Siemond, but he does serve the Kurem family in his own way. I was concerned about your dealings with the witch, and I asked him about the prophecies. He gave me this note. I have read it, and after what I have seen in Woldhom, I know we are coming into a time where we will need to exercise the utmost caution and tact. We need a unified Osmjornia once more. It truly does pain me greatly that I must do this, but I cannot risk the world dying because of my selfishness. You have fractured our lands; a man like you could never unify the people, and Osmjornia will never come together while you are still around. Everything you have done has soured our home. Your choice of love and your choice of faith have weakened us all. The people *hate* you."

Adar shook his head. He looked at the ground, clutching his chest. It felt as though his heart was rotting with grief. His eyes beckoned him to weep, but he refused. He would not show his older brother his tears. He did not want to give him the satisfaction. Instead, he mustered whatever saliva he could and spat at Geder's foot.

"You are masquerading under the guise of duty and honor. You are justifying this sin by using a cause you do not care for. You have never been a selfless man, and I am disappointed that I could not see that fault until now, as I near death," Adar said. "I have given up every ounce of myself for the sake of Kurembrog, and I have given up even more for the sake of my family. I never thought you would ever do this. I thought you loved me, Brother. I respected you dearly, and I respected how you stood resolute in the face of every obstacle life has given you. You knew I looked

452

up to you. You knew I would have done anything for you, Geder, and yet you choose to fabricate a charge against me."

Geder put his palm up to Adar. "No, that was all Hedmond and Jergi."

"I doubt that. The way you stand now paints you as the orchestrator."

"I had nothing to do with the counterfeiting nonsense," Geder said. "Although you were right about the embezzlement. Jergi was taking some of your coin and pocketing it. He would send the coins over to Belar and have them smelted down in a forge; allowed by Hedmond, of course."

"What do you get out of telling me this?"

"I just need you to know I had nothing to do with it. This was Jergi's plan to save his own arse."

"Yet you grip that maul as if you plan to kill me."

"I feel ashamed that I must."

Adar flicked his wrist at Geder. "You've never been one to feel ashamed."

"Maybe, Brother. Maybe you are right. But I know for certain that you will never be able to rally Osmjornia; and for that reason, you must go."

Geder walked over to Adar, raising the Molotokdar slightly.

"What of my children—your nephews?"

"They will not inherit," said Geder, raising the maul.

"Siemond and Mikhail will not accept this."

"Siemond already has."

Adar shot a glance at Jergi. The steward grinned. Adar looked up at Geder.

"Oh, Geder, how far from grace you have fallen. You will be forever known as Geder the kin—"

Geder slammed the Molotokdar into the crown of Adar's head. The world went dark, and his skull burst with excruciating pain. His broken body crumpled to the ground. He could feel the blood vacating his head. The ground was cold. His ears rang.

He mustered the last bit of strength he had to move his lips.

"—slayer."

The Molotokdar struck him once more, ending the reign of Count Adar Kurem the Superstitious.

Abba

bba grimaced in pain. How could he have let himself be so open? His opponent whacked him over and over with his sword. He tripped over his own feet, almost falling. In the distance created by his stumble, Abba stuck out the tip of his blade in the hope that it would discourage his opponent's advance. To his luck, it did, and for the moment they did not swing at one another, Abba's eyes strayed over to the stands.

His father was being carried down the steps by his uncle. Surely it was for something reasonable. Maybe he was relieving himself.

Abba forced himself to focus on the fight at hand. His opponent swung from up high, so Abba blocked the sword. Strike for strike, they exchanged swings of their swords to little gain. Abba was growing tired. It was his first match; how could he already be tired?

His opponent lifted his guard up once more and swung. Abba rushed to block, immediately hurrying to bind their handles together. The knight tried kick him away, but Abba shoved him forward, forcing him to awkwardly hop as he kicked. The kick did not even push Abba. Instead, it made contact with his chest and got stuck while Abba moved forward. Abba grabbed the foot, swung his arm under the leg, and then kicked the knight's feet out from under him. His opponent landed square on his back. He exhaled violently; he must have had the air knocked from him when he hit the ground. Abba pointed the tip of his sword at the eye slit of the knight's helmet. The announcer rushed over to Abba.

"Cease!" yelled Hedmond.

Abba sheathed his sword. He extended a hand to the knight, and the knight accepted it; although his posture hinted that he was quite dissatisfied with the outcome of the fight. The announcer raised Abba's hand and announced him the victor. Abba grinned, scanning the crowd for his parents. Adar was still not back in his seat.

Worried, Abba hurried over to the stands. He climbed up the steps to his mother, who was looking displeased and anxious. As soon as Ser Mikhail noticed Abba, he walked over.

"Good work, lad," said Ser Mikhail.

He sounded disinterested—or, rather, distracted. He did not have the same anxious expression as Abba's mother; he was tense. It felt as if Abba had walked in on something he shouldn't have; like they all knew something he did not.

"Where is my father?" Abba asked.

Ser Mikhail waved his hands in the air before he spoke. "He is dealing with a matter—"

"That thieving snake has been arrested," interrupted Hedmond.

"What?"

Ser Mikhail grabbed Abba by his shoulder and pulled him close. "Just worry about your fight. This matter is nothing. It is only a misunderstanding."

"My father has been *arrested?*" Abba said.

Ser Mikhail patted him on the back. "Just watch the fights."

Ser Mikhail and Abba sat down. Hedmond rocked forward with glee. A knight wearing the Kylns' blue walked out onto the tournament grounds, his expression unflinching. The knight held his helmet in his hands; he was the spitting image of Hedmond. His opponent stood across from him. There was nothing notable about the opponent, for his tabard was plain yellow. Hedmond commenced the fight, and with an impressive display of swordsmanship and athleticism, the knight in Kyln colors beat the fighter in yellow almost immediately. Hedmond shot up from his seat with his hands raised into fists.

"Good work, Hofstaad! Cease!" yelled the Regent.

Just then, Maric walked up the steps. He sat next to Abba, placing his hand on his older brother's shoulder.

"Good luck, Brother. He looks quite skilled."

Abba looked down. "Maric, Father was arrested."

Maric stood up. "What?"

The others looked over their shoulders at Maric. Abba pulled his brother back down into his seat. Maric stared at Abba with wide eyes.

"What was the charge?" whispered Maric.

"I do not know—Ser Mikhail wouldn't tell me—but Hedmond said something about a theft."

"That is a horseshit charge. Father is too proud to steal."

"He'll be alright, Uncle Geder went with him. Ser Mikhail said to just focus on our fights."

"Knowing that our father is jailed will make it hard to focus."

Maric patted Abba's arm, stood up, and went to leave the stands. Abba watched as he went. His brother went toward the practice area where several pells stood lined in a row. Abba's next duel would not begin for quite a while, so he elected to watch a few before he went down to get ready. Duels started, and duels ended. Very few of them were spectacular. One duel lasted an extraordinarily long time, but there were moments that were entertaining despite both competitors looking inept with the sword. Abba thought he would have been beaten in his first bout, but after watching all these fighters, Abba realized there was not too big of a skill difference between himself and them.

A mangy-faced soldier climbed up the steps, marching straight for Hedmond.

"Ah, just when I thought I was done looking at you. What is it, Frud?" Hedmond asked.

The soldier pulled out a letter from his satchel. "I have a letter from Duke Freihei."

"Open it."

Abba glanced over to Edit and Ser Elseharde. Both of them leaned forward to listen. Frud opened the letter and held it up, beginning to read aloud.

"Dear Hedmond Kyln, please apologize to my daughter on my behalf, for I have been delayed. I will arrive upon the night of the tournament. I wish for Ser Elseharde to travel down the southern road to Belar to meet me halfway, for I am traveling alone. He ought not to worry about the Lady Edit, for she is safe under the care of Adar and Anita Kurem. Once more, with sincerest apologies to my daughter, Duke Venceslaus Freihei," read Frud.

Frud leaned over to whisper something into Hedmond's ear. Ser Elseharde leaned over to Edit with a frantic look on his face.

"Ser Elseharde! Venceslaus requests that you meet with him," yelled Hedmond.

Ser Elseharde furrowed his brow, whispered something to Edit, and stood up. He walked over to Hedmond.

"Travel on the road that heads south from Belar. I will loan you a detachment that Frud will brief. Ride quickly."

Ser Elseharde turned to look at Frud, staring at the man for a moment. He nodded and went for the steps with a concerned look on his face. A few moments after he departed, Edit stood up. She walked past Anita and Ser Mikhail to sit next to Abba.

He leaned over to her. "What do you think happened?"

"I do not know," she said. "Father never travels by himself. He always has at least a dozen or so men with him on the road. The letter said nothing of his champion, either. Ser Groent would never let him travel alone."

Edit's eyes went wide. She placed her palm to her mouth.

"The Great Chancellor was assassinated right before I left on Geder's boat. If Ser Groent is dead…"

She stood quiet. Abba was unsure of how to comfort her. The Great Chancellor being assassinated was news to him as well, for she had never mentioned it.

He patted her forearm. "Your father will be alright. Ser Elseharde is heading over to retrieve him."

After a few more duels had concluded, Maric walked onto the dueling grounds. He had a cocky grin on his face. Instead of wearing a light blue tabard with two white serpents like Abba, he wore a gray tabard with two blue serpents. Abba recalled that he had requested this because he wanted to differentiate himself from his brother, and Adar had quickly obliged the request of his favorite son. His opponent was a boy a little older than Maric. He was dressed in the same green that all the other Pelesgebic nobles seemed to wear. Abba leaned forward.

Hedmond commenced the fight, and the two engaged one another. This particular Pelesgebic boy was larger than Maric; Abba knew that if he had gone against him, then he would have surely felt some anxiety. Maric's posture conveyed no fear, but

Maric never showed fear, daring as he was. Maric readied his sword. The larger boy swung, and Maric stepped just out of range. The boy kept swinging, but Maric simply refused to be hit. He was much faster than the boy, and once the boy realized this, he slowed down. The boy cautiously took a step back. Maric thrust his sword forward. It did not connect, for the boy slapped the blade away. But Maric did not falter and continued to engage the larger boy.

For quite a while, they paced around, gauging their distance. Maric struck forward again, and the Pelesgebic boy slapped his blade to the side once more. This time, however, Maric moved the blade with the slap and spun it around to swing at the boy's head. The boy did not stumble, but he was caught off guard. Maric used his non-dominant hand to grab his own sword on its forte and thrusted it at the boy's neck, sending him stumbling in order to catch himself. Maric grabbed his sword with both hands on the blade and slammed the cross-guard into the boy's helmet. He slammed it again and again until the boy crumpled to the ground. Abba stood up and raised his hands, cheering for his brother. The announcer ran over to break them up, waited for the Pelesgebic boy to recuperate, and stood them both up.

"Cease!"

The announcer raised Maric's hand. Abba stood up and hurried down the steps. He met his brother at the gate that allowed entry into the dueling area. Maric removed his helmet, and on his face was a wide grin.

"Good work!" Abba said. "He looked like he was strong."

Maric smirked. "He was, but all it did was slow him down."

They chatted while they moved away from the dueling enclosure. The initial rounds were finished, and the next round of the tournament was soon to begin. Abba and Maric went over to the pells, each grabbing a waster. The drilled strikes at one another, flowing and chaining their swings.

Eventually, one of the Kyln servants called for Abba. The servant led him back to the dueling enclosure. Maric followed his brother and leaned over the fence in anticipation. Hofstaad Kyln stood in the center of the dueling enclosure with the same unflinching expression he had in his first match. Abba stood resolute.

"I have heard he is quite good—but you will do fine. You trained with me, and I am much better than him," said Maric.

Abba shook his head, smiling as he put on his helmet. He walked onto the tournament grounds, ready to defeat the Kyln boy. The announcer led them to their spots, and Hedmond commenced the fight.

Hofstaad was the first to step forward. He took confident steps, but his surety did not dissuade Abba from stepping forward, too. Abba circled around a bit, waiting to see what Hofstaad would do.

Hofstaad swung his sword immediately. Abba had not expected him to be so prompt. Narrowly parrying the first strike, Abba failed to protect himself from the second. Hofstaad's blade struck Abba right in the neck, causing a jolt of stabbing pain. Abba reached for his neck. It *hurt*. It felt as if someone had struck a hammer at the back of his neck. Hofstaad hit him again with his sword, sending Abba into a stumble. Fearing he would get hit again, Abba reflexively whipped his arm between him and Hofstaad, and, in a stroke of undeserved luck, he stopped Hofstaad's next strike.

But that did not matter. Hofstaad grabbed Abba and lifted him up. Abba's feet dangled in the air, and he was thrown to the ground. The landing made the pain in his neck worse. Abba lay on the ground for a moment. He was ready to lose, but Hofstaad did not rush for him. Confused, Abba lifted his head.

Hofstaad was on the ground, too, apparently in no hurry to fight Abba. He tried to stand up, but as soon as he put his weight on his right foot, he froze. Abba kicked him in his right foot, and Hofstaad *squealed*. An irreplicable sound of pain came from Hofstaad. *He was hurt.* Abba frantically pulled himself back up to his feet. How had he hurt himself? It must have been when he had thrown Abba; had he rolled his ankle?

Hofstaad used his sword to pull himself back to his feet. Abba, his neck still aching, held up his sword. Hofstaad shambled forward. When he grew nearer, he attempted to thrust his sword, but he took too small of a step. His ankle must have really pained him. Abba felt bad. Hofstaad had been winning, fair to the rules. Why should he not win the bout?

Then Hofstaad's sword struck Abba in the face. Abba immediately swung back. His sword connected, hitting Hofstaad in the chest. Abba swung again, hitting Hofstaad in the head. Hofstaad stumbled, and Abba tackled him to the ground. He dropped his sword in the process. Hofstaad tried to get away from him, but Abba slammed his fist into his helmet. Abba grabbed his sword, stood up, and pointed the tip of it at Hofstaad's visor. The announcer ran over to get in between the two competitors, and Abba heard the voice of Hedmond yelling for them to cease. The announcer pulled the two of them to the center, Hofstaad limping, and raised Abba's hand.

When Abba exited the dueling enclosure, he noticed Maric waiting for him. He had a wide grin on his face, and he held his hands in the air.

"What has possessed you, Abba? You have never fought with such ferocity before!"

"I don't know," Abba said. "I was just acting. I wasn't doing it deliberately."

"Ah, so you know how to fight now. You better keep it up, because your next opponent is that skinny fellow in brown."

"He is going to be tough. He moves quickly."

"I'll be up soon. One of the tournament coordinators told me that my next opponent is a fellow from Belar with a teal tabard. I'm going to go watch for him."

Maric hurried off to the fence of the dueling enclosure, Abba following not far behind. When they got there, Maric immediately looked around. Abba guessed he was looking for his opponent, so he followed where he looked. Maric watched his opponent, refusing to take his eyes off of him. He was surely sizing him up. Hedmond yelled for the fight to cease.

Maric sauntered over to the center of the dueling arena, meeting with the announcer and the other competitor. This opponent was taller than Maric, too; but Abba knew Maric was not concerned. His younger brother was fairly short, after all, but Abba reckoned he would grow sooner or later, getting a growth spurt much like the one he'd had in the past few months. The duel started, and Maric walked forward. He led with an aggressive barrage of swings until his opponent got out a swing of his own, but Maric blocked it and kicked the knight. Maric swung and swung, moving closer to his opponent with each step. His opponent attempted to give Maric a kick of his own to no avail, for Maric smothered his kick by getting close, dropping his sword, crouching down, and wrapping his arms around the legs of the knight. He lifted him up and slammed him down. They rolled around in the dirt like pigs, grappling one another in an attempt to win. Maric tried to rip his opponent's sword away from him, but the knight refused to let go. For quite a while, it was much of the same, so the announcer went over the two and stopped them in order to bring them back up to their feet. Their longswords were returned to them, and the announcer resumed the match.

Maric inched closer to his opponent while he pointed his longsword forward. When he got close, he held the longsword's handle with only one hand while he kept his other hand hovering in front of him. Abba could tell that his brother was getting ready for something, so he leaned in to watch. Maric thrusted the sword forward, and when his opponent went to smack the thrust away with his blade, Maric grabbed the cross-guard of his opponent's sword and threw his own to the ground, wrapping his arm around his opponent. His opponent yanked back, but instead of preventing Maric from throwing him, he stumbled and pulled Maric on top of him while he tripped over his own feet. Maric slammed his elbow into his opponent's helmet, stripped his sword from him, and pointed its blade at the competitor's visor. The announcer separated them, and Hedmond ceased the fight. Maric's hand was raised, and he left the enclosure.

"What a great fight! You did quite well!" said Abba, patting his brother on his back.

"I could have done a bit better. I was going to throw him, but he yanked me," Maric said.

"I saw that. You really are gifted at this. You make all these other competitors look like it's their first day swinging a sword."

"I shouldn't get ahead of myself. There's always someone better," Maric said. "I've been watching that skinny lad all day. He doesn't have anyone with him, no tent or servants to aid him. He never practices with his sword; he just sits around the fence, waiting for his next bout. He is a scary one. Good luck with him."

Abba looked around in search of the thin fighter. He could barely make him out from all the brown rags in the crowd. His eyes did eventually cross over him. The lad seemed to have had the same idea; he was watching Abba from afar.

A few more fights took place, and it was Abba's turn again. He walked toward the announcer.

"Hello. I believe I am next."

"Aye, you are. Thank you for coming early," said the announcer.

"If I may ask, what is the name of the lad in brown?"

The announcer stared at the paper, squinting his eyes. "Er, it is an unusual name. I think it's pronounced... Ado?"

"Where is Ado from?"

"Low Beak, I believe. Why?"

Abba looked at the lad. "I only wish to know who I am going up against."

The announcer called Abba and Ado out to the dueling area. Abba tried to maintain his stoic demeanor, but Ado outdid him with how loose he was when he walked. It seemed like all his muscles were relaxed, as if he did not fear the outcome of this duel. This worried Abba; it reminded him of how Ser Mikhail had walked out to fight him. He must have seen Abba as no threat. Abba was tense. His hands squeezed his sword handle like a vise. He swore under his breath.

He looked up. Ado was coming straight for him. Had he missed Hedmond's commencement of the fight? Abba turned his head to the announcer, who was now stepping away to do his duty in watching the fight. Lifting his sword, Abba attempted to defend from Ado's oncoming swing. A volley of several slashes came at him, but Abba defended against them all. The strikes felt odd. They were just light taps on his blade. Seemingly, if the strikes were to connect, Abba reckoned that they would not have done any damage at all. This unnerved him. Ado must have been going easy on him. Abba could not understand why he would not just end the match immediately instead of wasting time. Perhaps it was just a game that he was playing. Maybe he only wished to toy with Abba, and then he would go on to his final match.

Ado was not in front of him anymore. Abba spun around, and he saw his opponent's sword hand slam into his face. Abba's body fell to the ground. His head spun, and he felt a weight bear down on his chest piece. He looked up to the sight of Ado's blade tip stuck through the eye slit of his helmet.

"Cease!"

Abba's heart pounded, and Ado pulled his sword away. He extended a hand to Abba, and Abba accepted his aid. They stood at each side of the announcer, and the announcer raised Ado's hand. After the two exited the dueling enclosure, Abba called out for Ado, but he did not acknowledge his calls. Abba sulked, feeling disappointed in himself. He looked for Maric. His brother was already prepared for his next fight; Abba must have passed him when he left the enclosure. Maric stepped into the dueling enclosure. It was not a quick fight, but Maric was not outdone. He finished the fight, and the announcer raised his hand.

His father would only know that Abba had lost. He never saw any of Abba's fights, any of the bouts that he'd won. Nothing was going to change; Adar was still going to be disappointed in him. Abba put his foot over a rock and pressed on it, pushing it into the dirt.

Someone wrapped their arms around him. He looked over his shoulder and saw that it was Maric hugging him. Abba hugged him back.

Maric pulled away. "I am really proud of you. I never would have thought *you* would beat someone in a fight."

Abba shook his head, smirking. "You said I should be proud earlier; where was the disbelief then?"

"I had to make sure your head was in reality," said Maric, chuckling.

"Well, you have a chance to prove how good you are. You're going up against Ado next."

"Ado is his name? I've never met an Ado. Sounds foreign."

"Aye, he is from Low Beak."

"Well, I will avenge you, Brother. He may fight well, but I will beat him!"

"He is quite good. I do not know if I can say that he rivals Ser Mikhail, but he is no lousy fighter. He was taking it easy on me in the beginning."

"Abba, taking it easy on you is not a good gauge of skill."

Abba punched Maric's shoulder. Maric laughed.

"Maric, I am serious," Abba said. "He is skilled. At one moment, he was in front of me; and the next, I was on the ground."

"Alright. I will keep that in mind."

There was an intermission between Maric's match and the final. The announcer notified the crowd that they could take a break, for Maric and Ado were to be granted a moment of rest before the final match. Maric did not pace, and he did not look concerned. Abba envied his composure. He did not wish to interrupt his brother at this moment. He trusted himself. Abba wondered if this confidence would be enough, for his opponent was far more skilled than the other duelists that had competed in the tourney. Ado was quicker than anyone Abba had ever fought; quicker than Ser Mikhail, even. He moved like he already knew where his opponent would step before they moved at all. He was like a finely tuned machine. Abba had never seen someone fight like him before. From a distance, he looked no different; but fighting him was strange. His mistakes felt like they were planned, already written. Abba looked around for Ado and saw that he was staring at Maric the same way he had been staring at Abba before their match. Maric watched him as well. Two bells rang. The announcer beckoned Maric and Ado out to the center of the enclosure.

Hedmond stood up, raising his hands to the crowd. They fell silent.

"Hear me! I thank you for attending this festival, and I wish for everyone to enjoy the final match of our duels. We have two fighters here who have proven their skill with the sword. Maric of Kurembrog in the gray tabard! But sixteen years of age, and he has proven his prowess with the sword! And Ado, a lad from Low Beak who is visiting Osmjornia! It is a joyous occasion to have him here, for he is truly a formidable fighter. Now, I do not wish to delay this undoubtedly exciting match any further. Ready yourselves. Maric! Ado! Commence!"

Neither Ado nor Maric lunged forward. Ado stepped to his left, and Maric did the same. They circled around the center, patiently watching each other's movements. Ado was the first to break this pattern, swiping down at Maric with his sword. Maric parried, but he did not riposte, preferring to keep his distance. They circled the center again, but this time Maric was the one to break the pattern. He thrust his sword forward, which Ado promptly parried. He turned his failed thrust into an upward strike. This too was parried, and Ado responded with a riposte. Neither of them could gain any ground on the other. They seemed to be equals at that point. They never hastened their strikes, and every attack seemed thoroughly strategic. Abba could tell that both of them were deep in thought underneath their helmets.

They ended up in a fit of just swinging at one another. None of their strikes were committal, for both of them seemed to prefer playing it safe. Ado grabbed Maric by his visor and yanked him to the ground. Abba squeezed his hands into fists and leaned over the fence to watch. Maric did not fall on his arse; instead, he only dropped to his knees. Ado walked forward, and Maric grabbed him by the heel and used his free hand to push him at the hip. Ado hopped on his free leg, refusing to be pulled down. He slammed his pommel repeatedly onto Maric's helmet. He tried to trip Ado, but he continued to refuse Maric's takedown, twisting, turning, and stepping in a way that prevented Maric from getting him to the ground. Maric released Ado's leg and kicked him away, giving him enough time to retrieve his longsword. Ado marched forward. Maric did, too. Ado held his longsword's guard near his cheek, sword tip pointed up. Maric raised his own sword even higher.

Ado thrust forward at Maric's exposed neck, but Maric swung his sword down at Ado's. Ado's sword now pointed down, touching the ground. Maric stomped on the tip of the sword. It bent. Ado did not try to yank it back. Instead, he released the sword, but Maric had already tackled him to the ground. While Ado lay with his back to the ground, Maric sent his elbow into his helmet. He slammed and slammed before he grabbed one of the swords. He probably wanted to be sure that Ado was sufficiently battered. Maric pointed the sword tip to the slit in Ado's visor.

"Cease!"

The announcer pulled Maric off of Ado, aiding the lad up to his feet. Standing them both at his sides, he raised Maric's hand. Abba noticed Hedmond gazing at the crowds. He had a less-than-happy expression on his face, gritting his teeth while he prepared his voice for a final announcement.

"Maric of Kurembrog is the Midsummer champion! Come, Maric! Come to the nobleman's stand to receive your prize."

Abba ran over to hug his brother, and Maric received it graciously. The two of them walked over to the nobleman's stand. Ser Mikhail stood at the bottom, waiting for them. When his eyes met Maric's, they gleamed with pride. He widened his arms in preparation to embrace the boy.

"Congratulations lad! I expected no less."

Abba stood, awkwardly playing with a pebble under his foot.

"Oi!" Ser Mikhail blurted, beckoning Abba over. "There's a hug for you, too. Your father would be proud."

Abba smiled and hugged Ser Mikhail. Maric went toward the steps that led to where the nobility sat. Hedmond sat with the prize resting on a table to his side. Maric smiled when he looked at it; but when he sought to grasp it, Hedmond halted him.

"Are you and your brother not partaking in the melee, Maric?" asked Hedmond.

Maric looked to Ser Mikhail.

Ser Mikhail laughed, shaking his head. "They are."

"Well, in that case, I ought to keep the prize by my side. For safekeeping."

"No, that is alright. I can hold it," said Ser Mikhail, sticking out his hand.

"I have made up my mind," Hedmond said. "Besides, if Maric's side wins in the melee, then it would be an even grander moment when I hand it to him. Do you not agree?"

Ser Mikhail grimaced. "I see what you mean."

"Wonderful."

Ser Mikhail turned around and put each of his hands on each of the boys' shoulders. He led them away from Hedmond and brought them over to the steps.

"I did not mention that I was putting the two of you in the melee because I wanted Abba to be focused on the duels themselves," he said. "Do not put too much thought into this— just try your best. Both of you did very well in the duels."

Ser Mikhail patted both of them on their shoulders, then walked them over to the dueling grounds. The announcer was leading the competitors over to their respective sides. The Western Osmjornish were on one side, and the Eastern Osmjornish were on the other. Abba and Maric joined the Westerners. Abba wondered where Ado would be. He gazed across the field, but Ado was nowhere to be seen.

After a boring wait, Hedmond commenced the melee. The two sides rushed each other like waves at sea. Once contact was made, the lines stopped. No ground was given, and no ground was taken. They whacked at each other with their blunted weapons. Clubs would have done more damage.

At some point, a large number of the Easterners clumped up in the middle of the melee. Maric was at Abba's side, swinging at the Easterners; then, suddenly, he was yanked into the group by one of the knights in the line. He was being held down. Abba rushed in to knock the knight off of his brother, but he was grabbed from behind. Abba squinted his eyes. They were behind the Easterners' line, and a knight wearing the Kyln blue walked over with a dagger.

"Hofstaad? Hofstaad!" Abba said. "Tell that knight to get off of Maric, he is already on the ground!"

Hofstaad walked over to the knight and made a waving motion with his hand. The knight got off of Maric, and Maric climbed to his feet. He reached out toward Hofstaad to give his thanks.

Then Hofstaad grabbed him by the visor, tilted his head back, and slit Maric's throat.

Abba's hearing grew tinny and narrow. He could hear his heartbeat in his ears. Maric reached for his neck. Dark blood spurted out from the wound there, reddening his gauntlets. He took a few shaky steps toward Abba, his face frighteningly pale. Then he dropped to the ground.

Abba stared at his brother. Blood had puddled beneath Maric's helmet. His visor was still up; Abba could see the whites of his eyes, the strange pallor of his face. Abba looked up at Hofstaad and tried to say something, but no noise came out; his voice was too weak to speak.

Hofstaad walked over to Abba. A few of the rings that made up the palm of his mail gloves were split, revealing a wound underneath. He grabbed Abba by the visor and lifted up his head.

"Your father can tell you how proud he is when you see him in Gol," Hofstaad hissed.

Then Abba's throat was cut open, too. He felt it fill with blood. Like Maric, he fell to the ground, choking. Warmth soaked the front of his gambeson.

The melee erupted into a battle. Abba narrowly saw the onset of this; the Western side had noticed the East's initiation of real bloodshed. He reached for his brother while the world spun around him, his vision fading to black.

Meara

ver the past three days, Meara had learned how quickly rations could run out. Her first decree as new leader of the orphans was to double the amount of food each child received; but as a consequence, the food had run out much sooner than usual. She immediately shrank the size of the rations again, though she still gave out more than Luka ever had. But the children still protested when she lowered the rations. This frustrated her. She did not feel that it was right to beat them, but that was how Luka had kept them in line. To dissuade further outbursts of dissent, Meara, knife in hand, pointed to the sack that held Luka's head. She kept it around mainly because she didn't know where to toss it, but it also allowed her to remind the children that *she* was in charge. She was the one who had brought the most food to the group; she deserved to lead them.

They generally did look to be happier, probably because their stomachs were fuller than they had been the week before. Food was still a struggle, but the festival had brought many opportunities to steal. For the first time ever, Meara had access to as much food as she could eat. But she shunned such an idea. She was *not* Luka. The children feared Meara in a different way. With Luka, they kept quiet, afraid to arouse his impulsive wrath; but with Meara, they spoke more freely, while still keeping an eye on her. She assumed that they were trying to gauge what brought about her own wrath. Luka was predictable because of the fact that there was nothing to predict: he was always going to beat someone. It was smart to keep quiet and be in the background, for those in the foreground of Luka's mind were the ones most often harmed. Although, from what Meara knew, Luka had never killed anyone directly, choosing to instead beat them severely and leave them to die on their own. Meara had killed someone.

As early as the second day of her being in charge, a couple of children had tried to steal some extra food. They were testing her. When she caught them, she saw them turn pale with fear. After that day, she started giving the most loyal of the older and larger children more food in return for protecting the store. This struck fear into the smaller, peskier children who still remembered losing to those same larger kids in Luka's forced brawls. It worked immediately. The risk-taking orphans eventually stopped eyeing the food altogether.

Two of the kids started to tussle. On the ground, there was sack, its contents of bread and fruits spilling out onto the ground. One of Meara's older kids grabbed the two boys, bringing them to kneel in front of Meara. Meara shook her head with disappointment.

"Luka is gone. Our days of fighting for food are over. You will take your share, and you will not protest or attempt to steal from anyone else."

One of the two boys huffed. "But I am bigger than him! I need more food than he does!"

Meara stepped forward, staring down the boy. "But do you produce more than him? You may be larger, and that may have helped you in Luka's pit fights; but did you *do* anything that makes you more deserving of food than him?"

The boy attempted to respond, and one of Meara's older kids smacked him.

"No, you have not," Meara said. "You have repeatedly whined about how much food we have given you, but you have brought very little back to the group. Some days, you bring nothing. How can you complain that you are not receiving enough food when you do not care to bring anything at all?"

The boy stomped and kicked, so the other child smacked him once more. Meara turned back and sat down on her throne. She enjoyed sitting there. She could see everyone, and she felt less uncomfortable. At times, she wondered if they would try to get rid of her; but she eventually realized that they probably felt like they needed her. She would make sure they were fed, and she was the best at getting food. If they ousted her, they would starve. The atmosphere, at least for Meara, was far less anxiety inducing with Luka gone. Her limbs had gotten less bony, and she was in the best mood she had ever been in. After all the beatings she had received in the past two weeks, she was finally starting to feel like she was getting her strength back.

Meara felt happy for the first time in a long time. She had felt unsafe for so long, but now she could sleep knowing that no one would mess with her. When she walked down the alley, she felt like a queen.

There was a tournament going on that day. Mutterings from the streets had spread to the mouths of the children. Some of them wished to go and watch, but Meara kept them from leaving. To Meara, there was no purpose for them to seek out a place where there would surely be guards, knights, and nobles. Certainly, that man—the one who had threatened to chop her hands off—would be there.

"Gol, keep watch here," Meara said. "I am going to take a few of the children to the town square. The merchants will likely be watching the tournament along with everyone else, so I think it will be a good idea to see what I can take from whatever goods they may have left out."

Gol nodded. He walked over to Meara's throne and sat down. Meara beckoned to a few of the children and told them to follow her. Together, they strolled down to the town square.

But in all honesty, Meara did not care for the town square at all in that moment. Her eyes were dead set on the merchant's house. She gazed around. The town square was nearly empty, with just a few people wandering the streets. The children scattered about, searching every box and crevice. One guard was stationed, but his eyes could not track everyone. When he would go to approach a child to apprehend them, another child would take it as an opportunity to snatch anything of worth and run off.

The mask stall was gone. This was strange, for the festival was nowhere near over. There was at least another day or two for the mask peddler to make some coin. From memory, it looked like his stall was the only one that was not present; every other stall was still there.

Something told her to check the house. It was not a gut feeling, but rather a strange draw from her whole body. She walked straight toward it and climbed up the steps. Stopping for a moment, she stared at the handle; it was unlocked. She opened the door.

Inside, there was a man. He was dressed in plate armor that was covered with a brown tabard. He sat on his knees, resting his weight on his heels. Meara approached him cautiously, leaving the door open behind her.

"Who are you?" asked Meara.

"That is a more complex question than you realize," said the man.

Meara looked back out the door to the empty street. She thought of leaving, her hand still lingering on the handle.

"I can assure you that I am no threat," said the man.

"You look like quite the threat at the moment," Meara said, eyeing his armor.

"A threat requires intention. I have no such ill intent toward you," said the man. "I know you are not a trusting girl, but look at the wall to my right."

She recognized his voice, but she could not place the memory. On the wall, there was a wardrobe that she had not seen before. Why had she not noticed it upon entry? She supposed that the presence of the strange man had blinded her from obvious new addition. The wardrobe was open; behind the door, she could narrowly see that there were masks inside. She stepped forward. There were even more masks at the back of the wardrobe. She paused to observe the man. He stared at the ground while he sat in what was probably a prayer.

"Your voice. I recognize your voice," she said. "Are you the mask salesman? Why are you in this house?"

The man lifted his chin up to look at Meara. Placing his hands around his helmet, he slowly lifted it off of his head. With a start, she recognized him. His skin was beige, and his eyes were brown. He wore a skull cap that covered the majority of his head, including his ears. It was the Low Beakish merchant.

"I could tell you my name, but it would do little good for either of us. I am a friend, and you can refer to me as such," he said. "You said you recognized my voice, but what of my face?"

Meara stared at him, her eyes wide with shock. "But... I thought you left! You removed all your belongings, and you were nowhere to be found!"

He laughed. "Men and women alike wear many masks throughout their lifetimes without even realizing it; I know that better than most, but it is still something I find to be damaging. People so often shun reflection. They should know who they are, and they should understand why they do the things they do. It is a tragedy for one to succumb blindly to one's own impulses."

He stripped his skull cap from his head and revealed a bandage that kept his hair compressed.

"Strictly speaking, I should not be revealing what I look like, or who I am; but I feel as though only pain can come from you not knowing. I see things. I know things before they happen," he said. "But do not worry, Meara. I have enough courtesy to not read everyone."

Meara stepped backward, pointing her feet to the door. "I never told you my name."

"I will not force you to stay. You may of course leave if you wish, but I am sure your curiosity will halt you in your tracks once I unwrap these bandages from my head."

He reached his hand for the end of the bandages, slowly unraveling it. At the lower edge of the wrapping, he undid another end, and the bandages spun around his head while it loosened. Meara halted in disbelief. After he dropped the bandage on the floor, he revealed two spear-like ears. *He was an elf.* She stumbled back, reaching for the door handle.

"Don't run," he said. "I know the orphans need food."

"I can feed them myself."

"You have made enemies. One of them is dead, yes, but the other two are far more powerful, and they know your face. Are you going to live your life snatching food until you lose your hands?"

"And what if you are another enemy, you spear-eared devil?"

He laughed. "You are right, I am a devil. I lied to you and said I was from Low Beak when I clearly am not. I have taken on many masks, none of them my own. I could have helped you with all your problems, and I did not. But your plights were not mine to solve. If I had saved Gol, then you would have never earned your bravery. If I saved you from Hrodert, then you would have never

472

attained your resolve. And if I had killed Luka, then you would never have felt secure in leading the children."

"You left me to suffer just so I could learn a lesson?"

"No, I looked at your future. It was against my own creed, but I was concerned. I saw enough to know that you would be alright. If I had seen any threat to your life, then I would have intervened."

"*Did* you intervene?"

"I do not think that is fair to say from my end. You have no ability of verifying if what I say is true, so I do not think it is right for me to make a claim like that."

"So why are you here?" Meara asked.

"I need your help. I cannot reliably prove the past, but I can prove what will happen. I need you to trust that what I am telling you to do is safe," said the elf. "There is a balustrade that overlooks the tournament grounds. I want you to go there now, and by doing so, I will prove to you that I can see the future. I need you to make sure certain things happen. If they do happen, I will make sure the orphans are fed until they can reliably feed themselves."

Meara furrowed her brows. "You have an oddly grand way of asking me to do a task. Why would you feed them for that long? Many of them are young; for how long do you require my aid?"

"Maybe a year? It is hard to gauge. I see winter." The elf put his hand to his chin, pondering. "My foresight for the near future is almost perfect, but when I peer further, the foggier it becomes."

"Then how can you be so sure that the *thing* you want me to see will happen soon, if your foresight is not perfect?"

The elf closed his eyes. "Today is the tournament day. The sun will be a bit low in the sky. The sky will be graying with heavy clouds. And the two Kurem boys will be killed in a brawl. I just let the younger one win only a moment ago, so the event obviously has not happened yet." He opened his eyes. "I can go on about how I deduced when it will happen, or you can go see it for yourself."

Meara looked out of the door. "I will go. I think I know the place you are talking about; it isn't far from the keep."

Meara turned her head back to the room. The elf had disappeared, and so too had the wardrobe. The bed was all that was left. A note and sack sat where the elf had knelt, and Meara walked over to them. The sack was full of food. The letter was sealed with an unbranded wax stamp. She opened it.

A child of yours is dawdling outside the house; hand him the sack of food and tell him to bring it back to the orphans. He is good-natured and will not take it for himself. After doing so, go straight to the location we spoke about.

A friend

Meara shook her head with confusion. Had he prepared this letter before their conversation? She walked outside, the sack of food slung over her shoulder. The elf was right: an orphan was loitering just outside. She handed him the food and told him to run off back home. Meara stared at him while he went, thinking about the strange elf. She shook her head, trying to free herself from her thoughts.

When she arrived, everything was as the elf had described: the sun was low, and the sky was gray. She leaned over the balustrade and watched the tournament. There was what looked to be a big brawl happening, but everyone was so far away that she could not see the details. But it was obvious when the event that the elf had alluded to finally occurred. Crowds of people began flooding onto the tournament grounds, the fighting surging up into the stands. People began to flee, shrieking.

As the panicked crowd dispersed, Meara spotted two crumpled bodies on the ground. The intense spectacle of death ended with raindrops and an empty coliseum.

Edit

 drizzle of rain tapped Edit's nose. She looked up at the heavy clouds above. It would rain soon; she would probably have to return to safety beneath the overhang, where the nobility sat. Ser Mikhail stood by the part of the tournament grounds' fence that was between both lines of melee competitors. Edit figured Ser Mikhail had moved there to get a better view of the fight; and while she understood his motivations, she still thought the view from the stands would have been more enjoyable. Despite this, she still felt more comfortable around him than she did in the stands. Lady Anita was there, but she had gone quiet after Count Adar's arrest, and Edit had always felt uncomfortable consoling someone under distress. Ser Mikhail did not talk much in general, but he was kind, and Edit could tell he cared about those around him. If he did talk, it would not be about something distressing.

Kyln banners were waving fiercely in the developing winds. The stands were packed: more packed than she had realized. Mothers led their children up the steps. Young boys stared attentively at the the competitors, waiting for them to begin fighting. Older women gossiped while their husbands jested with each other. She faintly heard Hedmond commence the tournament behind her, and everyone turned their heads to give the melee their full attention.

Edit had never really enjoyed tournaments. She had seen many of them; this was just yet another. She found it much more interesting to watch the people in the stands. Most of them refused to talk while the fight was underway, fully focused on the melee before them. The nobles were more prone to chatter; although, it should not be said that the more martially inclined among them did not give the tournaments the respect they deserved. Edit sat, thinking about why the commonfolk would be more interested than the nobility, and while she did, the intensity of the drizzle increased. Edit looked to the sky.

"Fuck! So soon?" shouted Ser Mikhail, throwing his hands up in disbelief.

Edit turned around, attempting to peer past the line of people hacking at each other on the field. She tried to see what Ser Mikhail had, but she simply couldn't discern through the mess of people.

"Did something happen?" asked Edit.

"Only that they're surely subdued. I saw one of them get dragged down, and the other went to get him. They're surrounded."

"At least Maric won the tourney," Edit said. "And Abba did not do too badly himself. That can be enough glory for today."

Ser Mikhail turned his head to Edit with a confused look on his face. "Glory? I am not concerned about glory. What they just did was stupid, and it would have gotten them killed in a real battle. I am going to have to hammer that into them when we are back home."

Edit did not know how to respond, so she just stayed quiet. Ser Mikhail's look of confusion hardened. He leaned forward, concern growing behind his eyes. He took a lurching step, walking along the fence-line. He said nothing, and his steps grew faster. Edit followed behind. He kept a hand on the fence and his eyes on the fight.

Suddenly, he stopped. He swore once, loudly, then he hopped over the fence and drew his blade.

"What happened?" yelled Edit.

Ser Mikhail looked back at her. "Go back to the stands, now!" he yelled, running off to the melee.

The melee erupted into a brawl. Edit turned around and stared at the crowds. They were cheering. She turned back around and watched the melee. There was a different level of violence here:

the competitors did not stop swinging when their opponents hit the ground. It had turned into a real battle. Before she knew it, guards began to push through the crowd, running for the tournament grounds. At around this same time, a commoner was bumped into by one of the hasty guards. That one must have been a rowdy fellow, for he immediately pulled out a knife and began to shove the guard, who was only equipped with a bludgeon. A few of the other guards tried to grab the man, but he swung his knife, keeping them at bay. It worked until one of them hit the commoner in the back of the head with a bludgeon. The guards beat him. The aftermath was unavoidable at that point. The commoner's sons noticed, and launched themselves at the guards. A riot was breaking out, she realized, and she was watching the whole thing unfold.

She snapped out of her trance once someone was pushed into her from behind. Edit fell face first into the dirt. She hurriedly turned her head. People were running in her direction. In a frenzy, Edit crawled back to her feet and ran. Edit learned quickly that she had to hold up her skirts so that her feet wouldn't get caught in her hemline. She wanted to look back and see what Ser Mikhail was doing. He had pulled out his sword. Something had to have happened to Abba or Maric; why else would he have drawn a weapon?

People poured out from the stands, the area between the field and the stands becoming overwhelmingly crowded. Edit tried her best to keep trudging forward. Someone grabbed her arm. Yanking it back instinctively, she turned her head, but she was unable to figure out who had done it. At that moment, she realized she was unprotected. If Ser Mikhail or Ser Elseharde had been here, then they would have immediately come to her defense; but at this moment, there was no one around to defend her besides herself. Her heart began to race. She tried to push through the crowd, but it refused to budge. The fence was to her right. She hurriedly climbed under the rail and ran through the opening, toward the stands. A few of the guards noticed her and tried to apprehend her, but one of them recognized her face and allowed her to move through the field.

When she made it to the stands, the rest of the nobility—including Anita and Hedmond—were being escorted away by a number of Hedmond's men. She hurriedly ran for the safety of their party.

Lady Anita beckoned her over. "What is happening? Did you see anything?"

"I think something happened to Abba or Maric," blurted Edit.

Hedmond glanced over. "What? What makes you say that?"

"Ser Mikhail hopped over the fence and drew his sword."

Hedmond whispered something to Frud, and Frud departed from the group, taking a few men with him. Lady Anita nodded her head, but there was worry in her eyes.

"They will be fine. Ser Mikhail will make sure they are fine," she said.

Edit looked onward. Hedmond's guards made a circle around the nobility, pushing the commonfolk away as they marched through the crowd. The rowdier part of the crowd was yards away, but they still ran into plenty of trouble when trying to move forward. There was a gap between two stands with a crowd of vacating burghers already there. Trying to move the group through the crowd was like trying to put a dowel in a hole that did not fit, but Hedmond's guards had no trouble in *making* room. These guards were not just some levied townsmen, but rather well-armored professional soldiers. When they walked through the crowd, the crowd did its best to part.

One of the town guards, separate from Hedmond's guard, called out for a wagon. He yelled that there were dead in the tournament, but he did not say who or where from. A number of people had come out from their houses to watch the ruckus unfold. People flooded into the town square, and a number of townsfolk began to rummage in the stalls. Edit turned her head around to the sight of a line of guards yelling at a group of peasants. The peasants were raising their arms, shouting. It was not long until a crowd obstructed her view of them, but the last thing she saw was a guard swinging his cudgel.

They made it to the gates of the keep. As expected in times of riot, the gates were closed; but at the sight of Hedmond, they were promptly raised. The nobility dispersed. Some went to the keep, and others stayed around to peer through the closing portcullis behind them. Anita walked toward the keep, so Edit followed her. Hedmond went off to talk to one of his guardsmen. He looked stressed, tapping one of his feet while he complained about something. Edit could see the disappointment clearly on his face. At one point, his father came up to him and looked to be asking for something, but Hedmond shooed him away like a dog.

In the keep, Anita peered around. Edit imagined she was looking for the dungeon. With her children out there, Adar was the only member of her family that she could presently reach. She found a doorway that opened to a set of steps leading down, with another barred door at its base. Anita took a few hasty steps toward it, but she halted in her tracks, looking around to see if there were any guards. Edit turned around, too. Directly behind the both of them was Hedmond.

"I reckon you've come to see your husband, yes?" asked Hedmond.

"Yes," said Anita. "Is that alright?"

"Of course. I was going to offer you the opportunity, but you've evaded my asking. Go on down."

Anita's gaze darted over to the door. She went down the stairs.

"You go down, too," Hedmond said. "Seeing her husband imprisoned will cause her some pain. She will need someone with her."

Edit dreaded the idea of having to comfort anyone, but she did feel bad for Anita, so she followed. The steps were dark, the stairwell devoid of any light other than the flickering of torches. She marched past a sea of reaching ne'er-do-wells before she caught up to Anita. Anita stood motionless, staring through the bars of a cell that Edit could not yet see. Geder was there, too, Edit realized, recognizing him with a start; and the hammer that Adar was obsessed with leaned on the wall.

Edit leaned forward, peering into the cell. There was a bloodied body on the ground. For a moment, she couldn't tell who it was. The only facial feature that still resembled Adar was his jaw; everything above it had been caved in. Edit stumbled back, but when she turned around, a guard was blocking her exit.

"What happened?" asked Anita, her voice strangely calm.

"He was going to die—"

Anita lunged at Geder, swinging her fists at him with frightening speed. "You killed him!" she screamed, her voice unrecognizable. "You killed Adar!"

Geder pushed her off of him and slapped her, shoving her into the cell with Adar's body. He shut the door and locked her in. She spat at him, hitting him on the chest. He grabbed a cloth and wiped the saliva off of himself. He threw the rag to the ground, then pointed at the guard and Edit. The guard walked over to Edit and grabbed her. She screamed and thrashed, but she could not break free of his grip. The guard threw her into the cell across from Anita's, and Geder locked it.

"As I was saying," Geder said. "He was going to die anyway."

Anita did not respond. She knelt beside her dead husband, holding her fingers near his skin but refusing to touch him. She looked like she was *afraid* to touch him.

"I put him out of his misery," Geder said.

Anita looked up at him, tears shining in her eyes. "Adar is too stubborn to end his misery. You *killed* him."

She touched Adar's chest, then quickly pulled her hand back. She began to weep.

The cell that Edit was in was incredibly clean, the bedding far too lavish for a peasant's hovel, let alone a dungeon. A spot on the ground was warm, similar to how her floorboards would get after a servant removed a bath from her room.

"Was this Jergi's cell?" asked Edit. "Where is he?"

Anita looked over to Edit, then to Geder.

"He forced my hand," Geder said.

"You planned this," said Anita. She got to her feet, jabbing her finger at Geder. "There was no trial. Hedmond let you kill Adar in his cell, and you let Jergi go. You are a conniving plotter."

Then she stopped.

"Where are my boys?"

Geder did not respond. He looked away.

"Did you plan the riot, too?" she asked, her voice close to a whisper.

"No."

"Then *where are my boys?*"

Again, Geder did not answer. Anita grabbed the bars, choking them.

"Ser Mikhail is going to kill you when he finds out what you've done," she hissed.

"He will never make it to me."

"He's still out there, you fool," Anita said. "He was down by the tournament grounds, watching Abba and Maric. He didn't come back with us. If you didn't plan the riot, then—"

She went silent.

"Did you plan something else?"

Geder did not answer.

"Did you plan to harm my boys?"

Again, Geder did not answer, but he must have given Anita a look that was telling. She lunged at him again, reaching her arms through the bars in an attempt to grab Geder. She screamed at him. She kept on yelling about how she was going to kill him. Geder just stood there while she went rabid. It took a while for her to run out of energy, but eventually she did. Her posture crumpled. She slouched over while her arms rested on the bars in front of her. Anita looked as though her soul had been ripped from her. Edit could feel her sorrow. She remembered how she had felt when her mother had killed herself. She wanted to hug Anita, but the damned bars in front of her prevented her from doing so.

Geder wiped his eyes. "It had to be done. There was no other way. With what I saw in Woldhom... I knew then what Osmjornia needed."

"I don't want to see your false tears, you conniving wretch," Anita said. "You were *always* bitter. You did not come to visit Adar for years. And you think that I am going to believe that this decision was made so recently? You knew he loved you, but you did not care about him."

She spat at Geder again.

"You are the reason Kurembrog is weak. If it hadn't been for you, my brother would not have died. Adar became weak for *you*, bending himself right over so that your family could fuck him in his rear," Geder said.

"Go on and kill me already. I want to be with my family," she said, walking over and kneeling down beside Adar.

"I am not going to kill either of you," Geder said. "I plan on ransoming you back to your family."

"I will spread word that you are a kinslayer. My father will march to Kurembrog to put your head on a pike," Anita said.

Geder shook his head. "No, he will not. Your boys died in a tournament accident, and your husband succumbed to his own sins. That is the truth of what happened, and that is the truth that shall be spread. You know your father's hatred for Adar better than I do. He despised your spawn. Your father will only wish to bring you home safely."

"Then *I* will spread the word," Edit said. "My father will have no qualms with paying for mercenaries to dispense justice."

Geder's eyes shifted to Edit. "Your father is likely already dead—him *and* that knight that accompanied you. I never planned on ransoming you; your gift makes you far too valuable to lose. I will keep you comfortable in this dungeon and then comfortable in some tower of Kurembrog. Eventually you'll come to see reason, and we will marry. Adar was an idiot, but even an idiot could recognize that acquiring High Beak would be a smart move. I— *we* will grow very wealthy together."

Edit stared blankly forward. Hedmond had had his knights escort Ser Elseharde to meet her father. They were dead. How could she have not realized this? She walked over to the small cot and sat down. She stared at the ground. *What a cruel joke her life was.* Being betrothed to Abba seemed like a paradise compared to the proposal Geder presented. This horrid man had stolen her father from her. Like Anita, she had no more family—and this sick bastard wished to have her *marry* him? She would have sooner ripped the blanket into strands and tied it up somewhere in the cell to hang herself. She thought of her mother again. Edit had once had a brother, too, but she had been far too young when he died to even remember him. Like Anita said: maybe if she did kill herself, then she could see him again, both of them now grown and able. Maybe she could see her mother again. Surely such a thing would be better than living under the control of Geder.

She slouched over, her head resting in her hands. What was she even thinking of?

Venceslaus

enceslaus stared at the trees to the east, the sun beaming down from up above him. Ten days had passed since he had set sail from Nara, ten arduous days sailing upstream on the River of Nar. He did not stop to ask for the aid of another lord, especially in the first few days. He could not trust the lords of Nar, even if they were upstanding; the King had ordered him apprehended. He would be arrested, transferred to the King, and likely end up dead as a result of another assassination. He was growing paranoid. He could not sail back home to Bek d'Lifa; it would have taken too long, and Venceslaus did not want Edit to suffer under the threat of the *Serpentine* any longer.

The days had begun to blend together. The dense forest around him did nothing to occupy his mind. He was also always on edge, as it was difficult to avoid the ships of nobles on the River of Nar. The river was the primary means of travel to and from the capital by the majority of the lords, both wealthy and less-than-wealthy. Venceslaus kept his head down whenever he saw heraldry on a sail. He reckoned he was moving more quickly than any order the King could have given; but if the King was truly so eager to have him captured, then he surely would have thought to send out an order through magical means.

At one point, Venceslaus saw a ship with the Lord Loffreaux's heraldry: a wine-red field with a trapezoidal, or-tinctured charge.

He made doubly sure to keep his face hidden at the sight of it. Venceslaus had a decent relationship with the lord, but Loffreaux would not have thought twice about arresting Venceslaus and handing him over, especially not if it was at the behest of the King. When making a decision, the question Loffreaux asked himself was never "would this hurt another?" but rather "would this help me?" and this mentality showed clearly in how he handled his own domain. When Geder had suggested that the King ought to institute tolls on the roads, Loffreaux agreed. A week later, Loffreaux's lands had instituted their own tolls on road travel.

From Loffreaux's point of view, it was a genius idea. He controlled the two most important roads in all of Mjorn, roads that allowed for trade by land to the east. The forests to the north and south were difficult to travel through, and Edrovith's Plateau funneled foreign traders neatly onto the two roads that went east. The unavoidable tolls made him rich, but the villages further away from the River of Nar went impoverished, suffering a sharp decline in the quality of their living.

When the money from local trade dried up, starvation was not the only thing that was killing the peasants. There were beasts in the forests north of Loffreaux's lands. As a result of their impoverishment, the local lords were unable to train and kit capable hunters. Depending on the beast, villages were either slaughtered overnight or slowly picked off one by one. On the road south of the plateau, okr raids became commonplace once they learned that the villagefolk had only their farming equipment to protect themselves. Venceslaus himself had once seen what a feral okr could do while on a hunt near Avonsgatte: a group of them could certainly overtake any poorly equipped village. And in the chaos of it all, the local lords prevented their peasants from leaving, as they were not eager to let go of their last means of attaining wealth. With most unable to leave, and the ones who *were* able to slip by being unable to afford the tolls, they were left susceptible to slavers.

Loffreaux could have stopped this at any moment. Yet when Venceslaus urged him to act, he had looked confused, as if he were unable to understand why Venceslaus would make such a plea. Venceslaus knew Loffreaux could not be trusted. He was a blind opportunist.

But the farther north he traveled, the more Venceslaus traded his paranoia for loneliness and boredom. One of the ways he had passed the time had been to simply watch the boats and people on the roads that ran along the River of Nar. Now, there was nothing to do besides row a few times and make sure the boat didn't hit the banks of the river. Venceslaus laughed at himself. His wealth had made him too comfortable. He always had means. If he wanted something, he received it, and at that moment this fact was a burden. To have such consistent access to means of contenting himself made the boredom excruciating. But it was not that he missed objects so terribly; what he missed was the people around him. He missed his daughter. He missed his knights. He missed complaining to Ser Groent about about the state of the kingdom. He had spent every moment of every day surrounded by people attempting to talk to him. Here, there was nothing but the rustling of leaves in the wind.

To the east were Urbaed's lands. The Cannens were a kind family, and Venceslaus doubted that Urbaed would give him up to Asbyorn; but Venceslaus knew decisions such as this should not be made so hastily. Urbaed was terrified of the Terukians, certain that they would invade; and Asbyorn would use this fact to his advantage. There was safety to be gained from betraying Venceslaus that made relying on Urbaed unwise.

To the west were the Blykers. The Blykers kept to themselves. Due to some concession made long ago, they had never been proselytized by the Phoenicy. They were so isolated that the last time Venceslaus had spoken to a Blyker had been during the Yhournish War. He barely knew Beltxo Blyker. Despite their interactions going well before, such brief interactions were rarely ever indicative of one's character. It would be risky to trust them as well.

There were a few smaller fiefdoms that Venceslaus could seek help from, but he did not have a personal connection to any of them. He would have liked to have been able to assume that people would help others in need, but recent events had made him wary of assuming such a thing. Venceslaus elected to continue sailing onward until night fell.

When night did fall, Venceslaus docked his boat on the bank and set up camp for the night. He fished, catching a few decently sized fishes that staved off his hunger for a moment. When he grew tired enough to sleep, he grabbed his bag and pulled it under his head to use as a pillow.

His head hit the ground. It was light out. He turned over to see a man pulling the bag out from under him. Another man stood by the small boat, unmooring it. The man by the boat was gesturing for the man closest to Venceslaus to hurry up, but Venceslaus grabbed the fishing pole near him and whacked the man on the head. He retrieved his bag, but the man ran off. Venceslaus pursued, only to trip over his own foot while he rushed forward. He tried to get up to pursue the thieves only to collapse under his own weight. The thieves fled with his boat.

Venceslaus slammed his fist into the ground, cursing at himself. He should have done something. He should have camped somewhere more concealed, or hidden the boat under some brush. How stupid of him. After a moment, however, he began to think about what to do. Venceslaus knew that complaining would not bring him to his daughter. His leg hurt so severely that he had to use his fishing pole as a walking stick. It was awkward and short, but it helped him enough to reach a loose branch that performed better. Venceslaus tied his bag to the end of the fishing pole and used his new walking branch to take him north, following the thieves down the river.

Venceslaus hobbled for a long time. It was about midday when he first caught sight of a road, and the time that it had taken him to reach it left him questioning whether or not he was even heading in the right direction. The pain from his leg worsened; he wondered if it was broken. He thought for a moment to sit down and take a look at his leg to see if there was any swelling, but he knew with its pain that he would not be able to stand back up. The road ran from the west to the east, curving north. He took a deep breath and continued on. This walk was easier than the one before, and he thanked whatever was up above for easing some of his pain. Despite his disdain for the Phoenicy, it still felt good to thank something.

"Who goes there?" asked a voice.

The man who called out to him was speaking Tiuvich. Venceslaus turned to look to his left, tripping over himself as he turned. He dropped the fishing pole and caught himself with his walking stick. In front of him, amidst the brush of the woods, was a well-armored man wearing a red and charcoal cape. He was blond and gray-eyed, with a rough, patchy beard. He held a bow in his hand, and Venceslaus watched as he strapped it to his back, bringing his hand to rest on the pommel of his sheathed sword.

486

His sabatons clanged as he walked forward. He *looked* like a Blyker, Venceslaus thought, but he couldn't be certain; at the very least, however, he was obviously someone important in the employment of the Blykers.

"Are you going to answer me or just ogle at me?" the man said, now tapping two of his fingers on the pommel.

Venceslaus figured he should just answer truthfully. He could have lied and pretended to be an old, addled peasant again, but in this area, that would've only made him look like a vagabond. The knight would likely ask for his papers, and when Venceslaus inevitably failed to produce any, he would apprehend him. He sighed, hoping that his faith in this man would not betray him.

"I am Duke Venceslaus Freihei," Venceslaus said in his best Tiuvich.

The man looked confused.

"Are you, now? And do you know why that sounds strange?" he asked, now speaking in the High Beakish dialect of Narese.

"Aye, I do. You would never expect a lord such as myself to travel alone; but given my injury, I believe it is apparent that I am going through some misfortune," said Venceslaus in Narese. "I can prove my identity."

The man extended his arm forward, palm up. "Go on, then."

"There is a pouch in my bag. I cannot reach it in this state; I think I broke my leg."

The man squinted at him, sighing shortly after. "If you could back up slightly, it would give me the comfort of knowing that I would have a bit of space if you were to attack me."

Venceslaus nodded, hobbling away from the bag. The knight picked up the bag and rummaged through it for the pouch. He opened it, pulling out a stamp. He looked concerned. Venceslaus's heart began to race. The stamp should've proven his identity beyond any doubt; was the man finding something wrong with it?

The man put the stamp back in the pouch and the pouch back into the bag. He walked for Venceslaus with his arm extended, gesturing for Venceslaus to put his arm around his shoulders.

"I apologize for being so wary, Duke Venceslaus," he said. "You do not deserve that, and neither do you deserve the misfortune you are suffering."

"It is to be expected. Your Narese is very good; where did you learn to speak it? I know that Phoenic priests are not a common sight around these parts," Venceslaus said, as they began to hobble forward together.

The man furrowed his brows. "My father taught me."

"Wait," said Venceslaus, looking at the man's face. "Are you Iragar?"

The man smiled, nodding.

"Oh my, how you've grown! You were but a small lad the last time I saw you. You Blykers rarely ever show your faces in Nara."

"We show our faces just enough to stave off the King's begging," said Iragar, smiling.

"Ha! Iragar, how is Beltxo doing?"

"It seems he is doing much better than you," said Iragar, looking down at Venceslaus's leg. "I have a horse nearby. I shall help you up onto it, and when we get to Blydkop, I will have a healer examine your leg."

"Thank you. Also, apologies for my poor Tiuvich. I try to speak the Mjornish languages well, but it has been years since I have spoken to Beltxo; I've had very little opportunity to practice."

"Your Tiuvich is fine," said Iragar, shrugging.

It had long been an open secret that the Blykers were not happy with Narese rule. Venceslaus had never truly suffered from the financial laws the Harferd kings had instituted. High Beak would have likely remained independent from the Narese if Avon had not come around, for it was not dependent on the River of Nar. As for the Blykers, there were several other lords between them and the mouth of the river. They rested on no coast, and their land was the last to see the river delta. If they had traded to the south, they would have hit every river toll, making their best trade partner the Kylns to the north. Consequently, it should have been of no surprise to anyone that the people in Tiuv more frequently spoke Osmjornish as a second language over Narese.

They made it to the horse. Iragar aided Venceslaus up, then he tied the bag to the side of his saddle, as well as the fishing pole. When he finished, he tossed Venceslaus's walking stick into the forest. They rode through a few towns, and when the sun was at three-quarters of its journey to the horizon, they finally reached Blydkop.

In all of his years, Venceslaus had never been to Blydkop. It was a moderately sized castle that rested on a high hill. Instead of being whitewashed, it was the dark gray color of the local stone.

These stones grew more frequent the closer they made it to the castle, but abruptly disappeared once they neared its gates. When Iragar's horse had reached a distance of a few legs from the gatehouse doors, they opened.

The typical lord wanted to rub elbows with the highest of society, but Beltxo did not. The Blykers stayed in Tiuv, long having given up on the Narese ever acting in their favor. To the east, the Cannens controlled large swaths of land and were able to trade with Teruk. Not only that, they also had plenty of land along the River of Nar. They could circumvent many of the river tolls by simply moving goods to a more southern port. To the west of Tiuv, there was thick forest that made running a trade route a waste of time. It made more sense to make a trip Belar to sell any of their goods. Most of the furnishings in the courtyard of the castle looked to either be obviously Osmjornish in their design or not too far from it.

Iragar hopped off the horse and helped Venceslaus down, leading him to a bench that stood near the stables in the courtyard. Venceslaus looked around. He eventually eyed his bag that still hung at the side of Iragar's saddle. He knew people valued his word; if he gave Count Beltxo an IOU with his seal on it, then maybe he would aid him in retrieving his daughter. Soon, Iragar returned—not only with a healer, but with his father himself. The healer nodded his head to Venceslaus and knelt down, lifting the Duke's trousers until a big, swollen bruise was revealed on his leg.

"Well, it won't be too bad," said the healer in Tiuvich.

"Is it broken?" asked Venceslaus.

The healer nodded his head. He pointed at Iragar, then behind Venceslaus. Iragar sat on his knees behind the Duke and wrapped his arms under the Duke's shoulders, holding him tightly. The healer opened a bag that he carried with him and pulled out a splint. The splint was made from a wrap of linen that had wooden rods tied all around it.

"I have to set it back properly. From the looks of it, I figure it is a clean break. It is going to hurt for a moment."

"That is no trouble, I have had my share of broken—"

His shinbone roared with pain, but it soon returned to the ache he had felt since the breakage. The healer held his lower leg firm while Iragar let go of Venceslaus, and Beltxo helped wrap the splint around Venceslaus's leg. He cinched the leg up tight with the loose string, wrapping it several times around the splint. After lowering Venceslaus's leg to the ground, the healer stood up.

"I will retrieve you a crutch. Do not put any weight on that leg. When it feels better, wait another two weeks to make sure it is safe to take the splint off."

Venceslaus nodded his head, and the healer walked off.

Beltxo sat down next to Venceslaus. "Iragar, let Meliora know to set an extra seat at our table for dinner."

Iragar nodded and went off to one of the doors that ran along the walls of the castle.

"Thank you for your hospitality, but I cannot stay long," Venceslaus said. "I must go as soon as I can."

"You are in no shape to travel. You may stay in one of our spare rooms until you are recovered. I can send out a pigeon, if you would like to request aid."

"No, I cannot. I can pay you for a horse. I need to leave as soon as I can."

"If you go now, you're going to break your leg again," Beltxo said. "And in any case, my conscience couldn't bear it if you died."

Venceslaus never knew how to react to Beltxo's words. It was difficult to tell whether he was joking or serious, for he always spoke in the same tone. He did not smile, and he was not at all a warm man. Physically, he looked like an aged Iragar, with the primary difference being the gray in his hair. He sighed.

"How did you end up in such a state?" asked Beltxo.

"I was traveling to Belar, but I was robbed. In defending myself, I succumbed this injury."

"Alone?"

"Aye."

"Why?"

Venceslaus paused, trying to decide whether or not to tell the whole truth. Beltxo was a blunt man; Venceslaus figured that if he were not also blunt, then Beltxo might take offense.

"My bodyguard, Ser Merr Groent, died in my defense," Venceslaus said, electing to tell the truth once again. "The King's men killed him. I am traveling to Belar in an attempt to save my daughter."

"To save your daughter from whom?"

"Geder Kurem. There is grave danger coming. A terrible plot is afoot, and I need to save my family."

"The Master Treasurer? How interesting. I always thought he was a conniving fellow," Beltxo said. "He is no friend of mine. I will pledge men to aid you in saving your daughter; I am honor bound to do so."

"What? I owe you for your aid, not the other way around."

"Do you forget? Two weeks we were without food while we held the line in those Yhournish trenches. We were far out, encircled. While the other commanders deserted us, you did not. Yes, you were not in the vanguard, but the vanguard was never anything special. None of the commanders would have thought less of you if you left us there, yet you did not. Iragar and a company of three other men will escort you to Belar. You already lost a child to save me; maybe I can save your child by aiding you now."

Venceslaus thought of Edeslaus's death so often that he had completely forgotten it was also the day that he had saved Beltxo. He had just been doing what he was supposed to do. His role was to supply, so he supplied. He never really thought of it as *saving* anyone. At that period in the war, Matnus had given the vanguard the order to retreat to a more defensible line, but Venceslaus was given the order to use his discretion: he should choose who to aid in their retreat. He had never wondered whether or not another commander would have done the same. He simply did what had to be done.

Venceslaus's stomach grumbled loud enough to turn Beltxo's head. He stood up and aided Venceslaus to his feet, handing him his crutch shortly after. He led Venceslaus to the same door that Iragar had gone through.

Inside, there was a pair of open double doors. In the center of the room was the dining table, and around it sat a number of golden-haired individuals that bore resemblance to Beltxo. Iragar, still mostly armored, sat at the table with his gauntlets removed. Beltxo sat down at the long end of the table that allowed him to face the double doors. The seat next to him was empty, and he gestured for Venceslaus to take it. The smell of gamey meats and cooked hog filled the room as a blonde woman brought out several platters of food. She placed them onto the table. A number of other servants brought out different greens and fruits while Beltxo's family waited quietly. There was a momentary lull, so Venceslaus just stared around the room.

Soon, the blonde girl that had brought out the meats came back, wiping her hands and sitting at the table.

"Thank you, Meliora. Everyone, I wish for you to welcome the Good Duke Venceslaus of High Beak." Beltxo's eyes wandered off to a servant. "You there! Prepare Venceslaus a bath in one of our spare bedrooms on the ground level. I do not want to see him walking up any stairs. Venceslaus, you have already met my wife, Leonora."

Venceslaus nodded his head to Lady Leonora. She was blonde, much like everyone else in the room.

"That there is Darof, my youngest, and that there is Meliora. She takes a liking to cooking for the family now and then. She wanted to try her hand at some pork today."

"Well, the pork certainly has an appetizing scent," Venceslaus said.

"Aye, you are lucky Iragar was out there bowhunting boar. He's always eager to do so, and he seems to have a knack for it."

"It is nothing I do not enjoy," said Iragar, smiling.

"Alright, now. Eat," said Beltxo, grabbing a fork and knife.

Venceslaus cut into the pork that was on his plate. He removed a small piece of meat from the loin chop and tasted it. It was *good*. Meliora was generous with the salt, but that was fine with Venceslaus. Usually, he would have enjoyed his time with such a meal, but he could not waste a moment. He inhaled it, licking his lips and wiping his fingers. He looked to his left; Beltxo was still in the middle of his meal. Iragar was not finished, either; he was taking his time with his meal. Beltxo grabbed Venceslaus's forearm.

"You must be starving. Get him some more," ordered Beltxo.

"No, no. I greatly enjoyed it, but I must go. The bath, I will accept. But I will save you all from the explanation for my urgency."

"Of course. Take a left on your way out. Down that hall is where the rooms on the ground are. There should be a servant waiting for you."

"Thank you," said Venceslaus, bowing his head.

Venceslaus followed Beltxo's directions and found the servant. He opened the door, and there was a bath already warmed in the room. With the help of the servant, Venceslaus undressed and climbed into the bath. The servant asked if he wanted any help with scrubbing himself, but Venceslaus let him know that it would not be necessary. He made sure to keep his splinted leg out of the water. He quickly tried to wash himself with a nearby sponge. When he was finally almost done, someone entered the room.

"Venceslaus."

It was Beltxo.

"Apologies, Beltxo, I am not finished quite yet."

"Oh, that is alright." Beltxo sat down on a stool beside the bathtub. "I would like for you to tell me everything that happened. What was the cause of your misfortune?"

"I suppose you have already heard of Barnut's assassination?"

"Barnut was murdered? How long ago?"

"Around a fortnight. His passing was the beginning of all the tragedy."

"Was the murderer apprehended?"

A laugh escaped Venceslaus. He rubbed his face, shaking his head with frustration. "I do not even know how to answer that question. We discovered the identity of the man with Barnut's blood on his hands, but that man did not truly commit the murder."

"What does that mean? Who killed Barnut?"

"Be wary of Asbyorn, but do not hate him. I am only telling you this because you are a vassal of his, the same as I."

Beltxo had a confused look on his face. He placed his elbow on his knee, hanging his head down. He let out a huff before he straightened up his posture.

"Our King is murdering members of his council?"

"It is not so simple. He is being controlled. Each night, Ser Bertram binds him so that he may at least be kept restrained in the dark hours. Whoever is forcing him to do such things has caught on as well. There were... *worms* inside of him."

Beltxo turned his head, raising a brow. "This is all indeed very frightening, but how is Geder involved?"

"In his trances, the King wrote letters, one of which was written to 'the Serpentine'. The way it was worded could not have referred to anyone other than Geder."

"Your daughter is in Belar for the Midsummer festival, yes? Why do you fear for her safety? What would Geder want from your daughter?"

"I am in talks of betrothing her to Abba Kurem. The letter... it referenced a previous letter where the King, using the moniker 'the Ultimate', granted Geder permission to secure the lands once promised to him. I entrusted her safety to the Kurems. If Geder kills them all, then my daughter would be in the hands of a kinslayer."

"Have you any men up there?"

"Aye." Venceslaus looked down. His fingertips were beginning to wrinkle. He placed his hand up to Beltxo. "One moment. Would you allow the servant in? I need to get out of this tub."

Beltxo opened the door. The servant rushed in to aid Venceslaus out of the tub. After drying the Duke off, the servant shawled a robe over his shoulders and secured its tie around his waist.

"I do have a man with her. His name is Ser Elseharde. He is a young knight, but he is an upstanding one."

Beltxo beckoned the servant to come near. He whispered into his ear, and the servant left the room.

"I told him to retrieve a pen and paper," Beltxo said. "I think you should send a letter asking for your knight. Geder has friends in Belar; I have seen him mingle with Hedmond plenty of times. He will know the moment you enter the city. You will need your knight for information."

"That will leave my daughter without a bodyguard."

"I doubt Geder would hurt her in any way. It would be of no benefit to him. If anything, Geder will ransom her. She is just a girl to him; you are the one with the riches. He will try to swindle you for as much silver as he can. Ser Elseharde, however, will die if he is not told to leave. If you want to save your knight, order him to meet you on your way."

Venceslaus shook his head. "What would you have me write?"

"Tell Elseharde to ride south. He should not worry about the Lady Edit's safety, since you entrusted her to the Kurems. Hedmond is not the most caring fellow. I would be wary of any soldiers in the Kyln blue. You ought to set an ambush for your own safety."

"You've become paranoid," Venceslaus said.

"After the war, I should think that anyone who survived has become paranoid."

"But what if Hedmond has nothing to do with Geder's plans?"

"Then you'll have no reason to yell for Iragar to let loose his arrow. If you're sure of your safety, then tell him to reveal himself."

Venceslaus nodded. The servant returned, and Venceslaus beckoned for him to bring him the paper and bone pen. He also told the servant to bring him a smaller pouch from his bag. Venceslaus grabbed the items, taking them to a small table in the room. He lit a candle and dipped his pen into some ink. After he was finished, Beltxo came over and read the letter. The two nodded their heads in agreement, and Venceslaus sealed it with his wax stamp.

"I will head over to my dovecote and send this off," Beltxo said. "On my way, I will inform Iragar that he ought to handpick two men to go with him. I reckon you'll be able to reach Belar in six days."

"Six days? The tournament starts in three!" Venceslaus rubbed his forehead. "Do you have another piece of paper?"

"Why do you require one?" asked Beltxo.

"I am writing you an IOU."

"No, you owe me nothing."

"It is not for your aid. I am renting your best horses. Your domain spans just a bit south of one of the Kyln tributaries, correct? I imagine you'd have a fief nearby."

"I do."

"And do you have a fief that is a two days' ride from here in the same direction?"

"Aye."

"Tell Iragar to get his best riders. We will make it in three. At each stop, I will pay someone to return the horses, and I will receive new horses. Do you think a full suit of plate armor per four horses would be fair?"

"Three full suits? It would be fair if you were buying the horses! That is far too much."

"Yes, but the horses may be worth a great deal less after such a ride. Some may be ridden to their deaths."

Beltxo rubbed his chin. "Alright, I will accept. The fief at the border of the Kylns' lands is owned by a vassal of mine, but he should be sure to comply. Head off to the courtyard, I will go inform Iragar of the plan."

"Thank you."

Venceslaus wrote the IOU and stamped it as well, then handed it over to Beltxo. Venceslaus placed his hand on Beltxo's shoulder.

"Do come show your face more often in the south. Your absence makes others wary, but you do not deserve such skepticism. You are a truly honorable man."

"I would prefer not to. I forget about them, and they forget about me; that is what's best for us all."

Venceslaus shrugged and hobbled his way out the door. It was a quick shamble to the courtyard, and Iragar met them shortly. With him, he brought two men. They all said their goodbyes to Beltxo and retrieved the horses from the stablemaster.

The four rode out until nightfall, giving the horses a period of momentary rest. The next morning was a struggle. Venceslaus winced in pain each time the horse came into contact with the ground. Each impact reminded him that his leg was broken, but he could not stop. They would make it to their destination, switch out their horses, and then proceed onto the route. By the middle of the third day, they had finally made it to Kylndod. At some point in the evening, Iragar told Venceslaus to slow down. They stopped their horses, and Iragar directed his men to lead them into the forest.

"I will retrieve a stick for you to walk with," said Iragar. "I want you to stand in the middle of the road, and when you hear the party of men looking to rendezvous with you, I want you to walk forward. I will keep watch and see if they are up to anything nefarious."

"Alright," Venceslaus said.

Iragar ran over, bow in hand, in the direction of his men and the horses. Venceslaus stood there for quite a while, periodically looking up to the sky to see the position of the sun. A drizzle of rain peppered Venceslaus. He frowned. How long would he have to wait? He wanted to see his daughter.

Rain began to come down, so Venceslaus looked toward the tree line where Iragar hid. When he looked back to the road, he saw Elseharde with Hedmond Kyln's men, a horse pulling a cart behind them. Venceslaus hobbled forward. A man leaned over to Elseharde, and Elseharde nodded his head. Two of the soldiers walked forward, and one pulled a pair of shackles from his waist. Elseharde reached out, saying something to the man; but another soldier behind him pulled out a bludgeon, raising it out to swing. Elseharde spun around, moving to draw his sword.

But before he could draw, an arrow struck the Kyln soldier. Elseharde looked out to the tree line. Another arrow was launched, hitting another soldier. The two men that Iragar had picked came riding out on horseback, swinging their weapons at the soldiers below. The two guards that had come for Venceslaus rushed for him. While the rest of the soldiers were focused on Iragar's men, Iragar and Ser Elseharde rushed to Venceslaus's aid. The guards were dealt with promptly: one by Ser Elseharde's sword, and the other by Iragar's dagger. The Kyln soldiers were slaughtered on their own road. Elseharde looked around with a dumbfounded expression.

"We… We have to hurry back. How did you know, my liege? How did you know?" said Ser Elseharde.

Venceslaus patted Ser Elseharde's shoulder. "I will inform you soon. Has anything strange happened in Belar?"

"Lord Adar was arrested."

"Why?"

"Apparently he was counterfeiting."

Venceslaus scoffed.

"What?" asked Ser Elseharde.

"Then Geder is the one counterfeiting." Venceslaus rubbed his forehead. "He is already enacting his schemes, I see."

"Schemes?"

"Do not mind that. Let us head for the city."

"Where is Ser Groent?"

Venceslaus shook his head. "I will tell you once we return, boy."

Ser Elseharde, Iragar, and his men dragged the bodies off to the side of the road and hid them. Venceslaus took one of their swords to keep for himself. They released the horse from the wagon and sent it off into the forest. Iragar tied his own horse onto the wagon and manned the reins. With the help of Ser Elseharde, Venceslaus climbed into the back of the wagon. When the rain began to pour down, Ser Elseharde climbed up onto the horse Venceslaus had ridden, and they went on their way to Belar.

Althalos

lthalos watched as the killer and Emmer talked. They meandered about with their words for quite a while. Emmer pointed to a mob of people. The killer bowed his head and went toward it. He raised his voice and began to speak to them.

As he spoke, Althalos went toward Emmer.

"May I speak to you alone?"

Emmer smirked. "Sure, as long as you don't burn me."

"That man you were speaking to is a known killer, and the first thing I ever saw you do was murder a man. Why?"

"Why? Why what?" Emmer frowned. "Why do I kill? I'm a killer. You're a killer. Who is not a killer?"

"I haven't killed anyone," Althalos said.

"Yeah? Well, you will. Especially with hands like those."

"I would never. My life was ruined because of killers, and all the lives of my loved ones, too. I would never wish to deliver that fate to another person."

"Ha! Then you're naïve. Get out of my face."

Emmer shooed Althalos away; but just when Althalos took his first step, Emmer slammed his hand onto the table. Althalos jumped, turning to face Emmer. He was holding his head down.

"That priest, the one you know—he is being burnt at the stake tomorrow."

Althalos grimaced, storming off. Agathius was one of the few truly honest people he had met since he had fled Dorthu. The priest had a warm feeling to him. Althalos had not known him long, but it was apparent that he was a light of hope for the people of Fisk. The same people who had burnt down Dorthu now wished to set fire to Agathius as well. Althalos needed to find out more, so he wandered off into the streets. A town crier was yelling the news. As he got closer, he realized that the man was actually *crying*. Althalos moved closer.

"I know Agathius! He is a good man, a man with more faith than any of those lords! I served in the war with him, and many of you did, too. I try to be a good servant to my King, but this execution is *wrong!* Our leaders of faith and our King—or, rather, the reapers of what we have sown—have shown that they are not truly *leaders*. They have demonstrated that they will kill a man for aspiring to be as great as his forefathers. Aswold did not serve in the war! He sat comfortably in the citadel while good Narese men and women rebuilt the vandalized Academy—while our homes had just been ransacked! While our brothers and fathers and sons were *killed!*"

The crier went on and on, repeating much of the same. Eventually, he fell to his knees, tears now streaming down his cheeks. A number of people from the crowd patted him on the back in an effort to comfort him. He must have known Agathius well. The people here were different, more willing to put on a spectacle. There would have never been enough eyes in Dorthu to garner such attention. So many people were here. They all had their own stories, most of which Althalos would never know anything about. Althalos had known everyone in Dorthu. Here, there were too many people to know. It bothered him.

The rest of the day was lackluster, much the same as the day prior. It was filled with protesting commoners and brutal guards. Althalos walked back to the tavern and back up to his room. Gunter was there, sitting on his bed, all bruised and blue.

"Agathius is being executed tomorrow," Althalos said.

Gunter did not respond. Althalos shook his head and fixed his blankets. After a long period of staring at the ceiling, Althalos allowed himself to sleep.

They awoke the next morning to commotion outside. Althalos looked down from the balcony: the streets were filled with men, women, and children screaming in protest. Althalos had never seen so many people in his life. After putting on his cloak and hiding his axe, he ran down to meet them. Emmer was riling up a group of people; *what a shame that he was such an amazing speaker*, Althalos thought. The people roared when they heard him talk. His words carried weight.

Althalos looked off to the rest of the crowd and attempted to push through it. At first, he was unable to walk past those in front of him, but he was eventually engulfed by others trying to enter the crowd behind him. Eventually, he was pulled along by the rest of the crowd to a line of guards. They stood in a row that led from the portcullis of the citadel to a wooden pillar that seemed to have just been jutted into the ground. Behind the keep's portcullis, there was a cage cart. Althalos tried his best to make it to the front, only managing to take just a few steps forward. But he could at least see past the shoulders of the guards.

The portcullis opened, and a detachment of knights with gleaming steel armor exited on horseback. Strung on their backs were wings made of black feathers, and in their hands were long spears. Behind them rode an elaborately robed man. He had a platinum circlet on his head, and the expression on his face was one of obvious judgement. At his side was a man dressed in a red tunic who wore a gleaming white crown that was as bright as the sun itself. It was the King and Orator. Behind them was another knight who was also dressed in shining armor. He carried a white spear that gleamed just like the King's crown.

Althalos's eyes drifted back to the knights with the wings. Those were not just knights; they were Phoenic paladins. They were a sight to behold. Althalos had never seen such well-kitted soldiers before. Ser Ernest and Ser Ulrich rode with them, but Irold was nowhere in sight. He must have been tending to the wounds he had sustained from their torture. They rode forward with resolute expressions on their faces. Althalos made sure to keep his head down, hoping that they would not recognize him.

Agathius sat alone in the jail cart. He looked sickly, and his robes were covered in muck. His eyes were sunken. He stared at the sky, his eyes closed and palms facing up. In his last moments, he was praying.

The Orator's look of judgement remained on his face. He did not look pleased. King Asbyorn did not smile, either. He looked fatigued, like he had not slept in days. His body swayed whenever his horse's hooves met the road. Turning his head, he stared at the crowds like a lost mutt. There was an expression on his face that almost looked like confusion. The people booed him. They threw trash at him, but he was too far away to be reached. In retaliation, the guards would circle around the instigators and throw them behind the line, beating them viciously.

Althalos pushed through the crowd, following the cart. He watched Agathius, and Agathius opened his eyes. He looked over in Althalos's direction and smiled. *Had Agathius noticed him? Why would he be smiling so close to his execution?* They rolled him to the wooden pillar. Those on horseback surrounded the pillar, and the men riding the jail cart hopped off to open Agathius's cage. Around Agathius's neck was a chain, and one of the men yanked on the chain, pulling Agathius out. He flopped on the ground, his body landing with a thud. They pulled him forward, and even though Agathius tried to go willingly, they did not allow him the courtesy of getting to his feet. They dragged him through the dirt while he attempted to crawl forward. When he made it to the pillar, they lifted him and bound his arms around it, behind him. The paladins climbed down from their steeds and walked over to some bundles of firewood. They placed them around Agathius's feet, stacking them to his hips. Agathius smiled through it all.

The Orator, King Asbyorn, and his knight rode their horses to the side of the pillar. The knight climbed down from his horse, stood in front of Agathius, and slammed the butt of his spear onto the ground. There was an almost deafening roar. Even when the noise had ceased, it was as if it somehow still echoed in open air. The once-muttering crowd stood silent, watching the knight in a daze. The Orator held his head down, and the King rode forward, raising his hand.

"My fellow people of Nar!" the King called. "My fellow followers of the Phoenix! This is a terrible day! A downright foul day! I have been called—nay, *forced* to execute a man of the cloth. This man, once Elder of the Temple of Fisk, has been spouting heresy! He has refused numerous opportunities to recant his foul claims. What am I supposed to do? Am I supposed to let him get away with such actions? My ancestors swore an oath to protect the faith; am I to sit paralyzed while an attack happens right before me?"

One of the guards handed the knight a lit torch.

"It is my duty as a protector of this faith to execute its justice! Agathius's punishment has been deliberated upon, and what we have decided is righteous and true to tradition. He is sentenced to death by immolation."

Asbyorn looked at his knight, nodding his head. The knight tossed the torch. The firewood at Agathius's feet was lit aflame. Agathius once more found Althalos in the crowd. He nodded, still smiling. The flame crawled up, growing larger and larger, but Agathius did not react; he closed his eyes, his expression completely peaceful. A flame flicked up in front of the priest's face, and in that brief moment, Althalos looked at the knight who had tossed the torch. He was holding his head down. Althalos looked once more at Agathius, but the flames had gotten too high for his face to be seen.

He was dead.

"The King killed Agathius! The King killed Dorthu!" yelled Althalos, sticking his finger into the air.

The crowd stared at him. The guards stared at him. Soon enough, Ser Ernest and Ser Ulrich stared at him; but when they began to pursue him, the crowd began to chant. They repeated what Althalos had said, pointing their fingers and throwing whatever they could find over the row of guards. Most threw trash, but some started to throw stones. Althalos turned his head. He saw Emmer standing to his right. The widest smile he had ever seen was on that man's face.

"What is a king that starves you? What is a king who marches into a village of his own people and kills his kin? A bastard! Our King is a bastard!"

By now, only stones were being thrown. One hit a guard in the jaw, and to his misfortune, he only wore a skullcap. His body went limp, and the crowd began to pour through the hole in the line of guards. The King's knight hurried back to his horse, pointing his spear away from him while he led the King back to the citadel. The people around Emmer had hammers and other tools, and some were even handing them out to others. They engaged the guards, swinging their bludgeons and throwing their stones. Anyone important had already fled, and the paladins were nowhere in sight, but this did not matter now. A group of guards came to reinforce the line, and they had spears. People fled, but others continued to engage. Althalos, once standing in the midst of everyone, was now being pulled by those fleeing, and pushed by those choosing to fight.

Althalos did not want any of this. He wanted justice, not bloodshed.

Pushed by an eager rioter, he stumbled forward. At his feet was a dead citizen of Nara, his face caved in. In front of him, a guard lunged the tip of his spear forward, narrowly missing Althalos when he was pushed by someone that stood at his side. That man was struck by the spear. He looked down, shocked at what had just happened.

A clearing between the guards had opened, and Ser Ernest and Ser Ulrich were in front of him. Althalos turned around, trying to break through the crowd. He wormed his way between two people, refusing to look back. He focused on just going forward. Forward was the only direction he could go. The throng of people would surely slow down the knights. But what if they were right behind him? What if they grabbed him, and he could have stopped it? Forward—*he had to go forward.* He was going to be pushed and pulled, but he still had to go forward.

Althalos looked behind him. The people in front of him were fleeing. Ser Ernest and Ser Ulrich stood, weapons drawn, in front of a number of guards. Althalos grabbed the axe from under his cloak. Maybe Emmer was right; maybe he would have to be a killer. He surely was not going to let them kill him. Ser Ernest swung his sword down. With haste, Althalos lifted his hand up and blocked the cut. Ser Ernest's longsword bit into it, forcing him to pull it away before he could strike again. Ser Ulrich was circling around him, too, sword in hand; but before he could strike, peasants engaged him from behind and struck him. Ser Ernest stared at his knight for a moment, but then he turned and swung once more at Althalos. Althalos slapped away the tip of Ernest's longsword with his axe and ran off through a new clearing in the crowds. As he ran, he collided with yet another person and was sent stumbling to the ground. People ran past him. Althalos tried to roll away from their feet to avoid being trampled. He dropped the axe, but at that moment it did not matter. He knew he would lose to Ser Ernest in a prolonged fight. Althalos climbed to his feet and ran.

As he ran, an axe grazed his shoulder. It was his own axe, Hrodolf's axe. It hit the ground with a thud, thankfully harming no one. Althalos ran to it and picked it up. Turning around, Ser Ernest thrusted his sword. Althalos narrowly dodged, choosing to grab the knight's sword at the crossguard. Without thinking,

Althalos swung his axe. The axehead landed awkwardly into Ser Ernest's cheek. It cut, and it cut deep.

Ser Ernest stared down at the axehead that was lodged into his face with a shocked expression. Althalos's hand trembled. Ser Ernest punched Althalos, sending him into a stumble backwards. When Althalos regained his footing, he noticed Ser Ernest awkwardly ripping off a piece of his own cape in order to stop the bleeding. He stared at Althalos for a moment—perhaps he was choosing whether or not to continue fighting—but eventually he turned around and walked away in a hurry.

With his pursuer unwilling to continue on, Althalos took off running once more. The crowd had cleared somewhat, but then it thickened again. It was an incoherent mess of people coming and going. There were people running to attack the guards, people running away from the guards, people standing and watching the whole conflict go on, and people nestled in the alleyways. There were *guards* in alleyways. They had torches in their hands, even though it was daytime.

One of them turned around. With a start, Althalos realized the man was not a guard at all; it was Emmer, wearing one of the guards' uniforms.

"What are you doing?" asked Althalos.

"Creating a better story," said Emmer.

He threw a torch on top of a building. Almost instantly, the roof caught fire. Emmer and the other guards—or, more likely, the other men *dressed* as guards—continued to throw torches, aiming for the roofs of the surrounding buildings. In a panic, Althalos ran forward and snatched a torch. He threw it to the ground and tried to stomp it out, but Emmer slapped Althalos, and his goons grabbed him. Althalos recognized one of them as the killer who had been at the inn.

Emmer leaned in close to Althalos's face, smiling from ear to ear.

"Do you know how stories become stories?"

Emmer grabbed another torch and tossed it as far as he could.

"A story only becomes a story if it is worthwhile to retell. Horrible things happen every day, but we only hear of a select few. Why? Because they *don't matter!* They are bland! Without my influence, today would have been another one of those stories. Yes, there was an execution and riot; but we can make this story last forever, my dear boy! It can be a story told for generations. It will ruin the name of Asbyorn. No Narese man, woman, or child will ever forget the day he burnt down his own city."

"You are killing innocent people!"

"So too is the King! Is it only fair that we do the same, for the sake of our victory. How are we to win without using every option at our disposal? They are stronger than us, and they care nothing for *our* lives."

He grabbed another torch. Althalos's heart pounded. He tried to jump at Emmer, but he could not; the two men were using their full might to control his limbs. Althalos could not move, but he had to stop Emmer. Emmer threw the torch. Althalos used all his might to lunge free, but it was too late. The fire burned high around them.

But the fire was white. Suddenly, Althalos's hands were free, and the two men who had been holding him down were lit aflame. Emmer turned and stared at Althalos. He looked at the burning husks of the two men, and he smirked. He pushed Althalos to the ground and ran away. Althalos cursed at himself. On his back, he stared at the sky. The roof of one of the buildings collapsed, and a burning patch of rubble dropped down next to him. He rolled to his side, picked himself up, and ran out to the streets. He looked behind him.

Every house was lit with white fire. People ran out of their homes. They screamed in panic. A woman ran into one of the houses. She was yelling someone's name, screaming *my baby*. Althalos fell to his knees. His breathing became labored. Flashes of Dorthu, memories of all those dead bodies, stabbed into his mind. He looked at his hands. He wanted to squeeze them into fists, but he was too weak to do so. They trembled, refusing to move the way he wanted them to. He closed his eyes and tried to think of other thoughts, but the entirety of his mind was consumed by the flames he *knew* he had created.

He felt a hand grip his shoulder. Opening his eyes, he saw that it was Gunter.

"Get up!" he yelled, pulling Althalos to his feet.

Althalos did not move, so Gunter pulled harder. He pulled him again and again, but Althalos did not react. Althalos faced Gunter, tears in his eyes.

"I did this. I killed those people," Althalos said.

"Althalos, get up and fuckin' *run!*"

In the far distance, the entrance to the Academy d'Ava could be seen quite clearly over the countless amount of people in the streets. In the distance, the bells chimed five times; and on the fifth chime, dozens of paladins came riding through the Academy gates. Gunter pulled Althalos up to his feet and dragged him in the opposite direction. The crowd would surely slow the paladins down, Althalos thought. For the sake of Gunter, he made himself run. The two ran into another thick crowd of people, and they were engaged with a large group of guards. Gunter raised his sword, blocking a strike from one of the Harferd men. He threw the man to the ground and thrust his sword tip into the man's neck. Blood splattered from the wound, coating his sword in red.

Ser Ulrich came walking toward them. His sword was drawn and, much like the rest of him, it was covered in blood. When Gunter noticed him, he pointed his sword down into a guard. Ulrich swung down, but Gunter blocked the strike and riposted with a thrust. Gunter's sword tip slid on the metal of Ulrich's cuirass, and Gunter, realizing he was overextended with his legs, stepped forward with his back foot and grabbed Ulrich's wrist to slam his pommel into the knight's helmet. Ser Ulrich reached for his dagger, but Gunter pushed him. With Ulrich momentarily unbalanced, Gunter used that moment to yank on the knight to pull him forward, but this did nothing. Ulrich stuck his foot out, preventing Gunter from unbalancing him any further. Using his hand that held the dagger, Ulrich tried to stab at Gunter, but the mercenary kept a firm grip on his wrist. The blade stabbed into Gunter's forearm. He released Ser Ulrich, cursing. Ulrich stabbed at Gunter again, and he cut his forearm again. Gunter's sleeve reddened with blood. Althalos desperately looked for something he could fight with, but there was nothing around. His eyes returned to the fight. Releasing his sword, Gunter grabbed the visor of the knight's armet and yanked it down while he used his bloodied arm to push at his hip. He stuck his foot out, and Ser Ulrich tumbled to the ground.

The crowd was dissipating, trying to avoid being engaged by the riding paladins. Althalos made eye contact with Gunter; and from how Gunter looked at him, Althalos realized that maybe they should be running, too. Gunter pulled Althalos in the direction he wanted them to go. They sprinted down the road. The buildings around them started to look familiar to Althalos, and soon he realized they were heading back toward the area where the sewer grate allowed them entry into the city. Althalos turned around.

"Stop fuckin' lookin' back!" commanded Gunter. "Just fuckin' run!"

They made it to the sewer cover. Althalos tried to lift the grate, but when he looked back once more, the paladins were only a dozen buildings away. Gunter knelt down, helped Althalos lift it, and hurried him down. He stood up, sword ready. He showed no interest in climbing down. Althalos lingered at the top of the ladder, watching as the paladins grew closer and closer. Gunter looked down at Althalos.

"The fuck are ye doin'?" He looked at the paladins riding toward them. "Go live, boy."

He pushed Althalos down. Althalos slipped on one of the rungs and fell, barreling down to the bottom of the sewer. He landed on his arm, and, looking up, saw the light of the sun fading as Gunter shut the lid. His arm ached, but he could not see it. He grabbed it. It felt raw, warm, and painful to the touch. His heart raced, and his movements became jerkier. He tried to remember what direction they had come from. He turned to the ladder, feeling it and the walls around it. The he hurried down the direction he thought he remembered them using to enter the city. As he walked, he questioned if he had made the right choice; but soon a soft light from the outside affirmed his decision. He wondered if he was being pursued, if the paladins or Ser Ulrich had decided to climb down the grate and follow him. Althalos figured the only way to prevent a possible pursuer from apprehending him would to be to just continue on forward. He ran out of the sewer and into the woods, threading between the trees like a string going through an awl.

Althalos looked down at his arm. It was as red and swollen as a forest berry. The sight of it made his stomach turn. His heart pounded harder, but he refused to stop running. He ran until his legs gave out under him. He hit the ground. His body felt cold, yet his arm burned with pain. As he grew weaker, he realized that he must have broken his arm. He had never broken a bone before. He tried to lift himself up, but even his capable arm was too weak to bring him to his feet. In the face of this inadequacy, he rolled onto his back. While he stared at the sky, he thought to himself, *why does this life torture good people?* Agathius was good. Gunter was not perfect, but he tried. The people of Nara did not deserve this pain. Dorthu did not deserve it. His *mother* did not deserve it. How many dreams must be foregone for the whims of tyrants?

A dark bird flew across the sky.

Althalos opened his eyes. It was night. His arm hurt him no longer; he lifted it up and saw that it was exactly how it had been before the injury, entirely devoid of any redness or swelling. He sat up. Face-eater stood a short distance away, grazing on a patch of green grass.

Epilogue

arm air entered through the wound in his neck. He was trying his best to fill his lungs. His vision blurred. His muscles were not just weak, he could not move them at all. He did not have the will to force his limp body up. Was this death? Objects that looked like splotches of paint moved around him until they diminished into nothingness. The sensation of what felt like smaller and smaller stones pattering him faded away. His sense of sound left him. He did not understand what was happening, but he did not feel inclined to speak or to move. The world urged him to accept his new reality, and while his mind fell deeper into this haze, he did not feel any compulsion to reject it.

Every so often, something that felt like a sack of potatoes fell on top of him. Had his sense of touch returned? He felt bumping underneath him. He could see again. He saw splotches of gray, but his eyes were too weak to make anything out. He felt hot; his skin was boiling. A heat escaped him, reaching outwards. His eyes shut like a slamming portcullis. This strength must have been momentary, a last sense of reality. He drifted back into nothingness.

He asked himself again: Was this death?

The smell of sweat and blood seeped into his nose. He wanted to gag, but his muscles were too weak to even bring about such a basal reflex. He felt like he was floating, but this could have been due to his inability to feel the ground below him. The only sensation that had not left him was his ability to feel heat. He was burning. It was such a potent feeling. He felt as if his body had been dropped into a bloomery. He had once known who he was, but he had forgotten. The only thing that he was aware of was the heat. He remembered he was cut, and the gash on his neck felt singed. Every breath he took gave him the sensation of molten steam searing his windpipe. His lungs burned. His stomach burned. His head and body burned. He wished that he would soon lose this feeling, just as he had lost all the others.

His sense of smell left him once more, but the agony continued. He thought he was crying, but he could not feel his tears. As more senses left him, the pain of the burning grew more potent. He wondered what he must have done to deserve this, but nothing that crossed his mind could answer it. He could not even remember what had brought him here, or why he existed at all.

He regained a sensation. He felt his insides churning as if he were being induced to vomit, yet it never occurred. It was a strange writhing within him, but he could once more feel where his limbs were. He tried to move his arms, but he could not. His insides continued to feel like a washcloth being wrung to release water.

Light flashed in front of him. It alternated colors with disorienting speed: red, then yellow, then white, then pink, then red again. He regained his vision, but everything was mired in a blurry haze. He could not discern anything other than a squirming foreground before him. His body, too, felt like it was squirming. He started to move. He tried to prevent his body from moving, but he could not. At some point, his body went limp once more, and he could feel his arms trapped in some sort of binding.

His vision grew less hazy, and a scene came into focus before him. The ground was red and beige, and purple stalks jutted into the sky. The sky itself was gray, its clouds spinning as if they were made of smoke. The scent of dead flesh was all that could be smelled. It made his eyes tears up. He could not see once more, and he wished to vomit once again, but the same force that had stopped him from using his own limbs inhibited his body's ability to release its contents. There were no flames around him, but the heat was still ever-present.

He suddenly grew cold—freezing, even. He never thought the heat would have left him so soon, but its total absence made him wish that it was still there. It returned. He felt both at once. His body swirled with excruciating heat and miserable cold. It was torture.

He could see again. His vision was better than before, and now he noticed that the ground was covered with red grass, or at least something that resembled grass in some way. He examined it further, and he realized that it was stiff, resembling a fungus moreso than grass. He knew nothing about flora, so he gave up on trying to identify the thing. The stalks looked like trees, and the sky was as smoggy as he remembered. He reckoned that the smog was the origin of the scent of death. There were swirls on the ground, fleshy tendrils that rolled around like dying snakes. They came for him, wrapping around his body. He realized that these must have been the bindings that held him down. He felt them pierce through his flesh and move within him. He cried. His only gauge for time was how hungry he grew.

A tall black figure crept toward him. It disappeared every so often, only to reappear a few trees away to the left or right from where it had last been. It had the shape of man with a cloak covering his shoulders. The tendrils avoided him, recoiling as if they feared him. They writhed as if they were in pain whenever he was near, but the ones furthest from him sought to get closer. The man came so close that his exhale could be felt. He had no face.

He felt the same discomfort that the tendrils must have felt, and his body tried to crawl away from the figure. The tendrils that bound him cinched tighter, pulling him down. He had nowhere to go, no means of escape. The figure grew so close that he felt his touch.

"Cease."

He immediately stopped his wriggling. The tendrils relaxed.

"Hello."

This place must have been Gol. He knew that he had died, and he remembered that he had knowledge of this place. This was the place souls went after death. This was the nightmare that those who had been sinful were forced to endure. The land of vice. But he could not remember what he had done wrong. He looked at his body. He was young.

He felt a hand grab his face. No, not a hand; rather, a talon, or some form of claw. He could not see it, but it felt like it was made from dry bone and flesh. He tried to move, finally feeling like he was once more in control of his body, but the claw kept him from even turning his head.

"Who... are you?" he managed, successfully forcing himself to speak.

"I."

He stared at the figure, confused. "Who am I?"

"*I.*"

He tried to shake his head. The claw was gone, but he could not move. He did not like the figure's answer. In fact, he was gravely annoyed with the answer. However, as he pondered longer, he thought maybe it was not too bad. It was alright. Actually, he rather liked the idea. He enjoyed the idea. It seemed *correct.* It *was* correct.

He shook his head. "Quit playing with my mind!"

"*My* mind."

"I did not agree with you, and you forced me to change my opinion."

"Why is that an issue?" asked the figure. "You believe it now. It is what you think is right, is it not?"

He felt compelled to agree. The discussion of beliefs was a dead end. It did not amount to any real answer. He looked behind the figure.

"Where am I?"

"A place, once."

As he should have expected: another non-answer.

"*What* are you?"

"Many things. Too much to describe to you. I used to be another. Many others. My form now comes from... a priest? Yes, a priest. A priest who knew many things. But now—now I know more than any other being. I know. All that I touch is mine, and all is I."

The figure touched his cheek with the talon, letting it linger there. When the figure removed the talon, he swiped his cheek, causing the young boy to bleed. It soon healed. He felt safe. He could not ever get hurt. He was safe. He cursed at himself and tried to leap out of the tendrils.

"Stop playing with my thoughts!"

The figure looked down at him. He felt its judgment, and the claw raised his chin up. "A thought that tells one to not use their own hand... strange. Such thoughts are rare, but I understand why they come. I do as I will. I do."

The boy screamed. He screamed as loud as he could. The pressure from the claw left his face. Everything returned to a blur, soon fading into nothing. He lost the feeling of the tendrils that had wrapped around his body. His smell, the ability to feel his limbs, and hearing all left him shortly after. He skirted near the edge of absolute nothingness, losing all awareness until his sight returned to him. He could only see light. It blinded him. He felt like was floating. He felt cold in all places except where his neck had suffered his fatal wound. His mind swirled in a daze, or maybe the world spun around him. He tried to lift his neck; but he felt that if he did, his head would fall from him. He *could* move his arms, but only barely.

He saw the sky, the sun. He felt something hit his hand. Was it another hand? Drops of water hit his face. What was this purgatory? What was his name? He thought about turning his head, but he stopped himself from doing so, still believing that if he did, then his head would fall right off. His eyes wandered. There were several bodies around him. One of them was familiar. He closed his eyes once more.

Tree branches moved in the breeze above him, and he was being pelted with rain. He felt sore and battered. The pain consumed him; it was the only thing he could think about. The trees moved, but it was always the same view: a storming sky and wind-blown branches. He heard muffled wails and cries. A sudden wave of sadness ambushed him. He did not know why, but he knew he had to mourn. Tears ran from his eyes, streaming into the water below him. He grew weak again, and his eyes shut.

He awoke once more. It felt like his lungs were being ripped from his body, like sharp knives pierced his chest. He gasped for air, and his whole body became hot again. He was being pulled. He looked around and saw the familiar body that had lain beside him also being pulled. He tried to see what he was being pulled by, but he lacked the strength to do so. There was shouting. His ears were too weak to hear clearly. In a blink, he was on the bank of the river. He felt two fingers putting pressure into his neck.

"He's alive! He's alive!" yelled a man's voice.

He looked around. Above him was a knight, and to the side of him was a man with a grayed ginger beard. He did not recognize this man, but he had an expression of utmost concern on his face. He was lifted up by his shoulders and feet and placed into a wagon. The old man and knight went for the other body. He watched the old man lift the body up and place the body next to him. He could see his face. His eyes wettened again, shedding even more tears. The face had nothing behind it, its jaw drooping in relaxation. Its gaze stared through the world, unable to focus on anything. The heat began to leave his neck, but it still lingered in his heart. There was a churning within him.

Someone had wronged him, and they would suffer for what they had done.

appendix

The Kingdom of Nar

Asbyorn Harferd, Ruler of Nar and King of All-Mankind

His Family:
Olena Dalnaf, Queen-Consort of Nar
Hrod Harferd, His Firstborn Child, His Firstborn Son
Ainta Harferd, His Secondborn Child, His Firstborn Daughter
Nema Ubbanwit, Queen-Mother
Matnus Harferd, His father, Deceased

His Retainers:
Ser Bertram Rowe, the White Spear
Malaina Rowe, Royal Seamstress
Loressa Lossefi, Servant Girl

His Crii:
Barnut Brind, Great Chancellor of Nar
Geder Kurem, Great Treasurer of Nar
Pol Donas, Great Marshall of Nar
Gaios Loffreaux, Great Dignitary of Nar, Duke of Edrais
Urbaed Cannen, Great Dignitary of Nar, Duke of Luron
Venceslaus Freihei, Great Dignitary of Nar, Duke of High Beak

His Vassals:
Harry Rowe, Baron of Wettay
Beltxo Blyker, Duke of Tiuv

The Duchy of High Beak

Venceslaus Freihei, The Good Duke, Duke of High Beak

His Family:
Edesa Linwit, His Wife, Deceased
Edeslaus Freihei, His Firstborn Child, His Firstborn Son, Deceased
Edit Freihei, His Secondborn Child, His Firstborn Daughter

His Retainers:
Ser Merr Groent
Ser Elseharde
Ser Jriton

The Barony of Wettay

Harry Rowe, Baron of Wettay, Lord of Fisk and Dorthu

His Family:
Iuda Mennin, His Wife
Irit Rowe, His Firstborn Daughter
Ser Bertram Rowe, the White Spear
Malaina Rowe, Royal Seamstress

Commoners d'Fisk:
Helwig
Ditwin
Agathius, Elder of Fisk

Commoners d'Dorthu:
Althalos
Agnes, Mother of Althalos
Hrodolf
Jethr
Marsi
Larmond, Elder of Dorthu
Cristof, The Miller
Adran
Viula
Adro, Son of Adran and Viula
Grita, Daughter of Adran and Viula

Commoners d'Wettay:
Lina, The Barmaid

Kuremdod

Adar Kurem, The Superstitious, Count of Kuremdod

His Family:
Anita Demenstin, Countess-Consort
Geder Kurem, His Older Brother
Abba Kurem, His Firstborn Son
Maric Kurem, His Secondborn Son

His Retainers:
Ser Mikhail, Marshal of Kuremdod
Siemond, Pyre Elder of Diplomacy, Court Elder
Madalbert, Dockmaster of Kurembrog
Tragileit, Bailiff of Kurembrog

His Vassals:
Jergi Hedden, Steward of Kuremdod, Baron of Heddi

Kylndod

Tedi Kyln, The Infirm, Duke of Kylndod

His Family:
Hedmond Kyln, Regent of Kylndod, His Firstborn Son
Hofstaad Kyln, His Grandson

His Retainers:
Frud

Commoners:
Meara
Luka
Gol
Hrodert
Leisa

The Phoenicy

Aswold, The Orator

Notable Prophets:
Avon, The Liberator, The First Prophet, Ascended
Ava, The Conciliator, Son of Avon

Pyre Elders:
Bolson, Pyre Elder of Restraint
Eframai, Pyre Elder of Justice
Siemond, Pyre Elder of Diplomacy
Udio, Pyre Elder of Patience
Paralabar, Pyre Elder of Charity
Cbatta, Pyre Elder of Harmony

Elders:
Bertram, Book-keeper of the Academy d'Ava
Larmond, Elder of Dorthu
Agathius, Elder of Fisk

www.ingramcontent.com/pod-product-compliance
Lightning Source LLC
Chambersburg PA
CBHW020645110726
47901CB00001B/54